BLOOD SLAVE

lovely to meet you! ♡

love

Eden Wildblood

The Complete series

#1 The Beginning
#2 Round Two
#3 Made of Scars
#4 Even in Death
#5 Carnival of Souls

By

Eden Wildblood

WARNING

Please note – This book is a dark paranormal story and is not suitable for those under 18 years old.

This book is dark. There will be moments you won't like and people you will hate. Know this before you go in...

BLOOD SLAVE

The Complete series

#1 The Beginning

By

Eden Wildblood

PROLOGUE ONE

"Fool me once, shame on you. Fool me twice, shame on me," Wynter told her very recently dumped ex-boyfriend, Dominic, before finally kicking his cheating arse out the door of her small townhouse. And she really did feel a fool. And ashamed.

He'd done the same to her months earlier and had come home grovelling with his tail between his legs, insisting it was nothing but a drunken mistake. That she 'meant nothing.' She'd tried her hardest to forgive and forget and had thought they were getting somewhere, but then he'd only gone and done it again. So, that was it. The straw that'd broken the camel's back, and her heart.

As she watched him beg for forgiveness, Wynter felt an icy chill run not only down her spine, but also into her heart as he pleaded for her to take him back. But it really was no use. She wasn't angry or upset with him. If anything, she felt indifferent to Dominic and his puppy dog eyes. There was nothing there anymore. No desire to try again and no fear of being alone. The last time, that was the only reason she'd taken him back. Being alone had seemed scarier than being locked into a relationship with a cheating bastard, but not this time.

She just guessed it was her way of coping, or some kind of defence mechanism getting to work on healing her from the inside out. Shutting off seemed the best way to deal right now. Closing that door and locking it tight was working, and she nourished that feeling of indifference. Part of her marvelled at how the human heart could close to someone it'd once held so dear, but hers really had. She wanted nothing more to do with Dominic, or any other man, right now. Wynter simply wanted to be alone and so shut him out.

But then she shut everyone out. In the aftermath of their breakup, the iciness set in and became permanent. It spread to all other parts of her life and Wynter had no idea just how much she'd changed. She failed to notice how all her relationships were affected, not to mention her love life. Besides, there was no such thing anymore, only one-night-stands and a beast of a dildo to keep her company on those nights she chose not to entertain the pretence of *real*.

She'd come to realise how her mother had been right. All throughout her childhood, she'd told Wynter how men were nothing but monsters. She'd been burned too many times. Been treated like an afterthought by those she'd loved and discarded so easily for the younger, newer model. By her early thirties, her mother had sworn off men entirely, and Wynter could finally see why. It was just a shame she had gone on to become bitter and twisted, and a recluse who'd never let another man come near her again. Even Wynter barely had a thing to do with her. She'd moved across the country for Dom, and for some reason had chosen to stay even after they were over. She and her mum caught up in their few and far between chats via text, and Wynter knew her mother liked it that way too.

She could see her life going in the exact same direction.

Those lessons had been hard to learn as a young woman, but even harder to overcome. As a teen, Wynter had somehow convinced herself she wouldn't suffer the same fate. She had done everything she could to work through the mixed emotions she'd had when it came to relationships and intimacy. She had wanted both and had followed her urges over the years, trying to have it all, but time and again the same fires that'd hurt her mother so damn much had burnt her too.

Men—they could all go to hell as far as she was concerned. Even her friends were selfish and self-centred. Her best friend only ever called or text when she needed something, but when Wynter had needed help, no one had been there.

She decided she was going to become like them.

Cold.

Manipulative.

Selfish.

She wasn't going to give anyone anything. Only take, and if they didn't like it, then all they had to do was look in the mirror to figure out why she'd done it.

PROLOGUE TWO

Blood. Rivers of it were cascading over him in waves of hot, thick crimson, and he could taste the various qualities in it. Emotions were distinguishable, as always. The sensations and undertones like subtle hints to the most deliciously flavoured wine he had ever tasted.

And to top it off, he could taste in the air the most delectable of scents. A woman with ice in her broken heart. He reached out into the ether and shared the feeling with her, like a dream that felt so real she would have to tell her friends about it the following day. She tried to fight it, unsure of what was setting her body on edge, but she was his to control, and so he would. Repeatedly.

Even in the haze of drunkenness, it would be the most wondrous thing she had ever experienced, and yet he knew she'd go home and tell herself it couldn't be true. She couldn't become this man's plaything. This monster.

But the dark man had forced her. Persuaded and manipulated every moment to bring her to this place where the world ended and darkness prevailed.

With a smile, he showed her a glimpse of the future. A time and place where eyes the colour of glowing sapphires haunted her.

She stumbled away, looking over her shoulder, feeling eyes on her.

He had memorised her scent, and Wynter knew he would always find her.

He would even prey upon those she loved to punish her if she didn't return. Maybe even force her to love him.

And to top it all off, she'd go willingly. Like a foolish little girl who had thought she was strong enough to outwit the most cunning creature who had ever lived, she would play his games and lose time and again.

ONE

"And finally, we have the boss's office on the fourth floor, which is where I leave you. Please take a seat and someone will be here to interview you shortly," the burly security guard, David, declared and, with a smile and a nod, he was gone again. And just like that, she was one step closer to the job of a lifetime. A chance to start anew and really get somewhere. To be someone else.

Wynter stood staring at the open doorway with a frown. This all seemed too good to be true. There had to be a catch. Jobs like this didn't just present themselves out of the blue.

Everything in her life had fallen flat, and there was no way this was going to be any different. The list seemed to go on and on, and to top it all off, there was that odd drunken dream she'd had the night before. Rivers of blood that tasted like wine… No, she wasn't letting herself so much as think about that right now. Too many vampire movies. That was the problem. She'd sworn off men and instead found herself fantasising about fictional anti-heroes and bad boys her psyche was trying to convince her could be saved. Or maybe she'd thought they could save her too? Jeez, this was exactly why she didn't like to let herself overthink shit like this!

Real life was bad enough without her somehow adding other strange woes into the mix. She'd broken up with Dominic two years before, who'd then gone on to marry the slut he'd cheated on her with. And all the while Wynter had simply grown colder towards men, rather than ever let one hurt her again. She'd used them up and spat them out before things got serious, or often only let them stay for one night to avoid any awkwardness at all. Her heart wasn't broken any more, but it was locked away. No key. Just a wall of rock-solid ice.

Her job prospects had been dwindling after being passed up for promotion in her current role as Junior Graphic Designer at *Marsden and Carmichael*—again, and that was why she'd jumped at the chance to start again somewhere new. How she'd ended up here, in a silent hallway waiting to be called in and scrutinised by what she presumed would be a panel of blank faces when she eventually got called through. But Wynter knew she'd play along if it got her the pay rise she so desperately needed.

She was alone and barely scraping by. The last thing she wanted was for some psycho to take the spare room in her two-bed home, but Wynter had also come to realise that without the extra money to pay the mortgage and bills, she was in danger of losing it.

She had attempted to drown her sorrows on the pennies left in her purse and dance through her woes at the nightclub the night before, where the same security guard who'd shown her around just now had approached her. He'd offered a job interview on the spot. Well, that wasn't entirely true. The offer of an interview had come after her having refused the invitation of the club's owner to join him in one of his private booths. He hadn't even bothered to come down himself and had sent his minion to do his bidding, and Wynter had laughed in the guy's face. She wasn't going to flutter her eyelashes and follow him upstairs just because his boss had spied her from his tower and had told him so before stalking away.

But then, the bouncer had intercepted her on the way out and offered her a different kind of invitation. The prospect of a job there had been much more appealing and while she'd played it cool, Wynter had readily accepted. She knew it couldn't be a coincidence that there was suddenly an opening available, though.

There was a reason *Slave* was one of the most prestigious and exclusive nightclubs Manchester had to offer. They never had open interviews or advertised for jobs, she'd checked, and while intrigued by the offer, she was not going to let herself be fooled into signing anything unless it looked legit. If the owner, Mr Cole, wanted her to work for him, then fine, but if he just wanted some whore on his payroll, then he was going to have to look elsewhere. She wasn't that hard up. Not yet at least.

After sitting for a short while, Wynter was eventually ushered inside another empty room, and she looked around the huge office. She'd expected to find other candidates sat waiting inside, but there was no one else. Just her, and so she took a seat and waited patiently for her interview to begin.

This was just the latest in a string of desperate attempts to turn her life around and, much like all the rest, she didn't expect to walk out with an offer above what she was earning in her current job. All she hoped was that they'd give her the chance to start at the bottom and work her way up. She'd work behind the bar if she had to or clean the toilets.

Something had needed to change for a long time. Wynter didn't know if it was the overbearing sense of constant rejection she'd felt from everyone in her life, or the iciness inside of her that was growing and growing with every pitfall she managed to find herself falling into, but she was scared. And tired. She didn't want to struggle any more. She wasn't afraid of hard work and was willing to push herself to whatever limits she needed to if it stopped her life from spiralling any further. If it made that downward curve turn the other way, even just a little, then she was willing to give everything she had to make it work.

And so, she was there and was ready and willing to hear what the illustrious Mr Cole had to say. She focussed on the inside of the club, thinking how it hadn't looked like she'd imagined. The walls had been white and the offices spotless. Almost clinical.

This one was different, though. The room she was in now had been decorated in blue and grey, and reeked of masculinity. There weren't flowers in vases or mirrors to brighten up the space, but stripes painted at perfect angles across the huge walls and even a collection of what seemed to be close-up photographs along one side. From where she sat, Wynter thought they looked like blood films. They were black and white but looked like various types of red cells. Some were flat, while others had clumped together. It was an odd choice, or so she thought.

Wynter wasn't waiting long but was surprised when a solitary man came in and nodded to her before closing the door behind him, rather than the panel from the HR team she'd expected.

"Good afternoon, Miss Armstrong," he said, his tone formal and his voice a deep, rumbling caress against her ears. He was certainly eloquent.

Wynter stood and shook his hand, taking in his appearance. He was in a charcoal suit that was clearly expertly tailored and probably cost more than she made in a year and had teamed it with a crisp pale grey shirt and deep blue tie. With his dark grey hair and the piercing blue eyes he was inspecting her with, he was interesting and well-groomed and had a powerful way about him. The man was clearly older than her by at least a decade, but he still had that sort of look about him she quite liked. He had to be in his early forties but was slim and tall, and he didn't appear to have let himself go over the years, either.

"Please, call me Wynter," she replied with a genuine smile, thinking how if he turned out to be the boss she'd turned down the night before, she was a fool to have refused him.

"Of course," he accepted with a courteous nod, as he took his seat behind the huge desk between them. "I'm Marcus. I oversee Mr Cole's numerous establishments across the world. He has asked me to outline his proposal for your employment and to seal the deal, so to speak." He then indicated for her to take her seat again, and Wynter frowned.

"Forgive me, I thought you'd need to interview me first?" she asked, but Marcus shook his head.

"No need. Mr Cole has already vetted you and made sure of your credentials. All that's left is for you to sign on the dotted line…" he then produced a folder from the drawer to his right and pulled a pile of papers from inside it.

They had been carefully arranged and collated, and she could see that someone had meticulously indicated various parts of the document using sticky tabs. The boss, Mr Cole, had clearly elicited a good few hours' work from whoever had put this pack together for him, and she found herself unsure. What was in that folder? Wynter suddenly felt uncomfortable with how fast the recruitment process was going and took a deep breath to steady herself.

"He can't possibly know enough to hire me without seeing what I can do?" Wynter insisted and was sure she caught Marcus roll his eyes with impatience. He clearly hadn't anticipated having to handhold her, but she wasn't going to sign anything until she had been fully informed of what would be expected of her.

"He does, and he has," he told her in a clipped tone, but then took a breath and fixed those bright blue eyes of his on her again. "Everything you need to know is outlined in this document." He plucked the top few sheets out and then laid his large palm atop the folder while he continued to scrutinise her.

Wynter sat back down, staring back at him. Marcus softened his features but continued to watch her, but she could tell he was trying to hide something. And was he really trying to woo her? To make her think she had a chance by flirting and attempting to make her go all giddy? Well, if he was, then he'd chosen the wrong lady to try that with. Wynter didn't do girly. She didn't get flustered thanks to a man's attention, nor would she foolishly sign her life away simply because he'd fixed her with those incredible eyes and insist she does so.

"And what exactly do you have there on me?" she asked, thinking the folder was far too thick to simply be a contract. If Mr Cole had some kind of dossier on her, he was obliged to show Wynter before she committed to a future with him. Either that, or he had a very meticulous way of doing business. If the latter, it appeared he was dead set on having a full agreement signed from the onset and proving all the ways in which she was expected to work beneath his administration.

No matter his way of having Marcus do things, it made her think he liked establishing power over his employees and proving he had the means to hold them to their promises right from day one. A way of ensuring no one backed out or walked away. Perhaps some kind of leverage over them?

Her mind wandered back to the night before. Yes, she'd been inebriated, but she remembered talking with the security guard, David, and asking if he liked working there. His answer had wholeheartedly been yes. He'd warned her it was the sort of job that took over your life, though, but in a good way. How he never wanted to leave and always arrived early and left late for his shifts by choice. Wynter hoped he had been telling her the whole truth, and not a lie concocted to get her on side.

Marcus waited a beat and when she didn't cave, he smiled to himself as though impressed by his new potential employee's ability to keep her wits about her even while under pressure. He clearly wasn't used to dealing with such headstrong workers, but she wasn't afraid to push him back. After all, the job was apparently already in the bag, or so he'd said.

"This is the standard contract all employees are required to sign," he finally answered.

"It's very large," she replied with an element of mirth to her tone and was pleased when she elicited a smile from Marcus, albeit a fleeting one.

"It is indeed very large, Miss Armstrong, hence the need to move forward right away. We have the usual outline of your job role and expectations anticipated of you therein, but then yours also has some special alterations and dispensations, as per Mr Cole's request. By the end of our meeting, I hope to have the contract fully completed and you ready to begin your probationary period right away."

"Probationary period?" Wynter asked, thinking it rather annoying that after not interviewing and yet hounding her to accept the role, the boss man would still appreciate the opportunity to get rid of her should she not live up to his expectations.

"Just in case," Marcus countered with a look of satisfaction on his stoic face, "it's better for everyone if you're given the chance to try the job out before you commit to anything."

Oh. That was a surprise. So, it wasn't for them to get rid of her, but the other way around? Wow, it really did seem like the sort of workplace that took over your life. David hadn't been kidding after all.

Wynter took a steadying breath and peered across at him. Marcus was powerful, she could tell. He liked that power and had an intimidating element to him she could sense. He didn't seem like he'd be uneasy in delivering their boss's demands. Not gentle and inviting, like David had been, but she appreciated that he might at least be honest with her, perhaps brutally so at times.

"First things first," she told him before taking a sip of the water she realised he'd poured them both without even asking her. "I'd like to know why he chose me? What made Mr Cole pick me out and decide to know more? And does he make a habit of hiring random people just because he finds them *intriguing*?" she asked, using the term David had relayed to her the night before when trying to lure her upstairs at Mr Cole's request.

Marcus grinned and leaned forward in his chair, where he linked his hands in front of his chin and rested it on them, all the while watching her with a devious twinkle in his eye.

"Mr Cole has very particular tastes when it comes to all aspects of his life, whether business or pleasure," he told her, "something about a person will grab his attention and he will not stop until he acquires them for whatever position he has in mind. As you may well know, there's no such thing as an opening within this company, Wynter. He creates roles for the people he wants to come and work for him. He dictates their working hours and their salaries. He makes demands of their time and effort in whatever way he sees fit, and not even one of his employees has ever complained or left his employment."

"Why?" she asked again, feeling overwhelmed. There had to be more to it. In what world would she be plucked from a crowd and given an offer that might change her life? This sort of thing didn't happen. Not to her, anyway.

"Because he can read people. Know what they need and how hard they're willing to work to get it. He saw it in you, too. And when you work for him, everything changes. You become one of the elite few who can walk on water simply because his name gives you the power to do so. He opens doors others only close, and it's like a drug. One each of us wants more and more of."

His comment hung in the air, making the silence tense and yet seductive.

Could it really be so amazing working for one man? And who in the hell was he? Wynter was still scared, but knew she had to find out.

TWO

Wynter reached her hand forward and held it out to Marcus. She was hesitant but also curious and wanted to find out just what this strange new boss had in mind for her. Plus, it couldn't hurt to look at the proposal. Nothing was set in stone and wouldn't be until she was ready to sign. She would walk out of there no problem if the deal and its terms weren't right but hoped that wouldn't be the case.

"Then let's see what he has to say about me," she told him and was met with another of Marcus's devilish grins. Those eyes of his were mesmerising and when teamed with that smile he was dangerously mysterious. He was hot, she couldn't deny it, and Wynter quickly found herself wondering what the rules were on inter-office liaisons.

But first, she had to keep a clear head and see what she was potentially getting herself into.

Her interviewer handed her the file, and she read the first few pages. It was indeed some kind of dossier, and within was a brief overview of her current career path and income at *Marsden and Carmichael*. The phrases 'face doesn't fit' and 'lacks the proper reputation' jumped out and were like a kick in the teeth. They were there in black and white, taken from copies of emails sent between her boss and line manager. The pair of them had discussed her personal life at length and called her a 'cold and distant sort. Not right for a position higher up within the company.'

If she weren't so cold and distant, Wynter thought she might be upset reading their words. Part of her was, but like any emotion, she pushed it down and turned the page.

It didn't get any better. Whoever had delved deeply into her life had pulled up her bank records and gone so far as to plot her sorry state in a graph. It had her current net worth in bright red letters at the bottom with a minus sign before it.

Further down, it got even worse. There were bullet points. Her personal life outlined so simply. So coldly.

Relationship status – single. Never married. No children. No prospects.
Casual sex – yes, frequently plus masturbation.
Uses sexual protection – yes, condoms and pill.
Number of sexual partners – approx. 30-35 in the past year.
Medical history – nothing significant.
Allergies – none.
Current medications – oral contraceptive. Past – anti-depressants.

Wynter went through a range of emotions at reading through her file. She was angry, ashamed, and then disgusted. How could they know some of these things? And what about her medical background, unless they'd hacked into the records held by her GP? And even worse, how could they possibly know about her sexual habits and number of partners, unless they'd snooped on her social media and perhaps even her phone records?

This was worse than trying for a job at MI6, or so she believed.

She wanted to shout her mouth off and storm away, but then took another look at the whole sum of her life's efforts. No family. No husband. Just a life of proclivity and crippling debt. The only person she should be angry with was her. She had let herself get that way and now, sitting opposite her, was her chance to change all that.

Wynter let out a sigh and lifted her gaze back to Marcus. "Wanna know my shoe size too?"

"We have to be thorough," he answered without a hint of an apology.

"Why?" she demanded, albeit half-heartedly.

"I can tell you once you've signed the contract," he replied cryptically, "don't like it? You know where the door is."

Marcus then waited a few seconds, and when Wynter didn't take the offer to leave, he grinned across at her. "Good. The full dossier on you will be handed over once you've signed the contract. We keep only one sealed copy for future records."

More like for leverage, she thought, but realised they didn't have any on her anyway, so figured she wouldn't let it bother her.

Wynter let out a huff and flicked over to the next page. At least the invasive part seemed over with. On the second page was a summary of her proposed job role. It was finally some good information and made her flush with excitement to discover that she would be given an office of her own, and the title of Marketing Manager.

She would apparently be working alongside the IT department to produce materials for both public viewing, and those accessing the club's exclusive member's only sites for the specialty themed nights in between. This was interesting, but at least it explained why the nightclub was only open to the public on a weekend.

She wanted to know more, but there was nothing about it in the role description. Wynter guessed perhaps there was a dark underbelly to the nightclub scene that wasn't common knowledge to those outside of certain circles, which included her as long as she still hadn't signed off on the job. It intrigued her to know she would find out the truth about what was going on behind the closed doors of the club during the week, though, and she could tell she was moving closer to accepting the job offer already.

The document then went on to describe how she'd also be moderating private groups and begin building an online presence for both the club she was in and Mr Cole's many others across the globe. Plus, she'd oversee the marketing campaigns as well as dressing the club in whichever colour schemes she saw fit for whatever occasion.

Now that sounded perfect. Putting her web design skills to use while also being the head of the marketing team was a dream come true. No more monotony of sitting behind a desk working on nothing other than simple designs while those above her got to do the exciting work, and of course take all the credit.

Wynter was ready to know more and turned the page where she found her anticipated working hours.

"Seven days a week?" she asked in surprise, and looked up at Marcus, who nodded.

"Absolutely. You'll be working from six o'clock in the evening until two-am every night. We all work those core hours, but others come in during the day as well to do overtime at Mr Cole's behest. He has asked that you add some specially designated hours to your working week, but they are outlined later," Marcus replied, still seeming utterly at ease with the terms of her employment, and just how much was expected of her.

"And what's the setup there?" Wynter replied, thinking how working every evening was going to be hard work, especially if she had to be up and out again for nine-am to work at her other job. She needed as much money as she could get, but it was doable, at least for a short while. She'd be able to work both jobs until she had enough money saved, or until her probationary period was over. Once she knew whether she wanted to stay with Mr Cole, she could easily quit one job or the other.

"Later," he insisted, and Wynter dropped her gaze back to the page, figuring it'd be pointless to waste time pursuing it when all she had to do was keep reading.

She took a moment to let the details sink in. The job seemed wonderful. The hours long, but acceptable. The club was prestigious and after working here, she'd have her pick of future placements. *Slave* was somewhere everyone she knew would die to work in, and she'd kick herself for not jumping at the chance to work there. Even the people were lovely, or at least the few she'd met so far.

Wynter knew there had to be a catch somewhere. She had to keep looking. Keep reading between the lines. She turned another page and frowned when she found more details regarding the level of commitment expected by the company.

"No sick days and no annual leave?" she asked, shaking her head. "Surely it's the law to provide those things?"

"Not if mutually agreed," Marcus countered. "Mr Cole wants to know every corner of his domain is covered at all times and doesn't want to have to employ temps or cover absences. You're to turn up every day without fail, or else face dismissal. Your salaried pay will more than make up for it. Keep reading."

Wynter didn't like the sound of their absence policy one little bit, but she held her tongue and did as Marcus had asked and carried on through the lengthy contract.

When she reached the next page outlining her proposed pay, she was surprised to find the box blank where her yearly wage should be.

She looked up at Marcus and frowned. "This part is up for negotiation," he informed her before she could ask. "How much do you think you're worth?"

Wynter gulped and gawked at him, but it appeared he was entirely serious and was ready to hear her answers before providing his counter offer. She knew she had to propose more than she'd anticipated to allow for some room to barter and so doubled her current salary and then doubled that too, just for good measure.

"One hundred thousand pounds per annum," she announced, thinking it ludicrous, but without hesitation, Marcus fixed his immense gaze on hers again and nodded.

"Done," he replied, before throwing her a pen. "Write it in there and initial it." Wynter grabbed the pen and went to do it, but then looked back to him and chewed her bottom lip for a second while trying to figure out the best way to ask if she ought to have demanded more. She didn't want to appear greedy but figured she might as well get the best offer she could. "Something wrong?" Marcus teased, and it was clear he knew exactly what was on her mind.

"How much do you think?" she replied, her voice a little shaky.

"I'm glad you asked," he said with that smile of his again. "The budget is two hundred thousand. As long as you said there or beneath it, I was advised not to negotiate."

"Perhaps I could make a counter offer then?" she asked him, mirroring his smile.

"I think rounding it up to two hundred would be more than acceptable, but don't tell Mr Cole I told you so," he told her, having known exactly what she was going to say.

Wynter wrote the numbers and initialled it with a shaking hand. She couldn't even begin to imagine what it'd be like to earn that kind of money, but she clung to the idea all the same. This might be happening. It might really be real.

She was about to turn over onto the final page when Marcus reached forward and put his hand over hers so fast it was like a blur. Wynter would normally pull hers away whenever someone touched her like that, but this time, she didn't. Instead, she peered up into his eyes again and took a steadying breath.

"What's wrong?" she asked him, her voice a mere whisper.

"I've a feeling the final page is going to make or break this decision for you," he said before leaning closer, seeming worried. "I want you to be aware before you read it, and know that, like the rest of it, everything is up for negotiation."

He lifted his hand away, and she turned the page, not knowing what on earth she was to expect to find there. Wynter couldn't imagine in a business that seemed to thrive on making its employees a fair offer, she would find something terrible there, but the look on Marcus's face told her there was some kind of powerful demand awaiting her. Something that, if she agreed to it, would mean a complete change in how she was going to view her new job proposal.

THREE

Marcus released Wynter from his gaze and sat back in his seat, watching her read over the final page with an enforced blank look on his face, but inside his guts were churning with need for her. Would she say yes? Or would she refuse the final proposal and storm out?

Might she like the challenge he'd set out for her and rise to it? He couldn't tell, but he wanted her to see it for what it was—a promise as well as a test. He knew she was special. There was no doubt about that. He could smell her from across the room and practically taste her scent in the air. Wynter was to be the perfect addition to his now thriving team, and he couldn't wait to make her his. And all she had to do was sign on that final dotted line.

It wasn't like he had lured her in, either. Far from it. She'd been drawn to his club for a reason. Perhaps one she herself didn't yet know, and while it pained him to have to wait patiently for her answer, he also knew he had to remain calm and let her have time to react to the specifications outlined on that final page. He'd let her say her bit, and then hopefully she'd tell him yes and sign her life away.

Would they have offered her enough money? Enough security? Had he been a gracious enough host during their time together so far? He damn well hoped so, because he knew that if he failed today, he'd be done for tomorrow. Fresh blood had needed recruiting, and he was damn sure that with her beneath him, their businesses both legitimate and otherwise would get the revitalisation it so desperately needed.

He was counting on her. That sweet and desperate little thing who so needed what he was more than willing to offer. Wynter was cold and lonely. Shut off from the rest of the world because she'd been broken too many times. But he was going to change all that. Marcus was going to give her somewhere to belong, but only if she agreed to give him what he needed in return.

***

Wynter read and reread the page to make sure she was clear on what would be expected of her if she agreed to the final terms of her employment.

'The employee is expected to undertake extra duties as laid out by her employer when called upon and shall set aside the hours of 2:01 to 17:59 every Saturday and Sunday to facilitate all tasks as and when given to her by Mr Cole directly. Overtime benefits are negotiable and will be paid accordingly, as well as added benefits for the extra time spent at the companies' behest.'

"What does that mean? I have to work overtime at weekends?" she eventually asked Marcus, whom she caught glowering over at her from the opposite side of the desk.

It was ever so odd. He seemed poised, like he was ready to pounce or something, and was having to force himself back against his seat.

He let out a gruff sigh and ran his hand through his dark grey hair, clearly disgruntled, but Wynter couldn't understand why. It seemed clear enough to her; she was just asking for clarification? "I'll gladly work extra. It isn't a problem!" she assured him, and then peered down at where she needed to sign and complete their deal.

Wynter waited for a reaction from him before signing the page off but was met with still stony silence and stared back down at the page. Overtime wasn't any hassle, plus it was still outside of her other job so would be fine. She could attend some meetings or do extra work if it was required of her and knew this was what she wanted. No part of her felt ready to refuse this epic deal just waiting to be done, and so she signed her name, completing her contract with Mr Cole and making it final.

Wynter then ran her thumb across the embossed paper and marvelled at the finery of it, but then hissed when she caught the edge and was rewarded with a small paper cut.

A single drop of her blood fell onto the page and was soaked up in an instant, having dried before she could wipe at it, and Wynter pushed her thumb into her mouth in a bid to stop any more from messing up the contract. She was about to offer Marcus an apology when she felt a wave of nausea wash over her.

She suddenly felt incredibly off. She came over hot and cold and was then filled with a strange awareness of her own body like she'd never felt before. Every inch of her skin was on fire. It was itching, aching for something, and she didn't know what on Earth it could be, or at least that was until she looked up at Marcus and felt drawn to him like a magnet. As if he were the cure to her sudden onset of desperation.

Wynter somehow knew that wherever he went, she wanted to follow him, and how she'd do whatever it took to stay there by his side. She didn't even know the reason or understand why she felt those things, but she did. And she hoped to God he felt the same way about her too, otherwise things could get awkward damn quickly.

His expression told Wynter he at least felt something. It didn't matter his age or the powerful position he was clearly in. She liked him and wanted to explore her feelings when appropriate and when they were, hopefully, reciprocated.

"I'd like you to take a copy of this home with you. Make sure you read it again and are happy before your probationary period ends in one week's time," Marcus told her after a few seconds of silence, before he took the signed contract and secured it in his desk drawer. "But for now, it's time you were shown to your office and given the full details about what other exploits we cater for here. Some will come as a shock, but you're one of the team now, so I'm sure I can trust you to keep your wits about you and use your discretion when it comes to being open-minded."

"Sure," Wynter answered with a shrug. Sounded to her like the club seconded as something secretive and perhaps illegal. Maybe involving men and women for hire? Or perhaps feeding extreme sexual appetites? She was no prude and figured she'd seen a lot and done plenty when it came to exploring her sexuality. There couldn't be much that would shock her. Or so she thought.

With a nod, Marcus then led them out and across the corridor to an awaiting elevator. Inside, Wynter felt herself gravitating towards him. She still felt that odd attraction to him, as if he had something she desperately needed. She wanted to tell him, but she caught her breath before she made a fool out of herself. Even if being away from him made her ache to get closer, she wasn't going to give in. There was no part of her that wanted to make a fool of herself on day one.

They went down to a set of offices she'd seen on her tour and came to a stop outside the one marked Marketing Manager. Her office. Wynter could've jumped for joy just thinking about it.

Marcus produced a key from his pocket, unlocked the door, and led her inside. He then handed the key to Wynter, who immediately secured it to her set of house keys.

"When you're out of this office for any reason, you lock the door," he demanded. "In fact, lock yourself inside when you're alone as well. Security is top priority, even with your co-workers. Not everyone is trustworthy, Wynter. You never know what people might try and snoop on when your back is turned or come in and watch you work with their prying eyes. In fact, go ahead and lock it behind us now. I'd like a moment alone before we get down to work."

Wynter felt strange locking them in together. She did as Marcus asked, but she couldn't deny feeling uneasy about being alone with him in her new office. It felt sordid. Like they were going to develop a name for themselves already and while she couldn't deny still finding him attractive, it didn't mean she was ready to jump his bones within minutes of signing her contract.

"Marcus, I…" she began, but he held up one hand to shush her.

Against all her natural instincts, Wynter couldn't help but obey, and she watched as he looked her up and down, that salacious smile back again.

"You agreed to do whatever tasks were asked of you during your overtime periods," he said, reminding her of the strange clause at the end of the contract. He then checked his watch, reminding her that, with it being Saturday afternoon, they were smack bang in the middle of those overtime hours. "But what kind of work do you imagine it to be?" he pressed her after a tense silence and Wynter gulped. "You need to go into this job with your eyes open. You'll be making more money than you ever dreamed while gaining the respect of your bosses, peers, and subordinates alike. But it will come at a price."

Wynter shook her head. She'd made it clear to David the night before that she was no whore, so if Mr Cole had put that clause in there because he expected her to perform for him or entertain his guests, then he certainly had another thing coming.

"It doesn't say in the contract what the overtime work will entail," she answered after remembering those few lines again. That was when it properly dawned on her. It didn't say she would be working extra hours to complete her usual work. In fact, it didn't say anything more than how she would be expected to add time to her weekend at the behest of Mr Cole. It could technically be anything he asked of her, and she wouldn't have a leg to stand on if she tried to refuse.

She opened her mouth to snap some snide remark Marcus's way, but he shushed her again.

"Before you go demanding to rescind your contract because of your probationary period, I want you to at least try things our way. If you leave before the week is up, you can never change your mind and come back. It'll be like you were never here. All will be lost and no amount of begging will change that, so why not at least give this place a go? Like I said, I only want you to go into this job with a clear head."

"Why?" she asked, feeling lost. Nothing was making sense, but she realised she'd been right about one thing. The deal had been too good to be true. Wynter had been offered everything she'd ever dreamed of. Money, a title she felt she deserved, and the chance to reinvent herself under a new boss and in a new life. This job was her opportunity to step out from the darkness she'd shielded herself in for far too long, but, of course, there was a price.

"Give me one week to sway you, Wynter," Marcus replied, stepping closer.

She stepped away, but he kept on advancing and soon her back was against the locked door and she had nowhere else to run. Marcus placed a hand on her cheek, ignoring her trembling, and she couldn't deny it felt amazing to have him touch her. "You may walk away at any point in the next seven days, but I believe that by the time we reach this same moment next week, you'll be begging me to let you stay."

"And why is that?" she asked, feeling penetrated by his powerful gaze. Wynter could also feel herself starting to thaw. She had a week to decide. Seven nights of work to see this place in all its glory and gore, and she was going to use them wisely. Get the lay of the land and figure out what the hell she was dealing with before she made her final decision.

"Because what Marcus Cole wants, Marcus Cole gets…"

Wynter started to laugh uncontrollably. Why hadn't she realised sooner? Of course, it was the renowned Mr Cole she had been dealing with the entire time. Who else would've had the power to offer her such an intricately planned out deal? He would never have trusted someone else to procure his next prize, not when he seemed to enjoy the hunt so damn much.

"And what do you intend to do with me for the next seven days, Mr Cole?"

"Teach you," he replied and then leaned closer so that his lips were right by her ear. "I've promised to give you everything you ever wanted, so now I'm going to deliver it. And all while you learn about my life and my work. How I run my empire. What I like and dislike. And of course, how I expect my women to behave…"

"You've got another thing coming if you think I—"

Marcus silenced Wynter with a kiss and while she tried to fight him off at first, it wasn't long before she began to melt against him, her senses suddenly overwhelmed.

Her body was strangely awakened, as if every one of her true hormonal responses and carnal desires had lain dormant and in wait for the right man to stoke those fires back to life, and properly coax them out of her.

Nothing compared to the rush she felt. No one else's kiss had ever made her feel the way Marcus's was. Her memories of other lovers were null and void after just a few seconds of his mouth on hers, and Wynter was suddenly feeling rather forgiving about his devious approach at getting her to sign that contract.

When he pulled back, she felt bereft. With him so close, she could feel the heat from his body radiating against hers and couldn't focus on anything other than her need to have his mouth on hers again.

Marcus licked his lips, and that was when Wynter saw the slightest shade of pink staining them. Was that blood? She didn't feel like her lips were bleeding or anything, but when he grinned again, his teeth were a dazzling bright white. It had to have been a trick of the light, she presumed. She'd been lost in her lustful haze and had seen something that wasn't there. Yes, that was it. It had to be.

"You're very lucky," Marcus warned as he dipped his head down again and placed another kiss against her cheek. "I don't usually kiss on the first date, but with you I simply couldn't help myself." He then let out a small laugh before stepping away. She felt lost all over again and slumped against the door behind, feeling vulnerable and drained. What the hell was that? With him close by, she felt whole, but when he was gone, so too were those rekindled hopes and dreams.

"Tell me more about what you want from me, Marcus," Wynter begged, "explain that clause at the end of the contract and why you warned me about it?"

He walked around the room like a ghost. He brushed his fingertips over the desk and chair with only the slightest of touches and didn't seem to disturb a thing. He stopped only once he'd reached the solitary window that Wynter could tell looked out onto the nightclub below.

"I expect the men and women who work for me to undertake extra work at my command," he answered, still looking down at what she assumed was the now empty club. Wynter knew that already but decided against saying anything more just yet. Instead, she crept closer. "Every employee has a maximum of two set days per week in which they cover that workload. My clients pay well and frequent us often, and that extra money is shared between myself and the employee who does my bidding."

"So, you do whore us out?" Wynter replied with a frown. She felt sick at the sheer thought but didn't stop her approach.

"No, I do not," he answered curtly. She moved closer still, watching his face from the side as he continued to stare out the window. "Everyone has needs. Some make sense to others and some don't, but that doesn't make them any less real. Myself and others like me require regular top-ups from those in our employ. By regulating it, I help to avoid causing a scene or doing any damage to our reputations while taking what we need. What we must have to survive."

"Regulating what?" she whimpered, watching him intently.

Marcus had seemed to go impossibly pale, yet his eyes were somehow shining even brighter. She could see his reflection in the glass and it was as if she were staring at a skeleton, not a man made from flesh and bone. His eyes darted and caught hers in the reflection, and she felt her entire body go icy cold. As if death himself was peering at her through the void of time and space. Like she had crossed over through the veil at the reaper's invitation.

"The blood-letting," he answered her in the same calm monotone he'd used earlier in the interview. "If we must take it, surely you agree it is better that we do so with willing donors?"

Her head began to spin. No, she couldn't have heard him right. No way.

And yet, Marcus remained perfectly still as he watched her take it in and process what he had said. His impossibly bright blue eyes still bore into hers through the reflection in the glass, and Wynter felt as though her heart skipped a beat.

"What are you?" she asked. "What world have you lured me into?" Wynter added before breaking the eye contact and slumping down against the desk.

"A world where blood means more to my clients than money. One where you and everyone else here holds the key to our very survival itself," he answered, and then he turned to look at her. Wynter was relieved to see Marcus as he had been before, not the ghoulish form she knew she never wanted to see again, and yet wasn't able to forget.

He stepped closer and, for some strange reason, she didn't try to clamber away. This time, she held his gaze and remained rooted to the spot, eager to know more.

"When you kissed me…"

"It was because I had to taste you," he answered with that same devilish grin she'd come to dote on in just the couple of hours she'd known him. "I had my suspicions that you would be delicious, but only recently did you begin to outshine all the other frequenters to my club. I needed someone new to join my specially chosen team and last night it was as though I could smell you before you'd even walked through the door." Wynter gulped. He could smell her?

"And that's why you sent David down to get me?"

"Yes, but you weren't playing, were you? I had to come up with a new plan. A better one. My desire for you overshadowed everything else, and so I did my research. I found out what you needed and offered it to you."

"And here I am," Wynter recollected, shaking her head at her own naïveté. She then realised he hadn't answered one of her questions from before, and so asked it again. "What *are* you?" she asked as she moved closer without thinking.

Marcus took Wynter's hand and lifted it to his nose, where he drew in a sigh and smiled to himself. He seemed pleased with his newest procurement and, while part of her was flattered by that notion, there was also a bigger part that was disgusted. And although she already knew the answer, she needed him to say it.

"Some of our kind call themselves vampires. Nosferatu. Creatures of the night who dine on the blood of humans to keep themselves immortal. I suppose that is kind of apt," he said, confirming her suspicions. "But to be something so widely fantasised about and immortalised in fiction seems uncouth to me. I wish to remain more mysterious. Better the myth than the cliché."

Wynter wanted to make some joke about the way he'd passed his reveal off like some suave and sophisticated aristocrat who hated labels. She wanted it all to be a joke, and yet, she could say nothing. Marcus was touching her again and, like before, she was desperate for more. She was drawn to that touch and wanted him to tell her more just so that she could hear his penetrating voice while they were still connected. "Against all odds, you want to give yourself to me, don't you, Wynter?" Marcus asked, and it was clear he knew exactly what she was feeling towards him.

"Yes," she hissed, nodding.

"You're already so compliant. So willing. I'm afraid I shall have to accept sooner than I'd anticipated," he replied as he turned her hand over and pressed the inside of her wrist to his nose before inhaling deeply. "But don't you want to know more first? Aren't there answers you still seek?"

"Of course," she told him, panting, "but still, I feel like I want to give you what you need first." She couldn't understand why she even felt that way, or how the scenario itself was somehow so erotic and enticing, but her entire body was screaming for Marcus to take a bite.

She wondered if perhaps the media and its obsession with romanticising the supernatural had affected how she saw him after all. But then and there, Marcus really was beautiful. The most stunning creature she had ever seen, and she was more than ready to give him all of herself. Every last drop.

Wynter grew curious as she waited. She wanted to see him take the bite. To prove to herself that this was real. But also, she was desperate to feel it as he took her blood inside of himself and let out a little soft sigh of relief when he finally opened his mouth.

She expected teeth, like in the movies, but instead it was his tongue that first made contact with her flesh, and she was surprised to feel him lick her. As he pressed the tip of his tongue down onto her skin, it was like shards of glass were piercing her flesh. Strangely, she enjoyed the sting of it, which was quickly sucked away when Marcus closed his mouth over the wound and began taking long draws of her blood.

Wynter cried out as a head rush hit her, but her shock was quickly outlived when it was suddenly replaced by sheer euphoria.

Her body came alive, and she felt powerful. Like she'd just been given some kind of epic high no other substance could remotely match. She counted four gulps and then he slowed his pulls and eventually lifted his head away, licking the wound clean before turning to look back at her and breaking their contact.

Wynter had that same feeling of emptiness she'd had when he'd stopped his kiss earlier, and a small voice in the back of her mind told her it had to be part of his power. He was able to lure humans to their deaths not only willingly but also begging for it.

And now she was under his spell, too. "Tell me," she croaked as she inspected the cut left on her inner wrist from his bite. Wynter had expected bite indentations or perhaps a graze from his glass-like tongue, but instead there were only the tiniest of marks. Like a papercut. "Tell me more about what you are, and why you've chosen me to be part of your empire?"

Marcus set his gaze upon her again and began a slow meander back over to the window, and once again she saw his eyes burn brightly, boring into hers.

Wynter felt like following him, the desire to be close again almost claiming her, but she forced herself to remember who she was and what she'd come to his club for. She'd gone there for a job and the new life that came with it. She had come to change her entire future and had gotten her wish. With or without her infatuation with Mr Cole, she needed to know the rest of what he'd been so willing to tell her before she'd unceremoniously thrown herself at his mercy and begged him to bite her.

And so, she sat back and waited for him to reveal all. With a clear head at last, she was ready to see the bigger picture. Not just what he wanted from her, but what he expected of their future together.

"Every one of my employees serves my customers at least one day of the week. Like with you, they're contracted to remain in the club after their shift finishes and work right through until the end of the following evening," he told her, and had retreated so far she could almost think straight at last. "Most of them work their overtime during the week, when we are visited by anywhere from two hundred to a thousand vampiric creatures. We have specialised evenings, but the highest level of Blood Slave is savoured. Taken slowly and enjoyed, rather than rushed. Each vampire can be allocated a suitable companion based on their preferences of blood type and such, or choose one themselves, before they're offered a private room and some alone time with their purchase."

"How many employees do you have in total?" Wynter asked, thinking that if every single one had to do their duty on their prearranged days of the week, then there would have to be well over a thousand to accommodate their visitors. That or, God forbid, they would be expected to see to more than one customer per day.

"A minimum of two hundred are here on any given workday," Marcus answered. "The schedule is staggered over the day to ensure they don't lose too much blood and allow them to get some sleep. It is an arduous schedule, but one easily managed once every employee gets through their probation and understands what is needed of them."

So, it had been the second of her two presumed arrangements. Wynter wondered what it'd be like to have to go from one vampire to another and letting them feed on her. Would she experience the same euphoria as before with each of them? Would that high make it all worth it? She remembered back to David's comment about how she'd want to come into work more than her scheduled hours. How she'd want to stay late and arrive early. Was he addicted to the rush, and that was why he felt that way? Was he more than willing to be someone's meal because he craved the feeling it gave him? Her instincts told her yes.

And then fear gripped at her gut. Had Marcus done more to her than just lure her in? Maybe he'd already arranged clients for her, and if so, she knew she had no hope of escaping them.

Wynter gulped and ran her hand over the small cut where Marcus had already taken her blood, and remembered shamefully she had been so damn willing.

She imagined having cuts like that all over her body and suddenly felt afraid.

"So on a Saturday and Sunday, I'll be scheduled to feed them too? Like you did with me a few minutes ago?" she asked and jumped in shock when Marcus turned his intense blue eyes on her and they were full of fury.

"Absolutely not, Wynter. Those Slaves are dirty and tainted. But not you. No…" he growled, "you were selected specifically because I wanted you myself. Each of my managers were chosen above all others because I was drawn to them for one reason or another. I made them the same promises I made you in my office and that I am making you now—no other of my kind will ever feast on your blood. You are mine and mine alone," he demanded, and the commanding power in his voice made Wynter tremble.

Was this really happening? Had he actually just said those words, the same ones the vampire anti-heroes in her stories always told the object of their affections? Wynter knew the answer was yes, but still, she wasn't completely sure she wanted his company in return. She was scared for him to want her so much. Scared to fail him or displease him. Terrified of not being good enough, or him changing his mind.

Maybe she should walk away before her probation was complete? It'd be easier to bear it if the loss was on her own terms, rather than suffer the shame of being cast aside.

Marcus watched her, and she wondered for a moment if he could read her mind because his frown only deepened and his eyes burned cooler. "You want to know if we can make this work? If you can actually live your life beneath my shadow?"

"Yes," she answered honestly, "and, why me? Why now? Why this way?"

"I told you earlier that I could practically smell you last night before you'd walked in the door," he told her, and Wynter nodded. "It's true. I could sense your desperation. Smell your despair. It was intoxicating."

"That's not exactly a compliment," she replied with a frown. It wasn't exactly how she'd imagined it. He could've complimented her in any way, and yet he was still honest to a fault.

"It isn't meant to be."

Marcus went to her and came to a stop just inches away. He then reached down and stroked her long chestnut hair around his deft hands. He curled a piece around the end of his finger before lifting it to his nose and breathing her in all over again. "My kind can sense emotions in ways humans cannot. I can taste your fear or excitement in your blood. I can smell your happiness or your despair. Like any other predatory creature, we have our likes and dislikes. And I simply adored it when a certain young woman turned up at my club, exuding hopelessness in droves. While hiding it well in front of everyone else in the room, there was no hiding it from me. I could sense you even from floors away and knew I had to have you. And now, you're mine, and I intend to make sure of it that you stay."

FOUR

Marcus's words left Wynter feeling even more disheartened. It was as if all her merits and skills had been overlooked in her hiring. And all because she'd simply had the perfect amount of despair and hopelessness that'd oozed out of her in waves so powerful a vampire had picked it up in an instant. Like a shark with the drop of blood luring it from the depths. She was his prey. His so easily procured new gift to himself. Even if he kept her alive for another sixty years and she died an old lady of natural causes, she knew she'd always be his.

Already, her future suddenly seemed inevitable. Two days every week for the foreseeable future, she was breakfast, lunch, and dinner to Marcus. Nothing more. She couldn't be, or else he would've told her so. He would've called her beautiful or sexy. He would've kissed her again and held her close, but instead he simply stood there, watching her come to terms with his awful announcement.

He sniffed the air and grinned at her, and Wynter knew she was giving off the exact scent he'd warned her was his favourite. He adored her sadness and even though she wished she could defy him; she couldn't stop herself from wallowing in her misery. And it wasn't like he was going to stop her anytime soon. After all, it was apparently what he liked about her so much, and right now, all those methods she used to hide her emotions away seemed to have gone completely out the window.

"So, what's the plan? How will our weekends work?" she eventually asked in a bid to pierce the heavy silence.

"Like I told you before, you're to remain here for the full two days. I will feed from you as I please and you're free to do some work or enjoy the time however you wish," he told her with his air of aristocracy Wynter figured had been perfected over many years, maybe even hundreds. "You don't have to remain by my side, but close by. Ready to serve me."

"And what if I refuse?" she asked, suddenly feeling brave.

Marcus beamed and let out a throaty laugh. He then fixed those icy blue eyes on her again and, without a word, had Wynter up on her feet and walking towards him with her hand outstretched and eager to feed him.

"As if you could try," he answered as he took her hand in his and lifted it to his mouth. Wynter thought he was going to bite her again, but instead he simply held it to his nose, soaking up her scent. He was right, of course, and Wynter felt a pang of rage spear in her gut. It was quickly replaced with adoration, but she knew now how that was fake. Merely masking her true feelings.

"Am I under some kind of a spell?" she enquired, thinking how no matter what, she'd still wanted him to taste her. Her fears had diminished the moment he'd lured her over, as had the shock at finding out vampires weren't only real, but also there in her city, and in her life. All she could think about was Marcus, and she felt her body gravitate towards him again. She'd soon pressed herself against him and was savouring his scent too while enveloping herself in it. In him.

"It's more of a curse," he whispered. He then ducked his head and offered Wynter a small kiss. "You gave your life to me the minute you signed the contract and sealed it with your blood. It was no accident, trust me, but then you were rewarded with a curse of my own creation. You're linked to me now. You will grow older as normal, but your life will only go on as long as mine does, plus you will serve me without question. Every natural survival instinct in you can be overridden by my need to feed, and should I decide to drain every drop of blood from your body, you won't even try to stop me."

Wynter wanted to scream and push Marcus away, but instead she grew hotter and was overcome with the desire to rip off his clothes and beg him to make love to her.

"I can sense what you need," she whimpered, realising how it wasn't she who needed to fuck, but her new master. She was emulating him. Mirroring his needs so that he might take from her what he so desired. "Do you sleep with your other managers, Marcus? Do you let them make love to you while you feed?"

Marcus pushed Wynter away as if she'd just offended him, and the moment the contact was broken, she felt ashamed for having been so brazen. It wasn't really like she'd been all that hot for him, but when their bodies had been pressed against one another's, it'd felt so right she hadn't been able to fight it. Like she'd wanted to offer everything on a plate to him, just as she had when it'd come to giving him her wrist to drink from. "I'm sorry," she tried, flushing hot with shame.

God, none of this was like her. Wynter had always separated work from all else, but here it was different. Marcus had cast his spell on her and while she wanted to maintain her distance, she simply couldn't.

"I absolutely do not fornicate with the others, Wynter. And I shan't with you either," he corrected her. "You're here to serve my one need and that

31

alone. The rest is off the table. I don't care who you sleep with, but make sure you do not propose such a preposterous notion to me again," Marcus then chastised.

Well, maybe if you weren't so gagging for it, I wouldn't have felt your desire, she thought, scowling over at him. Wynter wanted to say the words. She wanted to shame him like he had her, but she knew it wouldn't be worth the backlash. He would surely punish her for acting out, and she wasn't sure she was ready for it just yet.

"Hmmm," Marcus teased, grinning again as he inhaled the air between them deeply. "You're even more delicious when you're angry."

His remark had the desired effect, and Wynter was instantly riled. He wanted angry? She'd show him angry!

"Do you kiss the others like you kissed me then?" she demanded, unable to help it. Marcus shook his head no. "Then don't pretend you aren't interested in me sexually, and don't try to shame me for acting on the urges you've called up in me." She was pointing her finger at him and quickly dropped it. Where had this come from? She'd never dared tell one of her bosses off before and didn't know what to think anymore. She was disgusted both with her actions and the situation she'd found herself in. Too good to be true, she'd told herself before coming here. This job was turning out to be far worse than that!

"I do whatever I want, Wynter. If that means kissing you when I feel like it, then so be it. Just because I won't fuck you doesn't mean I wouldn't like to taste every part of you..." he countered. She flushed but forced it away, clinging to her rage. That was real, not the alternative. Not the desires still welling within her to creep closer. To touch him. To fuck him...

"But you'll only kiss me while you feed?"

"Of course. Why else?" he answered, closing the gap between them again.

Yeah, why else indeed, she thought, feeling dejected again. Wynter was about to pull back and attempt to walk away when Marcus seemed to decide against letting her go.

He moved the hair away from her neck and dipped his head is if to kiss her there, but Wynter was a fast learner and knew better than that. She could tell what was coming and sucked in a breath to steady herself, and it wasn't long before she felt that same sensation of razor-sharp shards cutting through her skin. As if a dozen tiny knives had just swiped her, the sharp sting was a shock, but was quickly replaced by euphoria.

Marcus drank deeply from the wound he'd made. She couldn't count the gulps this time as he took so many, and it was mere seconds before Wynter felt blissful again and as though she were drifting on clouds that made her entire body sing. She was also climbing a wave she knew all too well. One that usually ended in a crescendo of pleasure when she was with the right partner, and she began to pant, eager for her climax.

How could a bite feel so good and promise such a pleasurable culmination? But there it was, and it was building fast. She wanted the release so badly her entire being ached for it, but Marcus refused her yet again. He lifted his head right before she could explode with the strange release she was craving, leaving her so unsatisfied it hurt.

"No," he told her, evidently entirely aware of how she had been feeling. "Never."

Wynter wanted to demand to know why. She felt like shouting and begging for him to at least let her have her ecstasy, but he had told her no and her body obeyed even if her mind resisted.

He let her go and Wynter slumped against the desk, feeling woozy. It made sense, given the amount of blood he had to have just drained from her, and it wasn't long before she felt herself losing all strength in her legs.

She was fading fast, and so welcomed it, when Marcus lifted her into his arms and carried her from the office and back out into the hallway. She was a puddle in his arms, but it didn't matter. He had her held tightly against him. So close she could smell his scent. Like lavender and lemon. No, like roses and wildflowers. All her favourite smells wrapped in one.

Wynter watched as he ignored the few workers they passed on the way and she turned her head, not wanting them to see her so frail and in need of his help. She felt ashamed and embarrassed, and not just because of the sorry state she currently found herself in.

She was actually pretty ashamed of everything that'd gone on since she'd arrived at the club that afternoon in general and couldn't even begin to focus on processing it all.

The job wasn't worth this battle. She had to find a way to back out, and tried to tell him, but her voice came out as nothing more than garbled groans.

Marcus ignored her pleas as he took her back up to the top floor in the elevator to his huge office. There, he carried her a short while more before setting her down on a soft sofa that'd been laid out with cushions aplenty and a fur throw. "Rest now, Wynter. Sleep," he cooed, as if he cared.

She didn't have the energy to answer back though, and so just nodded and curled into a ball, snuggling into the warmth of the huge throw as the exhaustion of the day overwhelmed her and sleep carried her away.

The sun was low when Wynter awoke and it took her a few moments before she remembered where she was, and why she was sleeping in the daytime. She took a good look around in an attempt to get her bearings and groaned when the events of the day all came rushing back.

She sat up and looked around, realising how the entire fourth floor had to be extensions of Marcus's office. Then remembered how he'd returned them there after his last bite.

The living area had been sectioned off, and this part was set up like an apartment, with a kitchenette to one side and a bathroom beside it. She was in a kind of living area that connected them both, and then, on the opposite side of the room, sat Marcus at his desk. She could just about make him out because he was hidden behind a frosted glass wall that had offered her a little privacy while she'd slept, and Wynter was glad of that, if not much else.

She also wondered if this might be where she'd be expected to stay during the weekends when Marcus needed her close by to feed from and got her confirmation when she sat up and found an elegantly handwritten note on the table beside the sofa.

I trust you are well rested, Wynter. Please make yourself at home here. This is yours on a weekend, so help yourself to something to eat from the kitchen and use the facilities as desired, and then come to me. We still have much to do before six-pm arrives.
MC

Wynter did as he'd instructed and started by devouring a pre-packed sandwich she'd found in the fridge and two bottles of water, before washing up and brushing her teeth with the new toothbrush she'd figured had been left especially for her use. When she emerged, she heard Marcus talking to someone in his office area and took a few tentative steps over to where the glass wall separated them.

"I can still give you more, master. I'm perfectly well enough," she could hear someone saying.

"I know, Patrick. But that doesn't mean a thing when I can taste the death creeping in around you. There isn't long for you now, plus I have Wynter to serve my needs," Marcus replied coolly, and she heard the other man, presumably Patrick, give out a groan.

She decided against eavesdropping any further and so stepped through the open end of the glass wall and nodded in greeting to both Marcus and his guest. She realised right away what the problem was. The man was old. Probably in his mid-seventies, and yet it was evident he was one of Marcus's specially chosen few he fed from. One of his managers, or so he'd called them.

Marcus watched her with apparent intrigue, and Wynter felt her cheeks flush red beneath his powerful gaze. She wanted desperately to go to him, but knew it was his spell making her desire him so, and instead went to the other man and put out her hand for him to shake. "Speak of the devil. Patrick, I'd like to meet my new Marketing Manager, Wynter Armstrong."

"Good afternoon," she said, feeling relieved when Patrick shook it. "It's nice to meet you."

"And you," was all he replied before bidding them both farewell and heading for the lift to go back down, presumably to the third floor where their offices sat side-by-side.

"He doesn't seem too impressed that I've been recruited," she asked when he'd gone and she was alone with Marcus.

"He loves me, as do the other two," he replied with an air of nonchalance Wynter found amusing.

"Do you even care how much you affect them?"

"Them?" he countered, though not denying she was right. "You too, Wynter. You can feel it, can't you? The devotion you have towards me. The unyielding pull that gravitates you in my direction? The other employees feel this plus the raw and powerful euphoria a bite gives them with none of the strings attached because numerous vampires take them over and over, however you're afforded a single master. One solitary pull and one goal—to satisfy my needs. You'll come to love me too and, like I do with the other three, I'll let you. I'll even entertain your whimsy if the mood takes me."

"And how might you do that?" she asked, ignoring the nasty way he'd decided to describe the utter devotion three human beings had dedicated their lives to showing him. Instead, she decided to be selfish, focusing solely on the rewards she hoped to receive. "Money? Presents?"

"You'll see," he answered, giving nothing away. "I will readily give those things, but I can offer so much more as well. Money means nothing to me, Wynter. I have lived thousands of years and accrued power and wealth beyond anything a single human on Earth possesses. The only thing of worth is what runs in your veins, and I am willing to give you whatever you desire in order to obtain it."

"I don't doubt that," she told him honestly, "but what if I want something other than material things? What if I want my freedom or the chance to be loved in return?"

Marcus didn't answer, much to her annoyance. Instead, Wynter sensed him call to her and felt her feet start to move in his direction against her will. She was by his side in a couple of seconds and found herself staring down into those mesmerising blue eyes again. "Well?" she tried, earning herself a sly smile from her cruel boss.

"Sit," he commanded, and she looked around for a chair. There wasn't one. "Here," Marcus reiterated, pointing to the spot on his desk that sat right in front of him.

The desk was made from heavy old wood and was high. So high she had to jump up onto it and hitch her skirt a little, but Wynter did as he had commanded and was soon sitting directly before him atop the beast of a desk.

Marcus grinned and licked his lips as he moved closer. "Open your legs," he demanded, and Wynter quickly did as she'd been told.

Despite what he'd told her more than once already, a spark of hope rattled through her and she hoped that maybe, just maybe, Marcus was about to give her what she so powerfully craved. She felt like begging, but the devious smile curling at his lips told her he expected that. She imagined he was far too used to dealing with humans and their pitiful desires to care that he'd led her on while delivering nothing yet. Not a touch. Nor a single taste of him in return.

And now she was just one of the many who were under his spell. Well, the four in particular whom he favoured and yet never gave any part of himself to in return for their lifetime of servitude. Wynter thought it unfair. That deep voice inside of her reared itself and told her to run. To get away and invoke the power the probationary period gave her, if only she could find the strength to use it.

Wynter was about to try and snap her legs closed and jump down again, when Marcus lunged for her, seemingly ravenous for her blood again even though he'd already taken so much. With a hiss, he drew in a deep breath, and ran his palms across the insides of her thighs.

The moment his hands were on her, there was no need for him to pin her legs in place or still her. She obeyed his silent commands and leaned back, placing her hands flat on the desk behind while he lifted her skirt even higher.

He then took a quick glance at the clock on the wall to her right and she followed his gaze. They had ten minutes. Six hundred seconds and he'd have to leave her be for a few hours or else break his own rules. Wynter couldn't wait. She needed some space from Marcus already. Some time to heal and to rest. And of course, the chance to do the actual job he had brought her here for.

Marcus grinned up at her. "There's plenty of time," he said, before leaning down and closing his mouth over the inside of her right thigh. She felt the now familiar sting of his tongue against her flesh and the blessed wooziness his bite had delivered each time. Her high was imminent, and Wynter welcomed it as he drank, her body arching up off the desk involuntarily while Marcus continued to devour her. He yanked her towards him, deepening his bite, and she cried out as a wave of pleasure accompanied the pain.

The sudden 'ding' of the elevator then snapped her back to reality, and she turned to watch as a woman sauntered through the doors without a care. She had a stone-cold expression on her face but couldn't hide her surprise at finding their master still feeding just moments before their working day was due to begin. The woman didn't even seem to see Wynter. She was utterly fixated on Marcus and, like her, their intruder was panting and flushed with heat Wynter knew was resonating from within her, rather than from an outside source.

"Master," she whimpered, "it's almost time."

Marcus reacted quicker than Wynter could even comprehend.

One moment, he was still drinking from her, taking languid sips rather than deep gulps now, as though he were savouring every drop. And the next, he was across the room and he had the woman pinned to the wall by her throat. She was up off the floor, her stiletto heels more than two feet beneath her where she'd been yanked from them in Marcus's grasp.

The woman was choking and sputtering, but she didn't try and speak or fight him back. She simply let him do it, as though she knew she had done wrong and was more than willing to pay the price for her foolishness.

"There's plenty of time yet," he growled, "especially if there are no more interruptions."

Marcus dropped her and the woman then took off for the lift, which was thankfully lying open in wait from when she'd arrived. And all without even retrieving her shoes.

Wynter began to tremble and suddenly felt cold. She looked down at her thigh and saw that blood was oozing from the wound Marcus had made there. He had yet to close it, so her blood was pooling on the desk beneath her, making her head spin.

"M-m-m Marcus?" she sputtered, watching as a drop fell over the edge of the desk and onto the floor. The sight of the blood turned Wynter's stomach, and she felt her arms begin to give way beneath her. *No, don't pass out,* she told herself. *Stay alert. Stay strong.*

It was no use. By the time Marcus was back and he was cleaning her up, as well as the puddle on the tabletop, Wynter was losing consciousness fast and felt herself fall back on the desk. She turned her head to look at the clock and watched as the hour came to an end.

Three seconds to go… Marcus took his final draw and Wynter felt her body roar with heat.

Two seconds to go… With a dark laugh, he licked her clean and whispered about how she was such a lucky girl.

One second to go… Wynter exploded in an immense and unbridled climax that emanated from deep within her core and took her breath away. It was like a million fireworks were going off inside of her. Every nerve ending was alive and exploding with pleasure. But the most immense pleasure was where it mattered most. And all without him even having touched her.

By the time she'd come back down, six o'clock had arrived and Wynter was a wreck. She was hot and then cold. Light and then heavy. Awake and then being dragged into forced sleep. *No,* she thought. *I can't sleep now! I need to start work.*

But it was no use. It took her by force and without a care. Nothing but blackness and ice.

FIVE

Marcus watched Wynter sink into oblivion and then listened as her heartbeat slowed to a speed that was rather dangerous to her life, and yet he did nothing to rectify the situation. It intrigued him to see whether she'd survive her first day of work with him. Not even a day, in fact. Just a few hours in and she was already on the brink of death. What a fascinating little thing she'd turned out to be. He knew he should get to work, but he couldn't tear himself away. All he wanted was to watch her. To see the soft rise and fall of her chest as she breathed precious air into her lungs. To listen as her heart fought hard to keep on beating.

She was pale and beautiful. And his. The newest prized jewel in his crown.

Like all the others he'd ensnared to work for him, Wynter had succumbed to the curse her signature and blood oath on that piece of hexed paper had brought upon her, but she was still fighting his complete control over her, and Marcus liked it. The game was on, and he was more than willing to play. Even if that meant her calling his bluff here and there.

It had almost always disgusted him to so much as think of having sex with a human, but couldn't deny that when she'd propositioned him, it'd taken every ounce of his strength to refuse her. And now, when she'd climaxed just after he'd drunk more of her life force down, it'd broken him entirely. If Wynter hadn't passed out afterwards, he was sure he would've been inside of her a second later. Fucking her over his desk while the evening's work started beneath them, like some uncouth young fool who couldn't keep his dick in his pants.

But, thanks to whatever forces had taken her into the abyss of unconsciousness, he'd been saved the hassle of sex and intimacy. She would be sure to fall even deeper in love with him if he ever let her near his naked body, and the thought of her having the sort of power over him a lover instinctually possessed made Marcus want to strike her. But instead, he shut himself off to her lure. Forced himself to feel nothing at all. No rage. No lust. No desire. Only necessity.

His kind didn't fornicate with humans, anyway. Not unless they were planning to turn them into one of their kind and mate with them. That was their law. One he himself had helped the vampire elders write hundreds of years before when it was decided by all that he, along with a chosen few, would govern the lives of their immortal peers. The rules they created had been put into place and forcefully adhered to, even centuries later. The system worked, and so Marcus backed away from the sleeping woman atop his desk, lest he find her once again calling to him.

He instead plucked his phone from the cradle and dialled his assistant, whom he knew would have clocked in at six-pm sharp, and was undoubtedly already following up on his emails and admin. But tonight, he had another sort of task for him.

"Bryn," he barked when the young man answered. "Get one of the nurses and then come up here. And inform Joanna I will be visiting her office presently." Marcus hung up before Bryn even had the chance to respond but knew his subordinate would do exactly as he had instructed and without delay.

As he waited, he considered again how Joanna had dared come up and offend him so. His Finance Manager had pushed her luck by walking into his office unannounced and Marcus was still reeling from her foolish display of jealousy she had offered his new employee. He was going to see to it she knew to treat Wynter with nothing but the utmost kindness in the future and wasn't against delivering her a punishment or two to prove just how much he meant it. He had endured Joanna for long enough. Her undying love and reckless abandon when it came to offering herself to him. She had quickly become his most obsessive of the three managers and he'd always put it down to her girlish whims. He'd often left her to her fantasies, but after today, he was raging.

Marcus had gone so far as to entertain those notions of hers and encourage her to remain celibate because, as Joanna had always told him, if she couldn't have him, then she'd have no one at all. It had been a fun game to toy with her emotions and the consistently horny high she had never let herself come down from. But not now that she'd gotten above her station. Joanna needed to be put back in her place, and Marcus was more than ready to make sure of it.

Bryn, his scrawny but strangely strong assistant, arrived within mere moments of Marcus having ended the call, and as soon as he walked into the room, he took one look at Wynter's unconscious body on his desk and nodded. The boy had worked for Marcus for over ten years, and ninety per-cent of the time, he knew exactly what his boss needed and when, without having to ask. This was one of those times.

He lifted Wynter into his arms and took her back to the room behind where the glass partition would hide her from view. The nurse Bryn had enlisted followed him, and Marcus could hear them getting to work on making Wynter comfortable and hooking her up to an IV. She was going to be late in getting started on her real work, but really, he couldn't be angry.

Marcus knew he'd taken too much. That he should've shown more restraint, but she'd tasted too good. Even now, he could still taste her on his lips. Could still smell her blood from when it'd dripped down onto his desk.

It was intoxicating.

His eyes scanned the old wood, and he located the small smear of it she had left behind. With a grin, he then leaned down and licked it clean. He lapped at the remnants of her until it was all gone and then Marcus straightened, made sure his suit and tie were perfect, and strode to the lift. He then took it down one floor to where most of his minions worked.

It was time to get the working day officially started.

***

When she awoke, Wynter found herself back on the sofa, where she had napped a while before. This time, though, she woke with a pounding headache and a general sense of exhaustion that her short rest hadn't even remotely cured. Her arm also stung, and she looked down at it, discovering that an IV had been put in and a bag of fluids was being administered via it.

"Ah, you're awake," a new voice told her, and Wynter looked up to find a man standing guard over her by the open end of the frosted glass wall. "And alive."

Wynter took him in. He was tall and broad, and she could see in the dim light how he was older than her. Maybe in his early forties. He had dark hair with grey all down the sides over his ears and a warm enough smile that she didn't feel too threatened at waking up to find him there.

"Just about. Although I think our boss was going for the alternative," she croaked, and was pleased to see him chuckle at her lame joke. He might be another stuffy guy in a suit, but at least he appeared to have a sense of humour.

"No way. He hasn't lost an employee in more than twenty years, although it is unlike him to take three bites in such a short space of time. You clearly are his new favourite," the guy teased before dropping his smile and turning serious. "Mr Cole has had to step out on some business, but he asked me to watch over you and make sure you're okay. If I didn't know him better, I'd think he was concerned," he then added as he approached and took a seat on the chair beside her.

The notion that Marcus could possibly care intrigued her, but Wynter already knew better than to get her hopes up. Right now, she'd settle for just getting her arse up off that sofa without keeling over. She managed to sit and figured it'd do for now.

"I'm late for work, right?" she asked, looking out the window at the dark sky.

"Yeah, it's already after nine. You've been out of it a while," the man replied, but he didn't imply that she was in any trouble for it, which made her feel somewhat better. "I'm Jack. The HR Manager," he then told her. "Here to do my bit and make sure the humans are well cared for."

"Wynter, the new Marketing Manager," she replied with a small laugh.

"Oh, I know," Jack said with a sly smile, "you're quite the talk of the town this evening, Wynter. Hired on a whim and then took up the boss's entire afternoon since. Highly unusual. Plus, Joanna's in deep shit for coming up here unannounced and interrupting his feed."

Wynter gulped and cringed. So that was the woman's name.

"Will he punish her?" she asked, and then let out a groan when he nodded his head yes. "How?"

"Put it this way, our master happily drinks from us on our chosen days without much scheming or nonsense. He takes what he needs and only toys with us if he thinks we deserve it. But on the days we aren't his to have, he takes what he wants in other ways. And he isn't shy when it comes to making sure we remember who's boss. How much has Mr Cole told you about his preferences with his chosen Blood Slaves?"

"Mostly that, given the chance. He likes them desolate and full of despair," she answered.

"And terror. Fear is one of his most favourite tastes, and so he will instil it in Joanna in droves until he is satisfied she has learned her lesson."

"Poor woman," she whispered to herself, but Jack shook his head and leaned closer.

"She deserves it," he demanded, his face holding no hint of emotion. "She came up knowing that today was not her feeding day. She knew you were here and wanted to intrude so she could come between the pair of you."

"Why?"

"Because she loves him, of course," Jack sniggered. "We are both blessed and cursed to be his chosen ones, Wynter. The four of us are some of the only humans who get to have just one master. We're saved the humility of giving ourselves to one vampire after another and falling foolishly under their spells thanks to the power each one has to seduce humans into letting them feed. And all without so much as an afterthought about how they're left feeling once the feeding is over."

"I can't tell if we're lucky or not..."

"It doesn't matter. This life is what it is, and it's all you have to live for now. Patrick has worked for Mr Cole for more than fifty years. Joanna and I have been here for around twenty. We both fell in love with him before the end of our first week. You'll be the same."

"I hate how he can control us so much. How susceptible we are to his power," Wynter replied quietly, being careful in case they were being listened in on. "But at the same time, I crave his touch. I want him to bite me. I even propositioned him for sex."

Jack burst out laughing and then quickly put his hand up in apology, shaking his head as though she'd amused him beyond belief.

"I'm sorry, it's just that we each did it, too. You're not alone. That's the perfectly logical response to how he makes you feel, but just try to remember that it's not going to happen. He will never accept you for anything more than the blood you can give him. Your new friends here at the club can help satisfy those other needs and don't worry, he won't get jealous. I know he'd approve of his managers sticking together as well…" Jack informed her, and the look on his face told her he was more than interested in taking over whenever Marcus had gotten her all fired up and left her hanging.

Oh. So, Jack would be there after every bite to give her what he thought she needed. Sure. Such a selfless hero. She wanted to roll her eyes at his obvious come on.

But Jack was wrong. Marcus had given her something. He'd let her orgasm. Something he'd told her was never going to happen in his presence, and yet, it had. He'd told her to go elsewhere but then had still let that happen, and she couldn't fathom why.

"That's what Marcus said too," she eventually replied, feeling confused. "He told me I'm free to do what I want with whoever I want just as long as he gets his feeds on a weekend. But right now, the last thing I can think about is sex."

Jack's face turned cold and at first Wynter thought it was because she'd turned him down. She was about to give him hell for coming on so strongly at all, when he stood and walked back over to the glass wall as if to leave.

He stopped himself right before going through the opening and turned back to Wynter.

"He lets you call him by his first name?" he demanded, and it dawned on her how he'd referred to Marcus as 'Mr Cole' every time he'd spoken about him. And of course, how that woman from earlier, Joanna, had called him 'Master'.

"He introduced himself as such, so I called him by it," she answered defiantly. "I didn't feel the need to ask for his permission."

Jack seemed angry, but he quickly forced his rage aside and offered Wynter a look of concern instead.

"Please just be careful," he implored her, "it's all well and good being strong and defiant, but if you're not cautious, he'll get bored of it and suddenly all the fun and games go out the window. Hold your tongue, Wynter. Don't forget who you're dealing with."

"A vampire, I know," she bit back, and Jack shook his head.

"A creature older than the history books themselves. A being who roamed this Earth before man even came up with the concept of God or Satan. Death personified and with an evil streak that has resulted in stories which puts the old tales of heaven and hell to shame."

And with that bombshell, Jack apparently felt he had done his bit in taking care of Wynter.

He walked away, and she heard him take the lift downstairs, presumably to his office, leaving deafening silence in his wake.

SIX

When she felt up to it, Wynter carefully removed the line connecting the IV to her arm and placed some gauze and a plaster she'd found beside it over the tiny wound. She did feel better, thanks to the fluids, but still grabbed another bite to eat from the small kitchen area and helped herself to a tall glass of water before then taking the elevator down to the third floor.

There, she headed straight for her office, where she found a man sliding her name into what had been the empty space beneath her job title on the door. Marcus was overseeing the operation, and he grinned at her as she approached, eyeing her every move.

He didn't have to say a single word, just the headiness of being close to him almost knocked her off her feet. Wynter managed to keep it together in front of the workman, whom she thanked before ducking into her office, where she made sure her handbag and things from earlier were still safely located.

Marcus had an entirely different air about him when he joined her and closed and locked the door behind him. While Wynter still felt there was much they needed to discuss what he was and what he wanted from her, she realised quickly how there was a complete difference in their work time to their extra-curricular hours. There was a palpable change in the air, and she visibly saw as Marcus changed his tune when he spoke to her.

"It's unfortunate that you lost so much blood you were unable to start work on time, but at least I had longer to get everything ready for you," he offered, and Wynter rolled her eyes. He really wouldn't apologise, would he?

"You mean because you drank so much that I passed out? No need to apologise," she countered with a sly smile curling at her lips.

He didn't so much as rise to the bait, and simply took the seat beside her at the new desk and leaned over and fired up what looked like a brand new top of the range PC on her desktop. He made contact with her shoulder and she felt herself flinch thanks to his touch but wasn't entirely sure if it was with attraction or dislike. Her emotions were always in turmoil when it came to him, always conflicted, and she found it annoying how she could never truly decide how she felt about all of *this*. One thing was for sure, though, she couldn't feed him. Not so soon after what'd happened the last time.

"This is work time, Wynter. I won't ever ask you to take care of my personal needs during these hours. Trust me," he said, peering down at her with a softness to his stare that made her believe him. Wynter nodded and told herself to remember that promise at all times and make him stick to it. She was there to work, not to swoon over the boss or feel herself growing reckless thanks to his proximity and her new inherent need to feed him.

He seemed to sense her acceptance and smiled as he passed her the mouse. "I'd like to work closely with you tonight. If that's all right with you? Show you the ropes," Marcus then asked.

"It's perfectly fine," she answered, nodding a little too enthusiastically. "I've got a lot still to learn."

"That you do."

The two of them then spent a short while in front of the computer while Marcus showed her the real business he did inside his nightclub. It was a strict front for his bloodletting service. A complete cover business that not only employed hundreds of people, but, in turn, hundreds of his prized walking blood bags.

It was the perfect system, and Wynter knew that like all the others in Marcus's employ, she was just another source of food to him. One he had decided to favour above the others for some reason, but she was still expendable should he grow tired of her. Maybe Jack had been right to warn her.

After showing Wynter the real schedule for the upcoming week of member's only nights, Marcus stood and walked over to the window that looked down on the bustling club below. She caught him watching the crowd and couldn't help but want to ask him some more questions. It was her first day, after all, so she hoped he might afford her some extra time to settle in.

"Do you ever go down there?" she asked from her seat.

"Not at weekends, no," Marcus answered, still staring down at the crowd. "I can't stand the noise, or the smell. Filthy, sweaty humans all crammed into one space and writhing around against one another. Not my idea of fun."

"I always quite enjoyed it," she answered in a playful tone, and was glad to see Marcus picked up on it.

"I noticed," he said with a small laugh. And then, still without looking at her, summoned her to his side. Wynter felt him calling for her and stood without a second thought. When she reached him, she took his hand and let Marcus lead her in front of him so that she too was looking out of the window down onto the crowd with him pressed tightly against her from behind. "I've watched you more than once, Wynter. I've seen the men you took home with you. The short skirts and the carefree attitude. You were always just one step away from garnering my full attention, but then last night, you were truly broken. It was mesmerising."

He then brushed her dark hair away from her neck and leaned his head down to place a soft kiss against her neck. "But now that you're with me, you'll stay up here where it's clean and the men down there can't get their stink all over you. You will be cared for, here, Wynter. Where I can watch over you."

Wynter gave out a small sigh and tried desperately not to swoon over him but couldn't deny how Marcus sure had a way with words, and she knew she was falling further under his spell.

He didn't bite her this time, though, and she was glad he'd kept his promise. He'd already taken too much as it was. Even in her haze, Wynter knew it would be dangerous to lose more blood yet.

"I thought you didn't mix business and pleasure, Mr Cole?" she whimpered, her eyes on the glass but not watching the partygoers. She was watching him in the reflection. Lost in those bright blue eyes.

"I like to spend my time doing whatever I feel is entertaining," he answered matter-of-factly. "And usually, work is what entertains me the most. But not always." He pressed another kiss to her neck and Wynter felt a shudder go down her spine. She was scared that he was going to take more blood. To finish her off, but at the same time, everything inside of her was urging her to let him. It was the strangest sensation to be welcoming death with open arms, only as long as it was he who delivered it. "And please, call me Marcus," he added.

"Jack told me off for it," she informed him, but he just grinned against her skin and Wynter could tell he already knew. Perhaps he'd been spying on them? Or maybe his curse gave him insights into his underlings' doings, no matter whether they were near or far? "I got the feeling he was jealous."

"Yes, of course," Marcus agreed. He then lifted his head and stared back at Wynter in the reflection, his face serious. "The three other managers can be your best comrades here and worthy allies but be careful. Each is only looking to serve whichever purpose will ultimately get them closer to me. Their jealousy will drive them, not their integrity. Joanna was envious of you and tried to come between us. Patrick was resentful of you, so tried telling me it was too soon to have hired you. Jack is offended because he feels he and I have the strongest connection. As though we're friends, while I have always been nothing but business about our relationship. Don't trust them to have your best interests at heart. Only trust me. I will guide you."

Wynter turned to look up into Marcus's face and she frowned, thinking how odd it was that she trusted him at all after he'd lured her into the job under false pretences and then almost killed her, but she did.

It was the curse. It had to be. There was no one else she trusted like this.

No one else she cared for so strongly. Marcus was all that mattered…

"How old are you?" she asked him. "How did you become what you are?"

"Later," he said before stalking away, clearly not interested in divulging any more.

The moment the contact was broken, Wynter saw clearer. His power over her was strongest when they were touching. So strong it overrode every other thought and feeling she had. Marcus could say and do anything and she would let him, but when he was gone, her true thoughts were able to creep back in. Away from him, she knew better than to believe him or to blindly trust he was telling her the truth.

"No. I want to know now. I deserve to hear more," she demanded, shocking herself with the outburst, and instantly enraging Marcus. He was across the room in a flash, like she had seen with Joanna, and he had her by the throat in the same way a second later.

Marcus sneered down at her and shook his head.

"Keep fighting, little girl. We'll see who wins," he growled. "You want to know how old I am? Put it this way, you've been on this earth twenty-five years, and I have been on it three thousand years longer than you. I was born when the world was nothing and the people were soulless barbarians. Only the powerful survived, so I became a leader. A ruler. A man with more wealth than I could ever need while those around me begged for the scraps from my table."

Marcus then let go of her neck and forced her against the desk behind, his entire body pressed against hers. Wynter felt faint, but not thanks to any loss of blood or lack of oxygen. Marcus was overwhelming every one of her senses. Invading them one by one. "And when I was old enough to realise my days were numbered, I went to a shaman for help. He told me of the monsters that lurked in the shadows, feeding on the blood of the living to make them immortal. And so, I demanded he make me one of them. That he find a way to give me their immortality."

"And he did?" Wynter whimpered, her eyes wide with shock and awe.

"He did," Marcus confirmed. "I offered him and his kin my protection and untold riches in return for his gift. Those from his bloodline remain by my side to this day, and theirs is the power that hexed you this afternoon. They bound your life to mine and made you my perfect little slave."

His wicked grin irked her, but Wynter was instinctually calm. His spell was overriding every other response, thanks to his body still being pressed against hers, and so she found a stray independent thought and grasped at it.

"If I was a slave, you wouldn't have had to force me to give you anything," she countered, her smile matching his. "When, in fact, you're the one who just gave me what I wanted, Marcus." Wynter then arched her back, pressing herself against him tighter, and she could feel his hard body beneath his three-piece suit. "And yes, I will keep fighting. Even if I don't win, it'll be worth it just to know I'm getting under your skin a little."

SEVEN

Damn, she was right. Wynter had just gotten her own way despite him having told her no, and while Marcus was impressed, he was also livid. It took everything he had not to strike her or force her on her knees and to submit to him.

"One-nil to Wynter then," he simply said, leading her to believe the matter was over with when it wasn't even remotely. He would win. He always won. Marcus would not allow her to have any kind of victory over him and decided he would see her fall from that pedestal she had placed herself upon by the time she left his club and went home after the following night's shift.

As if on cue to break their tense silence, his mobile phone buzzed in his pocket and he stepped away, leaving her there, looking shocked and more disheartened than victorious. The look on her face left him wondering, had she meant what she'd said? Or was she just toying with him? If so, Wynter was soon going to learn that no one played games with him. Quite the opposite.

He pressed his phone to his ear and heard Bryn's voice come across the line.

"Sir, your input has been respectfully requested in the design department. The heads have called a meeting to finalise the upcoming Christmas themed special events," he said.

"I'll be there in two minutes," he barked before ending the call and turning back to Wynter, who had sorted herself out and was now fiddling with the items on her desk awkwardly to busy herself.

He made to leave but decided he would instead take the opportunity to introduce her to some of the other employees. "Come, Wynter," he commanded as he opened her door and strode through it.

She followed without hesitation, and he smiled to himself as he watched her lock the door behind them. She'd remembered his order without needing to be reminded. Clever girl.

They then walked down past the elevator doors and through to the reception desk that led into the rest of the huge building Marcus called both work and home. He barely left the premises other than to go to his other clubs around the world and adored the domain he had built for himself in the city he now called his. He revered this building too. It had been nothing but an empty shell of an old warehouse when he'd taken possession of it, and he had built the offices up around the centre that'd been purposely constructed to create a hollow space in the middle. It doubled as a completely private dance floor on a weekend and veritable cattle market during the week.

The heads of his workers all turned up in greeting as he passed them. Marcus knew every one of them had sensed his arrival and it wasn't long before he started to feel aware of the all-consuming desire they each had to serve him. To worship at his feet like the God he was. He ignored them all. They were nothing but fodder. A product he sold to the highest bidder without a care.

He stopped only when he and Wynter had reached the offices where the design team were situated, and he paused to open the door and allow her through it—like a true gentleman.

She thanked him and went in ahead, where they found ten humans eagerly awaiting Marcus's arrival.

She didn't need to introduce herself or tell any of them why she'd come along to the meeting. Even without Marcus by her side, the news of their new manager had spread among the teams and she was the only new face there. By process of elimination alone, they would know it was her who had completed his elite team.

"Good evening, Mr Cole, Miss Armstrong," his Head of Design greeted the pair of them.

"Good evening, Marcella," he answered, and Wynter imitated him. "As you're aware, Wynter here is still settling in, but I thought it pertinent that she meet your team and see what it is you're working on."

"I agree, sir," Marcella replied, ushering them both forward. "Please, come and take a seat and we will begin showing you the final concept for the winter designs."

He did as she had asked and shook his head when Marcella offered him his usual tea—a concoction of his managers' blood and hot water tinged with spices.

"I've already been well fed, thank you," he told her, and then revelled in the team's reaction as they all turned to look at Wynter. She turned her gaze away and immediately tried to hide the small scratch marks on her neck and wrist, only serving to draw attention to them. The flush on her cheeks was positively delightful and the scent of her shame only added that bitter edge to her scent he so adored.

He wanted her again already. How was that possible? He never took so much.

The members of the design team each continued to watch Wynter as they took a seat with them. The group was silent, but she accepted a coffee with a shy smile, and then she seemed to steel herself and sat higher in her seat. She'd clearly told herself to be more self-assured.

Marcus had to wonder if she had just given herself a mini pep-talk and got his answer when Wynter got stuck in with Marcella and the team, watching as they played some slides outlining the colour scheme and décor that were going to be used once the autumn campaign was over with. She jotted down a few notes and took charge, while Marcus remained silent until the end, when he simply offered his approval and then stood. He was acutely aware of the time and how much of the night he had wasted flirting with and focusing solely on Wynter. They had all the next day to talk about those parts of the job still playing on her mind, so he knew it was time he said goodbye. He needed to head back upstairs and finish the evening with Bryn before she came to him again. "Very well," he said, nodding to Marcella.

Next, he turned to Wynter and indicated for her to join him, which, of course, she did. They then left the meeting room and when they were alone, Marcus turned to her and lifted a hand to halt her in her tracks. "Stay here. I have work to tend to in my office. I'll send David down to collect you and show you to the IT department. You'll undoubtedly be spending a great deal of time with the engineers there, so it is important you meet them sooner rather than later."

"Okay," she whispered, looking sad at having to part from him, and Marcus was glad to see it.

"Come to me at two-am. Not a minute later," he added, and could sense her anticipation at being there to satisfy him again. It was invigorating, and he wanted to stay longer and enjoy her some more, but he forced his own reactions aside before turning and stalking away.

***

As Wynter watched Marcus leave, it felt oddly bittersweet. Nice to have some time away from that power he had to drive her insane, though. She didn't seem to know what she wanted first but was filled with the desire to please and serve him when in his company, so much so that she was having trouble focusing on her actual work. His leaving was also awful though, because try as she may to fight it, she was so incredibly drawn to him.

The other members of the design team then began to file back out of the room she had just left, and she turned back to them all with a polite smile every one of them returned. The red-haired woman in charge of the team, Marcella, was last out and Wynter fell in line beside her, thinking how they'd seemed to get on well before and that she was looking forward to seeing more of her and the others as they began to work on new marketing strategies in the future.

"So, how are you finding things?" Marcella asked when they were alone in her office and she'd grabbed them both a bottle of cool water from a small fridge beside her desk.

"Good," Wynter answered honestly after she accepted the drink and thanked her. "Strange though, and freaky at times, but still good. I love my office and the job is turning out to be perfect."

"It's just the blood feeding thing that's still taking a bit of getting used to?" Marcella then enquired with a knowing smile.

"Yep!" she replied, laughing at how easily the subject of being drained had slipped into conversation, and how she had hit the nail right on the head. It felt good being so open and honest with someone, like there might be a friend here for her after all.

"Trust me, you'll be over all of that before too long. It's not human nature to simply accept the supernatural, but before you know it things will feel easier. It'll come without a fight. We all go through this in that first week, but no one ever leaves."

"I hope you're right," Wynter answered honestly, "because as it stands right now, I don't even know which way is up, let alone what I want."

"At least you just have one master to satisfy. Me and the others can have up to ten a day. They use their powers to control our emotions and feed from us while working up that frenzy inside, leaving each of us so empty and alone in the aftermath it's often painful," Marcella blurted out, and while she was shocked, Wynter also found she wanted to hear it. She needed to know the truth, no matter how rough. "I hated them at first, but now I crave the seduction of the bite. I look forward to my overtime days because it's empowering, knowing I have something they need to survive. That without me, they'd go hungry. I have also learned to go and take care of the desires within me with the other Blood Slaves after it's over."

It was refreshing to hear about it so candidly from another human, and Wynter was glad she'd hung back to chat with Marcella more. She liked how direct she was.

"The bite works you up into such a sexual peak, doesn't it?" Wynter replied, feeling glad it really seemed to be the same for everyone. "I was utterly desperate for him to take me. It was embarrassing! Do you get together with others doing overtime and use the private rooms on the first floor afterwards?"

"Yep. Anywhere we can get a little privacy, really. Before I came to work here, I was reserved when it came to casual sex, but now, it's just another part of my working week. In many ways, it's horrible to have that reaction to their bite, but in others, it's freeing to let yourself explore your sexuality with others who need it just as much as you do. I can't imagine what it must be like for those who are in relationships and have to wait until they get home. Or those who are celibate, like Joanna," Marcella told her.

"She's celibate?" Wynter asked incredulously.

"Yep. So, in love with Mr Cole that she refuses to take anyone else to her bed. I've only been here a few years, but apparently she's grown worse as time's gone on. I think it's because she's getting older and he still won't have her. People have seen her coming out of his office in tears after repeatedly throwing herself at him during his feeds. Poor thing."

Wynter actually felt sorry for Joanna. She knew that feeling all too well and had only had to endure it a day, let alone for twenty years. Marcus was a tease, though. He knew exactly what he was doing and had told her himself that he loved breaking their hearts. He had been teasing Wynter in the office just before they came to the design brief, and something told her he would continue doing so when she went to him in a couple of hours to begin her second day of overtime.

"I've got a horrible feeling I'm going to end up going the same way. I can already sense him creeping in under my skin. Wooing me with no intention of seeing it through."

"My advice? Don't fight it. It's easier if you just give in," Marcella replied despondently and while Wynter could understand it, she still didn't want to succumb so easily. She wanted to keep fighting. To figure out a way to refuse him. To keep some of her own thoughts and feelings safe and to not always give in.

A sharp knock on the door ended the conversation, and Wynter was glad she hadn't had to answer Marcella's final comment. Her brain was in turmoil, and she wasn't sure she could trust her enough yet to tell her all the gory details about her feelings for Marcus, or the strange back and forth they'd had so far. She'd keep her thoughts to herself, at least until she knew who she could and couldn't trust among her new work colleagues.

After a second, one of the men who'd attended the design meeting popped his head around the door and directed his attention to Wynter.

"Sorry to interrupt, Miss Armstrong. David Tyler is here to escort you at Mr Cole's request," he said, and seemed pleased when Wynter nodded in understanding.

"Yes, thank you. Please let him know I'll be out in a second," she replied, and then turned to Marcella to wish her goodbye. "Thank you for making me feel so welcome. I'm sure I'll be able to come by and see you again soon."

"I don't doubt it. And me too, Wynter. It was a pleasure meeting you," she said with a smile that seemed genuine enough. She had a youthful face and was pretty too, but not just on the outside. She had the sort of eyes that lit up when she smiled, revealing warmth beneath the surface. Wynter felt safe in her company and hoped she was right to.

She left and found David waiting out in the small group office for her. He seemed strangely on edge and awkward when he greeted her, and led the way without a word, which wasn't like him. He'd chatted loads during her tour and wasn't the shy or retiring type.

"What's eating you?" she demanded when they were alone and waiting for the lift, and David waited until they were safely inside before answering.

"I wasn't sure if you'd be angry with me for having been the one who lured you here. I hope you know I had to do it. Mr Cole isn't someone I could refuse. When he told me to go get you, there was no alternative. And when you refused his advances, he commanded I get you back here by whatever means necessary," he said, his face pale and his light hazel eyes unable to meet hers.

In the cold light of day, she could understand why David was so worried. If he hadn't told her the things he had or made her believe this job was worth it, then she would've been saved the fate that'd now befallen her and taken over her life. Wynter would've been free. Still skint and panicking about the state of her life, but free nonetheless.

David hit the button marked 'B' and the lift began to descend.

She watched him in silence, still fighting her inner unrest. But it was true. He was to blame. It didn't matter that he was cute and sweet and trustworthy. He had delivered her to the monster who'd sealed her fate, and now that she thought about it, she was angry.

Wynter stepped forward and struck him across the face as hard as she could manage. David was clearly shocked by her lashing out like she had, but he took it without even looking like he wanted to hit her back. And as if he was actually glad she'd decided to punish him. "I'm sorry. I never wanted to be the one, but he knew."

"Knew what?" she cried.

"Knew I liked you. He saw me looking at you on the camera and chose me to be the one to approach you at the bar. After you'd point blank refused to go upstairs and meet him, he told me to flirt with you and make you feel good. Make you want to come back. And it did, didn't it?" David replied with a frown.

Wynter stared into his sad eyes and nodded.

"Yeah. You worked me over all right, and… you like me?" she asked, her anger turning into something else entirely. Something carnal and raw. A need that Marcella had reminded her was completely her choice in whether to tend to, and that it had nothing to do with their vampire boss who she chose to enlist into helping her. Marcus had preyed on her weaknesses and sent his errand boy to do his dirty work. The coward. He'd dragged her into this world of his and almost killed her once already, and so Wynter decided she would do whatever she wanted when it came to blowing off some steam. Marcus didn't want her, so she would find someone who did. Someone who just so happened to be standing two feet away.

She stepped closer and pinned David to the mirrored wall of the lift. They only had seconds, surely, but she didn't care. Wynter planted a kiss against his lips and delighted in the groan David gave her as he returned it. Their lips were still locked when the elevator doors opened again and Wynter forced herself away and out of them in case someone was there waiting and would catch them. They were blissfully alone, and so David kissed her again, deeper this time.

"I want you so much," he whispered against her lips, "I want to give you everything you need."

"Do you have a place?" Wynter asked, and David simply nodded before leading her a few doors away to a small bathroom. He locked the door behind them and watched her with hungry eyes. "Protection?" she asked, and he shook his head no.

"There's no time. Just let me take care of you, Wynter. We'll be together another day," he answered, watching as she jumped up onto the counter beside the sink and opened her legs without a care. This wasn't her first time getting off in a bathroom. It wasn't romantic or seductive, but she was sure he would do the job nicely and if he wanted to make it quick, then that was fine, too.

David's lips were back on hers a second later and his hand was between her legs almost immediately afterwards. He then pushed her knickers aside and played with her clit a little before sliding two fingers deep inside. "So ready for it," he groaned and then ducked his head down to suck on the bud still swollen and, like he'd said, so ready. David's fingers worked fast while his mouth delivered glorious pressure where she needed it most. Wynter was quickly writhing against him and pressing the back of his head towards her core. He let her command him and sucked harder, his hand still pumping in and out faster than she could ever manage when home alone with her dirty thoughts and desires. Wynter came in a hurry and was glad when he didn't stop. There was more to be had, and she was ready for it. The second orgasm was even deeper, and it had her crying out for him with unashamed passion and appreciation for how he had chosen to make things up to her.

"We can definitely do that again sometime," she murmured as he backed away and wiped his mouth clean with a delighted expression on his handsome face. Wynter then hopped off the counter and straightened her clothes before checking out her reflection in the mirror. She was rosy cheeked and wearing a look of utter satisfaction she couldn't hide, but she didn't care. It felt too amazing to have let off some of that much needed steam.

"We'll definitely be doing that again, Wynter. And more," David replied with a dashing smile, and she nodded. Nope, she was sure not going to argue with that.

EIGHT

Wynter only had an hour until she had to be back upstairs, so once she and David had made themselves presentable again, he checked the coast was clear and then led her all the way down the corridor to where a door would let them inside the offices of the IT team. They had almost the entire basement level for themselves, and it quickly became apparent why when the pair of them were buzzed through the security door and found no less than thirty men and women working furiously at the first line of desks, while others were running around maintaining the vast number of servers and other equipment that made up the huge mainframe for Marcus's business.

She peered down the enormous floor and could see rows and rows of the electronic towers, and it wasn't hard to notice the cool and carefully sustained temperature in the room. It was the perfect hub, and beyond anything she had ever seen before. Wynter realised incredibly quickly how there had to be an immense amount of data stored here. What she was looking forward to finding out was why.

The open-plan room itself was bustling and chaotic. There were people everywhere, and they were all rushed off their feet. David came to a stop next to a glass partition where one lone worker had some privacy. He had to be the head of the team, and Wynter looked through into his makeshift office to find the guy pacing up and down while bellowing into the speaker on his desk. Whoever was on the other end didn't have a chance if his body language was anything to go by, and she found herself watching him for a few seconds before she tore her prying eyes away and focussed instead on the others close to them.

A few of the IT personnel were standing a few feet away around a piece of equipment they'd stripped down and were evidently trying to fix. By the sounds of it, each engineer had a different idea of how to do it and was willing to argue their case profusely. It made for interesting listening, and Wynter found herself intrigued.

She went over to look and found they all fell silent.

"Yes, I'm the new girl," she joked, offering each of them a smile and an awkward wave. "What are we arguing about?"

"Well, I told Palmer over there not to open the tower because we might be able to claim it as still under warranty, but he went ahead and did so anyway," the woman beside her answered after a tense pause. Wynter nodded and looked at the man she had said was called Palmer.

"But it's lapsed, so I went ahead and opened the tower up. The motherboard is fried and was defective. We know that much. Phoebe just doesn't want to admit that I was right to look deeper," Palmer retorted.

"And what does Mr Chalmers say?" Wynter asked, recalling the Head of IT's name from when she'd looked at the list of employees on Marcus's vast list.

"He says to bin the bloody thing and buy a new one. It's in the budget," came a deep and booming voice from behind them. They all turned to its owner and Wynter found the man she had seen pacing the small office standing with his arms folded and his shoulder leaning against the far wall.

He looked mean. Like someone she wouldn't want to cross in a hurry. He was wearing a suit, but didn't seem too impressed about it, given that his shirtsleeves were rolled up to reveal his heavily tattooed arms, and his tie had been discarded. It didn't look right on him. He seemed like he'd be more at home in a checked shirt and a pair of jeans. The dark beard that covered his jaw was thick, as were his eyebrows and lashes, the impact of them hiding his face behind their dominating features.

"Sounds like a good plan to me. I second Mr Chalmers's decision," she answered with a smile. "I'm Wynter Armstrong," she then said, after bidding the others goodbye and walking over to join him.

"I know," he answered coolly before turning on his heel and going back into his office. She followed, as did David, but he was quickly shooed away. "She doesn't need any guarding here, Davey. I'll see to it she gets back to the boss on time."

David left, but begrudgingly, Wynter could tell. She offered him a gentle, appreciative look and was glad when he returned it, before he sent a scowl in her host's direction and shut the door behind him.

Chalmers watched him go and then peered across at Wynter. After a beat, his expression softened a little, but he still seemed aloof. "So, how can I help? And please, call me Warren."

"Well, firstly, I wanted to come down and say hello. I gather we'll be working together a fair amount and I figured it'd be nice to see where all the geeks hang out," she answered with a soft smile she hoped might thaw him.

Warren simply shrugged and fixed his dark eyes on hers, but Wynter didn't look away. He was large and heavy set, plus his demeanour was incredibly standoffish, but she wasn't about to back down. It felt like he was trying to intimidate her. Establish dominance.

Marcus had told her to keep on fighting, though, and she sure was going to. She was his superior, after all. "And, I have a request."

Warren sat back in his chair, rolled his shoulders, the material of his shirt stretching over his impressive array of muscles. Wynter got the feeling he was trying to show off his body in another bid to distract her, so she kept her eyes on his, rather than ogle at his muscular physique, like she guessed all the other women around the place often did. It wasn't that there was anything wrong with him, of course. There was plenty to look at, but she knew she needed to keep things purely focussed on the job if she had any hope of fitting in with Warren and his team. Plus, it helped that Wynter had just been satisfied moments before meeting him. Good old David and his magic touch.

"Fire away," he eventually answered when he saw he wasn't getting any reaction from her. She finally looked away and eyed up his filing cabinets before then focussing back on him.

"Well, everywhere I've been today, people seem to know who I am and the job I've just been given to do here. That's great and all, but I need to know where I stand, and I'm guessing there are some here who will know more about my private life than others," she said as she took a seat opposite him at the desk. "I'd be flattered, if it weren't for the fact I know you have a dossier on me somewhere down here. I'd like it destroyed please," Wynter added, making it clear that this was not just a request, but also an agreement between the pair of them. A way of creating a foundation of trust. If Warren kept her private life away from prying eyes, then she would always know she could trust him, and she would be sure and make the same show of faith in return.

She needed as many allies as she could get and was willing to do whatever it took to get them. That way, should anything go wrong, anyone who tried to take her down would face an army of loyal comrades—or whatever analogy better fit the predicament she'd now found herself in. Wynter was going to watch her back, and certainly wouldn't let people like Joanna ever get her into trouble should her jealousy get the better of her judgement.

"Sure," Warren agreed, breaking her reverie. "I did the work myself. Top priority, as per Mr Cole's request. I'll admit it was an interesting read, Wynter."

"Hmm, I bet," she answered, but figured she didn't really have anything to hide, so still wasn't too upset about the whole thing. It was good to know that only one person had worked on it, though. And that she was looking right at him.

Warren seemed to relax then, as if he had sussed her out and was satisfied. She was about to say something more when a wide smile crept over his face and he leaned forward. He finally dropped the grumpy guy routine, and Wynter appreciated the new view far better than the man she'd seen so far.

He finally appeared real, and she not only relaxed a little herself, but she let her walls drop a bit too. "So?"

"I'll delete the lot, but only if you tell me honestly, did you really date the Prime Minister?" he asked, shaking his head when she nodded hers. She had indeed. "No way! Before or after he was elected?"

"Not long before," she answered. "We started it up when I was at university. He was in his final year when I'd started my first. He spotted me at a fresher's party and offered to show me the ropes…"

"Yeah, euphemism much," Warren joked, and Wynter nodded. "What's he into?"

"Vanilla mostly. We did have a threesome with some Earl's son, though."

"Nice!" Warren replied with a snort that showed his geeky side. He seemed genuinely impressed by her story, and Wynter was glad they had developed such a quick rapport. She had the feeling she was going to enjoy working alongside the burly nerd.

He then turned serious and dropped his voice, watching her with his dark brows knitted together. Warren looked like he might be about to say something, but then stopped himself, as though he were trying to find a way to be both honest and tactful. And then he finally spoke, his voice softer and quieter than she'd expected. "You understand what you're getting yourself into by working here, right?" he eventually asked.

"I think so," Wynter replied with a shrug. "Marcus has been gentle, so far, but I'm really just looking forward to doing my actual job. I've never been recognised for my real talent before. Never been allowed in the big boys' club. But now, I'm hoping all of that is going to change."

"Oh, it is," he answered with a grim expression. "You're going to get everything you've ever dreamed of, Wynter, but only if you're willing to pay the price to get it."

"I am. I can do it," she replied, showing him no fear, because actually, she no longer felt any.

"Good," he said, his smile creeping back in. "And when that bloodsucker is finished with you, you come and see me and my guys. We'll look after you."

Wynter was about to groan and tell yet another sleaze to back the hell off when Warren picked up on how his comment had sounded and quickly corrected himself, much to her appeasement. "And by that, I mean we'll feed you and give you somewhere safe to rest. We'll make sure no one comes creeping while you're coming down from the bite. You're a manager. One of the boss's favourites and so a prime target now, Wynter. The perfect notch on any of the losers' belts that work in this godforsaken club, but we don't work that way down here. We take care of our own by keeping the wolves locked away outside."

"And I'm one of your own?" she whispered, suddenly feeling a little overwhelmed at the thought of having such a great team to work with.

"Damn right," he replied, and then checked his watch. "And it's clocking off time for you soon so that can mean only one thing—Mr Cole is going to need you back upstairs."

NINE

Marcus watched Wynter on one of the numerous video cameras he'd had installed around the building. There wasn't a single place where someone could hide from him, not even in the bathrooms. After all, that was where all the good stuff happened, wasn't it? It certainly had a couple of hours earlier when Wynter had taken David up on his most generous offer of making things up to her.

It had been a pleasure to watch. A sight to behold, Wynter had sat atop that counter with her legs wide and her body on show. What wasn't to like? And, of course, it wasn't like Marcus was going to do anything but continue to watch her. Yes, she was beautiful and sexy and certainly alluring, but she was also a bit awkward, and she liked to joke around. He had no time for nonsense like that.

There was still nothing about that young girl which made him want her for more than her blood. But then, why was he more than ready to call David up to his office and snap his neck like a twig for going near her? It wasn't like he cared. He was a three-thousand-year-old vampire, he didn't get jealous.

Marcus turned his attention back to the array of footage options he had in his sights and clicked on the elevator, watching as Wynter took it up to the third floor and disembarked. He checked his watch. Still five minutes to go. Five minutes and he could feed. He was more than ready. His body was aching for the nourishment she was going to bring him. He could taste her already. Smell her.

He drew a deep inhalation and realised he could still smell her scent from his desk. Not the subtle tones from far away, but close by. Wynter had left part of herself behind.

Marcus's senses immediately heightened and his adept nose found the source if the scent within a second. He stood and then crouched down on the floor before kneeling and pressing his nose to the ground beneath his desk. There it was. The single drop of blood that'd dripped down from her perch atop his desk. It had dried, but that didn't stop his tongue from darting out and taking back what was his.

Satisfied for now, Marcus then stood and made sure his suit and shirt were perfect. That his hair didn't have a single strand out of place. Everything had to be perfect, as usual.

And then he walked to the elevator, where he stood and waited for Wynter to arrive.

***

"Shit, shit, shit," Wynter groaned as she jumped in the lift and hit the button marked with a number four. It was bang on two-am and she knew she had just one minute to get up to Marcus's office and be ready to feed him. She'd cut it close. Too damn close. It wasn't even Warren's fault, either. She'd decided to check her phone and had to answer a string of messages from her friend Cossette and the time had just run away from her.

Ding! The elevator chimed, marking her arrival. Wynter checked her watch again. She still had thirty seconds and so let out a sigh. She was going to be okay.

The doors then opened to reveal her master. He wasn't sat at the desk like she'd imagined, but instead he was standing right beside the lift doors like he was either about to get in with her or he was lying in wait, ready to yank her out the second she arrived. Wynter wasn't sure which one he was going to go with, so she just stepped forward and smiled.

"Good morning, Marcus."

"Right on time, Wynter," he answered and then offered her his hand, which she took and let him lead her into the private area behind the glass partition she'd been in a few times now. It felt odd being so at ease with him, someone she barely knew and yet had already shared so much with. And yet, she clung to the hand he'd graciously let her hold, like it was the most precious thing on Earth. Marcus came to a stop beside the bathroom door. "I'd like you to take a shower."

"Sure," she answered, figuring it wasn't an unreasonable request. She'd been there almost an entire day already and was feeling a bit icky herself, so welcomed the chance to get freshened up. "Do you have products for me to use?"

"Everything you need is in the cabinet, plus I have clothing I'd like you to wear for me afterwards. Your work clothes will be washed and pressed ready for this evening," he replied with a smile that both terrified and beguiled her. She suddenly wanted to kiss him. To have his arms around her and his lips on her neck. His tongue lapping at her vein…

Wynter forced those thoughts away and knew she was only thinking them because of Marcus's power to control her and make her believe that was what she wanted, when in fact, she didn't. Not really. It took every ounce of effort she could muster, but Wynter steered herself away and instead opened the door to the bathroom.

She then walked into the huge room and was surprised when Marcus followed her in. "Undress," he commanded when she turned to look at him inquisitively.

She did as he'd asked and was even more shocked when he mirrored her actions.

As she slid off her jacket, Marcus did the same.

When she unbuttoned her blouse, he removed his shirt, and so on.

Wynter couldn't keep her eyes off him. Yes, he had that distinguished look about him on the surface, but beneath the suit was the body of a god. He was slim and perfectly toned, and his skin was impossibly smooth. She desperately wanted to touch him, but kept her hands to herself, remembering her shame from before when she had dared try to seduce him. She was learning, or so she hoped, and tried not to make any more of a fool of herself.

When he was completely naked, Marcus then walked further inside the bathroom and turned on the overhead shower jets. And that was when Wynter noticed how it was a twin shower. Two heads were built into the ceiling and water cascaded down from them so that two people could shower side-by-side and still have their own space, rather than be squashed into one cubicle like she'd been used to in the past.

The two of them entered at the same time, and Wynter hissed as the icy cold water hit her. She jumped out of the spray and glowered at Marcus, who was already standing under his own cold stream, seemingly without a care for the shocking temperature.

"Don't mind the cold, huh?" she groaned, whacking the heat up on her controls. Marcus peered out at her from beneath his wet lashes and grinned.

"I feel nothing, Wynter. It surprises me you still need reminding," he said, but she didn't believe him.

"Liar," she replied as she grabbed the shampoo and got to work on soaping up her dark brown hair. She then rinsed and opened her eyes, going in search of the conditioner, but instead found the face of her master just inches away. She went to jump back, but Marcus grabbed her and pulled her to him, crushing her against his chest.

"I have no heart, no conscience, and no soul," he growled. "What makes you think I feel a single thing other than the desire to fulfil my need to survive?"

She still didn't believe him. Bravery reared its head inside of her again and before she could stop herself, her thoughts came tumbling out of her mouth.

"If you were a heartless monster, then you'd never have created this business. You like to be entertained, Marcus. You have a need to facilitate in the survival of your own kind, but rather than create farms full of humans to expedite the bloodletting, you chose to create an empire. A place for hundreds of us to come and worship you. If you felt nothing, then you wouldn't need power or your cult following of humans under your spell. You'd simply take and take and take without a care."

Marcus let out a growl, and he thrust Wynter against the cool tile wall, moving her as though she weighed nothing at all. He closed the gap in a millisecond and bared his teeth when she dared to smile. She knew it was stupid to antagonise him, and yet, she couldn't seem to help it. "Did I hit a nerve? One you apparently don't have?" she teased, but knew she was pushing her luck.

Wynter hadn't known what'd come over her saying those things, but something just kept on snapping within her, and she couldn't help but bite back, so to speak. She knew it'd get her in trouble, but she didn't care. Just as long as it meant she'd keep some of her independence, she was willing to keep pushing him and decided she would take Marcus's punishments. Or at least she hoped she could.

He stared into her eyes as if he was looking into her soul, and Wynter was shocked to find he didn't appear to understand her at all. Marcus seemed lost and confused in that moment. Like he had no idea how to react. One second, he looked like he wanted to throttle her, and the next, he seemed like he was about to kiss her. Maybe even more.

Their naked bodies were against each other's, after all.

Strangely, though, Wynter didn't feel horny for him just then. She wanted to be close to him, yes, but not to make love. Not to jump his bones, either. All she wanted was for him to understand and to take care of her. To accept her for what she was willing to give, but also what she wanted to keep for herself. "No more games, Marcus," she whimpered, feeling lost herself now, too. "Let me feed you."

He pushed away like she'd offended him and stormed back to the other showerhead, where he ducked underneath and finished getting cleaned up without a word.

Wynter hurried through the rest of her wash routine and then followed him out of the cubicle, where they both dried up in silence and she applied some moisturiser and deodorant. She also ran a brush through her hair and left it down around her shoulders to dry.

When he was done, rather than stick around, Marcus left the bathroom, stalking naked into the living area. Wynter kept her towel around herself and followed, where she found him pulling on a pair of casual black trousers and a simple blue t-shirt. It was strange seeing him dressed that way. Even after only knowing him a day, she had already become accustomed to the perfectly tailored suits and crisp cotton shirts.

"Your clothes are in there," he told her, indicating to another set of drawers to his right. She went to them and pulled open the top drawer, where she found nothing but a single white dress. It was like a modern take on the nightgowns women used to wear in the olden days, nothing like she'd choose for herself, but she slipped it over her head without argument. The dress fell right down to her feet and swamped her, feeling less than flattering, but Wynter still didn't grumble. If this was what he'd wanted her in, then so be it. She'd riled him up enough for now without also adding a further insult about his choice of clothing for her.

"Marcus," she then hummed when there was nothing but silence between them. "I'm ready."

"Sit down on the couch," he demanded, and she did, thinking he'd take her wrist, but he evidently had other plans. "Open your legs and lift your skirt…"

Again, she did as he commanded. Wynter hadn't ever been one to shy away from men when it came to showing off her body, but with Marcus she felt like she was only revealing what was his. That, somehow, by covering herself, she was denying him of what he rightfully owned. It felt oddly good to be naked in front of him.

Marcus climbed down and lifted her left knee up, hoicking in over his shoulder so that his face was level with her thigh. She could feel her skin prickling, ready for his bite. Her heart was racing, pounding loudly in her ears, and she began to pant. How could she want it so much? This was insane.

"Please," she whimpered, but Marcus simply placed a kiss against her skin.

"Please what?" he asked, looking up at her with a wild kind of wickedness to his stare that made Wynter tremble.

"Drink," she answered, and he seemed surprised.

"Is that all you want?" he enquired, his eyes darting to her uncovered and fully on show pussy that was mere inches from his face.

Wynter thought about it for a moment. Yes, she was horny again now. But truly, she didn't want him. She didn't even want David. All Wynter wanted was for her duty to be done so she could rest. She willed the time to pass and for Marcus to take what he wanted, and realised it wasn't for any reason other than because she was ready to get away from him. That deep down, she despised him for what he had forced her into.

Marcus appeared to sense the cold wave of hate that flooded through her, and he grinned. "Yes. It is all you want, isn't it? To let me drink so you can be free."

Wynter simply nodded. Damn him and his tricks. "Then fight me. Tell me no. Make me force you."

"I can't," she groaned, and it wasn't for a lack of trying. Wynter's instincts were telling her to run, but the spell he'd put her under was working to override those reflexes and she could do nothing but sit there, vulnerable and at his utter mercy.

"Then I shall take my time. Make it excruciatingly slow for you until you can endure it no longer, Wynter. You think you can wind me up and there won't be consequences?" he growled, and there it was. She'd known he'd punish her somehow and cursed herself for having been so reckless. But at the same time, she knew she'd do it again if given the chance.

"I knew there would be consequences, but I also knew they'd be worth it. I might be your slave, Marcus, but I'm not your puppet."

"We'll see about that," he replied before pressing that razor-sharp tongue of his against the artery inside her inner thigh.

Marcus caught the initial gush of blood as it began to flow and then stemmed it, taking just a trickle into his mouth rather than the deep gulps like he had before. He was indeed teasing it from her, taking just a few drops at a time, and Wynter felt wonderful and horrible both at once. But then, with every drop, her burdens lessened, and she fell further into her ecstasy. Punishment or not, her body still roared with pleasure at his bite, and before she knew it her instincts to run and fight were quietened and all she had left was her need to serve him.

It was dawn before Marcus closed the cut to her thigh. Wynter was writhing and arching up and down on the sofa before him, her body seeking comfort in arms that simply weren't there. Release in the lover that wouldn't give her it. And when he finally closed the wound and moved away from her, she shoved the dress back down and curled into a ball on the sofa.

Reality set back in and brought with it that same sense of shame she continually fought when she was with her vampire boss. Tears sprung from her eyes, and she hugged herself tighter as they began to fall. When she had finished her mini-meltdown, Wynter unfurled and pulled the throw down over herself, willing for him to just leave her alone.

Sleep took her in an instant and while she needed it, her body also continued to cry out for its gratification. Her dreams were full of dark, sensual things. Of sex and desire, and of eyes that watched her, burning her soul as her body roared with heat.

She woke to find her hands between her legs. Her fingers swirling the aching bead atop her thighs. She worked it harder and harder, getting closer to her release, and then screwed her eyes shut when her orgasm took hold and she began to shudder and spasm in the wonderful rhythm her body had so desperately needed.

During her high, she saw one man's face. Warren's. She remembered his dark, brooding expression, and the words he'd spoken that morning.

He was going to look after her. Take care of her. Make sure she wasn't manipulated or taken advantage of. He was her knight in shining armour and Wynter quickly realised how what he'd promised was the hottest thing anyone had ever offered her before. No matter how hard she'd tried not to notice him, he'd gotten under her skin, and she knew she wanted more. "Finally. I thought you'd be there forever," Marcus's voice pierced her post-orgasmic haze, and she cringed at him having watched her in the throes of her self-pleasure.

Wynter jumped up off the sofa and found him sitting in the chair opposite. She glared across at him but found he didn't seem to care one little bit. He was just watching her inquisitively, but then held out his hand. "Come to me," he said, but she'd already been up on her feet and was moving toward him, anyway. His magnetism had drawn her closer, not his words.

She climbed into his lap and let Marcus hold her close. He pulled her against him, and she inhaled his scent and moaned dreamily.

"I feel so confused," Wynter told him with a sigh, "I don't know what to think or feel."

"We all tried to warn you," he answered, as if she was just being too foolish for her own good. "You will love me, but that doesn't mean you will always like me. No one else here has ever had the guts to express it, but I understand the way the hex works." Marcus shifted her so that Wynter could look up into his face. "What you feel isn't real. How you act and what you give me is by force. But I don't care. Trust me when I say so. All I give any kind of a shit about is fulfilling my needs and taking care of my business. The rest is just coincidental."

"I don't believe you," she countered. "I can't. If I did, I don't think I could bear being here for another second."

Marcus answered with a grin that told her he'd like that. To have to come and get her from her home and drag her to the club. To punish her for defying him.

"And yet, I can taste how broken you are. I can smell the misery on you, even still. I know there's nothing out there in the real world for you, just like there's nothing out there for me either."

"And what if I chose to burn this place to the ground? Where would you turn then?" Wynter groaned, not meaning it as a threat or any kind of promise, just a last ditch effort to get her life back again, even as crappy as it might've been.

"I've always got other options, but you don't. Plus, I'd make sure you burned along with the club and all the other humans in it, Wynter," Marcus answered with a sneer.

He then plucked her hand up and pressed his lips against her wrist, where he began to drink again.

TEN

After the day spent feeding from his new prize and then rewarding her with just a small amount of sleep each time, Marcus decided it was finally time to let her get some proper rest. He blocked out the afternoon sunshine using the fully blackout blinds he'd installed and then left her to sleep while he got some work done. He needed the time to catch up on the bits and pieces he'd neglected the night before anyway, thanks to him having been too wrapped up in his newest obsession to dedicate the time he had needed to them. What was it about her that had him so worked up? Even now, after languishing at her various veins for hours, he still wanted more, and had to stop himself going to wake her up again.

Instead, Marcus forced himself to focus on the reports on his desk. Or on the budget for the upcoming quarter. On anything at all that didn't involve that damn girl, but his mind kept on going back to her. To how he wanted more than just her blood.

No. They weren't going there. She was just exciting and new. The novelty would wear off soon. Yes, that was it. Wynter was his first new manager in twenty years, so it stood to reason that she was exciting him more than any other new acquisition. The other new employees had gone straight into the pool of blood letters, ready for the taking by his many clients. But not her. She was his and her blood was fresh. New. Delectable and delicious.

Wynter was like the young summer lamb, while his other managers were mutton. She'd soon lose her appeal, of course.

Yes, Marcus thought. He would indulge in the newness to the fullest because it surely wouldn't be long until it was nothing more than business as usual between them. Just another professional arrangement like any other, and so he endeavoured to enjoy her while the high lasted.

***

Wynter stirred and let the sounds of the world around her creep into the void between asleep and awake. Her head hurt, but she felt rested enough, and it was a relief when she looked at the clock on the wall and realised she still had an hour before her working evening began. It would be nice having some time to get ready without the rush this time.

She sat up and looked around for Marcus. He was nowhere to be seen, and so she headed for the shower again, but thankfully in private this time, and then brushed her teeth. She also found makeup and hair products in there ready for her to use, and every item was her usual brand and shade. She had to wonder if this was thanks to Warren's scrupulous background checks on her. Did they go as far as knowing the purchases she regularly made? Quite possibly. He undoubtedly had dug into every inch of her life and knew things no one else did. In some ways, though, that made her even more attracted to him. If he could look at her warts and all and not run away, then maybe things wouldn't be so bad here after all?

After she was clean and made up, Wynter then found her clothes also hanging neatly in a dry-cleaning bag that told her they had been sent to get washed and prepped, just like Marcus had promised. She slipped the clothes back on, finding it odd to think how some poor laundry worker had just dry-cleaned her knickers and bra too, but figured she was at least spared the embarrassment of collecting them and nodded to herself as she took one final look in the mirror.

She looked like her usual self. Back to normal, or as normal as she could be under the circumstances of her new role. And of course, after all that Marcus had taken from her during the past thirty hours. Her freedom, her life, and her blood. How the hell was that suddenly normal?

Her two days of extracurricular obligations were almost over with and come two-am the following morning, she would be free at last to head home. Back to her own bed and free from the advances of her three-thousand-year-old boss. Yeah, in what other world would that make sense? She wondered if her friend Cossette would even believe her when she told her about the new job. But then again, was she even allowed to? Wynter hadn't signed a non-disclosure agreement and hadn't been issued any warnings about revealing her boss's identity to anyone on the outside, but of course nothing here was as it seemed, so she decided to ask Warren when she headed down to his office a short while later.

It was strange. Warren seemed to be on her mind a hell of a lot. Now there was a conundrum. Someone she'd actively not pursued or flirted with in a bid to remain professional. She hadn't even fantasised about him after meeting him, but then he had turned up in her thoughts at that pinnacle moment of her climax and completely thrown a spanner in the works. Was it because he had been so chivalrous? So outspoken and ready to take on the 'bloodsuckers' as he had called them? He was strong and seemed to be fighting the curse as best he could, and Wynter liked that about him. In fact, there seemed to be rather a lot she liked there.

She checked the clock again as she emerged. There were fifteen minutes to go. Fifteen minutes and she would be heading back down to work for a normal night of meetings, arts, and design work. No biting. No games.

She could hardly wait.

Wynter sensed Marcus before she saw him. He was sitting at his desk and wasn't even looking at her as she crept out from behind the glass partition, but she felt him pulling her to his side, compelling her forward. Her body obeyed his call and within a few moments, she was on his lap and completely at his mercy, just like before.

She was under his alluring spell again and kissed him the moment he peered down into her face and was surprised when Marcus kissed her back rather than push her away. He then began opening the buttons on her blouse and she gasped when she felt him dive inside and capture one of her breasts in his warm palm.

After all the times he'd told her no, she was finally gaining the strength of will not to throw herself at his sexual mercy, and then here he was making all the moves? He truly did love playing his games, and she was powerless to refuse him—not that she wanted to.

After a few seconds spent fondling her, he pushed her bra aside and started massaging her nipple into a peak.

"Marcus," she groaned, his name a question as well as a pleading cry for more. She needed him to take what he wanted, desperate to please him, and having his hands suddenly on her was intoxicating beyond anything she had ever imagined.

He didn't respond. Not a word passed his lips as Marcus dipped his head and sucked the nipple he'd just been working into his mouth. It felt amazing. "Oh, God," Wynter croaked when she felt the sting of his tongue press against her flesh. Heat bloomed within her core in reaction to his bite, and Wynter grabbed the back of Marcus's head, pushing him deeper, even as she sensed him begin to drink. It felt amazing, and she wasn't ready to let him stop. Not even when Marcus lifted his head back and licked her cut closed. "No," she whimpered, "don't stop."

"Time for work," he answered with a teasing smile, and Wynter peered across the room to the clock, watching as the final second ticked by and six-pm arrived.

She wanted to scream!

Marcus laughed when she scowled up at him and pushed herself away in a bid to get up, but then held her back for just a second so that he could button up her blouse and give Wynter one last lingering kiss.

"You're making me late," she hissed against him, seducing another gruff laugh.

When she finally pulled away and made for the elevator, Wynter felt the iciness descend between them and knew before she'd even left how he'd broken whatever bond had just blossomed to life between them. She no longer felt the need to go to him. All she wanted to do was get away, and so she didn't even look back as the elevator doors closed and she descended one floor to her office.

David was lounging by her office door and when she reached him, he raised an eyebrow in questioning.

"Well. How was it?" he asked when she said nothing, bouncing on the points of his feet like he was excited to hear about her first proper day as Marcus's Blood Slave. Wynter groaned at him and shook her head. She knew exactly what he meant by that and understood Warren's comment about the vultures who would descend on her and try and claim a notable notch on their belt.

"Exhausting," she replied as she slid the key into the lock and opened the door. David went to follow her inside the office but she turned back to face him, shaking her head. "Not now, okay? I need some time by myself." She didn't mean to be harsh, but just couldn't play nice. She didn't have the energy or the patience.

He left, albeit begrudgingly, but Wynter didn't care. Yes, she was horny as hell and Marcus's last bite didn't help matters, but she wasn't going to be some sure thing David could just swing by and take a ride on. She remembered the warnings Warren had given her and decided she wasn't going to give into her lustful urges. She wasn't going to be *that* girl. And so, she would hide away and distract herself for as long as it took for her to forget those needs and quiet those desires.

Wynter locked the door closed behind her and slumped into her chair. She then took a few deep breaths, stretched, and let out a loud yawn before firing up her computer and getting down to some work. She remembered her quick and annoyingly vague run through from the night before and tried her best to answer the emails waiting in her inbox, but knew she needed to get her head in the game if she had any hope of properly getting to grips with everything.

It was slow going thanks to her lack of concentration and made even harder when she tried to log into the club's website as an administrator and was denied access, even when she checked and double checked that she was putting in the password that'd been left for her.

Wynter swore at the machine and then shoved herself back in her seat. This was no bloody good.

She was going stir crazy, and it wasn't even an hour into her night's work, and she started to feel herself growing angry. At the situation she'd found herself in. At Marcus for having lured her into his domain as well as his arms. At herself for having fallen for some of the oldest tricks in the book. And yet, there she was. Locked inside her own office and doing as her vampire master commanded, even though this was meant to be her time to work and fulfil her role as best she could.

Wynter was beginning to understand why the other managers were such solitary creatures. Why Jack and Patrick locked themselves away and remained private. Why Joanna wore her heart on her sleeve, but only for the man who would never love her in return, even if she couldn't see it herself. But Wynter failed to understand her own place amidst their odd quadruplet. She was a social animal. A lover of dance and music, and of fun and adventure. Wynter was the sort of person who wouldn't do well being locked away, and so she grew itchy. Desperate to leave the stifling office behind and be with likeminded people. Those who understood her and were on the same page. Those who had made her feel welcome…

It was glaringly obvious where she needed to be, and so she decided a change of scenery would do the trick. Wynter grabbed the brand new laptop Marcus had left her and shoved it under her arm, along with her notebook and pen. She then checked the coast was clear of unsolicited visitors and locked her office door behind her before taking the lift down to the basement and walking the long corridor towards the entrance to the IT department.

The doorway was just within her reach when she heard the buzzer sound that indicated the door had been unlocked from a switch somewhere on the inside. They'd obviously seen her coming and had opened, ready to receive her.

It suddenly dawned on her she really was welcome there. Wynter felt like she might cry. Who in the hell were these people, and why had they so quickly accepted her? She needed to know. To understand why they were being so nice.

"Hey," Warren called to her from his small sectioned off corner of the huge office the second she'd walked through the doors and headed inside. He came to the entrance to his office area and was smiling this time, rather than scowling, and his arms weren't crossed but down by his stomach. He was fiddling with something Wynter couldn't see, and so she moved closer to find that it was a Rubik's cube he'd completed.

"Hey," she said, "I just wanted to come and check in. See what's going on…"

"Any time. Hey, come and grab a coffee with me," he added, and she knew exactly what he was getting at. He was doing as he had promised. Keeping her safe in the aftermath of her first couple of overtime days.

Wynter did as he asked and followed him into his makeshift office, where she found Warren already pouring two steaming cups of black coffee from the percolator. "If you want milk, you'll have to make do with the powdered stuff," he told her, and grinned when she shook her head no.

"Black is fine, thanks," she replied before taking a long inhale of the caffeinated air.

Wynter then took a seat and watched him as he stirred a teaspoon of sugar into his brew before joining her at the desk. Warren eyed her up and down, clearly checking that she was okay before he started with his questioning.

"So, how are you?"

"Fine."

"Not good enough," he demanded. "How are you, really?"

"Knackered. Wired. Angry. Horny. What else do you wanna know?" she told him and was surprised by her own honest answer.

"How many bites?"

"In total over the day?"

"The weekend."

She mentally counted them and frowned.

"Seven," she eventually answered, and found herself scratching at the tender mark on her neck Marcus had given her the day before. It was beginning to itch, which was a good sign really as it meant it was healing, but she hated the reminder of what he had taken from her.

"Want some magic cream?" Warren asked, and Wynter giggled, but she nodded in answer. He then threw her a tub of ointment from his desk drawer, and she peered down at it with a smile.

"Nappy rash cream?" she asked with a frown.

"Trust me, it'll take away the itch as well as help it heal quickly. Here, let me help you," he told her as he stood and wandered around to her side of the desk and plucked the tub from her hands. He then scooped a small bead of the ointment out and rubbed it between his fingertips before pressing them either side of her neck where the scratches were.

It was like heaven. Wynter peered up into his incredibly dark eyes and forced herself to remain calm. To not remember how he had invaded her thoughts at the most inappropriate moment. To not feel like she had to tell him all about how he had featured in her dreamy fantasy, and now was on her mind for more than just how kind and helpful he had been. No, Wynter steered her thoughts out of the gutter and looked up at him as a protector. A powerful ally. A friend.

"Let me guess, they frequent the same drinking spots?" she asked while she did the same and took care of the two marks inside her wrists.

"Yep. Thighs too?" he asked, and when Wynter nodded Warren turned away and walked to the window so he could look out at his team, and to give her some privacy to rub some cream onto the two wounds inside the tops of her legs.

Wynter also unbuttoned her shirt and rubbed some of the cream onto her tender nipple and was just removing her hand when Warren turned back around and glared at her in horror. She quickly buttoned her clothing again and flushed with shame, while Warren just continued to stare at her like she was a ghost or something.

"What is it?" Wynter asked timidly, and he suddenly seemed to snap out of his moment of contemplative disgust.

"It's just not right," Warren answered, his voice merely a whisper. "None of this is right."

"No, but it isn't like we have much of a choice. Is it?" she replied with a frown. "The curse has me, just like it has all of you. The more we fight, the more they like it. The more *he* likes it. I tried, Warren. I was cold and cruel towards him, but I'm pretty sure that only made him want me more. He drew it out. Savoured the taste of my hatred rather than turn away from the bitterness I hoped he'd sense in me."

It felt strange being so open and honest, but she was glad to be able to speak her mind at last. To be able to say the words rather than hide them any longer.

"I know that feeling," he then answered dejectedly. "I have to work Friday and Saturday's and I dread them each and every week. I hate every second of the feeding time and while I know they love it I fight back, I just can't help myself. I fight for me. Not for them. I do it because, if I stop fighting, then I'm scared I'll never start again. I'll be lost. Another mindless lover of those bloodsuckers and the euphoria their bites bring." His words made so much sense to her it was insane, but he was right. She had to keep on fighting, and not because Marcus wanted it, but because she needed it.

"Why does the euphoria happen?" she asked, thinking how great it was having someone who was so willing to give her the god's honest truth.

"There are many theories, but I think it's because our natural instinct is to survive. Even the biggest thrill-seekers in the world wouldn't knowingly put themselves in the path of certain death. There would be a safety harness. A plan-B. Not here, though. Not with them. They are the harbingers of death, and yet we are lured to their sides like the sirens of the sea. Their bites bring passion and ecstasy, rather than pain and fear."

"It feels so good," she answered honestly. "I would've gladly kept on feeding him so I could get to my release. Even if it meant death."

"Never, ever let yourself go over that precipice while Marcus is feeding from you," Warren demanded, his face turning cold again. "Your body will rush with endorphins and the blood will pump into his mouth in droves. He will be driven wild by your frenzy and will take it all." Wynter gulped and stared back at him in horror.

"So, if you reach that climax, you die?"

"Nine times out of ten," he replied, and then noticed the awkward look on her face. "Did you do it? Did he make you come?"

"Yes. He had closed the wound already, but my body was lost to the sensation, and it happened before I could control it," she answered, suddenly feeling dirty. Wynter wasn't sure if it was because Warren looked even more horrified than before, but she hated that she'd disappointed him by letting Marcus elicit an orgasm from her. She hadn't been in control of her own mind, let alone her body, but Warren seemed appalled. Like she had somehow betrayed him. "Don't be angry with me."

"I'm not angry with you, Wynter," he answered, the look of hurt and shock so prominent on his darkly handsome face that she couldn't bear it. "I just can't believe he's taken so much from you in just two days. It isn't right."

"I know," she replied. "I know."

ELEVEN

Marcus watched via his camera systems as Wynter went about her night's work. She seemed lost. Like she didn't quite know what to do with herself. He considered going to her, having realised he'd never properly shown her the ropes the evening before, but eventually decided against it. She needed to find her own way. Even if it meant him leaving her to fend for herself so he could watch and enjoy the journey.

She hadn't lasted long in her office. Wynter had needed company and clearly wasn't a lone wolf like his other managers, so had taken herself off to the IT department. She had then stayed down in the basement for a long time, and he found it strange she would want to associate herself with the riffraff of the team down in the depths of the club.

Her decision irked him. Marcus had steered her towards his chosen employees to befriend and wanted to know why she wasn't doing as he had planned for her. Why she had denied Jack's advances when he had specifically put him in her path the day before. Why Wynter had been interested in his second choice, David, but not taken the bait, even when he'd ensured he was served up on a plate. And of course, why his new prize hadn't found solace in any of the friendly faces he had introduced her to himself. Not even Marcella, with whom she'd seemed to strike up an instant friendship. Wynter was a conundrum to him. A true enigma. But still a code he would crack. A puzzle he would solve.

Two-am soon arrived, and she left for home, leaving Marcus feeling somehow empty. He'd known it wasn't her day to feed him, so didn't know why it bothered him. Mondays and Tuesdays were Jack's responsibility, but still, Marcus had hoped she would stick around a while longer. Or perhaps she might've chosen to at least come up and say goodbye before running out the door.

He couldn't make her stay, either. Or could he? Perhaps she would be less inclined to leave if there was something keeping her at the club? A home there, like he had. That would work out nicely, and especially if he could orchestrate it in a way that she wouldn't know it was his doing until it was too late. There would be no more upper hands offered to her, not after she'd got her own way, not just once or twice over their initial weekend together.

Marcus vowed he would find a way to ensure Wynter remained there with him as long as possible, even if he had to work her to the bone to do it. He would formulate a plan and knew he had to study her some more and figure out the best way, so watched the various recordings of her back. He needed answers that were still beyond his own reach, though, so knew it was time he tapped into a wholly different power.

The ancient vampire lowered his head and focused on *her*. Not his new prize, of course, but the embodiment of the one powerful bloodline which had served him for centuries. The same one whose mastery was behind his curse he'd had placed upon thousands of employees across the world. Marcus called to his priestess and willed her to come to him, and in a second, the powerful young woman appeared. The witch was covered from head to toe thanks to her red cape, her tiny body shielded from view and from the various forces all around them. He knew why she shrouded herself. After all, the Priestess was not an elemental witch, but one of ancient power. A force taken from deep within the Earth itself. Supremacy, no one creature should've ever been able to tame, and yet it had been harnessed by only one powerful coven. The same coven that had served his needs without question or argument ever since turning him into a vampire all those years ago.

There was no doubt Marcus was the most powerful of his kind. He was their most prominent leader, the oldest surviving vampire and a wiser one than any he had ever met before. Their kind looked to him to guide them and so, of course, he did. He'd provided them with feeding stations across the globe, negating the necessity for the innumerable predators to hunt out in the open. Marcus was as strict with his own kind as he was with the humans in his employ. He commanded respect, as well as the adherence to his rules, and the belief that should anyone step out of line, his punishment would be swift and merciless.

His dear Joanna had been reminded of that fact the day before, thanks to her jealous reaction to Wynter's presence. Marcus had delivered her with ten lashings himself and had savoured every second of her pain and torment during her atonement. But he knew she would do it again, and that he would punish her over and over. She couldn't help herself. All any of these humans ever seemed to want to believe was that the bad guy could turn good. That he could be tamed thanks to love. Joanna had believed so for two decades now, and yet he'd never once given her any reason to chase that fruitless dream. She was nothing more than a romantic fool.

The woman standing before him was the most recent in the only line of women he'd ever cared for.

"My lady," he whispered in greeting to his priestess, bowing his head in respect.

"My lord," she replied before she took a step closer to his desk and inspected him. Marcus could feel her eyes on him. "You are burdened this morning. Tell me what ails you."

He didn't answer and knew he didn't need to. His witch reached into his mind and plucked the information from him anyway, and he didn't even try to stop her. The information delivered to her all-seeing mind; the Priestess inhaled sharply and then ran her fingers over his desk before licking the tips of them. "You desire her. The scent of her arousal drives you wild and you wish to take her."

She paused to gather her thoughts and then reached for Marcus's hand, which he gave her without question. He also didn't so much as flinch when she produced a blade from the bag at her hip and sliced his palm open. The Priestess then scrutinised the small pool of blood that gathered in his hand and whispered to herself as she worked out the meanings behind whatever it was she somehow saw there. "The full moon... blood will spill... wars will be won and lost all at once..."

"Tell me more, wise one," Marcus implored. He had been through this with the Priestess and her ancestors many times before, so knew her visions could go on like this for hours, but that a little prompting didn't hurt to remind her he was waiting.

"She's strong," the Priestess replied. "She will fight the curse. Fight you." She then dipped her head and lapped at the blood still sat in Marcus's palm, her tongue darting down into it like a cat's. "This girl will both adore and despise you, but you are capable of making her yours. If you don't, she will find love in another's arms."

"Then we shall continue to fight, and she will love another, because I won't do it," Marcus demanded, thinking she had to be mistaken. He'd relished drinking from Wynter and had let himself enjoy her company. It was true, but not enough to have anything more with her. "I have never taken a bride or created another like me. And I never will."

"Stubborn fool," the Priestess hissed, but he sensed her flinch with fear when she felt his anger spike within. "When the moon is full, it is time to choose. Change your mind later and it will be too late. The girl will never love you."

"Not unless I force her," he groaned. "Or you cast a spell."

He withdrew his hand and licked the last of the blood clean. Marcus could taste Wynter's scent in his own rich blood. Her essence was a part of his now, and he shuddered as a wave of arousal struck him.

"No force or spell would be needed if only you followed your instincts..." the Priestess answered, and then she gave out a shrill cackle and staggered back towards the centre of the room. Marcus thought she was about to leave, but instead she held on. He was about to ask why when she clutched at her stomach and let out a low moan.

"It's time," Marcus said, not in question but in knowing. He'd been through this hundreds of times already and knew the signs. The witches of her coven were always female, after all. Always in need of a male to help further their line, and when the time came, both Marcus and the Priestess serving him knew about it. And the forces demanding an heir weren't exactly gentle about letting them know it.

The coven leader would wrack with pain until the dark need was satisfied, and it appeared the current priestess was ready. Patrick had helped her mother and delivered the seed unto her belly, which had given life to the Priestess standing before him now. Her father was never far away and yet she had never cared to know him. Never wanted anything to do with him. Only Marcus. He was their eternal father—the caregiver for every generation—and it didn't matter who had been the one to procreate with the Priestess before them. They were nothing more than a donor.

Marcus knew who to choose for her, and so he summoned Jack to his office, who appeared within a couple of minutes and was understandably surprised to find the Priestess there. He fell to his knees before her and bowed his head, having met with her many times before during his time as Marcus's Blood Slave and so knew what was expected of him.

"My lady," he said, but she didn't answer.

"Come, I am in need of you," Marcus commanded as he climbed up from behind his desk and joined the two of them. Jack was ever the willing and obedient servant, so he did as he was told and immediately offered his master his wrist to drink from, but Marcus refused. He instead nodded to the Priestess, who was standing utterly still, watching them from beneath her hood. Jack followed his gaze and frowned at the hidden girl. The one whose face he had still never seen. The woman as precious to Marcus as the child he'd never get to have, well, at least until her daughter grew up and came of age before taking her place, and so on. The cycle would continue like it had for centuries, and to do so, Marcus needed the seed from another loyal subject. "Congratulations," he told Jack as he took his offered hand and led him towards her. "You have been chosen."

"Master... I don't know..." Jack tried, but then he fell silent thanks to the sight of the Priestess lifting her skirt to reveal slim, womanly legs and a natural tuft of dark hair atop her thighs. Marcus wondered if he'd expected her to be old beneath that cape, but Jack seemed impressed to discover the Priestess was, in fact, just a young woman.

"She's untouched. Ready for you to be her first," Marcus whispered in Jack's ear before running his tongue down the nape of his neck to the vein he regularly fed from there.

His actions had the desired effect. Despite them never having entertained any sexual kinship, Jack was hard in an instant. It didn't matter that Marcus hadn't actually bitten him, either.

He let out a soft moan, unbuckled his trousers and let them fall open at the fly. Jack would do whatever was required of him without much in the way of hesitation, and they all knew it. Marcus was once again pleased with him and told him so.

"Where, my lady?" Jack asked the Priestess, who lifted her hand and pointed one delicate finger towards the couch they all knew was behind the glass screen. She then went to it, her skirts still gathered around her waist, and waited.

Jack followed and Marcus directed him to remove his clothes and sit down in the centre of the couch. He did as he'd been told and was soon ready, as was the Priestess, and Marcus watched as she readied herself to mount him. He knew she was not to be touched, other than the obvious, so he stood behind Jack and held his hands behind his head to stop him from trying.

To then further his compliance, Marcus pressed his lips to Jack's wrist and unsheathed his razor-sharp tongue before pressing it against his vein. A trickle of hot blood reached the back of his throat a second later and he felt Jack relax into the euphoria of his bite.

Marcus smiled and sucked at the wound, desperate for more, and was rewarded when Jack's heart began to pound in his chest with sexual need. The Priestess felt it too. She knew the time was right and Marcus watched as she sunk down onto the rod protruding up from Jack's waist.

Because of their bond, he sensed her pain at the initial intrusion, signifying the removal of her innocence. But she remained silent, and Marcus watched as she let her instincts guide her through the rest of their encounter. He kept her lover in place while the Priestess rode him, being careful not to drink from him too much as Jack climbed the wave of ecstasy. Because of course, he was finally going to be allowed to unleash it.

His minion cried out when it happened, but the Priestess did not slow or put an end to their lovemaking. She carried on and on, taking more than another few orgasms from him, as well as having many of her own. It took all Marcus's strength not to drain Jack dry each time, but the wants of his priestess outweighed his own craving for blood, and so he remained calm. He took slow, languid laps at the vein and focussed on her needs rather than his own.

When she was finally satisfied and her body open to his offerings, not a word was spoken as she climbed up, dropped her skirts, and then dematerialised into thin air.

Jack was ready to pass out with exhaustion, and so Marcus simply helped him lie down and then he wrapped the covers up around him, tucking the man in like a father might do his son. He then went back to his desk and stared out the window at the night's sky.

It was as though the Priestess had never even been there for her visit at all, but Marcus felt her absence strongly and wondered why. He'd never felt lonely in his entire existence before.

But then it dawned on him how he didn't miss her, but another. The woman he'd been forewarned was going to try and make him love her.

Wynter...

TWELVE

The alarm clock was already on its third lot of snooze time, and Wynter knew she was cutting it way too fine. Why on earth had she thought she'd be able to cope with juggling two jobs? She felt like she'd had around two hours' decent sleep and was somehow now expecting to head out for an eight-hour day job. It was insane. Already too much and she wasn't even out of bed yet.

Wynter dragged herself anyway and tried desperately to function. She opted for topping herself up with copious amounts of coffee and hiding away as much as she could, but it wasn't long before her boss noticed something was up.

"Not being funny, but you look like shit," he told her, and all Wynter could do was nod.

"I feel like it," she answered with a yawn.

"Go home and get some rest. You're clearly coming down with something," he then told her, and Wynter wanted to kiss him. The thought of going home and getting some more sleep was heaven, and so she leapt at the chance and promised to come back the moment she felt well enough. It was a lie. Wynter already knew she would be quitting and working solely for Marcus. It was inevitable, so she decided to get a resignation email typed up and ready to go for when she got back from the club the following morning.

She was home less than half an hour later and dived right into bed. Her head had barely even hit the pillow, and she was out like a light, and thanked god she'd set a second alarm ready to alert her at five-pm, otherwise she had a feeling she might've slept in, and she didn't even want to know how much trouble she would be in if that were the case.

Wynter got to the club with plenty of time to spare and she headed straight for her office, where she bumped into a very pale and sour-faced Jack coming out of his own one. He looked the way she herself had felt earlier that morning, and Wynter was pretty sure she knew why. Marcus had spent the day feeding on him, after all.

"Everything okay?" she asked, receiving just a nod from her fellow manager, so she let him be. Not everyone wanted to talk about it. Not even her, to some extent.

Wynter just wanted to get on and work. She wanted to do the job she'd been employed to do and nothing more. That wasn't going to happen when Saturday morning rolled around again, though. This new job had its perks, sure, but then there was the other side to the work. The part she hated and yet strangely wasn't in a rush to give up. At least now she knew exactly where she'd be spending her weekends for the foreseeable future. Not partying in the club, but behind the closed and tightly locked doors of it.

What about the probationary period and the clause? her inner voice reminded her. *You can get out of this. All you have to do is send that letter of resignation to Marcus instead. Be strong. Fight the curse and you can be free again...*

In her heart, she knew it was what she wanted. The weekend hadn't been terrible, and she had made some good connections at *Slave*, but Wynter still wanted to be free to control her own life again. And so tried her hardest to do it. She wrote the resignation letter out in full to her other employer and then changed the addressee to *Marcus Cole* at the last minute without a hitch. That part was easy, but then it took her until the tenth copy before she could sign her name at the bottom properly thanks to her hand shaking so badly. This curse certainly wasn't making it easy on her. But there it finally was. Her resignation. Ready and waiting for her to hand it over to Marcus whenever she was ready to invoke the power the clause gave her.

Wynter stashed the letter in her briefcase and then stood, figuring she'd head down to IT and see the team for a while before burning her bridges and leaving them all behind. But then she began to doubt herself. Was she really going to do it? Could she walk away just because of a curse, which had given her so much while only taking very little? It wasn't so bad there, was it? She had herself in knots all over again and let out an anxious moan.

Could she really go back to *Marsden and Carmichael* and continue the way she was? The answer was no. Wynter knew she needed more from life, but she also wasn't entirely sure Marcus was the man to give her it.

With a huff, she grabbed her laptop and headed for the door, and found Marcella on the other side with her hand raised, like she was about to knock on it.

"Oh," she cried, and they both laughed at how they'd made one another jump. "Hey, Wynter. I was just coming to see how things are going? I wondered if you'd like to come grab a coffee and we could talk some more about the autumn campaigns?"

"That'd actually be great," she answered, and put her laptop down again. Hers sounded like a much better alternative to finding solace in the basement with the IT guys again.

"Were you going somewhere? Don't let me keep you," Marcella asked as she watched her, and Wynter thought it sweet how she hadn't wanted to intrude. It was a kind gesture to even say so, and her sweet nature made Wynter like her even more.

"No, I was just going down to IT. I still need to go through some of the system management options, but it can wait," she told her with a nonchalant wave of her hand, dismissing the idea entirely. Wynter then joined Marcella in the hallway and, after locking her office door shut behind her, they were soon off towards the main open-plan area to where the small corner office awaited them.

She and Marcella chatted for far longer than Wynter had anticipated, and two coffees later they had covered all the work stuff as well as some of the personal. Wynter felt like she could really open up to her and even felt comfortable enough to ask some more questions about Marcus and his kind. But when it came to the harder stuff, Wynter fidgeted and hesitated. She wanted to believe she was safe to ask the questions raging within, but still wasn't sure she could without raising any suspicion.

"Ask me anything, sweetie. I'll always tell you the truth," Marcella told her, clearly having noticed her unease.

"Well, I was just wondering… Has anyone ever broken the curse?"

Marcella was understandably surprised, but then a sly smile crept over her face, and she leaned closer, dropping her voice.

"As far as I know? Nope. Not a single soul." She shuffled closer. "Why, do you want to try? Do you believe you have the strength of will needed to be allowed to walk away?"

"I don't know," she answered honestly, "but I guess I have another few days to figure it out."

"Don't be too hasty," Marcella then warned, surprising her. "You're in a wonderful position here, one any of the men and women around you would fight tooth and nail to get to. You have the attention of the most powerful man I've ever known, and he won't share you. That's a blessing in this business, not a curse."

Wynter got it. She could see it from Marcella's point of view, but when presented with the chance at escaping her new life and having back her freedom, it was just too big of a deal to then let it go simply because, in the eyes of his other employees at least, she was Marcus's new favourite and ought to be grateful. She would find happiness elsewhere. Not in her old job. Perhaps not even in this same city.

Wynter figured she could start anew. Go back to basics and begin again. Reinvent herself.

Marcella seemed to understand things from her side, and she didn't want to keep talking about it, so was glad when the conversation then naturally moved on. They were soon laughing and joking again, and it wasn't long before another hour had whiled itself away.

Wynter then jumped when the telephone on the desk began to chime and was still giggling when Marcella plucked it up and answered. "Yes, she's here. Of course, I'll send her up, Mr Cole," she said, looking at Wynter with a frown. "Yes, sir."

She replaced the receiver and dropped her voice back to a whisper. "He wants to see you in his office."

"Oh, God. You don't think he's been listening in, do you…"

"No, of course not," Marcella answered, but then they both looked around the room as though they might spot the glaring presence of a camera or a bug. "No. Definitely not."

"I'd better go find out," Wynter answered, and she felt a surge of anxiety echo through her at having to go up to Marcus's office alone. She made quick work of getting on her way though and was in the elevator within minutes of Marcella having ended the call.

She half expected to find Marcus waiting for her at the lift doors like he had before, but instead she found his assistant Bryn there. He was shuffling awkwardly, as if he didn't quite know what to say or do, and his demeanour put Wynter even more on edge.

"Please, take a seat and Mr Cole will be right with you," he said as he ushered her inside and to the chair opposite Marcus's at the desk. Wynter thanked him and took it and was then left alone when Bryn disappeared back down in the lift.

She waited and waited and began to grow impatient. What was taking Marcus so long? In fact, where was he? Wynter looked around and she listened, hoping to hear him in the back room or something, but heard nothing at all. Not a peep.

She eventually stood and took a few tentative steps towards the glass wall and was about to peer through it when she decided against snooping and turned away, figuring she would have to wait it out in the chair. Whatever Marcus was playing at, he seemed to want to unnerve her, and she was determined not to get too riled up.

"Miss Armstrong, please take a seat," Marcus's deep baritone echoed through the room when she turned, and Wynter jumped as she found him sitting at his desk, as if he'd been there all along.

"You… you kept me waiting a long time," she said as she approached and nestled back into the hard-backed chair.

Wynter had tried to sound authoritative, but instead she cringed at how cowardly she had come across. She knew she was going to have to grow some serious balls if she had any hope of getting anywhere within his company. And certainly if she hoped to gather enough strength to ensure she got away from him before the weeks' end.

"The delay was unavoidable," he answered without even a hint of an apology. "Wynter, I called you here because I would like you to work an extra overtime day of each week," Marcus then told her, getting right to the point. "Patrick has been struggling for a long while to feed and although I'm rather fond of the old fellow, I simply cannot drink from him any longer. You're the youngest of my manager's and with the freshest blood. It stands to reason you should be my first choice."

"How flattering," she mumbled, hating how coldly he had worded his request, and thinking how she wanted desperately to refuse him. To deny Marcus a third day with her and save herself the hassle of enduring him another sixteen hours of overtime each week. She steeled herself and took a deep breath, fighting every urge within her to tell Marcus yes. To please him and do everything he commanded. To be his willing slave.

No, if he wanted it, he would have to take it. "I'm afraid I shall have to decline," Wynter then told him through gritted teeth. "I have my other work, as you know."

"Ah, yes," Marcus replied, looking totally unperturbed. "The same job you have resigned from this evening?" he then added, as he plucked a piece of paper from a closed file on his desk. It was her letter of resignation. The one she had printed, signed, and then left in her locked office downstairs. Wynter gulped. In the same briefcase was the amended one to Marcus. He had to have seen it. Whether he'd listened in on her conversation with Marcella or not, he knew she was planning on leaving him. And yet, he didn't seem to care.

"I haven't sent it yet," she answered.

"I took the liberty of doing it for you," he replied with that smug grin of his. "You will not be expected to return, not even to clear out your desk. I've sent someone to do so on your behalf."

"Such a fucking gentleman," she scoffed and turned her face away.

Wynter was filled with the urge to lash out at him for invading her personal space. For trying to force her to stay with him. For daring request that she give him one more precious day.

No. Enough was enough. She was going to do it. "And of course, you must have seen how there were actually two letters of resignation in that folder?"

"Sure," he replied with an air of arrogance that only served to make her angrier. "But unless you physically hand that to me and explain your reasons why, I shan't accept. A piece of paper serves nothing more in your attempt to break your curse than a wooden steak would in endeavouring to smite me." Marcus then took out the second resignation letter Wynter wasn't surprised to find he'd taken along with the other and balled it up in his fist.

He then offered her another smile before throwing it into the fireplace behind him, where the flames disintegrated it within seconds. "So, Friday.

Come to me at two-am and I'll make sure you're rewarded handsomely for the overtime," he told her, as if the matter was settled and she'd accepted. "You may go," Marcus then said, adding insult to injury.

Wynter stood, and not because he had dismissed her, but because she couldn't wait to leave. She glowered at Marcus for a moment, rage boiling her blood.

His satisfied inhale made her want to throw something. Preferably something heavy and expensive.

He was getting off on making her angry. Enjoying every second of it.

Well, she figured, two could play at that game.

"I'm busy Friday," she demanded. Marcus didn't react. He focused on the papers in front of him and began jotting down notes as if she weren't even there. He might be ignoring her, but there was one thing Wynter was acutely aware of and was going to use to her advantage. He wasn't commanding her like he had during their days together the weekend before. Marcus was simply her boss, hex or no hex, and tonight he wasn't seducing her using his lure or controlling her with his bite. "I'm not staying Friday, Marcus. And that's that. Are you listening to me?"

He said and did a whole sum of nothing in response, and Wynter had no choice but to walk away. She was beginning to feel like a fool standing there shouting when he wasn't even acknowledging her existence. Shame crept in around the edges of her rage and she stormed out, hoping Marcus couldn't sense it. That he wasn't enjoying her even more now that she had given him exactly what he'd evidently wanted.

THIRTEEN

Wynter's scent lingered long after she was gone, and Marcus savoured every morsel of it. Damn, that girl really was delectable. He'd had to play it cool when she'd been shouting and demanding her freedom, because it really had taken every ounce of strength he'd had not to pounce on her and drink his fill. Jack's blood hadn't been enough. Joanna's wouldn't be either. The sheer idea of drinking from Patrick again turned his stomach, and Marcus smiled to himself.

Friday couldn't come fast enough. He would have her when he said so, not when she deemed it convenient, and he was going to show Wynter just how much power he had over her and her measly little life.

Marcus then turned and glared into the flames where he had thrown her resignation letter. She was stronger than he'd thought for being able to so much as garner the strength to write that, and there was a part of him that felt afraid. He had put the probationary period into the contract for the fun of it, and not a single human had ever been able to break his spell and claim their freedom. Was she going to be the first? If so, Marcus knew he would not allow it. Not her. Of all the humans he could acceptably lose, it would never be her.

He called out with his mind to his priestess, and she had appeared by the time he'd turned his head away from the flames. She was enrobed as always, but he sensed her trepidation and knew she was still in a great deal of pain.

"I shall summon Jack for you again, my lady," he told her, and she offered him a simple nod. "And this time, I shall not let him stop until the deed is done."

"Yes," she answered, her voice like a wisp on the wind. "And I've found the act itself eases my suffering as well as delivers his seed unto my belly."

Marcus smiled at her. His precious young witch was a woman now. A man had taken her body and, after remaining pure her entire life, just as her obligation to her coven had dictated, she knew the sexual gratification the act of love could bring. She wanted more, he could tell. Wanted to explore her body.

The thought made Marcus hard at the waist. He imagined himself being reckless and letting Wynter ride him the way his Priestess had taken Jack upon that sofa the day previous. She had commanded his body and elicited moans and pleasure from him like a woman who'd known what she was doing, rather than a virgin he'd kept under lock and key since the moment she was born.

Wynter did know what to do, though. She knew her body well and wasn't afraid to use whatever tools she had to hand to get her satisfaction. Marcus had seen so on that footage of her with David in that bathroom, and while it'd made for interesting viewing, it hadn't held a candle to watching her in person writhe against her own fingers while still half asleep on his couch. She'd made herself climax without a care for who might be watching. Her needs had taken over and Wynter had seen to them. She knew what she wanted and took it, just like she was trying to do now with obtaining her freedom.

"And what of my needs?" Marcus asked his priestess, forcing his sexually charged thoughts away. "Wynter intends to leave me. How is that possible?"

"I told you, my lord," she answered softly. "She's strong in herself and her will, and she also affects you in ways you still refuse to acknowledge. The girl weakens you. She challenges you in ways you refuse to acknowledge."

Marcus stood and was across the room in a heartbeat. He soon had the Priestess in his grasp, and he pinned her to the glass wall, glaring into the eyes he could just about see beneath her dark hood.

"Do not ever call me weak," he demanded.

The Priestess answered with a low cackle.

"Then do as your body commands and take her. Make it so she will never even think of leaving you. Mark her. Make her yours. Merge your soul with another after three thousand years of loneliness."

"I've told you, never."

Marcus let go and recoiled. That was the end of it. Conversation over.

He then walked back to his desk and pressed the intercom. "Bryn, send Jack up, will you?"

***

Wynter stormed into the IT department and flung herself into a chair behind one of the spare hot desks. She needed to lose herself in something. Anything. So, she logged into the encrypted system on her laptop and tried once again to get her head around what she was seeing. Behind the basic webpage she herself was going to start work on updating, sat a series of the intricate ordering systems Warren and his team had in place. Clients could log in, pay their fees, and then choose a Blood Slave and a time slot. As if they were ordering a fast-food delivery, they could browse the humans and sort by any number of factors. If a vamp wanted a certain blood type, they got it. If they wanted specific personality traits, they were there. The information was incredibly specific and invasive, and included things like whether they were vegetarian, how much they exercised and their body mass index.

"Who knew vampires had so many options when ordering their liquid lunches, huh?" a voice asked from over Wynter's shoulder and she turned to find Phoebe standing there, the woman she'd met when she'd first gone to the IT department a few days before. She was dressed in jeans and a tight geeky t-shirt and had teamed it with a chunky cardigan and heavy boots. Wynter liked her style and even liked her bright pink hair. It was edgy. Fun. Not like her in the corporate gear she had to wear, thanks to being based a few floors up. But now wasn't the time to be inwardly wishing she could be more like Phoebe and express her own style. There were far worse things going on than her lack of outfit choices.

Wynter simply looked back at the screen and frowned.

"The site makes for an interesting read. Do we really have so much information on every employee?"

"Don't be naïve, Wynter. He doesn't just keep tabs on his employees. More like every man, woman, and child in this country. The vampires are all registered in Mr Cole's database, too. He likes to catalogue them. To watch them and keep tabs. The IT teams at his every base across the globe do the same."

"So, our boss effectively runs the world?" she asked incredulously. There was no way that was possible, surely?

"Something like that," Phoebe answered with a frown, "he knows everything, including how to manipulate anyone into doing exactly what he wants because he has the details close at hand." Phoebe then took a seat and turned the laptop towards herself, which she typed on impossibly fast before hitting enter and turning it back to Wynter.

A picture of Warren was on the screen, and she could see the venom in his eyes as he glowered back at the camera. She then looked down and read his bio. They'd marketed him as a fighter. A challenge to any vampire who was looking for someone who wouldn't go easily. "He had to write that bio himself. To make himself look good to any vampire who didn't already know his name. Imagine having to write your own advert."

"It's disgusting," Wynter answered, reading down to where it said about Warren's height and weight, and even information as specific as how he wasn't currently sexually active. Now, that was taking things too far.

"All we can do is look after each other," Phoebe whispered. "We're all in this for life, and that includes you now, Wynter. We'll take care of each other. And of Warren, just like he takes care of us."

She felt terrible. There she was, planning her escape, and all while people like Phoebe and Warren were planning to look after her and make her one of them.

They took care of their own. She'd heard it said more than once now, and now they counted her among them. It hardly seemed fair that while they were doing all of this, she wasn't giving them anything in return.

She was so confused. Conflicting emotions rattled through her and Wynter wished she could just go back to the Friday before and just stay at home. To not go to the club. To not reek of despair so much that Marcus desired her so. To refuse David when he delivered her such a tempting offer.

Something clicked inside of her as she continued to stare at Warren's photo, and she suddenly realised how this could be so different to everything else she'd tried and failed at so far. The people were different. She was different, and she couldn't leave them behind.

Yes, she knew she'd continue to try and fight Marcus and his curse, but also that she couldn't desert the others. She owed them more than that.

"I've gotta go do something. I'll be back soon," Wynter suddenly announced, and while Phoebe frowned, she didn't try to stop her. She simply closed the laptop and took it over to her workstation for safekeeping, while Wynter headed for the door.

Once through it and on the other side, she couldn't get away fast enough. Something powerful had urged her out the door. She needed air and to be alone with her thoughts a moment, and so walked right to the end of the hallway, then out what she'd hoped was a fire door.

But it wasn't. Instead, she found herself in the main floor of the nightclub. The same one she had once loved dancing in, but not anymore, and definitely not on a Monday night when it was far from the fun and frivolity the weekends had to offer. She cursed Marcus and his incredibly designed building. The damn insulation had muffled the sound so well she hadn't realised she was walking towards the muted music, not away.

Wynter looked around at the dark club and immediately began to panic. There were people everywhere. Far more bodies than were usually crammed into the lower-level dance floor on a weekend. She pressed herself against the door she'd just come through, her hands fumbling all over it in a bid to find a way back in. There wasn't one. It was accessible only from the other side.

In a bid to get her bearings, Wynter looked up and realised they were indeed beneath the mezzanine floor where VIPs overlooked the dancers below on weekends. It was more like a cattle market on nights like this, though. Humans were dancing and writhing against each other while vampires watched them from above. They were there to pick out the one they wanted and then would send one of the waiters to go fetch.

Wynter had read the blurb on the website just hours before. She knew

Monday nights were a free-for-all. She also knew she needed to get the hell out of there and so ducked her gaze back to the floor ahead, looking for the best route out and back upstairs.

She then spied the door to where she knew the smoking area lay beyond. It was a direct enough path for her, albeit straight through the centre of the throng, but Wynter decided she could make it. That she'd force her way through if she had to, but she wasn't going to just stand there any longer.

She pressed forward, having assumed some of the people there might move out of her way, but instead they seemed to close ranks. The ones closest looked like they were completely out of it, as if they were on something, and not a single person looked her in the eye or so much as registered her presence.

With every movement she managed forward, it was like they resisted her, and she was squeezed tighter by the crowd and forced back. Wynter tried again and again and could soon feel herself starting to panic with a sudden onset of claustrophobia. She felt lightheaded thanks to the lack of fresh air, and anxiety speared in her gut. All she wanted was to break free and yet the people there were dragging her back repeatedly. As though they wouldn't let her go without a vampire's say so.

She begged and cried out, but none of them seemed to hear her, and soon she was screaming and crying. Feeling lost and afraid.

And then, she suddenly felt their constriction wane a little. Wynter used what she could get and pushed herself onwards. She moved a few feet and looked up in search of the door, which was when she locked eyes with those icy blues she'd come to both adore and despise. Marcus was standing at the edge of the dance floor, and he moved forward with his hand outstretched, his presence seeming to part the sea of people without him even trying.

Relief washed over, and Wynter cried his name into the crowd, hoping somehow he could free her.

"Come to me," he whispered, and yet she could hear him all too clearly. Marcus left his hand out for her and when she finally reached the edge of the crowd, she took it, and then held on for dear life. She let him drag her from the cesspool behind and clambered into his arms the moment she was finally free. She'd never thought she'd be so happy to see him.

"Thank you," she whimpered. "Why did you do that?"

"I sensed you were upset and in danger. It's my job to look after you now, so of course I came to your assistance. There's no need to thank me," he told her, and his words came as a shock. Wynter hadn't expected that. She'd anticipated some snide remark about her having to be more careful in the future, or for him to tell her off. But not for him to be nice.

"You'll look after me?" she asked him and could feel herself trembling in his embrace. "But you told me you didn't care?"

"Sometimes I say things, but it doesn't always mean I meant them, or that

I don't care. You can trust me, Wynter. I'll always keep you safe, even if I'm angry with you."

She got it now. Marcus certainly did like her weak and despondent, and so he'd said those things to hurt her. But now he was showing the true empathy he was capable of. The real and caring side he had to him, and probably rarely showed unless necessary. "Look to me for guidance, Wynter. Come to me when you're in need and I will always help you."

It was too much. She didn't know whether she was coming or going, and Marcus wasn't helping matters by being so chivalrous suddenly. She still needed her space. Some time to think things through.

"Yes, I will. Thank you," she told him, and then sidestepped away. "I'd like to take a few minutes and get some air if that's okay?"

He nodded and then lifted his hand in a wave to beckon someone over to them. Wynter knew who was coming to keep her company before he'd even arrived, but she didn't mind so much this time.

"David, see to it that Wynter gets some fresh air and then please kindly escort her to her office," Marcus ordered, never once taking his eyes off her.

"Yes, of course," David answered. He, too, eyed her curiously, as though checking she was truly all right, but seemed happy enough when she offered him a weak smile.

Marcus was gone again before Wynter could turn back to thank him, and so she instead followed David out onto the patio and took a seat beneath one of the heaters, but it wasn't enough to stop her shivers.

Her watcher joined her, and Wynter stared at him with a frown.

"I'm sorry I've been so cold towards you. My head is all over the place and I couldn't even begin to process what was going on between us," she told him honestly, "so I pushed you away."

"It's fine, Wynter. We had a bit of fun and while I'd love to do more, we can keep things casual," he answered with a soft smile, and she felt a weight lift off her shoulders. That would be perfect.

"Maybe even become friends?"

"Of course," he told her, "so tell me, why are you so confused? Isn't the job turning out okay?"

"The job is fine. It's Marcus who is driving me insane. I can't get my head around that guy."

"You're not meant to," he replied with a gentle laugh. "He keeps everyone on their toes, Wynter. It's his job to own us and—his managers excluded—hire us out to his buddies. I doubt it's glamorous or an exciting role, and so he plays with his toys to keep himself occupied."

It was Wynter's turn to laugh.

"Yeah, that sounds about right," she agreed, "it's definitely a crazy world I've found myself in, and strangely, money is suddenly the last thing on my mind."

"Yep, and we won't do a thing about it because we all love him so damn much," he answered with a shake of his head, and she was glad to see it confused him just as much as it did her.

"But that's another thing I don't understand," Wynter replied. "Why do you love him, David? How was he capable of doing that to you? Don't get me wrong, part of me wants to adore him and do everything he says without question. But then there's another side of me that wants to fight the curse. Wants to lash out at him and play games right on back. Wants to walk away."

David seemed surprised, and Wynter cringed. She'd gotten swept up in the moment and had let herself get carried away and regretted it almost immediately.

"That's the side of yourself that you need to fight, Wynter," he told her with a frown. "You can't say those things. Can't think them. He will punish you for it."

"I know. I hate myself for thinking it, but I can't help it. And then, he turns me around again by being tender and kind. By making me want to trust him. Perhaps even love him," she mused, and then flung herself back in her seat. Wynter ran her fingers through her hair and scratched at her scalp with rough strokes. "I'm losing my fucking mind," she groaned.

"Welcome to the club," David replied with another small laugh. "We've all lost our minds here, so at least you're in good company."

That sounded about right, and Wynter tried to smile, but then remembered back to their first meeting with a pang in her chest. She thought again how, if only she hadn't come to the club that night, she wouldn't be in this mess. Wouldn't have caught Marcus's eye…

Wynter had taken a break from dancing and was approached by someone exactly her type. He was tall, good looking—albeit obviously—and going by his three-piece-suit he was wearing, she decided he had to be either a businessman or a gangster. She was more than willing to find out which.

"You look thirsty," he teased, clearly having noticed she had no drink on the go. Wynter grinned.

"Yeah, but I'm okay for now. I'll grab a drink later…" she replied, playing it cool. She didn't want to admit she barely had a tenner to her name, and it was still another week until payday.

The man turned to the barman to order two glasses of water, and that was when Wynter noticed he had an earpiece in that went down into his shirt via one of those curly wires. He had to be one of the bouncers, and she wondered why she'd never seen him there before. She would've noticed someone like that on the door.

She thanked him for the drink but couldn't hide how she wasn't all that impressed by his choice of beverage. She could've asked for a free glass of water herself. Gin would've been much preferable.

"I've noticed you around here before, but usually you're not being so thrifty. Everything

okay?"

"Funds are a little low this month. Is that a crime?" she retorted, trying not to lose her temper. Whose business was it but hers if she wasn't flashing the cash? Not his, that was for sure.

"No, but we're not in the business of charity, Miss..."

"Wynter. And I'm not a charity case, I'm just conserving funds until I figure out what I'm gonna do about the lack of a housemate I have going on right now."

She didn't know why she'd answered honestly but didn't bother to try and take it back or explain herself further. The man smiled to himself and nodded, and Wynter had to wonder if someone had just said something into his earpiece from afar.

"My boss would like to know if you'd care to join him for a drink?" he suddenly asked, confirming her suspicions about the voice in his ear.

"Oh really, and just how did that come about?" she replied teasingly. The bouncer laughed and shook his head, his cheeks flushing a little as if he found being the go-between embarrassing but had no other choice.

"He's been watching you too and said to tell you you're an enigma, Wynter. And how he finds you intriguing and would like to meet you."

Wynter mulled his proposal over. She didn't think she was in the right frame of mind to get involved with whatever illustrious boss the security guard was talking about, especially as she'd never seen the guy or heard a thing about him. This was surely how young women like her got trafficked, or worse, involved with suspicious gangster types by their own accord?

"And your boss, is he intriguing and enigmatic too?" she replied with a smile, shaking her head. "Tell him thanks, but no thanks. I'm not the kind of girl who'll fall for some kind of mystery man scenario just because I'm a little bit down on my luck." She turned and started walking away, figuring it was time she went home after all.

As much as she'd once loved watching those romance movies depicting the billionaire businessmen getting the girl of his dreams, she hated the clichés of said girl being downtrodden or in need of a rescuer. Wynter certainly wasn't in need of anything or anyone, least of all some secretive club owner who had sent his henchman down to fetch him a companion for the evening.

The bouncer reached out and grabbed her hand in a bid to stop her, and Wynter turned and glared at him. "Take your hands off me," she demanded, and he immediately let go.

"Sorry, I just wanted to offer you another option. There's a potential alternative to you finding another housemate. Do you have a job, Wynter?" the man asked, and she nodded. "Full time?" she nodded again.

"Nine-to-five. What's your point?"

"And would you consider working evenings?"

Wynter rolled her eyes.

"What, behind your boss's bar?" she answered with a snide edge to her tone. If she was honest, it was the best offer she'd had all night and knew a second income would solve all her problems, but she still stopped herself from taking back what she'd said. Her ego simply couldn't allow that.

The guy gave her a second, smiled in a gentle way that told Wynter he knew exactly what was going through her mind, and then stepped forward. She watched him twitch his neck and knew that the voice in his ear was making more demands, so figured it wouldn't hurt to hear them out.

"You could take a job behind the bar for barely more than minimum wage," he told her, "where you'd be ogled at all night and rushed off your feet, but at least you'd get to keep coming to your favourite club…"

"Or?" she replied. His eyes flashed as if to say, 'clever girl' and she knew she was right. There was a better offer on the table. She just needed to hear it.

"Or you could be behind the scenes doing a real job. Some proper work that you'd be paid handsomely for. Care to know more?"

It was a strange question, or so Wynter thought. Of course she wanted to know more, and she nodded, but then stopped him before he went to deliver the rest of his boss's proposal.

"But I'm not a whore, nor will I strip or anything," she said with a frown, making him laugh.

"I can assure you, we already have plenty of those kinds of employees," he replied with a wry smile. "What you'd be doing is more up your street. Mr Cole requires someone with a keen interest and skills in graphic design to completely revamp both his portfolio and his behind-the-scenes profile. The club is open to the public each weekend, as you know, but during the week he caters to a variety of other clients with any number of necessities. He has secret online message boards and member-only sites that need a consistent eye for detail and continual moderation. Mr Cole has looked you up, Wynter, and he likes what he's found. He wants the right person in the entirely new role and is willing to offer you the chance to take it. Not only can you make it all your own but also move up into a job that'll far surpass the benefits of your current role."

It sounded good, but Wynter knew there had to be a catch. People like her weren't just handed jobs like this on a plate. There wasn't a time when she'd not been overlooked or pushed aside so that one of the big boys could move up, even though she'd worked her socks off for her current employer. He only ever seemed to want her to remain where she was.

"I find it hard to believe your boss is so ready to offer me the chance to single-handedly run his online empire when he hasn't even met me," she countered, thinking the entire proposal seemed too good to be true, so it more than likely was.

"Come back here tomorrow afternoon for a formal interview then," he responded, and the expression on his face was one of complete and open calmness. "You can see the offer in black and white and make an informed decision."

She believed him.

Wynter thought about it for a moment and figured she had to at least give the idea a proper think and maybe see what the boss had to say during her interview. She was being petulant in remaining frosty to the very insinuation that someone in high places might've noticed her and had to hope it wasn't purely because this Mr Cole wanted to get in her knickers.

"Sure, I'll come back tomorrow. What time?"

"Noon."

"I'll be here," she replied before sauntering away without looking back, and then

heading straight home.

And of course, she had gone the next day. She'd accepted the job, much to Marcus's satisfaction.

FOURTEEN

Marcus listened in on Wynter and David's conversation via his hidden cameras and smiled to himself. His minion was doing well in steering Wynter in the right direction. Not like that impossible lot down in IT. Marcus guessed that was what he got for employing true intellectuals. They were incredibly good at what they did and had maintained his epic database without incident, but at the same time, their higher brain function seemed to have a negative effect on the hex his priestess had created. They could fight back, albeit only to a small extent, but their influence on Wynter had shown over the past few days.

David, on the other hand, he was a true airless wonder and Marcus liked having him as his puppet. The boy was drawing Wynter in and helping to sway her. Coaxing her further into her curse to ensure she caved.

She was breaking down. His plan was working, and she was losing in their game. She didn't know which way was up, but she was starting to see the true north. The direction of her inner compass should always point her to—him.

There were forces against her she couldn't fathom, but Marcus had and would continue to use every one of them to his advantage. Like down in the nightclub just minutes earlier. His Priestess had worked her magic on the crowd at his request. She had made them close in on Wynter and saw to it she was panicked and desperate, and ready to be saved. Marcus could've ended her suffering any time he'd wanted, but it had been fun to see her suffer. To sense her despair. It'd even been amusing to toy with her in the aftermath. And what fun to discover just how desperately she had craved that gentler touch. To see him as her saviour because it was no doubt easier to let herself fall for the man she hoped he might somehow be underneath it all, rather than the monster it was clear he truly was.

***

Wynter finished her night's work in the quiet solitude of her office. She'd had enough of being around people in general and just wanted to be alone, so when two-am came, she waited a short while before leaving. She gave it a bit longer in the hope that most of the others would have gone and was rewarded with a quiet and almost empty office when she finally emerged, locked up, and made for the exit. There was still the security staff there, and some cleaners had gotten to work, but overall, it was still. Almost peaceful.

She headed home and fell into bed with a heavy pit still welling in her stomach. Nothing felt right, but then again, it somehow didn't feel wrong, either. She was being pulled in two incredibly different directions. All she had to do now was decide which side made the most sense.

The phone by her bedside woke her far too early the next morning, and Wynter answered it with a groan.

"What?" she demanded and was rewarded with the throaty laugh of her best friend, Cossette.

"Where have you been and what the hell are you doing? I feel like I haven't seen you in ages and of course I need all the gossip on the new job. But also, I needed you and couldn't get hold of you. Simon's been a right dickhead all week and I need to offload!"

This was typical Cossette. She'd left Wynter in the lurch by moving out to live with her fiancé, and ever since then she'd not stopped whingeing about the poor guy. Wynter hadn't heard the end of it, and had always half-heartedly listened, but not now. She needed to talk to someone herself and tried to find the words to tell Cossette how shit she was feeling, but it was like she'd forgotten how to open up. She didn't even know where to begin and instead let out a sigh and pretended, like always, that everything was fine.

"Are they asking about me at work? Did they receive my letter of resignation?" Wynter replied and knew by the loud laugh she got that her old bosses had indeed been made aware of her change in circumstance.

"It's all anyone can talk about. Some are speculating you were wooed by a tall, dark, and handsome stranger and ran off with him. But I set them straight," Cossette clucked, "told them you got a better offer in a multinational company and took it."

"Good, thanks," she replied, and then tried again to open up a little. "The hours are hell, but I think it's worth it. I'm still figuring out my place there…"

"What's that mean? Is it too hard? I had the same at my old job, do you remember? That boss of mine tried to shag me and when I refused him he made my life hell." There she went again, making it all about her. Wynter wanted to scream down the phone. To beg her friend to help her, but she was still harping on about herself.

"It's just really draining," Wynter eventually answered, and then figured she'd try and tell Cossette a little more about the ins and outs of the new job. Like she'd realised, there had been no non-disclosure agreement signed, so figured why not. She opened her mouth to say more. To tell her best friend how she'd spent her weekend being sucked dry by her vampire boss. But she couldn't utter a word. No matter how she tried, Wynter was incapable of forming any sound at all, while that was what she wanted to tell her. *Damn that curse,* she thought, both impressed and astonished by the intricate nature of it.

"Well, you just rest up, okay? Take it easy and get some more sleep. I'll try and remember not to call until the afternoon," Cossette replied, and Wynter promised she'd do just that.

They then ended the call, and she snuggled back into her pillows, eager to get some more sleep before it was time to start all over again at *Slave*, thinking again what a marvellous name Marcus had chosen for his club.

The next few nights went by in a blur. Wynter was kept super busy with what felt like a hundred requests for assistance from the different departments, plus her input via emails that'd come from all over the building, as well as from Marcus himself, even though he didn't put in much of an appearance in the flesh. All their correspondence was done via email, and she quickly became comfortable liaising with him online thanks to the lack of pretence and any form of strange ups and downs like she often found when dealing with him in the flesh. He was to the point and precise with what he wanted when over electronic mail. All business, which suited Wynter perfectly.

When Thursday night came around, she still hadn't confirmed with him whether she was willing to take on the extra day of overtime, and yet Marcus hadn't asked her again either. Did he just assume the matter was settled, and she'd be there? Wynter hoped not. She had no intention of staying whether he asked politely or downright demanded it. And still, she found herself turning up on Thursday evening with some spare clothes in a suit bag over her arm.

Wynter told herself it was all just part of her plan to keep a change of outfit at the office in case she spilled a drink or required a new set of clothes sometime. Of course, it had nothing to do with Marcus and his proposal that she remain at the club for the next three nights straight. No sir.

Halfway through her shift, she got a call from Bryn and immediately plucked the receiver from its cradle, placing it to her ear.

"Hey, Bryn. Everything okay?" she asked.

"Yes, thank you, Miss Armstrong," he replied, regarding her formally, no matter how many times she'd asked him to call her Wynter. "Mr Cole has dictated a few paragraphs for you to put on the website. He has asked me to send it directly for your attention to type. Are you happy for me to bring the Dictaphone down?"

Wynter rolled her eyes. Oh, so now she was his secretary too? He had some nerve.

"Sure, why the hell not?" she replied, figuring it wasn't fair for her to rant at Bryn about their boss's gall.

He ended the call and was at her office within a couple of minutes, the electronic recorder in his hands at the ready.

"I'm sorry," he told her, "but when he gives me specific instructions, I have to follow them. And he said you alone were allowed to hear what's on this tape."

Wynter felt sorry for Bryn. She wondered how long he had endured working directly for Marcus and just what he'd had to do in that time. In some ways, his role could possibly be deemed worse than hers. At least she got some respite from their boss, whereas Bryn was with him every night of the week without fail. It couldn't be easy.

"No problem," she told him, and Wynter also placed a gentle, reassuring hand on his shoulder. "I'm on it."

She then locked herself back inside and took her seat, all the while glaring at the recorder on the desk. She wasn't going to rush listening to it. Marcus could wait. And yet, it was all she could think about. Wynter had to know what was on it and why and soon found she couldn't focus on her other tasks, so knew she'd just get it over and done with.

With a huff, she hit the play button and opened a blank document on her screen, her hands poised over the keys at the ready.

"Good evening, Wynter," Marcus's deep and warming voice began to chime from the machine beside her, and she felt her body break out in goose bumps at the sound. She had barely heard his voice in days, and suddenly realised she'd missed it.

No, she scorned herself internally. *You didn't miss him. You don't even like him. Fight, Wynter. Always fight.*

"I would appreciate you adding an update to the members' only part of the website," he began, and remained ever so formal throughout. "As follows: Thank you for your recent feedback. To all members who have expressed an interest in my providing new premises within the UK, please rest assured I have taken your requests under advisement and have set up a series of meetings to that effect. I shall update in due course but do trust these changes are afoot and will come with exciting new elements to the regime."

Wynter typed as he spoke, before adding the update to a small text box she'd opened on the site. Nice and easy. A two-minute job.

She began to wonder why Marcus had sent the machine down rather than email the information to her and was about to turn it off when she heard him begin to speak again. "There's more, but this is just between you and I," his deep voice told her. With a frown, Wynter turned away from the computer and focused on the Dictaphone, her hands flying to her mouth so she could chew on her fingernails anxiously. "You never answered me before when I requested your assistance on Fridays in Patrick's place. I have therefore taken the liberty of making arrangements for us, regardless. I want to feed, of course, but I would like to give you the chance to earn a reward from me. To get your bonus, I first have a task for you…" he paused and Wynter leaned in closer, as if she might have missed it. He let out a small sound, almost like a shy laugh, and then continued, his voice sending another wave of goose bumps across her skin. "It would bring me great pleasure to watch someone fuck you," his recording continued, and the way he'd said *fuck* made every nerve ending in her body tingle.

Wynter went cold and then hot, and an ache she knew all too well sprung to life in her belly. Damn, Marcus had a way with his words.

He'd both shocked and aroused her, and while the stubbornness in her made Wynter still want to refuse him, she couldn't deny he was getting under her skin. Making her want what he wanted and need what he needed. "Male or female, it's your choice, but I want you naked and screaming with pleasure while I feed from you. I'll gather my chosen suitors. All you have to do is give me a name and I'll make it happen. If you're in my office when the clock turns two-oh-one tomorrow morning, I'll accept that as your way of telling me yes."

***

Marcus called a heads of department meeting at one-am. Each one of his most loyal subjects was issued a demand that they attend, and he used every bit of power he had over them to ensure they obeyed. Marcus never usually called a meeting so late, but he had something he needed to obtain. Not just Wynter's body at his command and her blood coursing through his own veins, but also her compliance. For her to experience at last the loss of a fight and for the realisation to strike that she would not win against him again.

It was going to be marvellous.

Jack and Patrick were the first to arrive. Ever the leaders of his merry little clan, they took their seats at the large meeting table and looked straight to him rather than sit chatting or fiddling with the paperwork before them. There was nothing for them to talk of, anyway. No life outside of his club or their duty to Marcus himself. They were both just half a man each. Nought but a single whole between the pair of them.

Jack was pining for his priestess. He missed her already and was yearning so strongly for something, it made the air around him palpable. Perhaps to know whether their exploits together had done the trick? To discover whether he was indeed about to become a father to a child he would never know. Yes, that was it. Marcus inhaled the scent deeply and licked his lips. He liked Jack so desolate and decided to play with his loyal servant some more. To give and take from him over and over for the fun of it, because he could. And gladly would.

Patrick was just as pathetic. A hopeless mess now that his services as Marcus's blood slave had come to an end. He hated not being used and missed that high already, but Marcus had bigger plans that no longer involved Patrick or his blood that had been soiled by the cancer running through his veins. Plans for a different future. Ones that involved someone knew at the helm.

As if on cue, Wynter then arrived, and she went to sit beside Jack, but Marcus shook his head and patted the seat to his right. She didn't want to obey his beckoning, he could tell. She hesitated and frowned like she was attempting to come up with a reason for her taking one of the other seats, but it was no use. Marcus pulled her to him by force, and Wynter let out an angry sigh as she flung herself into the chair.

"Good morning, Wynter," he told her with a smile.

"Morning, Marcus," she replied, looking everywhere but at him, and her coyness made him smile. She'd listened to his recording and clearly didn't know how to handle what she felt about his demands. Did she think he was bluffing? Marcus hoped so. It was going to be fun playing with her.

Joanna, Warren, and Marcella were next to arrive, and like the others, they each took their seats and sat in silence while they waited for the remaining few to arrive and for Marcus to get started. The lift brought the last four department heads, and they took their seats as well, and with a smile, Marcus stood and surveyed his motley little group.

He sent out a silent wave of power, exerting his sway over each of them to ensure they did exactly as he commanded, and then lapped up their looks of adoration and desire. Each one was his, through and through, but still the same one stood out in defiance. She was looking up at him like the others, but he wasn't sensing the same affection as them.

Wynter was steeling herself. Holding onto her strength because, as Marcus presumed, she was planning to defy him yet again. She was going to attempt to leave on time and he simply could not allow it. He had to be the victor in their new game and he would have his spoils, even if he had to play dirty to get them.

FIFTEEN

"I have called you all here to reveal my plans to open some new nightclubs," Marcus began, and Wynter watched in horror as the faces of his department heads all lit up, as though they wanted this. Wanted more locations, meaning more new employees, and more slaves for his friends to feed from. The sheer idea made her sick. "We have this club as well as the London establishments, plus two upcoming clubs in York. I'm thinking Dublin, Edinburgh, and Cardiff. What are your thoughts?"

Each of the department heads and managers then painstakingly gave their input and Wynter found herself watching the clock, willing them to hurry it along, but it was no use. The time was rapidly passing and as two-am approached; it didn't seem as if the meeting were remotely over with. Marcus had clearly timed his get-together, so that she was stuck there. His captive and, therefore, his new Friday blood bag. But there was another caveat to his request. He wanted her to do the unthinkable, and fear suddenly raged within her.

Wynter didn't want any kind of public show, and all she could do to settle her fraught mind was to look around the table at those he had invited along. To scrutinise his obvious choices.

His words from the recording were echoing around in her head. The others had been chosen to attend not only for their advice on the proposed new clubs but also for her to choose a fuck buddy for the morning from. Marcus had told her so, and now it was all she could think about. The group continued discussing the plans for this newest endeavour, of which Wynter had the sneaking suspicion was already in the pipeline anyway, so the meeting was nothing but a ruse, and she continued to watch them all in silence.

"London has been an incredibly successful venture and there is plenty of hype around the new club in York. I don't see why creating more would be an issue," Marcella was saying, "create a national branding. Do you have any premises in mind, Mr Cole?"

Wynter wanted to throttle her. She'd just opened the conversation further, and Marcus jumped right in. He began projecting photographs onto the far wall with the help of a device on the desktop and every head turned to look as a slideshow began to play.

It was like they were mesmerised or something, because every one of them were silent and still, doing nothing but stare at the point on the wall where Marcus demanded.

Wynter wondered why, but then quickly got her answer when he took his seat and leaned close, his lips just an inch or so from her ear.

"Ten minutes to go, Wynter," he whispered. She followed his gaze to the clock on the wall and saw that he was right. In just ten minutes, she would be his once again. She knew, deep down, that she didn't want to stay. She wanted her freedom and felt anger and anxiety spear in her gut just thinking about being forced into submission yet again by her strange new employer. Wynter also wanted to stand up and slap Patrick for being so old and feeble. How come he was getting off the hook? She glared at him but could see for herself how he was diminishing. Patrick had to be dying. That was the only explanation.

"And what happens then?" she enquired, instead of lashing out.

"I shall begin to feed," Marcus answered, as though it was obvious, "and they shall watch."

Wynter shuddered and shook her head no. She turned to peer into his icy blue eyes.

"No, please," she begged, but could see Marcus wasn't going to budge. He had trapped her there and forced her to comply with his first wish, but then he was going to add to that defeat by making her entertain him with one of her colleagues. The sheer thought of it made Wynter want to be sick.

"Then choose quickly," he replied with a sinister smile.

"I don't want any of them," Wynter told him, shaking her head. "Please, I can't do it."

"That's a lie."

He was right. All she could think about was Warren. How she wanted him to be the one to take care of her like he had promised. She couldn't deny finding him attractive and had been spending more time down in the IT department because of that pull. Wynter had hoped that one day they'd reach a point where things might've moved forward between them, but that wasn't the only reason she felt drawn to Warren now. Regardless of her true feelings towards him, he was the only one she trusted not to take advantage of her when she was vulnerable. The only person there who wasn't a vulture, as he'd called them.

Like always, Marcus could tell what she was thinking and seemed to know she did, in fact, have someone in mind. With a wide smile, he then turned back to the team and garnered their attention once again. "Very well," he told them. "I will visit these locations in due course and choose accordingly.

Thank you for your input."

Wynter listened, thinking about how he hadn't taken any real advice from them. She'd been right. He had made up his mind already. His conclusion further confirmed her suspicions that the meeting had been a trick just to get her in his office for when two-am arrived.

She stared at the clock while he spoke, watching the seconds count up to the change of hour. When two-am came, she let out a defeated sigh as she slumped back in her chair. The deal was done. Marcus had won. No matter what she'd said or done, he had won. She had to accept her third day of overtime no matter her reluctances. And it wasn't about to end there.

He didn't even look at her as he reached down and plucked her closest hand from where she'd cradled them in her lap. "Before you all leave; I have one last order of business."

As if he had mesmerised them again, the room fell silent, and all his chosen minions watched intently as he began to drink from her. As if it were nothing at all out of the ordinary.

Wynter's heart was pounding in her chest and she had to look away as she felt her body flush with heat and desire as he began to drink. She rubbed her thighs together uncontrollably and let out a moan when he drew in a deep gulp. The world was spinning, but he stopped before she could get too lightheaded and then closed the wound, offering Wynter her wrist back with a wink.

Marcus then looked around the room, surveying each of them, as if he were reading them in the same way she often felt he was reading her. "Tell me, which of you would like to stay behind and help Wynter to better serve my needs?" he asked them, and she watched as whatever spell he'd put them under waned and they were allowed to respond.

"Master, they should not be allowed to feed you. If she's not adequate enough, then you should call upon one of us, not them," Joanna demanded, pointing to the others with nothing but contempt. In fact, she was staring at Wynter in just the same way, and she felt like getting up and throttling her.

"Come now, Joanna. I've warned you against petty jealousy already this past week," Marcus replied casually, but Wynter could tell he was seething. "Don't make me have to teach you another of my lessons." She paled and sat back in her chair, looking flustered. "In fact, you three may leave. This doesn't involve you," he added, and then shooed them away. Begrudgingly, Jack, Patrick and a very sour looking Joanna all got up and left, leaving the rest of them behind.

Wynter watched them as the remaining few waited with achingly painful patience for him to reveal his intentions, but instead he turned to her and a broad, devious smile spread across his lips.

Before she could ask him what he wanted of her, she was moving. Climbing up out of her seat and onto the table against her own will. She knew it was Marcus doing it to her, but also that she had no other choice but to comply. His power over her was growing stronger, or at least it felt like it.

The vampire surveyed her as she moved into a seated position before him, just like she had on his desk before, and then he pushed back in his chair so that Wynter's legs could dangle open in front of him. Her heels slipped off her feet and onto the floor, but he didn't seem to care.

She could see him looking up her skirt hungrily and felt herself flush with heat again. Something inside of her wished he were looking at her that way because he wanted her physically. Desire for him burned brighter than ever and even though Wynter knew he only wanted the blood coursing through her veins, not the rest of the packaging, she still yearned for him in ways that shocked her. She was no fool. In the back of her mind, she still knew those feelings were the work of the curse and nothing more, and yet, something made her wonder if she was beginning to cave. To love him, just like he and the others had warned she would.

"Marcus," she hummed, "I want you, and you alone." Wynter's voice was quiet and soft, but full of yearning, and she watched as his eyes flashed with something. Some kind of emotion or comprehension, she couldn't be sure, but her words had seemed to surprise him. He shook it off almost immediately and let his cool and calm iciness fall back into place.

"I invite one of you to stay behind and see to it that Wynter is given her fill of orgasms," he told the others, having ignored her plea. "Who would like to volunteer?" Marcus then added, and Wynter saw each and every one of her colleagues' hands go up.

She was about to turn around so she could speak to them and apologise to explain that this wasn't her doing, but it appeared Marcus had other ideas. He stood and grabbed her by the knees she'd had open in front of her and then yanked them skywards. The move forced Wynter to fall back on the table, and she lifted her head just in time to stop it from crashing against the hard wood.

She went to cry out and give Marcus what for, when he parted her legs further and pushed her skirt up around her waist. He was so quick that by the time she went to react to each of his movements, he was already onto the next, and so all Wynter could do was lie back and let him do as he pleased. She got the feeling that was precisely the point. He was giving the others a show to lure them in, but also making it clear that Wynter herself had no sway over his actions, or how their day together was going to go.

Wynter locked eyes with Warren just as Marcus unclipped the stocking from her left thigh and began to remove it. "Choose," he told her before pressing his lips to her exposed flesh. She kept her eyes on Warren's even as Marcus cut into her skin and began to drink.

She let out a mewling sort of cry when the first wave of pleasure overtook her, and opened her mouth, ready to say Warren's name.

Humiliation overwhelmed her when he frowned and shook his head no before she could choose him. Wynter was mortified beyond anything she had felt before and knew Marcus could sense it. He let out a deep, rumbling growl and gulped harder from her vein, and she knew he was enjoying her moment of utter shame and despair.

She turned her face away from Warren and instead peered up at the ceiling, wracking her brains with whom to choose next, when she felt someone take her hand on the opposite side. Wynter looked for the culprit and found Marcella watching her with a gentle, innocent smile. Far from the friendly and relaxed way she'd had when they'd spent time together the few occasions Wynter had gone to her office.

It was a relief to find someone willing. And she trusted Marcella, like she thought she had trusted Warren. She was genuinely pleased to have her friend come through for her in the end. Wynter even began to wonder just how much Warren had meant it when he'd made her his promises and found herself recoiling from his direction on the table. She arched towards Marcella and smiled back at her, her body roaring with ecstasy and desire, but not for Marcus this time.

"I've chosen," she whimpered, and felt it as he closed the cut he had made before releasing her from his steady hold.

Free from his grasp, she clambered up onto the table and settled herself in front of Marcella, who had kept a firm grasp of her hand and was now holding it to her lips.

She didn't know about her new friend, but Wynter had never been with a woman before. She figured it would be just the same as with a man, though, minus the obvious, and was more than ready to give it a go. Her hormones were in frenzy and Wynter didn't hesitate to kiss Marcella when she turned her sweet face up towards hers. It was a gentle kiss, but also one of mutual acceptance and respect. Anything seemed possible with her, and even felt right. Far from the forced choice their entire encounter had initially seemed.

Wynter felt ready to indulge in a fantasy she'd not humoured before and was pleased to sense the same emotions emanating from Marcella via their kiss. They were both eager, yet willing to be led by the other. And, of course, by the dictator who had instigated the entire thing.

***

Marcus licked his lips, watching the two women with a salacious smile.

"Everybody out, bar Marcella," he commanded, and his order was obeyed immediately and without question. Just the way he liked it. The team of department heads moved for the lift as a collective, each emanating the same sense of disappointment, but one of them was giving off regret and despair in droves. It was calling to Marcus's senses, and he decided it was time to play one more game before indulging his new pet and her fantasies.

He left Wynter and Marcella to collect themselves and chased the disparaged IT guy down. Marcus held Warren back as he tried to follow the others into the elevator and then thrust him against the wall so that he would have a full view of the two women on a mission to satisfy both him and themselves once they were all alone.

Warren tried to fight against him, and Marcus had to smile at the foolish boy's attempt to defy him. He almost respected him for it.

"Please, Mr Cole. Let me go. I have to work my overtime today," he demanded, as if that would sway him.

"They can wait," Marcus answered without a care for the vampires who had booked Warren's services and would be waiting for him downstairs. They were going to be angry, but it would be Warren who would have to deal with it, not him.

And then he remembered just why this little minion in particular was so popular. "Although, that's exactly what they want, isn't it? To be allowed to punish you. To watch you suffer and pay for keeping them waiting."

Warren groaned and fought against Marcus again, and he surprised the old vampire with the display of strength he had when faced with the very creature who owned his body and soul.

He and Wynter were kindred spirits indeed, and it suddenly dawned on Marcus what his priestess had told him just nights before. Wynter was going to fall in love with another if he didn't stop her. She was going to break his curse and blood would spill by the next full moon.

Well, Marcus was determined to make sure that didn't happen. He could feel for himself how Warren was indeed torn. He needed to leave and yet had wanted to stay, so why had he refused her?

"Please," was all he replied, and Marcus found himself letting go.

"You're a fighter, Warren," he told him, "so fight."

"Fight who, sir?" he replied, and all Marcus had to do was nod his head in Wynter's direction to give him his answer.

"If you touch her, I will end you," he threatened through gritted teeth. "I will gut you and skin you alive, little rabbit, simply because I can. And then I'll serve you up in pieces to all of my friends."

Warren shuddered but then took a deep breath and stood taller, as though desperately trying to show dominance rather than cave beneath Marcus's threat.

"We're just colleagues. I promised I'd look after her whenever you're done lapping at her veins and I meant it," he then replied, but Marcus could still sense the despair oozing out of him. And the lust. He was watching the two women kiss and fondle one another intently, desperate to go and join them. Warren couldn't tear his eyes away and Marcus knew it was because he regretted his decision to refuse her.

"You had your chance, and you blew it. The next time she comes to see you, I suggest you tell her straight away that you're not interested in being her friend or her lover, or whatever the hell she wants you to be. She belongs to me and I say who and where and how. Got it, little rabbit?"

Warren saw red and Marcus revelled in the rage coming off him in droves. He'd taunted him on purpose and was delighted by the foolish man's reaction.

"Call me a fucking rabbit one more time and I swear to God I will find a way to hurt you," he growled, and Marcus simply burst out laughing.

In one fluid and controlled move, he then grabbed Warren by the back of the head and slammed it off the closed elevator doors. He fell to the ground, leaving a smear of blood in his wake, and clutched at his face as his nose began to pour with blood. Marcus contemplated taking a taste, but then recoiled. The fool was tainted and ruined. His blood marked by all those who had fed on him before.

"Let's see you fight back now, little rabbit," he ground, his lips curled back in a sneer. "And if you want to try coming after me, then do it, but be prepared to fail time and again before I eventually decide it's time to end your pitiful life."

Marcus then used his power over Warren to stir his senses and stoke the fire inside of him that loved him and would always do as he commanded. Warren fought the feelings, even in his pain and anguish, and Marcus laughed again. "You don't like it, do you? Being forced to adore me and be my slave for hire."

"No," Warren agreed. He just about managed to get to his feet and Marcus delighted when he stepped closer and Warren recoiled in fear.

"You'd best get used to it because you're my new favourite. The one I'll be keeping a close eye on to ensure you don't step out of line again, as well as the one I'll be recommending to all my new clients."

He then pressed the button to call the lift and stepped away with a devious smile. Warren looked a wreck and felt even worse, he could tell, and Marcus felt a sense of victory come over him as he watched him leave. It was just too easy.

SIXTEEN

Wynter watched Marcus and Warren fighting out of the corner of her eye and while she hated seeing him get hurt, she found it was rather satisfying. And kind of a chivalrous move from the ancient vamp. Warren had hurt her feelings and her pride, but Marcus had avenged her in his own odd way. He had questioned Warren and punished him, and even though Wynter knew there had to be a bigger reason than just to discipline him on her behalf, it still felt good to see him scuttle off with his proverbial tail between his legs.

She and Marcella were working each other up nicely and had been kissing and touching one another in a bid to get all those frenzied hormones buzzing, even after Marcus had finished his initial feed. She was already desperate to climax, her body aching to be touched, and she couldn't wait for the three of them to get started again.

"Wynter," Marcella whispered, breaking her heady reverie, "I want this. I want you," she added, along with another kiss. "But I'm not as experienced as I made out before. I don't really know what to do."

Wynter pulled back and looked into Marcella's warm eyes with a smile. So, she'd given her some false bravado that time when they'd discussed their sexual proclivities following a feed. Surely most people would've done the same in a bit of a bid to impress their new friends, though? She couldn't begrudge her a bit of over exaggeration and so kissed her again while scooting closer on the table and then wrapping her legs around Marcella's back.

"We can just show each other what we like. Where we like to be touched and how, and then the other can follow. This is about me and you, not him…"

They were still pressed against one another, Marcella standing between her open legs, when Marcus returned and then sauntered past the pair of them with a cocky grin.

"Shower," he told Wynter, who had guessed that was to be the case, anyway. He'd been the same the previous Sunday morning after her evening's work, and she could tell he liked his prey clean and fresh. Ready to tend to him.

But this time, it was going to be different. There was a third party involved, and Wynter was surprised by how calm and unnerved Marcella seemed to be. Anyone else and Wynter was sure they'd be all over Marcus in a bid to get in with him, but she was focused solely on her.

She led her behind the glass panel and into the bathroom, where they mirrored one another as they each undressed. Marcus watched them from the doorway, eyeing Wynter with a sort of reverence she found difficult to process. He seemed to be ignoring their guest, too. Just like Marcella, he was focused on her alone and it was odd having two sets of eyes on her as she stepped under the left set of jets and began washing her hair and body clean.

When she was done, she looked to her right and found Marcella had just finished up too, and she was about to shut off the water, but Marcus seemingly had other ideas. "Join her, Wynter. Keep each other company while I wash up as well."

She did as he'd commanded and stepped over to where Marcella was standing timidly beneath the warm jets. Without her clothes, she had a petite body Wynter was envious of. There wasn't a single stretch mark, nor a blemish in sight. She had breasts that were small, but seemed swollen, and she groaned appreciatively when Wynter cupped them and trailed her tongue around her nipples. She then ran her hand down over Marcella's stomach to her hips and laughed when she elicited a ticklish giggle from her.

Marcus watched them, and then removed his suit and underwear, and Wynter found herself watching his every move as he walked towards them, but then headed under the other shower. He was beautiful, and she studied him as he washed. Watched his delicate hands and the way they tended to the wash routine she herself had always taken for granted as a boring deed. But when he was touching himself and massaging that soap into his palms and then over his body, Wynter was mesmerised.

Marcella seemed to sense it and she reached for her, running her hands over the places Marcus was massaging on his own body. Her top-heavy frame had left her with a big set of boobs and a tiny waist, and Marcella didn't seem at all fussed by their differences in shape and size. Her fingers swirled across Wynter's nipples, and she worked them into peaks before gently pinching and kneading them, sending pleasure through every inch of her body.

She then followed each of Marcus's movements, even when he cleaned between his legs, and he then turned to the pair of them with that same smile that always dazzled her.

He continued to rub himself, his hand going back and forth in ways she had seen many a man do in the past. However, none of them had been this beautiful. Wynter wished she was touching him but knew she would have to settle for the alternative offered to her. Marcella's hands were magic. She was somehow gentle and yet still penetrating her deeply, both at the same time as she delved between her parted thighs and stroked in and out to the same rhythm Marcus was working.

His eyes were on her pussy just as hers were on his cock, and with a jolt, they both came at the exact same moment. Wynter cried out and began to pant with the force of it, while Marcus shuddered and released his climax, letting the water wash it away.

In his moment of release, his eyes burned a brighter blue than Wynter had ever seen them, but by the time they were both done, so too had that strange inner flame. He was cool and composed once more, and Wynter yearned for the return of that look in his eye. The sense of something deeper. Something real.

He turned and looked up into the jet of water, letting it cascade down his body while she continued to watch. In fact, she couldn't peel her eyes away. Not until he'd finished up and left her and Marcella behind. She watched him go right until the last moment and then snapped back to the here and now with a sigh. It was the first time they'd parted, and she hadn't been glad, and it felt odd to miss him.

"Was that okay?" Marcella asked her once she'd given Wynter a little space to come back down from her high. "Was it what you wanted?" she added as she shut off the water.

She was so gentle and timid Wynter wanted to laugh, but instead she stepped closer and placed a deep, appreciative kiss against her lips, her still wet body crushing against Marcella's. She was so odd. Like she really didn't know how to be with another person sexually, and not just with women. Everything about Marcella was different now that she was exposed and laid bare. Her bravado and the funny woman Wynter had gotten to know before was gone, and all that remained was a sweet and pure young woman with innocence like that of a child.

"It was perfect," she answered when she finally released Marcella from the kiss. "You are perfect."

Marcella blushed and smiled coyly but said nothing in response before then leading them out of the shower cubicle to where warm towels awaited them. Wynter moaned appreciatively as she wrapped one around herself. They were huge and like heaven against her sensitive skin. She let out a contented sigh before getting to work on drying off and fluffing her hair as dry as she could get it. Marcella did the same with her deep red shoulder-length hair and then helped her plait it and weave the braid into a bun, and soon they were laughing and joking at how inept she was at trying to style Wynter's far longer hair.

She loved spending the time with her though, and Marcella was so sweet it was endearing. Her lithe fingers were gentle, but she kept forgetting herself as she leaned across Wynter's back, their semi-naked bodies moving against each other's and the edges of their towels catching one another's, threatening to fall loose.

Marcus hadn't so much as bothered to wait for them as he dried off. He'd just left the women to it, and Wynter caught him watching the two of them through the open doorway with a scowl. She wanted to ask him what the problem was. To demand some kind of explanation. But instead, she smiled at him.

The games could wait. This, what was happening here between the three of them, was the best thing she could've hoped for. Marcella was tending to her with a tactile sort of grace she found she adored, and Marcus, well… he was being his usual brooding self, but still, she quite liked it.

***

Marcus watched Wynter with a frown, thinking how odd it was that he'd so easily entertained the idea of mutual voyeurism with her, when he'd never once done it before. Especially not with a human. He was a creature of habit and had only tended to his sexual needs with one woman in all his years. The vampire Camilla was marginally younger than he and the pair had come to an arrangement centuries before, so that whenever either of them needed a lover, they would make themselves available immediately. No matter where or when, Marcus had been there for Camilla, and vice versa.

His body grew restless and in need of release perhaps once or twice per human year, and she was the same. In fact, most vampires were. Their bodies worked slower than their human underlings did. They were creatures without much of an appetite for anything other than the blood coursing through their Blood Slave's veins. But, now and then, the mood would strike for something more than just the satisfaction a feed would give them. That was when vampires called upon one another to satisfy that urge. It wasn't that they respected humans too much to defile them, not at all. Far from it. If anything, most vampires saw them as too lowly to be worth their affections, plus there were risks to taking human lovers. It had to be real love or else there were severe consequences.

There was plenty of his kind that had found someone they truly cared for, of course. When a vampire fell in love, they fell hard, and so were often forced to turn their lover into one of their kind anyway, thanks to a kind of ancient oath each of them had readily taken in order to accept their vampiric transition. Like with all the other elements to their immortal existence, it was magic that had done the deed in creating them. Not God, a demonic force, or a curse, but an undertaking they'd had to accept. A blood pact with the ancient covens and dark mystical forces they were beholden to from the moment they were turned to their eventual demise.

Blood was a necessity, but anything more was by choice and wasn't to be taken lightly. It was why he'd refused the Priestess's insistence that he take Wynter and make her his. Should a vampire make love to a human, their souls would merge and their immortal life would be tied to the other's fleeting existence. The human would be protected and magically warded, and when they eventually died so too would their loved one, for the witches decreed that should the one you love perish, then surely any true soul mate would wish for the same fate rather than live on without them.

Instead, vampires turned their lovers before they could grow old, and they would enjoy immortality together as one. Many unions had been forged and whole families of vampires created over the years, but never for Marcus. He'd always remained alone. Never sired a single progeny. Never fallen in love or mated with another.

Times had changed, along with the morals and values of the humans they fed on, but still, the fundamentals remained the same. If a human wanted to become like him, they could ask for such a change. If accepted by a witch or warlock, their transition would be slow and their actions measured to ensure they were right for the gift being bestowed upon them. The oath was not taken lightly and would override even the most potent Blood Slave curse. The new vampire would be free from the chains of servitude and overnight would become one of the many predators feeding upon the humans in Marcus's employ.

None of Marcus's Blood Slaves knew this truth, though. It was one of their most absolute laws not to reveal how the transition worked, but in the throes of passion, even the strongest of vampires could reveal all to their lover. In a show of the ancient magic, their eyes burned brighter when they gazed upon the one they loved. Their soul, the only link to their former life, and that which had so readily been locked away, would come to life in that moment. Especially during their carnal release and the few seconds afterwards. Then they were helpless.

The act of making love was sacred to the witches, and they had kept it so even centuries later.

Even today, a vampire could only take a human to their bed if they truly loved them, and the oath they'd each taken had made it so they could not deceive their soul mate once the deed was done, even if they weren't yet turned. Any curse a human might be under would be broken. All manipulations would come to an end. The covens believed that to truly love another, then each party must be laid bare, and were willing to force it if necessary.

Marcus continued to watch as Wynter smiled up at her new friend. One she now knew intimately. She was so free with her sexuality it was a pleasure to see, and yet he couldn't help feeling covetous. He felt like sending Marcella away but knew he couldn't without looking like a jealous fool. And so, he forced his feelings aside and locked them tightly away.

This was dangerous ground, and that was the safest place for them, after all. Like the storybooks always said, true love was the greatest power of all and could break any spell. Falling in love was the biggest risk a vampire could take and was exactly why so many only ever had sex with those of their own kind. Like Marcus, they wouldn't take even their most prized Blood Slave to their bed. They would let them tend to their needs themselves in private or with another human after the feeding was over, while they ignored those desires and focused only on the needs that must.

And that was how he'd come to this decision to have another person service his new obsession. Of all the people Marcus had wanted to watch her be with over their day together, though, it was strange that Wynter had chosen Marcella—his undercover priestess. She was the same young girl he'd watched grow and change into a woman under his care and guidance. Someone who had only recently learned what it meant to have a lover touch and pleasure her. And now she was learning new lessons. Changing all over again and exploring her body, giving into new wants and needs.

It was becoming apparent to him very quickly how the witches didn't count lesbian love affairs as breaking their sacred oath never to make love to someone they weren't intending to procreate with. It made sense, given how every witch he'd ever known had been female and only ever used a man to further their bloodline. Never for fun, love, or a long-term liaison.

Plus, it was something he was now going to bear in mind during his alone time with Wynter. If foreplay wasn't enough to create an unbreakable merging between them, then he was damn sure he wasn't going to waste any chance he got to pleasure her. Himself too, just as long as he kept away in the aftermath when he felt weak and his soul was rising to the surface, ready to be laid bare.

He had felt it when he climaxed in the shower. He'd wanted to go to Wynter and bury himself inside of her, but his willpower had won, and Marcus had held himself back. He was sure he could do it again. Just as long as she didn't touch him, then all would be well.

He continued to watch as the two women he still couldn't quite believe were together left the bathroom and positioned themselves upon the sofa. Marcella was letting her cover slip. She was showing Wynter her true self, and yet there didn't seem to be any hurt feelings or upset from the latter.

Wynter seemed open and accepting of her, regardless of her daring and the demeanour of the independent woman she had falsely portrayed to her during the times they had met over the past week. In fact, he sensed no malice in her, only lust and desire. It was almost as if she liked teaching Marcella the intricacies of the female body, and Marcus wondered whether this kind of treatment was exactly what Wynter had needed to ensure she finally felt comfortable at *Slave*. Every time he had pushed her, she'd fought back, but with Marcella it was different. Wynter was the one pushing. She was doing the leading and appeared to be in her element with having someone so ready to follow her.

As he watched, Marcella climbed up higher on the sofa so that she was kneeling behind Wynter, and she leaned over her from behind, kissing her neck. Her hands danced over Wynter's supple breasts, and she shot Marcus a look that spoke a thousand meanings. She was enjoying this and knew he was, too.

Marcus wondered if she had planned it this way. If she had swayed Warren into refusing Wynter's request and then had swooped in to claim the prize she too had been drawn to? Was it inevitable that they all might love Wynter in the end? His Priestess had issued Marcus with a forewarning to take her as his own or lose her forever in the arms of another. Would it be to Marcella herself? Would they fall in love and his powerful witch would defy him after all her coven had done?

As he stood there deliberating, she climbed down and soon had her mouth between Wynter's parted thighs. Marcella was lapping at her, building another impending orgasm, and he could sense her desire building as well. She wanted Wynter to return the favour but was too shy to ask her for it. Sex, or at least the semblance of it she now knew could exist between two women, was something Marcella apparently wanted, and especially with his most prized possession.

After Wynter's next climax, she didn't hesitate or ask for permission to return the favour. Marcus watched as she took charge and soon had Marcella panting and writhing against her mouth atop the sofa. The atmosphere was heady and tense, and when the powerful witch cried out with her release, it wasn't just her eyes that grew brighter. Her entire body seemed to shine for a moment, and he was glad Wynter hadn't appeared to notice.

Damn, that woman was a sight to behold, though. She was bent over Marcella and was stark naked, her body completely on show to him. And still she had all the power. He would not touch her there. He couldn't. It was too dangerous.

Marcus felt as though he was running around in circles again, trying to piece it all together. Marcella had foreseen something. A life-altering change was on the horizon, and all centred on Wynter. He wished he knew more than just the fragmented prophecies he'd pieced together with his own thoughts and the experiences he'd had with her under his wing the previous week. There was still much for him to learn, but overall, he knew he had to trust that Marcella would make him proud.

He didn't know where their future lay, but he knew he would be a fool not to cherish every moment he had with both his coveted new slave and his powerful ally. She would come through for him in the end. His Priestess always did.

After all their years together and him having entertained her request to live as a human and work for him, Marcella had become a woman in just a matter of days. While still in her ceremonial robes, she had taken Jack over and over again until the pains within her had subsided, signifying the conception of the next generation of witch. Her human lover adored her now and pined for the woman he hadn't even been allowed to kiss, touch, or see while she'd taken him. Jack would never be the same again, just like Patrick hadn't been after conceiving Marcella with his old priestess.

And yet already, she had moved on. Little had Jack known that he was making a child with the same woman he had worked with for almost two years, but there was no point in him revealing the truth. Marcus knew Marcella had no intention of showing her true self to him. She was now released from the virginal binds that had once shackled her, and it appeared his priestess was eager to indulge her womanly needs in as many other ways as she could.

And while she took care of those needs, so too would he. Wynter had been given a long enough reprieve.

It was time he fed again.

SEVENTEEN

Wynter woke up late that afternoon with a big stretch and a loud yawn. She expected to find Marcella still lying beside her on the sofa where they'd eventually fallen asleep together, but she was gone and Wynter looked around for her in a panic. Marcus wasn't there either, and she immediately clambered up and pulled one of the thin cotton nightdresses from out the nearby drawer. As she was pulling it on, she heard a pair of voices and halted, listening intently.

"Unlike you, to succumb to the pleasures of man. Or should that be, woman?" Marcus was saying, and she heard Marcella laugh.

Wynter froze and listened closely, desperate to hear what Marcella had truly thought of their time together. She herself had enjoyed every moment of it and would gladly do it again sometime, but then again, she also knew she wasn't gay. While it had been fun, she didn't want to lead Marcella on or make her think there was anything to it, other than them having spent a day following Marcus's orders and her friend having come through for her when it'd mattered the most.

"It was time," she replied dreamily, "and she was worth it. Just a bit of fun with a beautiful woman who gave me everything I needed and more."

Wynter sighed in relief. Yes, it'd been fun all right, and she was glad Marcella thought of it the same way. It was nice knowing there would be no hurt feelings now that their liaison was over.

She also couldn't stop her thoughts from going to Warren and his embarrassing refusal to help her. God, she was mortified. She wasn't sure she could even face him that evening when it was time to work again and looked at the clock, wishing the time would slow a little.

What a change in her, she thought. Just days before, she had come to love her night-time work and hated the days she had spent feeding Marcus, whereas now she was exactly the opposite. Had he done it on purpose? Had he somehow known to push her and her friends and watch them crack?

Wynter told herself it was impossible, but then again, nothing was impossible where the devious vampire was concerned.

"Yes, just a bit of fun…" Marcus was saying, and Wynter got the feeling he was interrogating Marcella somewhat. "And something worth repeating or not?"

"Perhaps, if my lord commands it," Marcella answered, and Wynter thought it odd how she'd addressed Marcus. How old fashioned.

"And what of the baby?" he asked, making Wynter freeze in shock. Marcella was pregnant? She hadn't said anything before, and she just hoped their exploits wouldn't have hurt things in any way. Surely not, given how much they had both enjoyed themselves? Not once had Marcella had to stop or ask Wynter to be gentle, so she had to have been sure.

"She will come, as babies do," Marcella answered him with a teasing edge to her tone, "but I assure you, I am quite well and the pregnancy did not get in my way."

"Oh, I noticed," Marcus answered, "now go, get some rest."

Wynter heard Marcella leave, and she waited, listening to see if she could figure out what Marcus's next move was going to be. She got her answer when he appeared behind her as though he had moved as fast as lightening.

"Shit!" she cried, making him laugh, "you scared me."

"That's what you get for snooping," he replied.

"I didn't mean to…" Wynter stammered, "I woke up and didn't want to intrude."

"It's fine," he told her, batting the subject away as if he truly didn't care. "It was nothing private. In fact, it's better that you know of Marcella's condition."

Wynter nodded and then found herself stepping closer to Marcus, suddenly needing to touch him. To have him hold her. He reacted just the way she'd dared hope for and wrapped her in his arms. She then nestled herself against him and breathed him in, thinking it strange how he was neither warm nor cold, but almost imperceptibly temperate, and how still he remained. Like a waxwork model or something.

"What's wrong?" she whimpered. Wynter then pulled her head back and peered up at him. "Were you not pleased with us?"

Marcus answered by brushing the stray strands of hair from her exposed neck thoughtfully, stroking his way across her skin more times than had to have been necessary, but she didn't mind. It was nice to have him touch her so delicately.

"Yes, but you were both more focused on pleasuring yourselves than pleasing me, Wynter."

Her first instinct was to pander to him. To beg Marcus for forgiveness and ask how she might make it up to him, but then another voice in the back of her mind reminded her he had pushed for this. He had forced it upon her and she didn't need to ask his forgiveness in the slightest. The second voice won the internal battle to control her response and Wynter let out a small, forced laugh.

"I came, and you drank, over and over," she reminded him with a smile. "That was what you wanted, and I delivered it. The rest was up to me to do as I pleased."

A smile curled at Marcus's lips, and Wynter felt a pang of fear echo through her when he let it spread across his entire face.

"And so, you became my whore," he countered, and her heart sunk. He was right. Not even one week previously, she'd told David that she was not going to whore herself out to the boss talking in his earpiece. And now look at her, still reeling from a day spent fucking one of her colleagues for that same boss's enjoyment. "Shall I show you what I do to my whores, Wynter?" Marcus asked, but he didn't wait for her answer.

He pushed her away and charged for the chest of drawers she'd plucked the nightgown from, where he opened the bottom drawer, pulled out a day dress and tossed it to her.

Wynter yanked the old-fashioned nightie off and threw it to the floor in a huff and then waited for him to throw her some underwear. He didn't. Marcus simply watched her with a scowl, his brows furrowed atop those impossibly bright blue eyes.

She couldn't hold his gaze, and so looked down at the cotton dress in her hands. She wanted to cry. She'd seen the pattern and style before and knew exactly where he'd bought it. *Madam Brigitte's*. Her favourite boutique dress shop and the place she had frequented in a former life. She'd only been able to window-shop there for months due to her lack of funds, and at some point in the last week, he'd sent someone to buy her clothes from there. He'd known she'd love them and had bought them for her, and now she'd tainted his gift by being rude.

"Thank you," she mumbled, stroking the soft fabric. "I'm sorry. You don't have to show me anything. I was wrong, and you were right." There was no part of her that wanted to fight him, but that didn't seem to matter.

"Too late for saying sorry, Wynter. Just put the fucking dress on."

She hated how he could go from one extreme to the next. One moment he'd been so sweet and kind, but now he was back to being impossibly cruel again, and she loathed his ability to turn his emotions off so easily.

Fighting back her tears, Wynter pulled the dress over her head, letting it fall around her, and then buttoned it up at the front. The vintage style was perfect for her shape and size. It cinched in the middle and was low cut enough to be provocative without being slutty, and the sleeves fell in a delicate cascade over each shoulder before tightening around the tops of her arms. Luckily, the dress was long enough that she didn't feel exposed, given her lack of underwear, and when she was done, she turned away from Marcus so she could slip on her shoes.

The moment she was ready, he had her back in his grasp and was soon leading Wynter over to the elevator. Every move he made had her jumping out of her skin. He went to press the call button, and she flinched, and when he yanked her into the lift and pinned her to the mirrored wall, she cried out and shook her head. Wynter knew he was going to punish her. Was he going to force her into bed with someone? Turn her into a proper whore without any of the choices being her own this time? She couldn't stand not knowing and began to tremble and cry.

"Please, Marcus," she whimpered, "let's just spend this time together. Let me feed you," Wynter tried, and against all her inner commands to run or to fight him off her, she curled her body against his and placed her hands up on his shoulders, her fingers lightly rubbing his neck just above the collar of his polo shirt.

He pressed an urgent kiss to her lips in answer and then grabbed her behind so roughly Wynter knew it would bruise, but she didn't care. She gave herself to him and forced herself to be silent as Marcus lifted her up into his hold and then perched her up on the wooden handrail that went around the middle of the wall. He could have whatever he wanted, just as long as they remained alone.

He pulled away just long enough to press the stop button and halt the elevator's descent, locking them inside and somewhere between floors. And then he was on her again. Wynter was left panting, and she flushed with heat, but desperately tried to force those feelings away. Marcus needed to know it wasn't about sex, but about her willingness to be one of his special slaves. One of his chosen few that were his alone and he didn't share.

Shit, she thought. That was exactly the point. He'd wanted her to have some fun, but then had to have been jealous in the end because she'd had too much fun. Marcus didn't want to share at all, and he was willing to scare her into not wanting to go elsewhere, either.

Her legs opened wider at his command and she then did exactly as he directed, without question or argument. Marcus was calling the shots, and she knew she had to let him. The curse aside, Wynter's sense of self-preservation was doing the leading, and she was more than happy to let it.

She expected him to bite and feed, but Marcus surprised her again by burying his face in her pussy, rather than over his usual spot on her thigh. Wynter squealed and writhed when he lapped at her clit, and even when she felt the razor-sharp sting of his tongue cutting her down there, she continued in desperation and need. His careful licks changed to deep sucks as he began to drink from her, and Wynter became like a woman possessed. She cried out and reached down, unable to stop herself from pressing Marcus harder against her. He responded by taking more and more of her, and she gave it perfectly willingly.

When she came, she felt as though she might pass out. She saw stars and was in a euphoric high, but then reached the other side of her climax with a thud. Her head was pounding and her core ached, and she peered down to find Marcus still feeding from her. Panic rose in her chest, and she tried to squirm away, but his hold was absolute, and he wouldn't stop drinking. She screamed and called his name over and over, but he paid her no attention at all. He was lost, just like she'd been warned he would be, and death would soon be the only option left for her if he carried on this way.

A question entered her mind. Was she willing to give him everything? Would she happily die right here and now if he decided to drain her dry?

The answer was no. The curse was working on her yes, but not fully enough that he'd won, and she was done for. She was still her own person and wasn't going to let her life come to an end like this. "I resign," she mumbled, and then took a deep breath and forced herself to speak up, ignoring the blackness behind her eyes threatening to drag her under. "Marcus Cole, I wish to invoke my rights to resign and terminate my employment."

With a hiss, he pulled himself back and then clambered away, as though she'd struck him. He shook his head repeatedly, staring at her in shock. But Wynter was having none of it. She could feel his curse breaking somewhere deep inside of her and knew she was on her way to becoming her own person again. Not his slave. Not even his employee. Just Wynter. Penniless and miserable Wynter, but at least she'd be free. And alive.

"No," he cried, peering up at her in surprise. As if he couldn't quite believe she'd managed it. Marcus looked weak there on his knees, and she felt sorry for him. Part of her wanted to stay, but Wynter knew it was foolish to want it. Just because she'd felt safe there and loved the work didn't mean she could overlook the rest of the awful nonsense that went on inside Marcus's club.

Ignoring his pleas, Wynter pushed the button that restarted their descent and the lift shuddered back to life. They arrived on the first floor a few moments later and Wynter stormed out, but Marcus was hot on her heels. Plus, she was weak from her blood loss, and he was still far stronger than she'd ever be, and before she could get more than a few feet away, Marcus had her up off her feet and in his arms.

Wynter fought back and didn't stop. She was her own person again, and he had no sway over her, and she saw the handful of security guys watching her in surprise from the doorway that she knew would lead to her ultimate freedom.

"No!" she screamed, "get off me. Let me go." Marcus didn't listen to a word. He carried her further into the club and through the huge double doors that led to what would later be the dance floor. Where writhing bodies had once enveloped her was instead a set of leather beds, and atop each were two humans who were fucking like their lives depended on it. They were bound to each other at the waist, ensuring they couldn't part their bodies from one another, and each wrist had been cuffed to the bedside in readiness for the next feed. It was the most awful sight Wynter had ever seen, and she wanted to scream.

Marcus let her go and when she turned away, he whisked her around, so she was forced to see them in all their sexually depraved glory. They were people she knew or had seen around the offices, and she cringed and tried again to look away, but it was no use. Marcus had her face in his grasp from behind and he kept her looking forwards by force.

"Whores," he then growled in her ear, as if she hadn't already guessed. "I have whores by the plenty, Wynter, and while they fuck each other my clients drink from them." As if on cue, the next round of patrons were positioned by each wrist and they immediately began to feed. The people on the beds didn't seem to notice. They simply succumbed to their euphoria and closed their eyes, smiling to themselves as they rode the new high.

"I won't be your whore, Marcus," Wynter demanded, earning herself a gruff laugh.

"No, you won't," he agreed, his voice sending a shiver down her spine. "But you will be my slave. You may have, by some miracle, broken the curse, but I can still force you to do as I command. I have other methods at my disposal."

"Just admit you've lost," she replied, feeling braver by the second now that his curse had indeed lifted. "I'll never be yours again. I'm going to leave here and never come back."

Marcus didn't respond. She sensed rage rolling off him in waves, but he didn't bite, so to speak. Instead, he lifted Wynter off the ground again and carried her away. He stopped only once they'd left the main dance floor and had gone into the smaller one at the back, which was used as a chill-out room when she'd been there on a weekend night.

He settled Wynter back on her feet and it took her a few moments to decipher what it was she was seeing. A boxing ring was in the centre of the room but she couldn't properly see what was going on inside thanks to the huge array of onlookers who were shouting and calling to the people inside.

Then, as if Marcus had somehow willed them to part, the vampires each moved out of her line of sight and Wynter saw at last what it was they were watching. Warren was in there and he was laying punches at someone curled into a ball on the ground. Hope speared through Wynter's gut that it was a vampire he'd successfully fended off, but then she saw the guy's face and recognised him as one of the security guards she'd come across during the past week.

A whistle blew and Warren retreated right away, but the poor guy on the floor wasn't quite so lucky. He was then dragged out of the ring and straight into the arms of an awaiting vampire, who didn't waste a moment in getting her fill of his blood.

"Friday's is humans battling it out. Winner stays on, loser feeds," Marcus then explained to her, and Wynter cringed. She peered up at Warren and could see he was struggling with what he had just done. He couldn't even look at the man he had won against. "Your boy hates to win. But losing makes him feel worse. Like he's less of a man to have a bloodsucker taking his strength from him while he can do nothing to fight back."

"You quote him like you know," she retorted.

"I know everything," Marcus answered, as if it should've been obvious. "Such as how you have feelings for him, and he you," he added, and while Wynter felt butterflies spring to life in her belly, she still shook her head.

"He refused me. He walked away even after he'd told me he was going to help. I can't trust him, and I don't care for him."

"Liar."

Marcus was right. Seeing Warren up there, half naked and dripping with sweat and blood from what had to have been numerous fights, he was masculine, dangerous, and hot as hell. Wynter still wanted him, even if he had let her down. "Warren refused because he cares too much about you to accept your body in such a disrespectful way. He didn't want to have me feeding from you while he made love to you. He wanted it to be special. Real…"

"Now who's lying?" Wynter countered, but Marcus shook his head and smiled.

He was telling the truth. Warren did want her, but in the right way. She could see it now and felt awful for having thought of him so badly whilst with Marcella. Their liaison had truly meant nothing, while time with Warren would've meant everything, and evidently to them both.

Raw emotion flooded Wynter's spent body, and she knew it was more than lust or passion, but something meaningful. Something that would last long beyond that day or any other. Perhaps it was even a spark of real love? It was the first time she had felt anything for anyone since her ex had done his damage, and Wynter despaired at the thought of leaving Warren behind should she do as she had threatened and walk away from *Slave* without ever looking back.

She peered back up at him and watched him ready himself for another fight. His mind was gone, his gaze empty, and Wynter knew he'd gone onto autopilot in a bid to do whatever he needed to in order to survive his overtime shift. He would sacrifice the others to save himself being fed on, and Wynter couldn't blame him.

"He might win every fight today and get through it without having to feed, but tomorrow it's Warren versus any vampire willing to pay for a fight with him. He always loses and they always feed. Stay with me and I'll make sure they're gentle. Leave, and I'll give them permission to take more than just their fill. I'll let them drink him dry and leave him for dead. And all because you chose your freedom over his life."

"No, you can't do that!" Wynter croaked, and Marcus yanked her away, twisting her to face him. He then dropped his voice and pulled her closer to him, but this time, she felt none of that old spark between them. All she felt was hate. Disgust. Loathing.

Marcus looked positively delighted and shook his head, breathing her in.

"I can end his life anytime I want, and I will. He's disposable. They all are," he corrected her.

"Then why not kill me too and be done with this pretence? Surely I'm an embarrassment now that I've successfully broken your curse?"

"Because I wasn't talking about you," Marcus answered, and she caught him eyeing her darkly. He was somehow pleased with himself. Far from the embarrassed loser she'd expected after having been bested. "You must realise by now that you're different?"

"I got the hint, yeah," she replied snidely. Wynter tried to walk away, but Marcus grabbed her hand and yanked her back into his hold. He breathed her in again and smiled. His eyes even flashed brightly for half a second, just like they had previously.

"Why hadn't I thought of it before? To have a real captive, not someone under my spell, but someone who fights back? Someone whose blood ripples with hate and anguish, yet who cannot ever leave me?"

Wynter began to tremble. She shook her head and pulled back, her sorrow eating her up inside. Marcus let her go long enough for her to turn and look back at Warren, who was back to beating up his next victim in the ring. She couldn't take her eyes off him.

Could she live with walking away in the knowledge that Marcus would surely take out his loss on him? The answer was no. No matter how cold her past experiences with men had made her, she simply couldn't live another day if Warren was dead because of her.

Wynter turned back to Marcus and glowered at him.

"Don't tell him," she spat, "don't tell any of them."

"An interesting proposition," he replied, and rubbed his chin thoughtfully, his smile never faltering. "What are your terms?"

"I'll continue to work for you and will stay here the three days we'd previously agreed, but won't be shackled or treated like a prisoner. Only you and I will know the truth about the curse."

"And my priestess," he replied, and Wynter frowned. She had no idea who that was, but figured it had to be the person in charge of his vile hex and the reign he had created using it. She shrugged and nodded. "What do I get in return for allowing you such freedom?"

"What?" Wynter demanded. "You're getting to feed from me and treat me like a slave, even though I'm no longer under your spell. What more do

I have to give?"

"Your unending loyalty," Marcus answered, "love me or hate me. I will have your compliance and your devotion. If you try and run, I will kill your precious Warren. And then I'll move onto other people you care for. Starting with your dear friend Cossette, and then your mother..."

EIGHTEEN

How hadn't he seen it before? Hadn't realised just how sweet the victory would be to have a true slave at his disposal? No curse that made her mask that pain with love, but pure hatred, and all of it directed at him. Marcus was enraptured with her. Wynter despised him with every breath she took and didn't even attempt to hide it, and he savoured that flavour more than if she were the most splendid morsel who ever had lived. In fact, she probably now was.

Their deal struck. He led her away and back upstairs to his office. Past the guards who were watching them both in intrigue, wondering to themselves what it could possibly be that they had seen before when he'd charged past with her slung over him like a ragdoll.

Marcus sent a wave of power their way. A renewed sense of devotion washed over each of them and the team of guards soon forgot what they'd seen. Like Wynter had said, only the pair of them would know the truth. She would keep the secret because to her, the alternative was worse. Even worth truly enslaving herself for.

Marcus knew he'd drank too much before, but in that elevator he had turned wild with lust and greed for Wynter and her delectable blood. He'd thought he could handle anything, and then in a second, all of that had changed. He was lucky she was even still standing after everything he'd taken. But it was her own damn fault. She'd climaxed for him against his orders, and his predatory urges had well and truly kicked in. The ancient vampire hadn't been able to control himself and knew he wouldn't have stopped without force. Luckily for them both, Wynter had gone into survival mode and, because of her creeping closer to death, she'd been able to take charge of her fate at last. She had fought him off and lifted the curse, and her body had then pumped with enough adrenaline to keep her on her feet in the aftermath. But now, her strength was waning.

Her body, lacking in its essential blood cells, was doing its usual thing of crashing after a feed. Wynter was struggling to keep up with him as he

THE COMPLETE BLOOD SLAVE SERIES

marched her back upstairs, and so Marcus yanked her up into his arms again and held her to him. She struggled against his hold, only serving to make him smile wider and so he held her closer, but then she succumbed to the rest she so desperately needed and was asleep against him before they'd even reached his office.

There, he let her sleep. They had time and he could drink some more before their working night began, and so he got to work on a new plan. A brand new arrangement that would ensure she stuck to her word and wouldn't try to defy him again.

After all, that was the second time now that she'd gotten her own way. Anyone else and they'd be good and dead, but with her, Marcus couldn't stay angry. He had suffered a minor defeat, but had gained something even better. All the hexed, willing slaves in the world couldn't match up to what he now had at his command.

***

Wynter woke with a start, having felt what seemed like a hand pressing down against her chest. Judging by the force of it, she felt like she'd just been punched, but when she shot awake to fend off whoever was apparently attacking her, she found herself alone and in total darkness. Wynter felt immersed by the blackness though, as if it wasn't natural, and felt panic beginning to rise in her chest. Was she dead? Had her body crashed so hard she'd slipped away into the abyss of the afterlife?

Tears pricked at her eyes and she rubbed the aching spot on her chest. She felt real. Still alive, at least.

"Marcus?" she whimpered, and was met with nothing but icy silence.

"He's gone, for now," a deep, ominous voice eventually whispered. The sound was otherworldly and resonated as if it were both in her ears and across the room at the same time, and Wynter wrapped her arms around herself in an attempt to shield her body from whoever it had come from.

"Are…" she replied in a shaky whisper, "are you his witch?"

"His Priestess?" the voice answered, sending another chill down Wynter's spine. "Yes, of course."

She clutched at the still aching spot between her breasts and frowned. "Did you hurt me?"

"A simple tracking spell, my love," came the voice again, and Wynter shuddered but then quickly became annoyed. How dare she? After everything Wynter had agreed to do and carry on doing for Marcus! "You don't approve?" the Priestess mused, laughing to herself.

"Of course I don't approve," Wynter snapped, "I made him a promise and intend to follow through with it."

"And of course, you're a woman of your word, Wynter…"

"What's that supposed to—"

"You lie to everyone, including yourself. You pretend you don't care. That you're happier being closed-off and alone, but it's all a lie."

Wynter bristled and tried to look around again. She was quickly growing less and less fond of this priestess and was about ready to tell her where she could shove her assumptions.

"Everyone does that," she retorted, "so I suggest you realise what the fuck century you're living in and deal with the fact that every human in it is a walking disaster."

Hands were suddenly wrapped around her throat and Wynter struggled, clasping in vain at them to try and release their tight grip. She pleaded and begged, and then tried to fight back, but it was no use. The Priestess had a mighty grasp, and it appeared she wasn't against using it, even on Marcus's favourite Blood Slave.

"We've seen you," she whispered in Wynter's ear, and her voice sounded like that of twenty different people all rolled into one. As if it weren't one woman talking, but many. "Seen your future, Wynter. It isn't pretty."

As stars glittered in front of her eyes, Wynter was aware of her mind slipping away, and yet a vision came to her. Clearly, and as if she were seeing it for real.

Blood was everywhere. On the walls. On her. In her mouth. Wynter could taste it and instead of recoiling, she let out a satisfied moan and licked her fingertips clean. Then, at the sound of the lift arriving, she turned to find Marcus as he strolled in casually from the open doorway.

He laughed and shook his head playfully.

"I forgot just how hungry new vampires are."

"I need more," Wynter groaned, and she lunged for him, biting playfully at the hard skin on his neck.

"You'll not get any satisfaction drinking from me, my darling," he replied, peeling her away.

"Then bring me a slave," she replied.

"I have," Marcus told her, summoning a guest she somehow hadn't sensed was there from the waiting elevator. It was Warren who stepped out, his face contorted with rage, and yet Wynter could smell the fear rolling off him in delicious waves.

"So it's true? You really are one of them? A bloodsucker," he chastised, and Wynter lunged for him. Without a care, she drank and drank. Gulped every last drop down and then lifted her head just in time to hear the last beat of Warren's heart before he finally slipped away.

"Yes, and you're nothing but the dinner," Wynter teased his lifeless corpse before peeling herself away and jumping up into Marcus's awaiting arms. She kissed him tenderly and then peered into his eyes, the hues of them turning brighter and more vibrant as he looked back at her. Their souls were one now. Their fates united. Merged. Forever.

Wynter came back around with a garbled cry. Her strange dream. Snippets of that nightmare had been the exact same as this vision, and now they had been pieced together. It was real. How hadn't she realised before? Why hadn't she seen how it was not a dream at all, but a foretelling? Something that she ought to have considered a warning, rather than just a strange hallucination.

She tried to speak, but there was nothing, and as a second vision invaded her senses, Wynter realised how her future couldn't necessarily be so clearly laid out for her. Perhaps there was a choice. An alternative.

The full moon shone overhead, and Wynter was in the arms of a dark figure. His features were indiscernible, but he was holding her close, like he loved her. She then turned and peered up into his face with a smile. She loved him, too.

"I choose you," she then told him, "only you. Let's run away."

"He'll never let us go," the man answered her, "he might kill us for trying, but I'm willing to do it if it means we can be together."

"Me too…"

Wynter came back around again with a frown, and then watched as whatever darkness was covering them lifted to reveal a completely shrouded woman. The Priestess. She no longer had her hands around her throat. She was simply watching her from beneath her cape, her face and body entirely hidden from view.

"You will either be his saviour or his undoing, Wynter Armstrong. Whichever path you take leads you to heartache, pain, and loss in one way or another. Neither will be easy."

"I'll never let that happen," Wynter groaned, still feeling tired and uneasy. "If there are variances, then it means my future isn't set in stone. I can change it," she tried, but the Priestess said nothing. She just walked away and then disappeared out of sight before Wynter could so much as clamber out of the makeshift bed atop the large sofa to confront her further.

***

When six-pm finally rolled around and Marcus released her for the night, Wynter was even more of a mess than she had been earlier. She'd earned her freedom and then lost it again within the hour, but that wasn't what was playing on her mind the most. It was that awful vision of her as a vampire. Why had that priestess shown her it? To stop it from coming true? Or perhaps to show her that it was inevitable and she would remain Marcus's possession even if the day came that he gave her immortality?

Either way, Wynter felt like she was done for. She contemplated ending it all, but was too much of a coward. She wanted to talk to someone, anyone, yet didn't know where to turn. All she could do was lock herself in her office and cry. The tears came, and they didn't stop for the longest time. Not even when she could hear someone pounding on the door from the other side. And not when her phone rang over and over again on the desk.

Eventually, she stood and went to look out of the window at the clubbers below. She envied each and every one of them and wished for a different future.

Seven days before this, she too had been down there, innocently going about her business and trying to enjoy herself, regardless of her limited funds. She'd been yearning for something to change. An opportunity to present itself. Never had she thought that opportunity might come in the form of a new vampire boss who would dominate every moment of her days and nights since.

"Your wish came true, you silly bitch," she chastised her sour reflection in the glass. "So now what? Choose Marcus and become that monster you saw? Or choose anything else and bring his punishment down on you and everyone you love?"

"Or you can choose option number three..." a voice told her from behind, and Wynter spun around to find a woman there who had somehow managed to get inside her locked office. She went to her, but the woman disappeared, like some kind of a foggy apparition.

"No, don't go!" Wynter cried, "tell me, please."

The woman reappeared, but this time she was over on the other side of the room where Wynter had initially been stood.

"Follow him, your tormentor, and he will lead you to me. But do not let his soul merge with yours. When his eyes glow, it means he's calling to you, and your body will be powerless to refuse him, as will your soul. You will become his immortal bride if you do not escape, and there's only one way to do that. You must sever your connection with him completely."

"How?"

"I will show you, but not yet. Bide your time. All you have to do is follow him, for now..."

The end of book one in the Blood Slave series...

BLOOD SLAVE

The Complete series

#2 Round Two

By

Eden Wildblood

ONE

Thud, thud, thud!

The strange apparition of the woman vanished as quickly as she had appeared, leaving Wynter alone in her office once again. She'd evidently chosen to come when all her hope was lost, and her thoughts were still reeling as she turned towards the doorway and frowned. Only this time, she wasn't sad or afraid any longer, but instead filled with determination. The odd woman had told her there was another option on the table. She didn't have to be turned and wouldn't necessarily have to run either. All hope was not lost, after all. Or so she held onto that belief.

She continued to watch as the door was being pounded on so hard she thought it might be about to come off its hinges and then began to panic. Was Marcus onto her and had come thundering down to put an end to the strange conversation she'd somehow just managed to have with a kind of spectre? Was she in trouble for not having gotten straight to work on time and instead been wallowing in self-pity? Wynter honestly didn't think anyone cared enough to come chasing her down for personal reasons, so figured it had to be him.

Her blood ran cold at the thought. And how different those feelings towards him suddenly were. The curse truly was lifted, and rather than feel any sort of pull in her vampire boss's direction, she wanted nothing more than to run away.

She forced herself to calm down and remember the promise the strange woman had given her. There was a way out. All she had to do was be patient, and so she unlocked the door and inched it open to find Warren glowering at her from the other side.

It was a relief to see him, despite the anger reddening his cheeks.

"What?" she hollered, and then let out a shriek when he barged his way inside and flung himself down into the chair she had been sat crying in just minutes before.

"Lock the door, Wynter," he then demanded, and she watched as he rolled his sleeves up, showing off his extensive collection of tattoos, while also revealing fresh cuts on the inside of his wrists. So, he'd lost a fight in the end, after all. Served him right.

Wynter didn't know why, but she was glad. Pleased to see that he'd had to whore himself out to the vampires in the end, after all. Glad that after refusing to help her earlier that morning, Warren had been forced to fight and had eventually lost. Even if his denial had apparently been because he had wanted something real, rather than a show for Marcus's amusement.

Did he regret denying her? He didn't seem to. In fact, he seemed to have regretted letting her get close to him at all.

She did as he had asked and locked them inside, but then turned back to him with her arms folded and a hard expression on her still tear-stained face. Two could play this game, and she'd had more than enough practice at being a frosty bitch over the years.

"What do you want?" she asked with an icy edge to her tone she knew she had to thank Marcus for. He'd taught her well, it seemed. "To help me? To protect me? Because, of course, I'm one of you. And you take care of your own…" she mocked, reminding him of his promises from before.

"I came by earlier and all I could hear was you crying, Wynter. It broke my heart to hear you that way. To know I had caused some of that pain when I left you behind and refused to help you. I'm sorry," he groaned in response, not even arguing back.

Warren suddenly looked lost. He seemed more than just hurt or tired, he looked broken.

The visions the Priestess had given her returned by force and she felt an ache rattle through her chest. Warren was going to end up either dead at her feet or running for his life if she chose him over Marcus. She hadn't seen the man's face in her second vision, but it had to be him. There was no one else she cared for enough to run from their oppressive master with. No one that mattered enough to try.

She knew she had to push him away. This couldn't get in the way of her plan to escape, and so she quickly realised she had to force him to back off. It was the only chance she had to save him. And potentially herself.

Wynter finally had options, albeit ones which were far from optimal. She could become a vampire and Marcus's immortal bride, which meant she'd gladly drain and kill even those she cared about, including the man sitting opposite her. Or she could run away and still risk their safety for her own selfish means. He hadn't lied when he'd told her who would die first for her foolishness, and Wynter knew there would have to be another way.

Which, of course, there was also option number three now. To follow Marcus and let him lead her to the witch, as the woman who had appeared to her had stated. He would apparently take Wynter to her given a bit of time, and there she would be given an alternative to her, either becoming a bloodsucker or a runaway.

She knew she'd do whatever it took to try for a future other to that in which she was Marcus's soul mate, and eventually did the unthinkable and murdered Warren. The only man who meant a thing to her. The one she had given her freedom up for. He didn't know it, but he was the only reason she was even still in Marcus's godforsaken club at all. She would've been long gone if he hadn't issued her with an ultimatum. Him or her freedom, but the price of it was Warren's life.

"I don't care about you, Warren," she lied. "I wasn't crying for you, but for me. I'm looking out for myself now. I'm not one of your friends or on your team. I'm your boss and as far as I'm concerned, you can stay locked down in your basement day and night. I'll email you when I need an IT guy."

It broke her heart to say those words, but Wynter felt she had to. She knew he had been telling the truth about being sorry and that just made it hurt even more. Warren hadn't meant to upset her by saying no earlier that morning. He cared deeply for her, and Wynter knew it, but so did Marcus. His adoration came with dangerous consequences for anyone who tried to get between the pair of them, and so her budding relationship with the burly geek had to be over. She would put an end to this before it even began because, if she were sacrificing her freedom to save his life, she would go one step further and save him from a broken heart. Even if that meant her having to rip her own to shreds to find the strength to make it so.

"Sure. Whatever," he answered as he climbed back on to his feet. Warren then cracked his knuckles and stormed over to the door like the brute she'd always thought he was, but then he faltered at the last step. He turned back to her and showed the pain in his eyes as he took her in. He knew she didn't mean it but seemed to agree that this was for the best for now, and so stayed silent as he finally ducked out of her office and disappeared into the night without so much as looking back again.

Wynter kept herself locked away all night long after she'd kicked Warren out. He called up an hour after having left and was clearly still raging, she could tell, and he somehow managed to convey using his tone of voice alone how he didn't believe her. That he was indeed the fighter she had seen in that ring and he wasn't going to back off. He was going to keep on coming for her.

Even more reason to follow the apparition's instructions and follow Marcus into whatever darkness he intended to lead her. She would play the game. Play nice.

She had to.

When two-am came around, she was out the door and heading up in the lift without hesitation. But this time, thanks to the lack of a hex dragging her to him by force, she decided it was her God-given right to have her say.

Rather than throw herself at Marcus like she had the mornings previously, Wynter stormed over to him and slammed her hands down on the desk he had strewn her over on more than a couple of occasions.

"Good morning, Wynter," he told her with that bright, devious smile of his, "so wonderful to see you."

"Remove it," she growled, ignoring his greeting. Marcus's eyebrow flicked up in question, and Wynter saw it as a challenge rather than a show of his confusion. He was always completely in the know about his employees. Especially her—his new favourite. And she was a fighter too, just like Warren. That was what Marcus had said he so liked about her on more than one occasion, and she was determined not to ever stop fighting him.

She unbuttoned her blouse and let it fall open, ignoring the passion in his eyes as he swept his icy blue gaze over her exposed flesh. She had intended to show him her chest where the Priestess had touched her, placing some kind of spell on her.

"Ah, if you're that eager for me to feed, you only needed to elaborate, my sweet," he told her as he stood and stalked around to her side of the desk. Then, with what appeared to be no effort at all, Marcus grabbed her by the shoulders, plucked Wynter off her feet like a child, and then deposited her on the wooden top.

She tried to fight him off, but he was far too strong, of course. Marcus had her pinned down in an instant and he leaned over her, and she hated how helpless she was to stop him.

He then placed a gentle kiss against Wynter's lips, ignoring her writhing, before working his way down to her neck. There, he pressed his razor-sharp tongue down, which broke the skin over her artery, and a second later he began to drink.

Wynter felt her body rush with the usual endorphins that were a result of the feeding process. Like a bittersweet way of blocking out the gore and eliciting a carnal response, Marcus's bite still made her desirous for more, regardless of her having broken the curse he had placed her under the day he'd hired her. She was under an entirely different kind of spell when he fed and found she relaxed in a heartbeat. Despite all her strength of will and desire for independence, she shoved her hands in his dark hair and pulled him closer, reacting to his deep gulps with moans and sighs of pleasure.

God damn it. She was torn all over again. Questions were running through her mind at an alarming rate, her head spinning with them.

Why couldn't she just stop all of this and walk away? Why did she have to be so foolish and not jump at the first chance she'd been given at a different life? Why did she have to enjoy Marcus this way? Enjoy his touch. His smell. The feel of him against her skin…

When he sealed the wound and lifted his head away, he grinned down at her, and Wynter found herself smiling back. She even stroked his stubble covered chin and let her body curl towards his, like he was some kind of a magnet.

"Marcus," she hissed, and clutched at the lapels of his wool jacket, keeping him close.

"Yes?" he whispered back and then licked his lips clean of her blood.

The feeding was well and truly over though, and she snapped back to reality and remembered what she'd come in demanding.

"Tell your witch to remove her locator spell, or so help me God I'll..."

"You'll what, fight her? She'd crush you like a bug, Wynter. You could try and run, of course, but that wouldn't end well," he teased, laughing to himself as she shoved him away.

However, Marcus did focus his gaze on the exact spot Wynter had felt the Priestess mark her, and he looked thoughtful for a moment, as though considering her request. "The locator spell remains intact until I can trust you not to run from me."

She let out an angry shriek and sat up, and then proceeded to button her blouse back up in a bid to hide her body from him. She'd even worn trousers, just for the occasion, so she could keep his prying hands at bay, and so curled her legs up and sat with them crossed in front of her.

"What's it gonna take?" she then asked, and Marcus positively beamed at her readiness to negotiate.

"Your soul," he replied, before tilting her back down and then ripping her trousers clean off her legs and waist. He had his mouth over the vein on her thigh a second later and Wynter quickly felt herself falling under his mesmerising spell before she could stop him, not that she thought she could if she wanted to. However, his words rung in her head, and she remembered the warning from the strange apparition she'd seen in her office. If a vampire's soul merged with a human, then they were done for. Bonded for life. If he did so with her, Wynter would be done for too.

She peered down her half-naked body and frowned at the man lapping at her vein. However, of course, he was no man at all, but a monster. One whom she despised. And yet, Marcus had also been gentle at times. He had made her feel protected and comfortable, and had let her orgasm, even though all the others she had met had told her it was forbidden.

She was in complete and utter turmoil, but he didn't seem to care. All he wanted was his satisfaction, and she was about to beg him to stop feeding so she could keep some of her strength, when his hand reached up her opposite thigh and began caressing her sensitive flesh.

He crept higher and before Wynter could make a sound, Marcus had pushed aside her flimsy knickers and was stroking his way inside her molten core. Shit! She wasn't ready for that and let out a garbled moan, feeling beyond, ready for more. She opened her thighs and arched her hips, eliciting a laugh from her predatory master.

Marcus continued to push his long fingers in and out, and it wasn't long before she felt the usual tension building within her that signified her impending orgasm. It was all too much. The bite and his wonderful touch all at once weren't something she could fight, not that she wanted to. Not really.

She tried to stop it. Tried to call to him to stop feeding as she was so close, but it was no use. The orgasm burst forth and she shuddered with bliss as the wave overcame her, her body writhing against Marcus's fingers greedily as he continued to take her. She initially sought a second climax thanks to his relentless probing but, in a moment of clarity, opened her eyes to check whether Marcus was in a feeding frenzy or not. If he were, the best thing she could do was scream bloody murder and hope someone would come and pry his mouth from her vein before it was too late.

But instead, she was already safe. He had closed the wound without her realising and was watching her with a bloody smile. His gaze then lifted to hers and she saw his bright blue eyes seem to radiate with light from within. It was mesmerising.

Wynter stared into them, and imagined how if they switched off the lights in the room they would undoubtedly still shine like two icy beacons, and was about to laugh, when she remembered the reason why they shone like that. His soul, or whatever remained of it, was calling to hers, and she had to refuse it, or else.

"Marcus, your eyes," she whimpered, and then cried out when he yanked her off the desk and sat on his chair, pulling her onto his lap so she straddled him. His fingers continued their exploration between them and her body couldn't help but remain so ready for his touch. He coaxed her further towards her coveted second climax, and she was desperate for it, albeit utterly foolishly.

Wynter rode his hand like a woman possessed, and she kissed Marcus with reckless abandon while doing so. She could taste her blood on his lips and knew it ought to disgust her, but she felt beyond all of that now. All she cared about was herself and the needs she, too, had to satisfy.

She felt like she might finally be succumbing to the cold nature she had pretended to have and had Marcus to thank for that. He had taught her a trick or two about being selfish, and so she took a second orgasm from him without asking or begging. It was empowering, and probably the hottest dose of foreplay she had ever received in her life.

As she came down, Marcus let his hands retreat. He even covered her back over with her soaked knickers and watched her with his usual smile, but with an extra glint in his still luminescent eyes.

"Do you have any idea how much I want you, Wynter?" he growled as he pressed her body against his. She could feel his raging hard-on beneath her and let out a laugh.

"Yeah, I think I do," she replied, "but you can't, can you? Not unless you want to merge your soul with mine."

Marcus seemed surprised that she could possibly know so much, but he didn't say so. He just offered her a nod before standing up and letting her feet fall to the floor. Wynter then watched as the light emanating from his eyes waned, and by the time she had gathered her composure, it was gone completely.

Their moment was over, and she felt odd in the aftermath. The hex he had put her under a week previously might have been broken, but his bite still brought forth feelings that neither of them wanted to address once it was over.

Wynter felt awkward and still ever so confused. She wasn't sure what to say or do, so scooped up her ripped clothes and tossed them in the bin and then started walking towards the glass panel that partitioned the huge room. "I'm going to take a shower."

Marcus said nothing to stop her, and so she left without another word.

TWO

Marcus waited until Wynter was safely out of the way before summoning his priestess. She appeared within seconds and kept her head bowed in respect beneath her shrouding hood and cape. He couldn't see a single piece of flesh beneath the red cloak, and not even her long auburn hair was billowing out like she sometimes wore it.

"My lady," he said in greeting.

"My lord," she answered, "what might I do for you?"

"Well, you can start by telling me why you decided to place a locator spell on our dear Wynter?" he replied and knew there was a snide edge to his tone but didn't rectify it. Marcus had hardly shouted at or had to raise his voice to his priestess before, but when it came to his new favourite, he was ready to do whatever it took to ensure she remained his.

The Priestess had gotten close to her though. She had made love to her as he'd drunk from Wynter's vein. She had kissed and fondled her. Tasted that glorious body and elicited orgasms while having plenty of her own. Marcus knew it had been odd, the Priestess coming forward for such an explorative task, but she had. And, in the form of her usual guise, Marcella, she and Wynter, had sparked quite a connection. One Marcus hoped was for his benefit, and not his Priestess's.

"I don't trust her," the witch answered. She had always been honest with Marcus, often brutally so, and he had no reason not to believe her still, so he waited for her to elaborate further before he spoke again. "She will return to you each night and remain here the three days you've agreed, but I do not believe she will have your interests at heart in the days between. I have seen numerous visions of her future. Some catastrophic. Others wondrous. I do not know for sure which path Wynter will take, but I am certain I must keep watch."

"And will you take action should I need you to?" Marcus demanded, stepping closer. He gave her some credit; she did not step away. Not even when he was so close, he could hear her heart pounding in her chest.

"Always," she answered honestly, "and I will watch her on your behalf, my lord. I shall guide her to do your bidding and remain loyal."

"Then how is it she knows about the merging?" Marcus bellowed, his hand shooting up to her throat. Again, his priestess did not back away. He felt nothing but her servitude and steadfast loyalty emanating from her, and she even lifted her hands to remove the hood shrouding her face.

Her deep brown eyes drank him in, and Marcus yanked his hand away from her neck as if it had been burned. He then placed it upon her cheek with a gentle hold. "Tell me why you showed her."

"She is entitled to see, just as you are, what the future holds. I showed her but two potential outcomes of your liaison. The first was the one I hope for the most."

"A future in which our souls have merged, and she has been turned?"

"Of course. I will perform her ceremony myself."

Jealousy flooded through him, and Marcus had to fight the urge to lash out at his priestess again. Did she want that solely so she too could remain by Wynter's side? Did she have plans to steal her away and keep her for herself?

Marcus went to open his mouth to ask when she cut him off. "Stop this charade, my lord. You want her, so take her. None of this is for my own personal desire. Wynter is yours and yours alone, but only if you accept your fate."

"And what of the lover you warned me she would choose over me?" he growled.

"A *male* of merit, my lord. Not I, nor any other female. Be warned, should their souls merge, you will forever regret it."

His Priestess then bowed and left him, leaving Marcus seething.

Warren. It had to be him. No one else had turned Wynter's head. Not a single human had made her feel anything more than passing attraction. Not David. Not even Marcella. But with that burly geek, Wynter was a bundle of mixed emotions. He'd been able to sense them himself and knew the feelings were mutual. Warren wanted her too, but the foolish boy didn't know that she had given up her freedom for his sake, and Wynter had made him swear to it that he never would.

That didn't mean he couldn't toy with him, though.

Marcus left the office before Wynter had even emerged from her shower. He trusted that she'd stay there and use the time for a well-earned rest, and so headed down to the same club floor he had taken her to the previous day. His clients were lining up at the ready for their feeds, and each nodded to him respectfully as he passed. Some reeled with admiration for his stature, while others were envious, perhaps even violently so. He simply smiled. They could try and overthrow him if they so pleased. Marcus had thwarted many a foe over the years and, of course, more arose with every passing decade. Their kind all wanted power. They craved it over their prey and coveted it in their everyday lives. Marcus was one of the only vampires who made a fortune feeding them, while not having to pay a single penny for his own Blood Slaves. He was master of all that he saw, and then some.

He was also clever and cunning. He had files regarding the lives of every vampire in his extensive list of clients and would find ways to bring them down should they so much as try to revolt against him.

But not today. Right now, there was only one person he wanted to bring down. He knew where he wanted to go. To the same ring as before, and to the same slave.

"Mr Cole, what a pleasant surprise," one of his burly human guards said in greeting. He had a device in his palm that held the timetable for the day's bookings, and Marcus put his hand out for it. It was the man's and the other day staffs' job to oversee the successful deliverance of the slaves for his kind to feed from, and they had been briefed never to relinquish the device to any vampire, all except him. Many of his kind coveted their technology, and so the guards themselves were warded. Their blood was poison and if any vampire took so much as one drop, they would die a slow and painful death that no witch on Earth could provide an antidote to. It was his safeguard, and yet the boy had handed it over to his ruthless ruler without hesitation. He knew better than to argue with the master of his fate, after all.

Marcus grinned and peered down at the list. Today was Warren's lucky day. He had two vampire opponents lined up for later that morning, followed by a nice big gap so that he could rest. Well, that wasn't going to happen. In fact, he was going to need the rest sooner than anticipated because Marcus had plans for him.

"Send Warren down now," he barked, and the guard relayed the message via radio to the team who looked after the slaves on the first floor of the club.

He arrived just minutes later and approached the pair of them with a frown.

"Mr Cole?" he said and was right to be uneasy. "Has an extra fight been added?" Marcus nodded and then ushered Warren towards the boxing ring. He climbed in and went over to his corner, and then silence fell as Marcus climbed up after him.

"Yes, little rabbit," he taunted him while wearing his most wicked of smiles. "I told you you're my new favourite, didn't I? So, let's have some fun together."

Marcus removed his jacket and unbuttoned his shirt.

"Sir, I can't fight you," Warren pleaded, but Marcus continued to prepare. When he was ready, he stepped into the centre of the ring and used his power over Warren to lure him closer.

"Try," Marcus whispered with a bright smile, even though he knew it would be torture for Warren to do so. "Try for me. For your wounded pride. For Wynter and everything I have stolen from her…"

They were nose-to-nose and yet still, Warren refused to strike, so Marcus threw the first punch. With a blow strong enough to break a lesser man in two, he sent the boy flying backwards into the ropes, where he crumbled into a heap and curled into a ball on the floor of the ring.

Marcus grinned, but found he wasn't all that satisfied. The hex was too strong. He wouldn't fight back, not unless the Priestess lifted it, and Marcus wasn't about to go that far just to get a good fight out of him.

Delivering him with a good beating would have to do instead. He summoned Warren back to him again and then rained down blows upon him, leaving him covered in blood and bruises, but still breathing. Still alive. For now.

***

Strangely, Wynter wasn't tired after her shower. She got changed into one of the horrendous frilly nightdresses Marcus always stocked and gave her scruffy hair a few scrunches into messy waves, and then she padded out into the office but found he had left her alone. She wasn't expecting that, so thought for a minute what she could do to pass the time. Marcus wasn't exactly the type of guy to have books at the ready or a television, so she decided she'd go down to her office instead and retrieve her handbag so she could catch up with her friends via her mobile phone. She'd only be gone a few minutes and wouldn't leave the building, so figured it'd be okay.

Wynter was as quick as possible. In and out in a minute, but still made sure to properly lock her office behind her on the way back out to the lift. She was just finishing up when she turned and found David watching her from down the hall. He had a sort of smug smile that made a shiver creep down her spine. And that was the perfect word for how he was coming across—like some sort of creep.

He approached at speed, and Wynter groaned and moved as quickly as she could for the elevator. There, she hit the call button and then lifted a hand in an attempt to stop him from getting any nearer.

"Not now, David," she tried when that didn't work. What happened to their agreement to put things between them on hold and remain friends? He came to a stop just beside the lift and when she climbed inside, he wedged his foot in the way of the sensor to stop the doors closing behind her. "Please, I need to get back upstairs," she begged, hugging her body in an attempt to cover up. Damn, she wished she'd gotten changed into something more appropriate than just the nightdress. It was thin enough that he could probably see right through it, and the last thing she wanted was for David to still believe he might have a chance with her.

"What were you doing? Sneaking around?" he asked her with a snide edge to his tone. So, all niceties were clearly out of the window now that she had given him the brush off all week, but she wasn't going to let him upset her. She'd dealt with creeps before and scowled up at him in the same way she always did with those who'd tried it on with her in the past.

"In my own office?" she retorted and added an eye roll. "Gimmie a fucking break."

David laughed her remark off and then actually seemed to relax a little. He still had both hands on either side of the elevator door though, blocking it entirely, and he leaned back and looked up and down the corridor behind him. It appeared as if he might be about to walk away, but then he apparently changed his mind. A dark look swept across his face as an idea seemed to come to him.

Using his grip on the frame, David propelled himself into the elevator with Wynter and he had her pinned to the wall behind in a second, licking his lips while staring down into her face. This wasn't what she wanted. Not in the slightest. Being stuck down an otherwise empty corridor in a lift that was about to take them up to a just as empty office was not what she'd ever imagined could happen. Not on Marcus's watch. But it seemed this was happening, and when the lift began to ascend, Wynter panicked.

David's boyish charm was gone. The soft and tender way he'd had with her at first was long forgotten. All that remained was a predator, and one who she didn't particularly feel like entertaining the advances of. "Back off, David. Give me some space."

"I did," he growled and then pressed himself even tighter against her, invading Wynter's personal space on more than just an overbearing level, but a dangerous one. "I left you alone all week and instead of you getting your shit together, you just grew closer to him," David added, pointing upwards. She knew the gesture meant Marcus, and she wanted to laugh at the sheer stupidity of the man. Everything she and their vampire boss shared had been thanks to his hex. Even now, their only tender moments were because of the affect his bite had on her, and she knew there was no real love between them. There probably never would be. "But you owe me, Wynter. I took care of you, now it's time you took care of me—"

He then gripped her hands and held them by her head as he lunged for her, kissing her roughly while prodding her with his rock-hard cock in the belly. Wynter tried to fight him off, but he was stronger than she'd imagined, and by the time the lift arrived on the fourth floor, she was firmly in his grasp.

David emerged, holding her by the throat, and he looked around, clearly checking to see if Marcus was lurking there. He was still gone, and Wynter cursed him for being absent. The one time she needed him and he was nowhere to be found. Go figure.

"He'll kill you for this," she spat, but David didn't seem to care.

He flung her face down onto the rough carpet floor and lifted her flimsy nightgown to reveal her nakedness beneath. Wynter kicked and screamed against his roving hands, trying desperately to fend him off, but he just held her down by the back of the neck and pressed her cheek against the hard ground.

She couldn't move.

She could hardly even breathe, and cried out when the realisation hit that there was nothing she could do to stop him from doing whatever the hell he wanted to next.

But then, he was gone. His harsh hold on her suddenly absent. Not just let go but ripped away as David was plucked from atop her by force. It was as if some kind of giant hand, like a grabber in one of those arcade games at the beach, had ripped him up into the air and taken him away.

Wynter was sure it had to be Marcus having come to her aid at last, and she clambered up onto her knees and scooted forward so she could get out of their way. Trembling, she scrambled over by the wall and tucked herself into a ball as she tried to hide and block out what would surely be about to ensue, but then all she could hear was the thumping of her heart in her ears. Nothing else. No fight. No telling off. Just nothing...

When she eventually lifted her head and peered around to try and figure out what was happening, David was no longer there, but neither was Marcus. And it didn't appear to be some cruel joke or a ploy from David to make her think the ordeal was over. He genuinely had been removed from the situation, or so it seemed.

A garbled groan then alerted her senses again, and Wynter began to whimper. Of course, he couldn't have disappeared entirely, and she began looking around for any sign of him, but there was nothing.

"Help... please," then came a clearer groan, and Wynter finally managed to follow the sound. She peered up and found David at last. Like something out of a horror movie, he was stuck to the high ceiling right above where he'd just been holding her down moments before. That was the only way she could describe it. He was lying flat against the dark ceiling tiles against all laws of gravity and looked like he was being crushed up into them by force. Wynter whimpered and gazed up at him, but she didn't move or try to help him. All she could do was stare in absolute horror.

David had to have been propelled up there by some serious force. He was bleeding from his ears and nose thanks to the impact to the back of his head, plus his right leg was bending the wrong way, clearly broken. He had to be in so much pain, but she had no idea what to do, or whether she was capable of doing anything at all. Or if she even wanted to.

He opened his mouth like he was going to plead for help again, when he suddenly went flying back down to the ground with an almighty crack, as though whatever forces holding him up had let go just as suddenly as when they'd first grabbed him.

Wynter heaved at the sight and knew the awful cracking sound she'd heard had to have been that of more of bones breaking, and she full on gagged at the sight of his crumpled body laying still on the ground. Her instinct was to rush to his aid, and yet there was another voice echoing through her skull. One that told her to let the son of a bitch die. That he deserved it.

She made a lame attempt to sit up and move toward him, as though that would make her feel better about wanting to leave him to die. As if she could convince herself she'd tried and how her conscience was clear.

Before she could move another inch though, David was launched back up to the ceiling, but he didn't remain there. A second later, he plummeted back down, and so on. It was as if he were inside a box that someone was shaking. Up and down his body flew, crushing a bit more with each impact, and Wynter could do nothing but watch in horror as his life slowly drained from him.

When he was nothing but a broken mess, the rattling finally stopped, as did his punishment. Silence descended, and Wynter clambered backwards as far as she could. She didn't stop until she was sat against the far wall and there; she shook back and forth, unable to take her eyes off the bloody mess before her.

"That's what the locator spell was for, my love," the deep, resonating voice of the Priestess then chimed from across the room, and Wynter looked up to find the cloaked woman standing at the open end of the glass wall. She was covered from head to toe, like before, so Wynter couldn't see her face, but she somehow knew the strange woman was smiling. She was pleased with herself, and Wynter couldn't even begin to understand the mind of someone who'd think nothing of taking a life so violently.

"You sensed I was in danger?" she mumbled, thinking about what the Priestess had just said.

"Yes…"

"So, you killed him?" she cried in a shrill tone, her throat closing as she tried to breathe and fight back her tears.

Shock was clearly setting in, and Wynter felt herself trembling harder. The cold was seeping into her bones through her thin nightgown. Invading her, just like David had wanted to do. And just like the Priestess had successfully done with her spell.

"Yes…" the witch replied, "you can thank me later."

Wynter began laughing hysterically, which then turned to tears and wailing sobs. She couldn't speak but knew there were no words to convey how sickened she felt.

The Priestess simply stood and watched her come undone and didn't try to engage her or come closer to offer any form of comfort or apology. She simply observed her for a few seconds before disappearing back into the nothingness.

A blink of her eye and the woman was gone, and Wynter was immediately aware of how she was stuck in Marcus's office with only a bloody and pretty much unidentifiable corpse to keep her company.

She opened her mouth and let out a blood-curdling scream. The loudest, most painful shriek she had ever cried before. She didn't stop until she was hoarse and delirious with shock.

But then, she was acutely aware of a pair of strong arms picking her up off the floor and holding her close. Someone was shushing her and sharing their warmth to help soothe her, and it felt amazing.

Wynter was so glad not to be alone with David any longer that she clung to her saviour harder, expecting it to be Marcus, but when she peered up into his face, she found the hard set of a different man's jaw. His was chiselled and strong, and beautiful. She saw blond hair instead of his dark grey, and then the most incredible grey-blue eyes that locked on hers and held them.

"It's okay," the man told her in a heavily accented voice, "we can take care of 'dis."

THREE

The elevator then arrived with a *ding,* and Wynter felt the air in the room suddenly go ice cold. It was as if someone had just turned on the air conditioning full blast, and every inch of her went back to being frozen. She knew it was Marcus and could sense his rage emanating out of him in waves, but for whatever reason, he wasn't making a show of force against the man holding her. And he wasn't running over to release her from his grip.

The room was silent and still, everything at a standstill, as if time itself had stopped. Wynter knew she had to do something, and so tried to wriggle out of the grasp, still holding her tightly. It was no use. The man just pressed her harder against him.

"What is the meaning of this, Jakob?" Marcus shouted, and her odd saviour stopped dead. He didn't so much as draw a breath, and after a second, he seemed to decide on his course of action.

The man holding her turned and, as he did, Wynter could see Marcus properly at last. His gaze locked on hers and her stomach lurched. Was he angry with her for accepting the strange man's help? Did he blame her for what had happened to David? She couldn't read him at all but knew one thing for sure. She was going to be in some serious trouble if she didn't get away from the man who had scooped her into his arms. Jakob, or so Marcus, had called him. The name sounded foreign, which matched his accent. Perhaps Russian?

"While you were distracted, your slave was attacked, old friend. It's a good thing your priestess arrived in time to save her," Jakob replied in that same accented tone, his voice deep and gruff. It was alluring, and she stared up into his face again. He really was an admirable sight, and the lack of emotion on his face only made her more attracted to him.

Jeez, she really did have a type. And a hell of a lot of issues.

Wynter shook it off, figuring it was just another vampire and their captivating way they had about them. The magic lure they had that made you go willingly towards death. He would undoubtedly drink her dry given half the chance, just like the rest of them.

Marcus stepped closer to the pair of them but didn't seem in any rush to come and get her. Maybe he was proving to his guest that he was still in control and so didn't need to fight him. Or maybe the message was to her. Either way, she could tell the gory scene he'd just found in his office had mystified him. Wynter guessed he had been expecting to find it empty of all but her once he returned, and yet he'd walked in to find her in the arms of another vampire while another of his blood slaves lay dead on the ground.

"I knew my Priestess would handle things in my absence," Marcus replied with an air of nonchalance Wynter almost believed, if it weren't for the remarkable chill still lingering in the air between them. He then put out his hand, his palm up. "Come, Wynter," he told her, as if she was still under his spell and he was summoning her to him. As though he still had the power to force her movements.

She knew she had to play along. To pretend she was still hexed. For whatever reason, Jakob had to think she was beholden to Marcus for purposes other than bribery and forced submission, and so Wynter gave it all she had to try and wriggle free from his hold.

With a huff, he finally let her clamber out of his grasp, and Wynter made for Marcus as quickly as her shaky legs could take her. She was sure to go in a large arc around the crumpled body, still lying in a heap in the centre of the office, his blood now dark and congealed. David's face was almost unrecognisable and Wynter had to look away from the awful sight or else she had a feeling she might be sick.

She focused instead on Marcus's outstretched hand and ran the last few steps to take it and let him pull her to him. Wynter tucked herself under his arm and tried to focus solely on him, but then she turned her face and caught Jakob staring at her.

He was too intense. Too knowing. He was watching her with a look that said he was reading her like a book, and she didn't like it one little bit.

Marcus bristled and held Wynter closer. "Please take a seat, Jakob. Allow me a moment to settle my slave and I'll be right with you."

Without waiting for the go ahead, Marcus then led Wynter away and behind the glass partition. With her still tucked under his arm, he took her into the bathroom and then held her at arm's length, eyeing her up and down.

"I'm s-sorry," she mumbled, looking down at her nightdress that was covered in dirt and blood from her altercation with David. Wynter knew Marcus liked her clean, but now she felt more than just dirty. She felt broken. All she could picture when she closed her eyes was David's face, and the dark look on it as he'd eyed her and forced himself into her personal space. She could still feel his hands on her, and a shudder echoed down her spine.

"Take it off," Marcus answered with a frown, and she immediately did as she was told. "Did he hurt you?" he then asked, and Wynter nodded.

"Where?"

She showed him her neck and the friction burns to her knees and elbows. Marcus said nothing as he then inspected her body thoroughly, checking each bruise and scrape David had given her. He even parted her thighs to check he hadn't caused any damage there and seemed satisfied enough that she was still in one piece and hadn't been violated. "Get washed up and dressed and then get some rest. I'll be back shortly."

Marcus then turned to leave, but Wynter grabbed his hand. He twisted and scowled at her, but she refused to back down and stared into his eyes pleadingly.

"Please don't leave me," she implored.

Marcus's eyes flashed with that iridescent brightness at her plea, but he seemed lost for words. Wynter used the silence to her advantage and stepped closer to him, nestling her cold and naked body against his before planting a soft kiss against his pursed lips. "Please, Marcus. Stay."

"No," he eventually groaned before gently pushing her away.

Wynter knew he had to get back to his guest, but the rejection aroused venomous feelings from within her and she lashed out. She slapped Marcus as hard as she could manage and then tried for a second one, but he was too quick. He grabbed her flying hand and stopped it with ease and then frowned down at her through hooded eyes. "You get one, Wynter. Don't push it. Trust me, if David wasn't already dead, I'd have him strung up so I could butcher him slowly. Take pleasure in his pain and torment. And all in vengeance for his crimes against you, my sweet."

A sob burst from her chest and Wynter shook her head franticly as she crumbled once again.

"Liar," she cried, "you don't care about me." She then wrenched out of his grip and stumbled away, catching herself just before she went crashing into the glass door to the shower cubicles.

"Yeah, keep telling yourself that if you think it'll help," Marcus retorted before heading for the door.

"Fuck off," Wynter croaked, but then her heart sank when he opened the door and did exactly that.

By the time she'd cleaned herself up, Wynter was already a lot calmer, but she still hated the idea of being alone. She'd been in the bathroom a while and hoped to God that Marcus's meeting with the strange and yet enigmatic Jakob was over, so she didn't have to be on her own once she was back out in the living space behind the office.

She emerged in just a towel and went to the dresser, expecting to find another old-style nightie there, but instead she found black leggings and a fluffy jumper with stars painted on it. They were just like the ones she wore to bed at home in her cold house, and Wynter climbed into them both with a soppy smile. This was much better than the old-fashioned nightgowns Marcus had insisted she wear before. Warmth immediately spread through her, and Wynter felt tired at last. In fact, she was exhausted.

She went over to the sofa and sat on it, listening for any sign of Marcus and Jakob around the corner. She could hear them talking, however the conversation was too muffled for her to make out. But at least Marcus was there. He was close by. She pulled her knees up and hugged them, willing sleep to come, but it didn't. She was just too on edge. Too wired.

She stood and began to pace up and down in a bid to expel her nervous energy and was about to give up and run for the elevator when the Priestess appeared out of nowhere and blocked her path.

"Come," her deep voice whispered, and the witch held out her gloved hand. Wynter refused to take it, though. She was still wary of the strange woman, even after she'd saved her. Especially after that. Her chosen method was not what Wynter would've ever had in mind.

"Where?" she demanded, earning herself a laugh of amusement.

"To sleep," the Priestess then answered, but she dropped her hand and instead went to the couch, where she sat and nestled herself against one of the corners to get comfortable. She then placed one of the pillows on her lap and patted it gently.

"Just sleep?" Wynter asked, but she was already moving towards her, anyway. Already succumbing to her tiredness and the deep-seated sense of trust she somehow had towards the strange woman. Something about the Priestess made Wynter want to be near her. Want to touch her. It was like they were already part of one another. As if they had shared more than just a few fleeting moments together. Wynter couldn't put her finger on why, but she was already beginning to feel like she knew her.

"I'll protect you, my love. Watch over you," the Priestess insisted, and Wynter climbed down on the sofa, fighting a yawn as she went. She then put her head on the pillow and closed her eyes and couldn't deny she felt calmer than she had a few minutes earlier. Sleep was taking her, and Wynter let it.

She felt safe, kind of like her guardian angel was watching over her. The woman who had protected her from an attacker. The one who was there when Marcus had refused her. It didn't matter whether she agreed with her methods or not, what mattered was that the Priestess had been there for her when it counted. Even if she'd never seen her face, she was still the closest thing she had to a friend right now.

"Thank you," she whispered, and then let herself fall into a deep and dreamless sleep.

***

The pleasantries and small talk over, Marcus turned to Jakob and got down to business. He'd had enough playing nice and knew it was time they were honest with each other about why the dangerous and somewhat unpredictable vampire assassin had turned up at his club unannounced. He wasn't here of his own accord, Marcus knew that much at least, and so he fixed him with a knowing stare.

"So, she sent you to spy on me?" he asked, and Jakob nodded. They both knew who he was on about. Jakob's employer, Camilla. "And you came. You saw. Time to relay back about what I've been up to and why I've ignored her invitations to spend an evening with her. But then you showed yourself rather than slink away unnoticed. Why?"

Jakob's lip curled into a knowing smile, and it was all Marcus could do not to reach over and slap the guy. He'd been right. Jakob had been slinking around unannounced and hadn't intended on showing himself. It wasn't hard to figure out why.

"I 'vas intrigued by your slave. That man desired her so much he was willing to do whatever it took to have her. I could smell his desperation a mile away, and your priestess isn't much better. She wants her. And so do you." Jakob then rubbed his strong chin thoughtfully and readily revealed what was on his mind. "She has you all ensnared. Don't think I cannot see your affection for her," he told him, and Marcus didn't deny it.

He couldn't lie, especially not to a skilled interrogator such as Jakob. It was the assassin's job to figure people out. To spot the truth and catch his prey in their lies. And it was true. Wynter sure did have them all tied up in knots around her little finger. Thank God she didn't realise it, otherwise they would have a real issue with whom was in control here. Marcus would be forced to show her it was him, and deep down, he didn't want to offer her his firm hand. He wanted to protect Wynter. To care for her. To *love* her…

No, he told himself. To love meant being weak, and that would never happen.

"And so, what if the girl does have us spellbound? Her presence here is solely to feed me and entertain me, which she's doing a good job of. I don't see what business it is of yours, or your employer's?" he snapped.

Jakob shook his head, laughing to himself, and then he regarded Marcus with a smile.

"She gets jealous. You know 'dat. You've never given her a reason to be jealous before, but now, suddenly, you refuse to accept her invitation for an audience. Camilla simply wished to know why."

He didn't believe that for a single moment. She had to be more than just jealous to send Jakob after him.

"Indeed, and yet she and I have had the same arrangement for hundreds of years. Neither one of us forces the other to tend to their carnal needs. It is a mutually pleasurable affair, and one neither of us can claim to be exclusive or binding. Should I wish to refuse her and never take her to my bed again, I can without explanation. Please remind your boss of that," he countered.

"Surely you are not foolish enough to believe you mean nothing to her? To think she will let you go without a fight?" Jakob asked, but they both knew Marcus was neither a fool nor someone's boy-toy. He would take Camilla down in a heartbeat if he needed to and wouldn't so much as break a sweat in the process. But of course, that was exactly why an ancient vampire such as Camilla would have an assassin in her employ. A ruthless, cunning killer with no conscience and no soul, who would do his research well and find a way to end Marcus for her. She wouldn't even need to get her own hands dirty. Jakob had been her puppet for hundreds of years and while Marcus was still sure he would win in any fight, he knew one with him would be lengthy, bloody, and costly.

Jakob was notorious in his world. So famed for his wretched way of life that vampires and all manner of magical creatures knew his face in every corner of the world. If he arrived in town, they all knew someone was about to die, and just had to hope it wasn't their name on his list.

He'd torn apart entire families before finally ripping out his true target's heart. He'd broken apart souls that had been merged for decades, killing both parties in the process. And then there had been the business with the village he had laid waste to simply because their leader had offended him by cheating in a game of poker. Such violence in his wake. Such chaos. And all without an ounce of guilt. No shame in what he had done or the legacy of nought, but anarchy and death Jakob would undoubtedly leave behind.

Marcus wasn't willing to risk a war with him simply because his jilted lover had decided to take his dismissal badly. He knew an alternative had to be arranged. Or at the least, he would need to negotiate.

"Perhaps you should step up in my place, Jakob? You've remained loyal to Camilla for a long time and yet, as far as I can tell, have never been rewarded with more than your usual fee for serving her. Makes one wonder if there's something more than just your loyalty keeping you bound to her?"

Jakob frowned but didn't answer. He simply remained stoic, but he still bristled angrily and his reaction made Marcus wonder if he might be right. Maybe the heartless assassin was indeed a lover as well as a fighter. "You have seen for yourself how busy I am with my work. Tell Camilla I send my apologies, but I shan't be visiting with her again."

"You have a new lover in her place. Understood," Jakob snapped, and now it was Marcus's turn to have to hold back his anger.

How dare he presume that something sexual was going on between him and Wynter? Jakob had no place there with them, and Marcus was quick to tell him so.

"Speculating will only make you look weak. Like a gossiping little woman deciding on stirring up trouble where there isn't any. I took you for better than that, old friend…"

Jakob rose to the challenge. He stood and fixed Marcus with a venomous stare.

"I 'vill tell Camilla you are indisposed. You can explain the rest to her yourself when she pays you a visit, which we both know will be her next approach. Thank you for your hospitality," Jakob answered, his voice robotic and forcibly calm.

"Farewell," Marcus answered, and then he watched as Jakob disappeared into the night via the open window at the other end of the room, rather than the door.

He inwardly cursed the highly trained soldier for being able to come and go as he damn well pleased, and then locked the place up tight. Marcus also checked every inch of his office, and he decided then and there to hire some more guards. Not humans this time, but something more on the same level as Jakob. Something powerful enough to hold him off, should the day come that the assassin came to visit for reasons other than to check up on him at Camilla's behest.

When he was satisfied that his fortress was clear and he and his minions were alone again, Marcus headed into the back of the huge office, and he let out a contented sigh when he found his Priestess still watching over Wynter as she slept.

He'd hated having to leave her, especially when she had begged him not to go, but had been forced to keep up appearances for Jakob's—and ultimately Camilla's—sake. The assassin couldn't know how his soul had yearned to comfort hers in her moment of need. How desperate he'd been to stay with her. And how heart breaking it had been to have to walk away.

It'd already been abundantly clear how horrendous he felt when he'd returned to find her in Jakob's arms after the attack. He could've cut the tension in the air with a goddamn knife, and it'd taken everything he had not to storm across the room and forcibly remove her from the assassin's grasp. And so, he'd had forced himself to pretend. To act as though he cared not for the woman herself but only for the blood in her veins he'd rightfully claimed and was glad she'd figured him out and played along when he'd pretended to summon her back to his side. Such a clever girl, even when in shock following her awful traumatic experience.

He was also pleased to see that Marcella had taken it upon herself to fulfil the role of protector for him. There was no better person for the job. He knew that now. No one he trusted with Wynter's safekeeping more than his Priestess, and he vowed never to let himself feel jealous of her ever again.

His poor girl was curled in on herself protectively when he went to them. She had her head in the witch's lap, and she looked so peaceful it made his heart ache harder.

Marcus joined the pair of them on the sofa, having opted to squeeze on it by Wynter's side rather than take up one of the many other empty seats. He didn't explain himself, nor did he feel he had to, and the Priestess didn't say a word. She was still shrouded, concealing her face, but he knew she wasn't asleep. Like him, she never slept.

After a few minutes of silence, Marcus reached down and lifted Wynter's cold feet into his lap and frowned. Even in her fluffy pyjamas, she was still frozen. She needed somewhere proper to sleep when she came to him. A bed with a warm blanket made up only for her. Just for his special slave.

He rubbed the warmth back into them and then sighed. It was time he found out exactly what had transpired that afternoon between her and David.

"Did he rape her?" he whispered into the silence.

"No, but he tried," the Priestess answered. Marcus had thought as much, but he needed to know for sure. He had purposely put David in Wynter's path, after all, and it had backfired. Yes, he was willing to claim responsibility for the plan going awry, but he also felt guilty—an emotion he hadn't been plagued with ever since he could remember.

But the fact remained. Wynter had been attacked on his watch. She'd been hurt and would bear the bruises and marks of it for weeks to come, and Marcus wished he could take them away. Not only for her benefit but also his own. He didn't want to have to see them and be reminded of how he had failed her.

"Thank you," he told his witch, and the Priestess said nothing in response. She knew what the appreciation was for. She had saved Wynter while he was off playing his power games with Warren. Teaching him a lesson he'd thought was entirely justified at the time, when he ought to have been taking care of the woman he had insisted stay there with him. The woman he cared for, whether he was willing to admit it or not.

"I have the perfect protector in mind for her, my lord," the Priestess said, as though having read his mind about Wynter needing an official guard. Once again, they were on the same page.

"Don't say a shifter," he groaned. "We all know how frustrating they can be. And disloyal." The Priestess laughed and shook her still cloaked head.

"No, my lord. I was thinking of a jinni. A powerful and loyal presence that can watch over her day and night, but someone Wynter wouldn't even realise was there. And it just so happens I know where we can find one."

A grin spread across Marcus's face, and he nodded to his impressive witch. With just that one suggestion, she had outdone herself, and won back his favour. Jinn were notoriously reclusive and hard to command, but once someone was taken on as their charge, they were theirs and would protect their host until that person died, but then they were rewarded by being turned into one of their kind. It was either that, or the host was transformed into a vampire first, just like the Priestess had told him Wynter would be.

Their path, it seemed, was on course to that outcome like foretold. Marcus still didn't feel comfortable merging, but that aversion was already waning somewhat. As if it were being replaced with another fear. The fear of losing her, or of someone defiling the perfect creature he so enjoyed moulding and grooming to be his flawless companion.

Whichever way it worked out, Marcus was beginning to accept that she was soon going to have to turn away from her human heritage and become one of the immortal elite. And it was worth it knowing she would be safe from any other harm and securely by his side once she transitioned.

Damn, was this going to happen? It sure seemed so.

The Priestess had been given the go ahead and would undoubtedly have the jinni under her wing by dawn. She would see to it that he or she was delivered to the club without delay, and Wynter's protection would be in place before her next shift was even over.

The deed would be done without his darling young woman ever even knowing it, and she would be under the ruthless creature's magical protection from that moment onwards. And there would be no mercy for any creature who tried to come between a jinni and their charge. David's fate was nothing to that of an execution by Jinn. They were renowned for their dark forms of justice, and an even darker sense of humour. They often decapitated their oppressors and stripped the flesh from their bones before mounting them on their walls like macabre décor.

One notorious feud had ended with an entire household of vampires being strung up and drained of blood before being left to rot within a magical cage only the jinni could enter. After a decade of starvation, the patient captor had then relieved them of their skins and had them made into a leather chair, but he'd still refused to kill them. To this day, not a soul knew the rest of what'd happened to the family of vampires, but the story was an infamous lesson to any and all who dared make an enemy of a jinni.

This was going to be perfect.

FOUR

Wynter woke later that afternoon and, for a glorious moment, she forgot all about what had happened with David earlier that day. For just a few seconds, all was well, but then she shuffled on her pillow and felt the knees beneath it, reminding her of how she'd fallen asleep in the Priestess's lap. And, of course, she then remembered exactly why the strange witch had watched over her in the first place.

She turned her head to look up, expecting to see the same shrouded woman as before, but it wasn't her. It was Marcus. He seemed thoughtful and was looking off in the distance, as if he hadn't realised she'd awoken.

"Hey," she croaked as she rubbed her eyes and sat up. She figured the best thing was to compose herself and keep her distance, so she went to move down towards the opposite end of the sofa, but Marcus evidently had other ideas. He reached out and grabbed her before she could move away and then pulled her to him and held her close, his intense blue eyes swallowing her whole.

"Good afternoon, Wynter," he said with a smile. "I've enjoyed watching you sleep. It was very... peaceful."

Wynter's first instinct was to joke with him about being creepy, but she didn't. She just smiled and thanked him. It was nice to know she hadn't been left alone, even while she was out of it. Marcus and his Priestess had cared for her when she'd needed them most, and Wynter knew she wouldn't forget it in a hurry.

His breath then suddenly hitched and Wynter peered back into his eyes. She figured he wasn't used to having someone be genuinely happy to see him, and she shook her head.

"All these people who love you, and yet you're surprised when I offer you some real warmth?" she asked timidly.

"I understand how my curse works. I also accept their affection because I know it isn't real. But with you, everything *is* real. Often overwhelmingly so," he groaned, but thankfully didn't push her away. Wynter still needed the

161

closeness. In fact, she wanted even more. Her body ached all over from David's rough treatment, and she knew sex ought to be the last thing on her mind, yet she wanted Marcus to touch her. To make her feel good again and, albeit rather strangely, as though she was still desirable and untainted in his eyes.

She placed a gentle kiss against his lips and arched her body against his, and Marcus reacted exactly the way she had hoped. He held her tighter and kissed her back, softly at first and then harder. His lips were so forceful they bruised hers. His hands pressed into her hips so hard she knew he'd leave marks. But she didn't care. Unlike David's bruises, she welcomed them, along with the silent promises she could feel his body making hers.

Damn, this was so confusing.

When she eventually pulled away and sucked air deep into her chest, it was no surprise to see Marcus's eyes shining brightly from somewhere deep within him. They were the most beautiful things she had ever seen and Wynter knew she ought not to be drawn to that shining beacon calling to her from inside of him but couldn't help herself. She was meant to be following him to that woman in her apparition, not letting her soul merge with his. She was meant to be keeping a safe distance. And yet, all she wanted in that moment was for him to love her. To share his life with her, and his soul.

"Tell me what you want, Marcus," she croaked, "tell me what you need."

"I want you," he answered her, and pulled her closer still, "I need you."

Wynter thought about ripping off her clothes and throwing herself at his mercy. She had stayed away from having any real sex all week, but now all she could think about was having him inside of her. She yearned for it like an addict, but something still told her it was no use. He wasn't going to give her it, no matter what he truly wanted.

And he'd called her the fighter in their little tête-à-tête.

Before he even said another word, the shutters went down. Marcus retreated into his usual cold shell, and Wynter shuddered against the sudden chill that swept over the room.

She didn't need telling no. In fact, she didn't want to hear it at all, and so she climbed up out of Marcus's lap and walked over to the bathroom without another word.

Inside, she threw her pyjamas in the wash basket and climbed straight into the shower. Wynter turned up the heat and got to work on her wash routine, all the while telling herself it was better this way. She would remain free if he kept her at arm's length, and that was still the ultimate goal. To keep hold of the freedom, she had fought so hard to get back until she could get away from him completely.

After rinsing the last of the conditioner from her hair, Wynter finally opened her eyes and looked down at herself. It took a minute for her to take in the damage and attempt to get her head around what she was seeing. The bruises had now had time to develop. Her wrists were littered with cuts and were both purple where David had held them while he'd forced his kisses on her. Her legs had huge bruises on them too from where he'd thrown her down on the ground and wrenched them apart, and Wynter screwed her eyes shut, trying to force away the memory of her kicking and fighting him as he held her down and tried to force himself on her.

But it was no use. The memory was too fresh. The feeling of his hands roughing her up too real. Her pain too present. It was all just far too powerful to overcome.

Her knees hit the shower floor first, and Wynter let herself tumble down onto the ground without a care for the extra bruises it might cause. She felt lost and afraid all over again and let her tears flow. The world was suddenly no longer full of any hope or wonder like before, but an awful place and she knew there was no good left. There was nothing left to fight for.

She'd clung to her strength for so long, but the Priestess was right.

It was all a lie.

She wasn't strong.

Nothing was right.

She was alone and unloved.

Wynter didn't move. She just sat there and continued to cry her heart out, even when she was enveloped from behind and pulled into the strong arms of the vampire she knew would always hold her, even if he couldn't bring himself to properly love her.

Marcus was still fully clothed and his wet shirt clung to his chest as Wynter nestled herself against him, turning see-through. She started unbuttoning it, but he shook his head no. "I want you, Wynter, but not like this," he whispered. "I told you before, you're here to feed me. The rest is none of my business."

She saw red.

Wynter pushed herself out of his hold and clambered to her feet. She didn't care that she was naked. All she wanted was to get away. On wobbling legs, she grabbed a towel and then ran for the door, leaving Marcus still sitting beneath the cascading water.

She made it to the lift and threw herself inside the second it opened and thought for a moment she was going to get away unscathed, but then Marcus appeared and shoved his hand between the doors and forced them back open. He was dripping wet but didn't seem to care. Like her, he was clearly fraught and his emotions were all over the place. Wynter could read him that well, at least.

He looked a wreck, but he was also raging, and she pressed herself against the back wall of the elevator in absolute fear.

"I never thought I'd say this, but you win, Marcus," she then sighed dejectedly. "I'll never ask you for anything ever again. You can feed and then I'll leave to recuperate alone rather than let myself get even more confused by your mixed signals. These emotions within me aren't real, or at least you keep telling me so, and I'm finally learning not to trust my heart, but my head. I can't stand it any longer. I can't want you when all you want me for is my blood."

Wynter then looked up over his shoulder and saw the clock on the wall turn to six-pm. Her overtime shift was done. Their time was up. He knew it too and took a step back so that the lift doors could close at last, his eyes on hers the entire time, yet he didn't say a word. Marcus didn't even try to fight her on any of it, and she was left wondering if he'd ever actually cared at all.

**

The second Wynter was gone, Marcus unleashed his rage upon everything within his reach. He told himself it was for the better, but the pain and anguish resonating through him said otherwise. Why couldn't he just accept her? What was wrong with him to make him force her away like he repeatedly did? There were others who readily accepted love into their lives, but he just couldn't bring himself to say yes to her when she begged for him to love her. There was no reason he shouldn't take her, and yet he'd let her go, thinking he didn't care again, just like all the other times.

He couldn't fathom why he was so averse to letting their souls merge, but figured it was a power thing. To give part of himself over was a fate worse than death for a control freak such as he. And so, once again, he had pushed Wynter away. Told her no. Let her believe he didn't care for her. All he'd done was watch as she disappeared out of sight, rather than stop her. Rather than tell her he did care and wanted to love her but was scared.

And there it was. The true reason—he was scared.

That realisation only angered him further and Marcus picked up the nearest thing to him, a lamp, and hurtled it towards the glass wall that had until that second served as a partition to his top floor office. It shattered with ease, and Marcus didn't stop there.

He trashed the entire room. Ripped apart the sofa that still smelled of Wynter. Emptied the drawers of her new clothes and shredded them. Broke apart his huge wooden desk where she had perched naked before him and shattered it into a thousand pieces.

So, this was what it felt like to win?

He couldn't think of anything worse.

FIVE

Wynter had never been so grateful for her stash of essential supplies before in her entire life. She had the spare clothes hanging in her office closet and had even brought underwear and shoes in on the off chance she might need them. And now she needed them desperately. There was no hairdryer, so she had to leave her dark hair to dry in waves, but it wasn't the end of the world, and she made a mental note to bring in a spare for next time. Everything else was readily to hand in her gloriously private office and it wasn't long before she was dressed up, made up, and ready to start her usual night's work.

All was well, on the outside at least. Underneath the façade, she was a right royal fucking mess. What the hell else was new? She contemplated, but then forced all her emotions, anxieties, and pain away. She went back to adopting her utter coldness and fired up her computer before then busying herself with the usual admin of answering emails and moderating the website boards while updating each of their private sites.

Immersing herself in work was bliss. It worked a treat to distract her from the wreck of a life she had created for herself. After all, who needed therapy when you had procrastination and denial?

Hunger pains were soon niggling in her gut though, and after a couple of hours spent working solidly, she gave into them and poked her head out of her office door, checking to see whether the coast was clear.

There were workmen outside in the hallway, though. They were heading up and down in the lift to Marcus's office, and Wynter frowned. What on Earth were they up to?

She stepped out, locking the door behind her, and then approached one of the men.

"Hey, what's going on upstairs?" she asked with a gentle smile.

"Mr Cole has asked us to redecorate his office," he answered, and was about to head back into the lift when Wynter put her hand on his arm.

"I have some things up there. Would it be okay if I came up and grabbed them?" she asked, thinking of her clothes and her handbag that was still in Marcus's office from when she'd been down to get them that morning before running into David—someone she didn't want to be thinking about right now though so forced that thought away.

"No, Miss. The room has been cleared already and everything has been binned. It's now't but an empty shell," he replied, and then left in the awaiting elevator.

Wynter stormed over to the desk where Bryn was sat typing at his computer, and he turned to her with a smile, which dropped when he saw how enraged she was.

"Miss Armstrong, what's wrong?" he asked, his tone gentle in a practised bid to diffuse the tension.

"What's Marcus playing at?" she demanded, and then lowered her voice. "My handbag was upstairs. Please tell me it's not been thrown out in all the rubbish?"

Bryn looked sheepish. He checked down the corridor to ensure they weren't going to be overheard and then leaned closer to her with a frown.

"If it was up there, then it left in pieces," he told her, "this was not a planned redecoration. Put it that way. It sounded like an animal had gotten loose in there." Bryn then looked her up and down, one eyebrow raised in questioning.

It was obvious he thought she had something to do with whatever had gone on upstairs, and Wynter knew he was right, but she wasn't going to say so.

"He was fine when I left," she lied, "thank you anyway."

Wynter then headed for the main stairs and she bounded down them to the basement. She told herself that she wasn't looking for a certain someone, but for the group of people she felt safe amongst. The team she was part of despite what she had told Warren the last time she'd seen him. She just needed somewhere safe to hide out until she could figure out what was going on with Marcus, but as she stalked down, a bunch of questions were whirring around in her head.

Had he trashed the office because of what had been said and done between them? Was his refusal of her all lies and bravado? Did he truly care?

His soul had been shining out at her from behind those pale blue eyes numerous times, and Wynter knew that reaction had been real. It wasn't a lie or something she'd imagined thanks to her raging hormones, but Marcus had still pushed her away, despite it all. He had let her go, rather than beg her to stay, and so he was to blame for however he'd felt in the aftermath of their fight. If he was angry enough to lay waste to his own office, then it was on him. She'd tried and tried to get him to stop hiding, so wouldn't let herself feel guilty about how he chose to unleash those emotions when her back was turned.

Inside the open-plan IT office, Wynter went straight for the kitchenette, and she poured herself a large coffee before grabbing one of the bagels from the cupboard and popping it in the toaster.

She then spied Phoebe across the room and offered her a wave and was pleased to see a welcoming smile on her face as she dropped what she was doing and came bounding over.

"Hey, where have you been?" Phoebe asked when she reached her, "we've missed you." Wynter gave her an awkward smile. She'd stayed away on purpose after her fight with Warren. She'd told him she wasn't one of them and didn't want to be, but it was all lies. Pain she had to put upon him to help her force him aside. It was nice to know he hadn't relayed her hurtful words to the rest of the team, though.

"Missed you too, Phoebe," she replied, and then gave her a small hug. "Things have been mental upstairs. Plus, I had a run in with Warren yesterday," she added, thinking a bit of honesty wouldn't hurt.

"Ah, so that's why he's been such a delight," Phoebe replied with a knowing smile. "I know he hates Fridays and Saturdays because of the obvious, but he's not usually such a miserable arse as he has been this weekend. I thought it must've been because he took a bigger beating both days than usual."

Wynter frowned. Warren was hurt?

She looked around for him, but he wasn't there. He wasn't even in his makeshift office behind the frosted glass partition. Surely he wasn't home sick?

"Is he okay?" she asked, and Phoebe shrugged. "Where is he?"

"He's still in one piece. We all have good weeks and bad. He'll get over it," she replied sullenly, "and he's up in marketing helping Marcella with something. He'll be back in a few minutes."

Wynter sighed in relief. She couldn't have handled it if Warren was in too bad of a state. Not after she'd seen for herself just how nasty it was in that ring.

They sat down and she started eating her bagel with a frown. She tried to pretend she didn't care, but truly did. She wanted to see if he really was okay, or if Marcus had somehow hurt him some more. She didn't trust that he would've left Warren alone while her back was turned.

She'd seen Marcus lash out at him on Friday morning after Warren had rejected her, but other than his fighting in the ring, as far as Wynter knew, they hadn't had any altercations. Unless perhaps Marcus had given him more vampires to spar with over the Saturday daytime? Had he given him a heavy workload in the knowledge that he wouldn't be able to cope, just to spite him, and Wynter? Had he done his best to make sure Warren was beaten and broken so that she no longer desired him so?

Wynter didn't doubt he would be capable of such things, and felt her despair surge within, as if it were a growing, living thing.

"And he's miserable? Or just in pain?" Wynter asked, and she couldn't deny the ache she felt in her chest when Phoebe reached across and put her hand over hers. It was such a gentle, tender thing to do, and still the gesture spoke volumes. Kindness. It cost nothing, and yet Wynter felt it was just another debt she owed. Another person she would have to fret over.

"Both," Phoebe answered, "and something tells me you're exactly the same."

Wynter burst into tears and didn't even try to quieten them when half the room turned to stare at her in shock. She even let Phoebe gather her in her arms and hold her. It was wonderful, but still her tears kept flowing, no matter how many minutes ticked by.

Her week had been hell. Wynter had hated her new life one day, loved it the next, and then feared it just enough to earn back some semblance of her freedom by the end. She was glad of her new job, yet her heart was now full of nothing but contempt for the vampire who had given her it.

"What the fuck?" Warren's voice permeated the chaos, but Wynter ignored him. She kept her face buried against Phoebe's shoulder and clung to her tighter.

"Back off," Phoebe replied, and Wynter heard Warren mutter beneath his breath, but he did as she had asked. He stayed away.

The sound of a spoon hitting the inside of a mug then reached her, as did the smell of fresh coffee. Next, she heard a chair being pulled out near to her and someone took a seat with a thud.

Gulp. Gulp.

Did he have to drink it so loud?

Gulp.

It took Wynter a few moments to realise she was no longer crying. To notice how she was listening for him, rather than pouring her anguish out onto poor Phoebe's blouse. She shuffled a little and turned her head just enough so that she could see him out of the corner of her eye.

Warren was sitting two chairs away, his back straight and his arms out in front of him on the table, a mug still cradled in his hands. He had cuts and bruises all over his face and neck, as well as on his knuckles and wrists.

Wynter could also see the feeding marks. So many littered his skin, not hidden even by the tattoos etched upon every inch of his flesh. And there were too many. It wasn't fair.

"Is that my fault?" she croaked.

Warren didn't even look at her. He just stood and stormed back over to where the pot of coffee was sat waiting.

"You guys want one?" he asked.

"Yeah," said Phoebe.

"Yeah," echoed Wynter.

He delivered them without any care for whatever sloshed over the side, and Wynter had to laugh. Warren certainly wasn't the delicate sort, so she wasn't surprised in the least. In fact, she smiled to herself despite the ache still radiating in her chest.

The three of them sat in silence for a while, and Wynter eventually peeled herself from Phoebe so she could pluck up her coffee and take a sip. It was perfect and made just as she liked it. Fresh tears threatened, but she beat them back and took a deep breath before finally looking up and over at Warren. He was sitting waiting patiently, and she appreciated him giving her the time to gather herself. He hadn't pounced, and he hadn't come in shouting or screaming either. He'd simply let her be.

"None of this is your fault, Wynter," he groaned, and then sighed, "don't ever think that." She didn't believe him. "Those bloodsuckers did this. Not you."

The air between them then suddenly heated and Wynter glared at Warren.

"Don't be so naïve," she demanded with a frown, "he knows I—" she hesitated, but knew she had to be honest. She had to tell him.

Phoebe seemed to sense that things were about to head towards the deep and meaningful, so she pushed back in her chair and deposited her mug beside the sink. She hovered there a moment, waiting for Wynter to give her the go-ahead to leave, which she did.

A second later, she and Warren were alone. He moved into the empty chair between them and took her hand in his, peering into her eyes intently.

"He knows what?" he asked her, "that I care for you? That I want you? He does know. Mr Cole told me himself."

"He did?" she cried, and Warren nodded. She softened and leaned into him ever so slightly, craving his warmth and comfort. "Well, I was going to say that he knows I care for you, Warren. He isn't jealous with any of the managers, and yet with me it feels different. He added the extra day for me to feed him, but there's more. He touches me. Acts like he wants me in ways I'm not sure I can handle."

"It's all part of his games, Wynter. He plays them with all of us, but just stay strong and be his slave when he needs you to be, and then be yourself in between. The curse can only invade us so much," Warren replied, and Wynter cringed. She was free of at least that one element, and being close to Warren now, she knew it was worth giving up that freedom for. He was alive, albeit a little battered, and it was all because of her sacrifice.

Totally worth it.

"I think I can manage that," she replied as she turned her face up to look into his. Warren was rugged and hardened. His features weren't soft, even hidden behind his beard and the dark eyes that now burned into hers. He had seen his share of evil and yet had remained a good and honest soul.

And one she wanted to know. Perhaps, even wanted to fall for.

Before she could say another word, his lips were on hers.

Warren's kiss was as wild as he was and his beard scratched at her face, but Wynter loved it. She put her hand on his cheek and kissed him back, and it wasn't long before their kiss turned feverish and full of longing.

She wanted him and knew now how he wanted her just as much. There was no question of their attraction to one another, and when he eventually pulled away, Wynter felt lost without him. This was dangerous, they both knew it, but she didn't care.

SIX

Warren stood and pulled Wynter to her feet with a grin. She quickly followed his lead and soon they were heading away from the kitchenette and over towards the back of the room where the pillars of servers were located, and she saw how their kiss hadn't gone unnoticed by the other members of the IT team. Eyes were on them and followed the pair as they passed, as well as the smiles and nods of approval. It was good to know their team approved of what had just sparked to life so publicly between them.

"This is where we come to rest or to get some peace," Warren told her when he eventually came to a stop, and he turned the handle on the door to what Wynter had assumed was a broom closet or an electrical cupboard. Inside, she found a small space that had been cleared of janitorial goods and they'd been replaced with cushions, blankets, and even a massive beanbag that she figured she might be able to fit her entire body on.

She let out a giggle and kicked off her shoes before clambering straight onto the beanbag, and then held up her hand to let Warren know how she wanted him there with her. He took it and obliged her, taking up the entire leftover space with his huge body when he joined her on the small makeshift bed.

"Hold me," Wynter whimpered, shuffling closer, and Warren did as she asked. He wrapped her in his arms and pulled her close. Their bodies were soon pressed tightly against each other's, and while Wynter wanted more, she didn't push for it. Fear held her back. Terror over what Marcus would do if he caught them. If he figured them out.

Warren let his hands roam over her back and up to her face, though, where he cradled it and pressed his lips against hers once again.

His next kiss was ferocious and somehow gentle at the same time. His lips caressed her mouth, his tongue delving inside and taking charge of her senses, and Wynter swooned. She hadn't felt like this since when she and her ex were first seeing each other. In fact, even before then. Back to when her heart had still been full, and she had been ready to love. Open to anything.

The endless possibilities and a determination to prove her mother's cynicism about men wrong.

And yet Wynter knew it was she who had been wrong. Her heart had believed in something that hadn't existed, or at least that was what she'd come to believe after nothing but heartbreak after heartbreak.

She bristled and pulled away, and Warren looked at her with a sorrowful expression. Did he feel it too? She thought he must do. Did he know their best-laid plans were fruitless in the face of the powerful and predatory boss they were both fighting against in their own way?

"This isn't over. He hasn't won," he groaned, confirming her suspicions, "we'll find a way to be together."

"He'll kill you if he discovers we're fooling around behind his back, Warren," Wynter croaked. She knew Marcus would do it, but she also knew something her beau did not. She was only still under his employ because of her deal with the vampire tyrant to keep Warren alive. If he went back on their deal, then she'd be gone, and Wynter hoped that'd be enough to ensure he never lashed out at him to spite her.

Marcus would always be selfish. Always put himself and his needs first, even if that meant having to keep Warren around, and that gave her a certain amount of control. It was only a little, but it was still something.

"Then we shall lie," he answered with a smile. "We'll still know the truth, but when he's around, we'll both hide how we feel. Keep it secret."

"Even if we have to keep our distance and hide our feelings, we'll know the truth," she agreed. "But what if he kisses me, or touches my body in the throes of the feed?"

"Then you close your eyes and think of me, Wynter," he groaned, and she felt heat rage from inside of her at the thought. "Imagine it's my hands on you. My lips," Warren continued, and she arched herself against him, desperate to feel his body crushing hers.

One day, she told herself. When Marcus was over his infatuation with her and he'd calmed down with his mind games. When she was free to live and work in peace through the week, and then feed without all the chaos at a weekend. That was when she and Warren could be together for real. When she could spend the day making love with him and being a normal couple. They might even fall in love and live happily ever after.

Maybe...

Thud, thud, thud!

"Guys, you need to wrap up whatever you're doing in there and get out here quick!" Phoebe's voice permeated their little bubble, and Warren jumped to his feet in record speed. He opened the door and reached down for Wynter, who was just climbing up onto her shaky legs. She felt exhausted and in need of some sleep, but the look on Phoebe's face told her they weren't going to be allowed any more quiet time. Her eyes were wide, and she seemed terrified, as if she had seen a ghost.

"What is it?" Warren asked her.

"It's David... he's dead," she replied, her voice shaking.

"Oh, God," Wynter croaked, holding her stomach that'd just begun to ache at the news, finally being out amongst the others at the club.

"Mr Cole called directly to inform me and to say he's going to come down and see me. There was some kind of accident and he fell down three flights of stairs," Phoebe explained, and then her knees buckled and Warren caught her in his arms, holding her close.

Wynter was frozen solid. She didn't know what to say or do and wasn't sure why Marcus had told Phoebe the news, or why he'd lied. There had to be a reason. She got her answer when Warren eventually turned to her with a grim expression on his dark face.

"Her cousin," he whispered, and she nodded.

"I know he had his moments, but he was a nice guy. Wouldn't hurt a fly," Phoebe said, still looking shocked, as if she couldn't get her head around the sombre news. "Oh my poor Aunt Nancy."

"When did it happen?" Warren asked.

"Sometime this afternoon while everyone was either out or working their overtime hours," she replied, and began to sob. "He was just found by some contractors because they were using the service entrance rather than the usual one. Everyone just thought he was off doing his checks."

Wynter couldn't listen to anymore. She put her hand on Phoebe's arm in a bid to be supportive, but all she wanted to do was escape. She couldn't bear to hear how he was such a great guy, when he was dead only because he'd tried to attack her. Marcus could play it off as an accident all he wanted, but she would always know the truth.

"I have to go," she groaned, before adding a robotic, "I'm sorry for your loss."

Warren opened his mouth as if to stop her, but Wynter just walked away. She couldn't stay and listen to this fabricated story any longer. She felt bad for what'd become of poor David, but at the same time, she was also angry. She had been attacked and no one would ever know it. They'd never learn just how horrible David had been or how much he'd hurt her.

She reached the huge open-plan office and ignored the quizzical looks from the engineers as she passed through the small group and headed straight for the door. The last thing she wanted to do was explain what'd happened between her and Warren or discuss what Phoebe had gone running to tell them both. Wynter just wanted to hide herself away again.

She flung open the door just as Marcus was coming through it and full on collided with him. He was like a wall against her flimsy human body, and she crashed into him and stumbled backwards.

He reached his hand out and caught her around her lower back; the move serving to not only stop her from tumbling to the ground but also yanking her flush against him.

"Tread carefully, Miss Armstrong," he whispered in her ear as he held her there, and she couldn't ignore the menacing tone to his voice.

"Or what?" she challenged, but Marcus ignored her. He let go and moved past her in a swift and fluid movement, holding the door open so that Wynter could escape like she'd planned.

She wanted to refuse him and stay, but knew she had no other choice than to leave them to it. He knew she was flummoxed, of course, and Marcus simply shut the door in her face with a sly smile, while all she could do was walk away with a huff.

***

Marcus was being petty, he knew it, but couldn't help himself. The look on her face as Wynter had collided with him had been thoroughly amusing. Her reaction to him shutting the door in her then shocked face, however, had been priceless.

She'd been trying to hide from him ever since their fight, but he wasn't really the kind to dwell. Yes, he'd lashed out in the moment, but his rage had quickly subsided. After he'd trashed the office, it had just been a few minutes before he was setting in motion a plan to have it back up and running again before the night's end.

The redecorated office would have everything he needed in it and then some, including a properly sectioned off area for Wynter to call home. A place where she could be locked away and stay safe from all others during the daytime.

The space was not for the additional managers, of course, but only her. He had offloaded his anger after she'd run from him and had now seen sense. He did want her, he couldn't fully deny it, and so had perfected a different kind of plan to make her stay with him.

Marcus wasn't going to let her leave, not even on the days she wasn't obliged to stay and feed him. She would fight his decision, sure, but he was ready for her this time, and of course he had three thousand years' worth of strategies at his disposal. She was no match for him and his superior strengths of both prowess and will. The sooner she accepted it, the better.

Wynter had, of course, admitted defeat, but that wasn't good enough. Marcus wanted her broken and completely at his disposal. He'd had enough of her evasion tactics, and even more so of her strong and independent woman routine.

She might not say so out loud, but she wanted someone to love her, and Marcus wanted to ensure she never found it. He was also going to make damn sure she never tried to get close enough to ask him again. The comfort and warmth had to go. He was determined not to give her anything else other than his usual attention while administering his bite. Wynter was his slave, not his lover, and it was time she learned that.

And yet, he couldn't force aside the memory of her body as it'd called to his. Not only with her words but also with her soul. She had wanted him to make love to her, and not for the first time. Was her soul really his for the taking? No, he reminded himself. She was only there because he had forced her to be. Plus, there was that little show with Warren at that table. And then they'd disappeared into the back together? Nope. Not on his time, or under his nose. The boy had been threatened before about touching what wasn't his, and Marcus wasn't against issuing him with a polite reminder.

He carried on inside the huge department and then sat with Phoebe and fed her his lies while also using his power over her to ensure she believed everything he said. She was smitten with him in no time and had soon forgotten any questions she might've had about her cousin's untimely demise. She believed it to be an accident. Plain and simple. Case closed.

That task over with, Marcus then turned his attention to Warren. He had spent the afternoon beating the little rabbit to within an inch of his life and then watching as his clients fed from him and had thoroughly enjoyed himself. Enough that he wanted to toy with him some more. To savour the flavour of the boy's defeat.

"What fun we've had today, you and I," he told Warren as he entered his small section of private office and closed the door behind him.

Marcus watched as he fought with his conscience about whether to answer him back. Anger flared within him, and yet Warren remained calm and collected. He couldn't deny that he was impressed. "But it seems you need reminding of a few things, little rabbit…"

"I haven't touched her," Warren barked, still fighting his urge to properly argue back. "I promise. Wynter came to talk with me and we did, that's all."

"All of it?" Marcus replied knowingly, and he watched with a satisfied smile as Warren squirmed under his scrutiny. He then took a seat opposite him at the small desk and grinned from ear to ear. "Shall I tell you what happened after I left you in that ring today? What I walked in on when I returned to my office?"

Warren squirmed and fear began oozing out of him. He was terrified of being hurt again, and given by how scared he was, it was a marvel that he was still standing.

"I'm sorry, sir. I'll keep my distance. She instigated the kiss," he eventually answered, and Marcus shook his head. Oh, how easily he'd sold her out. Tried to get her in trouble rather than accept it himself.

"That's not what I was talking about."

"Then what?" Warren asked, and while he calmed a little, he continued to shake with the remnants of his fear. It was utterly delightful.

"David... He loved Wynter. I knew it and she knew it. She tried to let him down gently, but then, she couldn't help herself. She loved the attention he kept on giving her and lapped it up, even when she knew it was wrong to toy with the poor boy," Marcus told him with a bogus sad look on his devious face. "When my back was turned, she lured him up to my office, thinking she could play with his emotions some more. She'd told him to keep their affair secret. To wait and pretend to everyone else that they were just friends. But all the while, she'd promised him that when the time came, they would be together. That one day they would be free to love one another openly."

Marcus watched Warren crumble from the inside out. So, he was right. She'd made similar promises to him. She'd reached out, and he had believed her when she'd told him they'd find a way to be together. Warren had trusted her, but not anymore. Not after what Marcus was telling him. They were utter lies, but the imbecile didn't know that, and thanks to the hex placed upon him that rendered his emotions never fully his own, he had no choice but to trust his forceful boss's word.

"No, she wouldn't. She couldn't love him," Warren croaked.

"Of course not," Marcus replied with a deep laugh. "She is incapable of love but is devious and selfish enough to pretend in order to get what she wants. Wynter likes to be adored and will do anything to have men falling at her feet. Women too."

Warren replied with a groan. He clutched at his chest and shook his head, still struggling with the news, and so Marcus pushed him harder. "David was in turmoil. She had him tied up in so many knots that when she sent him away again, he couldn't stand it. He threw himself down those stairs because he could bear it no longer. It's Wynter's fault he's dead. I saw the poor boy for myself. David's death was no accident. He committed suicide thanks to what she did to him."

SEVEN

Wynter headed straight for her office and threw herself inside in an angry and petulant mood. Marcus was toying with her, Warren was right, and she hated how she was letting him. Why the hell was he being like this? She'd already admitted defeat to him once today, and she was sure as shit not going to do it again.

No sooner had she locked the door behind her that a light cackling sound from behind her made her jump. She turned on her heel and found the Priestess standing over by her window that overlooked the dance floor below. Shrouded and hidden from prying eyes, as always, she was watching the crowd. Wynter went to her, drawn to the powerful lady by not only her magnetism but also the sense of trust that had already begun to develop between them. The Priestess had cared for her. Protected her. Kept her safe from harm when she had needed it most. The strange woman had earned a place in Wynter's good graces, and she hoped to one day call her a friend.

"My lady," Wynter greeted, using the same term Marcus always seemed to. "To what do I owe this pleasure?"

"My love, I wished to check on you. To make sure all was well, but you are fraught. Why?" she replied, her voice still that strange sound of mixed vocals all meshed into one. It always reminded Wynter of those horror movies where the young victim gets possessed and speaks in a demonic tone. There was nothing right about the sound in the slightest, but she didn't recoil like she had the first time. She was getting used to it, and to her presence and all-seeing power, or so it seemed.

"Marcus has cruelly toyed with me," she replied honestly. "He messes with my head and my heart. I can't stand it."

"Yes," was all the powerful witch replied. The Priestess was unequivocally loyal to him, Wynter knew, but she also seemed to understand her plight. She had to know what a pain in the backside he could be, even if she wouldn't betray him by saying so. "Here, I have a gift for you," the Priestess then whispered and reached out her hand. Atop her gloved palm was a jewellery box, and Wynter frowned down at it. Somehow, it felt like whatever it was inside might be about to make things worse. As if it were a dastardly trick Marcus was having the witch play on her.

"What's inside?" she asked, but the Priestess shook her head.

"You'll have to open it and see…"

"Did Marcus put you up to this?" she tried, and felt immediately relieved when the strange woman shook her shrouded head no.

"I made it for you. This token of my affection will keep you safe from harm, Wynter."

"More so than your locator spell?"

"Yes…"

She could bear the suspense no longer and opened the square box to reveal a white beaded bracelet. She reached forward and stroked the luminescent beads, and found it was made of the lightest and yet sturdiest stone she had ever felt. And the colour! It was like the fullest of moons on a clear, dark night.

It was as if the beads had been carved from marble, or glass, or… she had no idea. It truly was like nothing she'd seen before. Utterly extraordinary.

She inspected it more and found there was just one solitary black stone at the base, and as she took the bracelet and viewed it in the light, Wynter was sure she saw the blackness within the bead wisp and move, like mist. "My gift to you, my love. Wear it always and none shall be allowed to cause lasting or irreparable harm to you. Not even your master."

Now then, why hadn't she led with that? Such a gift would be perfect, if it was true.

Wynter did as she'd commanded and slipped her hand through the circle of beads, and felt a strange shudder pass over her when they clasped tightly around her wrist. She figured the bracelet had to have been empowered with some kind of protection spell and, while it was strange to be so used to such things nowadays, she thanked the Priestess.

She then watched the shrouded woman for a moment before looking down on the throbbing sea of partygoers below them. She'd forgotten it was Saturday night and felt a pang of longing as she watched the humans dancing and enjoying themselves at the club. So unaware of whose establishment they were in. So innocent of the danger all around.

Wynter envied them.

"I guess I'd better get some work done," she told the Priestess, eyeing the clock. It was one-am.

"But you don't want to, do you?" she replied knowingly. "You still want to rebel against him. To be disobedient and have a little fun."

"Yes, but I know he won't allow it," Wynter replied dejectedly.

"What he doesn't know won't hurt him…" the Priestess told her, and she could hear that she was smiling thanks to her jovial tone.

Someone then knocked on her office door, and Wynter watched as the witch disappeared in the blink of an eye, rather than be present when she opened it. She almost didn't but was glad she'd decided to because on the other side of her office door stood Marcella. She was grinning mischievously and came bounding inside without having to ask for an invitation.

"Hey, what's up?" Wynter asked, but Marcella just eyed her up and down, her finger tapping her chin thoughtfully.

"Lose the blazer and unbutton your blouse a little," she ordered, and Wynter did as she asked, her brow furrowed in questioning. "Great, much better. Come on," Marcella then commanded, taking her by the hand.

"What's going on?" Wynter asked again, still confused.

"We're going to have a dance," Marcella replied, throwing in an eye roll as though it ought to have been obvious. "I've suddenly got an urge to be naughty and go enjoy myself. Don't make me go down there alone…" she added with a pout.

Wynter had to laugh. She got the feeling the Priestess was behind this but wasn't the least bit angry or upset about it. In fact, an hour of bunking off work was exactly what she could do with, and she nodded to her new friend.

"Don't have to ask me twice," she told Marcella as she followed her out into the hallway and then locked the door behind her.

The pair of them sneaked down to the dance floor, where they danced and immersed themselves deeply in the throng of people enjoying their Saturday night out in the old town. Most of the men around them were drunk and a little bit handsy, but they each just batted any wandering hands or wannabe suitors away without a care. They weren't there to pull, but to simply let off a bit of steam.

Wynter was used to the craziness a Saturday night out on the town brought with it, though, and she let herself just be in the moment. She loved being back to her old self again and was under no illusion that she'd be in trouble once Marcus found out, but she didn't care. She was having fun for the first time in days and was enjoying every second of it. Plus, she had her new friend by her side and couldn't deny she was enjoying the company. The pair of them had spent those strange but hot few hours fooling around together the previous day, but it didn't seem to have unhinged their friendship in the slightest. All that mattered was how they were two kindred souls who enjoyed their carefree relationship. Wynter trusted her and knew the feeling was mutual.

Once they were finished dancing, Marcella called for a break and led her to the bar, where she ordered herself a glass of water.

"And I'll have a large gin and tonic," Wynter added, and the barman gave her a nod before getting to work on her drink.

She then turned to Marcella, thinking of the conversation she had overheard between her and Marcus before she'd left them the previous day. "So, you're pregnant?"

Marcella practically spat out her drink but managed to gulp it down in time, and Wynter laughed.

"He told you?"

"Nope, I overheard you two talking," she explained and then gave her a nudge. "It's okay. Just as long as you're fine?"

"I am, thank you," Marcella replied with a soft smile, "it's only early days, but he knew, of course."

Wynter nodded. Marcus must have sensed it on her, just like he could their emotions and such. He might've known before she had.

"And you're happy?" she asked.

"Ecstatic," she answered with a beaming smile, and Wynter believed her. She was glowing, and her eyes were sparkling. Brimming with happiness. The petite redhead was lighting up the room, and in a way, Wynter envied her. Marcella must have a life outside of the club. A world of her own out there and someone who loved her. But then again, she'd said she was single, so maybe not. Maybe she was just pleased that a happy accident had come her way, and why the hell not?

The barman then brought over her drink and Wynter went to pay, but he shooed her away and walked off without a word. She shook her head. Marcus. He had to know they were there and told them to give her free drinks. How else could the guy have known? Or did he somehow just know they were fellow members of the same slave vampire team? Were the barmen and women in on the charade, too? Were they all?

Wynter suddenly felt under the spotlight. One of the bouncers was standing at the end of the bar, and she caught his eye. She remembered him from her visits to the club before, but also from her nights spent there since joining the ranks of the Blood Slaves. He knew exactly who she was and Wynter realised as she looked around at the rest of the staff members, whose eyes darted her and Marcella's way, that they probably all knew. She was no longer just a face in the crowd, but a known entity. Someone to watch and report back on. Not free in any sense of the word.

She grabbed her drink and took a long pull on the straw poking out the top. It was strong—good. Just what she needed to calm her nerves. Wynter finished the drink in record time and then she jumped down from her stool and took Marcella by the hand, indicating that she ought to go back upstairs. She pouted again but nodded. It was the right thing to do, and so Wynter took the lead. All she wanted was to get out of there. Back to the quiet solace of her office.

"Thanks for that," she told Marcella when they reached the third floor and had come to a stop in the hallway. "I really enjoyed myself."

"Anytime, babe," she answered, and then the pair of them headed off in their separate directions to their offices.

By the time Wynter had unlocked the door and shuffled inside, she was feeling lightheaded. She just about managed to lock the door behind her when a wave of nausea hit and she had to quickly lie down on the small couch Marcus had thankfully placed there for her.

Her body suddenly felt heavy, and her arms and legs numb. Her eyesight even began to betray her, and she forced herself to focus on the clock above her computer. There were just minutes to spare until it was two-am. Marcus would surely punish her for turning up to feed him while drunk, but Wynter knew it would be ten times worse if she arrived late or not at all.

As she tried to sit up, another thought struck her. She'd only had one drink. A double or perhaps a tad stronger, but certainly not a skin full. Not enough to have her drunk and disorderly so fast.

Had she been poisoned? No, it couldn't be. But it was feasible that she'd been drugged. The barman. It had to be him, the bastard.

She somehow hoisted herself off the chair and to her feet, and left her shoes where she'd kicked them off on her way in. Wynter could barely stand as it was, let alone try to negotiate her way around with heels on, too. They could stay behind, no big deal.

She told herself over and over to move. To work on autopilot. To just get upstairs and prove Marcus wrong. He couldn't have one of his minions drug her just so he could punish her for being late. Nope. Wasn't going to happen.

Wynter just about managed to lock her office door closed behind her and then she stumbled across the hall to the lift, having to feel the wall for the call button as her eyes were now hardly working at all.

Once inside, she pressed the number four and then slumped to her knees. By the grace of God, she still hadn't passed out, but it didn't feel as if it'd be long. Sleep was calling to her and her body ached for it. But no, she had to move. Wynter told herself to just stay awake a little longer, and when the doors opened to reveal a freshly kitted out office ahead, she was forced to crawl out of the lift on her hands and knees.

"I like you this way," Marcus's voice spoke from somewhere ahead of her, but she couldn't see him. All she could see was the ground a couple of feet away as she clambered in the direction of his voice. "On your knees and at my command."

Wynter couldn't answer. She simply slumped to the ground and then curled in on herself protectively. What was happening? She hated every second and wanted to cry.

She tried to plead with him not to punish her, but her words were nothing but garbled groans, just making Marcus laugh. She then wanted to shout at him not to be so rude but had nothing left. No fight. No voice. Not even her last string of consciousness.

Drowsiness took her and Wynter let herself succumb to it, but somehow even when she was beneath that veil, she was still aware of herself and of her surroundings. She wasn't completely gone but was in no way in charge of her body. It betrayed every command she gave it to move or to fight and she wanted so desperately to scream but could do nothing even remotely close.

It was like she was trapped inside her own skin. Just another sort of prison Marcus had created for her...

***

Marcus chuckled to himself as he watched her slip under, and he leaned down, scooping Wynter into his arms like a baby. She was utterly limp and her body was splayed around him, his hold the only thing keeping her in place. He knew that should he drop her, she would tumble to the ground like a broken doll, and he contemplated doing so, just to show her what he was capable of. Pain was the best form of punishment after all, but as he peered down into her face, he knew that wasn't the right approach for his little fighter. He didn't want her to be in any physical pain. Only in emotional turmoil and anguish.

That wasn't so much to ask, was it?

But for now, he would enjoy her this way. She was gone from her body and yet still lucid. Trapped inside her mind thanks to the spell Marcella had cast upon her, like he had requested. Wynter was so trusting. So sweet and innocent at times. The Priestess wanted her as a friend and for her to join the pair of them as an eternal ally, he could tell, but that couldn't happen. Marcus had told her so no end of times already. But he'd still allowed the two of them some time together to show his loyal witch that her needs had meant something to him.

First, though, she had, of course, delivered her with the gift their new Jinn friend had provided to bind Wynter and her new protector. She'd remained shrouded and had chosen to carry on maintaining her secret identity, and Marcus knew it was partly because the Priestess enjoyed being her friend too much to reveal herself yet. She'd also played Wynter using both sides of her relevant personas, and Marcus had rejoiced in her devious tactics. She'd learned from the best after all.

Wynter sighed against him and he felt her innermost desires rise to the surface. He sensed her fear, but also her longing to feel safe. To have him keep her close in her hour of need and protect her while she was vulnerable. Damn, that was new.

Marcus had never been the saviour in the story before and he wasn't sure how to deal with it.

He leaned down to place a soft kiss against her forehead and could smell the club on her. Smell the other men whose scents had marked her. Detect the tang of alcohol on her breath and in her pores. "Let's get you cleaned up," he told her, heading for the bathroom.

On the way, Marcus took a second to admire his new surroundings. Gone was the glass partition and in its place was an actual wall. He had to open a door in the centre and walk through it to get to the area on the other side, adding some privacy to the otherwise huge open space.

In there sat a new pair of sofas that were deeper set and more comfortable than his previous ones, or so his interior designer had told him. They were to become his location for feeding during the week, as well as a place for quiet contemplation should his slave of the day require it. Unlike with Wynter, he usually dismissed Jack or Joanna once he'd fed and they would sleep it off in their offices, hence the couches each of them had and the necessity for locked doors. But all of that was going to change. The dynamics of their arrangement were going to be vastly different soon, and Marcus wanted to be ready for when he announced that change.

He continued through the large space and passed the freshly remodelled kitchenette to the fully equipped bathroom still on the left side of the second room. Next to that was a new set of drawers, but only the one. And only for his things.

Wynter's clothes were now located elsewhere—in the third new room, situated on the opposite side of the room, where nothing but the floor-to-ceiling windows had once been. They had now been blacked out and glued shut, giving her total privacy as well as no chance of escape.

Two more new walls now blocked that same corner off and made a bedroom just big enough to house a double bed, an en-suite and a small selection of furnishings. Inside of the drawers there were simple garments for Wynter to wear for him. Not the old-fashioned nightdresses he'd used to insist on, but more modern clothing. The tea dresses she liked and replacement pyjamas with warm, fluffy socks. She was going to become his captive now as well as his slave, but that didn't mean she had to wear rags or go cold.

But first, he needed her fresh and cleaned up. He wanted her body free from dirt, makeup, and perfume. Just with her natural look and freshly washed scent. She was his gift to himself, after all, and he wanted her to stay perfect.

Marcus ran a warm bath and peeled away her clothes, being gentle with her despite his urgency. He desired her incredibly and his eyes kept going to the vein at her neck, but he forced himself to wait. To be patient.

He would have his fill in due course and the anticipation only made it better.

Wynter sighed and her eyes fluttered open when he lowered her into the deep water, but she was still completely at his command. So at his mercy that he even had to slip his arm underneath her shoulders to lift her up from behind and stop her from inhaling the fragrant water. He then washed her with his other hand and he took his time, slowly running just a simple bar of soap across her naked flesh while caressing her skin and cleaning every inch.

Her eyes followed him and Marcus knew she was slowly coming out the other side of the spell. He didn't have long before she would find some motion again. Some feeling in her hands and feet, and eventually all over. And he had a feeling she wasn't going to be happy about it.

The Priestess had warned him her listlessness would be temporary. A slow building stun that would reach a climax and then ease off again, which Marcus could tell had already begun. And so, he moved slightly faster.

He finished up, pulled the plug, and dried Wynter off before wrapping her in a towel and then clutching her to him again. He then carried her out to the living area but did not dwell there. Instead, he unlocked the new bedroom and took her inside.

Wynter fit perfectly in the centre of the bed. Her dark hair was back off her face and her limp, naked body looked beautifully pale in the dim light streaming in from just the open doorway.

She opened her mouth and tried to speak, her eyes wide. Her lips then pressed together, and Marcus knew she was trying to say his name. "It's okay, my sweet," he told her as he climbed onto the bed alongside her. "I'm here. I won't hurt you, and I won't drink until you're better."

Her body convulsed ever so slightly and Wynter sucked in a deep breath. She then peeled back her lips and whispered three small words with as much venom as she could apparently muster.

"You. Did. This."

Marcus leaned down over her and pressed his nose to her cheek, where he inhaled the sweet, bitter taste of her rage. He willed the spell to wear off quicker. To lessen its hold over her some more so she could continue to defy him, and tried not to smile. Not to give the game away, but he couldn't do it. The ancient vampire grinned down at her and captured her chin between his thumb and forefinger.

"What are you going to do about it?" he whispered, challenging her, and then planted a deep, hard kiss against her trembling lips. He then kept his mouth against hers but let his hand rove over her body, caressing her breasts and mound while feeling as she responded at last and was finally able to start moving against him.

Wynter initially tried to pull away, but Marcus just gripped her tighter, and he pushed one knee between her thighs to pin her down. He kept on kissing her, even when she found the strength return to her hands and pushed at his chest and tried to fight herself free. Like he'd promised, he'd waited, but now that she was no longer captive in her own body, he unsheathed the razor-sharp edge to his tongue and let it slice through the tip of hers.

She had fought her way out of Marcella's spell, but within a second, she was under his. The power of the bite was no match for even the strongest of humans, and Wynter did a complete one-eighty. Just moments before, she was fighting him in a bid to get away, but now she was holding him to her and kissing him back like a woman possessed.

She gripped his thigh with her own and squeezed, and Marcus knew what she needed. What it was she was craving.

What she was always bloody craving. She certainly wasn't afraid of her sexuality.

But he wasn't going to give into her needs.

Not today.

EIGHT

Wynter was trying so hard not to let him make her feel this way, but it was no use. Marcus was in her head, in charge of her body, and invading every one of her senses thanks to his explosive kiss and his roving hands. She'd laid in that bath confused, scared, and then seething. He had done this to her, she knew it for sure now, and he'd clearly loved having her at his complete and utter mercy. It didn't matter that he'd been gentle and tentative with her bath, the fact remained that he had drugged her.

She closed her eyes and tried to think of Warren. To imagine he was the one doing this to her, and it worked for all a few seconds until Marcus's voice was ringing in her ears, their kiss having finally broken.

"I'm waiting, little fighter. I expected more from my favourite little pet…"

Oh hell no, she thought. There was no way she was standing for being called that.

Wynter knew it might be exactly what Marcus expected of her, but she did as he asked and fought back. She pushed him away and clambered from the bed, charging for the door regardless of her nakedness. There would be clothes somewhere for her to grab, surely. Or at least a towel or a new throw from on the sofa outside.

She reached the door and put her hand down in search of the handle, but there wasn't one there. The door was flat to the touch and no amount of pushing on it or searching for a handle made the damn thing budge.

The sound of mirthful laughter from behind her made Wynter's blood boil. She turned on her heel and glowered at Marcus, who was lounging on the bed where she'd left him as though he didn't have a care in the world.

"That door," he then told her with that wide smile she'd come to hate, "only opens if you have the key. And I have the only one."

"You can't keep me locked in here, Marcus," Wynter demanded. "We made a deal."

"Yes, I know," he replied nonchalantly, and she let out a huffed sigh.

He was incorrigible!

"Marcus, will you please just speak to me?" she begged, and then she started looking around the room, checking the drawers in the hope she might find some clothes to wear so she could at least cover her modesty. Each one was empty, and it wasn't long before the cold began to creep in, so it was clear she had no other choice than to climb back on the bed and under the heavy covers to get warm.

Marcus scooted aside but remained atop them, and Wynter was glad. She wanted him as far away from her as possible, even if that was just the other side of a duvet.

"What would you like to talk about, Wynter?" he then asked in a gentle, eloquent tone, "shall we discuss how you've betrayed my trust no less than three times in the past twelve hours? Perhaps you'd care to start by explaining why you left my office during the day and then invited David back up here with you?"

"What?" Wynter cried, shaking her head. That was not what'd happened, and he knew it. "He followed me up here against my will and tried to force himself on me. That was not by invitation!"

"And then you sat back while my priestess was forced to step in and take his life because of your ineptitude, before finding solace in the arms of another vampire. And let's not forget that embarrassing moment when you dared try and seduce me again," Marcus added with a roll of his eyes.

God, she hated him. Hated all the ways he made her feel so inadequate and unlovable, and even more so because even with all of that, he still wouldn't leave her be.

"You're the worst person I've ever met. Do you know that?" Wynter croaked, but Marcus didn't seem to hear her. He clearly hadn't finished berating her and wasn't going to be interrupted until he'd completed his chiding.

"You then ran to him, Wynter. You ran to Warren and told him all about your evil master. Told him you wanted to escape me. Let him make you believe you two could become something more than what I have allowed you to be."

Marcus leaned closer and tried to cup her face with his hand, but Wynter pulled away. She didn't want him to touch her, but he gave her no choice. He reached around and grabbed her damp hair, fisting it roughly in the same palm that just a second before had been so gentle. "After all that I have done for you, how is it I'm still the monster?

"You are a monster, Marcus. You drugged me and locked me in here against my will," she seethed.

"You decided to go partying rather than do your job. That's grounds for punishment if ever there was one," he replied with a dark, knowing stare. Marcus then dipped his head and pressed his mouth to Wynter's neck over her vein.

"I won't be your prisoner. You can't do this to me," she groaned.

"When all of this is over, you won't have to be a prisoner," Marcus corrected her, "because you'll follow me anywhere. Do anything I tell you. Be anything I want you to be…" his razor-sharp tongue then cut her flesh, and he began to drink.

This time, Marcus took deep gulps, rendering Wynter immobile in just a couple of mouthfuls, and she hated he was right. She was lost to him within seconds and was indeed his. No doubt about that.

Something told her getting away wasn't going to be quite as easy as she'd once thought.

***

Marcus had his fill of Wynter's delectable blood and stopped a little too close to being dangerously short of draining her dry. Unlike the last times, though, he didn't rush to tend to her or replenish her valuable blood stores with an IV bag. He simply sat back and admired the young woman who had him so smitten he wanted to scream.

The girl who made him want everything and nothing all at the same time.

Marcus knew the best thing to do would be to send her away. To be rid of her temptress ways and be free of her presence that lured him to her with every breath she took. Wynter was indeed like a drug to him. She was the perfect taste when he was in one of his sunnier moods, but also the right elixir to calm his fraught mind whenever the desire to murder or maim overwhelmed him.

The main problem, as it currently stood, was that she was the cause of a lot of such hungers. Her disobedience irked him to no end and yet he egged her on, while her coy ways enamoured him and he welcomed that sweeter side she used to toy with him.

He adored being with her, and yet she loved to defy him and rile him up. She enjoyed playing with the fire within him, and Marcus knew she did it on purpose. The Priestess had led Wynter into temptation without much more than a nudge of her rebellious side and had told him so too, but he'd already known. Wynter had been nothing but trouble since the moment she'd walked into that interview room, and yet, he simply couldn't be without her.

Desire swelled within him again, and he knew there was no denying it this time. He demanded satisfaction no matter how close his soul might come to merging with hers, and so he whipped back the covers and let his eyes rove over Wynter's naked flesh. She was so pale. So delicate. So beautiful.

Marcus leaned down and sucked on one nipple, relishing in both the clean taste of her skin and the natural sweetness her womanly pores seemed to ooze with.

He unbuttoned his fly and began to touch himself, just like he had when in the shower with Wynter and Marcella. He then built his climax in no time at all, thanks to the model on show for him, and before he knew it, he was covering her in his release.

When it was over, he sat back and let himself take a few calming breaths before deciding on what to do next. The chivalrous thing would be to clean her up and cover her over. To let her rest. But Marcus wasn't feeling in a particularly chivalrous mood. He wanted Wynter to know she had been taught a lesson, but he also wanted her to believe she had the upper hand.

Marcus adored playing these games with her and wasn't going to put an end to them yet, so instead of cleaning her up, he leaned forward and smeared her with his release, using his fingertips. He smoothed it over her skin like he was applying moisturiser, when instead it was a part of him blending with her of his accord. A part he was more than willing to share, but on his terms. Marcus even spread it over her breasts and into her belly button, and then to her thighs. Wynter's unconscious body still fought his oppression, and she snapped her legs closed, much to his devious amusement.

The ancient vampire laughed to himself, thinking how even in sleep, his new favourite was getting one up on him. She was winning, even though he had taken so much from her.

Anyone else would've been nothing already. Naught but a broken shell of a person, but not Wynter. She was his little fighter and Marcus hoped she would always remain that way, no matter what he put her through in the days to come.

NINE

Wynter awoke hours later feeling groggy and disorientated. She tried to remember everything that'd happened before Marcus had bitten her, and groaned when it dawned on her just how much trouble she was apparently in. The vampire who hadn't laid down any kind of law or outlined his rules had decided to punish her for simply being herself and having her own mind. Well, that simply wouldn't do. Wynter would fight him on everything, big or small, and hoped Marcus was ready for it. There was no way she'd be the timid little slave, no matter how hard he tried to break her.

But first, she had to figure out how the hell she was going to get through her current punishment in one piece while still being fundamentally free. Wynter opened her eyes and tried to look around but was met with nothing more than pure and utter blackness. She wondered for a moment if she had been blindfolded and reached up to check her eyes, but found nothing covering them, so figured the room had to have instead been completely blacked out.

Wynter hated not being able to see. There wasn't so much as a strip of light running down at the ground where she guessed the door had to be.

She clambered to her feet and stumbled forward, making slow progress thanks to her lack of vision and because she didn't know the room well enough yet to navigate it in the darkness.

When her fingers found purchase on what Wynter thought had to be the doorframe, she scrambled at it, trying to pry it open, but it wouldn't budge.

The darkness continued to envelop her, and she soon began to panic. She hated feeling trapped and tears started to prick at her eyes within seconds.

"Marcus? Are you out there?" she whimpered, calling to him even though she'd promised herself she wouldn't pander to him. That she wouldn't go crawling to him. "I'm sorry. Please don't leave me locked in here all alone and in the dark."

"Oh, the darkness isn't so bad once you get used to it," Marcus's voice whispered from right beside her, and Wynter screamed with fright. He was in there with her? That had to be it. There was no other possible explanation for how closely he had spoken, and Wynter shook her head furiously in a bid to make sense of it all. "And you're not alone, my sweet. I'm here. I'll always be here…"

She stumbled away from the sound of him and tripped over her own feet as she did so, falling back onto the bed with a thud. Thankful for the soft landing, Wynter then curled into a ball and tried to cover her head with the pillow. She then felt the bed dip as Marcus climbed over her and she tried to scoot away, but it was no use. He had her exactly where he wanted her. Ever the prey to the all-consuming predator.

He turned her onto her back and leaned over her. Wynter could feel his body bearing down on hers and she opened her eyes, looking frantically for a way out. And yet still, all she could see was the black darkness all around them. It shrouded Marcus and hid him from her, but she got the feeling he could see her just fine. A creature of the night, or wasn't that the myth? Maybe it was right, just like all the other dark sides of her new employer and tormentor that had been true to the lore.

Wynter shuddered and fear emanated from deep in her gut when Marcus spread her legs and nestled himself there, and she peered up to find two crisp blue orbs piercing the darkness from directly above her.

Marcus's eyes were doing that insane thing again where they glowed from within, as if a light had been turned on behind each of them, and Wynter knew what it meant. She knew his soul was calling to hers and that she had to steer clear of him when in this state, but she had nowhere to run. Nowhere else to look other than right back into those incredible blue eyes.

"Is this what you meant?" she whimpered, hoping she might talk him down instead. "When you told me I'd soon become your willing slave? Are you going to merge your soul with mine?"

Her words seemed to disgust him, and Wynter was glad of it when he climbed off her and backed up, his icy blue eyes still on hers.

"Never," he then croaked, "now, it's time to get to work."

Marcus then seemed to simply press on the panel behind him and it opened with ease, far from the absolute nothingness Wynter had got when she'd tried. As it opened and he left, a crack of light from outside hit her and she flinched, but then she sprang forwards to stop the door closing behind him and locking her inside.

Wynter was on her hands and knees before her master again, and she peered up into his amused face with a frown.

"Please let me have a key," she begged.

"This room is for your protection as well as a place to put you where I know you won't wander away. There is no other key than the one I carry.

You want the door open? Then I suggest you stick by my side. End of story." With that, Marcus walked away, and Wynter let out a scream in her rage. It consumed her and mixed with the fear still churning within to provide her with the worst kind of emotions she could imagine.

The fight-or-flight instincts kicked in, but they were joined by a third sensation. One of hopelessness. If she did either, then she would lose it all and end up not only with nothing but also with the weight of the world on her shoulders too. Marcus would undoubtedly kill those she loved, and all whom she had become close with at the club.

Warren would be taken from her first. There would be no running off into the sunset together. No celebration of their victory. No evading their oppressive leader. Just death and loneliness.

By the time Wynter had screeched herself hoarse and looked back up, the Priestess was standing over her and she had her hand outstretched, beckoning for her to take it. She did, and she let the small woman she'd still never seen without her hooded red shroud pull her up on her feet and into a gentle embrace. Wynter savoured the warmth readily given from another and leaned into her some more. It felt so good to be held she couldn't bring herself to pull away, so she rested her head on the witch's shoulder and slowly felt her fear and anger begin to dissipate.

"Be still, my love," the Priestess told her in that same deep voice with a thousand tones she always found incredible, and Wynter found herself doing so without even thinking of answering the witch back or defying her. In fact, she welcomed her guidance and felt herself starting to calm down pretty much right away.

The two of them stood like that for a few more seconds before Wynter eventually pulled back. She was glaringly aware of how naked she was, and in need of a shower, and she breathed in deeply to calm her nerves, planting a fake smile on her face.

"Thank you," she told the Priestess, peering into the darkness of the hood to try and discern some kind of face beneath the cloak. There was nothing but blackness. Almost akin to a black hole or something, she found no eyes staring back, or a mouth pulled into the smile she hoped the strange witch might be mirroring. It was the oddest sight. "I need to shower and then I have to find some clothes. Do you know where he put mine?"

The Priestess pointed her hand back to the room Wynter had just left, and she shuddered. The idea of going back in there made her want to scream again, and she shook her head. "Then I'll go down to my office wearing nothing but a towel if I must. I have spare clothes in there."

"I'll hold the door for you, my love," the Priestess replied as she ushered Wynter backwards, but she resisted. "You must hurry. You're late and will be punished."

"But—" Wynter tried, but she was persistent.

"No time to argue. He's on his way," the Priestess hissed, and Wynter had no other choice but to follow her command. She decided to trust in the strange woman to do as she had promised and hold the door open. It hadn't closed behind her anyway, so the likeliness was that the door wasn't going to close and lock her in, but Wynter still hadn't wanted to risk it. The thought of staying in there all night made her want to cry. She'd never been claustrophobic in her life, and yet the idea of being held prisoner there was terrifying. Something she hoped Marcus wouldn't ever do to her again.

Thanks to the light streaming in from the main room beyond, Wynter found the light switch and managed to turn on each of the three overhead lights. It was stupidly bright now, but she didn't care. She'd take that over the darkness any day.

Wynter then took in the small space Marcus had seemingly built just for her. There was the bed and the same small set of drawers she'd tried before, but not much else. She had plug sockets and space for her laptop, so hoped that if she ever was stuck in there again, Marcus would at least have the decency to offer her some form of entertainment during her captivity. And maybe some more lighting.

She turned to the Priestess with a frown and was about to ask her where the clothes could be, when she lifted her hand and pointed again, this time at the set of drawers that had been empty just a few hours previously.

Wynter ran to the unit and pulled open the top drawer to find underwear and hosiery at the ready, each of them brand new and exactly in the right size. She slipped into a pair of knickers and its matching bra and then tried the next drawer. That one had pyjamas inside. The bottom drawer only had casual clothing, and Wynter let out a disgruntled cry. They would have to do though, so she plucked out a pair of jeans and a t-shirt and threw them onto the bed behind her, ready to put on.

That was when she noticed how the full-sized mirror at the opposite side of the room had a handle on it. Wynter scooted around the bed to it and pulled, thinking it might open inwards, but instead the door slid to the side a little to reveal tracks at the bottom, and she carried on sliding it sideways until a small closet behind opened.

Inside were more than twenty whole outfits for her. More than half of them were dressed in either a fitted wiggle style or the floating tea dresses she liked, and the rest were tailored dress suits and blouses, just the type she liked for her working nights.

Wynter threw a skirt on along with its matching shirt and blazer, and then slid her feet into a pair of kitten heels that had been laid out for her at the bottom of the small closet.

"Marcus has really thought of everything," she whispered as she turned back to the Priestess and was pleased to find her still holding the door open like she had promised.

Wynter thanked her and then ran across the room to the bathroom so she could freshen up, brush her teeth, and apply a quick bit of makeup to her pasty, pale face. All the blood loss was taking its toll on her complexion, and she cursed Marcus again for taking so very much from her.

By the time she was done, she was over half an hour late for the working evening but didn't rush. It was Marcus's fault, after all, and so she emerged through the new doorway into his refurbished office with her head held high.

Wynter was all for going straight to the lift and leaving without so much as a single word to her boss but was met with no choice when she found the heads of departments all sitting around the meeting table in wait— presumably for her.

Just like at the last of Marcus's meetings, he had saved her the seat to his right, and he patted it with a smile.

"At last," he chimed, "I thought we'd have to wait all night…"

The others sniggered and their faces each turned to watch Wynter as she approached.

The majority wore fake smiles as they eyed her up and down, and she wanted the ground to swallow her whole as she moved forward on autopilot and then took the only available seat, but with her eyes anywhere other than on their vampire boss.

Wynter suddenly felt like she was on the outside of some playground clique and didn't know why. She began to wonder if they'd been talking about her behind her back. Plotting something devious to humiliate her or oust her further. Joanna was watching her with a venomous stare, and it made Wynter feel like an ant the older woman wanted to crush beneath her stiletto heel. Was she the ringleader? Had she whispered evil lies into everyone's ear so that Marcus's new favourite wasn't going to be liked by anyone but the vampire himself? Wynter could imagine her doing something like that. In fact, she could imagine him instigating such a thing, no doubt about it.

Bryn then piped up from behind Marcus and he read through the meeting's itinerary while Wynter turned her face away from Joanna. Why wouldn't she just leave her alone? Why the hostility?

She instead looked to the faces she hoped would be wearing kind and gentle smiles for her.

As she looked up from the pad of paper and pen by her hands, she found Marcella was indeed surveying her with concern, and it warmed her heart to know her friend still cared.

Their eyes met and Wynter gave her a half smile, but then grinned when she saw Marcella wink and slip Joanna a sly middle finger in the ruse of her scratching her nose. Wynter loved how she could just know what was eating her. How Marcella seemed to be able to read her without having to ask. It was refreshing to have found such a nice friend so quickly, and her gesture cheered her up tremendously.

"Sir, this project no longer involves the IT department," Warren's deep voice suddenly cut through Bryn's introduction without apology. The young guy was talking about how there was an upcoming takeover of a second club in their city, which had apparently been in the pipeline for quite some time, however Warren was clearly uninterested. He seemed almost agitated. "May I leave?"

The entire group turned to him and Wynter was pleased to see they were each as shocked as she was to hear Warren speak out of turn. She tried to catch his eye in a bid to get a read on his mood, but he seemed to be making a point of not looking at her. It was almost as if he was doing more than keeping his distance, like they had promised one another, but avoiding her entirely.

And then it dawned on her. Marcus had known what they'd said to one another while having their moment of solace in the closet. He'd taunted her about how she'd promised Warren they could be together. Wynter had presumed it was down to him having installed a sly camera or two inside of their hideout, but then she had to wonder if it wasn't that at all.

Maybe Warren was the one who'd told him those things. Could he really have betrayed her trust like that? She couldn't be sure, but knew she had to get him alone and figure out if so. And if he had, then that meant she couldn't trust him after all, despite what he'd told her about being his own person away from the curse and the bites. He'd told her he was a fighter and encouraged her to be one too, and Wynter had to wonder if everything truly was as it'd seemed these past few days.

She then turned her gaze back to Marcella and frowned. Was she deceiving her, too? Were they all just puppets in Marcus's game and he was utilising them to confuse her and break her down? He was certainly capable of being so dastardly.

Wynter felt him shift beside her and knew Marcus was so tuned into her emotions, he had felt them flip and change so quickly. He pressed a hand over her thigh to draw her attention to him, and Wynter's head snapped around. She was about to demand he take his hands off her, but then realised that was exactly what he was after. He wanted to know why she was suddenly so paranoid and had clearly hoped she'd give the game away by snapping at him, so she bit her tongue.

Two could play this game.

Marcus looked Wynter over, his eyes roving all around her face as if he were taking a mental picture. She quietly seethed, but knew he adored that, so forced herself to calm back down. To not give him the satisfaction of fighting back.

"Don't interrupt the meeting again, Warren," he then barked, still staring at Wynter, "in fact, I'd like you to stick around after it's over so I can have a word."

Warren didn't answer. He just sat back in his chair with a huff and folded his arms.

Wynter couldn't quite believe his behaviour. He was acting out without a care for his punishment, but why? What was he playing at?

Bryn then piped back up and began running through the details again before handing over to Marcus, who led the rest of the meeting with his hand still clutching Wynter's thigh. He squeezed here and there, but didn't move away once, not even when she tried folding her legs and squeezing him back as tight as she could manage.

THE COMPLETE BLOOD SLAVE SERIES

TEN

When the meeting was finally over, Wynter and the others were released, and they headed for the lift as a collective. She was eager to get away but still ended up holding back so as not to overcrowd the small space, and was joined by Joanna, much to her annoyance. Wynter tried to look busy as she fussed over her notes and made a point not to look at her fellow manager, but Joanna simply couldn't seem to let her out of yet another of her jealous taunts.

"You know, he was the same with me when I first started," she told her, "couldn't get enough of me. Always keeping me back for extra overtime and giving me gifts, as well as his personal time. He even took to touching me inappropriately in meetings, just like with you…"

"Let me guess, but he grew tired of you, so I should expect he'll tire of me before long too?" Wynter bit back. She couldn't help herself and hated how obvious Joanna was being with her envy towards the new girl. Yes, it was clear she adored Marcus and would do anything for him. Apparently, she'd loved him and chosen to live no life outside of the club all these years, even though he hadn't shown her any love in return. That was fine if it was what made her happy, but Wynter could see it hadn't. Joanna yearned for Marcus in ways she herself couldn't understand, but guessed it had to be the years of being under his spell. There was no other explanation for it. Surely no one could love such a monster without being forced to?

"He knows I'll never let him down. That I'll run toward him rather than away. With you, I can see you're resisting him. Not doing your duty. It's a wonder he's even kept you on," she retorted, eyeing Wynter as if she were just some foolish girl. If she were honest, she sometimes felt as if she was. Marcus had her head in a spin and her heart and soul in tatters. She was playing games she didn't even know how to play and always seemed to be on the losing side rather than making progress, but she wouldn't give up. Not now, not ever.

Plus, there was one victory she'd had that Joanna knew nothing about.

None of them did. Wynter was free. She was under no curse, just the moral obligation she had made to keep those she cared about safe. She could leave at any time, just so long as she was ready to face the consequences for doing so. Despite the dark repercussions, that knowledge gave Wynter a great deal of power, and a certain authority over people like Joanna. She might be the new girl, but she was no fool. She'd beaten the system and was the sole person able to say she'd done so.

As if to say, *I know something you don't know.* Wynter let a sly smile creep onto her face, and she delighted in Joanna's surprised response. She'd clearly expected her to come back with something just as foul, but instead Wynter remained silent. Her smile screamed with everything she'd left unsaid, and she could tell Joanna wasn't pleased.

She clearly wanted desperately to know what secret she hadn't been let in on. That thought made it all that much sweeter, and Wynter then happily rode down in the otherwise empty lift with her fellow manager without another word said between them.

They arrived at the third floor and Joanna got out, but Wynter remained inside. She hit the button for the basement instead and arrived in seconds. She then headed down the long hallway to the door, which buzzed open the moment she arrived.

Inside, she found Phoebe and some of the other engineers huddled around another piece of equipment like they had been the first day she'd come down. Wynter went over to them and saw that this time was different, though, and there was no argument over what best to do with an old piece of kit. Just silence.

The group of them were standing around a laptop, which was open and had a webpage up, and they were each reading it.

Wynter moved closer and tried to see what it was but couldn't make it out.

"What's going on?" she asked the man to her right. Palmer, she seemed to remember his name was.

"Mr Cole has split our team up. Half are heading to the new club after tonight and the rest will stay here. Bryn has just sent us a group email with the list," he answered with a frown.

Wynter was about to ask what would be so bad about that, but deep down, she already knew. These people had stuck together for years. Looked out for each other and seen to it that they were treated as family. None of them wanted that to be torn apart.

Her heart then lurched as another thought struck her. Was Warren moving to the new site too? If so, she'd hardly get to see him, and Wynter knew that would be exactly what Marcus would want. Maybe that was why he was so standoffish in the meeting? Why he was being so cold?

"That's terrible. Why doesn't he just hire new IT staff?" she asked, but then shook her head. She already knew the answer. Marcus had trust issues. He would never employ a wholly new team, and she knew it. "So, who's going?"

Palmer reeled off a few names and Wynter looked around at the relevant peoples' sour faces. They weren't happy, which was understandable.

"Plus me and Phoebe," he then told her, and Wynter's stomach dropped. As much as she hadn't wanted to hear Warren's name on the list, the idea of losing Phoebe was also a huge blow, and she looked over at her with a sad smile. Phoebe returned the gesture and then worked her way over to Wynter so they could talk.

"When Mr Cole came down to talk to me about David's death, he also told me about the move. I was sworn to secrecy until it became official, but I've been promoted to the Head of IT for the new club. We'll only need a small team there and I'll report directly to Warren so will be here for meetings and stuff," she then told her, and while happy to hear about the promotion and how she'd continue to see her new friend, Wynter was still sad about the news overall.

"Silver linings and all that," she groaned, and Phoebe nodded solemnly.

The door to the huge office then opened and slammed closed, and each of them turned to see Warren as he came storming towards them, clearly having been the one who had burst through it. He didn't say a word to any of them. He just charged straight for his small office and shut himself inside. Wynter went to go over to him, but Phoebe stopped her with a gentle hand on her arm.

"Give him a minute," she told her. "If we've all learned something since working with that guy, it's not to go barging in when he's in a shitty mood."

"I've a feeling his mood isn't going to improve by me being here," Wynter confided in her with a frown as she watched Warren pace up and down in his small space. "He seemed distant upstairs. More so than if he was trying to just playing it cool. Have I done something else to upset him?"

"Mr Cole did speak to him last night," Phoebe answered, and she followed Wynter's gaze to where her boss continued to pace like a caged animal. "He told me before how he'd been warned to stay away from you. Do you think something more was said?"

"I guess I'd best find out," Wynter replied with a shrug. She couldn't wait any longer. She had to know what was eating Warren and so walked over to his door and crept inside without so much as knocking.

He turned to her like he was about to rip her head off, but then stopped when he realised it was Wynter there and not one of his usual engineers. Warren just stared at her and then stormed over to his chair and flopped into it with a huff.

"So, how was it?" he demanded as she took a seat opposite him and Wynter frowned.

"How was what?"

"He built you a bedroom, Wynter. A fucking bedroom! Told us all how you were taking so long to get ready because he'd spent the day in your bed with you and the time had run over. I know you said he touches you, but I didn't realise things between the two of you had progressed to him spending the entire day in bed with you."

Oh, so that was why everyone had been looking at her like that. Wynter wanted to scream at Warren for being such a gullible idiot. She wanted to curse him and call him a child. But instead, she calmly straightened in her seat and took a deep breath before leaning closer and placing her hands on the desk between them.

"Firstly, he built me a glorified prison cell," she informed him, flexing her fingers in a bid to stifle the rage still bubbling within her. "And secondly, he always spends the day with me. That's nothing new. However, nothing happened between us. Not like that anyway."

"Then, like what?" Warren asked desperately, and she was pleased to see him calming down at last.

"Marcus is evil, Warren. He taunts me. Plays horrible games and watches as I fail with the biggest smile on his goddamn face. Whenever he touches me, it isn't to be kind or sensual. It's purely to get what he wants from me."

"I warned you," he replied, but there was no victory in it and Wynter could tell. "Why would he build you a cell?"

"Because I keep defying his orders and he doesn't like it," Wynter told him honestly, "he said he's going to lock me away whenever he pleases and that it's for my own safety."

"As if that makes it okay," Warren answered, and she was glad he seemed to be on the same page. Wynter nodded. "And he really stays with you all day when you're working overtime?"

"Yeah, bar when I'm sleeping. Although sometimes he does stay even then," she answered uncomfortably, but she knew she had to be honest. "Why?"

"I just know he never does that with Jack," Warren answered with a puzzled look on his rugged face. "He told me once how Mr Cole feeds and then sends him down to his office until he's ready for more. Apparently, he only feeds about twice or three times a day."

Wynter gulped. How on Earth could the others have it so easy? Was it the same with Joanna too? Surely not. Maybe just with the male managers.

"And what about the others?" she croaked.

"Patrick is obviously a different setup, but I think it's the same for Joanna. I always heard Marcus has meetings during the day, so they never stayed upstairs with him. I might be wrong though," Warren said, and he seemed to be growing further concerned the more they spoke. Like her, he was realising there was indeed a big difference to how Marcus treated her when compared to them.

"Shit," she whispered, looking around out the windows at the rest of the team. They were going about their business and not watching them, but still Wynter was anxious. "Do you think he really is different with me?"

"Seems so," he replied, leaning towards her and taking her hand in his. "Which explains why he tried to turn me off you last night. I think he's jealous."

Wynter wanted to laugh. She couldn't fathom how Marcus could possibly be jealous when all he had to do was take what he wanted and neither of them could do a thing about it, but at the same time, it made sense. He had been acting out a lot and been erratic too. Far from how he'd come across during their initial meeting.

"What did he say?"

"He told me about David," Warren replied, and Wynter sat back in her chair as an icy chill swept down her spine.

"Did he tell Phoebe?" she demanded, and Warren shook his head no.

"And I won't either. It isn't fair on her," he said, but then he looked away, as if he couldn't quite hold Wynter's gaze.

"Hang on," she asked, "what exactly did he tell you?"

"We all knew David fancied you, Wynter. It makes sense that he would've pursued you and maybe not have been able to handle the rejection. Did he really commit suicide after you turned him down?"

The very insinuation made Wynter so angry she wanted to scream, but instead she reacted by bursting out laughing. It was the crazy kind of laughter that was more shock than amusement, and yet she couldn't stop herself. Not until she put her head in her hands and let her tears come instead. How dare Marcus concoct such a vile lie? She was livid!

"David never went near those stairs, Warren," she told him when she'd calmed down enough to answer. "But I guess it was the best explanation for his so very many injuries."

Warren paled and put his hand over his mouth.

"What injuries?" he asked incredulously.

Wynter shook her head, trying to fight the barrage of images flooding back to her. Especially the memory of David's body flying up and down against the ceiling and then the floor, and the ceiling again. It wouldn't leave her, and she thought it might never.

"Have you ever seen someone die?" she asked Warren, who shook his head no. "It isn't quick, like in the movies. They don't accept their fate and get on with it. Death is more like a drawn out, obstinate thing. Something that you must commit to forcing upon its intended. The victim makes awful sounds as the pain wracks through them, and it seems to take forever before they're silent and it's over. I never, ever want to see that happen again."

"Marcus did it?" Warren asked, his face now thunderous.

"No," Wynter told him honestly, "David was indeed infatuated with me and he tried to force himself on me, but she saved me. The Priestess killed him to protect me."

"Who?"

Wynter frowned and went to laugh, but then realised he was being serious.

"The Priestess?" she repeated with a wide-eyed look. "You know, red cloak. Deep, weird voice… Marcus's number one loyal crone and all-round badass powerful witch?"

Warren continued to look at her blankly, and Wynter shook her head. This couldn't be happening. She was sure he had to know her. He just had to. "Seriously. If you're messing with me, I'm going to flip my shit," she told him, but he remained at a loss for words. He clearly had no idea who the Priestess was, and genuinely so.

"I'm sorry," he replied with a shrug. "I've never seen anyone like that around here or heard anyone speak of her before. That doesn't mean anything, though. Maybe Mr Cole only lets you and the other managers see her?" It made sense, Wynter guessed, and she nodded.

"I hope so," she then told him, "because it's either that or I'm going mad."

THE COMPLETE BLOOD SLAVE SERIES

ELEVEN

Marcus summoned his priestess to his office and got a delightful surprise when she appeared to him as Marcella and not in her usual robes.

"My lady," he greeted her with a gentle bow, "how lovely to see you."

"My lord, the feeling is mutual, as always." She stepped closer and hovered for a moment before deciding on having a seat opposite him at the desk.

"How are things going?" Marcus asked her, and he was pleased to see that Marcella knew exactly what he was getting at without him having to outright say it.

"Wynter is indeed an enigma," the witch replied with a fond smile. Marcus didn't know why, but that small smile irked him. Marcella wasn't allowed to care for anyone but him. Like with all his slaves, he was their number one priority, and he wanted to be sure that the same rules would apply to his priestess as well.

"You care for her," he said. It was a statement rather than a question, and Marcella offered him the slightest nod of her head in agreement.

"But my love is reserved solely for you, my lord," she appeased him, and Marcus immediately calmed. He could sense she was telling the truth and smiled, his eyes flicking down to her stomach and back again.

"And your child," he reminded her. Marcella beamed and nodded.

"Indeed," she replied, instinctively placing a hand over her womb. The baby was still nothing more than an embryo, and yet, Marcus could tell she was going to be a strong witch and a powerful ally in his never-ending crusade for power. Like her mother. And like Marcella, he would treasure and guide the child as if she were his own.

"Have you seen anything more of her future?" he then asked, his mind going back to Wynter and the prophecy Marcella had previously told him.

"I still see her running into the arms of another," she replied with a frown. She then settled back in the seat and stared off into the distance wistfully. "But I cannot see whom. I have made steps with Warren to ensure he stays away from her, but I can only assume it either isn't enough, or that it could possibly not be him."

"But who else?" he enquired, and Marcella shrugged. There was no one who Wynter cared for as much as the boy. Marcus had been forced to admit that much, and he had also used her attraction to his advantage to make her stay with him. The feelings between the two were mutual, and yet even Marcus could see they were in no rush to fall in love and plan their escape.

Her curse was lifted and he could see such a difference now between Wynter and the other members of his team. They all adored him, even if they also had undercurrents of loathing or fear, and Marcus liked it that way, however with her it was all just one big show. But the façade was not for him. No, the pretence was for the others. She was already an outsider because of the special attention Marcus gave her, but if the rest of his slaves found out she was also free from his curse, Wynter would undoubtedly be ousted entirely. They wouldn't trust her. Either that, or they would envy her. They certainly wouldn't be friendly anymore. Only civil out of courtesy. And then she'd be truly alone. Broken. Marcus smiled to himself, thinking how that might be kind of perfect. Something he could implement should the need arise.

"I put a spell on Warren," Marcella told him, her voice plucking him from his reverie, "so that he doesn't sleep with her."

"When did you do that?" he asked and was impressed with her initiative.

"I rang down on Saturday to ask him to fix my computer. There was nothing wrong with it, of course, but I took him into my office and cast a curse on him. No matter how much he wants her, something will always get between them. Such as yourself and Phoebe when they were hiding themselves away after he'd left my office, or perhaps an idea that will pop into his head and turn him off at the last minute. They'll never get together, my lord. Not as long as my curse still holds."

"But that won't stop her from wanting him, will it?"

"No," Marcella confirmed, "and you cannot kill him or send him away without her seeing it as an offensive move. One to which she will react in kind."

"Wynter cannot be allowed to leave me," Marcus ground. He knew that wasn't Marcella's intention, but she had given him a warning. One he knew without her having to have said the words aloud.

"Then merge with her," the Priestess implored. She then sat forward in her seat and stared into his dark gaze. "Do as your soul is telling you and take her as your own, my lord. You continue to fight your attraction to her and yet I can see it within you. I can sense your yearning."

"Then you are mistaken, my lady," he replied, forcing himself not to strike her or take any action that might result in hurting his darling priestess, or her child. "What you sense is lust. Nothing more."

"But, my lord," Marcella began, however Marcus cut her off.

"But nothing. I appreciate your candour as always, however you must learn to hold your tongue when you're proven incorrect," he chided.

Marcella did the right thing—she backed down. She saved them both from having an argument about who was right or wrong, and Marcus was pleased to see she'd not taken her place by his side for granted. He could lock her away just like he had her mother when the time had come for her to drift out of his life and leave the young witch in his care. He was her master. Her tutor. Her mentor. But more than that, he was her everything and Marcella ought to remember so. "What's next?" he asked, giving her the opportunity to prove herself to him again, and the Priestess did not disappoint.

"You're needed at the new club tomorrow to oversee the final arrangements, but that can be done in one day. Afterwards, why not take the opportunity to visit the other new sites? Take her with you. Let her know just why those of your kind require so many new slaves. Teach her why it's important she remains loyal to you, rather than be thrown to the masses."

"You mean, show her the hordes?"

Marcella nodded and a wicked grin spread across her lips.

"She'll soon come running to you once she sees the truth about what happens when the vampire race you so carefully control is left without proper guidance. Make it clear that if she runs, then it's towards a worse danger. Better she stays with the devil she knows, so to speak."

Marcus nodded, and he, too, grinned from ear to ear. The Priestess was right.

If Wynter saw for herself just how terrifying the truth was about the state of his kind, she would think twice about trying to evade him again. The vampires had needed a leader, and he had taken it upon himself to provide it, but at the same time only those of wealth were afforded the lifestyle his clubs allowed. The rest fed on the scraps their sires threw them, and they had become wild, feral creatures of the night because of it. Certainly, being no young woman such as Wynter should ever hope to come across unprotected.

It was indeed a case of her being better off sticking with the evil master she despised, and Marcus was determined to let her see so with her own eyes.

***

Wynter was just finishing up for the night when she got a knock on her office door. She'd hoped to find Warren on the other side, or perhaps Marcella like she had the morning before, but instead it was Bryn. He was standing tall and with that air of arrogance about him she had come to dislike, but Wynter still smiled politely and greeted him, regardless. Her personal opinion of him aside, the fact still remained that she would have to work with the guy for the foreseeable future. So, rather than groan and make a comment about how she was now officially off the clock, she beckoned him inside her office, but kept the door open.

"Mr Cole has asked that you go to his office before leaving. He has a favour to ask of you," Bryn told her, and this time, she couldn't fight her reaction. Wynter knew all too well about Marcus and his favours and wasn't too keen on walking into some kind of trap.

"What favour?" she tried, but Bryn just shook his head. He either didn't know or wasn't allowed to tell. Either way, Wynter knew there was only one option. She had to go up there, and with the best will in the world, told herself it really was just going to be for a minute or two before she'd be on her merry way again.

She wanted her home and her bed. Some peace and quiet and, most importantly, some alone time.

Wynter gathered her things and plucked her coat from the hook behind the door. Rather than put it on, she hung it over one arm and hooked her handbag over the other. Bryn was out the door and down the hall before she'd even finished locking up and had even had the courtesy to call the lift for her so it was sat open at the ready when she reached it.

She felt like calling him a job's worth. Felt like snickering and telling him to stop being such an arse kisser, but instead she forced herself to say nothing at all. Not even a polite thank you.

The lift arrived on the fourth floor within a few seconds and the doors opened to reveal Jack, who was standing over by the window, looking down at the street below. Marcus, however, was nowhere to be found, and so Wynter took a few tentative steps inside before leaving her things in one of the chairs around the meeting table.

She watched Jack, who had to know she was there, but hadn't turned to greet her at all. He seemed lost in his own thoughts and away with them a little. Nothing like the cocky and arrogant man she'd met when she'd first started the job. Something had happened to him. She just didn't know what.

The sound of the elevator arriving again then made Wynter jump in shock, and she turned on her heel to see who was just about to join them. Joanna stepped out of it and she had the smuggest of smiles on her face, but only until she saw the other two managers there as well. Wynter wondered if she'd thought Marcus had summoned her to feed him, and got her answer when Joanna shuffled nervously to button up her blouse and cover herself a little.

Wynter wanted to tell her she could have him. To inform Joanna of all the ways she despised their boss and would gladly never let him feed from her again given the chance. But she couldn't do it. She couldn't break her promise and also allow for her façade to be uncovered. She had chosen to live this lie and knew she couldn't go back on it now.

"Where's our master?" Joanna demanded, and Wynter ignored her. She instead went over to where a small fridge held bottled drinks and snacks to keep Marcus's workers hydrated and refuelled, and she plucked herself a bottle of ice-cold water. She was still gulping it down when he finally appeared from inside his now fully privately partitioned area and grinned around at them.

"So glad you could all make it," he then chimed, "please, follow me."

Marcus walked back to where he'd come from, and Wynter's stomach began to churn. She didn't want to go back there. She wanted to be back in that lift and on her way home already, and yet, there was nothing she could do to refuse him. Like always, Marcus was going to get his damn way, whether she agreed with it or not.

Joanna practically ran for the door while Jack's pace was far slower and matched Wynter's. She let the pair of them go on ahead and then hovered in the doorway, watching them from a few feet away while she made up her mind about whether to follow them or not. "Wynter, come." Marcus held out his hand to her, and she scowled back at him. He had no such power to command her body like that and they both knew it, but he was exerting a different level of control. One she couldn't ignore or fight against if she wanted to keep up with the pretence of her still being under his spell.

She did as he commanded and took the seat Marcus offered her beside Jack and Joanna on the new sofa. Only when they were each perched beneath his gaze did he speak again. "The four of us are going to be doing some travelling," he told them.

Joanna reacted with a shriek of delight, and she even clapped her hands excitedly, like some teenager who'd just been told the next school trip was to fucking Lapland. Jack simply nodded to Marcus and otherwise sat motionless and silent. Wynter shook her head but bit her tongue. What she wanted to say about his offer would be best done in private.

"When? Where?" Joanna asked, still bouncing in her seat.

"Tomorrow," Marcus replied, and he put his hand out for Joanna to take before pulling her up out of her seat. "Now, go home and pack some things, and bring them with you to work this evening. We leave this time tomorrow." Joanna nodded profusely and then skipped away, and Marcus then turned his attention to Jack, whom Wynter knew was working his overtime days so probably wouldn't be in any rush to try and go. She was surprised to find him quite the opposite.

"I'll make a list of the things I need and head home right away, Mr Cole. I'll be back in time to feed you before six o'clock."

"Yes, you do that," Marcus agreed, and then Jack left without another word.

Wynter was left gobsmacked. She knew for sure now how their vampire boss really did treat them each so differently. Jack was, for all intents and purposes, on duty for the day, and yet he'd been allowed to go home? That wasn't fair at all, and when they were alone, Wynter told Marcus so.

"Why is it Jack gets to go home during the day? I thought he was feeding you today?"

"Simple," Marcus answered with a nonchalant wave of his hand, "it's because I only usually feed from him once or twice. Perhaps a pint or so, nothing more. I only need a little really."

Wynter opened and closed her mouth in shock. How dare he take so much from her and so little from the others? Again, that voice was ringing in her head about how it wasn't fair. None of this was.

"So, it's true?" she demanded, recoiling when Marcus sat down beside her, pinning her in. "You treat the women differently to the men."

"I suppose," he answered without a care, nor did he seem to feel the need to apologise for it. "But Joanna is different as well. You know how much she cares for me, but it's so profound that her blood is sickly sweet. Some days just a sip will suffice."

Wynter shook her head, glowering at Marcus. All the bites he'd given her and all the blood he had taken. He'd almost drained her dry on more than one occasion and now she had to hear this? It made her sick.

"If only I loved you as much as she does," she mused aloud, "you might leave me alone too."

"I'm counting on you to never love me, Wynter," he told her with a small chuckle, "and if you ever do, I'll soon beat that love right out of you. That's what I do to Joanna when she's been naughty or has displeased me. I force her to fear me. I beat the sense back into her and then drink my fill while she's broken and beaten down. But I don't need to do that with you, do I? You despise me and reek of loathing and bitterness every minute of every day. It's intoxicating," Marcus added, and he breathed her in as if to make it clear he could sense her hatred even still.

All her instincts told her to run. To flee and never return, but anxiety speared in her gut at the sheer thought of running from him. Marcus wouldn't let her go. She knew this, but she would continue to fight, even if that was what he wanted.

"I'm going home, Marcus," Wynter told him as she fought her way out of her seat and to her feet. "I'll grab some things for the trip and bring them with me this evening, just like the others. And I expect to be paid overtime for while we are away."

Marcus burst out laughing and shook his head as though she'd not only amused him greatly but also surprised him. Wynter scowled down at him and balled her hands into fists. "Today is not my overtime day, and neither is tomorrow, or the next two. You cannot expect me to stay."

"It's not that," he explained, although still chuckling to himself. "It's just that you are too innocuous for your own good sometimes, Wynter."

"And what's that supposed to mean?" she cried.

Marcus was up and out of his seat in less than a second and he stormed forwards, closing the distance between them in a heartbeat. Wynter wanted to stand her ground, but she couldn't. Her feet moved backwards one step at a time in retreat and before she knew it, she'd hit the wall behind.

With a grin, he boxed her in with his hands on either side and then pressed his body against hers. He was taking deep, languid breaths, and she knew he was still relishing in her bitterness and fear.

"What I mean is that you *are* home, my sweet. This is your home now."

"No fucking way," Wynter cried, trying to fight his hold, but Marcus remained where he was and shook his head as though still highly amused by her.

"Your house has been sold and your things cleared out. I've taken the liberty of putting them in storage for you to sort later," he explained without even a hint of a care for having invaded her personal space and taking measures she had not okayed.

"You can't do that!" she screamed, punching her still balled fists against his chest in her angst. Neither her pleas nor her punches were getting her anywhere, though, and Wynter felt like crying. She wanted to scream and bellow at him some more for overstepping the mark by a huge amount, but she felt weaker by the moment. She was beginning to wilt under the pressure he insisted on piling up on her.

She was tired and angry, and tired of being angry all the time. All she wanted was some peace and quiet and space from him. Couldn't he at least give her that?

"I can do whatever I want, my sweet," Marcus countered with a smile. "If I say you're staying here permanently, then that's what you'll do. End of discussion."

"Then I'll run away," she tried, but it was an empty threat.

"And who would help you, hmm? The boy under my spell? The Priestess whose loyalty is pledged solely to me?" Marcus put his palms around her shoulders and squeezed, watching her intently with that sinister smile still lingering on his pale face. "Face it, if you leave, then I shall consider your actions as an act of war. Our deal will be broken and I'll go right downstairs and snap Warren's neck in front of all his subordinates and make them watch. And then I'll go after each and every one of your friends and family. My men will defile them and mutilate their bodies beyond recognition, and it will be all your fault…"

Wynter's heart broke at the sheer thought of it, and she knew Marcus could tell because his handsome face spread into another of his awful smiles. "There it is. See? I don't even have to torture you, Wynter. You think you're brave and tough but look how easily you break. Now, go to your room." He pointed to the bedroom she'd been confined to the day before, and Wynter shook her head no. She didn't want to be locked away in there all day again.

"No, please," she tried.

"Shall I make you?" Marcus challenged in response, but she shook her head again. She didn't have the energy to fight any longer and knew she couldn't handle being punished.

"I made you a deal and intend to keep my promise. I'll come back, just like I did last week. Please, leave me be. Let me have some freedom," she whimpered as a last-ditch attempt to sway him.

Marcus seemed about to cut her down again, but then stopped. He eyed her for a couple of seconds, as though reading more than just her emotions, and then seemed to make up his mind.

"I won't lock you in," he countered, "bar my comings and goings. The office door will remain locked and will not be opened again until six o'clock. You are to remain here and are free to use the facilities and kitchen, however I must insist you sleep in your bed and not on the sofa."

"And the bedroom door?" she had to ask, needing to hear him promise her that he wasn't going to lock her inside again.

"Will remain unlocked—for now."

This wasn't what Wynter wanted at all, but she was too exhausted to argue any more. She promised herself that when they returned from the trip, she would find a way to get back home and away from Marcus's reach day and night. She was entitled to her space and would fight for it, but not today. She desperately needed rest and was willing to concede if it meant she got it.

"I'll stay, for the time being," she told him, "but you're going to have to learn to trust me. I refuse to stay locked up in this club day and night. That wasn't the deal."

"We'll see…"

TWELVE

Wynter slept almost the entire day and while it was nice for Marcus to be able to get a decent amount of work done in the knowledge, she was safely locked away, he couldn't help but continue to think of her. He wondered what she might be dreaming of, or if perhaps those dreams were nightmares.

Did she really despise him through and through? She'd told him so and he'd acted in ways to ensure it, but there was still that niggling sense of wonder in the pit of his stomach that told him he was taking the harder route by refusing his feelings and not following his soul's desire by merging with her.

At least if he did, Wynter would be his until death parted them. No other would tear them asunder and he wouldn't have to try so damn hard to make her hate him, because he would instead revel in her adoration and return it tenfold. But it just wasn't his way. Part of him considered reaching out to Camilla and satisfying his carnal hunger with her in a bid to distract himself, but each time he reached for his phone to call upon her, he put it back down.

Jack arrived back at the office early as arranged, and Marcus led him through to the back rooms and deposited him on the sofa where the three managers had been sat earlier that morning. Wynter was up and in the shower, and while Jack was clearly surprised to find she'd stayed the day there, he didn't ask any questions. He was a good boy like that, and while he saw all, he also didn't feel the need to interfere. Just another reason why Marcus was so fond of him, even still.

Marcus joined him and snapped his fingers to command his Blood Slave to tend to him. He didn't need to say a word. Jack did as was needed and repositioned himself on the sofa so that he could offer his wrist to Marcus for feeding. He accepted and sliced through his flesh to the veins beneath before taking the first gulp of metallic goodness into his mouth.

He then swirled the blood around his tongue, savouring the taste and sensing all the innermost emotions Jack was dealing with. His slave was still yearning for the touch of his Priestess, but he would never know her body again and Marcus could tell Jack was struggling to come to terms with it. He wanted her and often thought of the virgin he had made love to, having imagined her tight body around his while taking care of his personal needs in private, rather than with their master watching over them. He, like Joanna, had no one he wanted enough to take her place. No one more than the object of his desire and so nothing else would do. Only masturbation and his days spent wallowing in his misery.

As Marcus drew a second gulp, Wynter emerged from the bathroom dressed only in a towel. She jumped in shock at the sight of the pair of them and looked like she might be about to apologise, but then evidently thought better of it and scuttled to her room without comment.

He drew a third mouthful and watched her with hungry, lustful eyes. He saw the smallest curve of her bottom as she passed them and ground his jaw against the flesh between his teeth.

Jack let out a cry of pain, but Marcus did not yield. He settled his slave with a wave of power through their bond, exerting control over his body with ease, and Jack fell silent. He was giving off fear in droves, though, only exciting the vampire more, and he took another gulp.

Marcus then looked up and caught sight of Wynter in her bedroom. She had the door wide open and was parading around in just a bra and knickers. Did she know they could see her? Marcus had to wonder if she'd thought she'd closed it enough to obscure her from sight, but it was the exact opposite.

Even so, he watched her, desperate to touch that flesh and to taste the delicious nectar coursing beneath it. He gulped harder and harder, ignoring the struggle from the slave beside him. Marcus was ravenous for more and would not relinquish his hold.

He took another gulp, and another, watching as Wynter slid a pretty dress over her head and then let it cascade down over her slim body. It bunched at her curved waist and she wiggled her hips to release it, making him laugh.

The curve of his mouth separated man from monster and Jack's arm fell into his lap with a limp thud. He had been drained to a dangerous point, but would live, and so Marcus left him to rest. Instead, he went to her, his perfect slave, and blocked the doorway with his huge frame.

Wynter turned to glare at him and then looked behind to where Jack lay slumped and half-dead on the sofa.

"I thought you said you only take a little bit from him?" she asked, her voice barely more than a whisper. "He looks half-dead."

Marcus licked his lips, and he saw her eyes dart to them. Her cheeks then flushed as some sordid thought went through her mind and he grinned. So, her dreams hadn't been nightmares after all. She was hot and giving off a needy vibe that told him she'd had dreams of a steamy variety and not offloaded any of that need herself while in bed or in her shower.

Why wait? He wondered, and then got his answer when he walked inside her room and closed the door behind him. Wynter tried to hide it, but she was scared. Not necessarily of him, but of the closed door. That was why she'd left it open rather than maintain some modesty after her shower, and probably why she'd not felt comfortable enough to take care of business after her long rest.

"You need something, don't you, my sweet?" Marcus asked, stepping closer, and he adored the flush of Wynter's cheeks as she tried to lie to him.

"No, now would you please open the door."

"No," he echoed, sauntering closer. Wynter backed up like she had earlier that morning and he advanced, closing the distance in no time at all and then boxing her into the corner.

Without a word, he then lifted her skirt and pressed the flat of his palm over her mound. Wynter groaned and sucked in a breath, like she was going to say something, but Marcus put his other hand directly over her mouth and pressed it closed. His thoughts were wild and frenzied, but his actions smooth as he slid his thumb under the waistband of her knickers and then pushed them down. The sheer fabric glided downwards and slid around her ankles with ease, leaving Wynter naked at the waist. She moaned again when he stroked his way down over her barely-there tuft of hair towards her clit.

Marcus shushed her and pinned her harder against the wall, teasing open her thighs by splaying his fingers wide, and Wynter followed his command without complaint. She even arched her hips to grant him easier access, and Marcus laughed to himself as he thought about all the times she had defied him. Told him she hated him. And now here she was, soaked and ready for him to be inside of her.

He started slowly, teasing his way in and out and then taking a second to rub her clit with each withdrawal. Wynter was breathing hard through her nose and began arching her hips in time with each of his plunges, as if she'd figured out his rhythm, so Marcus altered it. He pressed his long fingers all the way inside and pushed against her g-spot, making her moan and buck and tense around him, and laughed again. "I can do this for you every day if only you be my good, good girl," he whispered against her temple, running his teeth over the top of her forehead as his desire to take a bite grew stronger. He pushed in again and tickled that same spot, this time offering relentless pressure that he knew would force her over the edge.

Wynter's eyes grew wide, and she suddenly gripped Marcus by the wrist of the hand between her thighs and pushed it against her, deepening his intrusion. She writhed against it and then came, and he watched her with relish as she reached her climax and came utterly undone.

But it wasn't good enough. He wanted more. Marcus removed the hand covering her mouth and kissed her, ravishing her lips with his wild mouth, and then he bit down on her bottom lip, drawing blood. He then drank her down and continued to kiss her, while Wynter's body went into overdrive and she began to shudder with another almighty release. Her core clenched around him, but Marcus continued to push in and out at the speed Wynter still dictated thanks to her hands, doing the guiding.

When she was finally over that precipice and fully spent, her hands fell limply at her sides and she trembled against him. Marcus wondered if she would fall in a heap should he let go, and again he contemplated doing so, but then thought better of it. Instead, he ordered his hand to retreat from within her still throbbing body and pulled his mouth away from hers.

Then, he scooped Wynter up off her feet and carried her to the bed, where he laid her down atop the duvet and watched as she basked in the euphoric afterglow of her releases.

***

Wynter wanted to tell Marcus to leave, but not for any reason other than because she felt vulnerable and laid bare in the aftermath of what'd just happened. She didn't want to admit it to him, but she'd enjoyed that. Like, really enjoyed it. It'd been so long since her last proper session in the bedroom that she felt like she'd forgotten what a penis looked like but couldn't deny his hands had worked some serious magic in place of her having had a proper seeing to.

He'd been right. She had been horny as hell but hadn't known how best to deal with it. The bathroom had reminded her of her embarrassing attempt to seduce Marcus the week before, so she hadn't felt like getting herself off while in there, and so she'd figured the bedroom would have to do. But then she'd emerged and found Marcus feeding on Jack on the sofa rather than the privacy she'd anticipated. It was a strange sight and something which had stirred a variety of emotions in her. Yes, there was the usual shock and sense of *yuk*, but there was something else too. Marcus's eyes had been full of heat and she'd felt them on her, but there was also a certain kind of sexiness to watching him feed. Something she'd never considered before. He was powerful and like a gory king among men. Wynter had gone to her room and thought of nothing more as she'd gotten dressed and as soon as he'd appeared in the doorway, she knew he'd figured her out.

The big bad wolf had come to claim his prize, and for some reason, Wynter had wanted nothing more than for him to take it.

"You fed from me," she whispered, licking her swollen lips and breaking the silence at last.

"Yes, it appears I did," Marcus replied in a mirthful tone. "How very naughty of me…"

"You should be punished," she teased, watching him from under her lashes. Wynter felt tired again despite her having gotten an entire nine hours of sleep, but knew it was just her body's way of enjoying the aftermath of her sexual release. It would pass, and so too would their moment of playing nice, and so Wynter was determined to enjoy both while they lasted.

"I could drink from you every day," he replied as he lifted her dress and gazed down at her still naked core. "And I could touch you like that every day, too. If only you'd be mine and no others. And if you proved your loyalty to me and did everything I asked without argument."

"Never gonna happen," she replied with a smile, but then faltered when she realised he was being serious. Wynter lifted herself up onto her elbows and peered down at him, watching as he covered her back up and then plucked her knickers from the floor.

"Put these on," he ordered, and was back to being icy cold again.

Wynter did as he'd asked, and then she clambered off the edge of the bed and blocked the door, staring up into his immense blue eyes.

"Whatever you think and whatever you do, I will always be my own person, Marcus. What you must realise is that it's not a bad thing to let a woman have her own thoughts and feelings. You might actually like being part of the modern world if only you'd give it a try."

He moved her out of the way by physically lifting her up by the shoulders and placing her back down a couple of feet away.

Marcus didn't seem to be angry with her, but he also appeared to have considered the conversation over with, so Wynter let him go and she instead took off for the bathroom to freshen up again and do her hair and makeup. She also had to finish packing, so got straight to it, putting the thoughts of him and his promise of some kind of future aside, for now.

THIRTEEN

Wynter wasn't sure exactly what she'd expected of their trip, but a drive to the other side of the city in a blacked-out minibus wasn't exactly it. She had to admit, though; it wasn't a thing like the tin can style old buses she'd been in before. This one was state-of-the-art and more than comfortable enough, but she'd figured Marcus for more of a sports car type. Or maybe one of those huge, armoured cars she'd seen diplomats drive around in. Something exciting and that reeked of importance, not a standard *human* mode of transport.

She tried not to watch him as they drove, but it was hard given how they were sitting directly opposite one another in the back. Jack was to her left and Bryn to her right, but Joanna had been quick and had made sure she'd taken the seat beside their master before anyone else could.

Wynter hadn't minded one little bit, but now wished she had chosen another seat because all she could feel was his gaze on her. The look in his eye brought back all kinds of sordid thoughts and memories of what'd just happened in her so-called bedroom, and she found herself growing warm. Marcus had touched her in ways he hadn't ever before. He'd been soft and gentle, and oddly adoring. He'd touched her like a lover, not a controlling oppressor, and she'd come away confused and still scared, but also eager for more of that touch.

When they arrived at their destination—the location of Marcus's new nightclub *Bound*—they were each given a hard hat and a high-visibility jacket to wear and then were shown around the new club. It was so close to being done that they were already stocking the shelves behind the bar area, but upstairs there was still building and decorating work going on and the team trailed along behind Marcus as he led them around, pointing to each of the departments and offices explaining what they were to become. Wynter couldn't understand why he felt the need to, though, as it was almost an exact replica of the offices back at *Slave*. She knew before he told them which were the HR offices and such and recognised the four private offices along the hallway as soon as they arrived beside them.

"My dear managers," Marcus barked as he came to a stop, "you will oversee both clubs so might have to visit with me again on a regular basis. Here are your offices should you require some private space. Your key will open both locks."

"Master," Joanna jumped in, sidling closer and fluttering her eyelashes up at him. "Will we stay here some days too?"

"You, my darling," Marcus answered, and Wynter hated how she felt a twinge of jealousy in her gut when he placed a hand against the small of Joanna's back, "shall come with me. Wherever I am, you managers are to follow. Plain and simple."

"As will I, I presume?" Bryn asked, and Wynter had to hide her smile at the jealous edge to his tone. So, someone else had felt that twinge, too?

"Indeed," Marcus agreed, and then he led them upstairs to where the final touches were being put on his office. It was the same setup as he'd originally had back at *Slave* and Wynter had to swallow a lump in her throat when she looked down at the ground, at where David's body had lain in a crumpled heap in the other, previously matching office. Everything was exactly the same, and Wynter hoped Marcus would change it like he had the other one. She didn't much like being reminded of what'd happened, even if it hadn't been here.

"Ladies and gents," chimed a woman's voice from across the huge room and they each turned to watch as a tall brunette came sauntering towards them, teetering on ridiculously high heels, considering the place was still technically a building site. She came to a stop in front of their master and kissed his cheek. "Marcus, darling. I wasn't expecting you until tomorrow morning. I had intended to lay on a feast in your honour. My sire will be most displeased with me."

"You know as well as I do, Claudine that I do not feed from the slaves in my employ, only my managers." He beckoned to the three of them with his hand and Claudine, presumably a fellow vampire, turned to eye each of them in turn.

Wynter picked up on the woman's distaste for the four of them and refused to look away when under her scrutiny, like the others had done. As far as she was aware, she had no orders to act timid or fearful of the others of Marcus's kind. She would give respect to those who reciprocated it, but she wouldn't shy away. He'd protect her and keep her safe, she was sure of it, and so stood her ground.

"This one reeks of self-importance, Marcus," the woman told him with a sneer, "makes me sick."

"Yes," he replied without a care for the insult she'd just administered. "And Jack there is heartbroken and desperately lonely, while Joanna is an insufferable bore who adores me so much I can beat her within an inch of her life, and she'll always come back for more. They each serve their purposes, dear. Much like you serve yours."

Wynter felt like applauding him for the comeback but settled instead for the tiniest of smiles. She didn't want to push her luck, after all.

She then stared down at the bracelet still around her wrist. The gift from the Priestess. She'd never taken it off and didn't want to either, and thought it odd how it had just become part of herself. Something she was so used to, she forgot it was even there. It had to be magical. The black mist swirling within the single dark bead was mesmerising, and Wynter had often found herself staring into it. It was marvellous. Like now, was it somehow getting darker? It seemed so.

"Ah yes, back to the task at hand," Claudine then said, and Wynter snapped out of her reverie at the sound. She then watched as the vampire turned her attention back to Marcus and ignored both his answer and his slaves. "The last of the work is due to be finished well ahead of schedule and Camilla has agreed to your request for funding of her hordes' feeding days. She does wish to speak with you to go over the terms, though, and has requested that you visit with her immediately."

Wynter watched as a frown encroached on Marcus's usually so carefully stoic guise, and she got the feeling he didn't much fancy going to visit this Camilla, whoever she was. Wynter thought back to the apparition she'd seen, though. Could that be her? Or perhaps someone associated with her? She was willing to bet this trip had to be the first step in her being set free of Marcus, though. It was too much of a coincidence otherwise.

They were finally away from *Slave* and due to travel with him for however long he determined, and while things had indeed changed between them, Wynter still yearned to be released from his tight grip. Still wanted to meet the woman who had appeared to her and find out the truth behind her promise of an option-number-three.

Claudine then took the small group through the last of the walkthrough and finally, she ushered them all into a small office just inside the main front doors. There, the humans were offered refreshments while the two vampires talked in private over to one side of the room.

Wynter wasn't sure why, but something about the set up didn't feel right. She sipped on her freshly brewed coffee and stared out the window to the foyer beyond, watching as the workmen went about their business as usual. None of them appeared to be hiding anything or watching from over their shoulders, so she turned her attention back to the room and realised the source of her unease was in there with them. Claudine. She had been employed by Marcus to be Project Manager of the new club's opening, so he had to trust her, but there was something off about the vampire. Something that made Wynter's blood run cold whenever she looked at her.

As she continued to watch, an odd sensation began to creep up her spine, and she suddenly felt lightheaded. She tried to shake the feeling off, but then looked around at the others and realised that they, too, seemed to be reacting in the same way. It was like when Marcus had drugged her, using his cronies at the bar. One moment, Wynter was with it, and the next her legs were so tremendously tired they buckled and she slumped to her knees. The others each did the same as well, and it wasn't long before they were in a heap together on the floor of the office, barely fighting to stay awake.

The last thing Wynter remembered was watching as Claudine turned to them with a smile while Marcus was grimacing.

***

"About time," Claudine told Marcus, who was seething at her audacity but had decided to keep his cool, at least for the time being. "My witch cast that spell before we'd even walked into this office. Your humans are strong to have taken this long to succumb."

"And you are on dangerous ground," he answered curtly. "I do not appreciate my staff being mistreated this way. It's not how I like to do things."

"Oh, really?" Claudine responded with a smirk, "Jakob tells it a little differently…"

Marcus sneered. Of course, that little sneak was behind this coup. His information regarding what he'd seen at Marcus's office had clearly gone back to his mistress, who had now sent her witch across during his visit to ensure he accepted her request for an audience.

Only the same witch who cast the spell to knock his three slaves and assistant out could undo this sort of spell, and Marcus didn't need to be told so to figure out that her actions formed an ultimatum. Attend or have naught but a pile of sleeping humans to drag back across the city. The rest of them he'd willingly leave as such, but not his favourite little pet. Not Wynter. He wanted to curse and lash out at Claudine as well as his surroundings but forced his rage aside. He would save it for the real culprit. Camilla.

"Let's away then," he barked, but first did not pass up the opportunity to grab Claudine by her throat and pin her to the wall behind. "And if you ever try something like this again, do rest assured that I will not hesitate to rip you to pieces and burn the remains. I care not for whom you serve. When you're employed by me, you're mine to command."

She tried to loosen Marcus's grip, but he refused to relinquish his hold, squeezing tighter. He wanted her to know he meant what he'd said. It was no idle threat.

When he eventually let go, it was because he'd chosen to, and nothing more. "Now, take me to your sire."

FOURTEEN

When Wynter awoke, her head was pounding, and it made opening her eyes almost too difficult to even bother with. It was as if she'd been hit in the head or something because everything from the neck up seemed to hurt like a bitch. What the hell was in that coffee? And why had yet another vampire felt the need to spike hers and the others' drinks to make them go easily? Couldn't that bitch have simply asked?

She wondered though if the drugs hadn't been about getting the three of them to behave, but to garner the attention of someone else. Someone tall and handsome with those icy blue eyes. Thinking of Marcus only made Wynter's head hurt more, and so she buried it in the pillow someone had thankfully placed beneath her and groaned.

"The affects will wear off soon, Wynter," a deep and heavily accented voice told her, and she mumbled in response about how it wasn't wearing off soon enough, making the man watching over her laugh.

She knew the voice before she even had to open her eyes. It was that strange vampire from the night of David's death. Jakob.

"Where am I?" she asked when she was indeed beginning to feel a little better. "And where are the others?" she added, having noticed how quiet the room was.

"You are the only one Camilla is interested in, so the others were left behind to await Marcus's return. You won't be joining him," a second voice told her, and it was one Wynter recognised as well, but not from any meeting. No, she knew this woman from the night she had come to her as a vision.

She jumped up and looked to where the sound had come from, blinking away the sleep from her dry eyes. Lo-and-behold, the woman who had appeared to her before was indeed there with them. She was whole. Flesh and blood.

Wynter looked from the woman to Jakob and back, checking that she was safe to talk openly, and breathed a sigh when the woman nodded and offered her a kind smile.

"You're the one who came to me. You told me to follow him to you and that you'd separate us. Is that offer still on the table?"

"It is indeed," the woman confirmed with a knowing smile. "I'm pleased you were able to refuse his advances. It speaks volumes about your strength of will, Wynter. I intend to follow through on the promise I made you, but it won't come easily. You have to know what you're letting yourself in for before we attempt this."

She wanted to tell the woman a resounding yes, but then hesitated. Her feelings towards Marcus had changed over the past few days. She had changed. Him too. She wasn't as desperate to leave him as she had been before and couldn't offer the witch a definite answer. She needed to get her head straight first.

"We'll give you some time to think about it, Wynter," Jakob interjected, making her smile with the way he said her name as *Vinter*. "Marcus is busy for now, so we have time to allow the details to sink in."

The witch looked furious with him for having stalled the proceedings and Wynter frowned, thinking that if this really was all for her benefit, then what did it matter if they waited just a little longer? The woman's actions told her there had to be another motive at hand, and she wanted to know what it was before she acted out against Marcus and potentially lost her place with him forever.

"Yes, I'd like some time to think," she answered him and then turned to the witch, "will you tell me more later when my head isn't pounding?"

"Sure," she replied with an icy edge to her tone that made Wynter retreat even further. The witch then stood and stormed out of the room, and Wynter half expected Jakob to join her, but he didn't. He simply sat back in his chair and watched her with an amused smile.

"You gonna tell me what's really going on here?" she asked him as she lay back on the bed and stared up at the ceiling. Her head really was still pounding, and it was irking her, making her grouchy. "Why the rush? And what does she really have to gain by separating us?"

Jakob was quiet for a moment, as though deliberating on just how much to reveal, but then he shrugged and began to speak. It was as if he didn't care about the repercussions for telling her the truth, and while she didn't want him to get in any trouble, Wynter was glad of his candour.

"Lola works solely for the love of her mistress, like your priestess does her master. The vampire Camilla has asked her to separate the pair of you. Of course, she intends to follow through on her promise to deliver but cannot break his witch's spell by force. That's why she came to you when your soul was crying out for a way to escape Marcus's clutches, because you have to be willing..."

Jakob leaned forward, placing his elbows on his knees, and Wynter felt him glaring at her, reading her reactions in the same way Marcus always did.

He was so intense.

She wondered if perhaps all vampires could read humans so easily, and decided to be more careful which of them she put her trust in. Wynter turned and looked into Jakob's eyes and was surprised to find warmth in the deep blue hues. Far from the iciness behind Marcus's. He wasn't like him at all, and it was refreshing to discover how not all vampires were devious and selfish megalomaniacs like her boss.

"And now that things are different?" she asked him as she turned onto her side and continued to watch him.

"She's scathing. I believe she thought this was going to be easy," Jakob answered, and Wynter frowned.

"Why are you telling me all this?"

"Because I try to be beholden to no one other than myself and I made an oath not to lie," Jakob replied with a soft smile she was once again drawn to. "I get results, Wynter. Make no mistake about that. But I do it with honour rather than by being devious."

Jakob had a solemn look on his face that made her want to believe him. And to trust that he'd always be honest. She was reminded of him holding her close in an attempt to do the right thing by her once before. And of how he'd stared at her afterwards and had seemed to be peering right into her soul. Was it the truth he was seeking then, too? Had he found it?

"So, you'll tell me the truth about all of this? About what Camilla wants from me and why?"

"Of course, and I'd appreciate it if you did the same in return. Tell me the truth about what Marcus is up to in his tower. I snooped around that night I found you, but I would like to know first-hand what it is he's playing at. What his end goal is," Jakob countered, but Wynter shook her head.

"All I know is that he rules us all with an iron fist. He expects each of his slaves to behave and serve him without question. We don't get told the gory details."

"And yet you fight him, don't you?" Jakob replied with a knowing smile, "everyone else tells him yes while you tell him no. Did you break his curse?"

Wynter looked away. She'd kept that a secret and wasn't sure she wanted to confirm or deny it, regardless of Jakob's request for honesty.

He already knew the answer though, she could tell, and seemed to take her silence as confirmation, anyway. "Why do you stay if you already have your freedom? Do you genuinely care for him?"

Wynter knew he couldn't understand. She barely could herself and breathed a sigh.

"I don't know. There are times when he makes me feel good and shows kindness, but there are others when he's a monster who delights in tormenting me. I stay because I have no other choice," she eventually answered, and was surprised to find understanding on Jakob's face.

"Do you think he cares for you? That he could ever love you?" he asked.

"Sometimes. But if he did, surely he wouldn't be so cruel?" Wynter replied, and it dawned on her as she spoke the words that Marcus couldn't possibly love her.

It didn't matter what his eyes showed her when she got too close, his actions were what spoke volumes and he didn't treat her like someone he loved, but someone he wanted to control and have at his command. Just like all his other minions, and yet undoubtedly sweeter, because she wasn't under his spell like they were. A true prisoner, just like he'd always wanted.

"Did he threaten you to make you stay?" Jakob asked, continuing with his interrogation, and she nodded. "Who is it? Which life is at stake if you leave?"

"Everyone I care about," she breathed, and a tear slid down her temple. "But the first on his hit list is another of his slaves. Someone I've come to care a great deal about."

"Would this slave do the same for you?" the vampire pressed, and Wynter wanted to say yes, but she wasn't convinced he would, in all honesty.

Warren had blown hot and cold too and she had told herself he would only ever sell her out because of his curse but could never be entirely sure. He wanted out, it was clear, and Wynter wondered if he'd gladly throw her under the bus to save himself given the chance. "It strikes me," Jakob said, breaking her reverie, "that everyone seems to care for you, Wynter. You're likeable and kind, and of course very beautiful, but that's where the fondness ends. You've held back from getting too close to anyone for so long that you've become nothing but a shell. Someone unlovable because you have no heart."

His words hit her like a punch to the chest.

"Don't say that!" she cried and sat up atop the bed. Wynter couldn't imagine him saying anything more hurtful than he just had done, and she began to cry. "I'm not *that* closed off and I'm certainly not heartless."

He watched her come undone with a sad expression on his face, but Jakob didn't take back what he'd said.

"You care, it's true," he agreed, "but if you stopped shutting out your emotions, you'd see that real connections aren't something you should have to work so hard for. None of these men love you, Wynter. If they did, they would put you first without question. They would think of you with their every waking moment and want to spend it by your side. Not play games or leave you guessing whether they would make sacrifices to save you."

"So, what, I've got to accept that no one loves me and probably never will?" she answered despondently and hung her head in her hands.

"You can choose. Continue as you are and let everyone you care about walk all over you because they cannot see you for anything more than you already are. Half a person, and half a heart. Or open your heart fully and follow it. Don't give up on yourself and go forward in the knowledge that you're more than good enough. That you should be loved. That you deserve to be."

"Fool me once, shame on you."

"Fool me twice, shame on me," Jakob finished for her, and Wynter began to cry harder. She truly was the fool. She had been played time and again because she'd stayed too closed off to see what the people around her were doing. They were using her. Forcing her to do as they wanted by toying with her and manipulating her. And all the while, she'd let them because she hadn't wanted to get too close and let anyone hurt her again. Well, no more.

She was going to love with everything she had and was going to start by learning to love herself again.

Jakob stayed with Wynter for hours. They talked through her past with her ex, Dominic, and how she'd ended up at the club that night when David had approached her. She told him how Marcus had lured her in and then put her under his spell, but how she'd managed to get out of it again.

It felt incredible to finally tell someone. She felt she could trust him and knew that while her admissions weren't secrets he'd keep safe, Jakob seemed to understand her motives. He also appeared to want her to come out of this different and in one strong piece, and it was refreshing being open and completely honest with someone about what she'd been through and how it'd all made her feel.

She wanted to stay there all night, thanks to how comfortable and refreshing it was in his presence. But of course, thanks to the time that'd passed, it wasn't long before her stomach began rumbling and Wynter stood, heading for the doorway.

"I need some food, and quick. Are you taking me for something to eat or shall I see if Lola can bring room service?" she joked, making him laugh. With a smile, Jakob climbed to his feet, opened the door, and then ushered her forward with a wave of his hand.

"Please, after you," he said and then led her out into a dark hallway.

There, Wynter stopped dead thanks to the stark coldness outside. It was far from welcoming. There were doors all the way down the hall they were now in, but each was closed, presumably locked tight. All Wynter could see was the stream of moonlight coming in from the window at the end, and in its cool rays was the path to an exit.

The door she and Jakob had just left through closed with a bang behind them and she jumped, moving closer to him for safety. It was odd how after just a short period of time together, she already trusted him so much. But really, she figured, why not. He'd been the first person to truly be honest with her and not lie or cheat his way into her good graces, and he certainly hadn't manipulated his way in either. He was strong and seemed to know how to use that strength wisely, and she felt safer by his side.

She peered up into his face and took him in, and watched as the shadows clung to his strong, square jaw and prominent cheekbones. He was looking right back at her, his pale blue eyes roving over her face curiously, too. For a few seconds, they simply stood there, taking one another in, and Wynter couldn't deny feeling warmed from the inside out thanks to his closeness. Jakob truly was a handsome, powerful man. His blond hair and blue eyes might make anyone else think of him as a pretty-boy, but she knew differently. She could see the strength behind those eyes and the fierceness in his stance. He was old and wise and had seen his share of both good and bad. But unlike Marcus, he hadn't sought power or riches. He seemed to want nothing more than balance and peace, hence his openness and ready honesty. A true conundrum.

A shiver then swept down her spine. It was eerily quiet wherever they were and Wynter realised then how she'd quickly gotten used to the sounds of the nightclub around her day and night. She wasn't used to the silence anymore and wasn't all that sure she particularly liked it.

"Where to?" Wynter quickly asked, and Jakob shrugged.

"Where do humans like to eat?"

She giggled and shook her head.

"There must be a kitchen or something around here? Doesn't Camilla keep human slaves?" she asked, and then paled when Jakob shook his head no.

"She feeds and then gives the scraps to her hordes. Needless to say, we don't entertain much…"

"Whoa," Wynter replied, and it was hard to shake off the realisation of what Jakob had just said. Maybe there was such a thing as being too honest, after all.

She'd heard that term used back at the club, too. Hordes. What did the vampires mean by that? She wanted to ask him but was scared to hear his answer. Whatever a horde was, it couldn't be good. She guessed it had to be a group of vampires that weren't as refined as the likes of Marcus, but perhaps wilder. Maybe it was a term for collections of bloodthirsty vampires who lacked the sensibilities those others had? Those missing a conscience or a soul that couldn't be trusted to feed out in the human world, so had to be fed scraps from vampires like Camilla?

Wynter had the suspicion she'd just answered her own question. "So, she doesn't have any qualms about killing? And what about the laws?" she asked Jakob, hoping she might be wrong.

"She thinks nothing of killing. Most of our kind don't, but there are rules," Jakob told her, leading Wynter down the hallway towards what she could see was a fire door at the end.

She followed, wandering slowly beside him as he continued to chat with her, and was drawn to him once again thanks to his openness and decency. "Contrary to myth and fiction, we do not shy away from sunlight or can be deterred by garlic or crosses. We cannot be killed with wooden stakes or holy water. Our deaths are administered by decapitation or by us being burned alive."

Wynter wrinkled her nose at the gruesome information, but still nodded in understanding. She was getting a lesson she hadn't even realised she'd needed and listened intently as Jakob continued. It was fascinating to hear, and she still wholeheartedly appreciated the way he spoke with such refreshing honesty.

They went through the doorway and, like at the club, Wynter expected to find more corridors there to ensure they couldn't just escape, but was stunned to instead find themselves going straight out into the cool night air. She looked around and discovered that they were outside a service exit of some kind of stately home and turned back to look up at the huge house in the darkness.

"What is this place?" she asked, impulsively changing the subject.

"Camilla's residence. She lives at the front of the mansion while those such as Lola and I live at the back. She much prefers the prettier side," he replied with a playful roll of his eyes.

"While you prefer dark and cold?"

"More like practical and private," he corrected with a smile, and then led her over to a garage. There, he opened the huge door to reveal a bright blue sports car that was the exact colour of his eyes. Not that she'd noticed, of course. Wynter grinned and let herself have a moment to appreciate the beautiful piece of machinery. She didn't know much about cars, but she knew this was something special. And expensive—not that creatures like Jakob had to worry about it, of course.

"Understated, just like I expected of Mr Practical and Private," she teased as she climbed in the passenger side and buckled up. "Now, take me out for dinner," she added, and then checked her watch and realised that it was almost five-am, "or breakfast. Whatever. Just feed me."

Jakob watched her with a smile and then shook his head, as though surprised by something. Wynter wanted to ask what, but then remembered her promise to herself. She wasn't going to care what other people thought of her anymore. She was going to be herself and do what she wanted with her life. Those around her could get on board or get out.

Look after number one—that was the goal.

He sped away and in just a few moments, they'd turned out of the private driveway and onto a winding country road.

Jakob drove insanely fast and Wynter held on for dear life as he took the corners at breakneck speed and flew through lights as if he somehow knew they'd always be green.

She hated every second of it. She was not like those girls in the movies, where they always seemed to trust their driver and enjoy the fast ride. Nope, she was more the close her eyes and hope for the best kind of girl. Not one for thrill rides in the slightest.

When they finally came to a stop, it was outside a small shopping village set away from the nearby town and regular shopping areas. Wynter just hoped there might be an early-opening coffee shop, or at least an all-night fast-food chain there, so she could grab something. Anything!

"Will this do?" Jakob asked as they both climbed out and looked around at the empty parking lot. "I meant it when I said I didn't know where to get food."

As was expected, the shops were closed, but there was a burger-chain restaurant up ahead and Wynter ran for the door in the hope she might be in luck. She wasn't. The damn place didn't open until six-am. She cursed and stepped back, where she collided with Jakob, whom she hadn't realised had been hot on her heels.

He was quick to grab her, so she didn't fall, and she heard him take a sniff of her hair.

"Looks like I'm not the only one who's hungry?" she said, turning to face him, and Jakob seemed surprised by her reaction.

"No, I'd never feed from you, Wynter. You're not mine to taste," he replied with an awkward expression. As if he really and truly would never take from her what Marcus so readily did. It was odd, but also a nice thought to have a vampire companion who didn't want to devour her every five seconds.

"Like you said, people seem to like me well enough. I'm starting to see how I can use that to my advantage," she informed him, and then lifted her hand to show him the mobile phone she'd just taken from his jacket pocket while he'd been flummoxed momentarily.

Wynter grinned mischievously and then pouted when she tried to access the phone but was halted by his passcode. "Tell me your code, Jak. I'll pull up the maps and we can actually go in search of somewhere that's open."

Jakob moved over to her in a heartbeat and had his phone back in his grasp without so much as a struggle from her. She wasn't playing games, and so just continued to smile up at him and then looked down at the phone in his hands. "Hurry up, I'm getting hangry," she demanded, and delighted in his puzzled look.

Before he could ask her what that meant, she took off for the parking lot and skipped over to his car, perching by the driver's side. "How about I drive?"

Now that really made him laugh. Jakob was still bellowing out sniggers after he'd physically placed her in the car's passenger seat and buckled her in, and then he turned to Wynter, eyeing her with that same thoughtful look.

227

Again, he seemed surprised by her, and she liked it.

"I've found a food place that's open," he then said, before starting the engine and tearing away with a screech. They turned out of the shopping village and around the corner, and then it was Wynter's turn to laugh as the bright lights of a huge supermarket came into view. It wasn't exactly the greasy spoon or fast-food breakfast she'd thought, but it would do nicely.

She said nothing as he parked up and followed her inside, sticking awkwardly next to her. Wynter figured Jakob had never been to a supermarket before, and she enjoyed being the one to take the lead. She took him into the foyer and ordered for him to grab a trolley, which he just about managed after finally figuring out how to pry the metal carts apart.

She smiled to herself as she watched him, and then realisation struck her. She didn't know how long she'd end up being away and so decided she was going to stock up on supplies. Just the human essentials, but necessities nonetheless. And why not. The supermarket was pretty much empty and, she enjoyed the simple pleasure of just being free to do some shopping.

With Jakob in tow, she set about grabbing something to eat and some snacks and basics for her stay at Camilla's mansion. He followed her up and down the aisles with wide eyes and confusion that was so evident Wynter found it endearing. He really had no idea.

Jakob seemed quite sweet and while she could tell he wasn't keen on being away too long, he said nothing to hurry her as she browsed the store and made her selections.

It was fun. Probably the most fun she'd had in weeks, and by the time she'd hit the checkout, she was smiling from ear to ear.

FIFTEEN

When they were back at the mansion, Jakob carried the bags of shopping in while Wynter munched on some croissants she'd bought from the supermarket bakery. She'd devoured one after leaving the store before they'd even reached the car and had put the rest aside, not wanting to make a mess of Jakob's posh car but was already hungry again so hadn't delayed once they were back at Camilla's foreboding home.

The pair of them then went back to the room she'd woken up in, and Wynter sat down on the bed with a sigh.

"What's wrong?" Jakob asked with a seemingly genuine frown.

She wasn't sure she could tell him, but she was still so lost. Wynter suddenly felt like she didn't know what she wanted, not really. Put her in a room with Marcus and she knew she'd want him. The same would be for if she were with Warren. Neither one of them had really done anything to warrant her affection, though, and she wondered if she really was just a fool whenever it came to matters of the heart. Different men had done a number on her time and again, and yet she'd still never learned. And even after having convinced herself for years that she'd found the secret to surviving via her icy mind-set, it appeared she was still back to square one.

"All of this," she replied as she ushered around the room with her hand, meaning the situation she'd found herself in overall, not just the how and where of the current situation. "And I get the feeling you're not just spending time with me for my sparkling personality. Are you babysitting me?" Wynter asked with a frown.

"No," Jakob replied with a smile, surprising her.

She looked up at his handsome face and knew she was wearing that doe-eyed look of wonder girls often got when peering into men's faces but didn't care. His chiselled jaw and hardened stare were still intimidating, but when he smiled, Wynter was captivated. She remembered what it felt like to have him hold her and let herself indulge in her fantasies a little. After all, what harm could it do? She knew it'd never lead anywhere. He was just another vampire, and his kind did not fornicate with humans. That'd been well and truly drummed into her by now.

"But?" she asked him and knew there was indeed more to it when he bowed his head slightly, as though conceding.

"But I am guarding you. I've been asked to make sure you don't misbehave or try to escape."

"Oh. And if I had tried to run earlier at the store?" Wynter said with a determined look at the vampire she knew was not only stronger and faster than her, but also more cunning and clever. There would be no way she could outrun or outsmart him if she tried, but that didn't mean she'd have to like it.

"I would stop you," Jakob answered curtly, as if it were obvious. "I might not like it either, but I know what's best, and that's for you to stay with me."

"With you?" she countered, having found his choice of words a little odd.

"Well, I mean you must stay here and if it's me or Lola watching you, then you're better off with me. Camilla does not care for your safety, only that you comply with her wishes. Lola would not be an ally, but a warden. Someone who would merely keep you safe because she had been ordered to," he answered, but Wynter got the feeling he too was bending the truth a little.

"Tell me more about Camilla," she asked, opting to discuss the more important matter at hand—her official captor. "I need to know what I'm dealing with. Does she intend to kill me?"

"Oh, yes," Jakob answered with a jovial smile, but she knew he was telling the truth. "But only if you don't behave. She wants to take you away from Marcus first as punishment."

"What have I done?" she demanded, feeling hard done by.

"Not you," Jakob chided, "him."

"Oh. And how does she plan to do that?"

"Either by making him abhor you, or vice versa. She had hoped for an easy resolution, but your strength has made that somewhat difficult. You remember I told you we don't mind killing humans? Well, that was the old way. Times have changed and we're trying not to do so unless absolutely necessary," he explained, but Wynter was still confused.

"How?"

"We outnumber humans two-to-one. Because of this, we cannot kill them without facing the repercussions. Each human should be kept alive as a slave until they're no longer fit for purpose. Camilla has never entertained that idea, so she feeds at clubs like *Slave* and the numerous others Marcus runs, but she also commands an army of vampires she calls hordes. They're kept hungry and caged. The remains of their human minds broken and lost so that only the feral side is left. They are the ultimate hunting machines and were created as a contingency plan should humanity ever discover our existence and revolt against us. They are trained not to drink their fill, but to take a mere sip and pass their prey along so that the others in their pack survive."

"Oh, God," she replied with a gulp, the realisation striking that she had indeed been right to assume the worst about them. "And Marcus wouldn't drink from me if I have been tainted by the bites of others. He told me so before."

She cursed herself for being such a quick study and clutched at her aching gut.

"Exactly," Jakob replied, "she won't kill you, but she'll make him refuse your vein by having anything from one to a dozen vampire soldiers feast on your blood."

A chill ran down her spine at the thought.

"So, it's that or I escape him some other way?"

"Yes. I guess the only other way would either be by merging your soul with another vampire or becoming pregnant with another human's child. Either would be enough of a change to spare you his affection for long enough to ensure your escape."

The room suddenly started to spin. There was no way she could imagine herself going that far. No fucking way in hell. She'd rather stay with Marcus.

"But I don't want either of those things!" she bellowed. If she let any of the hordes bite her, Marcus wouldn't just turn her away, he'd throw her to the wolves with all his other slaves. She'd have to work in that club, feeding them in whatever depraved method he chose. He still wouldn't just let her go free. Nothing was ever that simple when it came to him.

And if she merged with another vampire, then surely that meant they'd have to love one another first? She couldn't give her soul to someone and become their willing slave, because she knew that was what would happen once she merged. There was no doubt her mind and body would no longer be her own. Not really different to her current predicament.

And then there was the third option. Marcella was doing it, she knew, but she couldn't bear to do the same. The idea of bringing a baby into the awful world she'd found herself in was deplorable. She couldn't imagine anything worse.

None of these plans would do. Not a single one.

Wynter decided she would fight tooth and nail with any man, woman, witch, or vampire who tried to make her do any of them. This was no longer about just escaping Marcus, but instead this was about her survival in general. She was up against threats from numerous sources and knew it was time she put her newest plan into place.

She would put herself first like she'd promised and not cave again.

Not even for a second.
Because now, her life well and truly depended on it...

SIXTEEN

"I shan't discuss this with you again, Camilla," Marcus snapped, before letting out an exasperated groan. How had he been so blind for all these long years? The damn woman was in love with him and yet he'd not seen it before. Not realised the extent of her attraction to him, while he'd taken their liaisons as casual rather than see how she adored him both in and out of the bedroom.

Camilla had indeed played a perilous game to get him to her home, and Marcus was livid that it'd worked. She'd moved her pieces into place while he'd been too distracted to see it, and now there he was, her captive. And Wynter too. She was in the belly of the house and was being held there while he played his part of the game. Marcus could sense her, but knew she was well though. Not currently harmed or under any duress. He knew his actions might alter that, however, and so treaded carefully whilst dealing with his hostess.

"Then send the girl away, Marcus," Camilla demanded, her voice shrill with jealousy. "Be done with her and things can go back to how they were."

He took a step towards her and fixed his icy stare on the ancient vampire he knew had the upper hand for now. Marcus approached and Camilla retreated, but not like Wynter did. Not out of fear. No, she was doing it to lure him towards the bed she'd made up especially for him. She wanted him to take her atop it. To make love to her and have her believe everything was going to be alright. But he couldn't bring himself to want her or desire the same body he'd been with countless times before. Things had changed.

Her actions had only cemented things for him. He wanted Wynter. He wanted to complete what he'd started a few weeks before and make her his. It was clearer than ever before, and Marcus couldn't believe it'd taken him so long to finally see it.

In many ways, he couldn't believe he'd wasted the time playing games and toying with her. She was the only thing on his mind, and he was sure now that he was ready to take the next step. He was ready to merge his soul with hers. He had Camilla to thank for pushing him, at least.

"I will not send Wynter away," he groaned honestly. The consequences be damned. He would lie and fight his way out of whatever Camilla threw at him, but he couldn't agree to anything that would damn his darling girl to whatever fate his vampire lover had in store for her.

Marcus knew what had to be done. That he would need to offer Camilla something in exchange for his precious prize and knew exactly what was needed of him. He had to agree to one more tryst. When it was done, he would take Wynter home and complete the merging process, but he had to do this one thing before he could take her and go.

To save Wynter, he had to lie. "I won't send her away because she means nothing more to me than my fondness for the blood running through her veins," he replied with a sour expression.

Camilla seemed surprised, but convinced, and so Marcus moved closer still, giving his ruse everything he had to make it seem real. To make her believe it. "You've let your jealousy get the better of you, my darling. But your fears are unfounded. Here, let me show you. Let me love you…"

And he did.

***

After two days of being stuck under the watchful eye of the strange Russian vampire, Wynter began to see their world in a whole new light. He told her many things as they passed the time together. About the history of his kind and just how many countries were pretty much ruled by them. Jakob talked for hours about the places he'd seen and the people he'd encountered, but he always seemed to hold something back. She wasn't sure why he insisted on it, but Wynter knew she was finally ready to know the truth. She wanted to get the whole story.

"What are you hiding?" she asked as she propped herself up against her pillows and relaxed against them, feeling tired. The days and nights had blurred together in their small room and while she'd had a decent amount of sleep, she hadn't ever slept for long at a time. Not with her guard always watching. Always seeming to be scrutinising her in ways she couldn't fathom. "Your stories, they always end abruptly, like you aren't telling me the whole tale."

Jakob shifted in his seat, seeming uncomfortable for the first time since she'd met him. That just made her more eager to get to the bottom of his unease.

"It's because with me, everything ends badly."

Well, that didn't make any sense. Wynter sat up higher and scratched at the nape of her neck where a chill had just swept over her that seemed to somehow be emanating from Jakob. It was the same when Marcus was in one of his violent rages, and yet Jakob still seemed at ease. Far from the fear-inducing iciness she felt around her master when she'd said or done the wrong thing.

"As in?" she asked in the hope he'd elaborate.

"Death," he eventually groaned, staring blankly through her. "I am known by many as an assassin. A butcher. A fiend," Jakob revealed with a frown, "the village outside Paris I told you about—I burned it to the ground and killed everyone after my visit there. Man, woman and child," he explained, knocking the wind out of her. "If you were to ask me what my trade is, I would answer that I am a reaper. I take those that are living and render them otherwise for hire, or for my own means."

"So all the places you've visited and the people you've known, they were all for jobs? You were there to murder someone?" Wynter asked, her heart pounding in her ears as fear suddenly reared its ugly head and wracked through her. Was that his current job as well? To end her life when he got the call from his mistress?

Jakob nodded, and he didn't even seem sorry.

"For Camilla, but sometimes for others who pay me well. Other times for myself, or perhaps professional curiosity," he said, as though reeling off a simple list of reasons, but Wynter was dismayed.

"Why?" she whispered, her eyes wide. She couldn't imagine taking another person's life, much less if she had to do it without any other reason than because someone was paying her to. It didn't make sense to her at all.

"Why what?" he dared ask, and Wynter shook her head.

"Why her? Why not say no? Why take those lives?"

"Camilla is my sire, Wynter. Vampires hold their sires in the highest esteem and, above all, others. We serve them and follow in their footsteps, just like any other mentor."

"And if she told you to kill me?" she demanded.

She climbed up out of bed and stood watching Jakob for his answer, her hands on her hips defiantly. "Would you do it without question? Would you even care for the life you'd just snubbed out? Would it matter that we became friends?"

"Yes," he answered, but Wynter didn't know which of her questions he'd meant it for. Either way, she wasn't waiting around here to die. What a cruel game, leaving her locked away, sitting and having nice long chats with the man just waiting for the go-ahead to end her miserable life. She wanted out of there and wasn't going to play nice any longer.

"Screw you," she croaked, and then pulled on her boots and jacket. "And fuck her. I'm not staying here to die."

Wynter stormed out and was surprised when Jakob didn't stop her. She made it all the way to the door at the end of the hallway before he appeared in front of her like some kind of goddamn ghost and scared the crap out of her. Damn them and their ability to move like that.

He stared into her eyes with that all-knowing look again, and then Wynter saw him flinch, as if he'd caught a scent from somewhere. She presumed her, but then his eyes darted behind her.

"No, 'dis way," he said, directing her back to the other end of the hallway. "We go 'dis way."

"Why?" she snapped, but Jakob didn't answer. He just took her by the wrist and led her away.

Wynter had no choice but to follow and had to pick up the pace as Jakob took her down and then through a door at the opposite end of the hallway.

Once inside, he turned to her and put his forefinger to his lips.

"Stay absolutely silent," he told her, and Wynter nodded.

She then looked around and realised they were now inside the main part of the house. Camilla's home.

He then led her deeper into the dark mansion and even though none of the lights were on, Wynter could still see that the foyer they were in was lavishly decorated and filled with ornate marble figures the size of behemoths. As they neared them, she saw they were depictions of roman gods and goddesses. Mythology personified in the artist's own way. She quite liked them.

Wynter spied what she assumed had to be the front door and made to go to it, but Jakob appeared to have other ideas. He instead led her up a set of wide stairs to where the only small sliver of light emanated from.

The pair of them then came to a stop outside the door that had been closed but not shut completely. A few inches of space remained, and through it Wynter could see two people thrusting and writhing against each other atop what looked like a huge chaise. She knew right away who the male of the two was. Marcus. He was slamming himself inside the woman beneath him, eliciting cries and groans of delight with every plunge. His suitor was transfixed on him, and she was clearly eager for more.

Wynter stood there, frozen. She was glued to the scene before her and knew she ought to look away. Or to give them some privacy at least, but she couldn't. She knew she should be embarrassed, but oddly, wasn't.

No, she then realised, she ought to be furious with him for having led her on so much the past few weeks and then coming here to fuck Camilla while she'd had Wynter locked away under the watchful eye of her personal assassin.

But she felt nothing. Not jealous. Not angry. Not even hurt.

The scene before her just proved Jakob right from before. Marcus didn't love her and never would, but she no longer had to wonder how he felt about her.

She watched him and felt the shutters go down on any feelings she might've once thought she had for him. Wynter knew for sure now how it was all nonsense, every kiss and fake bit of closeness they'd shared, and all the times he'd let those eyes of his shine brightly.

She meant nothing more than a slave to him, and that was fine. It would also make her decision to step away from both him and Warren all that much easier to stick to.

Camilla's cries bought Wynter back to the view before her and she watched as the stunning woman then wrapped her hands around Marcus's neck and squeezed. She grinned as he took the exchange as a challenge and mirrored the move as he continued pounding into her, and then Camilla let out an almighty scream as what had to be an orgasm ripped through her. It was the hottest thing Wynter had ever seen. Despite her coldness, a raw wave of emotion flooded through her and she didn't try and stop it.

Heat bloomed between her thighs and radiated to her stomach and up her chest. Wynter felt horny as hell and found herself leaning back against the vampire standing pressed right against her. Jakob responded the opposite way Marcus would. Rather than push her away in distaste, he took a deep lungful of her scent, and she could tell he liked it when he tilted down his head, buried it in her hair, and took another.

Marcus continued inside the bedroom. He didn't stop and Camilla didn't seem to want him to, and so the pair of them carried on, just as they had been when she and Jakob had found them. And Wynter wanted to watch some more. She put her hand up to her lips and instinctively thought of the times Marcus had kissed her hard, the way he was kissing Camilla. And of how he'd touched her and made her climax so very many times now, just like he was with her.

The memory of how his fingers had brought her such pleasure just days before invaded her thoughts, and Wynter was soon filled with even more desire.

Marcus's head lifted, and she knew he must've caught her scent, but didn't care. Part of her wanted him to find them there, watching him and Camilla fuck. She wanted to be caught while catching him in the act. Wanted to dare him to tell her off, when it was he who had closed those doors by giving into Camilla's desires.

She arched her back against Jakob's torso again and pushed herself into his tight body. It was wanton and sordid, but she didn't care. In that moment, she needed to feel something. Was desperate for someone to touch her and elicit those climaxes Marcus was drawing from Camilla. Jakob responded by pressing his rock-hard erection against her back before inhaling her scent again, and his hands grabbed her hips, pulling her tighter against him.

Without thinking about what was doing, Wynter then opened her mouth and emitted the smallest of gasps. The second it left her lips, though, the moment was over. Jakob shut down and backed off. He then wrenched her away and spirited her down the stairs so quick she couldn't even think about fighting him back.

Before she knew it, they were outside in the cool night air and Jakob was throwing her into the passenger seat of his car. He then sped away without another word and Wynter turned to watch him drive with a teasing smile playing on her lips.

"Let me guess, you thought you'd break my heart by showing me Marcus in the throes of passion with your boss?" she demanded and got no answer. "Perhaps you weren't counting on me not giving a fuck, hey? Or on me finding the show pretty damn watchable."

Jakob continued to drive in silence, and yet Wynter could sense how he was struggling to maintain his composure. He was driving like a maniac and taking the turns even faster than the last time he'd taken her out, but she wasn't exactly calm either and still wanted to say her bit. "Or maybe you're angry that you wanted a piece of what I was so willing to offer you? It's okay if you do, Jak. I'm not afraid to tell the truth about wanting you. No strings. No complications. All you have to do is take it."

Jakob tore the car off the road and drove up an overgrown side road before finally screeching to a halt at the peak of a hill overlooking the mountainous view ahead. Wynter even thought how it would've been a lovely sight in other circumstances, but not necessarily tonight. Not with the predator sat seething beside her.

Once he'd turned off the engine, he was out of the car and on her side in a heartbeat, and all still without a word. At least he'd seemed to calm down, but Wynter was still hesitant as she accepted his hand and let the silent vampire pull her from the car and lead her around to the front of the bonnet before coming to a stop at the grill.

He was brooding, she could tell, and so stared out at the view while letting him make up his mind regarding what he wanted to about what she'd said. After all, she'd been rather candid, and a little vulgar. Wynter felt she'd said more than enough. Done more than enough. Jak had to be convinced by now that she had no real personal tie to Marcus. That she'd meant it when she'd told him she was with him by force and nothing more.

She still wanted a way out, but she wanted an easy way. Not to be rendered disgusting by a horde of vampire soldiers each taking a sip, and not to be sold off to another vampire to become their soul mate. She might as well just stay with Marcus if that were the case.

She closed her eyes and pictured him and Camilla together. She was beautiful in that iconic vintage way Wynter herself loved, and she was envious of her curves and the ample breasts she'd caught sight of in that room. They made a stunning couple.

"You've called me Jak twice now, Wynter," Jakob finally muttered, and she opened her eyes to look at him. He was staring out at the world around them, and his features were soft, making him look young and almost innocent. "It makes me think of things I shouldn't. Remember, a time when I wasn't a vampire. When Camilla wasn't the only mother I knew."

Now that had come as a shock. She hadn't expected him to be reeling from such an innocent nicknaming, but figured it had to remind Jakob of a very different life he must've once led.

"I can stop," she offered. They had developed a rapport over the past few days. Perhaps even a friendship. The last thing Wynter wanted was to make Jakob feel uncomfortable, but at the same time, she wanted to know more about what he remembered of his human life. She hoped he wasn't about to take her up on the offer and turned to look at him.

He was bathed in moonlight and was beautiful. God, Wynter wanted him even more. In her quest to begin to love herself, she had also found someone for whom she was starting to feel something for. Something worth grasping hold of, rather than push away.

"No," he whispered, "don't."

"Then talk to me, Jak," she replied. "Tell me what you want."

His breath hitched, and then he was on her.

Jakob had Wynter up on the bonnet of his car with her legs spread and he nestled between them in an instant. He forced his lips on hers and his body was soon pressing against hers like before, his raging boner pushing against her core.

"You were right," he eventually groaned, "I do want you, and was shocked by how you responded. But I liked it. I like you. You're a fighter, Wynter. You're strong."

His words reminded her of the same things Marcus had told her, and she grinned at him.

That was much nicer to hear than the things he'd told her before.

"So, is there a way around the merging? Can you take me without the consequences?" she asked, reaching down his body so she could grab his hard-on from outside his jeans. It really was huge, and Wynter wanted to see it. To feel it. She was a wanton fiend and couldn't bring herself to care one little bit.

Jakob hissed and pushed himself into her palm, licking his lips. He then grinned and fixed his deep blue eyes on hers.

"Oh, don't worry," he said as he began stripping her with haste, "you can't merge if you have no soul, Wynter." He then laid her back and unbuttoned her jeans, sliding them down before pulling them off along with her underwear, leaving her naked atop the car before him.

The winter air pricked her skin, but she didn't care. She was so hot. Too hot. All she wanted was for Jak to make it better, and as he kissed his way up her thighs and then to her core, she was delighted to discover he wanted to help her, too.

Wynter cried out as his tongue delved inside of her and then swirled up and around her clit in perfect motions. She soon came for him and then could do nothing but stare in awe as he then removed his clothes and mounted her atop the car.

Every inch he pushed inside was like heaven, and she cried out as he took her body and made it whole at last.

Jakob was truly a stunning and virile man. More beautiful than any sunrise or sunset, and even better than the bright and very full moon that shone overhead as he pushed into her over and over. She was mesmerised by the stunning view and lapped it up as he continued to take what she so willingly offered.

SEVENTEEN

Jakob was wild and rough with her atop that car bonnet, and Wynter loved every second of it. He took her every which way she could imagine on one surface, and they both came repeatedly. Sometimes together, and other times to their own rhythm, but everyone somehow seemed more powerful than the last.

It was like nothing she'd experienced before. The power as he commanded her body was astounding. And the stamina? She thought he might never tire.

He threw her across the car bonnet on her stomach and was inside her again a second later, his hands fisted in her long mess of hair. Jakob then yanked her head up and back, arching her against him.

"Jak!" she cried, "please…"

He shushed her and yanked harder, her scalp burning with the pain.

"Stop that," he growled, "you're nothing, do you hear me? Nothing but an empty shell. You don't feel pain…"

She wanted to scream at him. To tell him off. But at the same time, she couldn't deny that it was true. There was an empty void within her that she slowly understood needed filling, and by being with him it was just the beginning. The start of her selfish quest to find herself again.

She didn't need to beg or plead with him to give her what she needed, either. He was giving her what she wanted freely, and so it was up to her to take it. To use him and fulfil her needs.

And so she did.

They only stopped when a light rain started to fall, making her finally shudder and begin to feel the cold. Jakob was attentive to her response to the elements and so lifted her into his arms and took her to the backseat, where he warmed her with his body before fucking her some more. He didn't seem ready to stop, and while she was beginning to tire, she wasn't ready either.

His mouth was back on her and never left. Either on her lips or breasts, and sometimes her neck and shoulders as he kissed and nibbled at her, but he never once drew blood. He was more dominant and predatory than bloodthirsty, and Wynter trusted him not to take that which Marcus thought nothing of drawing from her time and time again.

Jakob wasn't gentle, though. He wrenched on her hair with his fingers some more and commanded her by force, and not once did Wynter stop him, because she wanted it too. She loved being owned. Being taken. It'd been far too long, and she'd missed being fucked raw by an expert lover. Not a single one from her past compared to the vampire between her legs and even when her energy waned, she refused to stop because it was exactly what she'd needed.

"Jak," she whispered against him, "don't stop, please."

"Don't beg. Don't plead," he reminded her, and she nodded. "Who do you love?" he then groaned, watching her with hooded eyes and a dark smile.

"No one," Wynter hissed, and then she cried out when his hand shot around her neck and yanked her hard against him. He was such a brute, and she adored it. "No one but I," she then whimpered, and let out a satisfied sigh when he came deep within her and then removed his hand.

"Too fucking right," he croaked before kissing her again. But this time, he didn't keep going like before. Jakob began to slow his movements, and she had a feeling this was it. Their night together was finishing up at last.

Wynter didn't want their affair to be over yet though because she had a sneaking suspicion that when it was, she'd have to go back to that room in the mansion and act like nothing had happened. To go along with whatever plan that witch Lola had in store for her, or worse, Camilla.

When the sun began to creep over the horizon, Jakob let her come one last time and then slowed even more, and he then began to touch her with surprising gentleness. He'd been such a heavy-handed lover that Wynter had wondered if he'd forgotten how, but then his hands suddenly roved her body in tender sweeps and his plunges were deep and delicate, rather than hard and fast.

"Well, what a surprise you are Mr Big Bad Assassin," she teased, "I wouldn't be amazed if you could carry on for days."

"When the mood takes us, vampires can indeed go for days. It's you humans that cannot keep up," he replied with a smile, and then kissed her tenderly.

He then mumbled something she couldn't understand and when he looked into her eyes, Wynter that knew what Jakob had said wasn't for her, but for himself. He'd spoken in Russian instead of English and rather than fret, she smiled.

"Whatever it is, you don't need to worry, Jak," she whispered against him. "I told you. No strings."

He shook his head and whispered the same phrase again and this time, and Wynter frowned at him questioningly.

"It's nothing. Let's go," he grumbled, lifting her up. Rather than push him to tell her the truth, she just followed his lead without argument. She didn't want to end their night with a fight, so figured it'd be easier to relax and leave him be.

She pulled on her dirty clothes and then climbed back into the passenger seat, where she turned to watch him drive. Jakob was closed-off again, but he seemed relaxed enough and she smiled, thinking of their amazing night together. She hoped they'd be able to do it again sometime soon. "Here," he suddenly said as he turned to her with a boyish smile, and then lifted the centre armrest to reveal a small compartment. Inside were a dozen cereal bars and a couple of bottles of mineral water. "I remembered to feed you this time," Jakob added with a small laugh, which Wynter echoed.

She thanked him and helped herself, watching out the windscreen as he drove them away in what was now a heavy, thundering rain.

He was slow this time, though. Leisurely. Like he didn't want to rush back, and Wynter smiled to herself as she took another bite of her makeshift meal.

When she was finished, she shifted in her seat and peered out at the grey and wet morning but didn't care. Nothing was going to dampen her mood. They'd had a night to remember, and she didn't regret a thing. If anything, it'd been exactly what she'd needed and the perfect way to re-establish her new mantra. She'd done exactly as she'd wanted to do. Taken charge of herself and her future and had gone onto have the night of her life. And why the hell not? She was beholden to no one and had let her impulses lead her. No harm had been done, and she felt amazing.

Tiredness claimed her after eating and relaxing in the warmth of the heated seat, and soon Wynter was dropping off to sleep. She tried to stop herself, but it was no use. Her body had been thoroughly worked out, and now it was time to rest. She let out a soft moan and then felt a hand on her thigh. It was a gentle, reassuring hold, and she liked it. "Sleep now, Wynter," Jakob then told her, "we have a long drive ahead of us."

"Huh?" she grumbled with a frown, wondering why they weren't heading back to the mansion. He didn't give her an answer, and she didn't really care, so she just put her trust in him and let herself succumb to her body's need for rest.

When she awoke, it was late morning, and they were still on the motorway heading south. The rain had stopped and a bright winter's day seemed to lie ahead, and she stretched as best she could in her seat. Wynter hadn't slept particularly well, but she felt good, despite her having had just a few hours brought on by sheer exhaustion and didn't mind the warmth still resonating from between her thighs. The memory of her and Jakob's night together was so fresh she wanted to blush, but instead she just grinned to herself and took a few gulps of water from the bottle beside her. There was no doubt about it, their time together had been amazing, and she wasn't going to let anything make her feel bad for having let him take her repeatedly both atop and inside of the same car they were still travelling in.

She then caught Jakob watching her with a soft smile and couldn't get over how much she was beginning to like that damn face of his. And his company. She didn't crave space like she did with Marcus after their liaisons were over, and while it scared her to think of how much trouble those emotions could get her into, she also reminded herself of how she'd promised not to shy away anymore. Not to close herself off from her feelings. Nope, she was embracing them. Becoming a whole person again, not just an empty shell. So, she remained strong and attempted to be fearless in the face of her desires. Yeah, she liked Jak and wanted to be around him some more. Big deal. It didn't mean that anything between them was forever. Even if it was just for a few more days, that'd do nicely.

"How much longer?" she asked, her bladder having given her a sure signal that it needed addressing soon.

"We're almost there," he answered, and soon pulled off the motorway and down towards the coast. He was right, and it wasn't long until he'd pulled up at a tall red brick house that overlooked the ocean via some rocky cliffs with a beach further below them. The cool sunshine was beaming down on them, lighting up the epic stretch of coast brightly, and Wynter soaked up the view.

Jak then cut the engine and they sat there in silence for a moment. The wind seemed to be picking up outside, but there was still some lingering warmth, and she stared out at the scenery with a smile. It was truly stunning, and Wynter stopped and let herself admire it before she climbed out of the car with another stretch, but Jakob seemed intent on getting her inside rather than linger to take in the sights any longer. He hurried her along, and she decided against arguing, so headed inside behind her immortal companion without delay.

The interior of the quaint home was not a let-down. She was pleased to discover it had been not only cleaned and fully furnished ready for their stay but also seemed to be fully equipped with necessities and essentials, plus the food supplies had thankfully been well stocked by the looks of things. She had a quick look around, but soon followed Jak upstairs to a huge master bedroom rather than stay downstairs alone.

Wynter then watched him check every inch of the place, as if he was looking for bugs or something. Jakob even ran his hands over each of the windows and made sure their locks were secure. He clearly didn't want any unannounced visitors.

"What is this place?" she eventually asked, and then took a seat on the huge king-sized bed. There were clothes in a small pile atop the duvet, and Wynter picked them up and started to check each one out while she waited for Jakob to answer her. They were all her size. Someone had clearly been expecting her.

"Safe," was all he replied, but it was enough. A word that held many meanings, of course, but she trusted in his knowledge and expertise. And in his wisdom and guidance. If Jakob had brought her here to keep her safe, then she'd stay, and so she headed for the bathroom without argument and with a contented smile on her still tired face.

It was so odd how comfortable she felt with him, though. She even wondered if she was under some kind of new spell? But surely not. Jak wasn't the sort to do that to her.

Maybe she was just happy? Or whatever semblance of it she was capable of while still knowing what chaos lay ahead. Wynter couldn't deny feeling pleased with the erotic turn of events the night before. It had been nice to get away from the scrutiny and vile company Marcus often was. It was even good to get away from the club for a few nights, and even though things could go sour in a heartbeat, she didn't care. For now, she'd just settle for the happy little bubble she'd found herself in.

She used the facilities, brushed her teeth, and then took a long and hot shower. It felt amazing to get freshened up and when she emerged, she felt good as new as she finished drying off and slid into a pair of pyjamas she'd found among the new clothing that'd awaited her arrival.

Jakob was waiting for her, evidently having finished his checks. He too had washed up somewhere, and when she clambered into bed, he climbed in behind her, spooning around her while stroking her freshly washed skin.

Damn, that felt so good. He was warm and tender, and even though she knew she was in the company of a killer, she had never felt safer.

Wynter began to arch against him on instinct. How could she want him again so soon? But there it was, that flourish of heat blooming between them. The need that was building again.

He kissed and caressed her neck, whispering foreign words while enticing her body with his touch. Wynter didn't ask his reasons why, but knew he wanted her again too, and so she turned her body towards his and peered up into his impossibly deep blue eyes. They were a whole different colour to Marcus's. His were icy, while Jakob's were warm. Like the colour of sapphires.

"What is that you keep saying, Jak?" she had to ask, and was disheartened when he frowned, like he didn't want to tell. But then he sighed and pulled her closer.

"I keep saying to myself, and to you, that it'll be okay. I won't have to do it. There will be another choice," he answered, but Wynter barely felt any clearer.

"Do what?" she had to ask.

Jakob shuffled and looked away as if he were ashamed to say it, but Wynter put her hand on his cheek and pulled him back, locking their gazes again.

"Kill you," he then croaked, and she finally understood his unease. They really were in a lot of trouble, she realised.

"But if she says to, you'll do it without hesitation?"

He didn't want to say it, she could tell, but Wynter needed to hear him with her own ears. She had to know, and still wasn't scared. Foolish or not, she continued to have hope that things would work out somehow.

In fact, there was also a part of her preferred death as a way out. She didn't want to face any of Lola's offered alternatives other than being free to walk away unscathed, and the thought of dying when compared to either being turned, bitten, impregnated, or merged with someone she couldn't possibly love, didn't seem quite so bad.

"Yes," he confirmed with a pained expression, "you have no idea what it's like, Wynter. She's my sire, and that bond can never be broken. Not until—"

"I don't want to hear your reasons why, Jak," she told him calmly, and still smiled. "If I must die, then how better than by your hand? So, no more fretting over it, okay?"

Jakob stared down at her in wonder and then shook his head.

"You are a miracle to me," he told Wynter as he climbed over her, pulled off her clothes, and then positioned himself between her thighs. "One I shall admire long after our time together is over."

Wynter took the strange compliment as she hoped he'd intended it, and then readied herself for another round of his fierce fucking, but instead Jakob continued with his gentle, leisurely pace from before. He slid inside and nestled himself there, looking down at her admiringly as he took her, and Wynter basked in his adoration.

It was sheer heaven. No one had ever been so attentive with her before. So loving and caring.

I could die right now and go happily, she then thought as he made love to her.

Even as the night fell later that evening, Wynter and Jakob continued their exploits in the bedroom and only let up when the incessant ringing of his mobile phone was just too hard to ignore any longer.

She headed for the bathroom while he took the call, and Wynter could hear him barking down the phone in Russian to whoever was on the other end. She presumed either Lola or Camilla, and was glad to be out of the conversation, as she had the feeling she might not like what was being said between them. Presumably something vile about her.

She then diverted for the kitchen rather than nestle back under the sheets and was stood perusing the contents of the fridge when Jakob came down to join her.

"Who stocked up for me?" she asked, her head still in the huge door of the appliance. There was a bit of everything and some real thought had gone into it. Human thought. "And the clothes?"

"I have contacts," Jakob answered, and then he went quiet for a second as he watched her. "This house is cloaked by magic and is a kind of safe house for those who need some space from the elders of any kind. Vampires cannot enter without permission, and witches are completely unable to find it. A group of rebel humans use rune magic to create barriers like this, and they were the ones I contacted to give us some sanctuary for a while. I told them your clothes size and that you like to eat."

Wynter let out a laugh. Well, that was an overstatement. She needed to eat. There was a difference.

"And now that they've finished fucking, I'm guessing Marcus and Camilla want to know where we are?" she mused, plucking some ham and cheese from the shelf and a couple of eggs. Wynter then began chopping the meat, and she grated an edge of the yellow block, her focus on her task rather than on Jakob. She wasn't sure she could deal with too much dark and depressive right now. Not after the amazing couple of days together they'd just had. All she wanted was for time to stand still and for everyone to leave them alone. Let them have their time together. Let them be happy, even if just for a short while.

"I told them we went for a drive," he replied, watching her intently. "You're under my watchful eye now, Wynter. Camilla knows I wouldn't let you out of my sight and she is satisfied—for now."

"And Marcus?" she asked as she whisked the eggs in a bowl and threw them in a hot pan with the fillings.

"He's furious," Jakob answered with a smirk.

"Understandably."

"He demanded that I return you forthwith," he said with a confused expression. "Such strange words he uses."

Wynter laughed and finally gave Jakob her full attention. He was beyond cute, but it was obvious he was holding something back.

"Or else?" she guessed.

"He has nothing he can threaten me with," Jakob replied, but Wynter wasn't happy. She flipped her omelette over and then stared into the flames beneath the pan while the other side cooked.

"But I do," she hissed. "Does he know I went with you by choice? Does he know we're hiding away so we can have a dirty weekend without him knowing?"

"No," Jakob told her, "I was sure to let Camilla think I did this for the purely tactical advantages, when instead I did it for my personal reasons."

"So, you lied? I didn't think you ever lied, Jak?" Wynter countered as she shut off the gas and then transferred the omelette to a plate. But suddenly, she was no longer hungry.

She was afraid instead. Part of her wanted to demand they jump in his car and go back. She would appease Marcus in whatever way he demanded and go with him. Leave all of this behind—including her hopes that something might change. She couldn't risk the lives of those she cared about.

"I didn't lie, but I told part truths. I gave Camilla only what she needed, and not the full story."

Jakob then crossed the room and pulled Wynter to him. He smoothed her messy hair away from her face and watched her with his brows tightly knit in a frown. "But do not fret, Wynter. This is what she wants. You're out of the way and she can have Marcus to herself, and she will keep him busy. This is the best alternative for now."

"Until he resists her advances, and she takes her jealousy out on me again," she replied sourly, and wanted nothing more than for Jakob to shake his head and tell her she was being foolish. But of course, he didn't. She was right.

"That's why we're here," he assured her, "so she cannot make either of us do anything we don't want to. I took you far away from the mansion so that she cannot act against you without first having a clearer head. And also so he cannot come charging in after you and prove her right."

Jakob then planted a soft kiss against Wynter's lips and smiled. "And so, I can have you all to myself a while longer," he added, before pushing her still untouched food towards her, "now, eat."

***

Marcus was livid. After everything he had forced himself to do in that bedroom with Camilla, he still didn't have Wynter back by his side like she ought to be. Jakob had taken her away and not told a soul where the pair of them were, and Marcus believed Camilla when she said she had no clue where they might be. It was just like the devious assassin to steal his precious slave away and hide her. And just like his mistress, to have ordered him to do it.

He'd better not have dared taste her blood. Marcus seethed with just the thought of Wynter being tainted by his bite and could do nothing but pace the bedroom in wait for Camilla to reappear. She'd of course, offered for him to go home to the club and return to his other managers. She'd insisted she would send word when Jakob and Wynter were back, but that was not an option. He had instead told Camilla he'd wait with her a while longer.

If he left now, there would be nothing but a battle on his hands to get Wynter back. Camilla would feed him excuse after excuse and Jakob would be the same. They were playing him for a fool, and he wanted nothing more than to teach them both exactly who they were dealing with.

He needed a plan. A strategy.

His Priestess was the only one who could be trusted to give it to him. But she couldn't come into the mansion or else face the wrath of Camilla for trespassing on another witch's territory, and he couldn't have that. There was nothing else to be done but for him to act on this treachery alone.

He could wait it out and be patient, but instead, he wanted to give Camilla a reason to hate him. For her to see that she couldn't control him, no matter what she tried. Perhaps he'd set fire to everything she had built and make her watch it burn, just because he could.

In search of inspiration, he headed out of the bedroom and straight for the nearest set of stairs, where he caught the lingering scent of his darling Wynter. She had been here, in this part of the house. She hadn't been alone either, nor had she been afraid.

Marcus took a deep drag of the scent and cursed. Wynter had indeed been here, and she'd been horny as hell while she was at it. He could taste her pheromones on the air.

Had she seen him in the throes of passion with Camilla? Yes, she had to have witnessed the pair of them. And he knew exactly which vampire had led her to them. The Russian. Someone else who would now have to die simply because Marcus desired it so. How dare he bring Wynter up to watch them? What had he hoped to gain by it? Her compliance and disgust? But his plan hadn't worked. Jakob had hoped the sight would repulse her, but instead she'd been stirred up into a sexual frenzy by what she'd seen. She had enjoyed the view.

Marcus smiled to himself at the thought. Oh, how the tables had turned. His darling had watched him fuck another vampire and the fire she had for him had only been fanned, rather than put out. Had she enjoyed seeing him naked and going for it with Camilla? Had she wanted to touch herself because of it? Or perhaps yearned to be touched by the same vampire she had run both from and towards these past few weeks?

Yes, he was sure she had, and damn if that didn't make him want her back even more.

He was out the front door and around the side of the huge building in a heartbeat, where he stood and took stock of the situation at hand.

Camilla had spirited Wynter away and lured him to her bed, willing or not. Her chief minion had then taken steps to move his slave while they were too busy to notice them leave, and now she was gone, and Marcus knew he wouldn't rest until she'd come back to him.

As he stared out across the huge areas of land around Camilla's stately mansion, a plan began to form in his mind. There were a dozen or so underground bunkers lying head of him under the ground. They were shelters created for one purpose alone, to hide their contents. They were not a place to seek shelter should the threat of nuclear attack come, or a safe house for the slaves and their masters come the end of days, but quite the opposite. They were created to keep its occupants locked inside. Sealed away. Of course, they were the holding facilities for Camilla's hordes.

He sniffed out the group of most emaciated vampires from the collection of bunkers and approached the only entrance, a cover that was set in the ground above their nest. It was little more than a manhole, and he lifted it aside without any exertion at all.

Marcus then looked down into the hole and spied the fifty pairs of shining red eyes looking back up at him. To anyone else, it might be an eerie sight, but not to him. These men and women would soon become his brothers in arms. His comrades. His newest slaves.

Each of the naked soldiers was clambering closer to the small source of light and—most importantly for them—the prospect of food. They were nothing but wild animals taught and trained through starvation and fear, but today some were going to be freed. They would be enlisted to help him. Do him a service.

Exact his revenge.

Using his teeth, Marcus tore open the vein at his own wrist and then held his arm over the hole. He then watched as his blood cascaded down into the pit and gave it a few seconds before he healed the wound again and pulled his hand back. The soldiers below scurried to get a coveted taste of the precious life source, and soon he could hear them fighting over the remains.

"What are you doing!" a shrill voice hollered from the house and Marcus turned to the sound with the biggest of grins on his face. He then watched as Camilla's priestess, Lola, approached at speed. She was clearly terrified of what lay in the pit behind Marcus, and rightly so, but she still ran forwards regardless and he had to stop himself from saying anything that might reveal what he'd just done. She couldn't know until it was too late for both her and her mistress.

Lola soon reached him, and Marcus watched her eyes dart from his mouth to his wrist. She spied the blood he'd spilled and inhaled deeply, ready to scream and warn Camilla what he'd done, but Marcus grabbed his prey and placed his hand over her mouth to silence her.

"Now, now. Don't ruin the fun, little witch," he whispered in her ear before then tossing her down into the pit headfirst.

The scurry of the many for a drink from their solitary sacrificial lamb was audible, but it was, of course, only a special few who properly took their fill. The strongest and most cunning, and of course those who had already had some blood that fateful morning. His blood.

He listened as they drank Lola dry and then Marcus stood back, watching, and waiting for them to act. To seek out their freedom and obey a new master.

The first of the soldiers leapt up and out of the hole mere seconds later, followed by another, and another. When there were five immortal warriors standing before him, each of them covered in blood and lacking both clothing and hair, or even colour, Marcus nodded and smiled.

He looked at each of them and saw nothing but beasts. Creatures who were now ready and willing to do his bidding thanks to him having fed them his blood. It was an ancient rite that had bound them to one another and had brought forth a covenant between them all.

Marcus was their master now. Their new sire. The five had been born again thanks to his blood offering, and they would serve him until their last breath. "Welcome, friends. What say we have some fun?" he asked, receiving grunts from each of the huge men in affirmation.

A wide smile spread across his face. This was going to be fun.

He sent them a wordless order to follow him, and the biggest fell directly in line at his right-hand side. Marcus looked the alpha of the small pack up and down, watching as he moved with stealth and precision to every movement. The man was built like a bodybuilder. He was a behemoth, and Marcus was glad he'd absconded from Camilla's reign and joined him instead. This one would make the perfect leader of his unholy army.

Marcus led the handful of soldiers straight over to the mansion, where he pointed to the building and sent them another unspoken, yet clear, order.

Kill them all.

Hunt any stragglers down.

Bring me my darling Wynter, along with Camilla's head.

EIGHTEEN

Jakob's phone wouldn't stop ringing again, but this time it was interrupting Wynter's much needed rest, so she kicked him out of bed to go get it. She tried to go back to sleep but realised the moment he answered it that something was seriously wrong. He was shouting back to someone on the other end and Wynter could hear them screaming down the line at him from where she was still laid feet away.

"*Da*," he finally muttered in a stone-cold tone, and his body language changed entirely. The shutters suddenly went down, and he turned to Wynter, who saw him swallow hard.

Something life changing had just happened. Before he even said a word to her, she knew. It was over. Jakob hung up the phone and then physically crumbled onto the bed. She'd never seen him like this before and didn't know what to do, so just tried to comfort him while asking what was wrong.

"Please talk to me, Jak," she implored after repeatedly getting nothing back off him, and eventually he turned his wide blue eyes upwards at her.

"You were right. Marcus has retaliated because of your disappearance," he croaked. "Camilla got away, but she's the only survivor."

"What?" she cried, trying to fathom what that could mean. The only survivor? Out of how many? Jakob stared down at her and he grimaced.

"She's coming here. I have to tell her where we are. I have no choice other than to offer her safety with us."

Wynter leapt to her feet and began pacing. Her heart was pounding in her chest, and she knew before he said another thing about what to expect when Camilla arrived. The vampire might be coming to seek refuge, but once she had it, it would be the human who was no longer safe.

Camilla would do some retaliating of her own.

"She's your sire," she whispered, a tear rolling down her face. "You protect her and no one else. Obey her alone, no matter what you want for me."

"No," Jakob tried, watching her through hooded eyes. "I'll tell her you're innocent. That you don't deserve to die."

"And then she'll kill us both," Wynter told him with a sad smile. Jakob opened his mouth as though he was about to disagree, but he couldn't. They both knew what was coming for them, and it wasn't going to end up with either getting what they wanted. One would have to concede.

"I'll have to kill you, Wynter. Camilla will force me," he growled and sent a punch flying towards the nearby headboard. "You must run. Now!"

She shook her head no.

"You'd catch me. That or Marcus—"

"Then choose Marcus. At least that way you'll be alive!"

Wynter breathed a deep sigh and clutched her aching belly. Yes, that was a viable alternative, but she wasn't sure she could bring herself to go to him. Not after everything she and Jakob had shared and the decisions she had made to finally start looking after herself. She had a plan now. She was going to become whole and find a way to be free. A way to live her life for her a no one else.

And especially after how amazing things had been between them. Against all odds and them both having told each other it meant nothing, their liaison had indeed ended up meaning everything to her. She had felt free with Jakob and finally knew what it felt like to care again. To see the world without the cloud of hate and iciness looming over her. Wynter cared about so much again. She cared for herself, just like he had told her to, and didn't want Marcus to touch her ever again.

"His eyes glow when we're together," she told Jakob dejectedly, "his soul wants mine and if I go back to him now, we'll merge and then he'll turn me. The Priestess showed me my future before and I wanted to believe I could change it, but now I know for sure that if I go to him, what I saw will come true."

Wynter took a step towards Jakob and climbed to her knees before him. She then turned her gaze up to meet his and let her tears fall. "I don't want that because I want you, Jak. I think... I love you. And I choose you," she then told him, "only you. Let's run away together."

"He'll never let us go," the shocked vampire answered her, "he'll kill us for trying, but I'm willing to do it if it means we can be together."

"Me too..."

But then Jakob let out a garbled cry, and he shook his head furiously. He began scratching at the back of his neck with rough, deep gouges while muttering words in Russian she couldn't understand. Wynter wondered if he was trying to cause himself pain and reached up to stop him. She wrenched his hands away and held them to her cheeks instead.

"She won't let us go, either. I will have to kill you," he ground, "I'll have no other choice!"

And there, like a jolt to her chest, was the realisation that she had seen this before. Like sudden déjà vu, Wynter remembered the vision the Priestess had given her. Of her and the man she wanted instead of Marcus. The life she would try and choose for herself, even if it meant running from the vampire, who was clearly not even remotely ready to let her go.

And yet, there was no chance for them. She knew it now and was sure Jak had known all along.

Wynter decided enough was enough.

"Okay, but I want you to do it. Because who better to take me away from this world full of monsters than you, Jak? When the time comes, I need for it to be you. Promise me..."

As expected, Camilla arrived a few hours later and Wynter watched as Jakob walked to the edge of the property and invited her inside the magical perimeter. She could see the vampire do a double take, as if she'd seen nothing more than coastline before being given the power to enter the house through the magical warding and was relieved to see that the spell cloaking them was indeed working.

The pair of them then stopped just inside the boundary, and Wynter saw them talking in hushed voices. She wanted to shout and tell them they needn't bother on her account but bit her tongue. She wasn't after a fight and just hoped Jak could talk some sense into his sire. Plus, Camilla looked in a pretty sorry state. Someone had taken chunks out of her, and she was far from the delicate and dainty woman Wynter had spied on just a couple of nights before. She looked a wreck, and as if it'd not been easy getting herself away from whatever had gone down at the mansion.

She continued to watch them from the doorway and bristled when Camilla then suddenly approached her at relative speed. She stormed towards Wynter with a face like thunder and swiftly backhanded her, knocking her flying to the ground.

She screamed in pain with the sting of it, but still turned her face up to glower at Camilla.

"Let me guess, I somehow did something wrong, even though I was miles away?" she seethed, clutching her stinging cheek. "You brought this on yourself by messing with him. Don't try and blame me."

"You do not speak to me, you insolent little bitch," Camilla roared, raising her hand as if to strike her again, but Jakob got between them.

"No," he told her, making Camilla do a double take.

"No?" she demanded. "Where do you get off telling me no? Marcus has ruined me, Jakob. My entire life was in that house and now he's taken it from me, along with the hordes. He... he," she started to cry, "he killed Lola and then sent them after me. After everyone at the house. He won't stop until he gets his little whore back, so I'm going to personally see to it that he never does."

They all fell silent at her vicious words, each of them waiting to see what the other did like some kind of standoff.

"I take it you want me to kill her?" Jakob eventually asked her coldly, and while she'd told him previously how she wanted it, Wynter hoped it was a front. That he was just figuring out Camilla's game first.

"No, worse," the vampire answered with a sneer, "I want her to suffer like I have suffered. I want her to be broken and abused, violated and so far from the woman he knew he won't be able to stand the sight of her."

It was Wynter's turn to cry now. This was indeed a fate worse than death. She was starting to wish she'd run when Jakob had given her the chance.

"Then you don't need my services," he told his sire, shocking them both.

He said nothing else on the subject and simply walked into the house as if nothing were awry, leaving the two of them out on the front step, glaring back at him in disbelief.

***

Marcus grew closer. He could smell Camilla in the air and, as he tracked her, another scent began to invade his senses.

Wynter.

Her arousal had increased, and her scent was tangy with the fervour of it. She had been having her share of excitement without him, and jealousy flared within him. Was it due to a bite from her captor? For their sakes, he hoped not. But knew he'd find out soon.

They were close. His personal soldiers were hot on Camilla's scent too and together they ran beneath the full moon like proper creatures of the night, covering vast amounts of space with barely an ounce of effort. Just like the stories said, they were predators and would not stop until they caught their prey.

They had each fed well back at the mansion too, even Marcus, and had energy aplenty for the run. And more than enough for the fight that then would lie before them.

The suburban world their group was immersed in was chaotic, with many scents and sounds to sort from, but soon opened up to reveal the ocean ahead of them. They had reached the edge of the country and were now running along the coast and, for a moment, Marcus wondered if their prey had boarded a vessel and sailed away in a bid to evade him, but no. The scent of the wounded vampire stopped abruptly before a cliff edge. Not a harbour or a dock of some kind.

He moved closer to the edge and tried to pick out the smell of either female he was tracking. Camilla's scent had indeed come to an abrupt stop and then linger on the breeze, whereas Wynter's scent seemed to surround him, but from nowhere distinguishable at all. She was close by, but he couldn't pinpoint her location, like she was there but had somehow been hidden.

He edged closer still and felt that there was more than he could see and feel. Something beyond their reach.

A safe house cloaked in magic. That had to be it. Jakob had enlisted the help of friends in both the human and supernatural worlds to help him hide Wynter, but he hadn't counted on the foolishness of his sire. She hadn't covered her tracks at all and had led them straight to their hideout. It was the only reason he'd let her escape the mansion in one piece after all, but she'd still not seen it. Marcus shook his head. He'd given Camilla far too much credit over the years. It was a wonder they hadn't come to an end sooner.

He then sent a silent order for his soldiers to stand in a semi-circle around the source of Wynter's scent, and then lie in wait. To watch and not take their eyes away. To not leave for even a second. Not until he found a way inside, which was when they were to come in with him and take Camilla down. The others, he told them, were for their master.

He would rip Jakob to pieces and then take his prized possession back to where she belonged, and he would merge with her. And when she had turned, they would return to his newly acquired property and rebuild the house and business that Camilla had once owned.

He would make it in his image, though, and command the hordes forevermore, but this time, it would be with Wynter by his side.

It was going to be perfect. All he had to do now was to ensure the plan worked in his favour.

NINETEEN

Camilla was pacing.

Jakob was brooding.

Wynter was wringing her hands and trying desperately not to stare out the window at the veritable gang of scary as hell vampires standing vigil outside the property. Who were those other five? She'd never seen them before and couldn't bear to keep looking either. They were like vampire zombies or something. Each of them had pale, greying skin and red eyes. They were each bald and had been dressed in a simple shirt and jeans, but none of them had any shoes on.

They had to be the soldiers Jak had told her about. And if they were standing guard at Marcus's command, then that meant their allegiance had changed. Camilla was no help to her now, especially not after having lost everything to Marcus, whose power was undoubtedly growing.

"What's the point of us staying here if we have no means of escape?" Camilla eventually shrieked and Jakob jumped to his feet and glowered at her.

"Maybe if you'd thought twice about covering your tracks, they wouldn't have come within an hour of your arrival!" he spat, and then, in a surprise move, came and sat beside Wynter on the sofa. He put his arm around her shoulders and held her close, shushing her sobs and the pair of them tried to relax, but it was no use. Camilla was right. They needed a plan, and fast.

"Just let me go to him. I'll lie and pretend I was here alone," she tried, but Jakob wouldn't hear of it.

"Marcus knows Camilla is here, and he knew we were together. He won't believe you're the innocent captive," he reminded her, and Wynter nodded. She then looked over her shoulder out to where the six vampires still stood, patiently waiting for their prey to come to them.

"Give me your phone," she told him, and Jakob did as she asked, but it was evident by the sour look on his face that he wasn't keen on whatever idea she had in mind.

She dialled Marcus's number, thinking it was a long shot, but that it just might work.

Wynter then climbed up onto the sofa on her knees and faced the window, watching as Marcus reacted to the phone vibrating in his pocket and then plucked it out. He grinned down at it smugly and then answered the call before lifting it to his ear.

"You've given up quicker than I would've expected, Jakob. I'm surprised," his voice echoed down the line and Wynter let out a small cry at how deadly his tone was. How feral. Marcus had come to claim what was his, and she knew he'd kill anyone who got in his way. There was no way out of this for Camilla, but she knew she might be able to at least negotiate a deal for Jakob. After all, he had kept Wynter safe like he'd promised. "My sweet…" Marcus sighed, having heard her, and realised it wasn't the phone's owner on the other end. "I've missed you."

"And I you, Marcus," she lied, "have you come to take me home?"

"Indeed, I have," he replied, and Wynter watched as his smile began to widen at hearing her compliance. "Why don't you invite me in and we can be done with this farce?"

"I would, but I have made promises to Camilla and Jakob to secure their safety. She came here to ensure you no longer wanted me, Marcus. To ruin my body and mind as she saw fit, but I have struck a deal. My life for hers. Jakob's too."

"I will not honour any such deal," he ground, and she stared out the window at him, and his face was like thunder.

"Then I cannot leave," she told him, and then peered down at Jakob, who urged her to deepen the threat. He mouthed to her to go on. To make Marcus believe it and act on her warnings. "Jakob has me at his mercy, Marcus. He will kill me and has told me so on more than one occasion. The only way to spare my life is to meet his demands."

"Then it appears we are at an impasse," he replied before abruptly ending the call.

Apparently, he wasn't in the mood to negotiate.

Wynter then watched in horror as he walked over to a nearby parked car, lifted it up off the ground with ease, and then sent it hurtling towards the window she herself was watching from. Wynter shrieked and clambered away, but luckily the exterior of the house took the force of his attack, and the three captive housemates were kept safe, for now.

He was testing the forces holding them safely inside. Seeing what could cross over and what couldn't. This clearly was not a hostage negotiation, but a mission for vengeance, casualties be damned.

Wynter turned to Jakob with wide eyes and she climbed into his open arms, finding shelter there, and solace. He held her like he just might love her back. As if he feared losing her. Or at least she hoped so.

It would be nice to die thinking someone did love her.

"I can't let him hurt you," she whispered.

"And I cannot let him take you away. Not now," Jakob answered, and Wynter turned her head so she could peer up into his face. She was about to ask what he'd meant by that when she saw his eyes begin to change their hue. The incredible blues were resonating with waves of light and dark from deep within.

The sight was mesmerising, and she knew exactly what it meant. Jakob's soul was screaming to hers, and he wasn't even trying to hide it.

"So, you did lie to me after all," she whispered, stroking his cheek tenderly as she watched his eyes glow brighter still. "You do have a soul."

"Apparently so," he replied with a soft smile, his gaze still boring into hers. And she didn't look away, not even for a second.

"What now?" Wynter asked, thinking they were quickly running out of time and options.

"Come here," he said, holding her closer, and she couldn't deny that she wanted it. Wanted him. Unlike all the times when Marcus's eyes had shone like this, she craved the soul on offer behind the eyes currently staring into her own.

There was no denying that she loved him. No refusing his call, or that pull he had.

"No," Camilla shouted, and she tried to grab them and yank the pair apart, but it was no use. They both ignored her.

Wynter continued to peer back into Jakob's eyes and realised that what she felt wasn't about sex or the intimacy, but the comfort and the adoration she felt for him. And the love resonating between the two of them. It was real and unbreakable, and as she continued to stare into his impossibly bright eyes, Wynter accepted the vampire before her.

His soul reached for hers and she let it. The good and the bad, none of it mattered. All that existed was them, and Wynter realised then how she was already free. That she loved Jakob and was ready to accept whatever lay ahead, just as long as they were together.

Her soul merged with his in that moment of clarity and acceptance. It felt like an explosion in her chest, and was terrifying, but even when each of them realised what was happening, neither tried to stop it.

Jakob then kissed her fervently and smiled, watching her bask in his affection as they both ignored the world around them for a few seconds and performed the strange and unbreakable rite.

They were one now. Two halves of a whole and, against all odds, they truly loved one another.

She'd never been happier and felt her entire body ache for him.

Wynter had to admit, she didn't feel much different in herself afterwards, but she could see a difference in Jakob. The way he touched her and was aware of her every movement told her he had some instinctual need to keep watch over her. To have her close and safe, and even when Camilla approached them, he bristled and put himself between his sire and his soul mate.

"You don't speak to her, Camilla. Don't look at her. Don't try and hurt her. Not anymore," he demanded. "She's mine."

"I can see that," Camilla retorted with a sour look on her face, "but have you stopped to think what Marcus is going to make of this happy little union? I doubt he'll accept it, even if he has no hope of coming between the two of you."

"We will fight," Wynter answered resolutely.

"Then you will die, and so will Jakob," she countered, but then her features softened. Camilla took a proper look at the vampire she herself had sired and sighed. She touched Jakob's face with her hand and shook her head, marvelling at the change in him. "Or I can help you."

"How?" both she and him answered at the same time, and Camilla smiled to herself.

"I shall require Wynter's blood. And then, you two must jump," she told them, pointing to the back door that led directly out onto the cliff edge. Wynter couldn't fathom what she was getting at, but Jakob seemed to understand and he nodded.

"Thank you," he told her, before rushing to the kitchen.

He then returned with a knife and an empty mug. "Let me take some, just a little..." he asked Wynter, and took her hand in his. She nodded, watching as he ever so delicately cut her wrist and let the blood flow into the cup he'd held at the ready.

She felt like asking him why, but instead just accepted that what he was doing was for the best. Something deep within told her not to question Jakob's actions, and for once, she went along with what was happening and had no argument at all.

After wrapping the wound to close it, Jakob then gave the cup to Camilla with a nod. She drank it down and, without a backwards glance, walked directly out into the front garden towards her awaiting foes.

"She's sacrificing herself for you," Wynter realised, "but why me?"

"Because we are one, Wynter," Jakob replied with a frown, "and now, we must run. There isn't much time."

Wynter nodded and, without daring to look back in Marcus's direction, she followed Jakob towards the cliff edge and let him lift her onto his back. Once secured, she held tight and closed her eyes.

"Do it," she whimpered, and then felt the rush of air whizz past as Jakob stepped off and the pair of them went plummeting towards the rocky ground.

TWENTY

Marcus sensed so very many changes happening around him, and could smell Wynter on the air even still, but her scent had altered. Her lingering presence was gone, and only a part of her remained. He wasn't sure what it meant, but something suddenly felt wrong.

And then, suddenly, a figure stepped out of the nothingness and appeared like an apparition in the morning sunlight. It was Camilla, and she reeked of Wynter's scent. So, that answered at least one of his questions, but as Marcus approached her, he realised just why she smelled so strongly of his beloved girl. She had tasted her. Drank from her.

"You dare drink from my slave?" he roared as he advanced, pinning Camilla by her throat and taking her down onto the ground. "I thought you'd agreed not to hurt her?"

"I lied," Camilla replied, mocking him with a deep belly laugh that made his blood boil. "I drank her dry and then left her to rot. Jakob too. He was weak and refused to kill her for me, so I took care of them both."

"I don't believe it," Marcus roared, but then he searched for any other sign of her, and realised Camilla was right. He couldn't smell her or sense Wynter like before. The only lingering presence was the scent of her blood on the vampire in his grasp's lips, and for that, he ripped her head clean from her shoulders.

She was dead in an instant, and yet Marcus was still left unsatisfied. He needed to see the body. To know for sure that Wynter was gone. He turned to his horde and issued another of his silent commands.

Find a way in.

Failing that, you find whoever is responsible for this cloaking spell and break it.

He had to know the truth and see it with his own eyes. Marcus couldn't rest until he knew that she was dead. That he would never see her alive again. If it were true, he wouldn't rest easy, but at least he'd be able to move forward. Move on.

His Priestess was going to tell him more about what she'd divined. And maybe tell him off. Had she seen this coming? Was all this part and parcel of the prophecy she had delivered? The full moon has risen after all, and it was possible Wynter had done as Marcella had foreseen and gone into the arms of another. But who?

Warren was miles away, and Jakob wasn't capable of love. Camilla herself had told him how her progeny was soulless, so it couldn't be him.

Either way, he had to know the truth, and quickly.

He'd had enough of the guessing games.

***

Wynter and Jakob hit the rocky ground with a hard thud and she almost lost her grip on him it was so thundering. The shock of it was still reverberating around in her bones as she righted herself, but he didn't seem fazed in the slightest by the fall. She peered up at where they'd dropped from and couldn't quite believe they'd fallen so far without injury, and held Jakob tighter as it dawned on her just how much trouble they were in.

Marcus was going to find them. And when he did, Jakob was all but dead. Wynter wanted to weep. What had they done? Such fools, the pair of them. There was no doubt about it. They'd have to be clever and cunning if they had any hope of evading her oppressive boss, and she didn't even know where to begin.

"Jak, where can we go? What can we do?" she whispered in his ear, but rather than answer her, he put her down and turned to her with a frown.

"It's already too late," he told her, stroking her cheek with his hand. And then he placed a soft kiss against her lips. "They've found us."

"Who?" Wynter asked, but she got her answer before her soul mate could utter another sound.

Everything suddenly went still and eerily silent.

The wind came to a strange stop.

Even the waves seemed to take a step back, and that was when Wynter saw two unnervingly pale figures approaching from the corner of each eye. They were men, if she could call them that, and were advancing at breakneck speed, running directly towards them. "No. No. No," she muttered over and over, her head darting left and right as the vampire soldiers approached them. "What do we do, Jak?"

"Run!" Jakob screamed at her, shoving Wynter away, and she fell back on the sand just as the two soldiers collided with her beloved. The three of them began to fight, but then one of the soldiers stopped and turned to her, seemingly fixated on her scent as Wynter clambered back in fear. His deep red eyes burned into her soul, and then the vampire approached, his hands reaching out.

Wynter screamed and cried out as his icy hand touched her, assuming she would be dead a second later, but instead the vampire pulled her to him, his mouth open as if he were about to take a bite.

She pushed her hands against his huge shoulders and punched at him in vain, which was when she noticed how the beaded bracelet on her wrist was now somehow fully white. The black bead was gone, but the bracelet hadn't been broken. It was somehow still fully intact.

And that was when she felt the presence of another being beside them. The vampire holding her was then suddenly wrenched back by hands that were as black as the bead had once been. As he was thrown, Wynter caught proper sight of her strange saviour. It was clearly a man, but he wasn't like anyone she'd seen before. His body was wispy, like it might not really be there, and yet he was fighting the vampire soldier with ease as if he were whole. He was laying punches against his pale skin that caused blows as real as Jakob's were against the other soldier.

She could do nothing more than watch in shock as they continued to fight around her. Was this the protection the Priestess had told her about? No, surely it couldn't be? Wynter was sure she had to be overthinking things. Perhaps even seeing things in her shock. The bracelet was nothing more than a trinket. The man was just dark skinned and moving so fast she couldn't see him properly.

Yeah, and the two zombie-like soldiers embroiled in battles before her were just men.

Not to mention her vampire soul mate.

God, she really was fucked.

She continued to watch, and it truly seemed as if the soulless vampire killer who had grabbed her was no match for his new foe, and so Wynter left them to battle it out and focussed her attention back on Jakob. He was miraculously still alive and fighting the other soldier off, but it was clear his strength was waning, and Wynter decided she had to intervene.

These soldiers were Marcus's lackeys after all, and so she had to assume they weren't there to kill her, but to take her back as a hostage. Unharmed. With Jak, on the other hand, she was willing to bet there were no such caveats.

She saw the soldier rear back and then flung herself between them, and took the punch meant for Jakob directly to her collarbone, which snapped in two like a twig. She screamed in pain, but didn't regret it. The vampire stopped for the merest second to assess the situation, and Wynter used it as her chance to save Jakob's life.

There was no end of pain radiating from her broken bone, but Wynter's body also flooded with much needed adrenaline, and she used every ounce of strength she had left to climb back on her feet and face the vampire soldier nose-to-nose.

"You have one real objective, am I right? To take me to your master," she demanded of him and was answered with a sneer. "Then do it," Wynter added, before taking off in the direction of the dunes ahead.

She didn't get far before the soldier was on her, of course, but she managed to look back and saw Jakob had been left behind, just like she'd planned. He was still kneeling in the sand, watching her in shock. "Run you idiot!" she then bellowed and was pleased to see him follow her order.

Jak stood and charged directly into the ocean in a bid to escape before either soldier noticed her ruse, taking the one and only chance she was able to offer him.

He turned back for a second to shout to her before he let the waves carry him away, and as the soldier finally took her down, Wynter held onto Jakob's words like gospel.

I'll save you…

The end of book two in the Blood Slave series…

BLOOD SLAVE

The Complete series

#3 Made of Scars

By

Eden Wildblood

ONE

Wynter hit the sand hard, and she got a mouthful of the stuff as the vampire soldier tailing her took her down from behind. He might have been told to deliver her to Marcus in one piece, but he certainly wasn't being gentle about it, and the soulless creature seemed to think nothing of them tossing her over his shoulder roughly and carrying her back up towards the cliff above. And, of course, she was powerless to stop him. Her previous spike of adrenaline was already on the downward slope, and she cried out as the pain from her broken collarbone struck now that she was upside down and the blood was rushing to her chest and head.

She turned her head to look at the other soldier that had attacked them and found him still fighting with the strange black creature who had seemingly come from nowhere to save her from being the vampire's next victim. As she continued to hang there limply, Wynter wondered again who the black figure even was and why he'd intervened. She wanted to ask him. To ascertain why he'd stepped in, but of course she could do nothing of the sort. She could barely even move, and so she simply watched him from her upside-down position.

He was an odd protector of sorts, still made up of nothing more than black wisps. She could see them swirling around him, giving him the shape and form of a man, but evidently, he was nothing more.

Or maybe she was just imagining it. Maybe he was simply a man like any other? The bodyguard she'd been promised.

Wynter wasn't sure she could tell what was real at all anymore. The pain was really starting to set in now, plus there was this terrible ache in her chest. Like her heart was breaking. She wanted to scream and cry out Jakob's name. To holler for him to come back to her but knew there was no point. She'd done what she'd needed to do and helped him escape, so had to pretend as if she didn't feel like she might die now that he'd done exactly that.

He would return for her, though, and when he did, Marcus wouldn't know what'd hit him. She could hardly wait for him to have his comeuppance, regardless of knowing she'd have to concede defeat to him in the interim. To play the game of the doting manager, but all the while Wynter would belong to another. And soon, Marcus would discover her truth, but not until she was ready for it.

There was nothing else for it. She knew she had to be strong of mind and will. To take everything her awful boss would throw at her and not let it sway her resolve. She was going to get away from him, no matter what.

The vampire holding her repositioned her across him, gripping tighter, and Wynter cried out with the pain, coming back around from her thoughtful haze with a start. She got the feeling she had been moments from passing out and wished she had. At least that way she could save herself the embarrassment of watching the world from her upside-down position over the soldier's shoulder.

She tried, but couldn't move a single muscle, and then looked down at her arms that were now dangling before her limply. She couldn't move or try and get away. All she could do was hang there, and as the tears began to flow, she noticed again how the bracelet on her wrist was still white all over. Could it really be possible the odd man had come from there—a simple piece of costume jewellery?

She turned her head to watch him in continued to wonder. As soon as her captor began to storm away from the beach, she saw the creature seem to disappear into a puff of mist that dissolved into the air, and Wynter did a double take. Part of her was sure she must've imagined that too, but then she saw something else that made her cry out in shock. There were footsteps pressing down behind them in the sand. Imprints being made by no one at all. As if a phantom was hot on their trail.

Wynter looked around for Jakob but knew it couldn't be him. She knew it with all her aching heart that he was long gone. She had sacrificed her freedom to save him and trusted that he would come for her, but found herself already wondering when? And how? There was no way of knowing. All she could do was wait for him, and to say safe in the meantime.

The huge vampire holding her somehow scaled the rocky cliff with his bare hands, and they neared the top of the impossible climb in no time at all. Wynter gulped when he scaled the ridge at the top and she saw the other four soldiers that had then regrouped and gathered at the top of the incline in wait. They were watching her with wide, red eyes and she cried out when they began to close in around her as the one carrying her reached them.

Their cold hands reached forward, and they touched her hair and back, and she heard hisses and groans as the biggest one continued to carry her forward.

The handful of soldiers Marcus had employed seemed hungry for her, and Wynter realised why when she looked down at her arms again. She was covered in scrapes that were oozing with blood. Not enough for her to be in any trouble, but certainly enough to get the immortal gang's attention.

That wasn't the worst of her problems, though. The vampire they were approaching was—Marcus. Wynter felt his presence before she saw him, and she shuddered when the icy chill he was emitting reached her.

He was furious. No doubt with her, but she hoped it was more at the situation as a whole. And he also ought to be mad with himself, or so she thought.

She intended to tell him so, but felt herself starting to lose consciousness again thanks to the pain she was in. When the soldier bent forward and threw her onto the cold and hard ground, the air rushed out of Wynter's lungs and she could do nothing but lie there gasping for breath, winded with the shock of it.

She lay strewn there, desperately trying to breathe, while the soldiers and all the other vampires closed in around her again. They were indeed hungry for her, like a pack of dogs that had been given a sent to track with the promise of a taste when they hunted down their prey, only to discover they weren't allowed it after all. One's jaw snapped open and closed, his teeth echoing with the sound, while others were licking their lips and sniffing the air around her, as if relishing in her scent.

The five soldier vampires terrified her, but there was only one she focused on. The only one with any normal colour in his venomous eyes, and the one she knew she had to try and fool into believing she was still his perfect prize. That she could remain his and not be thrown to the wolves like he'd threatened her with no end of times before.

"Gentler next time, if you please," Marcus groaned to the huge alpha vampire, who grunted and then led the others away. Her master then leaned down and gathered Wynter up into his arms, where he checked her injuries with a frown. "Broken collarbone. How did this happen?" he then asked, and she tried to answer him, but instead she heard another voice do it for her. A deep and masculine sound that, while real, didn't quite seem whole.

"Ask your soldiers…"

She turned her head in the direction of the sound and saw nothing but emptiness, but then the void was suddenly filled with the wispy black form of a man. It was as if he had appeared out of nowhere, and the abrupt arrival made her jump. It was the same man who had come to her aid on the beach. He wasn't only real, but exactly as she'd imagined.

"What are you?" she whimpered but got no answer. The conversation, it seemed, didn't include her.

"She was in the behemoth's way, so he apparently thought nothing of laying a punch meant for Jakob on her. The smaller one then tried to bite her, so I was forced to intervene. Take control, Marcus. They need to know she's not fair game," he added, and she could see his black eyes dart to her and then back to the vampire still clutching her tightly. The dark man was brave to chastise him, and Wynter smiled to herself, but was sure to hide it from Marcus.

Her strange protector then raised his hand and touched her with it, and Wynter saw a band around what would've been his wrist should he be whole. It was made up of black beads exactly like the one she had on her own bracelet, and yet one of them was white. She could just about see it in the sunshine and frowned. The beads matched the ones on hers but were the opposite way around. Was that really how he'd known to come to her aid just at the right time? Was it the simple bracelets that connected them after all? It had to be, she was sure.

"Well, your service is commendable, Brodie. Thank you," Marcus replied in what appeared to be a genuine tone, and she was surprised to find him so ready to accept his advice. "You may go home," he then added, and as quickly as he had appeared, the man was gone again.

Wynter let out a garbled cry as she saw the black bead return to her bracelet the moment he was gone. At least that meant she was right about it, somehow magically connecting her and whatever the hell this Brodie was.

In fact, what was he? She tried to ask again, but knew she was fading fast.

Marcus shushed her and held her tighter to him, and Wynter was sure she heard him thank whatever God he might believe in for bringing her back to him.

She wanted to pull away. To fight him off her, but everything hurt too damn much. Every part of her body was weary. There was no strength in any muscle left. No fight left in her at all.

Her eyes rolled into the back of her head and the darkness began pulling her under. And this time, Wynter gladly let it take her.

When she awoke, it was with a pounding head and a great deal of heaviness behind her eyes. She tried to move and started to panic when she couldn't so much as sit up, thinking she'd been tied down. But then Wynter realised she was immobile only thanks to having been strapped up on her right side. Her arm was bent and then pulled up towards her neck, protecting the broken collarbone there and ensuring no further harm could be done while it healed.

Someone had worked on her while she was out cold, and they had secured her arm so that the damage could be rectified. Whoever it was had taken a great deal of care to make her comfortable, and she could tell they'd even bathed and dressed her in the process. Perhaps Marcus, if he were feeling compassionate enough to do so? The thought sent a shiver down her spine. She didn't want him touching her, not so intimate as that, but knew she couldn't show it.

Pushing the thought away, Wynter tried to get her bearings. To listen to the sounds around her and focus on what she could hear, feel, and smell, even if she was unable to see. She was propped up against some pillows in the pitch-black room, and instinctually knew without needing the light on that she was back in the bedroom Marcus had built for her at the club. They had to have travelled a long way, and yet Wynter couldn't remember a moment of it, and neither could she tell whether it was night or day, or how many hours it'd been since they were at the beach.

And then, of course, her thoughts went to the beach and what had happened there. How long had it been since she and her darling Jakob had last seen each other? She felt bereft without him and knew it was thanks to their merged souls. But Wynter knew she couldn't show how she felt. Not to anyone. No matter what, she had to remain true to herself and the promises she'd made to stay strong. She had to hide the truth, regardless of the consequences.

There would be a way out of this mess—all she had to do was find it.

But first, she needed to figure things out.

She had no doubt the door would be locked like always and so didn't even bother to climb out of bed to try it. She did, however, scoot sideways to where she had learned a lamp ought to be.

Wynter found the switch and breathed a sigh of relief when it turned on. She thanked God for the small things. At least she wasn't going to have to stay there in the darkness like she had on that first night Marcus had forced her to stay in his private prison cell. He'd taken everything away from her again, and now she was back in his keep. That she'd have to deal with, but being stuck in there blind would've been even worse.

When the sleep had cleared from her eyes and she had gotten over the shock of the sudden invasion of light, she moved back to her spot in the centre of the bed and looked around. It seemed unchanged from when she'd left it, but at the same time there was something different she couldn't quite put her finger on. It was only when she shuffled down and turned onto her good side that she saw what it was. Marcus had built her an even bigger en-suite, complete with bath and shower in place of the tiny washroom she'd had before. He'd given her that one thing she'd been missing to create the ultimate self-contained space for him to keep her in.

Oh great, she thought. Now he really could keep her locked in there day and night.

Damn him. She truly hoped one of those curses he threw around without a care would someday come back to bite him. Perhaps one day he'd get his just desserts, but she decided not to let herself fret over what was to come. Or to obsess about where Jakob was now, and if he was okay. Her heart yearned for him, and she knew it was not only because of their bonded souls, but because she really had wanted to run away with him.

It had been a wonderful dream.

One she had been so sure could come true.

Double damn him.

If Marcus hadn't gained the upper hand yet again, she would be with Jak now, when instead here she was. Locked away and so far from her soul mate, it made her want to die. And, of course, she was still waiting to find out what her captor had in store for her. She got the feeling he wasn't going to be best pleased with how things had gone down, but she wasn't going to let him beat her.

Wynter decided she would keep fighting no matter what he said or did, and she would lie through her teeth if she had to, just as long as it made sure Marcus didn't know the truth about her and Jak. He wouldn't forgive her for merging with another, and she knew it.

She eventually dozed back off, still thinking of Jakob, and dreamed she was with him. That they'd gotten away and were on some remote sandy beach together. It felt so real, too. She could feel the warmth of the sun on her skin and smell the salty air. It was a lovely dream, and Wynter woke with a smile, which faded as soon as she saw who was standing vigil at the end of her bed.

Marcus was scowling down at her, his arms folded across his chest and his rage palpable from where Wynter still lay a few feet away. She went cold as a shudder spread down her spine, her skin puckering with goose pimples at the sight of the dastardly vampire standing over her so creepily.

He didn't say a word, as if he was waiting for her to beg him for mercy or break down in tears, but Wynter wasn't playing this game. She was looking out for number one, just like she'd promised herself she would, and so pushed herself up into a sitting position and met Marcus's icy stare.

"Thank you," she forced herself to say with a soft smile, "for saving me from Camilla."

Marcus's eyes flashed and Wynter watched him soften just a touch. So, he hadn't expected that. Good.

She'd been right to appeal to his gentler side rather than instigate an argument. And to coax it out using her compliance and timid nature as bait. She might be faking it, but that didn't mean she wanted to fight. Not quite yet. Being a good girl was far easier, so she would continue to play along. At least until Jakob came for her.

"You tried to run from me," he growled, but Wynter shook her head. She tried for the biggest doe eyes she could manage and peered up at him in surprise.

"I was kept a prisoner at that mansion for days, Marcus. When we left, it was only because Camilla had allowed it. I needed food, so we had to go, plus she wanted me as far away from you as possible," she replied, and ensured her voice had a strong pleading edge to it. As if she was worried about upsetting him.

"Did Jakob hurt you?" he asked, and she shook her head again. At least he'd moved on from the accusations.

"No, but I knew he would have if she gave the order."

"But you still fucked him," Marcus bit back, and while it was a shock to discover how he'd known they'd been together, Wynter still didn't let him rile her. She could tell him some truths, and this one was quite a juicy little titbit.

"Yes," she confirmed meekly, "but you always said I was free to be with whomever I wanted? He told me himself he's a soulless killer and so it wouldn't matter."

"Indeed," he replied with a sneer. "And I have it on good authority he's been with many women over the years. Probably thousands."

Wynter knew what he was doing. He was trying to see if she got jealous, but she knew better than that. Along with his soul, she'd accepted Jakob for everything he was and knew that whatever his past, she and he were united now and that he would never take another lover. She wouldn't either if she could help it, but knew Marcus still had her in his sights, so would undoubtedly try and touch her like he had before.

But she didn't want him to, and in fact, the idea made her feel nauseous. She just hoped she might be able to fend him off the next time his hands roved over her body, or he had her in turmoil, thanks to his bite. She would simply blame it on her injuries and hope for the best.

"And of course you had a great deal of fun with Camilla too, before things turned sour?" she countered, but Marcus didn't seem surprised at all by her comment. He must've known she was there that night, or discovered so afterwards, and he shrugged it off as though his liaison with Camilla meant nothing at all. Nope, he wasn't getting away that easily. "For a vampire who professes to sex being sacred, you certainly weren't holding back with her. While watching you, I learned how you truly felt about me. How you hadn't been lying all those times when you pushed me away. I really am nothing but a Blood Slave to you, and that's fine. Tell me when and where and I'll be at your service, Mr Cole, but please don't pretend like there's anything else going on between us, and I certainly won't either."

Damn, there went her plan to remain timid and calm. Wynter's heart was pounding, and she waited for him to return with a snide comeback or to lunge at her and threaten her, but he didn't answer. Instead, Marcus continued to scowl down at her as if she'd said nothing at all. And then he left.

Wynter dived out of bed and tried to get to the door before it closed, but she was too slow. She was alone again in a heartbeat and while she welcomed it, there was still that niggling sense of anger and fear at her having been locked away again. Why would he do it? Why bother pretending any longer? She was desperate to find out, but knew she had no chance if he kept her captive.

She needed to get out of there. To rest and heal up fast so she could be ready, and so Wynter didn't scream her head off or kick at the door. She didn't beg or plead to be released. Nope, she simply pretended to be too weak to fight back and to welcome the solace.

After relieving her bladder and just about being able to move enough to freshen up, she then went back to bed and closed her eyes.

She didn't sleep right away, but just rested and thought of Jakob. Wynter tried to envision him in her mind's eye and call out to him, but he simply wasn't there.

He was gone, but not for long.

Or so she hoped.

TWO

Marcus paced up and down outside Wynter's bedroom for a while in a bid to gather his thoughts before he was due to attend the meeting he'd called of the department heads. His return to *Slave* had been bittersweet. He'd fed from his ever-willing Joanna and regrouped but had felt Wynter's absence everywhere. The last few hours without her in attendance had been torture but having her back and oddly indifferent to him somehow felt worse.

It didn't matter that she'd been upstairs for the past day resting up. She still felt lost to him. Like a closed book, when once he had been able to read her so well. Everything had changed since his impromptu visit with Camilla and while part of him was relieved that things had cooled off between them a little, he still wanted her the same. Still craved her as much as he had before bedding Camilla one final time. And he'd only done that to keep Wynter safe. To ensure his old flame's jealous wrath was sated before he planned to take his dear girl away and merge his soul with hers. Just like the Priestess had told him to.

But instead, everything had changed between them. She had come back to him different in many ways, but still the fighter he adored. And now she was fighting hard. Refusing him even after he'd saved her from those two fiends.

This simply would not do. Wynter was going to have to learn to be grateful for all the luxuries he was affording her, and he would start by reminding her who was boss. Yes, a firm hand was what she needed right now. And a powerful, fearless leader. He could be each of those things, and smiled to himself at the thought of breaking down those walls she'd somehow built so high again.

This was right, he could feel it. She would succumb to him once again and when she did, Wynter would be his forever.

He left her to rest up for a few more days, but then found he secretly enjoyed withholding her freedom and so added a couple more. And then some more. Enough so that she knew her incarceration was about more than just his way of keeping her locked away for her rest and recuperation. She was being punished, and solitary confinement seemed the perfect way of doing it. After all, Wynter never had been one for remaining alone. She was a social creature and being stuck within the same four walls had to be hell for her.

Marcus observed Wynter via the hidden cameras dotted around her room, and he loved watching her fall apart. So much so that he watched her day and night, suddenly no longer the workaholic he once was. There was a new addiction. A hunger he couldn't ever seem to satisfy. A darkness within him he knew he couldn't fight, and so was simply learning to enjoy instead. And it was all thanks to her.

He could almost always smell the tangy scent of her despair from anywhere in the club and couldn't help but toy with her more when it came to the many times he went inside her prison to visit with her. Marcus made sure to always be the one who took Wynter her meals and meds, and he stayed just long enough to watch her eat up before he'd then leave again, and all without saying a single word.

She had now been locked away for almost a week in silence and Marcus adored how hard she tried to remain strong in his presence, while always falling apart again the moment he left. But even the strongest fighters had their weaknesses, and she was finally beginning to break.

At first, Wynter would eat quickly. It was as if she'd wanted him to leave again as soon as possible, but after his extension to her captivity, she was slower now. She ate languidly and sometimes asked questions about his day or enquired after her friends downstairs.

Marcus never answered. Not even once. Instead, he watched her and took deep breaths of her intoxicating scent. His charming prisoner truly was despondent now, and she was growing worse by the day. There was nothing better.

It was time he had her at his mercy again. Time he had his fill of her delectable blood.

Marcus delivered her some breakfast the following morning and then helped her wash. They had developed a gentle back and forth during her clean-up routine, and all her fight was gone in those moments. She was almost childlike. Sweet. Innocent. Susceptible to manipulation.

It was reminiscent of the times he'd cared for his many Priestesses over the years, but with Wynter he craved her in ways he never had those witches at his command.

It was time he tasted her again.

After finishing up and helping her dress, he climbed behind her on the bed, where he brushed her hair and smoothed the now waist length dark waves into a bun.

Wynter remained silent as he tended to her. She seemed almost comfortable, as though she'd forgotten just how dangerous her protector was, and about his needs. The needs she was there to fulfil.

His mouth was on her neck a second later, and he pressed his tongue against her skin, piercing it with ease. Delicious blood flowed into his mouth, and Marcus let out a delighted groan as she relaxed against him and let out a soft hum.

He waited for her to react in her usual way. For her hands to rove across her body or her hips to start arching off the bed, but all Wynter did was lie still. She was euphoric as always but was somehow resisting the carnal side effects of his bite.

It was the oddest thing. Had she really been turned off after her long and lonely stay? Had she forgotten what it felt like to need him in that way?

Marcus began to wonder if he had pushed her too far. If he'd left her alone for too long and now she really did hate him. But of course, she'd said all those things before and had always come back to him in the end. Always desired him despite herself.

He released her and closed the wound he'd drunk from, and then he settled her back on the pillows where he took his place beside her, watching her relax into her bliss with a smile.

God, he still wanted her. He wanted her in every way he could imagine and began to feel that roar within him again. That rush of desire and a need to claim her. To own her.

But first, he needed to feed again.

***

Wynter kept her eyes closed and focused all her strength on not letting Marcus affect her like he'd used to. She'd been so lonely the past week, it'd been awful, and while she really hadn't wanted his attention in a desirous sense, she'd still found herself craving social interaction. And so, she'd welcomed him in when he'd come with her food. She'd taken her time and tried to converse with him, but Marcus had given her nothing. Not even a teasing smile or a hint at what he had in store for her. He'd stayed well away until today.

Today, he had come to feed, and so she let him. Wynter let herself enjoy the warmth of his body against hers and the ecstasy of the bite, but nothing more. Those other parts of herself had completely closed off to him now. Her heart wasn't yearning for anything Marcus had to offer her, nor did she feel desperate and ready to beg for it. No, she belonged to Jak and so held onto her thoughts of him as closely as ever.

She knew, deep down, that Jakob was no better than Marcus. He was a killer. A sociopath. A violent monster. But with him she had smiled. She had laughed and enjoyed his company, while trusting that he would always remain honest, and he had never once fed from her. It had been refreshing, and a much needed change from the company she currently kept. Damn, it was no wonder they'd both fallen so hard.

Marcus was never once honest with her. He always played his games and kept her in turmoil, and Wynter knew she would never do anything other than loathe him.

"My sweet," he groaned, nuzzling her neck as he placed soft kisses along her jaw, "are you still in there, my little fighter?" They were his first words in over a week and instead of being nice, he just had to taunt her? To ridicule her, rather than be kind or gentle, like she knew he could be. He really was the worst.

Wynter tensed and tried to ignore him, but his soft, gruff laugh let her know he'd sensed it. She was indeed still in there, and she was fighting with every ounce of her being. Her silence was an act of defiance. Her iciness, her form of revenge.

He clearly decided to push her harder, so then ran his hand down over her chest and began unbuttoning her pyjama shirt, but Wynter reached for him, her eyes fluttering open.

"No," she tried, but it was no use. He had it open and her body was quickly exposed without a care for what she wanted. Only for satisfying his needs. She tried to turn away, but Marcus pinned her down and captured her left breast in his palm.

"No what?" he teased as he kneaded her nipple into a hard peak. "No, I can't touch you anymore? Or no, you won't feed me?"

"No, you can't touch me. I told you before," she whimpered, and hated that she even had to explain herself. Surely, he knew he shouldn't be touching her without her consent. These were the fundamental laws of her time, and he ought to be adhering to them. "We aren't doing that anymore. You can feed and then you can leave."

Marcus answered by slicing his razor-sharp tongue against her breast, instantly drawing blood, and then he lapped at it with a smile.

"Then I shall cut everywhere I want while I drink some more," he groaned against her flesh, "just a drop at a time and against all the places I wish to touch, but you've decided are now off limits. You still fail to comprehend the complexities of our relationship, don't you, my sweet? I will always win. I will have things my way. And I will take whatever I wish from you despite any and all arguments you can muster."

And he did.

Marcus kept her at his mercy all day and by the end of it, he'd sliced into her skin more than thirty times to prove his point and have his fill, whether she agreed or not.

The worst part wasn't that his mouth was all over her, but that his bite brought with it that horrible, eager need. That was the one thing that hadn't changed between them. Like before, she felt heat bloom between her thighs and tension eventually begin to build there, regardless of not having been touched or so much as writhing against herself to relieve the pressure.

Wynter closed her eyes and tilted her head back, thinking if she wasn't looking at him or focusing on what was happening, she might just be able to block it all out. But of course, she was wrong. If anything, with her eyes closed, her mind wandered to her lost love, and only spurred her closer to the inevitable release she knew was coming if Marcus didn't cease his leisurely drinking session.

She opened her eyes again and went to look back at where Marcus was feeding from the vein at her thigh. She needed to remind herself it was him there and not Jak, and let out a garbled croak when she suddenly realised they were not alone.

The Priestess was watching over the pair of them from directly above her. Like some kind of creepy visitor, the strange and, as always, fully cloaked woman was staring down at her while she was pressed up against the ceiling. Just like with David, Wynter could see she was being held there by a strange force, but unlike him, she was there by choice and seemed somehow completely comfortable. She had materialised overhead so she could watch the pair of them during Marcus's feed, but why?

She tried to call out to her and ask, but the witch pressed her covered finger to her lips. Or at least where her lips would be if the cloak shrouding her face wasn't covering them. Wynter tried to disregard her command, and yet found she couldn't utter a single word. Not a sound passed her lips, and of course Marcus was too busy still lapping at her vein to notice or care. She could do nothing but stare back as she was held captive by not one but two creatures of darkness and fell further into her despair.

She tried to block it all out. To think of Jak and neither of her captors, but it was no use.

Her head was a mess and yet still, she bounced back and forth between fighting her urge to strike out and her need to cry. Her body still screamed for Marcus to touch her and finish what he'd started, and yet her heart was stronger and denied him every time. It still won the battle against her head, and she was somehow able to hold herself back. To resist him. It wasn't even that hard. Not now that things had changed so dramatically for her.

The Priestess, on the other hand, was a whole other story. Her presence there with them was disconcerting, to say the least, especially as all she did was watch them. She was like a ghostly manifestation, and Wynter suddenly felt afraid of the unknown. Of her power and of the strange woman, especially knowing what she was capable of.

When Marcus suddenly stopped his feeding and climbed up off the bed later that day, she breathed a sigh of relief and sat up with a wince at the pain radiating from her shoulder. The blood loss from her day spent as his personal buffet had taken a lot out of her, and the pain was back with a vengeance, too.

The Priestess disappeared in the blink of an eye then, evidently not having wanted their master to know she'd even been there, but Wynter was glad she'd gone. In fact, there was a huge part of her that hoped the odd witch might never come back.

She watched Marcus as he moved, her face a carefully crafted guise she hoped was hiding her disinterest in what the vampire was going to do next or what he had to say for himself. She just wanted him to leave. As much as she had craved some company these past few days, this hadn't been what she'd had in mind. Not in the slightest, and so she was ready to be left alone again.

Wynter had lost count of how many more bites he had given her over the last few hours. All she knew was that her skin was tender over every main artery her body had to offer, and then some. He'd kissed and lapped at her flesh in a bid to get a rise out of her, and while it was only a small victory for her not to have succumbed to the spell his bite always seemed to put her under, Wynter was glad she had at least managed that one thing.

One day at a time, she told herself, *let him feed, like you promised, but nothing else. He can have your blood, but he cannot have your heart or your soul. They belong to Jak.* A smile twitched at her mouth just thinking of her lost love, and Wynter could've kicked herself for being so careless.

Of course, Marcus had noticed. He had spotted the change right away, as if he had been studying her, and as he then approached, he put out his hand for her to take.

"Time for work," he told her, and Wynter frowned. She'd expected a challenge from him, and yet instead he was finally letting her out? Letting her go and do her fucking job at long last rather than keeping her locked away? There had to be a catch.

Wynter lifted her only free hand and let Marcus pull her to her feet without a word in argument. She wanted nothing more than to leave and so shuffled along close behind him and couldn't fight her elated smile when he opened the door and let her go free.

The homely area beyond was a damn sight for sore eyes, and she welcomed the chance to look out the windows at the city beyond the club. It had been too damn long since she'd seen the sky or breathed fresh air.

"What day is it?" she asked him, her voice barely more than a whisper. She truly had no idea, and it made her heart ache even more.

"Saturday," he answered, making her cringe.

"You've kept me locked in this room for an entire week?" she bellowed, her rage getting the better of her. "I fucking hate you."

Wynter moved away from Marcus and made straight for the main bathroom. She wanted a proper shower, not just the strip washes he had been giving her all week, and headed right for the glass cubicle where she'd taken many a long, hot shower since the start of her strange employment. Inside, she ran the hot water and managed to shimmy out of her underwear, but tried in vain to get out of her still open nightshirt. Of course, it was thanks to her broken clavicle that was still healing. These things took time, but she still cursed her weak body for not having done it already.

After a few seconds of huffing and puffing, Wynter just went under the cascading water, half dressed. She stood under it for a while, pondering how best to try and wash her hair and body, and realised just how little she could do given the sorry state that vampire soldier's punch had left her in. Her entire upper right side was still immobile, making every task a chore, and Wynter slapped her left hand against the wet tile with a roar. It was so damn unfair. All of it!

She cried out in shock and froze when she felt hands on her, but could tell it was her tormentor before she saw him or he said a single word.

This was Marcus all over, and it was then she realised how he was always close by these days. Always there to clean and bathe her. To bring her food and the medicine that took away her aches and pains for a blissful few hours. And because of all of that, she had come to depend on him. His touch didn't make her flinch or shy away like before. Had she gotten so used to his hands on her body that she was becoming desensitised to him? That, or he was breaking her down. Breaking through her guarded walls. She wanted to scream and cry at the sheer thought.

"Let me help you," Marcus whispered, "I'll be careful."

Wynter wanted to refuse, but instead she nodded. There was no use in fighting it. She needed him, whether she liked it or not.

He then removed her sling and shirt, and all while being surprisingly gentle, just like he'd promised. Her vampire master then lathered up her hair with shampoo and gave it the scrub Wynter had been desperate for, and she groaned appreciatively.

Marcus went through the rest of her wash in much the same way. He seemed to know how much pressure to use and what her body needed without her having to ask, and before long, she wasn't just clean and fresh again, but also relaxed once more.

She was quickly put back in a fresh sling and he helped her into some work clothes. She almost felt like her old self again, and by the time she was ready to head down to work, had an entirely new outlook on the way her awful life had gone since returning to *Slave*.

Wynter knew she was just getting through each day in the hope that Jak would come and take her away again, but that didn't mean she had to mope around in the meantime. She had rested up and now Marcus had deemed her well enough for him to feed from, so that meant she was strong enough to get back to work. And back to her old life.

She was getting stronger by the day and would find a way to escape him. With or without her noble Russian vampire coming to her aid. She didn't need saving, or so she tried telling herself repeatedly. Looking after number-one was the goal—everyone else be damned.

THREE

Wynter went down to her office and ploughed through her mountain of emails before doing her usual bit with the private online message boards and web pages she was tasked with moderating but had come to realise they basically took care of themselves. Like all the other lies Marcus had woven, her job was just another façade. No one had missed her this past couple of weeks, and she had to wonder if anyone had even noticed she was gone.

She decided to go see and headed for the basement the moment she had cleared her inbox and locked up her office behind her.

She got to the IT department a few minutes later and was buzzed inside, where she found it quiet and half-empty. She scanned around, looking for a friendly face, and then remembered that half of the team were now working from the new club. How her friend Phoebe had gone to head up the IT department there and taken a load of them with her.

It seemed odd down there without the bickering and the noise. Without the frenzy and chaos. Wynter didn't like it. She wanted the din and the bustle and the company she had been craving during her confinement.

"Hey stranger," she heard a gruff voice call, and turned to smile at the man she was glad to discover was still firmly in place in the bowels of the nightclub. Warren was his usual self. He was wearing a suit and tie and looked uncomfortable as hell in the thing. Like he would be more at home in trackies and a hoodie. Wynter noticed his beard was neater, though, as though he'd had a trim, and he'd cut his hair back too. She could see his eyes rather than just behind his usually unruly hair.

Wynter wanted to flush with heat at seeing him. She wanted to go all giddy and flirt with him like she had before. Wanted to feel something other than just the fondness she'd undoubtedly feel towards any friendly face right now. But she didn't. She was looking at Warren without her rose-tinted glasses and saw nothing but a man. Someone she had put her trust in, and yet he hadn't delivered on any of his promises to take care of her in return. He hadn't loved her when she'd needed him to and hadn't cared enough to put himself out in the slightest.

It had all been nothing more than a kindness. A caring gesture from a nice man, but nothing more. Warren wasn't the person she was destined to be with, no matter the promises they had made while holding each other close in that tiny room out the back two weeks previously.

Damn, had it really only been a couple of weeks? It felt like a lifetime.

Marcus had been right before. Warren was under his spell and wouldn't ever stand up to him on her behalf. In this place and amongst everyone who was beholden to that vampire's spell, she was truly alone.

Wow, as if she hadn't felt bad enough already, that realisation hit her like a blow to the gut.

Wynter swallowed the lump in her throat, shook it off, and took a seat opposite Warren at his desk, where she watched as he fixed them both some coffee and then joined her. He seemed relaxed, considering today had been his overtime day too, and Wynter watched him with a frown.

"How did your fights go?" she asked, before taking a sip.

"Oh, it was okay. Women don't punch as hard as the guys do, so it wasn't all that bad," he answered, but Wynter knew his defeat would've meant a bite or two and how he would've hated that part. However, Warren seemed totally at ease with himself, contrary to his usual gruff demeanour. He then started harking on about how quiet it had been with everyone across town setting up the new club and that he had been cracking on with all sorts of shit from his to-do lists.

Wynter tried not to get angry as she watched him going on and on, but it was hard. A hundred thoughts were going through her head and she was getting more and more riled up. What Jak had said about her being unlovable before was forcing aside her coldness and sadness that was at the forefront of her mind. And he had been right. Warren had liked her. He might have even fancied her, but that was all. There was nothing more between them, and never had been.

He hadn't asked after her or checked that she was okay. Warren hadn't so much as asked where she'd been the past week and a half, and Wynter wondered if he'd even noticed that she was in a sling. As Warren fell silent at last, presumably out of steam, she felt her blood boil and finished her coffee before slamming her mug down.

"Did you even realise I was gone?" she then asked her wide-eyed and so-called friend. "Did you notice? Or were you too wrapped up in your own shit to care?"

"What?" he replied and then scratched at his beard awkwardly. "You were at the new club with the others. Mr Cole told me."

"And so, you just left me to it? No quick email to let me know you were here thinking of me? No secret coded message for the woman you said you wanted to be with?" she demanded.

Warren looked dumfounded.

Wynter got the feeling he wasn't as used to dealing with women as she'd once thought, and she found herself scowling at him in much the same way as she often did with Marcus. He was infuriatingly pathetic, and she climbed to her feet, ready to leave.

"I just figured you were busy sorting out the marketing campaigns for the new club or something. Or whatever the hell it is you actually do," he snapped, only angering Wynter more. She wanted to bite his head off, but instead she just stared at him like he was the most stupid man alive.

"If I was working, surely I would've answered your emails? I would've called to ask for your advice or just to talk to my friend. But no. I was off having so much fun, I didn't have time to stop and get in touch. That'll be it," she groaned before walking away without another word or a backwards glance at him.

"Wynter!" Warren tried, but she just kept on going.

She needed to get away from him, or else she knew she'd end up saying something she might regret. It was awful to realise just how wrong she'd been about him and she felt like a fool for having given up her freedom to save him. For a future that would never come true.

All of this had been for nothing more than a hopeless infatuation with a man who didn't care. What an idiot she had been.

Wynter realised she'd been wrong about so many things and had made so many mistakes. All hope was lost, or so she felt, and so stalked out of the IT office and up the stairs in a daze, rather than take the lift. The world was heavy on her shoulders as she forced herself to carry on.

She wanted to hide, but then reached the ground floor and was about to carry on up to her office when the din of the music stopped her.

Wynter turned and watched as the night's guests were ambling inside, and she felt a wave of nostalgia hit her. It felt like such a long time ago that she had been one of them. That she would spend her Saturday night drunk and on the lookout for someone to scratch whatever sexual itch she currently had.

So much had changed in such a short amount of time. She was an entirely different person now to that girl from before and was saddened by the realisation that those changes weren't necessarily for the better.

She needed some air. After days and days of being cooped up, Wynter craved the cold night air in her lungs and she headed for the doorway, where she scooted through a gap in the crowd before anyone could stop her.

Once she was out in the street, she turned left to bypass the queue of punters waiting to get inside the club and walked as far as the street corner before losing her nerve.

There would be no going further. No running away. It didn't matter how much she still wanted to be free, Marcus would never let her go. If she tried, he'd do more than just lock her upstairs for a few days. He would make her pay for defying him, and Wynter knew she still didn't have the strength to handle that.

So instead, she just listened to the sounds of the city all around her and sucked deep breaths of crisp night air into her lungs. She could hear the trains whizzing down the tracks in the distance and some running water in the river close by. Hear the cars whizzing across the motorway a few miles away and the still awaiting socialites hollering and partying from the queue behind.

Life was moving on all around her. And without her. Wynter wanted to run, even still, but was as far as she could risk going, and yet she felt calmer already. It was just so good to have a few minutes of peace. It was nice to be out in the real world for a little while. To be in her city. Her home.

After a few minutes, she knew it was time she went back inside before she caught a chill, so she turned around, only to discover that a silent group of guardsmen had encircled her while she'd been quietly contemplating her fate.

It was Marcus's small pack of vampire soldiers. Each one had been dressed in a black suit just like the bouncers, and yet they didn't fit in at all. Not in the slightest. Their soulless red eyes stood out a mile away, even from behind their ridiculous sunglasses, and Wynter shuddered when she saw how they were each eyeing her like a prize they couldn't wait to claim. As if they'd been willing her to run just so they might be given the chance to hunt her down again.

She'd been right, at least. Well, she wasn't going to give them, or their leader, the satisfaction of hunting her. Not tonight.

"Calm down, fellas," she told them with a forced smile, "just getting some air."

Wynter then crept forward and had hoped they might part to let her pass, but they didn't. The biggest one simply closed in and glared down at her like he was about to strike, and she had to force herself not to freak the hell out. It was that, run, cry, or retreat, and Wynter forced herself to choose the latter. She sidestepped the huge vampire that'd already broken her bones once and made for the club's entrance as fast as her feet could carry her. She was almost inside when someone grabbed her wrist and spun her to face them.

"Wynter?" the culprit cried, and it took her a second to realise it hadn't been one of the vampires, but a human. One of her friends. In fact, her best friend.

"Cossette?" she replied before hugging her as hard as she could with her out of action right side. "What are you doing here?"

"Coming for a dance, of course! I was hoping I might see you, Wyn. Your phone has been going straight to voicemail for weeks. Where have you been? Someone else is living in your house too," she reeled off, going straight for the interrogation.

There was no way of answering her honestly, so Wynter just shrugged and tried as best she could to appease her.

"Yeah, I moved in with some of the guys here," she lied, "oh, and my phone broke, and I just haven't had the time to get a new one," she explained, skirting around the truth about how her vampire boss had trashed his office in a fit of rage, her handbag and its contents included, and yet he'd not replaced anything. Oh, and of course how he'd kept her prisoner and sold her house without her say-so. "I'm really sorry," Wynter added, and she felt tears prick at her eyes. It was the truth. She might not be able to tell her everything, but she could give her a little.

Cossette could tell something was wrong. Wynter saw her eyes dart to the entourage behind her and her face dropped.

"What's with the creepy hired goons? Wyn, is everything all right?" she whispered, but wasn't convinced when Wynter simply nodded her head yes. "You call me, okay? Any time, day or night. You speak to me. You can tell me anything."

"I know," Wynter replied, fighting back her tears. "Thank you."

She then went to walk away, but changed her mind and turned back to Cossette, gathering her up in another tight hug. She then whispered in her ear as quietly as possible but made sure she spoke clearly and sternly. "Don't come back here again, Coss. Stay away from *Slave* and the new club. Promise me."

Cossette tried to pull back, probably to glower at her and ask for an explanation, but Wynter wouldn't let her. She just held her even tighter. "It isn't safe. Promise me," she repeated before letting go and walking away without another word, and right through the gang of soldiers who had been watching their interaction from just feet away.

***

Marcus watched Wynter via the camera system and didn't quite know how to feel about what he'd just witnessed. She was broken and full of despair, which, of course, he loved, but there was still something that wasn't right about her. Something was off and he wanted to get to the bottom of it. He wanted to know what was said between her and that woman, who he knew was her best friend, Cossette. Wynter still needed teaching, and Marcus wasn't against forcing an answer out of his dear darling girl.

He reached out to his soldiers with his mind, connecting with the alpha of their group a second later, and relayed the vampire a message. An order for them to bring Wynter to him without delay, whether she wanted to or not. And then he watched on the screen as he nodded in answer.

Marcus then saw as Wynter charged her way through the crowds and away from his team of overseers, and he stiffened, urging for them to hurry the hell up and catch her. His worries were unwarranted though, and a few seconds later he could see that not only had she ducked straight into the awaiting elevator, but that she was also on her way up to him without the need for strong arming.

He closed the surveillance system down on his screen and switched to one of the spreadsheets he had been working on earlier. He wanted to look busy for when Wynter arrived, but then got a better offer when the phone on his desk rang.

"Yes?" he barked into it.

"Mr Cole, I have an urgent call from Dieter in the Berlin club. Do you have a moment?" Bryn's voice came through the speaker, and Marcus grinned.

"Of course," he answered, and the call was put through just as Wynter stepped out of the lift and took a few hesitant steps inside the office. Marcus could tell she'd heard him on the phone and didn't want to intrude, but he wanted her to, and ushered her over with a wave of his hand. "*Shön abend, Dieter. Alles klar?*" he greeted his German employee and the supervisor of his Berlin club, and Wynter crept closer as Dieter began running through some issue they were having with the local business owners in the same area. It was politics and a case of keeping the peace, but Marcus decided not to fob Dieter off with a snappy answer. He instead kept the man talking and didn't take his eyes off Wynter for even a second as she reached his side and stood there awkwardly. He adored how she didn't know what to do with herself and found himself wanting to hold her.

Succumbing to his instincts, he opened his arms wide, inviting her into his personal space regardless of them being in work hours.

In spite of herself, Wynter climbed directly into his lap and she curled into his hold like a child. She was exhausted and clearly in a tizzy, but she was here, and had come of her own accord.

Marcus grinned and carried on conversing with his Berlin office, but he wasn't really concentrating on what Dieter was saying. All he could think about was Wynter. He was enveloped by her scent and detected fear and sadness in her, but also some kind of strength of will, like she'd made a decision regarding something and felt good about it. Marcus wanted to know what it was but told himself not to rush. She would tell him, or he would find out himself. Either way, he wanted to just enjoy the fact she'd come to him willingly and not overthink her reasons why.

He continued on with his conversation, and all the while Wynter was gripping his shirt between the lithe fingers of her left hand, holding him closer. Anyone else and he might have found their neediness pathetic, but not her. All he truly wanted now was for her to grow irrevocably attached to him. To need him more than anyone else. Then he'd be happy, or at least that was what Marcus told himself as he held her back and rubbed his hand over her back and thigh.

He thought back to Wynter's actions over the evening since he'd released her from the solitude of her room. She'd hated being alone so had gone looking for company, just as he'd expected, but he wasn't happy that it'd been in the form of the Neanderthal down in the basement. At least all they'd done was talk, and she hadn't looked impressed when she'd left either. No kiss goodbye. No long, lingering glances. She hadn't even tried to sneak off with him to that back room. Why?

There was one logical reason. He was quickly reminded of the other male she'd spent a considerable amount of time with lately and wondered if being with Jakob had gotten to her. Could it be that she'd been satisfied aplenty by their exploits? Been given such a seeing to that no human would ever compare?

It was bad enough Jakob had fucked her, but he detested the sheer idea that she was also potentially so taken with the memory of being with him. That even now, she still thought of him and how she'd run off with the vampire in the night, and that they'd grown close enough for her to let him touch her and give her pleasure.

It was purely because of him knowing his own actions had caused the deed to happen that Marcus could forgive her for letting the Russian have his way with her. That didn't mean he had to like it, or that he'd forgiven Jakob, though. He wanted nothing more than to find the bastard and make him pay for being bold enough to touch his favourite slave. And he would. The assassin was skilled and had taken off after his sire had been bested, but he couldn't hide forever.

And really, he deserved to die simply for denying Marcus of his right to his Blood Slave's vein. But that wasn't why he was so angry. It wasn't because of his audacity at taking her away, but because he had done more than that.

How dare he have Wynter's body in all the ways Marcus would not? To touch and kiss what wasn't his and then make love to that amazing woman? To make her body sing and have her remember him so fondly in the days that followed.

The bastard.

Then again, he couldn't have gone too far. That was the one saving grace. Jakob wasn't capable of making love because if they had, their souls would have merged and he would've never let Wynter go. No vampire worth a shit would let his bonded soul mate out of their sight. It was too dangerous for one, because as the rumours said, it was also detrimental to each of them to be parted. They would each fester and wilt without the other half of their whole. One would eventually die of a broken heart, resulting in both ceasing to exist any longer. It was far too risky.

And anyway, Marcus was sure he would know if she had merged with another. Wynter would be different. She'd be eager to run back to her lover, when instead, here she was. She had clambered into his arms and not run away when she'd had the chance. She was lonely and scared and in need of his comfort, not skipping around like a lovesick teenager.

After Marcus wrapped up his call with Dieter and had said goodbye, Wynter let out a soft moan that let him know she'd dozed off in his arms. Her hand was still holding tightly to his shirt, and Marcus smiled down as he watched her.

And then he frowned. What was it he was just thinking about lovesick teenagers? He knew he was hardly one to judge because he was doing the exact same thing but was just glad they were alone and Wynter was fast asleep. No one would have to see this. See him.

Damn her. And damn the way she made him feel.

Marcus knew he loved her. Loved the way she felt in his arms and how she made him want to show her his love. There was no denying it, but he still wanted to wait. To bide his time until he could be sure about turning her.

The Priestess had delivered a prophecy that had proven to be wrong. The full moon had come and then went again without consequence. Wynter was still his, and he hadn't had to merge with her to ensure it.

All was well, and Marcus was sure things would remain so until he was ready to change them.

FOUR

Wynter woke from her nap with a contented smile. Yes, she missed Jakob with every inch of herself, but at the same time, she knew she was slowly starting to understand everything Marcus did for her. And actually, when he was being nice, it was impossible not to like him, hard as she might try.

She took in the sounds of her surroundings for a few seconds before eventually opening her eyes. Surprisingly, she was still in Marcus's lap. He hadn't locked her away or placed her on the nearby sofa. He had kept her close, and Wynter was glad he cared for her in his own way.

Things truly had changed these last few weeks, and she began to contemplate just what he had become to her. She'd never had someone keep her close and safe like he did, but also knew she didn't love him despite his caring turnaround.

Perhaps the old vampire was becoming like a father figure instead? Wynter had never had a male role model in her life, so had no one to compare him to. Her dad had disappeared out of the picture when she was just a kid and the boyfriends her mum had gone through were few and far between. Never enough to mean a stepfather was around permanently.

Wynter knew it was the most likely reason why she was always drawn to the wrong types of guys. And why they'd never loved her back or shown her the life she'd been missing. And probably why she herself hadn't known how to love in return.

But not now. Not since Jak had come into her life.

Wynter got it at long last. She finally understood about opening her heart and accepting love rather than mistaking lust for something real. And the differences between them. They were vast and many. She simply hadn't seen it before.

She looked up at Marcus, who was busy on his computer, and saw a man she could always appreciate and revere if he continued to care for her like he did, but also knew she could never love him. Never want him, not like that.

There was someone else in her life she felt the same way about, too. Warren.

Wynter knew she had to tell him so. Things needed ending, and she figured there was no time like the present.

"Thank you for letting me sit with you a while, Marcus," she whispered as she climbed up off his lap and rubbed the sleep out of her eyes. She then checked the clock. It was just after one-am. More than enough time to visit Warren, say what she needed to, and get back to begin feeding. "I've got a couple of errands to run and then I'll be back, okay."

He barely even acknowledged her, and Wynter guessed he was just playing it cool, but his iciness still irked her.

She felt like saying something but decided against it. He'd only lash out and perhaps punish her, and she wanted to get this conversation with Warren over with first.

She turned on her heel and left without another word and was down in the IT department within five minutes. There, she headed straight for Warren's office, where she found him making himself something to eat.

"Hey, I'm glad you came back down. Want one?" he asked, showing her his toasted muffin, and Wynter nodded her head yes. She then took a seat and watched him work.

There was no denying he was a gorgeous man. Someone any woman would die to get close to, but she knew this needed to be done. He had to know they were over.

"So yeah, I figured I could do a better job of explaining where I've been," Wynter eventually said, and he gave her an awkward shrug but nodded in agreement. "There's more to my absence than meets the eye and there's also something you need to know."

Warren sat down and pushed the plate with her muffin on towards her, and Wynter thanked him before taking a bite.

"And I have to say sorry. You're right, I just left you alone rather than check up on you like I ought to have. It was selfish of me," Warren answered, and while Wynter appreciated it, she didn't feel like letting him off so easily.

"Yeah, it was," she agreed. "You didn't even ask how I'd got injured or where I'd been. You just made assumptions, and that hurt."

"Then tell me," he demanded, but she didn't want to. Doing so would mean she'd have to explain about Camilla and the hordes, and Jakob. Nope.

Wynter shook her head no and shrugged.

"I'd rather not. And I've been thinking we should take a step back. Focus on being friends and nothing more," she told him, and caught the surprised look cross his face. Warren clearly hadn't expected that, but he didn't try to change her mind and Wynter was glad.

"Oh," he replied, his dark brows knitted together, "yeah, I guess friends will be better. Easier too."

"Yeah," she replied, and then rolled her good shoulder in a bid to scratch at an itch there. Warren noticed and jumped to his feet.

"You need some magic cream?" he asked, evidently appreciating the change of subject, and Wynter nodded. Her cuts were indeed a bit itchy, and she was glad of the chance to ease them a bit, and so accepted the small tub from him with a smile.

She tried, and failed, to get where she needed to and while it felt a bit strange, letting him run his fingers over her skin, Wynter then let Warren help her. It was when he was rubbing the cream on her neck, their faces just inches apart, that she knew he'd been lying about wanting to be friends. Warren's cheeks were flushed, and she could tell he wanted to kiss her, perhaps in a bid to make her change her mind, but Wynter moved away.

She'd meant it when she said they were over.

She was about to leave when Warren climbed down onto his knees and lifted the cream with a smile. "Come on. Let me get the rest of them and then you can go back upstairs."

Wynter hesitated, but then figured this was what a friend would do. Offer to help when she couldn't help herself, and so she accepted.

Warren was still kneeling between her thighs when the door opened and in strode Marcus.

She knew he was probably angry at finding them this way, and yet she didn't jump or tell Warren to stop. She knew they'd done nothing wrong and so grinned at him in greeting.

"Good morning, Marcus," she breathed, startling Warren. He clambered away as fast as his knees could scuttle and held up the cream, as if to prove to their boss he wasn't touching Wynter for any reason other than to help her out.

Marcus took them both in for a moment and she had hoped he'd see sense, but realised they were in trouble when a dark look crept over his face. He stalked back to the door and held it open.

"I want you both in my office, now."

"Mr Cole, we weren't doing anything untoward, I can assure you," Warren tried, but he was answered with a look that Wynter knew well. Marcus's death stare. He caved, of course, and walked out with his head down.

Wynter was raging. Where was his fight? His drive? If she hadn't already ended things, she would do now. The strong man she'd thought she knew was well and truly a myth. Warren was flesh and blood, like any man, and he had crumbled in the face of such a formidable foe.

She couldn't really blame him, either. Marcus was a monster, after all. It didn't matter what she'd been thinking just minutes earlier after waking from her nap. He would never change and didn't appear to even want to.

She didn't move a muscle. If Warren couldn't be strong, then she would be. She would stand up to Marcus for both of their sakes.

He let go of the door and stormed over to her, and Wynter put her left hand up to him in spite of her fear. She wanted to halt Marcus in his tracks, but he took her hand in his and used it to whip her to the side so he could scoop her into his arms.

She was up out of her chair and in his hold before she could even blink. This time, though, there was nothing comforting about it. The vampire was a walking ball of rage and venom. Wynter could feel it emanating off him in waves, and she shuddered.

"You don't have to do this, Marcus," she whispered as he carried her from the room and stormed out of the IT department without a word to any of the others.

Warren was right behind them and continued to stay silent, and Wynter knew Marcus had to be using his strange mind control power on him. He undoubtedly had no choice other than to follow them but didn't seem to be attempting to defy him either, the coward. "I came down here to break things off with Warren. We talked and agreed to just be friends," she tried, but he continued to ignore her.

Wynter then attempted to struggle free of Marcus's grasp and he retaliated in the worst way she could imagine. Not only was his dark stare boring into her soul, but he also seemed to decide to go one step further. Before she could try and get out of his hold, he pushed his hand beneath her sling and wrapped it directly around her still healing collarbone. "No, please, no," she begged, realising what he was intending to do.

With a sly smile, he gave the smallest of squeezes, but it was more than enough to send a wave of pain radiating throughout her entire body.

Wynter's mouth filled with saliva and she went icy cold as the pain took hold and rendered her helpless in a second. Marcus then released his grip but left his hand where it was, like he was ready to do it a second time should she try and worm her way out of his hold again.

Wynter got the despicable message loud and clear. She fought back her tears and opened her mouth in an attempt to beg him not to do it again. To spare her the agony of him feeling the need to show her more of his cruelty, but she was still fighting her nausea and fear and couldn't utter a word.

"That's it, my sweet. I was hoping you'd eventually learn when to shut the fuck up," he growled in response to her reaction. "It appears pain really is the key, and of course I'm not against delivering it should you speak out of turn again."

The three of them were out of the lift and in Marcus's office before Wynter could even get her bearings again, but she still tried when he leaned down to deposit her on one of his guest chairs. She used her good hand to grip his shirt and attempted to pull him to her. She even tilted her head in a bid to distract him with a kiss, but he was having none of it.

Marcus was gone without a sound or him even having wrenched himself away. It was more like he'd disappeared, but Wynter knew it was purely thanks to him having moved so fast she could barely feel it. Just another of his vampire skills that made this and every other fight with him unfair. He always had the upper hand. The advantage. And this time was no different.

Wynter dived off the chair and hit the floor on her knees. She tried to climb back up onto her feet but was then suddenly held back down on them by someone from behind.

She was facing Warren, who'd clearly noticed the new arrival, and she saw his eyes widen when he realised who had just appeared out of thin air and was now holding Wynter back. She didn't need to look back at who it was. The red-cloaked hands holding her still were answer enough, plus her senses were invaded by the soft, musky scent she had now gotten used to when the almighty priestess was close. Wynter cried out and tried to plead with the witch to release her, but she didn't budge.

"You're playing a very dangerous game, my love," she whispered in her ear in that same deep, multi-tonal voice Wynter now knew so well.

She refused to stop fighting her hold, though. Part of her even hoped she might be able to get through to her. That they were still close, like they were before. But, just like her, the Priestess had changed. Nothing about her seemed warm and her actions didn't give Wynter the impression she still cared for her at all. She hadn't even seen her properly in days, not unless she counted the odd voyeurism during Marcus's feed, and now that they were together, the strange woman wasn't acting in her usually affectionate way in the slightest. She seemed cold and bitter about something. As though she too was angry with her and wanted Wynter to suffer.

"Please. He's going to punish Warren for something he didn't do," she tried. "He and I are over. I don't want him."

"And who do you want? Your master? Or someone else?" she countered, silencing her, and Wynter realised she had to be careful. She knew she had to make the Priestess believe her intentions were always purely towards Marcus's wellbeing. To hide her love for Jakob, otherwise she'd surely be locked away again and never see the light of day so long as her soul mate lived.

"Marcus," she lied, but gave it all she had in a bid to convince her of her ruse. "In spite of everything he's done, I do want to stay with him. I want him to take care of me, and vice versa."

"You lie," the Priestess hissed, and she turned Wynter's head back so she was peering into her darkened hood. "You think I cannot see the changes within you? I no longer have the power to foretell your future, which means another's magic is at play…"

Wynter's stomach dropped. Shit. Yes, of course the Priestess would be able to see through her lies and call her out on them. Who did she think she was kidding?

And yet, Marcus hadn't seen those changes in her himself. The Priestess would surely have revealed her findings to him and if she truly knew everything, then there was no way he would have let her out of the bedroom and back to work. Wynter decided his witch had to be bluffing. Trying to figure her out in ways her magical abilities couldn't. If she knew about her having merged with Jak, then she wouldn't be threatening her. She would have acted already, rather than wait for confirmation.

"I have changed. You're right," she croaked, but then forced her voice out clearer and more resolutely. "I'm trying to be stronger. Looking out for number-one and not taking any shit from anybody. I want to be loved, my lady. Not just cared for or desired. I want someone in my life that truly loves me and would do anything to keep me. That's how I've changed, because I will no longer just sit back and let the people who have used and manipulated me for weeks carry on doing so. I will fight, even if I have to endure losing time and time again."

Now, that sure shut her up…

FIVE

Marcus did a double take at hearing Wynter speak out so strongly against not only him but also the Priestess. And even Warren. So, this was the real reason behind her having gone down to finish things with him. She wanted her freedom from every person she could feasibly take it from and so had indeed gone straight from his arms to Warren's office, but not for the reasons he had first suspected.

Jealousy had raged within him when he'd realised where she'd disappeared off to and he hadn't been able to help himself. He'd gone down there baying for blood and had intended on torturing the insolent boy for his foolishness, but now he had an altogether different plan.

Wynter wanted to be free of him, and so she would be. Marcus was going to remind her of his power over her life and surroundings in the most gruesome way possible.

"My lady," he called as he neared the trembling coward and stared him down. Warren was a wreck. He'd been fighting for the past two days and Marcus knew he was too tired to start all over again, but this time, the vampire wasn't going to simply deliver Warren a beating. He was going to take it all.

"Yes, my lord," she replied, and he could hear the smile in her voice. She already knew what he wanted of her, but for Wynter's sake, he spoke the words aloud. Dragged it out and made a show of it.

"Lift his curse. Give Warren the freedom Wynter so desires for him."

She followed his command without a sound and Marcus felt it as his minion was freed of his hold over him. Warren was indeed his own man again, and he stopped his trembling as a wave of anger spread through him too. Anger he could finally act on.

As well as resolve. And hate.

Marcus took a deep breath of his empowered scent and grinned. He was preparing to run. To do everything he could to escape Marcus and his club and never look back.

And all without so much as a thought for Wynter or any of the others. "My sweet, do you see?" Marcus asked, still peering down into Warren's determined stare. "Can you tell what he's thinking? Because I can."

"I can't, but I can guess," Wynter answered, and the smell of her bitterness hit him from across the room. She felt like a fool for not having done the same when she'd had the chance, but it was too late for her. It was also too late for Warren as well, but Marcus wasn't going to disclose that just yet.

"She fought her curse, Warren. Wynter won back her freedom," he revealed with a sneer, "and she stayed because of you. To save your life. And now look how you've repaid her. You've earned your freedom and what are you planning to do with it?"

"Run," he mumbled, and as much as Marcus could tell, it hurt him to be so brutally honest, Warren didn't appear ready to change his mind at all. He was still going to leave Wynter behind, no matter what she'd done for him.

What a sweet victory this was for Marcus. He'd just bested his little fighter and her new approach to life by having proven her so utterly wrong it had hurt her deeply. And now, he was going to take it one step further. He was going to manipulate her by having the audacity to avenge her honour when he himself was the cause of her pain. And he was going to do it by making Warren pay for his misdemeanours.

"So run, little rabbit," he taunted, "if you can…"

And with that, he kicked out Warren's legs and sent him flying to the ground, where he stamped on the guy's shin and didn't hold back. The bone gave an almighty crack and Warren let out a pained wail, while Marcus's face spread with a wide grin.

Warren's pain was like a drug to him, and he wanted more. A never-ending supply would be fantastic, but he knew better than to hope for such a thing. These frail humans never did last long when he really let loose on one of them, so better to enjoy every fleeting moment of it, or so Marcus told himself.

He walked away, leaving the boy to his sweet agony, and dropped to his knees so he could stare into Wynter's terrified face. Her dark eyes were even blacker now thanks to her pupils having dilated, and she too was trembling in fear, cowering before him. Marcus adored it, and he took the kiss she had offered him previously.

Wynter resisted but didn't fight. She let him take what he wanted and when he pulled away, he was surprised to find her nicely compliant— contrary to her usually so defiant nature. Marcus realised why when she tried to turn the tables and gain the upper hand. Just like her to try and win, even when it was so evident she wasn't even close to prevailing.

"Come, let's go and I can feed you. Leave him to his misery and to find his way out without our help," Wynter attempted, while also trying in vain to pry the Priestess's fingers from around her neck. His witch didn't let go, and Marcus knew why. She didn't believe her, and neither did he.

"Sure," he replied, and then planted another gentle kiss on Wynter's still trembling lips. When he pulled away, he couldn't hide his cunning smile though and she saw. Her breath hitched and that little flash of light behind her eyes gave her away—as if he hadn't already seen it, anyway. She was scared for Warren and thought there might be some way she could stop the inevitable from happening.

As if.

"Stop this, Marcus. He's done nothing wrong," Wynter tried, but the ancient vampire shook his head.

"He has vexed me, my sweet. Betrayed you and made your sacrifice worthless, and you still want to save him?"

"Yes," she mumbled, and then jumped when the lift arrived with a ding and his five vampire soldiers disembarked.

Marcus was hit with the true stench of Wynter's fear when she saw them, and his smile widened. He knew exactly what to do.

"Then take his place," he growled, issuing his horde with a silent order to descend upon her rather than the wounded sacrifice still writhing in pain on the floor.

The moment all five of them turned to her with hungry stares, Wynter shrieked and cried out incoherently. She tried again to wrench herself free, but his Priestess held her tighter, fisting one hand in her hair and pulling so that Wynter had no choice but to look up into the faces of death as they grew closer.

"No, no!" she cried, and Marcus held the horde off, but they were ravenous and he could see each of them licking their lips, desperate for a taste.

"Him or you, Wynter," he demanded, "and they're starving. I intend to let them have their fill. Now, will that be from you or from Warren?"

Silence descended on them all as she built the courage to answer him, and Wynter seemed frozen. Her eyes were unblinking and unfocused, as though she'd checked out entirely.

The snapping of one of the soldiers' jaws then seemed to stun her back into action, and Marcus watched as his darling girl finally summoned her strength and opened her mouth.

"Him," she ground, but that wasn't good enough. Marcus wanted her to say it properly. To seal Warren's fate once and for all. "Drink from him," she told the leader of his horde, whom Marcus also issued with the same order. The huge vampire turned and ushered for the others to join him, and together they drank Warren dry while Marcus and his Priestess forced Wynter to watch.

SIX

Wynter jumped awake in the pitch-black darkness of her room but didn't panic this time. At least she was slowly getting used to waking this way, but she still hated it, and immediately reached for the nearby lamp. She got the shock of her life when she found someone lying in the bed next to her, fast asleep. It thankfully wasn't Marcus, she could tell, but a woman. Someone with long, bouncy curls that Wynter could feel beside her as she climbed up and reached for the lamp.

When it came on, she gave it a second and then opened her eyes to find Marcella lying in the bed with her. Her first thought was to wake her and find out what she was doing there, but instead Wynter just laid back on her pillow and let her friend sleep.

She needed some time to think, anyway. Time to plan her escape at long last and track down her wayward soul mate to find out what the hell he'd been playing at rather than come get her like he'd promised. Plus, she needed a chance to process what had happened to Warren before she'd screamed herself silent and blacked out. She didn't even know how long ago that was or how many hours she'd been sleeping. But she knew one thing for certain, he was gone, and her mind was racing.

Would Marcus tell everyone it was her fault? Would he tell lies about her to all the others who already treated her like an outsider and probably wouldn't give her the time of day after this?

Everything was so all over the place. She didn't know which way was up, or what time of day or night it was. And really, she couldn't even remember what day of the year it was. It could be Christmas for all she knew.

Wynter felt as if she knew nothing at all anymore and had to stifle her tears as she leaned back and let the realisation of what'd happened wash over her. Warren was dead. The horde had fed on his broken body at Marcus's request, and there was absolutely no chance he'd survived. She'd seen him for herself.

The memory of his pale and exsanguinated body, and the five vampires in a feeding frenzy crouching over him, was ingrained on her skull now. His dull, lifeless eyes as he succumbed to his fate and let death take him away would haunt her.

It wasn't like David. Warren's death had been oddly peaceful and with barely a sound from him in protest. He had simply slipped away.

And yet, his death meant more than just a forced farewell. It meant Marcus had taken away the one person tying her to him and her job as his slave. He'd annulled their deal. He had nothing. Wynter would find his other leverage, Cossette, and run. She wouldn't look back, not until she found Jak, and then they would make a plan to come back and kill him. To finish him once and for all.

Yes. She vowed to be Marcus's undoing and wanted it more than anything else in the world. It was time the formidable leader was knocked down off his perch and taught a lesson of his own.

Jakob could do it. She'd seen for herself how uncomfortable Marcus had been by his presence at the club, and she was willing to bet he'd not only killed other creatures in his time, but his share of vampires, too.

Marcella let out a soft moan beside her and Wynter turned to watch as she slept. She wondered again why she was there and reached out to stroke her cheek tenderly.

"Marcy," she whispered, and was met with another moan before she slowly opened her eyes.

"Hey, Wynter," she replied as she stretched and yawned. "Sorry, I must have fallen asleep waiting for you to wake up. I'm tired all the time at the minute. Must be the pregnancy," Marcella added as she sat up and repositioned herself on the bed. "What's wrong?" she then asked, looking at Wynter's clearly confused expression.

"Why are you here?" she asked with a frown. "I don't understand it. Did Marcus lock you in with me? Are you being punished for something?"

"No," she answered with a small laugh, "why would you think that?"

"Because that's what he does with me," Wynter replied dejectedly, "so why?"

"He came to me and said someone had broken in and hurt some of the workers here. A vampire assassin called Jakob? Marcus said that I needed to come here and wait with you where it would be safe. Said you'd tell me what happened when you woke up."

Wynter sat and stared at Marcella blankly. Jakob had certainly not come to the club and hurt anyone. He hadn't been there at all, much to her disappointment. It was Marcus and the small horde that carried out his every request, and if someone had been hurt, it had nothing whatsoever to do with Jak. So why had he sent Marcella in here? What did he possibly have to gain by making her another pawn in his game?

"Nothing of the sort happened, Marcy," she told her, and then reached for her friend's hand. "But someone did get hurt. Warren."

"Warren?" Marcella croaked and Wynter nodded.

"You know, the IT guy," was all she could think to reply, and then wished she hadn't when Marcella broke down in tears and leapt off the bed so she could pace up and down the small bedroom.

"Of course I know him," she then cried, still sobbing into her hands, "he's the father of my baby!"

The air rushed from her lungs and Wynter went icy cold. He was the father? All this time and he'd never once mentioned having impregnated their colleague, but of course he'd thought it was fine for him to come onto her and promise her all the things he had. He'd clearly been playing her more than she'd realised.

Marcella then put her hand to her mouth and ran to the bathroom where she proceeded to puke her guts up and cry some more.

Wynter went to her but couldn't help. All she could do was rub her back and try to get her to calm down.

"It'll be okay, Marcy," she tried. "Marcus will take care of you and the baby. He'll make sure you're both safe."

"How?" Marcella finally croaked.

"I don't know, maybe get you a flat somewhere and—"

"I mean, how did this happen?" Marcella interrupted her with a screech, and Wynter paled. She suddenly realised exactly what he'd done and why.

Marcus had fed her lies in a bid to get her in this room with Wynter, so she'd have to be the one who spilled the beans of Warren's awful demise. But she wasn't going to lie. She wasn't going to be another of Marcus's puppets doing his bidding, and she certainly wouldn't protect him.

"He tried to run," she explained with a frown. "Him and I had grown close, but we decided not to pursue anything romantic and nothing ever happened between us. If I'd realised you two were involved, I would've never gone near him."

Marcella began to sob again, and she tugged off some toilet roll to wipe at her eyes and mouth. When she finally lifted her head out of the bowl, Wynter could tell that wasn't going to be the end of it. She needed to hear the rest. To hear how Warren had died.

By the time the awful tale had been told, Marcella was a wreck. She was lying on the bed in a ball and fits of tears just kept on coming, but there was nothing Wynter could do to stop them. All she could do was hold her and hope that she was bringing her some comfort. And that she didn't hate her for what'd happened.

**

Marcus watched via his hidden cameras as his priestess put on a bloody good show. The devious little witch truly did have a mean streak and while he knew she adored Wynter to some degree, he also knew she had taken after her mentor and showed that adoration in ways others didn't always understand or agree with.

Like him, Marcella wanted to manipulate and control the object of her affection and have Wynter hanging on her every word. To make her compliant to her wants and needs without the poor girl even realising she was doing it. And she was doing a good job in manipulating her. The lie about the baby's paternity had worked a treat and had truly woken up Wynter's softer side. She was empathetic and oozed with guilt and was opening up before his eyes.

Although, he had to wonder if his Priestess wanted some closeness so had concocted her lie, or if she perhaps had another motive for continuing to get close to Wynter and still not revealing her true self. Their friendship was split over the two separate personalities she had shown her. The two faces Marcella gladly wore and wore well.

"We weren't together as a couple, but things happened between us one night and he wanted this baby," he heard Marcella telling his darling slave. "We were going to try. To see where things went."

"I honestly didn't know," Wynter then replied with a frown, and it was clear she was beginning to second-guess her own relationship with Warren because of the lie. She was so quick to believe she'd been played. And all from someone apparently trying to better herself? She had the willpower of a crack addict who'd been promised a free fix. "But please don't worry. Nothing ever happened between us. I didn't feel that way about him."

"Why? How could you two go from being secretly sweet on each other one day and then stone cold the next? What changed?" Marcella asked, and Marcus beamed. She was trying to figure out what was truly going on with Wynter, too. They both knew something had changed in her, and Marcus had been forced to realise he couldn't coax it from her himself, nor was there a way of finding out using the Priestess's powers or forcing it out of her, so she was going for a different method. A more personal, tactful option.

Wynter shuffled awkwardly and stared down at her only free hand, which she was stretching open and then balling into a fist again. He'd seen her play with her hands before when she was on the cusp of revealing something that scared her, as though she was gathering the courage to speak up and needed something to focus on.

Marcella was so close, and Marcus silently urged her on. He was on the edge of his seat and watched, enthralled, eager for his witch to make sure Wynter opened up.

"Well..." she began, still staring at her hand, "that assassin you spoke of Jakob. He isn't what you've been made to believe. In fact, he and I spent a bit of time together while I was away last week. We talked a lot and even spent the night together."

Marcella feigned interest and surprise, while Marcus had to do everything he could not to scream with rage. He was about ready to storm in that room and give Wynter a proper beating for just mentioning her time with Jakob. Pain had made her comply before and he was more than willing to go down that route again. Softer touch be damned.

"So, do you love him?" Marcella asked, digging deeper.

"No," Wynter answered with a small laugh, but Marcus wasn't convinced. She'd been different ever since her escapades with him, and he would not stop until he found out why.

He stood and glowered at the screen; his hands balled into fists that he pressed down on the desk. His shoulders were flexing and tense with fresh rage. He wanted to hit something—or someone—and was just about ready for the next person he came upon to become his personal punching bag. It was that or strike Wynter, and if he was honest, he wasn't against the idea.

He guessed it all depended on what she told Marcella next, and so forced himself to pause. To take a moment and see what she had to say for herself. "It's just…" her voice permeated his silent rage, "I had the night of my life with him. Nothing compares to it."

Marcus proceeded to trash what little furniture he had around him and then fell to his knees. He had his head in his hands and was yanking hard at his short hair, relishing in the pain of it, when his Priestess's voice found him.

"You do love him then?" she asked, and Marcus peered up at the screen, watching as Wynter shook her head again. What the hell was she getting at? And why did he care so damn much? She was making him crazy.

"No, but he made me understand one thing," she answered with a sordid curl to her lip, and she waited a beat and then let her smile spread to a grin. "That no human man will ever satisfy me again. Not Warren or anyone else."

Marcus moved closer, his eyes still solely on Wynter as he watched her walls break down and finally speak the truth. She didn't want to be with any man thanks to Jakob. Only a vampire would do. She'd apparently made up her mind, and, by God, it was truly glorious to realise what that meant.

SEVEN

Wynter had given it everything she had to portray her lies. She'd forced herself to smile and pretend, because it was the only option she had left, and all because she knew Marcus would be watching. He had sent Marcella to her in a bid to extract the truth once and for all, and she knew it was time she gave him an answer as to why she had remained so aloof lately. So closed off. He had to believe it was for no other reason than her fear and love for him, and so placed her hand over her heart and steeled her strength as she gazed across at Marcella. Her friend, but also his slave. Just another person under his spell and one who she knew would betray her in a heartbeat.

"So what? You're going to be celibate like Joanna until you can spend the night with Jakob again? Or do you have someone else in mind?" Marcella asked, and Wynter shrugged her shoulders. She could work with that if it bought her some time.

Marcus wasn't shy when it came to touching her, and Wynter knew it wouldn't make a difference if she did or didn't want him to. He would do it anyway. At least if he thought her heart yearned for his, then perhaps he might stop playing his awful games and leave her alone? He'd wanted to be worshipped by a willing slave after all, and she intended to try that route to stroke his ego and hopefully gain a bit of headway.

"I've decided I'm Marcus's and his alone. If he wants me, then fine, but if not? I'll never take another lover," she lied, and while it'd been hard saying the words, she knew it was worth it. They both had to believe her. It was becoming a matter of necessity now that time was dragging along and she was still not free, and if Marcus believed she was his now, then surely it would appease his violent need to control her further.

"You're playing a very dangerous game," Marcella replied, and Wynter did a double take. Someone else had said those exact words to her just hours before. The Priestess. Was it just a coincidence that Marcella had said it too, or could it really be that she had been played? The woman who had spent an intimate day with her and taken her dancing, the one who had laughed with her and been there when she'd needed her. The friend whose shoulder she had cried on more than once.

Could she have been lying to her this whole time? Was Marcella nothing more than a hidden spy in the form of an everyday member of Marcus's staff?

It was entirely possible. She hadn't seen it before, but now it seemed obvious. Wouldn't that just have been perfect for Marcus and his desire to control all aspects of hers and the others' lives?

Wynter needed longer to piece it all together but was sure she'd figured them out. She decided not to call her out on what she'd said, but she was going to tread more carefully with her 'friend' in the future. She would watch and take note of the things Marcella said and did. And the same went for the Priestess. What a dangerous game indeed, but now the tables had turned.

"It's not a game," she answered her with another of her now signature forced smiles. "I want to be strong now. A fighter. But I will only fight for those who love me and I them. And I intend for Marcus to be top of that list."

***

Marcus shuddered at hearing Wynter's explanation. Could she really have grown to love him? He hadn't got that vibe from her at all, and yet she had indeed broken things off with Warren that morning straight after having found comfort in his embrace. Had she decided then that enough was enough so had gone to tell him? It appeared so, but he wasn't going to simply take her word for it. She would have to prove it to him. And he knew just how she could do it.

He went to the door of her bedroom and opened it up to reveal the two women sitting atop Wynter's thick duvet together, just like he'd seen on screen.

"Marcella," he growled, not even looking at her. His sole target was Wynter, and he couldn't take his eyes off her. She looked scared, and so she should be. "You may leave."

She did as he had asked and offered him a sly smile on her way. Yes, his priestess had done a fine job in getting Wynter to open up and reveal the truth about what she was feeling. She would be rewarded, but not now. No, he had another who needed his attention first.

He closed the door behind him and moved over towards the bed, where he came to a stop beside his darling girl. She peered up into his face and he watched her for a moment before leaning down and placing a hard kiss against her lips. She returned his kiss but continued to hold back, and that simply wouldn't do.

"Marcus," she whimpered, but he didn't want to talk. He wanted to act.

306

He shushed her and then a wave of brilliance washed over him as an alternative idea sprang to mind. It was time she was properly tested.

"Do not make another sound, my sweet. If you love me as you say, then you will bite your tongue and take what I have to give you…" her eyes flashed and her breath hitched and Marcus knew Wynter had thought he'd meant sex, but she didn't deserve his love yet. They had all the time in the world for that, but first, she still needed to be punished.

He shook his head and sensed her emotions transform from anticipation to a deep and resounding sense of trepidation, and she was right to fear him. He had a lot of anger still welling within his heart at how she had betrayed him and let Jakob try and run off with her. She hadn't fought the deviant assassin for so much as a moment of it, and Marcus had to know why.

Rage boiled within him again, and there was just too much to let him be kind or gentle with her. He had to offload first and was going to push Wynter to her limits in a bid to take away everything she thought she knew before and leave her with only him.

Her master.

Her mentor.

Her everything.

He started by flipping her over onto her stomach and wrenching down her pyjama bottoms to expose her perfectly round and white backside. Wynter was trembling, but she followed his order to remain silent as he ran his hands over her flesh.

She arched against him, but this wasn't the time for a bit of fun, and he proved so by slapping his hand against one cheek with a loud crack. Wynter jumped and hissed with the sting, but he didn't allow her the time to recover before delivering another smack.

He then removed his belt and curled it into a loop in his palm, which he lashed her with over and over. He sent his makeshift whip flying down on her rapidly reddening skin and with each slap she went to cry out but stopped herself just in time, proving her point.

Gaining his trust.

Earning his love.

Like the good little slave he knew she was.

EIGHT

Eight days earlier…

Jakob forced himself to move. To take the opportunity the few seconds' Wynter's sacrifice had given him to evade the huge vampire who had beaten him half to death. The behemoth had almost been on his way to besting the notorious assassin and they'd both known it, however his darling soul mate had been right. The soldier had one task. One focus. And Jakob wasn't it.

When she'd come between them, the soldier had faltered. Something in his brain had told him no, but he wasn't quick enough to stop himself from hurting her. Jakob would remember the sound of her bone cracking for the rest of his life. He had felt it too, like some kind of psychic link to her pain.

And yet his one true love hadn't stopped. Wynter had run away. She had taunted the mindless creature and given Jakob his freedom. The chance to get away while she sacrificed herself.

He felt like a coward for having taken it, but they both knew the only alternative was to let the soldier kill him or take him into custody, too. And then he'd be dead the moment the pair of them were delivered to Marcus atop that cliff's edge. He wasn't the type to forgive and forget, and Jakob had not only taken his favourite slave away but also merged his soul with hers. Something he'd never once thought himself capable of doing in his twelve hundred years.

Alone, Wynter might be able to convince him otherwise, but if they were together, Marcus would discover the truth. He'd see it in her eyes and read Jakob's actions and reactions like a book. It was true what they said about vampires who merged with humans. Once it was done, they were just as vulnerable as their human counterparts, and undoubtedly more emotional. Something inside of them clicked and lit a fuse that could never be snuffed out as long as their soul mate was alive. It was love in its truest and purest form. Something Jak had never succumbed to before and had pitied those who did. And yet now, he was broken without Wynter by his side. Desperate to pull her near and be complete again. He felt such loss without her it physically hurt and had wanted to take off after them.

But instead, she was being the hero. She would be taken back to Marcus, and he was powerless to stop it. All he could do was honour her sacrifice.

Jakob clambered to his knees and turned to face the second vampire soldier he had been sure would now come after him, but instead he found the foul thing locked in a fight with someone else. Or should that be something?

The black, mist-like creature was shaped like a man, but he wasn't flesh and blood at all. He was a manifestation in human form, as per the creature's design. Shit. It was a jinni. One of God's vilest entities to ever walk this Earth and something Jakob was not about to mess with. But why was it there? And who had summoned it? Perhaps Camilla? It couldn't be. She was dead now for sure anyway and her orders would be invalid, so how and why was there a jinni in their midst?

There was only one answer.

No, Jakob thought. It was worse than he'd imagined. Marcus really had done the unthinkable this time. He had rendered the services of a jinni and undoubtedly doomed them all.

He ran for the water, figuring his only way out was to the south, and stopped only to look back and check that Wynter was okay. He bobbed atop the waves as he focused on her—the other half of his heart and soul—and despite everything within him telling him to keep quiet and run, he called out to her.

"I'll find you!" he shouted in promise, still watching her as the feral vampire soldier slung her over his shoulder and made to leave. Jakob also watched as the second vampire stopped what he was doing and followed them, and as the jinni also backed off and disappeared in a heartbeat. That was when Jakob realised just how crazy Marcus was. He'd sent the horde after Wynter, sure, but to entrust her safety to a jinni? He had to be insane.

Yes, the jinni would protect Wynter at all costs and make sure of it that she never died or was hurt beyond repair, but he would also feed from her, just like Marcus did. The parasite would take root deep within and drain her life force while he was at it. They were nothing like the stories of wish-granting deities who lived within the confines of a lamp. No, real jinni didn't live inside a trinket, but was attached to a host. They lived off their strength and spirit while inhabiting their body. Feed from their energy, while diminishing that of the host.

The ancient creature would lie dormant until her life was in danger, which was when he would take form again like he had on the beach, but with each passing day Wynter would lose more and more of herself to him. She would grow weaker before long, which would eventually result in her death, turning her into one of the Jinn in return. Like some kind of thanks for having shared her life force with her freeloading guest.

And when that happened, there was no going back. She would be lost to them all forever, her human life over, and Marcus had to know this. So why had he done it? Why had he risked her soul just so that she would always have a protector on hand? He was beyond reckless.

Fearing the worst for his soul mate, Jak laid back in the water and let the current drag him further away from her. Every inch of him ached with the cold, his right collarbone hurting most of all, and he glared up at the clear blue sky while seething with rage.

It was because of the boy who had come close to taking her life. The deviant from his club that day Jakob had found Wynter beaten and bloody in Marcus's office. That had to be the reason.

Marcus had rendered the services of what was clearly a cunning enough jinni if he had falsely claimed he could depart Wynter's host body before he did any lasting damage. The vile creature undoubtedly jumped from one host to another, but they were never the same afterwards. No one ever truly survived a jinni's curse.

And so, Jakob now had two foes Wynter needed to vanquish. Each was as dangerous as the other, and he knew he would need some allies. Some others who despised their self-appointed leader as much as he now did. Marcus had killed his sire, but more than that, he had taken his merged soul mate hostage. Jakob would take his revenge, but first, he had to escape and put together a plan.

He let the tide carry him away as he formulated not one, but dozens of potential plans. The waves were rough, but it mattered not. The vampire needed no sustenance to survive or air for his lungs. No fresh water to quench his thirst.

He floated for two whole days with nothing but his thoughts for company before finally spotting a ship that was heading right for him.

It was a cruise liner, and the moment he began flailing around the ship slowed, and he could tell he'd been spotted. They fished him out of the ocean and drank up his lies about having turned over in a small boat. He kept thanking them all, and Jakob didn't even have to try hard to get into their good graces. The ship was full of humans enjoying their Christmas break, and they each welcomed him aboard like the trusting and innocent to the dark side of the world, people they were. Jakob didn't have the heart to tell them otherwise. He didn't even feed from any of them while he was on board either. He simply sat and stared out at the horizon, waiting for the ship to reach its destination, and wondering where his Wynter was. If she was safe. If Marcus was taking care of her.

He bloody well better had be. But it didn't matter, anyway. The ancient vampire was going to die at his hands regardless, and nothing he could say or do would change that.

***

Six days later

"It's now or never!" Jakob bellowed at his comrade, Nick. "We need to infiltrate the club and get Wynter back. I can't leave her there with him another week."

"I know," his old friend answered, his tone soothing and calm, and yet it did nothing to quench his desire for vengeance. "But we've been over this. As long as she's with Marcus, she is safe. He won't hurt her, plus she has the jinni on her side."

"Don't remind me," he growled, stomping away. Nick didn't get it. He couldn't feel what Jak felt or sense the iciness that was creeping into his body from the inside out. Wynter was dying without him. They needed to be reunited, and he knew there wasn't much time left. Planning and preparing was all well and good, but not when time was so clearly of the essence.

He decided to hit the gym. It was his only solace in these torturous few days since he'd arrived back in the blustery port of Southampton thanks to the cruise ship, and Jakob knew it was his way of dealing with having been parted from his soul mate.

The days were endless. The nights even worse. He'd bounced back and forth from plotting revenge and planning his attack to either working himself out until exhaustion hit or drinking himself into a stupor. Either one was preferable to the soul-crushing emptiness that enveloped him whenever he wasn't busy with one task or another, or the part of him cursed that human girl for having stolen his heart. Life would've been so much easier without her pulling him back to her.

Yeah, who was he trying to kid? She'd made him live again. Like, really come back alive, as if he'd been dead for more than a century. A walking corpse, until her.

Jakob would save her and had a plan all mapped out for once he got Wynter away from Marcus. He was going to place vials of her blood in random places across the globe while hiding her away with the help of his trusted friends. They too weren't fans of his and were ready to help Jakob take Marcus down a peg or two for nothing more than the sheer elation of knowing they'd had a hand in getting one over on him.

The problem that remained was just how he was going to get to her. Jakob had infiltrated Marcus's club before and was sure he could do it again, but he was no fool. Security would be tighter now. His vampire soldiers would be on the lookout and undoubtedly ready to pounce should they pick up his scent. And then there was the Priestess. She was not to be underestimated by any means, and in some ways, Jakob feared her more than any of the vampires standing between him and Wynter. Just like that boy she'd crushed into a bloody heap, Jak knew she would gladly end him should he cross her path again.

THE COMPLETE BLOOD SLAVE SERIES

NINE

Wynter woke to find Marcus drinking from her left wrist. She was lying on her belly exactly where he'd left her after beating her with that damn belt, and she knew there was no other choice but to remain where she was. The pain across her back was excruciating, but his bite was giving her that heady, needy feeling as usual, and Wynter felt a rush of desire flow through her, thundering in her core. She closed her eyes and thought of Jakob. Of the many times he had made her climax during their time together.

Not a single thought was for Marcus.

But those weren't her and Jakob's most wonderful of moments. No, it was when she had peered into his deep blue eyes and seen his soul shining back at her from within them. It'd had nothing to do with the sex, but of his true caring for her. Of his love. Jak had taken her body and made her feel something again, but his effect on her heart had been so inspiring she'd had no choice to love him back. To give him her soul in return.

There was nothing sexier.

An orgasm ripped through her without warning and Wynter buried her face in the duvet beneath her in a bid to stop from crying out.

She was then forced back to the here and now when she peered to her left and discovered Marcus still drinking from her vein, his frenzy more than evident now that he'd had another taste of her endorphin-laced blood.

Shit. This could be bad. Really bad.

Wynter internally chastised herself for letting her mind wander so far and cursed Marcus for not only his bite but also his ability to rule her emotions through it.

He had delivered her with so much pain she'd passed out, and all while she was trying her hardest to prove that she was loyal to him. He'd needed to hurt her so that he could test that loyalty, she knew, and just hoped he'd gotten what he'd came for.

But now, there were bigger issues at hand. She understood all too well that to climax while a vampire fed meant almost certain death for the human

313

being drained. She could already feel the effects of the blood loss and knew it wouldn't be long until she was out cold again.

When it'd happened before, there had been tricks she could try, but not today.

Wynter had nothing and knew she wasn't even remotely strong enough to try and fight him off. She was lying on her front, one arm strapped to her broken collarbone beneath her and the other stretched out to her side so she could feed the vampire lying against her pillow. Her legs felt numb and her arse so raw she wasn't sure she could even walk, much less run.

There was nothing she could do. No one she could scream to and beg for help. Nothing she could say to Marcus to calm his frenzy.

All Wynter could hope was that he would come to his senses in time and stop before it was too late and he'd taken too much. But it was already close. The light behind her eyes was soon dimming, and she held on as long as she could.

She cried out to Marcus and pleaded with him to stop before he killed her, but her screams seemed to fall on deaf ears. The last time this had happened, she'd shattered his feeding frenzy by breaking his spell. By inciting the power, she then had to annul their working contract and free herself from the spell the Priestess had put on her. That wouldn't help this time.

As a shudder ran down her spine, Wynter admitted defeat and closed her eyes. She was suddenly ready to go and could feel the death seeping into her bones. It was easier this time, though, and she knew it was because her fight was gone. Despite all her promises to herself to stay strong, Wynter realised she was the opposite. Nothing more than a useless human who had foolishly taken on the king of monsters and lost one time too many.

Jakob was in her thoughts again and she reached for him in her mind, desperate to go to him. To see her soul mate one last time before she was gone forever.

But then suddenly, the drinking stopped.

She forced her eyes back open and found nothing there.

Marcus hadn't just stopped, but he'd also gone, and she turned her head to scan what little of the room she could see.

That was when she saw them.

The black creature from the beach was back. He seemed more human than before, though. Like the mist he was made up of was denser somehow. And he was stood holding Marcus up off the floor and against the wall by his throat.

"Okay," Marcus croaked, pushing him away, "okay!"

"Get control of yourself or I will," her strange protector replied in a gruff voice, and only let go when Marcus nodded in answer.

He then glared at the creature like he was going to throttle him, and Wynter whimpered when his gaze fell on her. Marcus looked furious, and she had no idea why. It wasn't her fault. The other guy was right, and it was he who needed to learn some bloody self-control. Not that she felt the need to tell him that right now. It could wait until he was calmer.

He did a double take when he took her in, as though just realising the severity of the situation. Marcus seemed to sense her distress and the frail state he had left her in, and he immediately backed off.

He then stormed out without looking back.

Wynter let out another cry as she tried to climb up onto her knees with her free hand, but quickly failed thanks to her diminished strength and the loss of blood. "It's all right," the barely-there man told her as he took her hand and helped her up.

Wynter felt better the moment they touched, and she breathed a sigh of relief as he ran his hand over the cut on her wrist and somehow closed the deep, bruised wound Marcus had left her with. He had to be magical as well as mythical, or so she thought, and got her answer a second later when the black creature also reached up and unclipped the sling, holding her right arm in place over her broken collarbone. She winced as her arm fell free.

"What are you?" she asked, but he shushed her and ran his fingertips across the broken bone as though assessing the damage there. It was so strange, she felt him as though he were flesh and blood, and yet she could still see right through him. It was the oddest thing, but then things got even stranger when she suddenly realised that as he touched her, the bones mended. The deep, aching throb in her chest was gone, and she let out a garbled cry.

Wynter rolled her shoulder and felt no pain at all, and knew he had somehow healed her, just like he had the cut Marcus had left her with.

"There we go," he finally said, "all better."

Wynter stared into what she imagined were his black eyes and frowned. She couldn't even begin to envision what he was or why he had helped her, and so stared blankly at him for a moment before finally opening her mouth.

"On the beach, you saved me from the alpha vampire," she croaked, and he nodded, "and just now?"

"I stopped Marcus from taking your life," he confirmed. "It's my job, after all. My name is Brodie and I'm your protector. Hired by Marcus to watch over you and keep you safe should anyone try and do lasting harm. Including him. I can show myself or become invisible at will, but I am with you always, Wynter." He stroked her unruly hair and gave her what looked like a soft smile. "I see everything. Know everything."

Fear suddenly struck her, and Wynter felt her eyes widen in shock. Had he seen her and Jakob? Had he witnessed their souls merging and so knew all about how the two of them were bonded forever? He had to have, but for some reason, he hadn't betrayed her and told Marcus all about her wrongdoings.

That was a good sign, or so she hoped.

"What are you?" she asked again with a frown.

"A jinni," Brodie said calmly before placing one of his black wispy hands over her heart. "I live within you. I see what you see. Feel what you feel."

"And my thoughts? My desires?"

"I feel them too," Brodie answered with a small bow, "but fear not, they are kept sacredly secret between you and me. A jinni would never betray their charge."

"Never?" she demanded and raised her eyebrow in question. He had to know what she meant, and Brodie nodded again, which took a huge weight off her shoulders.

"Your secrets are mine to protect. No matter who hired me."

Good. That was very good.

Not once had Wynter considered Marcus having somehow put a spy inside her mind and body. Someone who had and would continue to snoop on every thought and feeling she had now that he had taken residence.

It was a strange concept and one Wynter wasn't all that comfortable with, but something told her there'd be no fighting it. She couldn't see him off, just like Marcus hadn't been able to.

Brodie was clearly more powerful than all of them, and someone not to be trifled with.

TEN

Jakob had tried two nights to get inside *Slave* under the radar, and nothing had worked. Marcus had thought of everything and no matter which window he tried or which stairwell he watched to seek out an opening, it never came. He started to despair, but knew he had to get inside and to her. His Wynter. It had been long enough. There was nothing else for it, and so he decided he'd go in the front door if he had to. He'd walk right up and ring the doorbell. Anything to get Marcus's attention and find his way inside.

Just as he was about to stalk up to the heavily guarded doors, a way in suddenly presented itself. An opening on the second floor caught his eye. Naught but a tiny window, perhaps a bathroom or kitchenette, but an opening just the same, and so Jakob willed his body to move. Against all human comprehension, his huge frame took flight amongst the shadows and became one with the air itself. Neither whole nor in pieces, he moved as one with the moonlight. It wasn't easy for vampires to transform in such a way, but he'd been doing so for hundreds of years. Just another skill the assassin had perfected as part of his chosen career.

He was inside the small gap a heartbeat later and hugged the walls of the tiny room he found himself in on the other side, becoming nothing but a cool draught. A silent whisper. The two people entwined and writhing against one another within felt his presence and he saw one of them, a female human, shudder.

"What's wrong?" her male counterpart asked, coming to a slow stop between her thighs.

"Nothing," she replied as she urged him to continue, "I'm just cold."

"Then let me warm you up," he teased.

"And close the window," she added with a nod, "you know we aren't meant to open them."

Jakob was gone before he'd even obeyed his lover's command, but knew the girl was right. And that her lover would act upon her warning. His way out was soon to be locked tight again. However, it didn't matter. He would get what he'd come for and leave before anyone noticed—even if he had to fly her off the roof to do it.

He reached the stairs a second later and found his way up to the top floor in silence.

It was quiet. Too quiet. Where was Marcus? And what of his men? Jakob could sense their presence and could smell Wynter's delicious scent upon the air, but she seemed cold. Isolated. Due diligence aside, Jak knew it was now or never. He had to go to her.

The room—her cell—was locked, but that didn't stop him. Jakob's nimble fingers made quick work of the lock and a second later, he was inside. He stormed towards the bed, where a huddled figure lay curled beneath thin sheets, and placed his hand on her in haste. But it wasn't Wynter. The woman turned over and peered up into his face in surprise, blinking away the sleep from her eyes.

Her bright orange hair fell in waves behind her, and Jakob cursed.

"Who are you?" she asked him meekly and reached for his hand as he went to walk away. "Have you come to save us?"

But Jakob wasn't that easily fooled. He could see right through her façade and knew without a doubt that he was in the presence of the same woman he had seen throw a man up and down the room like a ragdoll. She might've been under her shroud at the time, but he could sense that the female lying in the bed before him was not human. She was wrapped in sheets that still smelled of Wynter, but the scent was fading.

She hadn't been in them for hours.

That was when he noticed the vial of Wynter's blood hanging from a pendant around the woman's neck and scowled down at her.

Shit. Marcus had gone with the same plan Jakob was intending to go with. He'd planted a vial of Wynter's blood at the club and he had fallen for the ruse. He'd believed her to be there, even when he'd had nothing to go on but the scent of her essence, and yet, there he stood. Exposed and foiled in his attempt to save her.

"Where is she?" he demanded. "What have you done with her?"

The witch's timid expression faded in an instant and a devious smile curled at her lips as she climbed up onto her knees and faced him.

"What business is it of yours, vampire?" she asked, eyeing him curiously, "let me guess, you love her?" the Priestess added with an eye-roll.

So, she didn't actually know they'd merged? His Wynter was indeed more powerful than any of her captors had realised if she'd managed to keep their union hidden from them both. And Jakob was impressed.

He never should've doubted her. Of course, she would stay strong against Marcus and his oppressive means to rule her. And apparently even the Priestess and all her magical ability weren't strong enough to make her cave, either. Jakob had to fight the smile threatening to creep onto his face at the realisation.

"No," he lied, finding himself growing strangely used to the practice by now. "She and I made a deal. She put herself in the path of that vampire soldier so I could get away, but only in exchange for her freedom once I was able. I just came here to fulfil my end of the bargain."

"No, silly," the Priestess countered, and she gave a small giggle that Jakob might've considered playful on any other woman. But not her.

He bristled and readied himself for what came next. "You came here to die…"

ELEVEN

Wynter slept for a while after the jinni had gone, and she woke to find Marcus lying beside her on the bed. He was propped up on one elbow and had evidently been watching her sleep, much to her irritation. She just wanted to be free of him now and wasn't sure she could keep on pretending for much longer. Her mind began to race with potential escape plans, and yet there was no clear strategy. No obvious way out. She felt her chest ache with the emptiness she knew was slowly consuming her and it was all she could do not to cry.

"Your sadness is intoxicating, my sweet," Marcus whispered before drawing in a lungful of the scent Wynter knew she could not mask or hide. He would always know her overriding emotion and she endeavoured to give nothing away via her expression or answer. In fact, she said nothing at all, and Marcus grinned. "Aww, not talking to me now?" he teased. "Is it because I whipped you, or because I drank too much when you climaxed for me?"

Climaxed for him? As if. Wynter wanted to bite back and tell him where to go, but she didn't. She couldn't afford the backlash if she pissed him off now and so swallowed her retort.

"Both," she groaned in answer before turning over to her other side so she was facing away. Marcus simply let out a laugh and closed the gap between them, spooning Wynter from behind. He then ran his hand down over her backside and gave it a pat from atop the covers.

"Well, it appears you've miraculously healed. I assume you have your new friend Brodie to thank for it?"

She didn't answer. "This too," he added as he slipped his hand up and over her once broken collarbone. The same one he had squeezed in a bid to force her into submission before.

It was too much. All of it.

Wynter had taken all she could manage. Had more than enough of Marcus and his games.

No longer would she stand for it.

She jumped up out of bed and grabbed the closest set of real clothes she could find. She'd had it with the frilly nightdresses too and threw the one she'd been wearing to the ground without a care before sliding her legs into a pair of trousers and throwing on a chunky knit jumper that'd been beside them in the drawer.

Wynter looked around the room for a clock or some kind of indication of the time, but there was nothing, and she realised she'd lost all comprehension of night and day while locked away and sleeping only when Marcus had exhausted her during his feeds. He had a watch on his wrist, of course, but she wasn't about to ask him for clarification. She simply took it upon herself that it was time to go to work and climbed into her black heels.

Wynter then headed for the doorway and was met with another of Marcus's many obstacles. It was locked, of course.

"Open the door," she croaked without even looking back at her captor, who was still lying on the bed as though completely unperturbed by her reaction.

"Where are you going?" he asked with a mirthful tone that irked her even more.

"To work," she snapped, resting her forehead against the still closed door.

"No," Marcus answered.

"Then let me out so I can go and stretch my legs. Please, Marcus. I need some fresh air. Some time to myself. You broke our deal when you murdered Warren. I should walk out of your life for good after that stunt, but I haven't, so the least you can do is let me have some space."

Wynter waited a beat and when she got no answer, she pounded on the door with her fists until she finally heard it click open.

Of course, that also meant Marcus was right behind her.

He enveloped her and took her hands in his to stop her from hitting the door anymore.

"That's enough," he whispered in her ear, "if you want me to show you the world waiting for you outside these four walls, all you have to do is behave. Can you do that, my sweet?"

No, she thought, but forced her defiant side to take a back seat and instead nodded her head yes.

Marcus pulled her to him and then pushed the door open to reveal nothing but emptiness beyond her room. Not the usual living area Wynter was used to, nor the wall partitioning off the rest of Marcus's office. It was naught but a bare warehouse. Empty of all except a solitary desk and laptop atop it.

She walked out into the open space and peered around in the darkness. An icy chill went down her spine when she saw a skyline ahead she didn't recognise, and she turned back to Marcus and peered up into his frosty blue eyes.

"Where are we? And when did you move me?" she demanded, seeing red.

"This is one of my as yet unused locations across the globe. I decided it was time I kept you hidden, Wynter. Away from the other managers and from *Slave*. I don't want you working there any longer where they can taint you or come between us anymore."

"So not only have you taken away my friends and my freedom, but now my choices too? I refuse, Marcus. Do you hear me? I refuse to accept this life," Wynter bellowed as she stormed away towards the only exit she could find. One solitary green and white emergency light indicated the way, and even though she was terrified, Wynter went straight for it.

She tiptoed over the holes in the flooring and avoided the debris left behind after what had to be decades of dilapidation and eventually found the doorway. She opened up, half expecting Marcus to have come to stop her, and got her answer as to why not as soon as her eyes adjusted to the dim light, and she saw what awaited her on the other side.

Silent, motionless bodies were stood side-by-side in her way. They blocked the stairs leading all the way down and were each naked and lined up like some kind of firing squad were about to take them down row by row. But Wynter knew otherwise. She'd been told all about the hordes of mindless, soulless vampire soldiers Marcus now commanded thanks to him having killed Camilla and taken them from her sired vampire heirs.

The few dozen she could see seemed to be asleep, or in some kind of stasis, and Wynter guessed they were waiting on one of two orders from their master. To feed or to do his bidding.

She risked a step forward and peered down further into the bowels of the huge building and could see nothing but more rows of heads. It seemed never ending and Wynter shuddered as she brushed past one and felt the cold rush into her bones at his touch.

There had to be thousands in there, too. Each one a killing machine.

She stepped back, instinctively moving away from the creatures she knew would pounce should she dare take another step forwards, but found her way barricaded by another wall of vampire soldiers.

Marcus's chosen handful of guardsmen were blocking the door and she turned and glared up into the eyes of the alpha, who was towering over her. "Move," she hissed, and was met with nothing but his lifeless stare.

Wynter tried barging past, but it was no use. He was like a brick wall, just himself, but with the others huddling close, they were an impenetrable blockade she had no hope of getting through until they were ready.

She opened her mouth to ask again, when the huge vampire reached out and grabbed her by the throat. He was so quick she couldn't register the swift movement until he was already squeezing the life out of her and Wynter grabbed his hand, trying to pry herself free. The alpha responded by tilting her backwards and she began shuddering with panic as she teetered back on her heels and then further, directly into the sea of awaiting vampires.

The moment she was amidst them, those closest few sprung to life and started grabbing at her. Their icy hands ripped at her clothes and Wynter jolted with every contact their skin made with hers, and all the while she couldn't say a word thanks to the death-grip the huge alpha had around her throat.

It was only when he lifted her out again and flung her back through the door that Wynter realised none of the vampires in the stairwell had drawn any blood from her. They had to have been ordered not to harm her, but still, she was terrified.

Wynter curled into a ball on the dirty floor and began crying into her hands. She stayed that way until she heard Marcus calling to her from the door to her bedroom.

"Oh, my sweet. I have a gift for you…"

"I don't want anything from you, Marcus," she croaked in answer, defiant to the last, but then lifted her head to look at him.

That was when she discovered he was not alone. The Priestess was standing beside him, her red shroud back in place, and on his knees at her feet was a man who'd been bound at his hands and ankles. He had his head down, but Wynter knew right away who it was.

Jakob.

Her one and only love. He was here? She wanted to ask a hundred questions as to how and why but knew she couldn't give the game away. Not yet. Not while Jak was already in a bad way.

She needed him strong and ready to fight, and she would fight by his side if she had to. Wynter knew it was time. Now or never. She would be forced to do whatever it took to get away and would gladly do so, even if it meant doing the unthinkable and taking her life in order to sever Marcus's bond with her.

Brodie had told her he would appear whenever her life was in danger, but did that include suicide? She couldn't know, at least, not until the time came, and by then she had a feeling she'd want to end it all. That she'd be ready.

She only hoped the jinni would let it happen. That he'd consider his duty over and allow her to go.

TWELVE

Marcus watched Wynter unfurl herself and climb to her knees and then feet. She was wobbly but refused to lean on the vampire soldiers still within arms' reach as she returned to him. He'd been right to order the alpha to scare her. She was a frightened wreck and appeared to be in some kind of shock, too. Her eyes were wide, pupils dilated.

Why hadn't he thought of that kind of punishment sooner? She was damn near perfect in her sorry little state.

"He told us everything," the Priestess informed Wynter, who couldn't hide her surprise before daring to brush it off as though she had done no wrong.

"I'm leaving and neither of you can stop me," Wynter countered, but Marcus didn't quite believe it. She wasn't strong enough to leave. If she was, she would've risked climbing down those stairs through the horde below, but instead she had retreated.

Wynter reached them and Marcus watched her every move, waiting to see if she responded to Jakob's presence in the way a merged soul mate might do. She didn't so much as register him. Instead, she seemed focussed on his Priestess and Marcus watched enthralled as Wynter approached and went to her. With shaking hands, she then reached out and put her palms over the witch's belly. "I knew it," Wynter whimpered, having clearly felt the small round of her pregnant stomach, and Marcus grinned. He was reminded of the day he'd spent watching them enjoy their sexuality together. Two beautiful angels, and yet one who had hid a secret all this time.

When had she realised the truth behind who was truly beneath that shroud? Clever thing.

"What is it, my love," the Priestess replied. She hadn't put it together yet, and Marcus was surprised. Her intuition was usually second to none, yet it appeared Wynter was one step ahead of her this once.

"Yes, I am your love, aren't I? A friend. Someone who has opened up to you. Relied on you. And you betrayed me, Marcella. You played me."

Wynter didn't wait for a response. She simply reached up and pulled back the hood, hiding the Priestess's true features beneath to reveal she was indeed correct. Marcella was exposed, staring back at Wynter with a befuddled look.

"I saved your life too, don't forget," she countered.

"You also got me into trouble and even drugged me."

Marcella couldn't deny those things and so just smiled. All pretence was over, and Marcus watched as Wynter too forgot all about the niceties and considered her with a venomous look.

She then turned to him, and that malice grew stronger. More resolute. "And you," Wynter demanded with a scowl.

"Me? What have I done?" he asked, feigning innocence, but Wynter clearly wasn't playing his games any longer. She didn't hesitate, nor did she falter as she stepped closer to him and pointed a finger at his chest.

Marcus continued to grin down at her, but he could tell she truly was done with being scared. She'd crossed over the threshold where her fear still dominated her actions, and instead she was standing up for herself once and for all.

He'd be impressed if he weren't so fucking infuriated.

***

"You've beaten me and forced me to submit to your every whim, Marcus. But no more," Wynter told him, glowering up into his bright blue eyes. Something truly had snapped within her and she wasn't afraid to speak her mind. Not anymore. Not when he had her cornered and everything was on the line.

What was the worst they could do, kill her? She welcomed it.

Jakob had talked, or so Marcella had said, but she didn't believe that. He wouldn't give her up so easily, no matter what the witch had tried. He was undoubtedly used to the scare tactics and torture methods by vampires across the globe, and there was no way he would break. Not him.

As if he'd felt her presence, Jakob stirred and managed to shake off whatever fog was clouding his mind. He then jumped to action and made quick work of snapping the binds holding him down, before he then put himself between Wynter and Marcus, seemingly on instinct.

"You heard the lady. Back off," he growled, and it was all Wynter could do not to reach out and hold him. To put her hand in his and kiss him and welcome him home. She finally felt whole with him nearby. It was as if the missing piece of her heart was back again, and she yearned even harder for her freedom.

She would be leaving today. No matter what.

"Oh, she's going with you, is she?" Marcus demanded, and Wynter could see the pent-up aggression firing behind his eyes. He was about ready to explode, but she was ready, too. She wanted this standoff to happen more than anything, regardless of the repercussions. It was time this ended.

"I made her a promise. Her freedom in exchange for mine, and I'm here to make sure she gets it. This ends now, Marcus," Jakob replied, his body a wall of anger and power, and Wynter had to fight every urge within that was screaming for her to reach out and grasp him tight.

His words made sense now too, and the lie he'd woven was clear. Marcella thought she and Jak had simply come to some kind of arrangement. It was insane, though. All the stories she'd heard about bonded souls being so obvious, and yet they refused to see what was literally right in front of them. How did the formidable vampire and his priestess still not know they had merged? That they were bound to one another for eternity, and two halves of a whole?

It was insane.

"And if I refuse?" Marcus replied, just as she knew he would.

He was too smug, as usual. Too sure of himself. He always won, she knew, but not this time.

"And what makes you think you have any say in what happens to her, assassin?" Marcella asked, her face still cold and dark. She was far from the friend Wynter had thought she knew, and she felt a pang of sadness spear through her heart. She really had been alone this entire time. Been manipulated and used by everyone, most of all the two people standing before her.

The realisation made her desire to leave grow even stronger. She needed out of this hateful relationship and wasn't going to take no for an answer.

"Because in spite of all your efforts to break me, I'm still my own person. I'm still me. Not your puppet, and not your lover," she spat in answer to them both. Frustratingly, her words seemed to have little effect the old vampire. He simply watched her, glaring down into her face as he seemed to muddle over how he wanted to react.

"You think you can run off and be free? That's not how this works. Plus, even if you did get away, you might find yourself free of me, but not for long," Marcus replied, looking down at her chest, "you're dying, Wynter. Can't you feel it? Can't you sense the life seeping out of you with every passing moment? Are you that blind?"

She knew exactly what he was referring to and, while he was right, she smiled still. Wynter was no fool. She knew he was talking about Brodie. The creature living within her had to be taking more than his share of her life force, but she welcomed it. Readily gave him all of it. And why the hell not? If she couldn't be with Jakob, then she'd readily die at the hands of the jinni who had saved her more than once already.

He'd protected her when she'd needed it and had healed her wounds and had probably been kinder than anyone she'd met the past few months. Well, the only exception to that was Jakob, but he was currently in just as much peril as she was. They would not leave one another again, either by getting away or by letting death take them, but at least they'd be together.

"I welcome it," she hissed, "better death than be forced to stay with you any longer."

Marcus ignored her.

"Your only option to get rid of the jinni is to be sired as a vampire, my sweet. I can do that for you. We can forget all about this nonsense and move forward. Let me guide you. Be your mentor and master into the afterlife and beyond."

She wanted to laugh at his audacity. Marcus was fooling himself if he thought she would accept his offer, and she shook her head no. There wasn't a chance in hell she would let anyone sire her other than her soul mate.

"You're right. The only way to free her from the jinni's hold is to sire her, but I'll be the one to do it, Marcus," Jakob groaned, clearly thinking the same thing as she was. "It's time you let her go. You've taken more than enough."

"So, it's down to a choice, is it?" he answered with an amused smile, and Wynter cringed as she saw a flash of deviousness cross his face. He wasn't going to play fair, it was clear as day. "Me or you?"

"Just let me go, Marcus. Please," she tried, but he didn't so much as look at her. He was still glowering at Jakob and the pair of them looked like they were about to fight.

On instinct, she stepped away, but Marcella quickly moved and blocked her path. She gripped Wynter by the back of her neck, her lithe fingers yanking at her scalp, and it burned with the sting of it. For someone so small, she was stronger than Wynter ever could've imagined, and after one more yank that felt as if it were ripping the hair from its roots. She fell to her knees and looked up at Marcella through tear-filled eyes.

"You don't get to leave while we're in the middle of a conversation, my love. Not when it's about to get so very interesting..." she informed her, using that deep and ominous voice Wynter still found freaky.

She then released her grip and sunk into a crouch beside her so that she could whisper in Wynter's ear. "I've figured out your secret," she said, and Wynter's stomach dropped. "I had premonitions of your future, you remember? There were so many variances depending on which path you chose, but one in particular kept on haunting me. One I refused to believe."

She stroked Wynter's hair, so gentle, as if she hadn't almost ripped her scalp to shreds a few moments previously, and she shrugged her away. Wynter didn't want Marcella touching her. In fact, she didn't want her anywhere near her and tried to turn her face away, but the Priestess reached out and gripped her by the chin. She yanked her face back around and glared into Wynter's eyes, her face thunderous. "Marcus wanted to turn you, but I begged him to merge with you. The full moon was the turning point. I knew this, and yet it came and went without either of these things coming to pass. And so, I knew you had to have chosen one of the other paths I foresaw. My prophecy was right, wasn't it? The full moon came, and you ran into the arms of another man. You merged with him and fell in love. That's why Camilla didn't kill you when she had the chance."

Wynter felt like she was about to pass out. She couldn't breathe. Couldn't think straight. All she wanted to do was fight, but there was no way she would be strong enough.

"I told you, we just had some fun."

"Liar," Marcella growled before shoving Wynter away. She fell against the cold, hard ground with a thud and looked up as Jakob, having clearly heard her fall, turned his back to Marcus and reached down to help her.

He had to have moved purely on instinct, but Wynter knew it was foolish of him to turn his back on their two foes. It was too late for her to cry out for him to stop, though, and her eyes widened in horror when she saw Marcella's hands reach up around his neck.

It was like slow motion, and yet she was still powerless to stop it. Marcella was stronger than anything she had ever known, perhaps even Marcus, and crueller.

She seemed to sense Wynter's fear, but rather than put her at ease, she snapped Jakob's neck like a twig and all while watching her with a wide and sinister smile.

The sound of his head almost coming clean off his body was deafening, and when he slumped to the ground, Wynter began screaming uncontrollably. He couldn't be dead. He'd told her before it wasn't so easy to kill a vampire, and so she rocked back and forth on her knees beside him, waiting for him to jump-start back to life, but there was nothing. He was limp and lifeless, and now there was nothing to stop Marcus from having his way. She wanted to curse Jakob for letting his guard down, but knew it was her fault he had. She had made him weak.

When she'd calmed down enough to speak, she glared up at Marcella and then to Marcus.

"I will never do as you ask," she told him. "I'd rather die than let you sire me."

"Then choose death," Marcus answered with an unperturbed shrug, "but you shall remain my prisoner until that time comes. You will pass through to the other side unloved and with no one to mourn you. While I shall move on and forget you ever existed."

Wynter shook her head. She somehow knew he was lying. The realisation that she'd merged with Jakob had hurt him, but, of course, he'd never show it. Never just be honest and tell her the truth.

But there was one saving grace at least. One hope she could cling to. Wynter could tell how her soul was still merged to the lifeless vampire lying before her. If her instincts were correct, he was not dead. Only bested. He would come back to her in time, and so Wynter chose to let another of her instincts guide her instead. A voice within her was whispering words in her ear. Reminding her that there were laws regarding love and honour among the magical kind.

A vow had been made between her and Jak that could never be broken.

Plus, another deal had been struck with an even more powerful being who was still hiding himself away. Biding his time. And there was a strange urge rising to life within her. A new desire. The voice was calling to her. Guiding her.

She knew exactly who was doing the talking and what she had to do.

"You're an unconvincing liar, Marcus," she replied with a small laugh as Brodie's words in her head began to make sense, "because death is not an option for me, is it?"

He remained silent and still, but she saw the shock on Marcella's face and knew she was right. All this time, they had let her believe Brodie would drain her dry before leaving her to die, but it wasn't the case.

He was whispering truths to her as they continued their standoff, and at first, she thought it was from inside her head, but then she saw a footprint on the ground and remembered how he could disappear at will, like on the beach.

He'd done the same now and was there beside her, showing her the way. His whispers filtered into her ears and Wynter's heart began to race.

Could he really be serious? He had to be.

"Kill her, Marcus," Marcella cried, but the ancient vampire dismissed her with a wave of his hand. She wasn't put off and shook her head, her eyes wide. She was finally beginning to see what Marcus was too blind to accept. "She will never surrender to you and the jinni has too much of a hold. Have done with this now before it's too late!" she tried.

Her words worked in Wynter's favour and Marcus finally turned his attention upon the Priestess rather than his possession. He bellowed at her to leave, and the witch took a begrudging step away. Wynter thought it had to be for the safety of herself and her child rather than in submission, though. She had the impression witches didn't cower so easily before vampires.

While his back was turned, Wynter looked to her side where she could feel Brodie's presence and nodded her head in agreement with his plan. It was time they fought back. All of them.

She then watched as Jakob's still lifeless body was lifted off the floor by the invisible force of her jinni friend and was flung with incredible force at the window across the other side of the room. It shattered with ease and half a second later, Jak was gone.

Thanks to Brodie, he was finally away from Marcus. Away from his hordes and his priestess. She only hoped the force of the crash, or the resulting fall wouldn't do him more harm, but she trusted in his strength and ability to heal all ills. And, of course, Brodie's promise that her soul mate would survive the ordeal.

She, on the other hand, wouldn't be so lucky.

But Wynter didn't hesitate.

She shot up and took off across the room as fast as her feet could carry her, and before Marcus or his still retreating priestess could follow her or detain her again. Once she reached the wall of glass, she leapt out of the jagged opening Jakob had left at the ready.

Wynter jumped straight out of a fourth-floor window with the biggest of smiles on her face. She could see Jak lying in a heap below, but he wasn't dead, she could tell. The air was cold against her skin but felt refreshing and she breathed a deep lungful of it as she descended at speed towards the ground.

She felt not even an ounce of sadness. Just courageous righteousness. This was the right thing to do. She was free at last, and thanks to what came next, would remain so.

The ground was quick to claim her, but she didn't care. She had already resigned herself to such a fate and knew now how she'd been lied to. Death wasn't what was going to take her. It was instead a creature who caught her in his solid arms at the bottom. The man who was no longer made of black mist but somehow of flesh and bone. He was real. Alive. He had the darkest shade of black skin she'd ever seen and deep green eyes. He was whole. And beautiful.

"Brodie," she whispered with a smile before letting out a cry as the pain from her fall finally took its hold. Her body ached all over, as if every bone was broken and every nerve snapped in two. And then a wholly different sensation washed over her. She felt as if her broken body was somehow decimating piece by piece.

As it melted away, she felt herself changing, while her consciousness somehow lived on unaltered.

Wynter knew she was tied to the man holding her, and she found his heart calling to hers—or at least what was left of it. The calling promised her safety and a home at last. A place to recover from the pain and grow stronger once more. A chance to gain powers of her own and immortal abilities, the likes she couldn't believe. And that could only mean one thing. Brodie's mission was complete. He had taken what was left of her life force and utilised it as his own.

Of course he had, otherwise he would not be whole.

And good, she thought.

He deserved it.

Wynter lifted her hand in an attempt to see her flesh and bone one more time, but all she could see was that strange mist. Hers was white, rather than his black, and it was thin. More like a veil than a heavy haze, but she understood how it would become denser as time went on and as she grew stronger again.

Blissful clarity swept over her, and she realised then how there was no more pain. No more fog clouding her mind or judgement. She was utterly free from all the chains that'd once bound her, and she now yearned for nothing. Not life. Not death. Just more of this wondrous feeling.

And love.

Her love.

"Welcome to the world, young jinni," Brodie whispered to her with a smile, and his green eyes lit up as he watched her transform, "together we will do great things, just like I promised, but for now you must rest. Let me take care of you until you're strong enough to materialise."

Wynter knew what he meant. She needed to be patient and learn how to live as a jinni. She would have to follow his instructions and let him guide her, otherwise she would never be strong enough to show herself and reunite with Jakob in her new form.

She leaned towards Brodie on instinct, much like she would when needing to be held, but this time it was completely different. She seeped into his body until she found her place there within him, already waiting and open in invitation.

There was no bottle or lamp like the myth, but a place within his heart for her, and as soon as Wynter was nestled inside, she felt like she was a part of him. She could see through Brodie's eyes. Hear his thoughts and sense his emotions.

Was this what it'd been like for him when things were the other way around? It had to be. No wonder he'd known so much about her, and of course, known when to appear and save her life.

Wynter was awestruck as she watched through his eyes and saw Brodie pick up Jakob's even more broken body and carry him away at breakneck speed.

His mind was a chaotic array of different threads of thought as he spirited the three of them away, but one stood out amongst the others. Her host was making her a promise. He would keep Jakob safe. Keep him close. The three of them would travel together for eternity while Brodie and Wynter lived within each other's relative bodies to gain strength. While they shared one life force and made the union work, just like they had these past few weeks.

It was going to be okay. He was going to make it so.

But then there was another thought running through Brodie's mind that made Wynter wish she were strong enough to talk back. To set his new plan on another course. He couldn't hide it and stopped trying when he sensed she was onto him.

"No," she called, watching as Brodie peered down at the vampire out cold in his arms with an ulterior motive on his mind, "don't hurt him."

"I won't. Not right away at least," Brodie whispered aloud in answer, and she knew then he'd heard her plea. "But I will have my vengeance, Wynter. He has to pay."

He then opened his mind to her further, showing her just what kind of wretched life the jinni had been forced to live. He'd taken host after host, and always left them for dead afterwards rather than let them turn into one of his kind, and all because he couldn't bear sharing his life with someone new. Not after losing his soul mate over a century before. Like vampires, jinni souls could merge with those they loved and were bonded, however when one was taken, the other was forced to live on. Obliged to carry on without them, even if they're left broken in the resulting years of their immortal life.

"But why Jakob? What did he do to you?" she begged, and Brodie showed her another of his intense memories. One that made her want to cry, if that was even possible.

He'd spent ever such a long time hating vampires in general, but more this one vampire in particular. The vampire who had killed his bride.

The same vampire now unconscious in his arms and at his mercy.

The man Wynter loved with all her heart.

She wanted to scream in pain for them both and could see now just what Brodie had been through in the aftermath of losing the woman he loved.

Brodie had mourned the love of his life. He'd laid low. Bided his time. And now, he had the chance to exact his revenge. It hadn't been his initial plan, but after taking on the job of Wynter's protector, Jakob had crossed his path by some fluke or fate. He didn't know. Didn't care either.

And now Brodie was going to use what time they had to make sure he paid for what he'd done.

"You and I are one, Wynter. Two jinni's who now share power and are bound to one another for eternity. But we are not soul mates. We will take turns at sheltering each other, offering a place of solace while the other grows strong enough to become whole again," he said out loud as he continued to put as much distance between them and Marcus as possible, "but you are nothing more than a voice in my mind now. I am the driving force, and I shall do as I please. It's your job to understand my needs and support me, just as I did with you."

"But…" Wynter tried, however she knew she had nothing to argue with.

He was right. Brodie deserved his vengeance. She would have been the same. Hell, Jakob would've done the same if Marcus had eventually turned her rather than allow her escape. It was what you did when you were truly and irrevocably in love. So, who was she to try and stop him?

"Your soul merged with this vampire's, but mine didn't. I am not immune to his charms or oblivious to the things he has done. He will repay his debt to me, Wynter. I will control his fate until my cycle ends and it is your turn to become whole. And then the pair of you can have your time in the sun once again, when you can repair whatever damage I have done."

Wynter fell silent and then conceded, and she retreated further into the void in which she now resided so she could try and switch off while she focussed on healing herself.

She didn't want to so much as think about what was going to come next, much less see it through the eyes of the man intent on torturing her poor beau, but knew she had no choice other than to accept it.

They both owed Brodie a debt, one that would be repaid in full. And for Jakob, that time was invariably here.

THIRTEEN

Brodie took Jakob far away from Marcus and his witch. As far as he could manage in the initially tight head start he had. But he knew the vampire and his soldiers would be hot on their heels. They wouldn't be able to follow Wynter's essence now that she was hidden, but that wouldn't stop them from being able to track either his or Jakob's scent if they were cunning enough. He needed to get them either in the air or across the sea. Nothing else would break that trail.

It was a good thing the jinni needed neither sleep nor sustenance, and he didn't stop moving forward until he reached their initial destination—an airstrip off the west coast of Scotland. He'd moved from on foot to in a hire car, and every time the vampire in his grasp stirred as if to wake, he swiftly snapped his neck again to ensure there was no fight. And no engagement. Not yet, at least.

He wasn't ready. After almost a century spent in his dematerialized form, Brodie was finally whole again, and it felt rather strange. Almost alien. He'd survived by drawing just the right amount of strength from his many clients over the years, but never to fruition. And when he'd agreed to take Wynter on as a charge, he hadn't presumed this time would be any different. None had lasted long enough to see the process through until the very end.

None but her.

Like with all his other contracts, the Priestess had hired him on the proviso that it would never happen. He'd been assured that Wynter would be sired before he could drain her essence entirely and turn her into a Jinni, but the human girl had proven too strong for both the witch and her master. She had resisted them and taken a wholly different path, and now, because of that, she had given him true life because of her actions. Brodie could've never seen it coming.

He looked down at the bracelet around his wrist as he drove. The black beads were just trinkets, a symbolic ode to his black misty form, but the white bead was the key. It showed him just how strong Wynter was, and at present, the white mist within was barely even there. She had a long way to go before she would be whole, and Brodie would have to give up his human form so that she could live again. Plenty of time to allow him the chance to get some payback.

He stopped the hire car just long enough to switch to another hired ride, this one an executive saloon, complete with driver. He made out his friend was passed out drunk, and bundled Jakob into the back seat before their driver headed directly for the airstrip.

They sailed straight through the checkpoints reserved for humans and lesser beings without stopping. Those sorts of control checks and regulations were not for the likes of him. He might not have been wholly present for hundreds of years, but his affairs had always remained in order.

Brodie had no debts, only assets, and he had managed them well from afar with ease. It was precisely the reason he was headed to this particular airstrip in the first place. He owned a helicopter charter company outright and so ordered the driver to pull up right beside one of his most expensive choppers. This would do nicely.

Brodie liked the finer things in life. He'd always strived to have the best, and even though he hadn't been whole for an incredible amount of time, he still had everything he needed close at hand. The clothes he'd chosen to materialise upon himself were perfect. His black hair was, of course, quaffed to perfection, and while he was tall and slender, he made sure not to look down on anyone. Arrogance was not a fine trait in his eyes.

"Good afternoon, sir. Welcome back," one of the attendants said when he spotted him, and he greeted Brodie with a broad, practised smile. He'd never met the young attendant before, but the jinni knew exactly how the man standing before him, along with all the others who worked for his company, had been briefed for when the time came for the illustrious Mr Brodie Cruikshank chose to appear. They had been given a description of his appearance and knew not to ask questions other than to offer their help, or else face instant dismissal from their reclusive boss.

He was a phantom, after all. A ghost. He'd never been present during meetings, and except for the odd visit in his misty form when he'd remain invisible, Brodie would liaise purely via the telephone or on email. Humans weren't allowed to see the truth about what he was, and probably never would be. But still, Brodie had made sure that every single one of his employees knew his face and how, if he visited, they should approach only to see if he needed anything from them. And in this instance, he did indeed need one thing from the human standing in wait of a response, and so the jinni simply offered him a polite nod.

"I have some cargo in the back seat. Be a dear and load it for me, would you," he told the young man, who got the shock of his life when he opened the door and found what he clearly thought was a dead man laying strewn across the back seat.

He did the right thing and didn't say a word as he acted exactly as Brodie had ordered, and with an audible deal of exertion, he lifted the limp vampire up and out of the car. He then also heard his new aide breathe a sigh of relief when Jakob stirred and groaned as he was being strapped in.

He began mumbling something in Russian the boy didn't understand, but it didn't matter. One word stood out loud and proud.

"Wynter," Jakob croaked in his accented way of pronouncing her name. "Where is she?"

It'd be sweet if he wasn't continually being such a damn nuisance by waking up before Brodie was ready to deal with him. "Wynter…"

Brodie was still doing his pre-flight checks, so he shouted to his new assistant.

"Tell him she's alive. Tell him everything is going to be okay," he said, and then an idea struck him. Where they were going would be no humans for Jakob to drink from and that simply wouldn't do. He could survive months without it, but his body and mind would go into a sort of frenzy before he would then lose himself, becoming nothing more than a mindless brute. For Wynter's sake, Brodie couldn't allow that, plus he needed him sound of mind so that his torture wouldn't go on the back pedal to his hunger.

"It's okay, she's alive," he heard the boy saying, and Brodie could tell it was sinking in. Jakob was still very much out of it, but he was coming around, and fast. Back to a world in which his precious Wynter was no longer his human soul mate, but a jinni. A creature stronger and more powerful than even him—the notorious vampire assassin. The devil of the night who took any life if he was paid handsomely enough.

Did he so much as ask why? Did he even care? Brodie seethed just thinking about their shared past again and he moved faster. He wanted that vampire strung up and in some of the agony Brodie had been forced to suffer, and as soon as possible.

"Come with us," he then told the boy, whom he swung around to face him. The young man opened his mouth as if to answer, but he didn't let him. "He needs you to care for him in ways I cannot. We'll be gone for a while. Three years, five at the most, and I'll pay you handsomely for it."

Brodie could tell he was keen, he just needed one last push. And he was more than willing to give him it. "I'm talking millions. You'll walk away with more money than you'll ever need for just a few years of giving yourself over to a job I can assure you won't be like anything you could imagine. I have a secret task for you, and a way of helping your fellow man. What do you say?"

Desire flashed between the boy's eyes, and Brodie knew he had him. Men of this time always wanted to be the hero. They wanted to save the world, or blow shit up, and whichever way his mind was working, his new comrade was definitely on the hook.

"I'm in, just let me go home and tell my mum—"

"There's no time for that," Brodie cut him off. "You can call her from the chopper and I'll buy you everything you need. This is incognito, my friend. We're talking national security kind of stuff. Are you in or out Mr...?"

"Just call me Archie, and yeah, I'm in," he answered in his Scottish twang. He then puffed his chest as though the fate of the world had just come to his doorstep, and he'd gladly answered its call.

Brodie reacted with a smile as he gave Archie a leg up into the helicopter beside the still groaning Jakob.

"Good," he told him and then hesitated for a second before closing him in. "Now be a good lad, Archie, and snap his neck will you."

FOURTEEN

The chopper was low as Brodie piloted it out and over the Irish Sea. He headed south, and Archie stared ahead, watching as they headed out into the unknown. He still had no idea where they were even headed or why and was beginning to wonder whether he'd made the right choice saying yes to the billionaire boss he'd heard of and spoken with over the phone, but never seen before. The infamous recluse had finally shown himself after all this time, and he had certainly appeared with a bang. He had given him a mission. A purpose. And Archie had accepted, but now that the dust was settling and they were in the air and heading farther from home, he began panicking.

At just twenty-three years old, Archie had finished university a couple years before and wanted to become a pilot himself, but he'd lacked the funds to get himself there and so had taken a job at the airfield as a flight controller in the hopes of someday being given the chance to learn to fly without the two-hundred-grand price tag. So far, though, he'd never once been in a chopper other than when in the back seat. So much for living the dream.

Mr Cruikshank, having turned up unannounced, had been a surprise, but then he'd offered him a job just as long as he upped and left then and there. Cryptic and vague. It was definitely some kind of spy stuff, and Archie wondered if his boss might be some kind of MI6 agent or something. That would explain the secrecy. In a moment of daring, he had accepted, but still needed to know more.

He just hoped this was indeed the chance of a lifetime it'd been painted to be. The opportunity to finally get the recognition he deserved and, of course, the offered wages in recompense. Millions, or so Mr Cruikshank had said. That would be life changing.

Pointedly ignoring the unconscious man strapped into the back seat behind them, he turned to his boss and frowned. Was it the time or the place to start asking questions? He didn't know, so just opted for filling the silence at least.

"Mr Cruikshank, where are we heading?" he said into the microphone built into his headset, and almost gave up when he initially didn't answer.

"An island just north of Anglesey," he eventually replied shortly, "and please call me Brodie."

He wasn't sure about that, but figured it'd be best if they were on a first name basis.

"Sure. And what's there?"

"The next few years of your life, Archie. Now please, call your mother and tell her how an amazing opportunity has come your way, but do not tell her where you're going or who with. And then keep quiet," Brodie answered before throwing him a satellite phone, and while he was disappointed at being shot down, Archie did as he'd demanded.

So, Brodie wasn't the talkative type? That was fine. If this worked out, then it'd be well worth it, which was exactly what he told his mum when he eventually got through to her. She wasn't at all pleased with him for having run off without a word but agreed to let it slide and keep things ticking over for him back at home. He was still living with her and his dad, so there wasn't much in the way of admin to sort out, plus the only pain was that his car would need collecting from the airfield, but his dad would easily sort that out.

It was quite simple, really. So easy to walk away from his life. Almost too easy.

Archie was single and had no debts or ties to anywhere or anything. He was the perfect accolade for Brodie to have plucked from that airfield and he had to wonder if the powerful man had somehow known? No, that was impossible. People like him didn't do that kind of research into their employees. He'd simply been in the right place at the right time. That was all.

Archie ended the call and handed the phone back to him as directed, and Brodie stashed it in his pocket and just continued to stare ahead stoically. He forced himself to do the same and watched as the ocean slowly turned lighter beneath them. He could even see land to his left.

The helicopter descended a little and Archie didn't need to ask why. They were approaching their destination, which appeared to be a small cluster of islands cut off from the mainland and presumably private. There was a lighthouse on the biggest one, but they carried on past it and came to land in a small field on the next island over. It was only once they were there that he saw the small shelter built onto the side of the nearby cliff edge. The perfect hiding spot.

When Brodie had finished his final checks, the pair of them disembarked the chopper and Archie unbuckled their passenger. He was about to ask what to do with him, when Brodie slung him over his shoulder as if he weighed nothing at all, and then started off in the direction of the craggy cliff edge facing the ocean.

It was a challenging climb down the weatherworn path, but Archie didn't complain. After all, Brodie was still carrying almost a hundred kilos worth of unconscious weight on his back without moaning, and so he didn't want to come across as some kind of pussy just because he was wearing the wrong sort of shoes for a hike. And no coat. Plus, he had no water or food.

Damn, this wasn't looking good.

When they finally came to a stop by a small flat area of overgrown stone, Archie figured it must be for a rest at long last, but then Brodie turned and brushed away some moss overhanging an opening in the rocks. The move revealed a dark fissure, and a cold shudder suddenly swept down his back.

"Where the hell are we going?" Archie finally called as his guide disappeared behind and into what was presumably a cave beyond. This was getting silly now.

"Just get in here, dammit," Brodie barked in answer, and Archie knew he had no choice other than to follow him. He just hoped he wasn't about to fall to his death down some old, abandoned mineshaft or pothole. He'd seen more than his share of horror movies and knew it wasn't the best idea to go clambering around in dark caves.

He begrudgingly left the sunlight behind and moved into the damp cave, but then was surprised to find it quite light inside. The opening to the cave was small, but just a few feet in he found it opened out into a huge cavern and the many holes in the rock face were streaming with sunlight.

"Sorry," he muttered as he reached his scowling boss, and then didn't delay in following him deeper into the cave.

Up ahead, he could see something reflecting the sun's rays, and as they neared it Archie realised it was glass. Thick and presumably reinforced sheets of it were built into the cave, and as he took it all in, he also spied wrought iron beams and bars securing the structure from the inside. Was it some kind of underground bunker? Brodie had said back at the airfield how this was a matter of national security, and Archie envisioned a team of spies working on official secrets ahead or perhaps a safe house for bureaucrats and those under the protection of the government, or something like that.

It turned out it was nothing more than a kind of house. The building was still impressive, but as Brodie showed Archie inside, it soon became clear how they were actually the only people on the island. It was like some kind of secluded, forgotten habitat that had been separated from the rest of the world. There had to be a reason, and Archie was beginning to wonder if he wanted to discover it or not.

Behind the initial glass walls were proper dividers that created a strange layout inside. Rooms were built around the stone and glass, and while it was the strangest place he'd ever seen, it was still a homely structure all the same.

Inside, he found there was a state-of-the-art kitchen, and a decked out living room with a huge TV built into one of the walls, which was surrounded by speakers and high-grade electronics. Movies and books lined every wall and as Archie browsed the titles, he was surprised to find a ton of current choices. It was as if this collection was regularly updated, and yet the place didn't seem lived in at all. The house was spotless, though. Not a speck of dust in sight or a thing out of place. Someone had to have been taking care of it. Someone who was a fan of Harry Potter and Lord of the Rings marathons.

"The bedrooms and bathrooms are through there," Brodie then told him, breaking the silence at last, "choose whichever one you want. I'll be back later."

"Which is yours?" he replied, not wanting to inadvertently go for the wrong one and step on his boss's toes.

"I don't sleep," Brodie replied with a shrug, before turning and hauling the still unconscious man back over his shoulder out the way they'd came.

What did he mean, he doesn't sleep? Everyone had to rest sometime. Archie wanted to call after him again and ask for more details, but he already knew the man of few words wouldn't give him any. He would just have to bide his time and wait for the chance to get some proper answers out of him when the moment was right. But first, he guessed it was time to pick a room and then raid the kitchen for something to eat.

***

Jakob was consciously aware of his surroundings for a short while before fully coming to but couldn't move until his body had fully healed from yet another snap of his neck to render him immobile. He was about ready to throttle that fucking jinni, but of course had other things on his mind first. Wynter. He remembered someone telling him she was safe, but he didn't trust them, whoever they were. He needed to see her for himself. To hear her voice.

As the last of his bones finally fused together, he snapped back to reality and jumped up from where he'd been dumped unceremoniously on the floor. He sprung up onto his feet, like a jack-in-the-box at the end of its hiding song, but could go no further than the few square feet of space he'd awoken in.

He peered around, expecting to have found himself in a cheap hotel or some run down building. Somewhere Brodie had intended to hide them all for the time being, but instead found that it was a cave.

The blackness all around was initially intimidating, but Jakob's keen senses soon took over and he was able to see through it with ease. See down into the depths that probably ended at the sea one way, and towards a small shard of light the other. But he could go in neither direction thanks to the old iron bars built into the walls of the dark cave that were blocking his way.

They were enchanted and had to have been there for hundreds of years and, given by the stench of death all around, used regularly to keep people prisoner. Those who'd then never seen the light of day again.

He could sense them. Smell the desecrated remains of their flesh and bone and feel the anguish and agony they'd felt before passing. Something told Jakob that if he went exploring, he'd find a pile of bones somewhere to confirm his suspicions. Bodies of the dead for old for crimes he might never discover, but the vampire knew to trust his senses. And to use them wisely.

Something was very wrong, clearly, but he wasn't going to lash out at or try to run from his captor. No, he was going to reason with him. Or bargain. Whatever worked would be worth it. Brodie must want something, and if his soul mate's life was connected to his, Jakob was willing to negotiate.

"She begged me to keep you alive," a voice echoed through the darkness, and while Jak hadn't heard Brodie's voice much before, he knew exactly who it was.

"And so you did, jinni," he answered, looking around for the creature he knew was lurking somewhere out of his sights. "Freed us from Marcus and his clutches, as well as the Priestess. But why keep me incapacitated and then lock me in a cage?"

"Because I indulged her for her own good, but also partly for my own reasons. I would have gladly left you for dead at the hands of our previous employer, but like you, Wynter and I are bonded. She is one of my kind now and lives inside of me, and so I am sworn to protect her."

Shit. He hadn't wanted to hear that. She had become one of them. A jinni. His darling Wynter was no longer human, but a monster in the making. It didn't stop him from loving her, and Jakob vowed to himself that he would always lead her away from the darkness Brodie would lure her towards. Even Jinn were capable of good. All creatures were, if given the right guidance.

"You protect her, and that includes me too, I bet," Jakob finished for him, and the jinni grumbled in affirmation.

"But that doesn't mean you'll have it easy in my care. Especially after what you took from me," Brodie cried out into the darkness between them, and Jakob knew exactly what he was getting at. The assassin remembered every kill. Every life he'd taken. Each light snuffed out by his hand.

"I've killed only one jinni in all my years," he said into the pitch-black emptiness ahead, "a female. One who murdered women for sport and men for fun."

"Lies!" Brodie cried, appearing from the shadows, just as Jakob had hoped. He'd wanted to entice him out of the darkness, and it wasn't hard to know what would set him off.

Jak looked him up and down. He was a man now, or at least in male form. This meant he had garnered enough strength from his previous host to become whole, and there was only one way that could have happened. He hadn't been lying before. Wynter had indeed become one of them. She had died as a human, only to be reborn as a jinni, but she wasn't truly alive. She needed to recover from her death and the transformation. She was merely present, not necessarily living.

And yet, he felt her there with them. Sensed her as though she were standing just inches away, and Jak was drawn to the spirit he so adored. But it wasn't her, it was her host, and it appeared he was determined to make Jakob pay for a life he had taken a century earlier.

"I don't lie, Brodie. I saw her do it. Watched her seduce the innocent and tempt those who had already sinned into doing so again," he demanded, and then grabbed at the bars separating him from the jinni so that they were almost nose-to-nose. "You were blind to her actions, but that doesn't mean she did not do them. Your wife was corrupt. She was evil. And she had to be stopped."

Brodie turned to that black mist Jakob had seen him embody before. He did it just long enough so that he could move through the iron bars and then rematerialize inside the cell with him, and Jakob knew for sure then what the jinni wanted. He also knew he had no hope of stopping him should he decide that it was time for the vampire to finally die, but he just had to hope Brodie taking his vengeance would suffice, rather than him taking his life.

He could take any torture. Withstand being starved or beaten. He had been there, done that, and gotten the t-shirt—so to speak.

"Regardless of what she became, Ada was still my wife. My soul mate. And you took her from me," Brodie countered, and Jakob simply nodded. There was no use in denying it. "So you shall pay."

"And Wynter?" Jakob asked, and he peered down at Brodie's chest where, if the stories were real, his true love now lived.

"I'm forcing her to watch," he replied with a sneer, confirming Jakob's suspicions, "I control our lives for now. I call the shots while she gathers her strength, and I say you spend my cycle alone and suffering for your crimes. I will starve you, beat you, and drive you to the brink of madness. And only when I am convinced you've repented, will I release you from this prison and do the same with your soul mate."

"Then what are you waiting for?" Jakob chided, "I'm not going to beg or plead. Let's just get this over with. None of us are getting any younger..."

***

Wynter tried not to watch him exact his revenge. Not to scream and shout from her own prison as she saw the gory scene unfold through the only pair of eyes she could access. And the body she could neither influence nor command. Front row seats to the most violent and sadistic show she could ever imagine.

Brodie had been inside her heart for weeks and had showed her such kindness, but now the rose-tinted glasses were gone, and she could see he truly was a cruel and hardened soul. He showed no empathy towards Jakob, and no remorse for all the times he pummelled him senseless. He beat her darling black and blue and then watched as his vampire body began to heal itself before starting all over again.

And again.

And then again.

It was torture for her too, like some sort of never-ending loop.

No matter what bargains she screamed up into Brodie's mind, he refused her pleas, and she had nothing to negotiate with. No leverage. No case to plead in his honour.

Jakob had wronged Brodie and against all her once human instincts, Wynter knew she had to let him have his revenge. She retreated as far back into her confined space as she could and focused on getting better. On healing and growing stronger. This way she would be free faster, and in doing so could free her soul mate. She tried to drain as much of Brodie's life force as she could, being selfish and driven, but only because he'd forced her to.

And then, after two months of nothing but violence, something shifted in her soul. At first, Wynter thought it might be a sign of her renewed strength, but soon knew she was wrong when an ache began radiating from inside of her, and she was suddenly terrified.

She called out to her host for the first time in weeks, but Brodie didn't stop his beatings. He didn't release his grip on Jakob's bloody carcass. He kept on hitting him, crushing his bones with every punch, his rage still as prevalent as it was weeks before. He seemed lost to his vindictive need to punish him, and everything was suddenly clear.

Something sprung to life within her at seeing the horrifying scene unfold. It was primitive and raw. Something older and stronger than both the vampire lying beaten on the cold, hard ground and the jinni delivering the punishment.

"Stop!" she cried with force, and suddenly, she was watching the events from a wholly different angle. Not from behind Brodie's eyes, but from beside him. She had somehow left the confines of her home within him and was outside in the world for the first time since falling to her death and away from Marcus's hold.

She screamed to him again and watched as Brodie tried not to listen. He attempted to ignore her, but Wynter could tell he was losing his battle of wills. He had felt the change too and so dropped Jakob to the ground with a thud.

He turned to peer into what Wynter knew weren't her eyes but was still a sort of face. She wasn't whole, but she was still there with them. She was present and had somehow been strong enough to step in and protect the man she loved when he'd needed her.

"Don't do this, Wynter. Don't stop me," Brodie tried, but she shook her head no. She reached out a hand to her saviour and the friend she'd once thought he had become and saw for herself that she was just as she'd imagined—nothing but whitish mist. But she'd had to intervene.

Regardless of the promise she'd made to let him have his revenge, she wasn't going to let him kill Jakob, because she knew that was exactly where today's beatings were taking them. She'd felt her heart starting to break with the impending loss and knew it wasn't just a warning, but death coming for her too. No matter her new powers, their souls had merged before her transformation and so she knew that if Jakob died, she would follow him. And rightly so.

"You promised me," she whispered, and Brodie bared his teeth and answered with a growl, "he shares my soul and you cannot take his life without also taking mine," Wynter reminded him.

"I can control myself," he snapped, but she didn't believe it. He could, but he'd chosen not to. Chosen to let his primitive urges rule him, instead of seeing sense. And he'd let it go too far. Why else could she have summoned the strength to emerge from her cocoon if not to save Jakob in his hour of need? Brodie had needed to be stopped, and she was the only one capable of making sure he did so.

"Not this time, Brodie. I can feel my heart breaking. My soul is shattering because of you. If you do not stop, then you'll kill him, and me as well," she whimpered, having opted for a more heartfelt approach, but it didn't seem to be working.

Brodie reached down and gathered Jakob's limp body in his grip, as though ready to rain down more blows, but then he suddenly stopped and let out a sob.

"You think I don't feel it too?" he then whispered, shaking his head as though dismayed, and she was sure she saw his eyes welling with tears he'd undoubtedly refuse to ever shed over the vampire in his grasp. He was trying not to show it, but he felt remorse for what he'd done to him. She could tell.

He sighed deeply and then let out another pained growl. "When your soul merged with his, I was there. I was a part of you, Wynter. I felt it too."

"What are you saying?" she demanded.

She needed to know more but knew there wasn't enough time. She'd done her part and had saved Jakob's life. But now, her strength was starting to dissipate. She needed to return to her home and cursed her strength for being so quick to wane.

Brodie backed off and left Jakob to lie down on the ground again, and then he stared into her misty face, his green eyes still pained.

"I can feel my own heart breaking along with yours. It's as though I have been forced to care about him as well," he answered, and finally showed his surprise. He then stared at her as if she were whole, his brows furrowed, showing how the situation had him flummoxed for the very first time. But then another look crossed his face, like he was finally starting to see sense. "Either that or it's you. Your soul opened up and accepted his during the merging. Could it be possible it accepted part of mine at the same time? That we too are linked?"

"No!" cried Jakob, who appeared to be coming back around, "it's not possible."

"It would actually make a lot of sense," Wynter conceded, and she wanted to talk more but could feel herself beginning to melt away. She held on as long as she could, though, just long enough to reach for Jakob and feel his flesh against the palm she imagined was once again whole.

"I love you, Wynter," he demanded through his haze of pain, "only you."

"I know. And I love you too," she replied, her voice barely a whisper on the wind as she sunk back beneath the layers of flesh and bone within Brodie's chest. "Try it my way, please. Take care of him instead of this merciless cruelty. Become his friend and not his enemy. For all our sakes, find a way to forgive him," Wynter then cried out, her voice only audible to the one creature whose heart she had to call a home.

But he still didn't want to listen.

Brodie walked away without a word to either of them, but at least this way, Jak could rest. He could recuperate in peace rather than in anticipation of the next round of beatings, and she would work on her jinni friend.

FIFTEEN

Brodie didn't return to Jakob for weeks. He instead spent the time at the house, pretending to be busy so he didn't have to entertain the poor bored boy he'd invited to the island. It wasn't that he didn't like Archie, far from it, but he was too fixated on his mission for revenge to let anything, or anyone, else in. All he wanted was to head back down into the cave and end Jakob's sorry life, once and for all. The only thing holding him back was Wynter. Doing so would kill her too, so he'd have to endure Jak's presence. At least she had left him alone like she'd promised, but of course, was still there. Always watching through his eyes and reading his thoughts, just like he had when he'd been gaining strength within the confines of her heart.

It was just one of the factors involved when being a jinni. You became one with your host. No lies. No covering the truth, just complete and utter honesty, and of course a connection that, when cultivated over years, left the two Jinn inseparable. It was not only because of the necessity for one to shelter the other, but because a bond would form. And that was what was happening between them now.

Through the good and the bad, Brodie would have to let her in on everything he felt and thought. Even the vile contemplations he had of murdering her beloved. Or more recently, the sordid thoughts he was increasingly having about her, and the crazy fantasies that included both Wynter and Jakob with him in some kind of ménage situation. He still hated the vampire, but thanks to her, he was seeing him differently these days. Seeing him through her eyes and feeling what she had felt.

Damn her and the soul within him that was so in love with the vampire captive he had hoped to torture for way longer than just a few months.

"This is why I shouldn't have taken on a female client," he growled at his reflection in the mirrored glass one morning, talking to her, "you're making me soft!"

"Who are you talking to?" Archie asked from behind, and Brodie turned to him with probably the first smile he'd ever given the poor young thing. He'd barely said a word to him since they'd arrived and had left him to his movie marathons and training sessions while doing his own thing with Jak, but now he was purposely avoiding his captive and so had been spending a decent amount of time at the house.

And he'd found himself watching Archie, finding that he was interested in how he filled his days. He worked out a lot, and Brodie could already see the results for himself. He also couldn't blame the poor guy. It wasn't like he had much else to do, at least not while Jakob was still being denied a feed and while the housekeeper, Rafferty, was on hand to keep the island home neat and tidied.

Thinking of him, Brodie had to wonder if Archie had even realised there was someone else on the island with them yet. Surely he had seen for himself how the house was tended to? Always spotless and without a thing out of place? He wasn't sure, if he were honest, and then came to realise he'd never actually given Archie a proper run-down on just who he was living with and why. It was time he discovered the truth. Plus, Jak needed feeding as well...

"You want to know who I was talking to?" he asked and then laughed to himself, "well, I was talking to the woman who lives inside of me," he answered, and then grinned when Archie burst out laughing at the strange response. He clearly thought Brodie was joking, either that or going mad, and he eyed him like he couldn't be sure just which.

"No, really..."

"Really," Brodie reiterated, and he dropped his smile, turning deadly serious. "I never did tell you the real reason why we're here, did I?"

"No, and I gave up waiting, if I'm honest," Archie answered curtly, and Brodie had to give him some credit on that count. He really had been courteous enough to leave him alone, and he was quite impressed. Not many humans would just let something as important as that go for all these weeks. Their curiosity would've gotten the better of them.

"But you feel safe here? You trust that there's a reason for all of this?" Brodie replied, and he used his hand to indicate to the cavern all around them. Archie nodded resolutely. "Okay, if you say you're ready, then let's do this..."

Brodie led him into the kitchen, where he insisted Archie have something to eat. He then watched him prepare some porridge, and then eat it while he told him all about the two jinni's and vampire in his company. He seemed to think it was a prank at first, but then it appeared the story finally started to make sense. Archie's eyes suddenly opened wide, and he dropped his spoon into the half-full bowl with a gloopy clang.

"That was why you broke his neck, so you could subdue him? I did wonder how he'd survived that, and how you could carry him so far without breaking a sweat!" he cried, "and why neither of you sleep. Or eat..."

"Yeah, about that," Brodie interjected. "I'm gonna need you to start doing the job I brought you here for. Jakob needs to eat."

"Well, I'm living on ration packs, biscuits and berries and such. You want me to take him some?" he answered, and Brodie shook his head. Such a naïve young man his guest was.

"No, he needs human blood. Your blood."

"Ah shit," Archie grumbled, pushing his discarded food away.

How had he not realised the moment Brodie had told him what Jakob was? He blamed the media. The fool probably believed there was a substitute for the vein, or a choice. But there was none. Jak would either feed or starve to death, and as much as Brodie was happy to deny him too regular feeds, he knew he couldn't withhold it forever. "I knew there had to be a catch. Of course, I wasn't here to just chill out and do my thing, but I never once thought that might be the reason. Please tell me it's all just a joke?"

Brodie shook his head.

"And what did you think I wanted from you?" he enquired, genuinely interested in what the hell else Archie might think he'd offered to pay him so handsomely for.

"I dunno. I guess I thought you were a spy, and we were lying low while you interrogated your hostage. Maybe I'd be here to clean up your mess or be your bitch or something? Or become like a protégé…"

Brodie took another look around the spotless house and Archie followed his gaze, his brows furrowed. "Yeah, I can see for myself how this place is never dirty, but I didn't mean that sort of mess. How the hell do you even manage it?" he asked, and Brodie had to laugh.

"I don't do a thing. I have a man for that. Someone who has been here since long before you arrived and will stay for centuries more…"

"Another captive?"

"More like another employee, but unlike you, this one will never age and outgrow his purpose. His name is Rafferty and without him this island hideaway would never have become the safe haven it is today, or such a stronghold so that I can go about my business in peace."

"You are too kind, sir," a deep voice rumbled from the doorway and Archie immediately jumped out of his skin. Brodie knew then how he really hadn't had any idea who else was in the house with him and laughed again.

What a morning this was turning out to be!

***

Archie couldn't deny he'd wondered. Even back on his first night on the island, he'd used the kitchen to make some supper and had gone back later that evening to clean up, only to find the dishes already washed and put away. He'd been sure someone else was there, but for some reason they'd remained out of sight, and since then he'd tested the theory countless times. Leaving clothes strewn on the ground while he took a shower that had been moved to the washer by the time he'd finished. Moving ornaments and returning mere moments later to find them back in place. Someone was there with him, and while it'd both irked him and made him question his sanity at times, it was good to know he'd been right all along.

He turned around to look at the man who'd just spoken, and yet he saw nothing. Like always, not a thing was out of place and there were no clues as to whom had just replied to Brodie's glowing account of whose job it was to keep the island house up and running.

"Who said that?" Archie cried, and he began to feel riled when Brodie then started to laugh, seemingly at his expense. "Seriously!"

Brodie finally finished his laughing fit, and he looked behind Archie with a smile.

"Rafferty," he answered, "like I told you…"

Archie turned back and saw nobody there again, but then, as he continued to stare at the empty space, he heard the voice again. Someone spoke as if he truly was right beside him, and he jumped again.

"I'm afraid humans cannot see me, at least not when looking directly. I'm invisible to the human eye unless a witch or warlock has given you the gift of sight, and I realised when you arrived how you hadn't been. I'm afraid you will continue not to see me, which is why I chose not to speak with you either as I didn't want to put you on edge."

"To be honest, I'm relieved," Archie admitted, still looking around for where he thought Rafferty had to be standing. "I was beginning to think I might be mad!"

"Far from it. I shan't be silent now and will forewarn you of my presence in future," Rafferty replied, and then he seemed to direct his attention to Brodie. "Jakob needs nourishment, sir. I have just come from his cell and he's delirious with hunger now that he has healed from the interrogations."

Archie swallowed the lump in his throat and he looked at Brodie, watching as his face turned vacant for a moment. And then he sort of twitched, and it was odd to watch him.

"All right, dammit woman!" he then hollered and shot to his feet.

"Huh?" Archie replied, thinking Rafferty was clearly a male just as he was, and Brodie seemed to register his question without needing to be expressly asked.

"I told you, there is a female jinni who lives within me. That wasn't a lie. And the vampire you helped me stow away to this island is her soul mate. She's giving me hell in here," he said, tapping his head to intimate that she was somehow speaking to him inside of his mind.

This really was just getting weirder and weirder.

"So you don't live in little lamps like in the movies?" Archie asked with a hint of mirth, trying desperately to take Brodie seriously when all he wanted to do was laugh.

"Far from it. And don't get me started on the nonsense about us supposedly granting wishes! We're powerful, of course, but only for short periods of time. We are forced to live off the strength of another being. We reside within them until strong enough to become whole."

"So that's what she is doing with you, but now she wants you to help him?" he asked and then fell silent as he came to terms with what that meant.

"Yep, and that means serving you up for dinner, I'm afraid…"

Archie opened his mouth to argue, but Brodie lifted his hand to halt him. "Just a few drops. I promise. I told you, I'm keeping him alive, but that doesn't mean he needs to be fully satiated. In fact, I won't even let him take it straight from your vein."

He then grabbed a carving knife and a mug from the kitchen cupboard, and indicated that Archie go with him. He had the suspicion he didn't really have much of a choice in the matter, but went willingly anyway in a bid to prove he wasn't a coward.

He climbed to his feet and followed Brodie out the door and down into the darkness of the cave beyond the house. The only part of the island he'd not yet begun to explore.

As they descended, all he could think was how he was walking down there to go and feed a vampire. A fucking vampire! Like in the movies, but then not at all. There was no glamour. Just a real and bloody mess ahead. And blood.

His blood.

Archie stopped and peered back up towards the house, and then his eyes darted to the entrance to the cave itself. He'd been out there many times now. He knew the way up to where the helicopter was still stored safely away. Maybe he could run to it? Take the chopper and figure out what to do next?

A shadow passed him, and at first Archie thought it was a trick of the light, like a manifestation of his fear. But then the shadow solidified, somehow turning into a man.

"Christ!" he cried, staring up at Brodie in surprise.

"Come on, don't be a pussy," the jinni challenged, and a grin spread across his face.

"If I'm gonna do this, I want something in return," he replied, and then stopped him before Brodie could reply about money. "I clearly don't need the cash here, but I do want something."

"What? I'm sure it can be arranged?"

"Teach me to fly," he asked, "I know between torturing the vampire back there and actively ignoring me, you're pretty booked up, but how about we change that? Make some better use of our time?"

Brodie seemed impressed. He stepped closer and Archie felt his heart race a little. Yes, he was a little intimidated by him, but that wasn't why he'd responded in such a way. It'd been so long since anyone had gotten close, least of all a tall, dark and handsome stranger, and it was hard not to react to him.

"We'll see," the jinni whispered, and then twitched like he had earlier, as if the woman inside his head had just shouted something.

"Or you could just send *her* out? She seems chatty?" Archie replied and was relieved when Brodie saw the funny side. He creased up laughing and then clapped him on the shoulder.

"You know what? Maybe I'm beginning to like you after all…" he said, and then turned him back towards the darkness below. "Do as I ask and I'll give you your lessons. If you can squeeze it in between movie marathons with Rafferty, of course?"

SIXTEEN

Marcus paced the room and stared down at the carnage on the floor of his office at *Slave*. Dead bodies littered the entire storey and yet he cared not one little bit. Regardless of his usual preference for the untouched vein, he'd drunk his fill of tainted blood over the past few months since Wynter had evaded him. Since she had let herself die and be reborn as a goddamn jinni. He hadn't been able to stop himself, and yet nothing was quenching the desperate thirst he still had for her.

The stupid girl. The foolish, insolent little bitch. If only she'd let him turn her himself, they'd be together now, but instead, she had chosen to merge her soul with that loathsome boy. The assassin. He couldn't even bring himself to think his name.

In his rage he had lost all of his once precious humanity and had laid waste to almost the entire staff list in his employ at this club. Thanks to their cursed souls, not even one had denied him his fill, and it'd been so easy to drain each of them dry. His hordes had been fed well too, but now there were none left at *Slave* but his managers. Not Patrick, who had succumbed to his sickness a few days before and had offered himself to the alpha of his sired horde, but Jack and Joanna remained, and were the only two living humans in the entire building. Marcus would keep them, for now.

He would, however, burn the place to the ground and blame it all on an arson attack or faulty wiring. Whatever kept the insurance investigators sweet so he could make a claim and start over. All the bodies would remain inside, their deaths also put down to the tragic fire.

And then he would be free to continue his search. To push his hordes to trace even the slightest scent of her. To close in on Brodie's ties to the human world and find out where the hell that damn jinni had taken her. There had to be some clue they'd overlooked. A stone left unturned.

The human girl Marcus had ensnared was no more, that was clear, but it didn't mean this was over. Far from it. He wasn't the sort of person to let any kind of wrongdoing slide. And he sure had been wronged. He might even be broken hearted—if he had one—and found he missed everything about her regardless of his repeatedly telling himself not to.

He missed Wynter's company and the emotions she had stirred in him. Even the way he'd wanted her so. It'd kept him going. Made him whole.

Marcus also found himself wondering how could he miss someone who'd made him so crazy? An infuriating counterpart who challenged instead of feared him? Resisted rather than obey? And yet he did.

Regardless of her pertinence, he wanted her still and would do whatever it took to have her back. Dead or alive.

***

By the time Brodie made his reappearance by his cell, Jakob was clearly delirious after his extended isolation and seemed senseless with hunger. The moment he spotted the human standing by the jinni's side he lunged for the bars, his hand outstretched in the hope he might get his hands on the much needed nourishment flowing through his veins, and Brodie flinched, along with poor Archie behind him.

All games aside, it was clear he needed sustenance and that all niceties were completely out the window.

"Not so fast," Brodie teased, finding great satisfaction in watching Jakob squirm. He had to be starving. His eyes were wide, and he seemed quite feverish, as though he were sweating out an infection or coming through the final stages of some kind of sickness. But he couldn't be sick. Vampires didn't get ill. They thrived even when starving. They were strong and endured, and would find a way to continue to walk this earth long after humanity was done with it. Just like the Jinn.

Shit, there he went, feeling sorry for the guy again, and he cursed the voice echoing in his head.

Brodie turned away and walked back to the frightened human in his care. "I won't let him hurt you," he told him, but then plucked the knife from his pocket and reached for Archie's palm. "However, he must feed otherwise his body will shut down. He'll eventually go into a kind of stasis and if that happens, he'll lose all his humanity. He'd become nothing more than a monster who wouldn't hesitate to drain you dry."

Brodie then sliced a small cut in Archie's skin to open his vein, and then he placed the mug he'd also taken from the kitchen beneath to collect the small amount of blood trickling from the wound. To his credit, the young man didn't flinch or try to stop him. Archie understood what was needed and readily gave it. He simply watched the blood flow and fill just a quarter of the cup, but when Brodie released his grip, there was a clear sigh of relief as he pulled his hand back and applied pressure to the cut. "You can go back to the house if you'd like," Brodie offered, but Archie shook his head.

"If this is really happening, I need to see. I need to know what I'm dealing with."

"Very well," Brodie answered, and was impressed by his strength. He then handed the cup to Jak, who swiftly drank down the blood within and licked the mug clean. He then sunk back and onto the ground, watching Archie with a determined look on his face. He wanted more, it was clear, and now that he'd tasted him, they were connected in ways no one could possibly explain.

Brodie found the interaction intriguing. A cold-blooded killer was staring up at the one source of satisfaction he knew was available to him. He was desperate for more and could easily begin begging for it or plotting a way to escape so he could drain him dry, and yet something else seemed to be going through his head.

Jak wasn't soulless. Brodie knew that more than anyone now that he'd lived through watching him merge with his host, and a thought occurred to him. He perhaps wasn't the monster Brodie had always thought.

It appeared he didn't want to scare Archie, even though he had to be eager for more of his blood. Instead of using his predatory nature, he was instead remaining calm and seemingly at peace with the small offering Archie had given. Was he grateful? It appeared so.

He had more self-control than Brodie would've ever imagined.

"Thank you," he then whispered to Archie gruffly before staring up into his captor's eyes pleadingly. "Please tell me, is she okay?"

The jinni was taken aback once more.

"Why wouldn't she be?" he demanded, stepping away from the bars in surprise. Wynter was growing stronger every day thanks to Brodie, and Jakob knew that. He had seen her materialise with his own eyes. Felt her touch. Heard her speak.

The young jinni was a marvellous creature who would be ready to reveal herself to her lover again before long. He could feel it. The white bead on his bracelet was growing denser, too, as if he needed any proof.

"You know why…" Jakob ground, and his eyes flashed with rage.

Brodie turned and stalked away, dragging Archie with him. Yeah, he knew why.

In spite of her strengthening body, he could hear Wynter's wailing and feel her despair. She was not okay. He'd hurt her by hurting Jakob. By denying her his company while staying away, and it felt awful, but the guilt was just going to be something he knew he'd have to live with.

It didn't mean he was sorry, or that he wouldn't do it again should he feel the need to punish Jakob further for what he had done.

He didn't even care, or so he kept telling himself.

By the time the two of them had reached the house, Archie was swaying, and it was easy to tell why. Blood was dripping from the cut on his hand, leaving thick droplets that led all the way back through the dark cave. Strangely, denying Jakob those drops of sustenance and making him smell them from his cell didn't bring Brodie the satisfaction he'd anticipated. He kept wanting to go back and let the vampire have some more, but ignored those foolish impulses, putting them down—once again—to the feminine sensibilities he was now forced to endure.

"Let's get you cleaned up," Brodie told the human as they crossed the threshold and Archie lost his balance, falling directly into the path of the oncoming goblin, whose job it was to take care of the island and all its inhabitants.

Rafferty wasn't just in charge of their home there, but every inch of their little hideaway, and Brodie watched with a frown as he laid Archie out over the nearby sofa to rest while he tended to his wound and then set him up with an IV. Had he really lost that much blood? He sat down by the boy and could see he was indeed pale, but seemed well enough. Just squeamish, perhaps.

He then watched Rafferty fuss and tend to him, and could see his old friend with ease as he went about his business. Goblins were truly curious creatures. They weren't captured and put to service like some humans, often fictionalised, but were beings born with an innate need to have order and tranquillity despite whatever chaos arose around them. Some liked serving humans because they could remain out of sight and live solitary lives, as their kind often preferred to be, while others served the many other creatures of myth and legend that roamed the Earth for the very opposite of reasons. Rafferty was one such goblin. He wanted to be seen and was flamboyant and creative. He was a free spirit, which was unusual amongst their kind, but not unheard of. He liked music and movies, as well as books and art, and had great taste too.

Whether alone or with company, Brodie had found Rafferty watching others with intrigue. He always wanted to hear their stories and see the world through their eyes, while never once seeming to want to visit it for himself. Like he was born and bred to do, he simply stayed in one place and took great care of it.

"He'll be fine," Rafferty said, breaking Brodie's musings, "but next time, take a bandage with you!" he scalded, and then took off towards the bedroom Archie had chosen for himself. He returned with a pillow and the blankets from his bed, which he then tucked up around him like a father might his son.

"I should've known better. Sorry," Brodie croaked, and he went to walk away, but Rafferty stopped him. He stood and quickly blocked his path and, contrary to the myth, glared down at Brodie from his towering height.

"Yes, you should have," he echoed, "but more than that. You should've listened sooner. Should've tried harder not to be such a dick."

"All right, jeez!" he cried, but then couldn't help looking down at the poor lad, who was now completely out of it on the sofa.

Brodie did feel bad. He hadn't wanted Archie to get hurt but had lost his focus. He'd zoned in on Jakob and forgotten about the human he'd basically ignored since he'd persuaded him to leave on that chopper.

He knew he owed Archie more. He vowed to be better. To finally do right by all those in his care, not just Wynter, and knew that also included Jakob, whether he liked it or not.

SEVENTEEN

Archie woke with a pounding headache, remembering with ease just what was the cause. He opened his eyes and looked down at his hand, which had been cleaned and dressed, presumably by the invisible goblin he lived with. Jeez, he had to laugh at how that could possibly make sense, and yet he knew that all of this was indeed true.

Brodie was a jinni and had taken him to this island to be a vampire's breakfast, lunch, and dinner. Or however much he decided to give him, which hadn't been much more than half a cup full so far. He was his prisoner, and it'd been hard to watch the poor guy fighting his feral side, but Archie was glad he'd stayed. Glad he'd listened to the story of how the vampire, Jak, had been in love with a human. He hadn't once hurt her. In fact, they'd fallen in love, and so Archie had to hope he had been sincere when trying not to frighten him the night before.

All he had to give was a few drops here and there. He could do that. Sure… He just had to get over his fear of needles and knives first. And, well, the sight of blood, which always seemed to make him faint.

Urgh, great. Now he felt nauseous again.

Something stung his other arm and Archie reopened his eyes to find a small plaster on the inside of his elbow there. He frowned and went to pull it free, when a deep voice halted him.

"Please leave it. I had to put a drip in so you could replenish your fluids, but it's finished now. That plaster is just helping stem the fresh bleeding." It was that strange ownerless sound again, but at least now Archie knew who it'd come from.

"Thank you, Rafferty," he croaked and sat up. "I owe you one, mate."

"Think nothing of it, sir," he answered politely, his nonchalance making him laugh.

"Saving my life? Yeah, that was nothing," he joked, "and please, call me Archie."

"Of course," Rafferty's invisible form replied, and then things began moving across the room where the open-plan kitchen was. It appeared he was doing it on purpose so as to be seen when he was otherwise invisible, and Archie appreciated the gesture. He then laughed when two eggs floated into mid-air and wiggled. "Breakfast?"

"I thought you'd never ask," he told him, and climbed to his feet with a yawn and a good stretch. "Where's Brodie?" Archie then asked as he gathered up his duvet.

"He's taking some fresh air," Rafferty answered, and from his tone he got the impression they'd had some crossed words. He thought about asking what'd happened, but didn't want to pry. The three of them were finally getting somewhere and the silent house, thankfully, wasn't quite as quiet as it'd been before. He didn't want to ruin it.

He then left for a moment to deposit his bedding in his room and returned to find freshly made scrambled eggs and buttered toast waiting for him.

"Thanks," Archie said as he took his seat, but he got no answer and so presumed Rafferty had left to tend to his chores.

He ate with a great deal of haste, his body crying out for the nourishment, and let his mind go back over the events of the last two days. His still lingering hunger made him think of Jakob again, too. Brodie was keeping him prisoner for some reason, even though they were linked to one another because of the female jinni he'd told him was there with them. It was complicated to wrap his head around, but at the same time, he was intrigued by it all. By the creatures he'd once thought were nothing but fabled myths made up by their ancestors millennia before.

While he was deep in thought, Archie stared down at his empty plate, and when it started to move away, he jumped and reached for it on instinct. He felt the resistance from what had to be Rafferty's hold, but somehow he didn't sense the goblin himself. He didn't know why, but he'd presumed that should they touch he would be able to feel him, but instead, there was nothing.

"I didn't mean to make you jump, Archie. Sorry," Rafferty's deep voice chimed.

"Nah, it was me," he answered and let go, "it's easy to forget you're here and when shit starts moving on its own, it takes me a second to register."

"No need to explain."

"I want to," Archie insisted, looking up to where he was so sure the voice was coming from. "You and me can be friends. I want to be, and part of being friends is not letting the other fret unnecessarily. Explaining what's wrong and when. If I'm being truly honest, I was shocked to not feel your hand on the plate. You guys really are invisible to humans, aren't you, even to the touch?"

"Absolutely. I can tend to your needs as required, like when I placed the cannula in your arm, but if you consciously reached for me, you'd feel nothing," Rafferty replied, and Archie watched as he finished removing the plate and then put it in the sink to wash.

It was then that the front door to the house behind them opened and he turned to look as Brodie came in through it. He was muttering to himself, or at least seemed to be at first, but when his mumblings turned into a fully blown argument, Archie knew otherwise.

It was the woman.

"What's her name?" he asked, and walked the short length of corridor towards where Brodie was just kicking off his muddy boots. His black hair was dishevelled, as though he'd just been out in a storm, but he didn't appear to be feeling the cold at all. His black skin wasn't marred with goosebumps and his perfect white teeth weren't chattering. In fact, Brodie seemed his usual perfectly turned out self.

"Wynter," he answered, and Archie smiled.

He'd known a girl at uni called Wynter. They had used to frequent the local nightclubs together and people had always taken them for a couple, when in fact he'd still been in the closet and she had been a raging lesbian. Archie had been her wingman, while she had helped coax him to indulge in some of the urges he'd felt towards men over the years. Urges he'd always fought, but not anymore.

Archie was a 'guys guy'. He played sports and watched Formula-One on the TV. He drank beer and joined his friends whenever the Jäeger Train came rolling out, never having hit on any of them or made things awkward thanks to his sexual orientation. He went fishing with his dad and listened to rock music. Not once had he acted camp or pretended to be sassy. In fact, he didn't think he knew how to be sassy!

In his youth, he'd thought that was what gay men had to act like. He'd figured, therefore, he couldn't be gay after all, maybe just figuring himself out, but now he knew better. He'd lived in the real world and had tried the dating scene. It wasn't so bad. He was sadly completely off the market now thanks to his new job, but that didn't matter. He'd take a break from it all and go back rich and ready to find love. No problem at all.

"Nice name. Does she like rom-coms?" he finally replied, and then realised he was staring at Brodie a little too intently. He didn't know what he'd expected to see, perhaps another soul behind his stare, but all he'd got was those frowning green eyes of his glowering back. "I was thinking of putting on a movie, that's all. Figured she might like a break from the crazy, plus you're looking a bit frazzled. Might be nice to take a load off?"

"What do you know?" Brodie bit back, but Archie didn't let it get to him. He simply smiled and shrugged.

"I know she's hurting, and that it has to do with her being in love with your friend back there," he said, pointing down to where he knew the vampire was still being held. He then breathed a sigh and held up his hands, not having had to try hard to see Brodie was seething. "None of my business, for sure, but I still think it might be nice to take a break."

He retreated into the living area where he plucked down one of the many titles Rafferty's collection had to offer and pushed the disc into the DVD player.

By the time the movie had started, Brodie was sat on the sofa opposite, and Archie didn't say a word. He simply let him be and was pleased when he heard him laughing at the goings on in the film. He'd chosen well, and by the time it was over, the jinni seemed a lot more relaxed.

"So, you feel up to having a flying lesson?" Brodie asked when they were done, "I've got everything ready."

Oh, so that was what he was up to outside that blustery spring morning. He was prepping the helicopter, and in doing so meant he kept his promise from the night before. Archie was immensely pleased to hear it.

"Yeah, definitely," he answered, and couldn't hide his enthusiasm. This was exactly what he'd been after, and he wasn't going to refuse any opportunity he had to learn to fly.

It was slow going at first and it wasn't helped by the fact that Brodie wasn't the most patient of teachers. He shouted and seethed whenever Archie wasn't getting it fast enough, and not once did he tell him 'well done', but by the end of those first few hours, they had really gotten somewhere. Archie had grasped the basics and had even lifted their chopper up off the ground for a few seconds at a time here and there, but was reminded each time not to take them too high. They couldn't allow for the chopper to be seen from the mainland. Their presence was clearly a secret, and Archie found himself wondering, yet again, as to why.

They stopped their lesson only because the dark night that descended, and on the way down, he decided to broach the subject at last.

"What exactly are we doing here, Brodie?" he asked, and at first he thought his companion might be about to ignore the question, but then the jinni stopped outside the opening of the cave and turned back to him with a frown.

In the dark light of the descending sun, Brodie looked directly into Archie's eyes, and he felt like it was the first time the strange creature had really done so. He'd never properly looked back at him or seemed to consider him as more than a nuisance, and it was unnerving to finally have his attention after all this time. But Archie didn't wilt. He didn't fall back either. Instead, he joined him by the rock edge and stared back at him.

"There are things in this world that are worse than the cold-hearted jinni standing before you, or the vampire assassin held captive deep within this cave," he answered, and Archie nodded. It was the age-old story of there being a more oppressive danger, and regardless of it being the strange creatures involved, the threat was clearly very real.

"Who are we hiding from?" he asked.

"More like running," Brodie quipped, "from a vampire like no other who had Wynter in his sights. She was his Blood Slave and his favourite plaything. And she was flesh and bone, just like you. She was fragile, and so I was instructed to protect her. To stake my own type of claim on her human soul while he decided whether to turn her and make her his immortal bride."

Damn, that certainly put things into some sort of context.

"But she loves the other guy?" Archie replied, remembering how he'd seen their bond for himself, and all without ever actually having met her yet.

"That she does," Brodie concurred, "and so she was forced to run. She gave her life so that Jakob could live. And so that I could become whole."

Archie nodded again. He remembered how the story went, and knew she was indeed alive within their shared body, but was weak. She wouldn't be able to show herself until she had become stronger, and when that day came, it would be Brodie's turn to hide away and do the same.

"So, what now?" he asked, and turned to look out at the ocean ahead. It was a calm evening, but was quickly turning into a dark one. The sun was barely still with them, and yet the sky was lit enough for him to see for miles.

"Marcus cannot find us here, at least not while we lie low and stay hidden from sight by the mainland. Creatures like Jakob and I only leave the faintest of traces, and so I'm counting on Marcus to have sent his vampire soldiers after Wynter's scent and not ours. They will track her as best they can, but fundamentally she ceased to be before we'd even left his grounds."

"And what about locals? Won't they talk about this strange island and the inhabitants if this vampire comes looking?"

"This island is warded against humans and their prying eyes. Not invisible, but there are protections in place, thanks to Rafferty and his due diligence. Plus, there's no one close enough to see or hear us. The chopper, perhaps, but not our comings and goings on foot."

"But what about the lighthouse keeper?" he asked with a frown and pointed to the next island across where there had to be someone living. He'd seen the light turn on and off for himself, so knew someone had to be doing it.

"He is no one you should ever hope to meet, trust me," Brodie groaned, and he seemed to sense that wasn't a good enough explanation before Archie even had to question him further. "Vampires, Jinn, goblins… the myths and fables might be wrong, but the reality is true. You know this now."

Archie nodded and then stared back at the island ahead intently, looking for some evidence of what might be there. It was clearly some other kind of mythical creature.

"What is it?" he whispered.

"A werewolf. And not the kind who howls only at the full moon," Brodie ground, "his curse is to change every single night. As you can imagine, after a couple of hundred years spent ripping your own human body to shreds every night before transforming into a beast twice your previous size, there's little humanity left to cling to. He's a monster. They all are."

"And in the daytime?" Archie asked with a gulp.

"Still no better. They are creatures purely driven by instinct, even in human form. They take their land and mark it. Anyone who dares set foot there is classed as theirs for the taking, or so they see it. If you came upon a werewolf in its beast form, they'd undoubtedly attack." He then paused for a second, as though deciding whether to say the rest, but then seemed to think it was for the best. As if it was better, Archie knew the truth, so that he didn't take his warnings lightly. "They're known for dragging their prey back to their dens before fucking them half dead and then finishing the job with their teeth. By dawn, there'd be nothing left bar the freshly picked clean bones. When in human form, wolves are no different. The wolf on that island would gladly take unwanted visitors captive and have his way with them before the sun sets and then starting all over again in his other guise once transformed."

"Remind me not to go exploring," Archie replied, and he let out a whistle as the dark connotations of what Brodie had said made some pretty vile images come to mind. As he continued to stare across the water, he suddenly realised there was someone watching him back. Or something. He could just about see the dark shadow at the base of the lighthouse steps, but what was most disconcerting were the red eyes. They were so bright it was almost like a laser, and he suddenly felt incredibly vulnerable.

He stepped back and snagged his heel on the rock, and cursed as he fell back onto his behind on the mucky ground. On instinct, he put his hands down to absorb the shock of the fall, and then lifted both palms to find that each one was bleeding.

Archie clambered back up onto his feet, feeling embarrassed, and he saw Brodie look away. He then hissed something to himself and charged for the cave entrance before beckoning him to follow.

"You okay?" the jinni asked when they were safely inside and they had some light again, and Archie inspected his palms and nodded.

"Just grazes," he answered, and then paled when he saw the odd expression on Brodie's face. Was something wrong?

"Would... she wants to know..." he winced and Archie knew why. Wynter had to be giving him hell from within, and even though it had previously been Brodie's desire to see the vampire in his keep suffer, he seemed to be caving.

"If Jakob can have it?" he asked, and the jinni nodded.

He figured why not. All he'd do was wash it away and patch up any bleeders, so there was no reason the vamp couldn't have the few drops already starting to clot in his palms. He'd surely needed far more than the half cup Brodie had allowed before, so if he could have even this small bit extra, then Archie was willing to share.

He just hoped there wasn't much more than that, otherwise he was liable to end up in a crumpled heap on the floor again. He was well aware there was no reason for his squeamishness and yet every time he saw blood in droves, he had gone. Passed out like one of those women in the movies who placed the back of their hands against their forehead and then swept backwards in a graceful arc. At least their suitor would catch those women before hitting the ground. Archie was never so lucky. He'd wake up with cuts and bruises galore every time. Hardly graceful.

At least the last time he'd visited Jak, he'd made it back to the house before giving into his wooziness. Saved face a little.

Yeah, who was he kidding?

The pair reached the cell and Archie expected Brodie to approach the malnourished vampire first, but he didn't say or do a thing. He simply watched over them and nodded at Archie to go closer. He did, but he questioned his sanity the entire time. What the hell was he thinking? The guy could easily reach through those bars and drag him nearer before draining him dry, and yet here he was, clambering closer? It was sheer insanity.

Jakob was asleep, or at least appeared to be, but the moment Archie got close, his nose seemed to catch the smell of his semi-fresh blood and his eyes snapped open, making him jump. "Here," Archie whispered, his voice shaking as he reached between the bars of Jak's cell and showed him the grazes to his left palm.

Jakob didn't so much as wipe the cut to clean any dirt or debris away. He just leaned forward and Archie watched as his tongue darted out and he licked the cut clean. Not once did he grab at him or force his hand into his mouth to go in for a bite, and it occurred to Archie just how controlled he was. The vampire was showing such restraint it was actually pretty admirable.

He shuffled in his stance and pushed the other hand inside the cell, and watched as Jak did the same again. He didn't move anything other than his head, and when he was done, he finally fixed his intense blue eyes on Archie's face.

"Thank you," he whispered, but then frowned. "You're not afraid. Why? I could kill you even now. Drink you dry. I don't stop because of him, but because I choose to."

Archie knew he must be talking about Brodie and was sure there was no love lost there, but that it was another person Jak was doing this for. Wynter.

It was a love he himself couldn't fathom, and yet, he knew it was there.

The adoration Jakob felt for the woman trapped inside Brodie was shining out of him.

"Fuck you, bloodsucker," Archie then heard from behind him, and he turned to see the jinni was livid. He wasn't entirely sure why either but moved away from the bars when Jakob suddenly sprang into action and cracked his neck, like he was limbering up.

"No, fuck you. It's time we settled this once and for all. I'm ready, let's go," he growled, confirming Archie's suspicions, and then even had the audacity to put up his hands and then bend his fingers back in a 'come here' gesture.

"You killed my wife, Jakob! This will never be settled. I will hate you forever and would gladly beat the shit out of you every time I had to look at you," Brodie hissed, and then he approached the bars of the cell and glowered at the vampire. He wasn't at the locked door, and so Archie thought he was just planning on hurling insults at the guy, but then the unimaginable happened. Before his eyes, the man he'd spent the day with turned to smoke. It was like nothing he'd ever seen and he let out a curse in his shock.

The misty blackness moved forwards through the bars and inside the cell before transforming back into Brodie's usual guise, and the sight of him transfixed Archie. What the hell was that? Jinn really were nothing like the myths and legends had let on, and while he was horrified, he was also fascinated by what he'd seen.

"I'm not sorry and I never will be. She was a psychopath, but you were too blinded by love to see," Jakob bellowed, and he stepped closer, squaring up to Brodie. It was like something out of a movie, and while Archie was on edge, he couldn't tear himself away. Jakob had clearly had enough of being the captive and was ready to have his say, even if it meant sparking another fight between him and Brodie. "And where do you think the order came from, huh? Camilla? Not a chance she'd have the power to order that kind of kill."

Brodie faltered just a little as the thought seemed to finally occur to him about why this had happened, and while Archie knew only what'd just been said between them, he could tell Jakob was right. He'd been too blind to see it.

"Then who?" Brodie mumbled.

"The only power I truly answer to, and the only one who pays me no fee for my work…"

"Death herself, the Grim Reaper? But why?"

"Because she took too many. That's the Lady of Death's job and so, of course, she grew resentful. She needed Ada gone, but when it comes to the immortal creations born of magic, she often requests my help. And in return, she keeps me out of the underworld," Jak answered, and although it clearly wasn't what Brodie expected to hear, he still refused to back down. Refused to stop avenging the woman he still clearly loved, and Archie couldn't blame the guy.

Shit. This stuff really was serious. Whoever this woman was, Archie knew it was some next level kind of power and that Brodie needed to be careful. Him too. He'd been invited into their world without being told why until it was too late for him to back out. He'd be tied to the pair of them now, and Wynter included, should things turn sour. And if they pissed off some higher power, then surely he'd be the first piece of collateral damage to go. Humans always did seem to make the perfect scapegoats—or at least that was what happened in every movie he'd ever seen on the subject of man-verses-monster.

"Do you know what, fuck you both," he suddenly yelled, and his outburst seemed to surprise the two foes inside the locked cell. They both turned to him with questioning looks dominating their faces, each dumbfounded. "When's it gonna be enough, huh? When you kill each other, or when one of your many enemies finds you and does the job instead?"

Brodie scowled across at him, but Jakob seemed to agree. Instead of telling him so, though, he appeared to decide on a different approach. He head-butted Brodie right between the eyes and then proceeded to pummel him with punches that would have undoubtedly broken a human in two, but not the powerful jinni. He took the first few, but then roared with anger and unleashed his own kind of hell on the vampire. It was the bloodiest and most brutal thing he had ever seen.

Archie wanted to leave them to it and walk off in a huff. They clearly couldn't be helped or stopped, but actually, he couldn't tear his eyes away from the gory scene unfolding before him. Anyone else would be nothing but mush by now, but not them. They were clearly both seasoned fighters, and the show was better than any UFC or boxing match he'd been to watch in the past.

As the fight carried on, Archie actually wondered if all hope for them was truly lost, and that was when the third party apparently decided to intervene. Each of the two men were suddenly thrust apart by a bright white creature who appeared out of nowhere and took a human-like form between them. A womanly shape then seemed to materialise out of the smoky residue, and Archie watched in awe as she took form. He followed the curves of her back up to the hands stretched out to either side—each one clasped around the throat of the two men on either side of her.

"Enough!" she hollered, and Archie could only watch in awe as both Brodie and Jakob finally backed off.

Brodie retreated and then disappeared into the shadows in his smoky form too, and Archie let him skulk away from the cell rather than immediately follow him. The poor guy probably needed some time to cool off anyway, and he needed to process exactly what he was seeing. The misty woman no longer had her hands around Jakob's neck, but at the back of his head and she was pulling him towards what must be her mouth. They were soon kissing, he realised, and turned away rather than spy on them.

He went to leave, but then felt a hand on his arm and stared down at it in shock. He could feel her as though she were real, and yet the hand was made up of nothing but white smoke. It was messing with his head.

Archie followed the arm upwards and then realised she was standing between him and Jakob, the bars of his cell cutting her in two, and yet she didn't seem to notice at all.

"Wynter, I presume," he whispered with an awkward laugh. She giggled as she let go and returned to her lover, and Archie stepped closer, watching the strange entity intently.

"Nice to meet you properly at last, Archie," she answered. "Thank you for looking after Jak. I know it isn't easy coming to terms with allowing yourself to be fed on by a vampire, but please trust that he won't hurt you. And believe me when I tell you I will protect your life with my own. We owe you that and much more."

"I really haven't done all that much," Archie answered her with a shy shrug, but Wynter shook her head.

"I know what it takes from you, and so does he. That's why Jakob hasn't drunk directly from the vein, and he won't bite if he can help it. You're not yourself when ensnared by a vampire bite, trust me."

Archie simply nodded and then stepped back. He didn't know what she was getting at, not really, but decided to trust her. The entire situation was just nuts, but he reminded himself that only a few months before, she too had been human. Wynter had been trapped by the other vampire, Marcus, and had gotten away, having had to pay a huge price to do so. Things must've been really bad if he'd forced her to resort to such measures.

With a gentle smile and a nod to them both, Archie retreated. He decided to leave them to their reunion and so bid the white smoke lady farewell. It was a relief to have a moment to think, plus he had a feeling Brodie might need some company. Even if he didn't say so. He'd seemed to have clung onto his hatred for so long he might not know how to relinquish it, and so might need a friend while he worked through this new information Jakob had given him.

Archie found him just a short distance from the dank cell and came to a stop. He then pressed his back to the wall opposite and watched the still brooding jinni, maintaining the silence for as long as he might need it.

When the blatant sound of two people going at it reached them, Brodie finally laughed and shook his head. He then offered Archie a shrug, who grinned back at him.

"I can't go any farther from her," he explained, and then tapped his chest. Archie was reminded of how he was Wynter's host and so it made sense he could not go far when she was out in the world. Brodie had to understand these things in ways a human such as he wouldn't even begin to fathom. After all, he too had apparently survived the same way for hundreds of years and so would know the rules inside and out.

"Good of you to let them have some time together," he answered. "How does it work, the smoke, I mean?"

"It's weird, right?" Brodie answered with a smile, and for a second, Archie thought he seemed happier. As if he quite liked having the chance to talk about his kind to someone new. "All I know is that I feel the same now as I do when I've transformed, even though I'm nothing more than a shadow. I can touch things and move objects as though I'm whole, but then again, I can move through them without even thinking. The only problem is that unless we're whole, we cannot sustain it for too long at a time. Not like when I'm in this form," he added, indicating to his current stature. "Or, I can disappear completely," Brodie informed him, and then he vanished in the blink of an eye.

"That shit's insane!" Archie cried, staring into the blank space left behind. He then reached forward, thinking Brodie must've disappeared completely and that, like with their goblin friend back at the house, he wouldn't be able to touch him, but then he felt something beneath his fingers and grabbed it. A second later, the jinni showed himself again, and Archie realised he was holding onto his shoulder. He flushed and dropped his hand. "Sorry. I thought you'd be the same as Rafferty."

"No problem," Brodie answered, and for the slightest of moments, Archie could've sworn he'd seen him blush, too. Maybe he wasn't used to being touched, he didn't know, but it made him realise something.

"Listen, it can't be easy living with the pair of them," he said, and indicated to the cell where Wynter and Jak were still going at it. "If you ever wanna talk or anything, just shout. I'll even just sit with you if that's what you need."

Brodie said nothing. He went back to his usual brooding silence, but Archie still felt glad he'd said something. And, even though the jinni could be a douchebag and hadn't been the most gracious of hosts the past couple of months, he'd actually meant it.

EIGHTEEN

Marcus figured he'd never learn. He'd left *Slave* behind and burned it to the ground like he'd planned, and then he'd gone straight to his club in London and done the same there. He'd devoured more than twenty humans before the Priestess had stopped him and was now sat staring at her hooded figure across the room of the supervisor's office. Like some sort of naughty school kid who'd been called to the headmistress's office.

"So what? I'm just meant to move on? Get over my heartbreak and all that lovey dovey shit?" he demanded with a sneer, and then he shrugged. "I'm just hungry."

"No, my lord. You're not hungry. You're hurt and want to take it out on the world around you. Continue to do so and your empire will fall," she told him, and he knew without asking that she must've seen a vision of his future. He didn't doubt her newest prophecy could easily come true, and she was right. He needed to stop. To exercise some self-control and find a way to move forward.

But he just couldn't quash that yearning within him. The need that was still longing for what only Wynter seemed able to give him. And he knew exactly why.

"I love her, even still," he groaned, and realised it was the first time he'd said it out loud.

"I know," was all his powerful witch replied, and she stepped closer, offering him her hand. "And with any luck, she will find her way back to you, but until then, you must remain patient. The hordes are scouring every corner of the globe for her, and they will not fail you. And until that time comes, you need to show some restraint."

"You're right," he answered, taking her offered hand, "so let's away until then. Take me far from where I can drink like this. Teach me how to live without her. Or at the least, take me somewhere in which I can be miserable in peace."

"I know just the place," the Priestess replied, and then led him from the room and out to where his only two remaining managers awaited him. Jack and Joanna were both propped up on sofas and were fighting sleep, and Marcus couldn't blame them. He'd kept them at his beck and call for months now and it was finally time he got back to his preferences when it came to his feeds. The two of them would have to do, at least until he could control his thirst again.

"Come," he called as he passed them, and the two quickly fell in line behind their master without a word. They were his ever-loving companions. His trusted duo. All he had left of the legacy he had once built, and he vowed he would have it back. That he would put an end to all of this and move forward.

The four of them were on a plane within the hour and, after a short private charter to their onward location, arrived at Marcus's private island off the coast of Mauritius by nightfall. It was the perfect hideaway. No humans for miles, apart from the two he'd brought with him, and most importantly, no distractions.

Joanna was giddy with excitement and when they approached his manse at the top coast of the roasting hot island, she let it be known. She ran straight for the ocean, where she kicked off her shoes and let the warm water cascade across her toes.

While Marcus wanted to chastise her for being so childlike, he decided against it. Her joy gave him pause. The scent of her happiness wasn't as unwelcome as usual, and so he just watched her prance around like a silly girl, while Jack continued to stare longingly at the Priestess he still adored. She was covered from head to toe, as usual, and was pointedly ignoring him, as usual.

They were an odd quartet, but one Marcus didn't mind banding together for the time being. He needed to shut out the rest of the world for a short while, and there was nowhere better to do it than with two plentiful sources of food and his most trusted companion.

That night, Joanna tended to him and Marcus even let her lie close to him as he drank from her. He couldn't help but smile to himself when she began panting with need and started to clench her thighs and writhe atop the bed beside him. She hadn't been so wanton with him for a while, and he knew he had the island to thank for it. The change of pace had been welcome, and it occurred to him then how perhaps, just this once, he might give her what she'd wanted for so very long.

Marcus closed the wound he'd made on her neck and knew Joanna expected for him to leave, but instead he uncovered one of her small breasts and began sucking the nipple into his mouth and around his tongue. He didn't make a cut though, and it was a good thing he hadn't, because a second later the poor woman was climaxing and screaming like she was possessed.

She really had remained celibate for him. So much so that she was fit to burst.

He ran his hand over her skinny waist and then lifted her skirt, and all the way he was comparing her body to Wynter's. He couldn't help it, but still carried on regardless of feeling nothing but flaws. He needed a distraction and hoped Joanna might be the one to deliver it, and so forced himself to try and forget the other woman. The one whose skin felt different against his. The one who tasted different. Smelled different. Was just too different.

Irreplaceable, he thought, but then pushed it away. With his mouth still on her breast, Marcus pushed two fingers inside Joanna's soaked core and began to pummel her with them. He was being rough, he knew, but there could be no niceness here. No gentleness. Only savage, brutal need.

When she came again, Marcus reared up off the bed onto his knees and stared down at her, watching as she pleaded and begged him for more.

Instead, he wrenched his hand from between her thighs and rubbed them clean with her dress before reaching down and wrapping his hand around her throat.

"You're nothing, Joanna," he spat, and revelled in her sadness. "Nothing."

He then left her there, and without a word he stalked out into the ocean and ducked under the waves, where he screamed into the water with all his might in the knowledge no one would be able to hear him.

After a couple of weeks spent continuing to indulge Joanna's fantasies, only to then rough her up again afterwards, Marcus realised he was starting to enjoy her. Just a little.

The Priestess had stayed out of sight and she left him to his game, while Jack was still pining for the woman he couldn't forget, and kept looking for her around the island and in the huge house. Marcus had caught him sneaking into the many unused rooms in a bid to come across her, the mother of his unborn child, but he had no idea how her magic worked. She could be anywhere she chose to be, either visible or invisible. He wouldn't just happen upon her, she would have to will it so, but he was still interesting to watch. Still delicious in his agonising unrequited love.

In some ways, Marcus wondered if he and Jack weren't quite alike in their current situation. Did he too wear that same desperate look of a man in love with someone he could not have? Was he searching fruitlessly for someone who didn't want to be found, while everyone around him pitied him for it? He damn well hoped not, but knew if anyone had ever dared pity him, he would quickly lay waste to them for daring to do so. He was not the sort to be treated that way, even by those who meant well in doing so.

One morning, while Jack was preparing some lunch for him and Joanna, Marcus laid in the sunshine with his eyes closed and he opened his mind. He felt a niggle at the base of his skull and called out to the alpha of his horde, who came back with the most wondrous of answers for him. He'd caught a scent.

The most wondrous of fragrances.

Her…

Come to me, he called out in silent order, *come here.*

When he opened his eyes, he realised he was hard at the waist. Ready for Wynter to touch and for him to drive into her. Shit, just the thought of her had him so eager. So ready.

She was a jinni now too, far from the vulnerable human she'd been before, and he knew she could take a proper fucking. Oh, and how he would.

He gripped himself and closed his eyes as he stroked, imagining her body against his. He was beyond ready to have her back, his little fighter, and came quickly just thinking about the battles they would resume and the beatings she could take from him now that she was an immortal creature.

When he was sated with one thirst, he called out to Joanna to satisfy another, and to her credit, she was by his side barely a minute later. She offered her wrist, but Marcus was still feeling playful. He pulled her down on top of him and bit her at the neck instead. And, of course, it was a mere moment before she was writhing atop him, making him hard once again.

Desire flooded through him. Needs that had to be fulfilled. Cravings that would indeed be satisfied.

By his third gulp, Joanna was crying out for him to stop, but it was too late. She climaxed with her vein open and his mouth gulping at the delectable blood pumping from it, and Marcus drank her adrenalin full body dry.

She was dead in a matter of seconds, but he found he didn't care. Not as much as he might've thought, and he pushed her away and left her lifeless body slumped in a heap beside him on the sun lounger.

"Well, at least she died doing what she loved…" the Priestess told him as she appeared out of nowhere, and Marcus grinned.

"Not like you to make jokes, my lady?" he told her.

She said nothing in response, but he could tell she was smiling back at him from under her cloak. His eyes then drifted down to her belly, where her child was growing within. She was beginning to show a decent curve to her usually tiny waist, and she stroked her bump, clearly having seen him.

"Shit!" Jack then cried, and they both turned to watch as he ran from the house and towards Joanna, as though to check on her, but he stopped dead when he saw Marcus giving him a scathing look of reproach.

"She only has herself to blame," he told his minion, who was forced to nod in spite of his shock and fear.

"Always was an insufferable pain in the arse," the Priestess added and, for reasons Marcus couldn't fathom, she then lifted her hood and removed it, revealing her alter ego to his now sole surviving manager.

"Marcella?" Jack sighed, and he did a double take as he watched her reveal herself further. The Priestess removed her cloak completely, and she smiled when he dropped to his knees and stared at the ample round of her stomach. His child was indeed growing inside. Their daughter. "You... it was you. All this time?"

"Yes," she replied with ease, and then ushered for him to stand. He followed her lead and then began to cry when she took his hand and placed it on her belly. "Her heart is pure, and strong. She will do us proud."

"I thought I'd never know what became of her, or you. I thought you'd ignore me forever?"

"I wasn't ignoring you, my darling. I was merely waiting for you to be ready."

"Ready for what?" he whimpered.

"To love me, through thick and thin. You'll know what I mean, when the time comes," was all she replied, and then she took his hand and led him over to where her master was still sat watching them.

"My lady?" Marcus asked and watched as she climbed to her knees before him and then ushered for Jack to do the same.

"Do you bless us, my lord? Will you pronounce us married and bonded for eternity? As one, now and forevermore?" she replied indignantly, and Marcus couldn't hide his surprise.

Marcella had never given him so much as a hint that she harboured feelings for Jack, and in fact she'd seemed to actively avoid him, but then here she was asking for them to be wed? Something was afoot and Marcus went to argue the case, but then his priestess lifted her gaze to his and he saw pain in her eyes. Suffering.

His strong and formidable sidekick was hurting, and while he didn't know why, he knew she meant what she'd asked for. She had her reasons, and they were hers to keep secret should she wish.

Marcus turned to Jack and eyed him curiously. He wasn't afraid to accept her and was clearly aroused. Given the scent of him, he was fit to burst, and so was evidently impressed that the shrouded witch was, in fact, someone he'd worked alongside for years. Someone he had been attracted to before, and was even more so now that he knew the two women were one and the same.

"You have my blessing," he told them, and then watched as Marcella performed a binding ritual with the wide-eyed human. He couldn't tell what was going on, or if what they had was necessarily true love, but in that moment, they were both at peace. Marcella pushed aside whatever was paining her, and she smiled earnestly as she bonded her soul with Jack's.

They had shared a mind-blowing and life-changing time together a few months before and only now were they committing to more, and it made Marcus think again about how he had tackled things with Wynter. There was so much that he could've done differently. And he knew that, given the chance, he wouldn't mistreat her like he had again.

Hindsight, what a marvellous thing.

The alpha vampire and his group of soldiers arrived the next morning via Marcus's private plane, and as soon as he looked into the behemoth's eyes, he knew it was true. They had caught a whiff of his beloved. The tiniest of sparks had indeed hit his senses back on the blustery British Isles, and the huge male grinned at his master.

"Wynter," he hissed, his first word Marcus had ever heard him speak, and then he licked his lips. The beast had caught a trace of his prey, and so he was ready to hunt her down. The alpha wanted her, but it was his master who would reap the reward when they tracked down where Brodie was hiding her, and he would let nothing get between them. Not this time.

"Take me," Marcus replied, and within the hour, they were all back on the plane and heading towards his old home.

Back to the burnt-out shell that'd once been *Slave*.

Back to her...

THE COMPLETE BLOOD SLAVE SERIES

NINETEEN

Archie let out an exasperated sigh as, yet again, he failed to get the chopper more than three feet off the ground before losing control. It was like something was dragging them back down and, after ten hours' spent behind the controls, he'd had enough.

His stoic guide said nothing as they both climbed down and then performed their final checks, but on the way back to the cave, Brodie stopped outside the entrance and turned to him, much like he had the last time they'd actually talked.

"Would you mind letting him feed?" he asked, and Archie didn't have to ask who he was talking about. He just nodded and walked past the grumpy jinni, but he didn't go to Jakob's cell. Instead, he went into the house and to the kitchen, where he sliced a cut into his palm and then let the blood trickle into a mug.

"Here," he snapped, handing it to Brodie without even looking at him, and then he cleaned himself up. It was funny how the sight of blood wasn't quite so much of a trigger as before, but he guessed a daily offering would do that to you. He was certainly desensitised to it nowadays and guessed that was one bonus.

The scars would, of course, be permanent, but that was okay. He could live with them. It was the iciness he couldn't get to grips with. The stony silences and the cold-shoulder routine from Brodie. They were wearing him down, and so Archie slumped in front of the TV and set up the DVD player for another night of box-set bingeing with Rafferty.

The next morning, he decided he needed some conversation, and so went down to see Jakob. He took his cup of coffee with him and perched a safe distance away from the motionless vampire, but was glad to see he wasn't in too bad of a shape.

"You two stopped beating one another up yet?"

"For now," Jak answered with a smile, but then he turned serious, "I wronged him and he'll never forget it. Never forgive. And that's okay. I've made peace with my past, Archie. How are you managing with him for company?"

"Bored of the silence mostly," Archie answered him honestly.

"Hence why you came to me for a chat?"

"Yeah…" he said, and sighed, "I don't get it. He's crazy powerful and could easily take on this vampire who's after you, so why is he so worried?"

"Because it isn't Marcus who's the threat, but his hordes," Jakob told him, and Archie guessed his expression gave his confusion away, because the vampire continued without him having to ask. "He controls a vast vampire army. Soulless soldiers who follow orders and have no mind of their own. They cannot be reasoned or bargained with and are loyal to only one—"

"Marcus," Archie answered.

"*Da*. And one jinni might be able to take on a few without a problem, but against thousands? None of us would survive."

Christ. That explanation was more than enough to send a shudder down Archie's spine.

Jakob was brutally honest, as ever, and it was clear just how careful their small group needed to continue to be.

Archie knew he was just in a mood. Sulking for the sake of it, and he tried his best not to continue doing so. It wasn't in his nature to brood, and by the time he'd finished his brew, he was sitting taller in his seat, the black cloud above his head finally easing away.

"Okay, let's talk about something else," he mumbled, and then grinned, "like you telling me all about how you and Wynter got together?"

Now that got Jakob buzzing. He sat up in his seat and smiled back at his friend, and it wasn't long before he was regaling Archie with the story of how he had found her curled in a ball in Marcus's office the day a fellow slave had tried to force himself on her.

"But I held her to me. I was the one who calmed her, and even then, I knew she was special. Marcus pretended not to care. His Priestess disappeared rather than face me. But I saw the truth, and by the time I laid my eyes on that poor broken woman again, I knew she needed to be set free…"

***

Just a few miles away, at the top edge of the Welsh coastline, stood a gang of pale vampire soldiers. They were each sniffing the air, desperate to catch the same scent they had a few weeks before, and yet there was nothing to behold. Even though they'd manned their posts in strategic spots around the clock, using the darkest corners the countryside had to offer, Wynter was once again lost to them.

Marcus arrived in the back of his most prestigious limousine and he climbed out, cursing the wild winds as they swept around him from the sea. The breeze tasted of salt and smelled like shit, and he cursed the alpha as he led him to where he'd sensed her before. Ahead lay the ocean, and the only other close by option was a cluster of islands that were inhabited by, from as far as he could tell, a werewolf. The beast's scent was all over the damn place and was strong even from this distance, and Marcus knew he could go take the wolf out of the equation with ease, but he wasn't interested in starting a feud with the wolves.

Best settle this score first.

"The wolf might be hiding her," he said to the witch by his side, who was also staring at the lighthouse ahead in thought. She had ditched her cloak and her red hair whipped around her face in the breeze, her small rounded belly protruding nicely, and Marcus thought how she looked like some kind of formidable goddess of war standing there. It wasn't too far off. His Priestess's power knew no bounds after all, and he knew he'd be lost without her.

"It's unlikely he has her," she replied, "but we can wait here. My guess is that she took form momentarily nearby, which is why the scent was so fleeting. Perhaps they boarded a boat? Either way, we will keep looking for any other sign of her. But we cannot make our presence here known, otherwise she will run again."

"Yes," he answered, and then looked around at the few scattered cottages along the coast. One of them was bound to be empty, or better yet, for sale. Much more preferable to have heat and lighting wherever they took up residence. They would set themselves up there for however long it took, while his soldiers continued to lie in wait outside in the elements. But there would be no backing off now. He had to get Wynter back and wasn't going to pass up the chance to chase the only lead they'd had in months.

"What will you do when you find her?" Jack asked in a quivering voice from beside them, and Marcus watched as Marcella conjured up a coat to shield her husband from the cool coastal air.

Humans, they were so damn fragile.

"I will take everything she refused to give me willingly," he answered with a sneer, "or I'll just kill her and be done with all of this. I haven't decided which yet."

It was a lie, and he knew it. Marcella too, but she didn't say so. Despite her and Jack now being married, Marcus was still her master and she would remain loyal to him until her dying breath. She would serve his every need, he knew, and that also meant saving him from his own bruised ego should the need arise.

***

After a few more weeks spent finally mastering flying, Archie realised he'd fallen into a much better routine. He didn't pay any mind to Brodie's lingering silences and standoffish demeanour, not now that he and Jakob had built up a rapport during his regular visits.

At least he had someone to chat with, and he found the old vampire was actually pretty good company. He was well travelled and enjoyed telling him about all the places he'd visited, but was also a keen sports fan and a tech geek. They talked about cars and gadgets, and all the things Archie wanted to buy for himself when he returned to his real life. Whenever that might be, of course. But he had to admit, it wasn't so bad being cooped up with his strange little bunch of creatures for company. The experience had been eye opening, to say the least.

On their way back down to the cave one night, after a day of perfecting his take-offs, he decided to finally broach the subject of the captive vampire with Brodie.

"Do you not think it's time to let Jak out? Let him earn your forgiveness instead of being locked away and out of sight? Surely Wynter misses him?"

"He will never be forgiven," the jinni ground, confirming Archie's suspicions. He simply couldn't let go of his pain. It didn't matter that the torture was done with, and all Jak was doing was festering away in that cell. Brodie seemed to prefer him out of sight, but he clearly would never be out of mind. Not while Wynter was in residence within him. She must surely whisper to him daily about her soul mate? Must beg Brodie to release him?

"Perhaps he can simply prove himself, then? Find a way to get into your good books and show you he means to change?" he tried, and as they reached the doorway to the house, Brodie spun and glowered at him, but Archie refused to back down. He held his ground and stared him right in the eye.

"You think he's redeemed himself? Do you forget how much of a threat he will be to you if I set him free? Would you rest easy in your bed at night knowing a vampire is on the loose? One who has tasted you and whose survival hinges on him being allowed more?" he answered with a sneer.

"He has control of his hunger. I've seen so for myself," Archie replied resolutely. Yes, he knew it was a risk. Being near Jak always would be, but Wynter had been human, and she'd spent days with him without him harming her. She'd fallen in love with the guy, for heaven's sake! He couldn't be that bad.

"Put your hand through the bars and tell me you feel safe with him. Tell me he won't attack," he demanded, and Archie paled but didn't reply.

Was he that trusting in Jak that he'd put himself directly in harm's way? He decided to try. Brodie wouldn't let anything bad happen to him, even if he'd proven him right. He would stop Jakob, if for no other reason than to spite the vampire rather than let him feed.

His mind was quickly made up, and Archie went around Brodie and straight into the house and then through to one of the spare bedrooms. There, he grabbed a pillow, thinking it might be nice for Jakob to have something to lean on rather than the dank rock, and then he charged back out of the house and down to his cell without another word to the grumpy jinni.

"Hey," he said, and lifted the pillow to show him, "thought you might like this."

He then pushed it through the biggest available gap in the bars, his hands going through along with it, and he saw the starving vampire's eyes flash. The chance was there, and they both knew it. An opportunity to feed was within easy reach, but he didn't attack. All he did was thank him and then step away with his offered gift, and Archie smiled.

It wasn't very often he was proven right, and it felt good to know his instincts about Jak were correct. He liked the guy and actually wanted to see him be released. He would gladly keep feeding him when needed, but he didn't strike him as the sort to foolishly drain his only source of food dry. "So, I've been thinking about stuff. You really never once bit Wynter?" he asked, and Jakob seemed surprised by the question, but he didn't shy away. As always, he was honest with his answer.

"Never," he told him, "not even when I was fucking her brains out on the bonnet of my car. And in the back seat. And then again at the beach house. We did that a lot..."

"I gather," Archie replied with a shy smile, and Jakob beamed. He'd never had the sort of friends who were so open and unashamed about that sort of talk, and it was taking some getting used to. Especially all the details about women.

"Sex is sacred to most vampires, but I never had a problem with it. And I never went back for seconds before. Not until her."

"And then you merged?"

"*Da*," he confirmed, "but Marcus wouldn't let us enjoy our love. He took her away from me and it was torture. Worse than anything that fucking jinni would try on me," Jak demanded, probably for the benefit of Brodie's eavesdropping ears more than for him.

"Did he fuck her too? Marcus, I mean," Archie asked, and then almost apologised for overstepping the mark. He didn't quite know what'd come over him!

"No, but he took pleasure in biting her and then relishing in the reaction the bite gives a human. He thought she wanted him, but instead she lied to save us both, and let him believe she was still his."

"What exactly happens during the feed?" he asked, having also heard from both Brodie and Wynter about the effect of the bite, but he hadn't actually heard why it was so dangerous.

"You'd be riding a high the likes you couldn't imagine, and many humans then crave it in the aftermath. So much so they'd willingly beg for the bite again. And you'd be so sexually strung your inhibitions would go out the window. Not the most glamorous of experiences. Wynter never liked how he made her feel, and especially when she'd ended up climaxing because of him. It made her feel dirty. But with me, it was real. The bite was never part of what sent her from one orgasm to another."

Archie nodded in understanding. It made sense.

The bite brought with it an apparent sexual euphoria, and he was glad they'd all warned him not to let Jak do so with him. He'd prefer the cut marks from the blade to his palm than a deep sense of shame he knew would come with being transfixed by the bite.

They chatted for a while longer, but it wasn't long before Archie's stomach was crying out for something to eat, and so he said his goodbyes and then jogged back up to the house. Hopefully Rafferty had something at the ready, or else he had a feeling he might be about to raid his carefully organised cupboards.

On his way inside, he thought it odd how at home he now felt there. How used he was to the darkness and the cold, damp cave. And of his comrades, the four mystical creatures he knew not a single soul would ever believe had lived there with him.

He decided he'd just tell people he'd gone to work abroad for a few years. Tell them it was a covert mission for the government, like he'd originally thought it might be, and then say he wasn't allowed to tell them specifics. Simple. And how cool would that be? Everyone would be fascinated. He knew he'd be well impressed if an old friend had disappeared only to re-emerge years later with a secret story they refused to tell.

"Still in one piece, I see," Rafferty's voice permeated the silence once Archie was back in the house and had removed his boots and jacket.

He looked for the source of the sound, and saw one of the ornaments move a few feet to his left, which was Rafferty's way of showing where he was.

"Yep," he answered with a smile, "had Brodie warned you not to expect me for dinner?"

"He said you *were* dinner..." the goblin replied, and even though he might not be able to see him, Archie could tell he was grinning.

He laughed and nodded.

"Good one. You been reading joke books again?" he teased, and then headed further into the house so that he could grab a shower and get changed for dinner.

As the water cascaded over him, Archie couldn't help but find himself fantasising over the oddest things. He tried to imagine what he thought Rafferty might look like behind that invisibleness: he had no way of penetrating, and whether the goblin was the sort to entertain relationships and such. He was friendly and funny, and plentiful company, but it wasn't like you had girl goblins running around the place. Or did you? And did they even procreate? He wondered.

And then his mind went to the jinni he'd shared his days with lately. They didn't seem to have children either, but they instead took over human hosts and then made them one of their kind. Was it by choice? And if so, would he choose it? Could he imagine himself as one of them?

Yes, he could. But then, of course, that'd mean giving up his old life and becoming a misty apparition, like Wynter. Not that she seemed to mind. And neither did Jak. He'd told him they were big into fucking, and Archie had heard them going at it like rabbits that night when she'd appeared. He knew her altered state hadn't held her back from showing her lover just how much she still wanted him. And at least this way, they were both immortal and could be together forever—whether she was whole or not.

It was exciting just thinking about how it would feel to have such power and to be able to use it in whatever way he wanted, both in and out of the bedroom. What a thrill it would be to have strengths beyond anything a human could hope to possess. And such stamina too…

Great, now he was hard.

Archie was used to his nightly pause mid-wash, though. Just another part of his usual routine now that he was leading the single man's lifestyle. It wasn't so bad, but of course, it meant not being shy when it came to his daily masturbation routine. Hence the regular showers…

He grabbed his cock and began stroking it, pulling back and forth in moves that, like any red-blooded-male, he'd practiced many a time over the years, and as usual, his mind continued to wander. This evening, he fixated on the dark look in Brodie's eyes as he'd challenged him on the doorstep. He was such a grumpy git, and yet when that fury had flared behind those dark green eyes of his, Archie found he'd liked it. There was something about a bad boy, after all, and even he had to admit having been attracted to the darker side when it came to his exes. And he guessed he wasn't about to change type now.

Plus, there could never be anything between them. No one could want more with someone who never even spoke to him unless it was on their terms, or to tell him off. Archie didn't want someone who glowered at him the way Brodie did, either. Even if it was with that dark and brooding stare.

Yeah, who was he kidding? In his head, Archie imagined them going from such a standoff to then ripping one another's clothes clean off. And then some.

Maybe that was what made it such an indulgent fantasy then? The fact that it'd never happen, and so he could romanticise all he wanted and never end up being disappointed.

The next morning after breakfast, Archie took his coffee down to Jak's cell and chatted with him for a bit, and was surprised to have Brodie join them a short while later. He handed him a fresh brew and shrugged when Archie frowned in question. They would usually head straight out when he was done to go and fly.

"It's lashing it down out there and a storm is on the way," he told him, "so no flying. It's too dangerous."

"Damn it," he groaned. They were really getting somewhere now, and that was when a thought struck him. "If it eases, do you think we could go out, anyway? The storm will cover the sight and sounds of the chopper if we take it higher. Maybe go for a proper fly?"

"No," Brodie answered, and Archie let out a huff. He hadn't even entertained the idea for a second.

"Grumpy fucker," he answered, and Jakob laughed.

"What? It's true," the vampire added when Brodie turned to him with a scowl.

"I agree too," the seldom heard voice of his female counterpart added, and then she started laughing when the three men turned to her misty apparition in surprise.

Archie had to admit, Wynter looked denser than he'd seen her before, clearly having grown stronger the past few weeks, and it was nice to see her again. She went straight to Jak in his cell and was just placing a kiss upon his cheek when Brodie suddenly stiffened.

Archie began to panic when Jakob and Wynter then did the same. They both stood, and Jak sniffed the air.

"What's wrong?" he gulped.

"They're here," the three creatures all answered in unison, and Archie didn't need to ask who they were on about. Somehow, while they had been hiding away, thinking they were safe, the enemy had been closing in. How the hell had they known where to find them? And more importantly —

"What do we do?" he asked, and then ran out to the tunnel and looked up and down it, as though he might somehow be able to see through the darkness and find a way to escape the vampire he'd heard all about. He had no chance of evading Marcus, at least not without his magical friends, and so turned back to the three of them. "What are we gonna do?" he demanded again, panic rising in his chest.

"We fight," Brodie answered, and then he finally opened Jakob's cell to release him. It'd taken the arrival of their enemies to end their feud, and Archie wanted to scream at them both. Where were their defences? Their back up plans? And what the hell had Brodie been playing at all this time?

"I've got no chance against a horde of vampires!" he bellowed, and his heart sank when they all looked back at him with the same blank looks on their faces. "Shit. None of us do, do we?"

"No, but stay close to me and I'll do what I can, okay?" Brodie told him, and for the first time, Archie thought he showed some real caring for him. That he might be sorry for having dragged him into this war only to have then left him unprepared and without any chance of escape.

"Let's all stay together. Get to the chopper and either me or Brodie will fly us out of here," he offered, and the others nodded in agreement. It was their only chance, and when the sound of scurrying bodies scraping the wet ground began to resonate up from the depths below, Archie knew it was time to move.

He dropped his still warm cup of coffee and when the mug smashed on the ground, the sound sparked him into action.

Go, go, go, he told himself. *Don't look back!*

He ran for higher ground and reached the archway out of the cave in time to see a collection of horrific grey hands clambering over the cliff edge from the other side.

The vampires were climbing up the damn rocks.

They were scaling the island as well as invading it from the depths. Covering every inch of the place their little team had called home these past few months.

The vampires' heads quickly began poking over the top of the rocks a second later, and Archie knew he'd never forget the sight of a hundred red, soulless eyes peering at him through the grey morning light.

They were vampires, sure, but weren't like Jakob in the slightest. They were more like zombies, not men and women. Not even one seemed to have any semblance of humanity left in them, and Archie immediately went into fight-or-flight mode.

He went with the latter and ran up the small path to where he knew the chopper awaited them and was grateful for not only knowing the way like the back of his hand but also for having put in the work this past few months and having gotten his fitness levels the highest ever.

His heart was pounding in his chest, but he persevered and found he didn't need to rest or catch his breath at all. Especially not with those awful vampire soldiers so hot on their heels.

He didn't stop until he reached the small hangar that shielded the helicopter from the elements and breathed a sigh he saw that Brodie and Jakob were already on hand to help him get the blades cleared and the chopper ready to go.

He was about to usher Brodie into the cockpit, but he was already around the other side, and so Archie knew what he had to do. He climbed up into the pilot's seat and fired up the controls. His hands were shaking, and he had to force himself to calm down.

"You can do this. Go!" Jakob called from the back seat, and with a nod, he took a breath and then went for it. Archie managed to get them off the ground just as the wave of vampire soldiers clambered up over the cliff edge, and he pulled back sharply on the controls in a bid to hurry their escape.

Their group then watched in horror as the horde ran towards them, and he took off, hoping for the best.

They could do this. They could get away.

All he had to do was punch it.

But then his heart sank when he saw the vampires running in droves towards them, piling up on top of one another's shoulders below, where their chopper was just taking off. He was fixated on them, trying desperately to pull up in time to get away, but then a thud came from the opposite side of their craft and he spun in his seat, which was when he saw a second group of vamps who were careening over the top of the small hanger.

And then the front one reached over, his grey outstretched hand extending forward through the wet and windy weather…

"Shit!" Archie cried as he lost control, and knew they were done for when, instead of heading up, they were suddenly plummeting towards the ground, about to crash. The damn vampires had them, he knew. It had to have been the huge one at the front. He was bigger and somehow seemed more determined than the others, and Archie was sure he caught a huge smile spread across the vile creature's pale face as they careened towards the ground.

It was then that he turned to Brodie, his eyes wide, and saw the jinni shake his head solemnly. Their chance of escape was lost. They had tried and failed, but he was glad they'd tried at all. Better to die fighting than give up and go, anyway. Right?

A split-second later, Brodie transformed before his eyes, becoming nothing but smoke, and then the pair of them were somehow out of the helicopter and freefalling towards the ground.

Brodie was gone again in a flash, but Archie knew why when a black shadow then caught him in his arms to stop him from hitting the ground, rather than let Archie's frail body take the full force of the fall.

He knew exactly who was holding him. As always, no words were said, but Archie smiled to his friend, expecting for Brodie to drop him so they could run, but instead he carried him to the cliff edge and then flung him over the edge like he was tossing him out to sea for a mere swim.

"Head for the mainland… Only the mainland!" he called as Archie descended, reminding him of who lived on the other island, and to avoid washing up there or else become the werewolf's supper.

Archie hit the cold water a second later and immediately lost his bearings. He went into panic mode and looked back up at the island that was covered in grey naked bodies that were still clambering up out of the ocean and scaling the rocks. There had to be a thousand of them there by now, but there was one saving grace. At least they were no longer coming for him.

Their prize was fifty feet up in the air. Wynter.

A wave then swept over Archie's head, dragging him under for a second, and when he re-emerged, he was left clambering to regain his composure. He knew he was already going into shock with the cold and that he had to save himself. This entire situation was insane, but he had to move. Had to get away from them or else become their supper, too.

There was nothing he could do other than swim for it, and thanks to Brodie, he'd been given the chance of surviving Marcus's attack. At least he was in a better position than those he'd had to leave behind, and he wasn't going to waste his chance to escape the vampire invasion.

He swam towards the farthest land he could see through the darkening cloud and lashing rain, thinking it was the best bet at finding the mainland. The current seemed against him, but he pushed on. He used every ounce of strength he had left and hit the rocky beach what felt like an age later.

Archie was shaking from head to toe with the cold, but knew he could manage one more push. He could make it to safety, and so clambered up the beach in search of help.

Everything ached, but he forced himself on. Up he went, over the pebbles that cut his knees and through a patch of tall grass, only to find the lighthouse standing directly ahead.

Shit! He'd ended up exactly where he didn't want to be.

Archie curled into a ball and forced himself to scream silently into his hands. He knew he couldn't stay there. Not with the warnings Brodie had given him about the wolf who lived on the island. The creature whose territory he had just invaded by setting foot on the otherwise uninhabited land. He had no time to spare, and sat back up, readying himself to dive back into the ice-cold ocean.

"What have we got here then?" a voice from behind him then boomed, before Archie was struck over the back of the head, making him crumble in a heap with the shock and pain.

He rolled onto the ground and then looked up to find a huge, dirty man dressed in rags standing over him, and wasn't given the opportunity to respond before the man grabbed him and dragged him towards the huge white building ahead.

Inside, he hauled Archie up too many stairs to count, his back and hips thumping against every concrete step as the werewolf wrenched him higher up and into the towering building. It was agonising, especially when teamed with the pain wracking through his skull from the blow to the head he'd just been given.

When they came to a stop, it was only for the man to string him up by his wrists, which was when Archie finally got a look around.

He was in some kind of bedroom, and there were two women in it with him. Both of them were pale and dishevelled, and were clearly terrified by the return of their captor. They were cowering in a corner together and whimpering, and then seemed relieved when the man left again.

Archie's head was pounding, and it took him a few minutes to gather his senses, but he forced himself to stay awake.

"Please, help me," he whimpered, but the girls both shook their heads.

"He'll punish us," one said. She was a brunette with huge blue eyes. Eyes that were sad, like she'd seen too many horrors to recount. "You need to be good. Do what he says."

"How long have you been here?" he asked, thinking of how Brodie had told him the werewolf would've quickly claimed any prey and then had his fill before devouring them. He wouldn't keep them hostage, but the women had clearly been there for longer than a day or so. It appeared that when in human form, he had found a way to deny the beastly part of himself his feast. And in doing so had only postponed the poor girls' torture.

"I don't know for sure, but it's definitely been a few weeks," the other answered. She was blonde, not that he could properly tell from the dirt on her, and she seemed even more timid than the first girl. She couldn't seem to look Archie in the eye, and he didn't blame her. She had to have been terrorized these past few weeks, and was clearly suffering with some kind of trauma.

The man had kept them captive. Kept the girls for himself rather than let the wolf have them. He had to have some control over his animalistic side, or so Archie hoped. Perhaps he could even reason with the guy?

Yeah, that was clearly wishful thinking given the two hostages he'd kept at his mercy for weeks seemingly without a care. And now he had a third too. Archie wasn't sure which was worse, the vampires or the wolf.

"Our boat got into trouble so we headed for shore and towards the lighthouse, but then found ourselves in his clutches almost right away. He locks us in here each night so the beast can't have us, but most days I wonder whether that would be preferable," the brunette told him, still cowering on the bed.

"Always so dramatic, Rosalie. She's just still getting used to spending so much time with me, but you won't have to worry about that. Unluckily for you, I'm not into boys. The beast is though. I think I'll keep you until tonight and then let him have his fun..." the man said as he returned and placed down two plates of cooked eggs and berries for the women to eat.

Archie didn't answer. There was clearly no way to bargain with him, so instead he began hatching a plan. He knew now that he had the day to try and get away, because any longer and he would be done for. Night would fall and he'd be dead, and so he found himself wondering about his friends the next island over. Were they dead, too? He hoped not, and not only because he wished there might be a chance of getting rescued, but because he truly cared about them. Jakob had become a true friend to him, and while things had been strange between them, he was terrified for Brodie.

Was Marcus going to kill him for taking Wynter away?

It didn't even bear thinking about.

He swallowed the lump in his throat and watched as the girls scoffed down their food like they hadn't seen a proper meal in weeks. They probably hadn't, and he understood why they were so ready to accept the offer of a meal from their captor. He then expected the dirty, feral man to leave, but he didn't. The blonde hadn't so much as swallowed her last bite before he was on her. He grabbed her by the hair and then took her to the filthy bed across the room without a care for Archie's presence, and ignored her pleas as he then mounted her.

Archie did his best to look away and try to allow her some modesty, but when the brunette cried for him to stop hurting her friend and joined them voluntarily on the bed, he was surprised that the man did as she'd asked. But then the unthinkable happened. The vile man pushed the blonde girl away and kicked her in the ribs, completely ignoring her screams for mercy.

"You're no good to me broken," he spat, and then looked to Archie with a dirty smile. "It looks like she's just brought you some time, boy. Maybe I'll keep you around after all…"

TWENTY

Back on the island, Wynter was in her invisible form inside the cave, and Marcus had her surrounded by a wall of his creepy soldiers. Brodie was inside too, as was Jak, and her soul mate was looking seriously close to dangerous territory. She could feel her heart breaking already, and screamed herself hoarse, begging for Marcus to put an end to her torture.

Once Jakob was out cold following his numerous beatings, he was strung up over the alpha's shoulders like some kind of rag doll. She seethed and cursed the huge soldier, but he didn't so much as flinch. Why would he? He was nothing more than a beast for hire, and of course Marcus had utilised him well.

She turned her face away, and found four more of his soldiers pinning Brodie down on the cold, solid ground. Her jinni saviour had fought more than a hundred of them off. He'd stood his ground and bravely tried his best to succeed, but had eventually failed. The soldiers were too strong, and even though Brodie had demanded she stay hidden beside him, Wynter had known there was no way she could let his fight continue.

He couldn't pay for her mistakes.

"Come out, come out, wherever you are..." Marcus sang, and she reappeared in her misty form, but took the chance to throw a punch his way during her moment of surprise, and instead of lashing back at her, he simply burst out laughing. "My sweet, sweet girl. There you are."

He then stopped and eyed her up and down, his breath hitching, like he couldn't believe his eyes.

"Leave now, Marcus. I am not your slave any more and you have no claim over me," she tried, "I'm stronger and can beat you now. Strong enough to stop you."

"You can't help yourself, can you?" he teased, "forever my little fighter."

But she wasn't playing.

"Let us go. You can't win, we've proven this. There's no need to play these games any more. Plus, I need both of them if I have any hope of surviving and you know it!"

"Oh, him?" he asked, pointing over to where Jak was still out cold. He then went over and laid into him, dragging him down onto the ground before punching and kicking him some more.

Wynter stepped forward, acting on instinct to stop him, but it was Marcella who moved into place between her and Marcus, holding her back from intervening.

"Stop him, please," she begged, and the Priestess shook her head resolutely, making her see red. "You're nothing more than his little bitch, you know that? Don't you want your own life? To make your own decisions? I thought witches were meant to be more powerful than vampires, so why is it you just do everything he says?"

The friend she thought she knew was indeed long gone. The Priestess simply smiled timidly and then placed Wynter's hand on her belly.

"I need nothing more than what I have, my love. She knows you. Knows your voice and your spirit. She knows how good you made me feel that day we made love, and she knows how greatly I care for you. She misses you. I miss you too," was her response, and then Marcella suddenly kissed her.

Wynter tried to pull back, but then she realised she couldn't. She was rooted to the spot by magical forces, and even then, when the witch eventually pulled back, she was still unable to move a single wisp of her smoky form.

She glared at Marcella, but her eyes were shining back and were a pure, brilliant white. It was like something had overcome her too, and all Wynter could do was stare into her glowing eyes in shock.

Marcella then opened her mouth, and she recited a spell over and over again, using that peculiar multi-layered voice. They were strange, foreign words and even though she didn't know their meaning, Wynter started screaming at her to stop.

Whatever she was up to, she had the feeling it wasn't going to do her any good, and was proven right when Marcella then began to violently shake. It was like she was having some kind of seizure, but all the while she continued to recite her spell, and Wynter realised then how she could neither see nor hear anything else. It was as if time had stopped for the two of them and the world around them had ceased to exist. They were in their own little bubble, and nothing was coming in or out of it.

The spell freezing her to the spot was then suddenly broken and Marcella fell backwards, like she'd passed out. Wynter grabbed her before she could hit the ground, crying out for someone to help, but no one seemed to have noticed. She then looked up and found the witch had indeed created some kind of magical circle around them, and it was only when Marcella stopped fitting that she realised what'd happened.

She had hands and arms, legs and feet. Wynter was whole. Flesh and blood, or whatever jinni's had in place of what was once her human body. But it was real. Her heart was somehow beating in her chest and there was an incredible sense of strength within her that somehow didn't seem like it was there to be shared and then taken away, but given willingly.

She could feel herself drawing power from the Earth itself, like it was living within her, and it was as if something had somehow just been switched on inside of her. A button that'd taken her from a weak and feeble young jinni who needed the life force of a host to survive, to an all-powerful single entity who would never need a host again.

What at first felt marvellous then suddenly seemed like more of a curse when she looked down and saw the blood pooling between Marcella's thighs. It was flowing out of her in droves, like she was haemorrhaging badly, and Wynter screamed for help again. And, like before, no one came.

She pressed her hands over Marcella's stomach, only to find that it was flat.

The baby was gone.

Not delivered, but vanished entirely.

As if by magic.

"What have you done?" Wynter screeched, but the Priestess was still out cold, and as the magical circle then began to disappear, she could hear someone wailing from a few feet away. It was her old colleague, Jack, but she didn't know why. At least, not until he fell to the ground beside the pair of them and gathered Marcella up into his arms, where he whispered into her ear that everything was going to be okay.

She peered into his face and knew then how the baby had been his. "I'm sorry…" she whispered, but he didn't hear her. He was too lost in his grief, and she couldn't blame him.

"Yes! There is nothing on this Earth more powerful than the heart of a witch…" Marcus whispered from across the room, and Wynter was still attempting to figure out what'd happened when he then laughed. "Don't you feel it? And do you not sense anything else that's different, my sweet?"

She wanted to tell him no, but actually, something did feel different. And not in a good way. She was whole now, sure, but there was something missing.

Wynter looked up and over at him, and then watched in horror as he lifted up his right arm, showing off the decapitated head he held in his hand like some kind of trophy.

It was Jakob's. Her one and only. Her true love.

And he was in pieces.

Dead.

His blue eyes were dull and lifeless. His skin blue, blood pouring from every orifice.

Wynter retched and cried and wailed at the sight, but that didn't make it go away. Didn't make it any less real.

"No, no, no," she cried, tears falling from her eyes in droves. "This cannot be!" she screamed, clutching at her heart, which she expected to feel breaking, but it thundered on. It kept on beating without Jakob to make it whole, and she knew then how Marcus had somehow found a way to reverse their merging. Or rather, Marcella had.

"I took the risk and disposed of him once and for all during your new magical bonding with the unborn witch. And look, it appears your soul is free again, just like I'd imagined."

He then threw the bloody remains towards her and Wynter scurried back in shock, screaming her head off as she tried to get away from the awful sight of Jak's lifeless eyes that were left boring into hers.

She stood and tried to run, but the alpha soldier intercepted her, along with the thousand or so other vampires all crammed into the caves above and below them. He gripped her waist and glared into her eyes. And then he somehow whispered her name and fisted his icy hands in her hair, smelling it, and Wynter recoiled. But it appeared he hadn't had enough, because he then licked her cheek and sighed dreamily, smacking his lips.

"His first word was you, my sweet. I think he might be a bit smitten," Marcus teased.

It was only then she remembered she was not human and didn't need to worry about the alpha vampire touching or trying to taste her. Not anymore, and she certainly didn't need to fear him or the others, either.

"Don't touch me ever again," Wynter demanded, and then she shoved the alpha away. He went flying back into the wall of soldiers, and for a moment, she stood there in surprise, astounded at the strength she now possessed. Even the huge behemoth was no match for her now, but her revelry was short-lived when she remembered why and how this had all come about.

"Now, come and thank me for releasing you from the binds Jakob cunningly put upon you. And thank your new mother and father for sacrificing their unborn child to allow you to live without your strength ever waning again. You owe them. And you owe me…"

"No. Fuck you all," she tried, but it was no use.

She had no force behind her retorts.

No strength left to try and fight the magical forces Marcella had conjured in order to capture her using a different set of binds this time.

All was lost. It was over.

Wynter knew she couldn't escape Marcus this time, or probably ever again. He would continue to lay waste to those she loved if she dared try, and while she mulled over how best to admit careful defeat, Marcus watched her with an impatient stare.

"Very well, then I shall dispose of your jinni mentor too," he answered, and the vampires holding Brodie down lifted him up and then began to pull at his arms and legs. "Did you know, the only way to kill a jinni is by ripping them to pieces and then separating the parts so that they cannot merge back together? Quite brutal indeed, and oh so enjoyable…" he told her, but didn't stop them, and it was all too much for her to bear.

His screams were deafening, and Wynter ran to Brodie to help him. She tried to grab at the vampires holding him, but no sooner had she released one's grip that another would take their place. They were relentless, as was their master, and she knew there was no hope left for any of them. It was time she stopped fighting.

"No more, please. Don't take him too. I'll go with you, Marcus. I won't run anymore, but you let him go. He never wanted any part of this!" she begged.

"Oh, very well," he answered with a satisfied smile, and the vampires released Brodie without needing to be ordered aloud.

Wynter helped him stand, and then hugged him hard. This was goodbye and they both knew it, but it appeared he wasn't going to leave her without one more reminder. In spite of the danger, he leaned close and whispered in her ear.

"Don't trust any of them. And don't forget who you are. Jinni's are far more powerful than vampires, Wynter. Fight him. Fight for what you want and don't become his slave all over again. Call upon me and I shall fight beside you. Remember that."

She thanked him but shook her head no. She couldn't do it all over again. Marcus was too powerful and too merciless. She'd lost so much already, and couldn't lose Brodie too.

"Find Archie. Make sure he's safe. And for goodness' sake, show that poor boy how you feel," she demanded, and then went timidly to Marcus's side. She was trembling with fear at being near him again, but forced herself to stand tall and stare him right in the eye. "Let's just go," she pleaded, but it appeared he had other plans first.

With a smile, he took her hand in his and then turned to Marcella, who was still covered in blood from the waist down and only just about managing to stand by the looks of things. She'd regained consciousness in Jack's arms, but she was still a mess.

The Priestess stared into Marcus's eyes and was suddenly glowing with pride, as though she'd planned it this way, and Wynter gulped. The powerful witch had seen this coming. She had foreseen this and gone ahead with the attack, having known she would have to lose her unborn daughter in the process. "How could you?" Wynter whispered in surprise, but was ignored.

"My lady," Marcus insisted, and then nodded to her.

Before Wynter could ask what more he possibly wanted of her, his Priestess recited yet another spell in some ancient language she had no idea of, and then conjured some kind of magical bond around the pair of them.

A sort of golden thread seemed to settle around their linked hands, and she figured it was a kind of binding ritual. A way of him always being able to find her, no doubt. Her word never had been good enough, so Marcus was clearly putting some kind of hex on her, but she didn't fight it.

Everything was already lost, including her hope, and Wynter simply felt broken. An empty shell where a soul that had once loved and dreamed had been.

"You may kiss your bride, my lord," Marcella then said, and Wynter turned to her in shock. No way was that a done deal. They'd said no vows, and she certainly hadn't agreed to marry him, and she was about to tell them both so, when the Priestess used her moment of confusion to her advantage.

With a cunning grin, she lifted her hand and blew some kind of dust into her face from atop her palm, and Wynter felt herself fall back into Marcus's outstretched arms. Her initial confusion was followed quickly by nothing but blackness. She felt herself fade away, and not a single one of her magical skills seemed able to stop whatever potion Marcella had brought and had at the ready.

Her fight truly was over.

TWENTY ONE

The entire exchange was like something out of a horror movie. The bad guy had somehow won, while all the 'good guys' were left dead, scattered to the wind, or captured. Poor Wynter had also been forced to endure a transition from fledgling jinni to one of the most powerful forms their kind were capable of embodying, and Brodie still couldn't believe Marcus's priestess had sacrificed her baby to make it so.

There were very few Jinn around the globe who possessed the heart of a witch. Doing thus had not only given them an immortal existence but also a never-ending source of life force to live on. Their strengths depended on the type of witch, of course, but everyone knew Marcus had not aligned himself with a mere elemental coven. No, their power was drawn from the Earth itself and so their supremacy would last forever. Until the end of days, and then some.

Brodie only wished Wynter realised what that meant. She was now stronger than both Marcus and Marcella combined, but with that power came a curse, because she was connected to them, too. By magic, marriage, and also by blood. No power on Earth could part them now, especially since Marcus had also been sure to murder her soul mate while she was protected within the magical circle the Priestess had created.

The vampire soldiers began to disband, and Brodie could do nothing but watch as Wynter was carried away in the arms of that bastard, leaving him behind on the island they'd called home. He'd fought hard in spite of the never-ending string of vampire foes, but hadn't had the strength to carry on forever. He hadn't expected himself to either, but had been ready to die in battle if that was his fate.

However, after Wynter had pleaded for him to stop, he'd then forced himself to do exactly that and had gladly accepted the precious gift of freedom she had given him.

There was no choice in it for her, and perhaps there never had been. Marcus was clearly far too formidable an opponent. Too ready to watch the

394

world burn rather than let her have her own way, and even after all the months since they'd left him, he'd still come for her. Laid in wait and, of course, bided his time while they had become complacent.

They had been such fools to think they could simply hide and let things blow over.

As the sun then began to rise, he listened for any sound both above and below him, but the vampires truly had gone. Rafferty had hidden, and he didn't blame him. Goblins were not made for fighting. He wouldn't know where to start, and he too emerged and began the epic task of cleaning up while Brodie stood at the cave entrance and glared out at the new day, wondering where Archie was.

Had he made it to safety and left them far behind? He sure hoped so. But instead, when he reached out for the human with his mind, hoping to sense him somewhere on the mainland, it was to discover he was actually close. Far closer than he ought to be.

"Damn," he whispered to himself, and then followed the call to the ledge outside, where he looked across the stretch of sea and towards the lighthouse. The foolish boy hadn't followed his orders, and he cursed him. Either that, or the storm had swept the currents away from the mainland and taken him into the path of a different kind of danger.

He jumped straight off the side of the nearest cliff and turned to smoke before hitting the water. Brodie then travelled as naught but the breeze, invisible to even the most cunning eye, and he arrived at the base of the huge lighthouse within mere moments.

There, still in transition from werewolf back to man, was the island's sole permanent inhabitant. But that wasn't true now. Brodie stood watching him, and he picked up on three distinct scents. One was a recently deceased female, another a living woman, and a male. A wave of relief spread over him. Archie was somehow still alive, even after a day and night spent on the island, and Brodie knew he had to get him away from there post-haste.

He followed the now human werewolf inside the lighthouse without delay and saw as the man began making up some breakfast in the gully. But Brodie didn't linger there to keep watch. He instead went up to where Archie and the girl were being kept, and was outraged with what he found there.

He was strung up and clearly in pain, while the poor young woman was chained to a bed by her wrists. They were both in a bad way. The girl had been physically brutalised and taken advantage of, while Archie had been beaten and was suffering from clear hypothermia.

Brodie materialised before them, making the woman shriek in shock, but she quickly covered her mouth when Archie assured her he meant them no harm. He made quick work of releasing his friend, and tended to him for a moment, his heart pounding in his chest. A dozen dark thoughts were whizzing through his mind. What if the wolf had taken him? What if he had died and had been lost? Brodie didn't know what he would've done.

And there it was, the realisation of how much he really did cherish him. How he couldn't have handled it if the worst had happened to yet another person he cared about.

"Save her," Archie then groaned, and he managed to stay on his feet long enough to give Brodie a defiant stare. He was clearly pleased to see him as well, but they still had a fight on their hands. Still had to get back to the safety of their island and away from the wolf.

"Of course," he answered, and was just breaking her chains when the Were came in. He dropped the plates of food he'd brought up with him and quickly lunged for Brodie, but he wasn't at all in the mood to play any games. A far superior creature, he wrestled him to the ground with ease and then let his instincts take over. Let out his anger and rage on an adversary he could get away with bring down and tearing to pieces.

He leaned down and ripped a chunk out of the man's neck with his teeth, which he spat on the floor beside them. He then grabbed his chin and turned his face up to where Archie was leaning against the wall weakly. "He is mine, you fucking heathen," he bellowed, and the wolf-man nodded in understanding, but it wasn't enough.

Brodie had an overwhelming need to protect Archie, and so punched a hole straight through the guy's chest and ripped out his heart. It continued to throb in his hands for a couple of seconds, but his respite from death was short lived. Wolves were simple enough to kill, thankfully.

The girl still on the bed screamed in shock, but Brodie knew it was the right thing to do. They would all be better off with the wolf gone. Archie was his property, but as far as the wolf was concerned, that girl belonged to him, and he would've come looking if he'd left him alive. So, with their newest foe dead, he grabbed the two captives, and they ran out the door and down the stairs without delay.

He then used up an incredible store of his strength to carry them back to his island using his misty form, but it was worth it. There, they went directly back to what was left of the house, and he immediately called to Rafferty for help. Archie was shivering and seemed ready to collapse, and the girl began screaming like a bloody banshee. She had clearly been through an incredible trauma at the hands of the werewolf, and while Brodie wanted to help her, he felt inept.

He didn't know what she needed or if she even wanted their help, so just ushered her into the living room to rest on the sofa there and find her bearings. As he then watched the goblin strike a fire and deliver the two humans with blankets and hot drinks, all he could do was stand there, hovering like some imbecile who had no clue what to do.

And so he eventually took a seat beside Archie and tucked him under not one, but two heavy quilts.

With the fire now blazing in the hearth, the poor young man finally seemed to be warming up, and Brodie couldn't take his eyes off him. He knew then how he'd been nothing less than selfish. He had put himself first and let his ego stop him from getting close to Archie during their initial few months together. He'd foolishly stopped himself from moving forward with his life, like both Wynter and Jakob had repeatedly asked him to. And in doing so, he had almost lost everyone he'd come to care about.

He sat back in the chair and just continued to watch Archie warm through, while the poor girl cocooned herself in the blankets and eventually succumbed to her need for sleep. She had to be exhausted, and he didn't envy her the nightmares that surely awaited her. He would stay with them, he decided. Be there when either of them needed him.

"What did you mean, I'm yours?" Archie then whispered, and Brodie said nothing at first. He just stared back at him and then reached for his still icy hand, warming it in his.

"It means I'm sorry. That I do care and that I want you to stay with me," he then told him, but wanted desperately to say more, however he couldn't pull together the right words.

Damn, he really was bad at this.

"I'm guessing it's just us left, so am I finally here as your friend? Or are we still looking at this as a business arrangement?" Archie asked, and Brodie knew he deserved the icy edge to his tone.

He shook his head and then kissed the back of his hand. It was the most tender he'd been with anyone in a very long time and it felt so strange, but also like something inside of him had shifted and cracked open. Perhaps his old heart that he'd welded shut. He didn't know, but one thing he was sure of was that Wynter had been right. It was time he opened up and told Archie how he felt.

"I don't think we were ever actually friends, were we?" Brodie teased with a smile, "but we can be. In fact, I want us to be more than friends. I wonder if you might be able to forgive my bluntness and perhaps we can start over?"

"I'd like that too," Archie answered with a gentle smile, "and yeah, let's start again. Beginning with me saying thank you for saving me," he added.

"Anytime," Brodie replied, and then kissed him again, but on the lips this time.

***

Wynter came back around in a strange bedroom what felt like half a day later, and found Marcus watching over her with his usual stoic indifference. He had his arms crossed over his puffed chest and was emitting icy cold air in droves.

God, even after waging war to get her back, he still couldn't just play nicely? She wanted to scream. Or throw something. Maybe both.

"I don't know whether to kiss you or beat you," he eventually told her, and she climbed up off the bed and stood scowling back at him. Two could play these old games.

"Try either, and I'll rip your fucking throat out. I'm not the flimsy little human girl you can push around anymore. You want me to fight back, then expect a far fairer fight this time," she growled, and saw his mouth twitch with the smile he was trying to hide from her. He was enjoying this, and she inwardly cursed herself for bothering to answer him back.

"Sure we could fight, but of course you're my wife now and so you are obliged to respect and obey me. Plus, there's also the consummation of our marriage to consider," he answered with a smile, and she was reminded of the bonding ritual Marcella had performed before somehow rendering her unconscious. Was it true? Was she really his wife now? The thought made her want to cry, and the idea of consummating their union made her feel sick.

The unthinkable had happened, and Jakob was gone, but she still loved him. Still missed him. And she could feel the black hole in her chest that she knew was her grief just waiting in the wings. It would hit her soon, and when it did, she knew there would be no one who could help her through it. Like Brodie, was she going to hold on to it forever?

"That is never gonna happen," she demanded, but then she felt her heart pounding in her chest, pulling her towards him without her doing it. Wynter suddenly flushed with heat and desperation, and she shook her head profusely.

This couldn't be happening. He didn't have that power over her anymore.

The curse was long gone. She had broken that spell a long time ago.

Marcus watched her with a smile, and then he let out a satisfied laugh.

"Half jinni and half witch, my sweet. And the witch's heart within you beats solely for me. She will keep you strong and whole, but she is loyal to me implicitly. She loves me, as will you. And so you will learn from her. Because, like it or not, you are my wife, forevermore…"

The end of book three in the Blood Slave series…

BLOOD SLAVE

The Complete series

#4 Even in Death

By

Eden Wildblood

ONE

Everything felt different. From her now fully formed and always present body, to the rapidly beating heart deep within, it was suddenly all too real, and Wynter hated every second of her new life. None of this was right.

She shouldn't have a beating heart. No, she should be nothing but mist. She ought to still be following the usual jinni routine of learning and growing inside of her host while growing strong enough to finally become whole, but instead she was something else entirely. A creature far different from any of the lore Brodie had taught her about. And rather than with her creator, he had to be thousands of miles away. But it no longer mattered. She didn't need him to guide her.

Only Marcus.

Or so it appeared, seeing as she couldn't get enough of the guy nowadays. When with him Wynter felt like she was someone else, and he affected her in ways she had promised herself she'd never let him do. Especially after all the awful things he had done.

But it was like the heart she'd promised would never be his was suddenly screaming out for him, begging him to have her, and she yearned for more.

His touch.

His kisses.

His love.

The damn vampire had somehow forced his way into her good graces, and she strangely favoured him above all others, but there was something still niggling in the base of her skull.

She kept wondering how and why this change could've happened.

There were a hundred thoughts rushing through her mind when she thought back to that horrendous day, but Wynter knew it was the witch's heart Marcella had gifted her. It had to be because she was only under

401

Marcus's spell when she was near him. It was like those initial days in his keep all over again, but whenever she finally had some distance, her heart felt like it was breaking. She felt grief-stricken and so desolate it was torturous. Like she was broken from the inside out.

It'd only been a day since Wynter had woken up on the small island Marcus apparently had tucked away across the world, and she was still trying to get her head around what was going on within her. But one thing was for certain. She might be the driving force of her now immortal jinni body and in control of herself and her actions, but there were certainly two sides to her now that she had the witch's heart beating within her chest, as Marcus had described it.

An unborn baby had given her life in offering for this change, and now Wynter was convinced that she did indeed have two hearts. She was half jinni and half witch, and while the witch half sourced the power for the other, there was also a fair price Wynter had been forced to pay for it.

Her dignity.

Her integrity.

Her body.

Her will.

When she was with Marcus, the oaths passed down from one generation of Marcella's coven to the next immediately came into play. Their kin had vowed unending loyalty to him alone, along with their unbridled love and subjugation, and she could sense at last just why the Priestess had always remained Marcus's most loyal subject, no matter what he had done or what he had forced her to do for him. Every woman who had come before Marcella in the family tree had adored him and had taught the next to do the same. The child who had given her life for Wynter's included. However, she was just a single addition to the line beholden to the ancient mastermind. The last of thousands of generations of witch, and with so very many more still to come.

The child had been bred to serve him too, and so she was, and would forevermore. The only problem was how.

Wynter had been given the gift of the witch's heart, whether she'd wanted it or not, and was now paying the price for having been unwittingly added to his doting coven.

She still had her own will though, and so had actively avoided him the past day as much as she could, even though he'd been relentless with his advances. Whenever he approached, she retreated. When he walked in a room, she left it, but after the initial twenty-four hours, Wynter was in agonising pain that radiated from within because of that distance she had forced between them. If she obeyed him, she had the feeling the pain would go away. But she didn't want him like that, and of course, she downright refused to give into his desirous advances.

He'd won their awful war, and she had lost everything. She had admitted defeat, but that didn't mean she had to then hand herself over like some spoil of war he was then within his rights to enjoy at length. Wynter was determined to continue fighting him and wanted to keep some parts of herself after her violent downfall at the hands of the man she was now forced to accept as her husband.

And every time she remembered that fact, she felt like breaking down and crying all over again. In what world was this real? What had she possibly done to deserve this fate? To have been forced to endure his adoration.

Wynter hated how she had spent her entire life yearning for a love exactly like this. One powerful enough to overcome all obstacles and with a man on the giving end of it, who would do anything it took to make her his. But, like some kind of nightmare, the fairy tale had ended in the villain having his way—not the hero. A twist of fate, and a curse that could seemingly never be broken.

Wynter endured the pain of staying away, finding comfort in the agony. She soon found herself in her bedroom, where she pressed her back against the door, holding it locked shut. Better to keep the demons out, but not for long. He never let her stay away long. She readied herself as best she could, thinking he would come looking for her any second, but instead she was left to her fraught thoughts and adrenaline-spiked urges for a short, excruciating while.

Wynter began to wonder if he'd finally gotten the message and left her be. Perhaps Marcella had stepped in, or maybe Jack was offering his master a vein? Anything to take him away from her for a short while. Anything to give her some peace.

She wanted to enjoy it, but the pain was almost unbearable. It radiated from her chest outwards, like waves cascading across her entire being. Her head throbbed and there was an annoying whooshing sound in her ears, like when she'd stood up too fast as a human. She inhaled deeply and counted the seconds, holding it for over a hundred before finally letting go.

That was one bit of good news. At least she knew for sure she didn't need to breathe anymore. This immortality was an odd thing, but there were some decent upsides. Wynter was also glad she didn't have the ravenous hunger Marcus and the other vampires did. Or the necessity for feeding his kind was driven by.

She simply existed now. No need to find a host and have life cycles. Unlike Brodie, the Halfling would remain whole for the foreseeable future, and Wynter suddenly realised how there was nothing driving her forward anymore. No future with Jakob and no rotation of life with Brodie. No friends. No family. She was empty and had nothing to live for. She had no purpose.

Not a nice thought for an immortal creature.

Wynter knew she needed to find her reason for carrying on and focus on it. She had to figure out what was worth living forever for, or else this gift Brodie had given her would be entirely wasted, and the thought of that made her want to weep.

And then, suddenly, she realised wasn't in pain any longer. Somehow, she had been given a reprieve from the aching pull towards Marcus and the love he seemed so desperate to show her, and when she began to flush with heat, she immediately knew why.

He was close. Probably on the other side of the door behind her. But at least he was quiet, for a change. He wasn't taunting her or calling to her, and Wynter hated the realisation that it was exactly what she'd needed to calm her fraught emotions.

She closed her eyes and listened to her body. She was so horny she felt fit to burst, so desperate to be touched her skin felt excessively sensitive. Wynter kept telling herself to run from him again, but she couldn't. It was so wonderful to have a break from the pain and so instead; she turned and wrenched open the door, thinking she would simply ask him to slow down.

Or else they could fight. At least that way he would have his wish and she'd be giving him the attention he so craved.

She was strong enough to take him on now and was determined to do so.

Marcus was indeed standing on the other side, and rather than look her over with the glower she'd expected from him, he seemed to be admiring her with a gentle, as yet unseen by her, look in his eyes. She had opened up the door with all the will in the world to tell him off and beat him down, and yet the opposite seemed to be about to happen.

No, she couldn't let it. Couldn't give in.

"Please," she hissed, and wasn't sure exactly what she was asking of him. To go away? To stay? Shit, she couldn't make up her mind in that moment. All she knew was that her body was screaming for her to move closer to his, and yet she continued to refuse.

"I can't. I love you, Wynter," Marcus then whispered, shocking her further, and as he closed the gap between them, another realisation struck. He had never once said those words to her before. Never let himself be weak in front of her or show his true feelings. And because of that, he had pushed her away, letting her fall for another.

The look on his face was one of true adoration and love, and it was more terrifying to her than any of his usual dark expressions.

Wynter swallowed the lump in her throat and peered up into his intense blue eyes and shook her head.

"No, you don't. You can't love me. You're incapable of love…" she tried, but he was having none of it.

"I moved Heaven and Earth to find you, my sweet. I sacrificed everything I have spent centuries building, and all for you."

He came closer and was so fast she didn't have time to get away. Marcus wrapped Wynter in his arms, and as soon as their bodies were connected, she felt her defiance wane and her once insolent desires dissipate entirely.

It was wonderful, and for the first time in days, she finally felt alive.

"What spell have you put me under?" she asked, and Marcus shook his head.

"No spell. No hexes. Just love," he answered, and then leaned down to place the gentlest of kisses against her lips.

Wynter tried to pull away, but the moment he made contact, she was overcome with passion and need. The witch's heart within that beat just for him took control, driving her over the edge, and forcing her further into his embrace. She wanted more, but then forced him back, telling Marcus no. She wasn't going to let him have her, and so turned her face away.

She willed herself to turn to smoke and rush off. Begged her body to move, but it wouldn't listen. Marcus was holding her to him so tightly he was crushing her, but she didn't care, because they both knew she wasn't the same woman he had fallen for. She could withstand anything he threw at her, and yet she was still weak. Too weak to push him away. Too weak to say no and mean it.

Wynter let out a garbled groan when his mouth found hers again. How could he taste so good? "You're mine, Wynter. Don't fight it, and don't deny it," he whispered as he then placed kisses along her jaw and neck, lifting her up into his arms as he tilted her back further.

He then wrapped her legs around his back before clambering onto the bed, and she gripped him tightly, moaning and bucking as his torso made contact against her wanton core.

"No," she tried, but Marcus had already ripped away their clothes without so much as breaking their connection, and his skin felt so amazing against hers she felt like crying. It was like it was laced with a love potion or something, because she couldn't stop herself from wanting more of his touch. She knew she was no longer herself, and could feel a change happening within her, but couldn't stop it.

And she knew why. It was her body that wanted him, but it was not her soul or her heart.

It was the other one.

But still, she didn't fight it. She couldn't.

Marcus nestled himself between her thighs and reared back, watching as he entered her and began slowly teasing his way inside. He seemed captivated by the view, and as soon as he was all the way within, something seemed to detonate between the pair of them. His eyes shone down at her so brightly it was like they were on fire, if fire could burn blue like his were.

Her tormentor pinned her to the bed, impaling her from inside, and as he stared into her eyes, Wynter felt his soul calling to hers.

She wanted to refuse him. She'd already had a merged soul mate and had lost him only days before, so was sure there was no way she could accept another, but those eyes of his refused to look away from hers. His soul forced its way beneath the veils of her existence, and it took hold of whatever remnants she had left of her own soul. She didn't accept his, like she had Jakob's, but it forced its way in any way.

Wynter let out a cry, and she tried to wriggle away as realisation struck, but it was already too late. She and Marcus weren't only husband and wife. They were merged soul mates now. She could feel it in every ounce of her being.

And so could he.

Marcus grinned down into her wide-eyed face and rolled his hips, burying himself even deeper within, and it was like nothing she had ever felt before. Heat rattled through her, and it was somehow bringing with it a wave of pain to her core, like this was her first time all over again.

She tensed and grabbed Marcus's shoulders, digging her nails into his flesh. He hissed, but then laughed before finally pulling back and withdrawing from between her thighs.

But he wasn't gone long. Marcus plunged right back in, and she cried out as he hit that same deep spot within that was still resonating with heat. And then again, and again.

Her body quickly began to ripple with rhapsody as he indulged himself in a slow and steady rhythm, and all the while Wynter could do nothing but bask in the wonderful sensations as he made love to her. She lost herself to the moment, and soon kissed and touched him tenderly, all hate and pain forgotten while in his arms. And there, the two of them not only became one, but they secured the bond between them at long last.

Marcus's eyes continued to glow from within the entire time they were at it, and while it was completely different to all the moments when his soul had called to hers in search of a merging, Wynter still felt that deeper connection begin to strengthen between the pair of them. It was like she herself was transforming, but instead the change affected them both, like the act of finally solidifying their union had brought them together in ways beyond just the physical.

It was both a welcoming and terrifying transformation. Something she knew would take a long time for her to understand, and perhaps even longer for her to accept.

After all, Wynter had spent her days at *Slave* both loving and hating the attention her boss persistently gave her, so she was used to having him close, but never this close. Never in her bed as a lover, or in her heart as a soul mate. He'd instead spent their days and nights together toying with her emotions for the fun of it and had always left her wanting something she couldn't have. Until now.

And her husband was indeed a surprising lover.

She'd watched Marcus fucking Camilla back at her mansion the night Jakob had taken her away. He'd been brutal with his fellow vampire lover and had pounded into her without any fear for her safety or caring for what she wanted of him, but with Wynter, he was the opposite.

He'd not once slept with her back when she was human, but now she was his wife and he clearly revelled at having her at his mercy. They were making up for all the times he'd had to walk away, but the games seemed over with. Wynter was as strong as any vampire, perhaps even stronger, and yet Marcus was nothing other than gentle with her.

He made love to her for days. They stopped for nothing and no one, and Marcus remained attentive and loving the entire time, proving that his words of adoration really were true.

In many ways, Wynter could hardly bear it.

At least the rough and ready she could handle, but not the lingering looks and attentive lovemaking. And every time he told her he loved her, she wanted to scream.

After almost a week spent in bed together, she decided it was time for a break. Marcus wasn't overly keen on the idea, it was obvious, but he quietly conceded and so left to do some work while she took a walk on the beach. There was nowhere she could run to, or far she was able to wander, but Wynter felt it was worth pursuing the small amount of space just to have a breather and help gather her thoughts.

After all, everything had suddenly become incredibly intense between the pair of them, and she was still processing it all. Still coming to terms with what he had done. And what she had let him do.

Once away from Marcus, the desperation she had for his touch was gone. As she'd imagined, the spell was well and truly broken. Everything else was perfect, though. There was no soreness between her thighs and no tiredness dragging her down. Her energy levels were always at maximum capacity, and she knew it was thanks to the witch's heart she had been given in place of her Jinn one. Thanks to the Priestess too. Her magical knowledge had given Wynter a way out of the limitations to a usual Jinni lifespan, and she'd outdone herself with this particular spell. Wynter knew she could never escape Marcus now. She was bound to him by heart and soul, and it was clear she had no choice but to remain by his side, but that didn't mean she had to like it.

In fact, now they were apart, all her true emotions came flooding back. And the realisation of what all of this meant.

Wynter sat down in the warm sand and sobbed, crying into her hands while she hugged her knees to her chest. All her fears and pain were back with a vengeance, and she knew she was definitely in mourning. Jakob had been dead little more than a week, and while remembering him hurt like hell, she refused to simply let go. What'd become of him was a true injustice, and she owed it to him to remember. Not to let the memory die, even if her soul was no longer merged with his.

He'd want her to stay strong. To be herself and remember what he'd taught her—to look out for number one. And Wynter knew she had to, so she started by trying to figure out what the hell had been done to her and what it all meant.

She closed her eyes and focused on her body, becoming aware of how every fibre of her being felt. There was no doubt about it. She was in optimum health and could feel her heart beating steadily, and it wasn't as if she had two of them, but more like it was in two parts. And so, she tried calling to the magical half. She and Brodie had been as one while taking up solace in one another's bodies, and she wondered if the witch was the same. Maybe they could converse and come to some kind of arrangement if she appealed to her better nature and tried her best, but there was nothing. Just the power she knew had been readily given, but that could most likely also be taken away just as freely.

She cried harder, but then stopped abruptly when she felt someone behind her. Wynter knew it couldn't be Marcus, otherwise she would've felt her witch's heart race, so she figured it had to be Marcella or perhaps Jack. Probably sent to get her by their master.

When she turned to tell them off, it was a shock to find someone else entirely standing over. Someone dressed in his usual black suit, even given the hot climate, but it wouldn't even matter if he was wearing a fur coat. The heat wouldn't make any sort of difference to the cold skin or grey pallor the man had.

It was the alpha soldier, and while he was staring down at her with that same cold, blank expression as usual, he seemed odd. Odder than usual, if it were possible.

He opened his mouth and closed it and then did it again. It was like he was trying to say something, but only seemed able to hiss out one word.

"Wynter..." he croaked, and then flinched and seemed to be fighting with himself, and he proved her suspicion right when he then actively smacked himself in the temple with rage.

She didn't know what to think. It was like he was trying to tell her something but was inept thanks to his far from human-like state, but she had no idea what to even expect from such an exchange. And she didn't have the patience to try and find out.

"Oh, just leave me alone, will you?" she barked, and then stood and glared up into his red eyes. "You like me huh, is that what you're trying to say? Then you should protect me. Do my bidding, and not his," she tried, and again he clicked his mouth and seemed to try to form other words, but couldn't do it, and this time she saw him get properly angry with himself for not being able to answer her back. Whatever it was he was trying to tell her, she knew he wouldn't be getting it out any time today.

Wynter didn't stick around to watch him keep trying. She'd said her bit and was willing to see what the alpha made of her requests later, but for the time being, she knew there was no other choice. She would have to accept her fate and keep playing nice with Marcus.

She headed back into the house with the vampire hot on her heels and was intercepted by her captor. Her husband. Damn, she still couldn't get her head around that. With the flick of Marcella's wrist, the deed had been done and they were joined in goddamn matrimony. No vows, and no rings. Just their souls that had been bound by her spell, whether she'd accepted or not.

Marcus was dressed in his usual finery. He was in a fully tailored suit and vest and had even added his pocket watch to his ensemble for the day. As always, he had refused to let himself look unkempt, and Wynter looked down at her cotton dress and sandals, thinking how odd the pair of them looked together. They weren't a match, so why had he pursued her so? She went to ask when he cut her off with a sly smile.

"I don't think I like him following you around like some kind of lovesick puppy. Shall I kill him for you?" he asked, eyeing the alpha with his most vile stare, and Wynter watched the behemoth cower before him. He then started scratching at his temples, as though trying to rid himself of a voice in his head, and she knew whose it must be. She wasn't the only one Marcus had taken control of by force. Half of his empire now relied on the hordes at his command, and so, like Camilla seemingly had, he had to be ruling them using mind control. She'd hardly ever seen him give spoken orders to the alpha or his pack, and yet they always knew exactly what he wanted.

"No more killing, Marcus. There's already been more than enough," she answered, and kept her distance so she could also keep somewhat of a clearer head when talking back to him. The further away she was, the more of herself she remained, and for now, she wanted to keep things that way.

She then headed for the stairs, thinking it might be nice to get washed up and into some clothes that weren't rough with sand, and it was a blessing when he chose not to follow her. It was hard enough keeping her head straight when he was across the room, but far better when she had multiple floors and walls between them.

As she ascended to the top floor, she caught sight of herself in one of the mirrors there and frowned at her reflection. There was so much wrong with the woman looking back at her, and Wynter knew she had to get her act together. There was a lot she had to learn and do, and an entire world out there to see, but she was positive Marcus would never let her do any of those things unless she gave herself to him completely first. And not just in the bedroom during the blissful times when his touch made her transform into someone else entirely. The inner witch, perhaps? She had no fucking clue. But she certainly needed to get on top of her Jinn powers.

Starting with the sorry state, she looked.

Wynter was well aware of how she could change her appearance at will without the need to wear real clothes in order to do it. Or more accurately, she could simply conjure them up using her powers, but there stood her first hurdle. She had no idea how to do so. She'd seen Brodie do it on many an occasion, but of course he'd had time with his mentor. He'd had a host who had guided him along his path, whereas the two of them hadn't been given the chance for her to learn how to be a jinni, and now that she was going it alone, it was showing.

She simply sighed and carried on her way to the bedroom, and as she passed an open door, she was suddenly drawn towards it on instinct. Inside were Marcella and Jack. They were laid together on top of the huge bed and Jack was cradling her in his arms while she wept. It was clear that she was grieving. That beneath the exterior of the hardened loyalist to Marcus's cause, she was still a person. Marcella had lost her child, and like any woman, she was clearly bereft. Damn, that brought an entirely new ache to her chest.

It was comforting to see Jack with her, though. They really did appear to be in love, like Marcus had told her, and it seemed strange seeing the human man being the one to comfort the powerful witch. Marcella had always been so formidable. So strong. It pained Wynter to see her so wistful. So beaten down by the life she was forced to live. She wanted to blame Marcus for her friend's loss, but she could only blame herself.

Marcella noticed her then and Wynter offered her a smile, but rather than speak to her or invite her inside, the witch simply turned her stoic face away. It was Jack who got up and came to the doorway, and he shook his head forlornly.

"Not yet," he whispered simply, before shutting the door in her face.

Wynter was left standing there staring at the dark wood in shock, and part of her wanted to scream and kick the door down.

She hadn't asked for any of this either. Surely this was the time when they ought to be looking after one another, not creating more distance? Marcella had foreseen her daughter's future. She planned for things to end this way, and now she couldn't even bear to look at the result of those choices. Her chest felt heavy with sorrow, and she knew it wasn't just her own hurt that she was feeling. The heart within was mourning, too.

Rather than linger where she wasn't wanted any longer, Wynter turned and ran for her bedroom, where she found Marcus waiting for her.

"You seem lost, my sweet," he said, having clearly decided against leaving her be after all.

"Please don't," she begged as she pressed herself against the wall opposite him, but instead he came closer. The vampire closed the gap in a second, and as soon as she was in his arms, everything suddenly felt right again. All the pain and the hurt were gone, and in its place was a wondrous glow. A flame burning only for him. "What have you done to me?" she whimpered, but then started peeling away his clothes as desire flooded through her. She kissed every inch of him she could get to and jumped up into his arms before she let him carry her to the bed.

"I opened your eyes so you could see the truth and let me love you. I always loved you, Wynter. From the moment I walked into that office and got a proper look into your eyes, I was yours. And you were mine," he groaned, and then he stripped her bare and then made love to her.

She wanted to tell him no. To remind him she hated him. To push him away and tell him no more, but instead, she arched her back to deepen his thrusts and then let him have every inch of her for himself.

Wynter knew she'd regret it afterwards. There was no denying it but would gladly take him loving her over the oppressive and often violent way he'd used to show her his affection. At least now there was no bite and no games. He had her ensnared, but Wynter didn't care anymore. Against all odds, she was beginning to feel like less of a captive and more like his soul mate. No longer the slave, but the willing submissive. It was far easier to give in than keep fighting it, and she desperately wanted to stop the hostility. To rest her weary heart and mind, even if only for a short while.

"Do you truly love me?" she asked when they'd finally had their fill of one another and were laid watching the new morning arrive outside the huge window that overlooked the stunning ocean.

"I do," Marcus answered, "and I know now that I should've turned you on that first week when you tried to leave me. Marcella told me to, but I saw love as weakness and refused to let myself own up to how I felt. But I was a fool. It was only when you were gone that I understood how much you'd affected me, and I knew I had to get you back. No matter the cost."

A tear ran down her temple at his words, and while part of her basked in them, Wynter knew there would always be that other side to her that despised Marcus for what he'd put her through. And the life he'd taken to claim her.

She could never forgive him for that. Never forget.

The only option she felt she had was to learn to live with her pain and hatred towards him. To bury it down deep and hope that someday she might stop seething. Stop plotting his demise. And maybe even start to love him back.

TWO

Archie woke up with a start and then laughed as he rubbed the sleep from his eyes.

"I fell asleep again, didn't I?" he asked the jinni whose shoulder he'd found himself snoozing on.

"Yeah, but you're human, don't forget. Plus, you've been through a lot. You actually do need sleep," Brodie reminded him, and Archie nodded. He'd been surviving on very little since their return to the small island off the coast of north Wales and knew it was because he had been trying to spend as much time with Brodie as he could. They were connecting, and while Rafferty put the house back together in the aftermath of Marcus's attack, they had rebuilt each other, along with their friendship.

Plus, there was whatever had suddenly blossomed to life between them to focus on too, and Archie knew that was the real reason he was putting in so much effort to spend as much time as possible with Brodie. He'd told Archie he cared for him. The closed off jinni had finally opened up and shared his feelings, and so he'd not wasted a moment with him in the hope he might do so again. But of course, he'd gone back to his usual stoicism now that they were back home and out of trouble. He was avoiding the deep and meaningful stuff, but Archie couldn't let what Brodie had said go.

He was his. He belonged to the jinni, in whatever way that meant, and Brodie had saved his life. He had shown him gentleness and even kissed him. There were things that needed saying and doing about that. However, he would force it aside and focus on the important stuff.

For now.

After all, there was still the question of what they were going to do about Wynter, who had been dragged off to only God knew where with Marcus. Brodie had told him all about how that shit show had gone down after he'd swam for the other island, and while he didn't relish the idea of having another fight, Archie felt bad for poor Wynter. He wanted to know that she was at least okay. Marcus had taken her away with him, and none of them knew how he planned to keep her. Was he intending on wooing her into submission, or perhaps forcing her was more his style?

Part of him didn't actually want to know, but they couldn't simply leave her. They were a team, weren't they? They had to stand by one another and fight for what was right.

Plus, there was another part of him that felt sadder still. And angry. Jakob was dead. He'd never thought it could happen, not with the power their kind embodied, but somehow his vampire friend had been delivered to the Lady of Death thanks to Marcus and his jealousy. Archie felt the loss tremendously and knew he would always miss him. They hadn't known one another that long, but they hadn't needed to. He had taken a serious liking to him. He'd looked forward to the days when Jak planned to redeem himself and earn his freedom, and when he and Wynter would be together again in the flesh. He'd been excited for them, but now it was gone. Those hopes shattered. The future uncertain and without Jakob in it.

In many ways, he knew he was still coming to terms with the realisation that Jak had gone. He kept expecting to take a walk down to his cell and find him there, waiting to share anecdotes with him over coffee. But no. The vampire had been torn limb from limb. Murdered.

Would Wynter avenge his honour, like Brodie had done with the werewolf who'd trapped Archie and held him captive? He wondered but doubted she would be in any kind of position to fight Marcus, at least not yet, but maybe someday. Archie sure hoped so.

And, of course, they also had their new housemate to consider. The woman they'd saved from the lighthouse, Rosalie, had taken up residence in one of the spare bedrooms towards the back of the cavernous home and was refusing to come out. Rafferty was reporting back to them regularly, though, and it had been good to have a secret spy in the house only the pair of them knew about.

The poor girl had reportedly washed and dressed in the dead of night, but then she'd climbed back under the covers and had barely been seen since. He said he'd caught her creeping around the house on the search for food, but after raiding the cupboards had disappeared again, and now hadn't been seen again for over two days.

But they all heard her crying. The walls weren't thin, but there was no denying the unmistakable sound of someone sobbing their heart out day and night. Archie found himself regularly wanting to go to her, but he forced himself to back off and leave her be. To give her time. Maybe when she was through this phase of her trauma, they could get her to open up. Brodie could always offer to take her back home so she could be with her family. He didn't know where Rosalie's life was heading, but at least she wasn't alone. He and Brodie were there, ready and waiting for when she finally wanted their company. All she had to do was ask.

The same went for Wynter, too.

And until that time came, he knew he would have to carry on, regardless.

"I'm going for a shower and then to bed," Archie announced as he got to his feet and walked the short distance to the doorway, and then he turned back, suddenly feeling brave. "You're welcome to join me," he offered.

"I don't sleep," Brodie answered, looking sheepish, and Archie smiled. "I didn't say I wanted to sleep."

He then headed straight for his room without another word or a backwards glance and smiled to himself as he stripped off and climbed into the shower of his en-suite. He had indeed been feeling brave and got lathered up and washed in record speed. This time, he didn't even bother with his usually long shower that consisted of taking care of his sexual needs while beneath the warm jets. He wanted to see what Brodie was going to do first. To find out if he was going to act on his blatant attempt to get closer to him or not.

As he shut off the water, Archie found himself listening desperately for any sign, there was someone waiting for him out in his room. But he heard nothing, and so brushed his teeth and pulled on a pair of pyjama bottoms, thinking perhaps it was time for some sleep after all.

He was just climbing beneath his covers when the door opened and in walked the tall jinni. He too was dressed only from the waist down and looked as if he had just freshened up as well, but rather than go and keep himself busy somewhere else, Brodie had evidently decided to come and see Archie like he'd asked. This had to be a good sign, or so he hoped.

His heart raced as he watched him shut the door and then perch awkwardly on the opposite side of the bed. Brodie's dark hair was black and blended perfectly with the shadows beyond, and Archie couldn't help but also take a good look at his exposed flesh. It was the first time he'd seen his new beau without a t-shirt on, and he was surprised by how slim he was. Brodie was also black-skinned—literally. He was darker than anyone he'd ever met before, but he liked it. Unlike the other creatures he'd come to know these past few months, Brodie didn't blend in. He wasn't just another part of the crowd, and actually, Archie thought he did look kind of otherworldly. He also looked as if he hadn't eaten in months, which he knew was technically true with him being a jinni and all but was still surprised he wasn't more toned. Not after he'd seen for himself how easily Brodie had taken down the werewolf, keeping him and Rosalie hostage.

And yet, while he wasn't as muscularly built as Archie had become, he knew Brodie was a hundred times stronger. Even after having worked out hard these past few months, Archie knew he would be no match for him in a fight, visible muscles or not. However, the last thing he seemed to want was fight.

"Ever since I was turned, I've only ever had one lover," Brodie suddenly whispered, and he looked down at his hands as he spoke. Archie thought it endearing how inept he was at expressing his feelings and found it odd that he remained so shy after being alive for as long as he had been. It was like he really hadn't been able to show emotion without his lost soul mate to guide him.

"Your wife?" he whispered, and Brodie nodded.

"Ada. She was a jinni and when I was a human, she asked me to be her host, which was when we fell in love. I don't remember much about my life before her, but I do remember one thing. A man," he revealed, and then finally lifted his gaze to Archie's, "he was a lot like you, and I cared for him deeply. I remember his face and the way I felt with him, and I remember us being together in secret. In those days, you couldn't have relations with other men. It wasn't the done thing, and so we pretended not to care. Pretended to be friends."

"But you weren't. You were lovers?" he asked incredulously. He hadn't expected to hear this and was desperate to know more.

"I think so, but I don't remember much more. I don't even know his name, but I know how I felt, and I feel the same now. About you…" Brodie told Archie, and he felt his cheeks flush red. It was the most honest the jinni had been in days, and damn if it wasn't the hottest thing he had ever heard.

This also meant he hadn't been kidding before when he'd said he liked him. As in, like more than a friend. It was the best news he'd heard in days.

"We'll take things slowly. Find our way. I'm not going anywhere and I'm only young. We've got lots of time to figure this out," he replied, and wanted to kick himself for moving so quickly. But also had to remember, he wouldn't stay young forever. Ideally, they needed to make plans while they still could.

"Well, that was what I wanted to know. Do you still want this, knowing that I won't age? Would you be happy growing older beside me, or do you want something else?"

"As in, would I like to become one of your kind?" Archie had to ask.

"Yes, but then we'd be forced to live off one another's life force and so one at a time would remain whole. Or we can try another way, but it'd mean you becoming something else entirely."

"What do you mean?" he asked, trying to fathom how he could become his host while not necessarily dying himself. If that were even possible?

"Vampire…" he explained, and Archie paled. "Jinn are created via possession, as you know. We take the life force of another before sharing just that small snippet in return to complete the transition of the host. But vampires are created by magic. They embody it and feed the dark essence within them in return for immortal life. If you turned, I would be able to feed on that force and would remain whole as long as you fed."

Well, that killed his buzz a bit. Archie honestly hadn't thought of things that way.

He frowned and sat back on his pillow, and Brodie rearranged himself so that he was then lying on top of the duvet beside him. "If you turned, I wouldn't have to go back to being naught but mist, and we could stay together forever. No time limits. No growing older. No taking it in turns to live…"

"I don't know whether I want that life though, Brodie. I can't see myself as one of them, but I know I want to stay with you," he answered honestly. "How long do you have until you'll need a host?" he then added. The more time they had, the better really, and he would gladly wait it out before making any kind of a decision.

"A couple of years," he answered, and Archie let out a relieved sigh. That was plenty of time to decide, and they also had the chance to explore what their connection was too. Brodie wasn't ready for a big push, that was clear, but he'd made a good start and had opened up about what was on his mind, and Archie was glad.

He'd take that over stoic silence any day and turned onto his side to face him.

"So, we've got time," he replied.

Brodie turned on his side too, mirroring him.

"Yeah, we've got time," he confirmed. "I just knew I had to tell you sooner than later. I don't want you to ever think I've misled you or used you. If you don't want either of those options, then you're free to walk away, Archie. I'll never force you to stay or do anything you don't want to."

"And what if I do?"

"Then I'll be the happiest jinni alive," he answered with a smile, and Archie couldn't help himself. He leaned forward and placed a kiss against Brodie's lips. He'd tried to go in gently but had somehow ended up planting a serious one on him, and when he didn't pull away, Archie went for it. He leaned up over Brodie and it was a surprise when the jinni grabbed his hair and pulled him closer. Before he knew it, he was straddling him on the bed and they were rubbing up against each other, neither one daring to touch anything other than the other's face with their hands, while their bodies clearly had other ideas.

Archie was rock hard and was beginning to regret not having taken care of things in the shower. Brodie wasn't ready for them to take things too far. He hadn't needed to say so, but Archie could just tell. He had been honest about his lack of physical contact with anyone over the last few hundred years, and while it wasn't like Archie had been wild in his past, he'd still had plenty of experience in the bedroom and knew how he liked things. He had a feeling he'd have to guide Brodie. It was a good thing he was a 'top' and wasn't afraid of a little hard work.

But first, they needed to continue working on getting Brodie to open up.

"Put my hands wherever you want me to touch you. No bounds," he murmured against his lips, and his suspicions were confirmed when his beau placed Archie's palms back against his cheeks rather than on his naked chest or the erection he felt pressing against his thigh. "Okay, and now you touch me wherever you want. I've no qualms, so the same goes…"

Brodie began at his shoulders and then worked his way down over his pecs and stomach. They continued to kiss as he roved, and Archie enjoyed the simple act of making out and having a little grope and grind. He would've gladly settled for that, but then, in a surprise move, Brodie then slipped his hands beneath the waistband of his pyjama trousers and gripped his arse cheeks with both of them.

Archie let out a small laugh but didn't stop him. He'd said there were no bounds, and if Brodie wanted to touch him there, then that was perfectly fine. It did nothing to quell his desire, though, and he soon found himself wondering what sort of a lover Brodie would be.

Archie had always liked to be the big spoon. He would be the one doing the fucking, rather than the other way around, but knew he'd figure things out as time moved on. Lovemaking was about give and take, after all, but the jinni beneath him was sure in a brave mood. There was no ignoring their two huge hard-ons, but Archie kept his hands where they were and continued to kiss his new lover, even as Brodie swept his hands around his waist and to the front.

Archie let out a deep, rumbled sigh when he gripped him hard with one hand and began to move up and down with his lithe fingers and huge palm, and then felt it as Brodie smiled against him. But then he moved his head to the side and placed a kiss against Archie's jaw.

"I want to see you," Brodie whispered, removing the hands from his cheeks and pushing them down onto his chest instead, meaning that Archie was now bowed up over him. He followed Brodie's lead and then he peered down at his body, taking in the view.

His right hand didn't stop working his hard-on, and then with his left, Brodie pushed his pyjamas down off his hips and around his thighs. Archie was completely on show, but he didn't care. He was proud of his body and his modest sized little buddy, and when he saw the fire in Brodie's eyes as he took him in, he knew his lover liked what he was seeing too. "Beautiful," the jinni whispered, and it was all Archie needed to send him over the edge.

He warned Brodie to stop and grab a tissue, but he refused, and a few seconds later, it was too late. He'd passed the point of no return and was bucking against his hold, releasing his climax onto the slim, dark stomach beneath him with a groan.

Archie made quick work of cleaning up the mess, but he tried his best not to move away completely, not wanting to break the contact until he had to. Their connection was truly flourishing and the last thing he wanted was for Brodie to think he wanted to get away now that he'd shot his load.

When things were nicely cleaned up and he'd tucked himself back into his pyjamas, he gave Brodie the chance to take the lead again and stroked his hands across the jinni's bare chest.

"Show me what you want. I can do the same for you if you would like me to?" he whispered, but Brodie shook his head no.

"Can you just hold me?" he answered timidly, and Archie nodded. He then climbed beneath the covers behind his delicate lover, and there, he wrapped the jinni in his arms and cradled him. This wasn't like anything Archie had been used to before and he couldn't deny it was taking a great deal of patience not to push the limits. He expected for Brodie to move his hands lower, but no. The jinni simply wanted to be held, and so, with their hands entwined, Archie hugged him tightly. He gave him what he needed, and eventually fell asleep, and sensed Brodie with him the entire time.

Even though Jinn never slept, he didn't leave. He didn't move away either or seem to busy himself with some reading or anything. He just stayed there all night long and had Archie hold him close. Like somehow, they were already a couple.

THREE

When Archie woke the next morning, Brodie watched him rouse with a smile. It had been nice lying there with him, and he was pleased to see Archie seemed glad he'd stayed. The jinni had switched position though and was now on his back so that his beau was lying with his head on his chest. He watched as the human opened his eyes and, presumably on some kind of sleepy instinct, ran his hands over Brodie's bare torso.

It was a gentle, tender move. Nothing sordid, and yet, he wanted to clam up again. However, Brodie knew there couldn't be any more of that. Not after what'd happened the night before. They had started to share, and now there was no going back.

Archie knew about his past and how he'd lived since losing Ada. If he could call it living. And he also knew about the years before her. The time when he, too, was a mere mortal. A human with desires he hadn't indulged in for a long time.

Wanting more again after so long was terrifying, especially with a man, but Brodie was starting to feel ready to face that dread head on. He'd been beaten as a young man for wanting the company of other men, and so even now he struggled with the feelings he was developing for Archie. Times had changed, and those urges were no longer seen in the same way, but Brodie still remembered the lashings he'd been forced to withstand. And of course, the victimisation and the brutality he and others like him had endured.

It'd been a welcome relief to find a woman he cared for enough to help hide his true nature, and of course their life together had started as nothing more than a deal between a human and a jinni needing a home. She had given him protection and companionship in return for his life force, but that relationship had changed with time and, much like with Wynter, he had grown to care for her. But unlike his most recent companion, he'd begun to love Ada, and she had loved him back.

But then she'd been taken from him, and by the highest power of all—death herself.

The white-cloaked lady had decided her fate and enlisted the vampire assassin to carry out her bidding. It had been horrible to hear, but thanks to having discovered the truth at last, Brodie knew there would be no vengeance he could seek against the ancient creature of darkness. No justice. All he could do was accept it. The Lady of Death was, after all, the wisest judge of them all.

And while he was coming to terms with Ada's final judgement, he was also beginning to love again. Beginning to care. Starting to feel.

"Good morning," he croaked, and smiled down at Archie when he turned his pale brown eyes up to meet his gaze.

"Mornin'," he replied in his delectable Scottish twang. "You okay?" he asked, and Brodie thought it odd how it was Archie who was asking him. Of course he was okay, but it was nice to have someone ask. Archie was soon showing his true nature. It was clear already how he was the stronger one between them, and while glad to have such an intuitive partner, he was shocked by how in control he seemed to be. So dominant, despite his delicate mortal body.

"I'm fine," Brodie answered, "why?"

"You just seemed lost in your own head is all," Archie replied, and then he leaned up and laid a soft kiss against his lips.

"You know me, man of few words," he joked, "but yeah, I was thinking how glad I am to have found this."

"This? As in us?" he asked him, and Brodie nodded.

"Without a doubt," he answered, and then pulled him close again. He wasn't ready to let go in the slightest, and while things would have to move relatively slowly while he adjusted, he knew Archie didn't mind. It'd been so long since Brodie had let anyone get close, and it was going to take some getting used to. He'd vowed never to love another woman after Ada had been taken from him, and he'd stuck to that promise. Fundamentally, he still was, and knew that wherever she was, she wouldn't begrudge him the chance to love again.

They were still lazing happily in one another's arm when a timid knock came at the door, and Archie sat up in surprise. They both knew Rafferty wouldn't need to knock, but that he also wouldn't ever have a reason to disturb them, so there was only one other person left that could possibly be on the other side of the door. Rosalie. It'd been over a week since they'd last properly laid eyes on her, and it was agreed they would let her be until she made the first move and sought their company once again. She had a lot to deal with after all, and Brodie didn't envy her for the things she must see when she closed her eyes. Or the memories that had to be haunting her dreams, and probably would continue to forevermore.

"Come in," Archie called, and even though they were both covered, Brodie bristled. He didn't want Rosalie seeing him half naked and in bed with another man. That wasn't the proper way, and he quickly dematerialised so as to be invisible for when the door inched open.

Brodie then conjured up some clothing and reappeared in time for Rosalie rounding the doorway, but rather than place himself back in bed beside Archie, the jinni materialised into the small armchair across the room.

His new lover did a double take, but said nothing, however Brodie saw his brow furrow and give his reaction away. He was not impressed but hid those thoughts as he focused on their guest and smiled up at her, patting the duvet so that she might take a seat beside him.

Brodie wanted to tell him off. Surely the last thing Rosalie wanted was to sit beside an undressed man with merely a blanket between them? And yet, she readily joined Archie on the bed and smiled across at him, as though utterly at ease with his nakedness.

Times certainly had changed indeed!

"I just wanted to thank you both for everything you've done for me," she whispered to Archie, and then she turned her head and looked over at Brodie, who felt himself thaw when he peered back into her bloodshot eyes. Damn, he was growing soft after the past few months spent with Wynter in his head. "I couldn't have survived much longer there with him."

"You're very welcome, Rosalie. I'm only sorry we hadn't realised sooner," Brodie answered, and even Archie seemed surprised to hear it. He knew he hadn't exactly worn his heart on his sleeve, but he wasn't heartless either. He cared about those he held dear and after seeing the poor and sorry state that werewolf had left her in, he found he cared for Rosalie too.

"So, it's true? You live here?" she asked, and the two men nodded.

"Yes, and you're welcome to stay with us if you'd like? Or we can take you back to the mainland. It's your choice," Archie replied, and she smiled and nodded.

But then Brodie noticed Rosalie alter her position on the bed ever so slightly, as though she were uncomfortable. Anyone else might've thought she was simply getting cosier, but he could tell there was something else to it. The poor girl was trying to hide her secret, but the jinni could sense it a mile away. She was pregnant. Probably only one month along, but she knew it. Rosalie also knew she would need medical help before long and would have to return to the mainland to get it, and yet, something made her want to stay. And to keep quiet about her condition.

She then left without much more being said between the trio, and as soon as the door closed behind her, Brodie leaned towards Archie and told him the news. "Ah, shit," he groaned, "neither of us will know what to do when the time comes. Why didn't she tell us?"

"Because she's scared," Brodie answered. He didn't have to be in her head to decipher that much. "Which means she needs us more than ever."

"Okay," Archie agreed, and he climbed up out of bed, showing off his naked body without a care. Brodie felt his cheeks burn hot at the sight and couldn't tear his gaze away, and of course, his new beau noticed. "You can show off and materialise suits and ties out of thin air all you want, jinni, but you still can't hide your shy side, can you?" Archie teased him as he wandered over to his en-suite wearing nothing but his birthday suit and a smile, and Brodie tried his best not to stare at him and his perfect behind as he went.

Instead, he stood and then vanished for a second, before reappearing in the doorway to the small bathroom, blocking Archie's path. And this time, the clothes were gone.

"I don't do it show off," he corrected him with a smile. "I'm simply too good that naturally you're jealous…"

"Not jealous. Turned on," Archie countered, and then he stepped forward and crushed himself against Brodie before kissing him deeply.

***

Wynter decided she needed to get to grips with both her full powers and the limitations now added to the mix by the witch's power. She tried their most basic of tricks of disappearing or transforming into her white misty form, and had it nailed in no time at all, but couldn't get far from the house without some kind of homing beacon kicking in and forcing her back.

After her tenth trial, she began to wonder if it wasn't an issue with her power, but more that the heart she shared with the witch wouldn't let her get too far from Marcus. Not the house or the island, but him. Almost as if he had some kind of maximum radius around him in which she could go.

She tested the theory and knew her hunch was right when she remained invisible for hours and then as a white mist for even longer without any issue. The transformation was simple—like breathing—and wasn't at all hard to maintain, just as long as she stayed put and didn't dare try and have a fraction of independence, of course. God, she wanted to scream.

Marcus was no help, either. She caught him watching her from the house no matter which area of beach she materialized on. He seemed to enjoy watching her test out her powers, and when she went to him later that night as nothing but white smoke, he touched her misty flesh and seemed to marvel at what she had become.

"Stay like this," he said as he undressed and then pulled her into his arms. And of course, she gave into him. Gave him everything he wanted, and more.

Like always, once they were close to one another, she was no longer herself, but some other version he had groomed and moulded into being his perfect bride. The lover who was giving and generous, and the woman he loved that adored him in return.

In Marcus's arms, Wynter couldn't say no, but she also didn't want to.

She was spellbound and knew there was no going back. This was forever, and she had two choices.

She could fight and lose, time and again, and come to terms with the fact that the only way to escape him was to let death take her for real.

Or she could accept her fate and find some semblance of happiness in the strange new life Marcus had chosen for her.

The problem was, when she was away from him, she wanted one option, and when their bodies were entwined, she wanted the other.

The only way forward seemed one of embracing the unknown, and Wynter guessed it'd have to do.

FOUR

After an intense few days spent making love and not once leaving one another's side, an insistent ringing sound from afar began to irk the pair of newlyweds. However, given how adamant Marcus seemed on ignoring it, Wynter pretended not to have noticed while he seemed to grow more and more on edge with the interruption.

She wanted to tell him to go find out what was going on, but also couldn't bear to let him leave her. After all, the moment he did, she knew her shame and guilt would come flooding back and she would grow furious with herself again. That she'd soon then feel hard done by and miserable, and even though it was an obvious cop-out, she wanted to keep hold of her fake happiness instead.

"Please, don't go," Wynter tried when he began pulling away, and she actually grabbed his shoulders and wrenched Marcus back down onto the bed with her.

He grinned, and she saw his eyes turn that iridescent intense blue that meant his soul was rising to the surface and calling for her again. It was the third time that day alone and was a sure sign that the love he bore her was growing stronger and more intense now that they had somehow merged. It terrified her.

"I'll be back in just a moment," he promised, visibly forcing himself to retreat, and the moment their connection was broken, so too was the spell he had her under whenever they touched. Regret and grief flooded through her with breakneck speed. It hit her harder than ever and she knew Marcus could sense her emotions, so turned away so she wouldn't have to see the satisfied smirk on his face she was sure would be there. He'd shown how much he loved her and desperately wanted her to feel the same in return. That was undeniable, but he also loved it when she fought his adoration. When she was full of shame and despair.

Like now.

After he was gone, Wynter forced her hurt aside and climbed out of bed, thinking she'd go for a run or to practice her transformation techniques, but instead she found the doorway blocked by the alpha soldier.

"Move," she demanded, but he simply shook his head no. Wynter saw red. Had Marcus ordered for him to keep her there, like a pretty little wife who might do as she was told? Well, she wasn't about to let that happen. She simply ghosted directly through him as mist and didn't show herself again until she was already out of the house and on the beach as far away as she could get.

The alpha came running towards her just moments later, and she was surprised he'd found her so quickly at first, but then saw her footprints in the sand and knew she'd left an easy to follow trail.

Wynter felt a second wave of sadness echo through her at the sight. Brodie had done the same when he'd walked beside her on the beach back in England. On that god-awful day when she'd been forced to watch Jakob leave and had then been carried back to Marcus, strewn over the shoulders of the same vampire soldier who was now charging for her.

Not this time, though.

As soon as he got close, she balled her hand into a fist and sent it flying for his nose, which immediately cracked, and the alpha was sent flying backwards on the sand. Wynter didn't stop. Rage spurred her onwards, and she suddenly found herself laying into him, her fists flying over and over as she straddled him on the sand. And once again, it all came flooding back. "You stopped us. You took me away when all I wanted was to be free!" she screamed and continued raining down punches against the soldier's grey skin, but it wasn't enough. She wanted him to fight her and so reared back so she could look at the damage she'd done.

He was a bloody mess and seemed to be out cold, but he wasn't unconscious for long, and she readied herself for his attack. It didn't come. Even when he snapped back to consciousness, the alpha still refused to fight her, and he simply peered up at her with his creepy red eyes full of desperation and sorrow.

"Wynter," he then whispered, almost tenderly.

She reacted by reaching down and wrapping her hand around his throat.

"Fight back," she hissed.

"No," he croaked, and then he laid back against the sand as though more than ready to die for her. Talk about stopping her dead in her tracks.

It was the second word she'd ever heard the otherwise silent creature speak, and she was about to marvel at his steadily improving skill when he opened his mouth and uttered a third word. One that left her stunned and totally reeling. "Queen..."

She backed off in a split-second and clambered back on the warm sand, watching him with wide eyes. Did he really see her as a leader? Was that why he always remained close and had wanted to speak with her, but had failed miserably until now? No. He couldn't. Could he? As her mind processed the two small words, things suddenly began to fall back into place. Perhaps she was a leader, after all. That had to be it, and her anger was suddenly gone, replaced by dumbfounded shock.

And then something occurred to her. If she was his queen, that meant...

"Will you look after me?" she asked, and the alpha nodded. "Obey me?" he nodded again. "Kill for me?" he simply continued the up and down movement of his head. "Die for me?" there wasn't even the slightest hint he was going to stop, and Wynter climbed up onto her feet and peered down at him.

She didn't say anything more. Wynter simply headed back to the house, where she found Marcus waiting for her by the doorway, evidently having watched her exchange with the alpha soldier. She thought he might be about to taunt her about their odd altercation, but he seemed to have something more important on his mind.

"I'm going back to the mainland for a few days, my sweet," he informed her when she was close enough to hear, "and you will stay here."

"No," she replied indignantly, "I want to go home. I'm sick to my bones of this island and I need more. I want to get back to work. I want to live my fucking life."

Marcus was clearly surprised at first, but then seemed to sense that she wasn't going to take no for an answer. So, he went for the easier option and nodded.

"Very well," he answered, and then grabbed her hand and pulled Wynter into his embrace. "It's time you took your rightful place at my side, anyway."

"At *Slave*, or one of the other clubs?" she asked, and Marcus laughed darkly.

"All the clubs you'd ever set foot are now nothing but dust. I burned them to the ground, along with everyone in them," he told her, and Wynter felt a shudder echo down her back.

"Why?" she breathed.

"You know why," he answered, and then nuzzled her neck so that he could kiss her there. He didn't even seem sorry, while it was all she could do not to cry.

"Because I left."

"Yes. And because I was so empty and hungry without you. Thirstier than I've been in thousands of years and with a bottomless pit of rage to help fuel that hunger. To say that I was willing to lay waste to the world thanks to you leaving is a mere understatement."

Well, that certainly put things into perspective for her.

"And now?" she replied with a frown. God, he really had gone to the extreme when she had left him. Wynter knew she'd previously had no idea just how deeply he cared and how her leaving had affected him, but she still felt awful for the things she had done, and for the people who had suffered because of her.

"We will return and start again. Together," he told her, and Wynter nodded. She didn't know if it was because of their contact or because of her fear, but she vowed to herself to never, ever, leave him again. There was no telling what he might do a second time, and even if it meant her living a lie and hating herself every moment that they weren't touching, then she figured so be it. She would sacrifice herself and her freedom if it meant the world could go on turning.

They were packed up and back on Marcus's private plane before the hour was up, and as they took off, Wynter found herself staring out the window with a smile. They were going home. There was a lot of work to do if she had any hope of finding her purpose, but she craved it. The days were endless thanks to her not needing any sleep or sustenance, and without a reason to go on, there was nothing to drag her through each minute to the next. And so, she figured she'd find it.

Marcus took her hand in his from beside her and kissed the backs of her fingers tenderly, watching her.

"I want to be your equal," she suddenly whispered, and expected a fight, but instead her husband smiled.

"Of course."

"I mean it. I am strong enough and will gladly give every day and night to get our empire back up and running," she demanded, "but I will do it as your wife, not your captive."

"I have a vital role already in mind for you, my sweet. In fact, the alpha has been trying to tell you so for days," he answered with a sly smile. "He and the others aren't just mine, but they're your army now, too. Ours to command together, but yours to maintain. You will become their mistress. Their—"

"Queen?" she asked, thinking back to what the alpha had said at the beach.

"Precisely," Marcus agreed, and as Wynter stared back into his eyes, she was suddenly filled with hope. Things were about to change. She wasn't simply going to be Marcus's wife, or a slave he could keep from leaving, thanks to the witch's heart fuelling her from within. She was going to have a title and a job to do. An empire of her own to run.

Damn, was she actually getting somewhere? Was this going to happen? She sure hoped so. Wynter was terrified of what he was capable of and yet was addicted to that power he had if he could offer her such a thing so readily. He had two worlds at his fingertips and was willing to share one with her and, scary as that might be, Wynter was more than ready.

She then caught Marcus looking across the aisle of the plane to where Marcella was sitting with Jack, and at first, she thought he was looking to his Priestess for guidance, but instead revealed his reasons when her husband climbed up out of his seat and shuffled towards them. She didn't need to ask how or why. Marcus evidently needed to feed and so had summoned his only remaining manager to see to him, and Wynter didn't want to stick around to watch. In fact, she was going to use the time alone to her advantage, and so offered Jack her seat before then walking across and taking his aisle seat beside his wife.

Marcella tried to ignore her, as usual nowadays, but Wynter wasn't going to let her anymore. Enough was enough.

"Do you hate me?" she whispered to the witch, who continued to stare out the window, her back half turned to her. It was awful, but Wynter understood her reasons why. Seeing her had to be a constant reminder of what she had lost, and so she tried to approach things in a different way.

Wynter knew she'd not once appeared grateful for what Marcella had given her and decided to rectify that. "Do you regret giving me this gift, my lady? Because I don't. I'm glad you did it. I'm glad you shared her life with me because she is part of me now. She loves Marcus, so much so that she's making me love him, too. And she's not gone because she lives inside of here," Wynter continued, and placed her hand over her heart, "and she misses you."

Marcella let out a sob and curled in on herself, still refusing to look at Wynter, who continued on. These things needed saying, whether they had the desired effect or not, and so she knew she couldn't stop. "She loves you, Marcy, and I love you, too. And I miss you. I miss my friend."

The Priestess suddenly spun in her seat and finally looked at her. It'd been weeks of nothing but heartache and pain for the poor grieving mother, and when their eyes made contact, Wynter could sense her agony and she too began to cry.

But Marcella wouldn't let her look away this time, and it was as if she was staring into the depths of her soul. She gripped her cheeks and smiled through the tears still streaming down her face.

"I can see her inside of you," she cried, "and you're right, she's alive and she's thriving."

Wynter nodded, and it was a huge relief when Marcella finally stopped crying and seemed to move onto the final stage of her grief—acceptance.

"About time," Jack's voice broke their strange bubble, and Wynter peered up at him with a smile, which he returned. "I kept telling her to see for herself how our daughter is not gone, but she wasn't ready. I'm glad you two have worked things out." He then reached down and gave her cheek a stroke, and it was odd at first, but Wynter knew it was because he could somehow see his daughter there, too.

It wasn't like the pair of them had ever been close or anything, but it was a definite relief to have him on her side as well, and a wave of happiness swept through her, along with a thought that she someone knew wasn't entirely her own.

Family.

She didn't have to be alone or afraid ever again, and it was a welcome realisation.

FIVE

It was the following morning by the time their odd little group landed back on British soil, and Wynter couldn't deny feeling apprehensive. She had no clue where they were or how long a journey laid ahead. All she could do was disembark with the others and she followed Marcus's lead and climbed into the first of four huge armoured cars that had been waiting for them on the private airfield. She even snuggled against him as the driver prepared the rest of their convoy.

"Where are we?" she asked, but Marcus silenced her with a kiss, his hands roving over her body rather than stay away from her any longer. It wasn't like they hadn't passed the time together on the airplane either, but he seemed intent on having more of her, and Wynter was powerless to refuse his advances. As always. It was as if she could never have enough, and as they began to drive, she gladly climbed up onto his lap so that she could ride him.

She was still coming down from the last of her climaxes when the car eventually slowed, and she soon realised they were being let through a set of wrought-iron gates and into a private drive. Wynter lifted herself up off him and was still rearranging her clothes when she saw the tall building they were heading towards and paled.

It was Camilla's mansion. The place where she had spent a few days with Jakob not too long before. The fortress in which she had gotten to know him and they had developed a friendship, and more. It was also where she had watched Marcus fucking another vampire. She was far from jealous, and hadn't been at the time either, but she was loathed to visit the place where there were so many memories of the old days. The days when she was human, his Blood Slave, and had no control over her life.

So much had changed, and yet those days were no different to her life now. She was still trapped. Still broken on the inside, irrespective of her powers and utter transformation from human to jinni. Continuing her immortal existence as a dutiful captive seemed unavoidable, and Wynter figured perhaps she would remain so for the foreseeable future. It didn't matter whether they were on that island paradise, holed up in one of his clubs, or at the mansion. She knew she'd be confined to whatever perimeter Marcus set for her. Bars as unbreakable as the ones Brodie had locked Jakob inside, even if they were invisible.

Wynter swallowed the lump in her throat at the thought and watched him with a scowl as he climbed out of his seat and then walked around to her side. It was he who opened her car door rather than the driver, with his hand outstretched and a knowing smile curling at his lips.

She had to force herself out of the car, and knew Marcus sensed her unease, but he ignored it.

He simply kept her hand in his as he led her up the stairs and to the door of the huge house, using their bond to keep her compliant. He knew the effect his touch had and didn't seem to want to let her go. Didn't want her to think for herself or speak her true mind.

She wanted to throw every swear word she had at him. Wanted to refuse to go inside, but could do nothing of the sort, and soon she was standing in the most elegant entrance hall she had ever seen. She'd been there before at night, so hadn't noticed half the splendour of the place in the darkness. Hadn't seen just how grand the marble staircase was from the doorway. Or how it stretched up and around to both sides, showing how there was not just one, but two upper floors that lay either side of the centre. There was attention to detail everywhere she looked, and it was stunning, but still didn't feel like a home.

Outside, the weather was bright, and the mansion had been bathed in sunlight, but once they were inside, the house seemed cold and full of dark secrets. Evil. It needed a major redecoration if she had any hope of being comfortable there, and she reminded herself to tell her husband so when she was free to speak her mind again.

"You remember the mansion?" he finally asked as he drew her further into the house, and she nodded. It wasn't time yet.

They then passed numerous closed doors and stopped only when they reached a study that seemed to have been prepared for their arrival.

Inside, a fire blazed and yet Wynter couldn't feel the warmth from it. She felt cold from the inside out and knew it was because she was so empty. Wynter turned to Marcus with a frown.

"Why would you bring me back to this mansion?" she asked him, "of all the places we could go, why here?"

"Because this is our home now. I've gutted it of everything that once was and discarded all remnants of both Camilla and her dead progeny. I have even employed an entirely new set of staff to tend to our needs. You and I will live here, along with the hordes and, of course, the Priestess and her husband."

"And what if I don't want to?" she demanded and wrenched her hand from his in a bid to break their contact. Marcus was too quick, though. He closed the gap in less than a second and pressed himself against her, wrapping his arms around her back, but it didn't deter her. "What if I don't want to live in this house where I watched you fuck another vampire? Where I spent day after day locked away with…with…" she couldn't say his name. Not to him. He didn't deserve to hear how she was still grieving the loss of her true soul mate.

"You don't have a choice, my sweet. This decision has been made," he barked icily, and then kissed her cheek before finally letting her go.

Marcus then watched in what seemed like intrigue as she forced her true emotions to the forefront. As she pushed aside whatever magic made her want to adore him when they were touching and finally lifted the veil so she could give him a real piece of her mind.

"I will never love you," she hissed vehemently. "You've been so cruel to me and always so very selfish. I've seen the rage inside of you and the demons you can never hide from me again. Don't pretend that there was no other choice in this. You brought me here on purpose to spite me in some way. To hurt me. Always teaching me lessons, aren't you? The big, bad vampire always gets his way."

She didn't know what'd come over her, but truth was spilling from her lips in droves and Wynter couldn't stop herself. As silence descended, she was shaking and was terrified he would lash out at her but knew it would be worth it. He might think he'd won her over, but she was more than willing to prove him wrong.

"And the little fighter always gets beaten down, but that doesn't stop her from getting back up, does it?" he answered matter-of-factly, and then had the audacity to offer her one of his devious smiles. "You will do as you're told, Wynter. You'll stay and you will make this house your home. *Our* home. Every room has been emptied and is a blank canvas now, ready for you to put your own mark on it. A great deal of effort was made to cleanse this house of everything it once was, so don't be so quick to look a gift horse in the mouth. I could've forced you to live among Camilla's things, but I didn't."

Marcus then stormed away, leaving her there, and Wynter knew he was right. She didn't have any choice but to stay but would thankfully be able to make the huge mansion her own. And at least this way, the others would be with her too, including Marcella, who was finally speaking to her again.

She wasn't going to be alone any longer, which was a far better alternative to him having taken her somewhere to live, just the pair of them.

She looked around the room he had led her to, and at first wondered why this had been the only one decorated, but then she spotted the huge desk over by the window and it clicked. He always did like to keep her locked up in his office, and now seemed no different. The desk he'd strewn her over on many an occasion had evidently been painstakingly rebuilt following his brutality and was now here, and atop it stood one of his trusty computers. Work would evidently go on, but from the looks of it, he was planning to do it from the mansion now.

Wynter went over and stroked the old wooden desk and was met with a shock when she picked up on something there. Memories suddenly rushed through her. Scents and sounds filled her senses, and yet she knew they weren't happening in the here and now, but in the past. She saw herself lying there, legs wide, as a drop of blood rolled down onto the desk beneath her and found the spot with her fingers where the tiniest hint of a stain remained. Parts of herself had been left behind here. Her blood and tears were aplenty, and she was somehow able to sense them all. She could see the memories clearly, like a movie in her mind.

Wynter thought it had to be a strange new development to her powers, and one she wasn't entirely convinced was a Jinn thing. Perhaps it was her witch side that was growing? That would be a curious new advancement. There certainly wasn't an endogenous reason for this change in her, so perhaps the shift was indeed coming from an inside source? The most powerful supply she had ever known and yet ran through every fibre of her new being. It had to be a witch thing.

The sounds of voices reached her then, and Wynter retracted her hand from the desk so no one caught her tinkering with her new power. She also decided she would keep the visions to herself for now and figure things out on her own. Marcus had dominion over every aspect of her life, but he couldn't have it all. Some things she would keep for herself.

Still curious regarding the voices she'd heard, she turned invisible and went to investigate, but when she tried crossing the threshold of the doorway, Wynter found herself hitting what felt like an invisible barrier there. She couldn't cross through and out into the hallway no matter how hard she tried, and at first, she cursed Marcus for keeping her prisoner somehow. But then, as soon as she turned back into her human form, Wynter was able to cross through it with ease.

She was still stood staring at the doorway with a frown when Marcella approached from the other side and caught her trying to figure it out.

"Every doorway in the house is warded, my love," she told her, knowing as always exactly what was going through her mind. "Each magical creature must be in their human or equivalent form to cross through or else they are trapped. It's simple magic, but a security measure I find quite pertinent. After all, you were coming through invisibly with the intention to snoop, did you not?"

Wynter opened her mouth and went to lie and tell her no, but she knew it was no use. Marcella already knew and so she simply smiled and shrugged.

"Can't blame a girl for trying," she replied, and then looked behind the Priestess to the commotion going on there. Jack was seeing to his and her luggage, while the alpha seemed to be carrying Wynter's things up the huge stairway, and at the front of the house stood Marcus.

He was outside on the steps talking to a group of men Wynter had never seen before. They hadn't travelled here with them either, and so she went to go and investigate who had been so quick to come calling, when the witch beside her put a hand on her arm and shook her head.

"They are the High Committee of Vampires. You must not intrude on their conversation with Mr Cole," she demanded, and Wynter did a double take.

"What the hell is that supposed to mean?" she demanded, and then quickly followed Marcella back inside Marcus's new office.

"He drank dry hundreds of his Blood Slaves and then burned his clubs to the ground. He might be one of the most powerful vampires to walk the Earth, but he is still culpable for any actions that impact the future of his kind," she told her, and at first Wynter felt fearful for him.

But then that reaction was quickly replaced with hope.

Perhaps, at long last, someone might actually make him pay for his selfish actions. Might they imprison him? Or drag him away? She hoped so. At least that way she might be free of him thanks to the actions of this committee, and Wynter found herself once again wanting to go and eavesdrop on what the group of vampires were talking about on her new doorstep.

Surely, he would never let her get close enough to find out, though. Marcus had taken her to his office on purpose and had clearly sent Marcella up to keep her there, and so she knew she would have to change tactic if she had any hope of playing her husband at his own game.

Wynter started by utilising one of the skills she had finally perfected and conjured up the most perfect of outfits to wear. She closed her eyes and imagined it clearly. Something right out of the pages of the expensive magazines she had used to devour what felt like a lifetime ago. The long bejewelled dress and delicate heels were nothing like her usual either comfy or corporate style, and yet she moulded them around her body perfectly. Thanks to her own kind of magic, she could create anything her mind could put together, and within seconds Wynter was dressed to perfection and even the finishing touches to her hair and makeup were naught more effort than a snap of her fingers.

"There we go," she then told her companion, "the lady of the house should always ensure she greets her guests, after all," Wynter added with forced enunciation to make herself sound posh, and Marcella couldn't seem to find any argument with her new plan.

"Fine, but do not invite any of them in," she warned though.

"I thought that was just for in the movies?"

"Some of the myths are true, and that is one of them. Yes, you're allowing them entry, but give any vampire free access to your home and they will indeed utilise it whenever they wish—unannounced and unwarranted. Even with one another. Your husband will not want any members of the Committee being granted access to the house, and neither should you."

Part of her wanted to go out there and welcome them in just to spite him, but the seriousness in Marcella's tone stopped her.

"Why?" Wynter asked.

"Imagine yourself ten years from now. Perhaps you have rekindled your relationships with your family and friends and they're here to visit, only for them to come across one of those ancient vampires in the dead of night. You've refused to let Marcus claim them as his Blood Slave, so they're not protected. There's nothing to stop one of those vampires out there draining your mother, or best friend, dry."

Shit. She was right. All games aside, if this was going to become her home, then she knew she had to protect it.

"Okay," Wynter promised, and then she set off for the front door, gliding effortlessly on the tall heels that felt like air against her feet. Evidently gone were the days of forcing herself to wear shoes or clothes that were uncomfortable or that physically hurt her. The jinni was able to wear whatever the hell she wanted and didn't need a closet full of clothes to make it happen. That was much better.

She only wished Brodie was here to teach her more about this stuff. Wynter missed him terribly, and Archie, and just hoped the two of them were doing okay. But now was not the time to dwell, so she forced all thoughts of them aside. It was not useful fixating on those she had left behind. Not when there was so much she had to do if she had any hope of sorting out her own predicament.

"Ah, and this must be your stunning new wife," one of the vampires called in greeting as Wynter strode confidently out onto the front step of the house and joined them. Marcus turned to her, and his icy eyes burned into hers at first, but then even he could not seem to deny she had done well in dolling up and coming to greet their guests.

"Please forgive me gentleman, I was busy getting the house in some kind of order," she replied, and then took turns shaking each of their hands and exchanging polite kisses on the cheeks. "It's a pleasure to meet you," Wynter added, and was sure to make note of the five stoic vampires' names.

First, there was Mr Dickens. He was certainly not someone she would've hoped to come across back when she was human. Even though she was far from that now, his presence still irked her. He seemed to hold each of those beside him in utter contempt, including her. Not a nice man at all, or so she felt.

Next, she was greeted with the slightly warmer smile of a younger looking man named Mr Richards. Despite his youthful appearance, his pale eyes were cold and wise, giving up his true age. He seemed more bored than much else, but not so much of a threat.

She carried onto the next two men, who were identical twins who'd evidently turned on the same day. Both were named Mr Dawson, and one bore the scars of war on his face, while the other seemed to carry his perfection like some sort of trophy. His pompous manner only made her like him less, while the scarred brother seemed worldlier. Like he had lived a real and honest life before being turned. She wouldn't want to mess with either of them but didn't get the impression they were at the mansion to lay down the law, anyway. Much to her annoyance.

Lastly, a broad smile was her welcome and Wynter was pleased to finally be offered a Christian name, rather than a mere title and surname. It hadn't escaped her that the others wanted her to greet them formally, and yet they had each been wary of her as she considered them. She was a jinni after all. One moment of rage and each of their necks could be snapped like twigs, and even though they might all be older and wiser than she, the fact remained that Jinn were indeed the far superior race. Especially when at full strength, which she knew she would always be.

"Wentworth Mayweather, at your service, my lady. And what an honour it is to meet such a sublime young woman," he began, and then corrected himself, "I mean jinni, of course." He then placed a gentle kiss on one cheek and then the other and even offered Wynter a polite little bow. Now, that was more like it. She took an instant like to Wentworth and beamed back at him.

"The honour is mine," she answered.

"As you can see, gentleman. I do indeed have my hands full here. Please do rest assured I will make good on my promises before the year's end," Marcus then interjected, and the group turned to him as one, including Wynter. She wondered what he had promised them but knew she could never ask him outright. He'd never tell, even if just to play his games and taunt her.

She then went to his side and slid her arm around his waist as she forced herself to smile at the Committee members as they prepared to leave. So, her dreams of recompense were unfounded. Marcus wasn't necessarily in trouble at all, and in fact, he seemed to have the five of them wrapped around his little finger.

Maybe he truly never would be thwarted. She'd always known, and yet still hoped, that one day things might change.

Wynter knew she would never let go of that fantasy and was glad to still be herself underneath the bravado and with the witch's heart pulling her towards the man she still hated. It was a good realisation that she could be

THE COMPLETE BLOOD SLAVE SERIES

both, and it meant that at least while she was stuck there, she wasn't living a whole lie. She could indulge herself and give into Marcus's need for her, while secretly plotting his demise and hoping for a chance of escape.

Who said you couldn't have it all?

The matter evidently settled, four of the five vampires then climbed back into their chauffer driven cars and sped away, but Wentworth remained, and as soon as they were alone, he seemed to loosen up, as did Marcus.

Their remaining guest then turned to Wynter, and he clapped his hands excitedly.

"Well, my dear, it seems you really do exist. Marcus here has been spinning us story after story these past few months about how his soul mate was taken by a jinni and forced to become one of them. And, of course, how he was then obligated to avenge you and bring you home. I'm glad to see you two are back together at last, and that congratulations are in order!" he cried and was positively bouncing as he spoke.

So, that was Marcus's story, and the reason he had given for laying waste to hundreds of Blood Slaves and the clubs that had housed them. He wasn't just a wretched and selfish bastard, but apparently a brazen liar, too. And not only with her, but with others of his kind.

"Thank you," she answered, and went to offer Wentworth a fond farewell, but was surprised to find him following her and Marcus into the house. He'd been invited in? Well, she and her husband were certainly going to have words about that when they were alone.

Inside, Marcus made a song and dance of showing him around the almost empty house, and he even had the audacity to gloat about how he had killed Camilla and taken her hordes. He truly didn't care about anyone but himself, she thought, but then had to consider her own part in all of this. He did care about her. That much she couldn't deny. He had killed for her and would undoubtedly do so again if she forced his hand, which she would try never to do again. But at least it gave her an inside track to one day, hoping she had the skill to play him at his own games. Marcus was fearless and cruel. He had risen to great heights, and all because no one had been able to stop him. He'd had no weakness to exploit—until now. All she had to do was figure out how the hell she might go about manipulating the monster who adored her so. Hardly an easy feat.

Wynter left the two of them to their tour and was in the banquet hall with a pen and paper in hand when they eventually caught up with her again. Still dressed in her fine clothes, she'd simply been jotting down ideas for the décor, but genuinely didn't even know where to begin. She was just glad to have had some time to herself to try. As always, her demons roared louder when Marcus was far away, but at least she was beginning to learn how to ignore them. Slowly but surely that guilt and shame was waning, and Wynter thought maybe, just maybe, she might be on track to finding herself once again.

Marcus greeted her with a kiss when he reached her and he peered down into her face for a second, the intensity of his gaze making her blush. She was about to ask him what was up when he stepped away and offered her a wink.

"My sweet, Wentworth has been asking me all sorts of questions about you. He's desperate to know more about your kind and I wondered if you might be gracious enough to show him some of your skills…"

Wynter smiled sweetly and gave a small laugh, but she flashed her husband a look of disgust and saw his mouth twitch with the smile he was trying to hide. Marcus knew she wouldn't appreciate the insinuation that she was a circus act he could command, and it appeared he was more than willing to try and make her squirm. Did he think she wouldn't argue in front of his friend? Well, he had another thing coming if he did!

She turned her face away and moved towards their guest but didn't drop her forced smile. And Wentworth seemed to think she might be about to show him some of her tricks.

"Please forgive my husband's ignorance," she then told him in a cool and calm manner, and the vampire's eyes widened in surprise. He clearly hadn't expected her to decline Marcus's request, and Wynter took great pleasure in refusing them both. "I am not a performing monkey, and he knows it. And shame on you, Wentworth. I had hoped for better," Wynter added, chiding him playfully, and her guest paled.

"I meant no offence, Mrs Cole. Please forgive my ignorance. You are, of course, entitled to your privacy and I would never have asked such things if I'd realised it would intrude upon your privacy," he answered, bumbling, and clearly fretting. He obviously didn't want to upset her, and so Wynter took the opportunity to gain the upper hand.

"We all make mistakes," she replied, and then placed her hand on his arm gently. "Think nothing of it, and please, do not let this affect our budding friendship. In fact, I would offer you a place to sit and talk with me so we might get to know each other, if only I had some furniture."

Wentworth laughed, and Wynter joined him. She was glad the tension had eased between them, but was also pleased she had said no. After all, he wouldn't give her a show if she'd asked for one, so why think it safe to ask? She knew exactly why when she turned back to Marcus and found him grinning from ear to ear. He had clearly egged his friend on, and Wynter shook her head.

He truly was a damn fiend.

SIX

After spending the better part of the day still entertaining Wentworth, Wynter couldn't deny feeling more comfortable with him, and in some ways found him quite charming. He was well travelled and highly educated, and he had a story for everything. In fact, she'd lost count of the numerous tales he had told her over the day.

"Marcus clearly adores you," he told her when the two of them were alone. Wentworth had been marvelling at the marble statues Camilla had commissioned years before—the only things that'd seemingly been left behind of hers—and had asked for a closer look. Wynter knew now how he'd simply wanted a moment alone with her. She played along and nodded to him in answer, but then winced when Wentworth spoke again. "You two must be very much in love."

"He loves me very much, yes," she replied honestly, her eyes on the statue ahead of them rather than on him, but she saw Wentworth smile from the corner of her eye. It was clear he understood exactly what she was getting at and checked that the coast was clear before dropping his voice slightly and leaning closer.

"Which certainly explains his most recent behaviour," he said, and she nodded. "Then why stay? You're certainly strong enough to defend yourself."

Wynter felt a pang of grief hit her chest at the sheer thought of trying that route again and shook her head.

"I already tried, and it wasn't just his world he burned to the ground to get me back, but also mine," she whispered, and then turned to her guest with a sad smile. "I've accepted my fate, Wentworth. I'm making this future work, and actually, it's going pretty well so far."

"Glad to hear it," he replied, and then with a nod they moved on through the house and to the front doors, where she wished him a fond farewell and then left Marcus to say goodbye to his friend.

That afternoon, Wynter sat with Marcella for a while. At first things were awkward between them again, but it wasn't long before the Priestess began to thaw. She seemed about ready to open up and after a while, she placed a hand over Wynter's heart, as though sensing her lost child there.

"I was going to call her Mara," she whispered.

"Beautiful," Wynter answered, and then a thought came to her. "Are your names always a variant or have some kind of similarity to Marcus's?"

"Yes. My mother was Marsha, and my grandmother was a Mara. It's surprising no one ever seems to notice, but then again I am one of the first priestesses ever to live a normal life alongside our master."

"Times have changed, I guess, and you seemed to enjoy the work. Was it nice to have a human façade to hide behind?" Wynter asked and remembered back to all the times Marcella had fooled her into trusting her and believing she had her best interests at heart, when in fact the devious witch was always either getting her into or out of trouble.

"I adored it. I could see people from up close, rather than always watching from afar. I had friends and relationships, and of course was able to get to know you, my love," she whispered. "Without that closeness we shared, I would've never given my daughter's heart to you."

Wynter swallowed the lump in her throat and felt her eyes begin to sting with tears.

"Either way, if I had known what you were doing, I would've never accepted. Please know that, Marcy. I cannot bear that she is gone because of me, and watching you mourn her has been the worst experience of my life."

"She was fated to serve you, and at least this way, she will live forever. It was never your choice, or mine," Marcella replied, and Wynter frowned.

"Marcus. He made you do this," she hissed, and was surprised when the Priestess shook her head no.

"It was her, don't you get it? She would've never gone unless it was willingly. I saw her future right before we found you again, my love. I saw you, strong and whole, and knew I was merely a vessel. I was caring for her until she was strong enough to give you life everlasting, and when that time came, fate brought us together again," Marcella insisted, but Wynter still wasn't buying it. However, if this was what the powerful witch needed to tell herself, then she decided she wasn't going to argue with her. Marcella had been forced to give up something no mother should ever have to, and so Wynter decided she wasn't going to play the martyr or feel sorry for herself in her presence. It wasn't fair to her, or to Mara, whom she could sense was indeed thriving inside of her. Growing stronger and more resilient in what she wanted. Or more accurately, who she wanted.

Marcus.

She adored him and Wynter knew she had to be careful that love didn't take over them both. That Mara herself didn't take charge of her vessel and leave Wynter's soul, fighting to be heard. That they remained two halves of a whole and nothing more.

***

Archie knew he and Brodie were acting like lovesick teenagers, but he didn't care one little bit. They were spending day after day either making out on the sofa or working out in the bedroom, and while his jinni lover was still struggling to fully give himself to their new relationship, Archie knew he was all in. No more lying to himself. No more hiding how he felt. It was incredible.

Archie was patient and loving towards him, and Brodie was opening up more and more each day. It helped that they had all the space they wanted while Rosalie continued to hide herself away, but he was sure to check in on her often and had Rafferty to thank for keeping her fed and watered. She was getting there, but they all knew it'd still take a bit of time, and they were willing to give her all that she might need.

That afternoon, while the TV blared with a DVD the two of them were only half watching, he heard the unmistakable sound of a door opening and closing towards the back of the house. Rosalie was clearly up and about, and Brodie jumped beside him, clearly having heard it too.

"Any ideas on how to keep her this side of the door?" he asked, and Archie shrugged.

But then one came to him.

"Teach her about Rafferty, and about everything and anything. Give her the chance to see who we are, and to focus on something other than what happened to her," he suggested, and was glad when Brodie nodded in agreement. They'd tiptoed around Rosalie for too long already. She knew some about what'd happened to them and the creatures involved, but there was more than just darkness in this world. And more that they could teach her about finding the light.

They heard the gentle but unmistakable sound of footsteps out in the hallway a couple of seconds later.

"Hey, Raff. What's for dinner?" Brodie called towards the empty space on the sofa opposite them, and Archie followed his line of sight to where the goblin was apparently sitting.

"Barbeque chicken," came the deeply toned response from the exact location he'd looked at, and Archie's stomach rumbled in reply.

"Sounds good," he replied.

"Sounds really good," a soft voice chimed, and Rosalie's head appeared from around the doorway. She was smiling at first, but then frowned. She had clearly heard three distinct voices, but only found the two men there, and Archie knew it was time they told her about their invisible friend.

"Hey, Rosa. Come join us," he called, and shot Brodie a look when he stiffened, like they'd been caught in the act or something. He'd simply been sat with Archie in his arms, and yet still the ancient jinni seemed to think there was something wrong with people catching them together and showing one another affection. It was beyond frustrating, but an issue to be tackled at a better time.

Whenever they decided to leave the island, he vowed he was going to take Brodie out. As in, properly out. He was going to show him the gay scene of today and make him see that it wasn't something he should be ashamed of. Maybe he'd even take him to the next Pride Festival? That'd be nice. And good fun too. He'd been to a few in his time and was sure even someone barely out of the closet like Brodie would find the experience meaningful.

Rosalie did as Archie had asked, and it was clear she was still a little confused, so he got straight to the point. He told her all about Rafferty and how neither of them could see their friendly household goblin, and when she'd gotten over her initial shock, his voice chimed from the doorway.

"Dinner will be ready in ten minutes," he told them, and while Archie's gaze instinctively went for halfway up the wall, having assumed Rafferty would be small, he noticed Brodie's eyes dart upwards. He smiled and nodded, and that was when Archie realised just how wrong all the fictionalised goblins he'd seen in movies and on television had to be.

"How tall is he?" he asked his beau when Brodie turned back to him, and he laughed.

"Near enough seven feet," the jinni answered, and this time even Rosalie giggled. She'd clearly assumed the same, and it was just another surprise, but at least this time they'd both been caught out by it.

The three of them then chatted for a while, and Archie bided his time, but he had questions churning inside of himself. Things he needed to address, and he figured there was no time like the present.

"So, are you keeping the baby?" he asked over dinner, and Rosalie blanched, but she didn't deny her predicament.

"I want to keep it. What happened to me wasn't the baby's fault, so I'm going to show it how much I love it. Teach it to be good, rather than like him," she answered resolutely.

"Sounds like a bloody good plan if you ask me," he answered, making her smile, and they quickly returned to their meal, but Archie couldn't ignore the sour look on Brodie's face. He was across the room, so thankfully she couldn't see him, but he could.

Brodie was worried, and Archie knew why. The baby was going to inherit its father's nature, whether she wanted it or not. The time might come when Rosalie wouldn't have a choice or any input as to whether the child would remain innocent, but all they could do was hope for the best. Perhaps Rosalie was doing the same, and really, he didn't know what else they could do.

She wanted to keep it, so the half-werewolf child was going to come, and when that time came, he was going to make damn sure Rosalie knew she didn't have to go it alone.

SEVEN

With her new, decidedly brighter outlook driving her forwards, Wynter made an effort with everyone in the house. She spent day and night with Marcus, having no other choice, but she did her best not to hate him the entire time. Whether near or far, she tried to forget about the past and move forward. To become the wife he could be proud of, and the person she would feel proud to be, too. The elegant gowns stayed, no matter the occasion, and she was finally beginning to feel like she might belong by the stylish vampire's side. It was odd how just the small changes made such a difference, but at the same time, Wynter was glad of them. Without the small stuff, she knew she'd never make it through a day by his side, let alone an infinite lifetime.

Marcus seemed to enjoy her this way, too. Like always, he enjoyed ripping the clothes from her every chance he got, but he was disrobing her of finery these days, not the corporate suits and dresses like she'd always used to wear to her job at *Slave*. And at least now, the clothes weren't ruined thanks to his forceful need to get her naked in the swiftest way possible. The clothes she wore were merely manifestations from her imagination and transformed back into white smoke the second he removed them. They were like a part of her and appeared just the same way as her arms and legs did. Her true form was the smoky mist and remaining whole was merely an alternative. An easier one, sure, but Wynter felt she was slowly learning what it meant to be a jinni, and she was proud of her smoky self too. As cliché as she thought it might be, power was everything, and of course she now had this endless supply to draw from, so felt on top of the goddamn world.

Jack appeared to agree with her choices too, and he seemed happier, even if he was Marcus's daily feeder now that he had dispatched with the other managers. It was taking its toll though, and Marcella noticed her unease one night as Wynter watched her husband feed on Jack for the third time that day.

"He's fine, my love. Do not fret," she told her, and Wynter focussed on those strange mixed tones to her voice that came and went. Even after all this time, she knew she'd never get used to that sound. All those voices. All her ancestors coming through as one.

"Should I speak with Marcus and ask him to find some new managers?" she tried, but the Priestess shook her head no.

"Jack has his duty, as do you and me. He would feel like a failure if either of us got in the way of that," Marcella answered, and then Wynter saw her wince and curl in on herself. She tried to hide it, but failed miserably, and when a second wave of pain seemed to rattle through her, Wynter immediately went to her aid.

"What's wrong?" she demanded, but the witch refused her. She shooed her away and tried to change the subject. When Wynter insisted, she stood as though to storm away, but then clutched at her stomach and folded back in on herself again.

"My body has been telling me for a long while how it's time I conceived another child, but I'm not ready," she confided in her, and Wynter wrapped Marcella in her arms.

"What is it, period pains? I can get you a hot water bottle or some painkillers?" she offered, but the Priestess shook her head.

"A hundred times worse," she answered, "the pain is excruciating and will simply continue to get worse until I conceive. The previous priestesses of our coven usually experienced this once in their lifetimes, but for me this is the second calling."

"Because of me," Wynter answered, but she didn't dwell on things. Marcella didn't need to hear it either, and she simply smiled.

"I wasn't meant to have anything to do with Jack after conceiving the first time, but when I had my visions of what fate had in store, I knew I had to reveal myself to him and to secure his place by my side. My master must have his new Priestess, and until I conceive her, I will continue to suffer, but it's worth it."

"What do you mean?"

"The pain is comforting. It means I feel something physical. Something that actually ties me to this life, rather than lures me to the next like the agony in my heart does," Marcella explained, and Wynter wanted to cry. She pulled the witch to her and held her tightly again and suddenly found her mind going crazy.

Memories of their time together washed over her, both the good and bad ones, and Wynter was left feeling confused and overwhelmed, even more so than when it'd happened the first time with Marcus's desk.

Thankfully, Marcella hadn't seemed to notice, but she did seem to calm and warm against her. The Priestess then pulled Wynter closer still, and she tilted her head and offered the lightest of kisses. Wynter went to ease away, thinking this wasn't a complication either of them wanted, but instead she felt herself growing warmer too.

Instead of retreating, she instinctively put her hands on Marcella's flushed cheeks and smiled.

"Let me help you," she whispered, and as if on cue, Jack returned to them. He took in the clearly heady scene and even Wynter couldn't ignore the huge hard-on pitching a tent in his jeans. She remembered the effects of Marcus's bite well and knew Jack had to be gagging for it in the aftermath, and so decided to help them both. He probably had blue balls after his wife not having let him touch her, and rightly so after what she'd just been through, but it was time they reconnected—literally.

Wynter beckoned him closer, her arms still wrapped around Marcella, and then she was quick to switch places with him, but she didn't go far. She couldn't anyway, thanks to the Priestess having a firm grip of her hand, and so Wynter lingered, watching as Jack undressed his wife with a solemn expression on his tired face. He clearly loved her and was ever so gentle and was caring in his approach, not rushing a thing, and it was nice to see.

And then it appeared it was her turn. Marcus was suddenly on her too, peeling off her clothes and he was being his now often gentle self as well. Once he had her naked, Marcus did the same with his designer suit, and soon she was beneath him on the huge sofa she and Marcella had been sat upon, and the other pair were right beside them.

Marcus seemed to be mirroring them, and as soon as she heard Marcella cry out with Jack's gentle probing, she too felt her husband ease his way inside of her. He began to move, his mouth on hers the entire time, and Wynter felt her body begin to sing for him. He was so good at this. Too damn good. He always seemed to know exactly what she wanted, and soon she was fit to burst with her first climax, which he coaxed from her without apology, and of course carried on even after she had come back down from her high. And all while Jack did his best to satisfy his wife close by to them.

It was an odd undertaking, but one Wynter felt she had to see through. An heir needed conceiving, but it was more than that. Marcella deserved to hold her baby in her arms and give her the love she had been so ready to give her first daughter. She reached up and took her hand tightly in her own, and got the impression that Marcella needed to know it was okay. She had to feel not only Wynter's presence but also the approval from her, and her witch's heart.

Wynter readily gave her it and the witch held her back just as tightly, but otherwise they had nothing more to do with their lovemaking, and vice versa. It was strangely intimate, the four of them together, and by the next morning it seemed clear to them all that the shift had indeed occurred. Marcella was no longer in any pain, which could only mean one thing.

A new priestess was on her way.

That morning while Jack slept and Marcella rested alongside him, Wynter wandered the huge house. She went around making notes about what each room should be used for and the colours or wallpaper styles she wanted. She still had no clue what she was going to do with the huge house, but figured it was enough to simply be making a start.

"Darling?" she called and wasn't surprised when Marcus appeared around the doorway a few moments later. He might be busy with work, or so he'd told her repeatedly, but he never seemed to be far away. She wondered if perhaps she distracted him, like when they were back at *Slave* and instead of focussing on his work, he'd played his games with her. Toyed with her emotions and lured her away from the real life she'd foolishly been so desperate to change. And at least if the same could be said the other way around, then she'd gladly take it. Take any power over him she could muster.

God, she'd give anything to go back to that night at the club when David had approached her. She'd tell him no and walk out of there without ever looking back. Wouldn't let her dire situation and greed drive her into the employment of the dastardly vampire who had taken all that she'd offered and more. And all for what? She hadn't so much as looked at her bank account in months. Yes, there would be bountiful amounts inside, and yet she had no need for a single penny of it.

She peered back at him and had to force those thoughts away, like always. There was nothing she could, or would, do about it now.

"Yes, my sweet," he said, and in spite of her thoughts telling her one thing, her body reacted to him in its usual desirous way. She was drawn to him and soon found herself perched beneath his icy stare, her hands itching to touch him.

Wynter forced herself to take a step back just so that she could think straight.

"I'm going to make a start with the decorating. Any input from you on what you want where, or colours?" she asked him, and strangely, Marcus actually seemed relieved.

"No. I have my office, which is all I need. From there, I plan to rebuild my empire, while you rebuild this place. Make it your own and then we'll talk more about the hordes," he told her, and Wynter shuddered. It was easy to forget that they were all out there, buried in pits beneath the house and its grounds. But of course, she was meant to watch over them. To become their queen, or so the alpha had said.

"Sure, but don't come moaning to me when I go crazy and glitter paint the entire fourth floor," she teased, and Marcus smiled down at her, his gaze finally turning warmer.

"Glitter the entire house, if that is what you wish," he said, and then closed the gap between them and offered her a gentle kiss.

"You're under a lot of pressure, aren't you?" she asked, having somehow sensed he was stressed.

"The Committee needs me to put right what I destroyed. I broke hundreds of my own laws and need to make amends," he replied, and she was glad for the honesty.

"What can I do?" Wynter replied.

"Stop being so goddamn perfect and distracting me?" he answered playfully, but she knew there was an element of truth to his words. She was getting in the way of him running his empire, and there was a part of her that felt a great deal of satisfaction about it. At least she wasn't the only one who had to suffer the consequences for his attraction.

"Nah," she joked, and then backed away. "Now, get back to work."

He grinned and seemed like he might be about to defy her, but they both knew it was better he followed his own rules for a change, and Marcus took another step away.

"One month," he then said, and rolled his eyes when she frowned in confusion. "You have one month to have the house ready. We need to formally announce our wedding and unveil the plans for my new ventures, as well as outline the change in ownership of the hordes. We will host a grand gala to honour the occasion, so you must have it ready, my sweet."

He disappeared again before she could so much as grumble, and Wynter found herself more enthusiastic than ever about the task ahead. She had a deadline and a purpose. She might not like having to invite however many vampires Marcus wanted in her home, but knew it was inevitable. And if it was going to be the case of countless visitors to their home-come-office, then she was going to make damn sure it was on her terms, and in the perfect setting.

She started by grabbing a set of car keys from the numerous hooks by the door and then took off outside in search of whatever vehicle she'd happened to have the fob for. There had to be ten sat on the driveway out the front of the mansion, and so she was sure one of them had to match the key in her hands.

Wynter was still pressing the unlock button with her arm stretched high, hoping to come close enough to the relevant vehicle for it to bleep and alert her to its whereabouts, when the alpha vampire suddenly appeared from around the back of the house.

He beckoned her over, and with a huff she charged after him, half expecting to find Marcus there, but instead the soldier led her to where a garage lay. She pressed the button again and heard the distinct honk of a car from within its keep.

She didn't need to say a word. The alpha had the door wrenched open a second later, and she followed him inside, where they discovered a treasure trove of both classic and modern cars. Wynter grinned, and she went to each in turn, checking out their amazing condition and the absolute perfection all around her. Marcus hadn't destroyed all of Camilla's things, after all.

"Which one's my new toy?" she then asked her companion, whom she knew would be coming along on her little shopping trip. Marcus wouldn't have had to so much as lift his head from his desk to issue the order for his minion to accompany her, and she couldn't blame him. She knew there would be no going anywhere alone any longer, or at least until she had his trust, and of course, that might never happen. Not while she continued to seethe and hold on to her hatred towards him, and as it stood no matter how nice he was deciding to be, she had no intention of ever forgiving and forgetting. If she couldn't be free, then neither would Marcus, regardless of the connection they may share when in one another's arms.

Wynter pressed the button again and her face broke into a smile when the huge four-by-four at the end of the row flashed its lights and gave out a loud beep. She'd expected something small and nippy, but the big beast would be perfect. And practical. She was heading out with some serious intent, and just hoped Marcus was ready for her to take a chunk out of the fortune he had always been so quick to dismiss.

She climbed in and found a control for the garage exit on the dash, and by the time the metal door had lifted out of her way, both she and the alpha were in and good to go.

Wynter tore out of there without any fear and found she was incredibly aware of her surroundings while behind the wheel, anyway. Nothing like back when she had been human. It was almost as if the car couldn't keep up with her reflexes and the speed she felt more than comfortable cruising at, and her mind went back to the night when Jakob had driven them out these same gates and down the same country roads to take her shopping. Wynter smiled, remembering how uncomfortable she had been back then, and how incredible her driver had looked while careening around tight bends and whizzing through lights that had seemed to turn green at his command.

Damn, she still missed him.

Wynter shook those thoughts away and focussed on what she had set out to do. There was some sort of retail park close by, and after a mere flick of her fingertips against the built-in satellite navigation system, she had it programmed in, and they were on their way.

They arrived in no time at all, and the jinni was quick to change into a more 'every day' outfit, rather than her finest, but was sure to still look her best. After all, she figured what good was being able to alter any aspect of her appearance at will if she didn't also do it in style. Her companion, on the other hand, was still dressed like a doorman thanks to Marcus never having changed their dress code, and his pale skin made him look albino against the otherwise warm backdrop of a sunny spring day. "Keep behind me," she commanded, and the alpha simply grunted in response.

Wynter then stepped out of her hundred-thousand-pound car with a smile, and she watched as the other shoppers stopped and stared. They had to be wondering who she was and why she had a bodyguard with her. Perhaps she was royalty, or a celebrity? Well, they would never guess the real reason behind her apparent wealth, that was for sure, and so Wynter pressed onwards before anyone could even try.

EIGHT

After hours spent browsing the numerous shops on offer and finally choosing the first of her many purchases, Wynter had the alpha pack up the car and the pair of them then sped back to the mansion. But this time, she took things a little slower. She checked out the scenery and took a few minutes to figure out where the hell their new home was. The chillier weather had given the game away before, so she'd known they were high up in the country but was surprised to find that they were in Scotland. Wynter had her suspicions anyway after her having spoken with numerous members of accented staff back at the retail park but had to admit she'd had no clue before zooming out on the sat-nav's map to see where exactly they were.

When they were home, Wynter went room by room, where she painted square patches onto the walls using the many tester pots of paint she'd grabbed at the nearby DIY store. She also had wallpaper samples and carpet or flooring taster squares and was in her element as she began making her final decisions. She worked through the night and by lunchtime the next day, her plans were finally beginning to come together.

The house was eerily quiet, but Wynter didn't care what any of the others were up to. She had her jobs to do and was ready to make a start. She picked out the three reception rooms downstairs to be the first to finish. Each of them was to remain in the classic style, traditional to the house itself, and so she got to work. Wynter knew she could easily employ a team of decorators for the task but didn't want to. This was going to be her job to see through, and so she quickly acquainted herself with wallpapering, painting and even a spot of plastering where needed. It helped that she never tired, of course, and after a few hours the first room was done. Even though it wasn't perfect, she felt immensely proud of what she had accomplished, and couldn't stop smiling as she took a step back and admired her handiwork.

By the end of day four of working around the clock, she finally let the small group of Marcus's vampires start helping. The alpha led them, taking his orders from her before doing that strange silent hive-mind thing with the other four. And it was just a few days until every room in the house was decorated and ready for furnishing.

Marcus had remained locked away the entire time she had kept busy and as Wynter grabbed the keys to her new favourite car, about to head straight out, she found herself stopping by his office to check in on him. She told herself she didn't care, though. No, she was just being nosy.

"My sweet," he called when she opened the door and poked her head inside, "what a pleasant surprise."

"I just wanted to let you know I'm heading out for a while," she said, and knew it was a lie. She hadn't told him the last time, nor had she asked his permission for anything she'd done, and probably wouldn't ever if she could help it. The alpha was probably relaying her every move to his boss anyway, so Marcus wouldn't have to so much as wonder about her, and she didn't know why she'd come to him at all.

"Anywhere nice?" he asked, his eyes still on the documents splayed out on the desk before him, and she looked around his chaotic space. He had indeed been busy.

"The shops," she replied, and took a tentative step towards him. "I'd like to start ordering the furniture and there's a delightful store in town that sells handcrafted pieces that are one of a kind. I'd like to talk with the designer about doing some bespoke work for us."

"I'm glad you're getting somewhere with your decorating," he answered, and Wynter frowned. She moved closer still and saw numerous rolls of blueprints and plans beside her husband's desk. Had he drawn them up himself? Surely not? But at the same time, not a soul had come or gone from the house to deliver them to him, and she had to wonder if perhaps he truly was so dedicated to his work that he'd done everything it'd taken to build his empire.

Wynter reached his side, and she watched him work for a moment before answering him.

"It's for us, Marcus. You gave me a job to do and I am gladly doing it, but it's not just for me. Like I said, it's for us…"

She then went to turn away, thinking she'd leave him to it. He hadn't so much as looked at her after all, and Wynter had things she too needed getting on with. However, the second she moved away, his hand reached out to grab her by the waist and Marcus finally turned his face up towards hers. His icy blues bore into hers and she felt herself swoon.

"Oh, so there's finally an 'us' then?" he then mused, his lips curling into a smile.

Despite her better judgement, Wynter couldn't help but return it.

"I guess there might just be," was all she could bring herself to reply. Like always, she wasn't going to give into him too easily. "And maybe one

THE COMPLETE BLOOD SLAVE SERIES

day I'll be able to leave this house without a guard to watch over me."

Marcus simply laughed and then pulled Wynter down onto his lap playfully.

"That would take a great deal of trust, my sweet. And trust must be earned, of course," he told her, as if she didn't already know. He then cupped her cheek with his palm and offered her a gentle kiss.

By the time he pulled away, she was trembling with desire for him to do more than just kiss her, but Wynter forced herself to be strong. And to remember what she was meant to be doing. He didn't own her or rule her. He had a cruel and vicious side she refused to taunt nowadays, but of course, that didn't mean he wouldn't get bored of playing nice all on his own. And when he did, she knew she had to be prepared. To be strong enough to take it, or fight back, whichever the case may be.

"I intend to," was all she whispered against his lips.

"Good. Plus, don't forget you will only ever be able to leave for any extended amount of time when both the Priestess and I allow you to. Your vitality is thanks to her gracious gifts, plus your heart beats for me. You will never get farther away from me than necessary, and not a single step more than the front gates of this home if you had any ideas of running away once you breached them."

"Once a slave, always a slave..." Wynter ground, and she forced herself back to her feet and away from him.

"Marriage is just another form of slavery, don't you think?" he teased as she rounded the doorway, and Wynter stopped and simply scowled back at him rather than rise to his bait any longer. He couldn't just be nice and leave it there. He always had to goad her and remind her who was boss. Well, she'd had enough. And there was her thinking she could pop in to see him and walk away, having had a nice talk.

She stormed to the front of the house, where the alpha was stood waiting for her, and she passed him and stepped out into the bright sunshine without a word in greeting. But then she saw red. She turned and grabbed the vampire soldier by the throat and threw him to the ground, where she straddled him and peered into his bright red eyes.

"Just think. All those human shop assistants must believe you're there to protect me. Like I'm some delicate flower who needs someone to watch over her. If only they knew I could snap you and everyone else here like a fucking twig if given half the chance. My husband included," she hissed, and then let go and was back up off him in a flash.

Wynter then climbed in the driver's seat and threw the soldier a pair of sunglasses as he followed her lead. "Put these on. It's bad enough I'm stuck walking around with someone who looks like something out of a zombie movie, but those eyes simply will not do."

Damn, what had come over her? She truly didn't know, but decided it was time she bit her tongue. He hadn't done anything to her either, and Wynter knew it was Marcus she'd been trying to get her message across to, which it would, thanks to his psychic connection to the soldiers at his command. The job was done, and so she drove them away in complete silence. It was time she made this mansion perfect. Or should it be her prison that needed to be perfect?

That sounded more like it.

***

By the end of Marcus's one-month deadline, Wynter had done everything she had set out to do and more. She had decorated and furnished the huge mansion from top to bottom, and every room had a purpose as well as its chosen style and theme. She was beyond proud of everything she'd accomplished, as well as the personal steps forward she had taken while doing the work.

Through the hard work and busy days, she had processed her grief and had time to think and process those thoughts and feelings. The days weren't so dark now, and neither were her thoughts.

She had also found a way of connecting with the alpha and his soldiers in ways she'd never foreseen. Not in a telepathic way, but it was like they were more in tune with her needs and seemed to always be there, ready and waiting, before she even had to ask. The alpha watched over her day and night, and while she still had her odd moments of rage directed towards him, he never backed off. Never seemed to take it personally. It was like he knew she needed to offload, and it was nice to have someone around who was there for her without any games or the necessity for her to pay anything back.

Wynter had also fixed even more between her and Marcella, and while she remained a little closed off, she couldn't blame her. The Priestess was in early pregnancy and still had her work to do for Marcus whenever he needed it, plus she also had a husband to care for. Wynter hadn't failed to notice the regular visits Jack made to the office and how drained he still looked. They were all just doing their jobs, but at the same time, she couldn't help but think how it must be taking its toll on some of them more than others. Jack must need feeding and looking after too, and Wynter was surprised at how quickly she had forgotten what it was like to have to eat or sleep, or to wash and groom yourself. Those little efforts were what helped fill the day, but now she had needed to find other things to busy herself with and had to admit it was hard now that she had finished her task of beautifying the mansion.

Wynter was out the front of the huge house one morning, directing the gardener on some ideas she'd had for adding some colour to the façade, when the alpha appeared and beckoned for her to follow him. He wasn't usually the one to be doing any sort of leading, and she couldn't deny being intrigued. She followed him over to where nothing but grass lay ahead, but she knew better than that. They were standing over the underground storage vaults. The pits. Each of them filled with vampire soldiers like the behemoth standing before her.

The five Marcus controlled were different to the others though. He had told her himself of how he'd fed them his blood and so commanded them, but how she was to become their queen and watch over the rest of them. And there had to be thousands.

She could think of nothing worse.

Wynter remembered the awful day when she had tried to escape Marcus at his derelict warehouse with terrifying ease. Her last day as a human had been spent fighting and fearing for her life, which she had then given up to save Jakob. But before all of that, she had stepped out into a stairway lined with vampire soldiers. They had been icy cold against her skin and had then grabbed at her, desperate for a taste of her blood, and she could remember that horror like it was only yesterday. And then, of course, there was the assault on Brodie's island. They had been ruthless in laying waste to the place, and of course had been the only reason Marcus had won the fight against two Jinn and a seasoned fighter and assassin. In a fair fight, they would've taken him down with ease, but thanks to his seemingly never-ending supply of pasty-skinned and red-eyed soldiers, Marcus had thwarted them.

So, the last thing she wanted was to come face-to-face with them again.

The alpha had to know this, but still he drew her forwards. When they reached the first cover, he lifted it and peered down into the depths, his lips curled back in what she presumed was a smile.

A second later, he was gone. He'd jumped down into the hole and she heard him hit the ground below with a loud thud.

Wynter inched closer to the dark hole, and she let out a cry when she looked inside and found hundreds of pairs of red eyes looking up at her. Everything inside of her was screaming for her to run away, but she instinctively knew she had to do this. She had to follow him inside, no matter what horror awaited her in the depths below.

She transformed into white mist and billowed inside and hit the ground in complete silence before returning to her human form. For a few seconds, all she could do was stare at the naked men and women before her, and they simply stared back. They watched her just as she was watching them, and Wynter knew she wasn't hiding her fear well at all. She expected for them to pounce and readied herself to transform and rush away, but instead, they began to fall to their knees before her. Each of the soldiers put their heads down and their hands up, and Wynter didn't need any direction to know what they wanted of her.

She swallowed the lump in her throat and reached for the closest pair of hands. The man before her was pale and cold as she expected, but as soon as she made contact, something changed within her. Wynter wasn't repulsed or fearful like before. Instead, she felt herself flood with something else—devotion. The man was connecting with her on some sort of psychic level, and he was sharing his emotions with her. She could sense he was hungry, but that wasn't what was driving him. No, he was relieved to have her there. Comforted by having a mistress again, and that seemed more important to him than anything else.

The soldiers truly were unlike any other vampires Wynter had met since starting work for Marcus. They were primitive and almost childlike, and she could see now why they were the ultimate force to have at anyone's back. They had no ulterior motives and played no games. All they thought about was delivering true and proud subservience. And loyalty. It didn't occur to them to be disloyal and Wynter was quickly in awe.

She moved from one to the other, being sure to press her hands against every single one of theirs, and by the time she had been to each of the thousand or so vampires in this horde, she finally had some kind of understanding for who they were and why they had been created. These vampires didn't have lives to lead or loves to hold. They had once been men and women, just like she had, and yet they had evidently been given a choice. The hordes weren't simply vampires who had been left to go hungry or had suffered a curse of some kind. They had been turned this way because the magic behind their immortality had deemed it so. The soldiers had been bred and cultivated for one purpose—to fight for the vampire world should an uprising occur.

She suddenly understood how they were merely humans who had chosen this over death, and she wanted to help them. To give them the afterlife each of them deserved. And yet, they didn't want to be freed or to be given any other purpose. They only wanted to be taken care of. The soldiers in this horde had adored their previous mistress and had seen Camilla like a mother. They had missed her, and Wynter knew she was the right person to take over from her. Marcus could never show these soulless vampires that kind of love. He could barely love her, and so, as she stood beneath the opening and readied herself to go, she made them a promise.

"I will be your queen," Wynter called, and she sensed their approval in return. She didn't need to say another word, but instead felt their bond begin to form in her mind. They wanted her. This was what the alpha had been trying to convey to her for weeks, but she'd just thought he was trying to get closer to her himself, when he was more like their spokesman. He had been trying to make her see, and now her eyes were wide open, so at last she felt ready.

She transformed again and spirited herself up and away from the first horde and was followed by the enormous thud of the alpha landing on the ground behind her.

"Wynter is queen," he stammered after covering the opening again. She nodded to him and smiled.

"Yes. It appears I am," she answered, and then stepped closer to him. Wynter didn't know why, but she then climbed up onto her tiptoes and placed a gentle kiss against his cold cheek. "And you're learning to speak more. Why?"

He didn't answer, but she saw his gaze move from her to the house and back again and got the idea. Marcus had everything to do with the changes in them. He wanted his chosen few to be the ultimate soldiers. Not just the alpha, but the others, too.

Her husband probably also wanted his to be better than her followers, and Wynter shook her head as she stepped away again. If she was right, then it meant he was doing so for one of two reasons. Either he simply wanted to have soldiers that were superior to her hordes because he could then continue to have one up on her, or because he knew that should she command the soldiers effectively, they could end up more powerful than he could ever have anticipated.

Wynter wondered if she might be able to push them harder and prevail where Camilla had failed, and decided she wanted that more than anything. Another excellent job done by her, and even though she and Marcus were indeed a team now, she would still know she had gone one better than he had ever expected her to.

And she started by doing the same thing she had just done with each of the remaining pits of vampires beneath their grounds. It took hours, but by the end of it, she had connected with the thousands of soldiers now completely at her command. They were hers now, and she decided that while leaving them in the pits and in their sort of stasis wasn't the most glamorous way for them to live. There ultimately wasn't any other choice. At least in them, they were safe and contained, and as she wandered back to the house, Wynter thought of all the ways she could bring nourishment to them without the need for human sacrifice. Perhaps a sort of blood bank? Yes, that would make sense.

She was still deliberating when she reached the front doors of the mansion and found Marcus lazing against the jamb with a smile.

"My sweet."

"Good evening, Marcus. Have you finished your work?" she replied, and then she was suddenly filled with dread when his eyes flashed with something vile. He clearly wasn't in one of his better moods, and she didn't need to guess why. He had to be envious of her having connected with the hordes without his say-so. It was the only explanation. No matter his apparent love for her, he still had to rule her. Still seemed to need to control his bride, even in this strange immortal life she had been delivered unto.

"The plans are in motion for my new empire, but I will have to continue working on them during the implementation stages. I simply wanted to come and see you. To see what you'd done with the house," he answered, but Wynter wasn't falling for his nice-guy routine. Something was definitely off.

"And?"

"I don't like it," he told her, his smile fading. "So, I'd prefer it if you'd start again. The gala I'd planned is also to be postponed indefinitely…"

"I couldn't care less about your gala. And I do like it, so no I won't be starting the decorating again," she tried, and rather than respond, her husband simply stepped aside and showed her the carnage that lay behind him. He had laid waste to everything she could see. The wallpaper had been ripped from the walls and her carefully selected furniture was now in shards scattered across the marble floors. Marcus had done this to spite her. He'd clearly decided to waste her time and effort without a care, and he certainly didn't seem about to apologise.

Wynter wanted to scream. She wanted to curse him and hurt him back, but the damn forces inside of her wouldn't let her move so much as a muscle towards him in hatred. No matter what he'd done, the witch's heart beating within her was loyal to him and loved him so much she wouldn't lash out. Even when he'd done something this cruel and vile, and all because he wanted to get one up on her. There had been no reason for him to trash the place, but he had done so anyway, and she didn't need to see the rest of the house to know he would have done the same from top to bottom.

She turned and stalked away without a word to Marcus. Without giving him the satisfaction he so desperately seemed to want. She was desperate to know why he had done it. What reason he'd had for ruining all her hard work but knew the vile vampire would give her nothing but lies and torment. Never the truth. Perhaps she'd been right to think he was jealous that the hordes had welcomed her so adoringly. Or maybe he was simply angry because she'd finished her given task while he still hadn't completed work on his new empire. Whatever his reasons, Wynter was filled with renewed hatred for him, and so she put as much distance between them as possible.

She stormed down the driveway, her feet pounding the gravel path, and then after a few more metres, she transformed into mist and took flight.

A warm, dark night had fallen and so scattering into the wind felt like heaven, and she let the gentle caress of it sweep her away. The sensation felt freeing, and it dulled her rage, which she urged herself to let go of. It wouldn't do her any favours to detest him more than usual. It was what he seemed to want, for whatever reason, and so she fought it. Fought herself and her natural urge to fight back.

Wynter carried on floating away, but then suddenly it was like she'd hit a brick wall. She tumbled downwards and hit the gravel like a mist rolling across the hills and then took form where she lay. The gates that led to the mansion were right beside her, and she knew exactly why she had come to such an abrupt stop. It was the magic all around the house, and of course, the magic within her.

Even when up on her feet, Wynter couldn't take another step away from the house, and so she instead turned to the left and went for an impromptu walk around the gardens beside the house. As she returned, she found an old oak tree. An ancient and magnificent tree that she quickly scaled and then found the perfect perch in.

Wynter stayed there for hours, just watching the night's sky. She stayed there to watch the sun rise the following morning too, and still didn't budge when she saw half-a-dozen trucks pull up outside the house and more than twenty workmen clambered out of them.

She cursed them, her husband most of all, and stayed in her spot to seethe and spy on them as they cleared the debris Marcus had left in his violent wake. The first day was spent taking away everything she had meticulously put in, and Wynter didn't move a muscle the entire time. She remained there even as night fell once again.

But she couldn't stop from wondering why he'd done this. And why he'd been so ruthless in destroying everything she had worked so hard to achieve. Marcus had to know where she was, but at least he was thankfully leaving her alone, rather than keep rubbing what he had done in her face. Wynter guessed that was at least something she could remain thankful for, but she was also glad for not feeling the cold or the damp of being outside for two days straight. The tree wasn't all that comfortable, but she didn't have bones or muscles that needed stretching off, plus she didn't have a tummy that was rumbling and needed tending to. She could simply lie there and be still, and as she bounced between her various forms, Wynter forced all thought away and found herself starting to reflect back on her life. It was cathartic and a much needed exercise, and as she lay there meditating, the world simply carried on around her.

Days and nights passed in a blur, and all the while, she remained in her little bubble. She shut it all out and focused inwards. Deeper and deeper she delved, and by the time she had made peace with what she found there, she came back around to discover that not only had more than a fortnight passed, but that the house was alive and bustling with guests.

The driveway was rapidly filling up with newcomers, and Wynter knew it was time she finally headed back inside to find out what was going on. To return to the life, she'd chosen to embrace and back to him.

She transformed to mist and wafted over to the house, where she could see Bryn standing in the doorway. So, he had survived the fall of Marcus's empire. One of the chosen few, no doubt, and he was ushering people inside like some kind of butler. There was no part of her that wanted to be seen going in the front like a guest, and so she drifted over to the back of the house instead, where she took her human form and this time opted for one of her old corporate outfits. If Bryn was here, then that had to mean this meeting had something to do with Marcus's new plans and so, still technically being a member of his staffing team, she decided to join them for the unveiling.

Wynter opened the back door and knew before she'd even set foot inside what she'd find there. It was the same back entrance she had come and gone through with Jakob, and as she passed the small room she'd been held in, a pang of nostalgia hit her. They had laughed and joked in that room. Built a friendship. There would never be a day that she didn't miss that bloody vampire, but Wynter was glad she had worked through her grief during her meditation. She had chosen to let Jak go, and so smiled as she thought of him, but didn't dwell on it. She simply pressed on and headed through what were undoubtedly the servants' quarters before coming up into the main entrance hall of the mansion.

Damn him. Marcus had spared no expense in redecorating their home and while she was still annoyed about his way of doing things, Wynter couldn't deny he had chosen well. But one thing this new décor lacked in abundance was love. She had done the work herself and put her love into every selection. Every stroke of the brush. He, on the other hand, had probably just hired an interior designer before ducking back in his office and finishing off his master plans. Had he even cared, or okayed the plans ahead of time? She very much doubted it but refused to seethe any longer. She had plans of her own to see through, and in order to get there, Wynter knew she had to make amends with her reprehensible husband.

She followed the small crowd of people through to the greatest of their halls, which had been kitted out with rows of chairs all facing towards a small stage. Inside, Wynter looked around, and she could see nothing more than a sea of humans. No vampires or witches, just Marcus's new team, and she wondered how many had been recruited during these past few weeks. Had they already signed their lives away? Did they know what they were getting themselves into? Or perhaps tonight was his big reveal? As they each took a seat, she followed their lead and sat amongst them. Hiding in plain sight, even though he probably already knew exactly where she was.

Wynter sat in silence and waited, and as she did so, she looked at the array of faces all around her. Each of them was staring forwards like they were under some sort of spell, answering her previous musings regarding their contracts having already been initiated, and as she glanced around, she immediately spotted a plaited pink braid a few rows in front.

Could it be? Could her old friend phoebe have survived too? The geeky girl who had given her more than just a shoulder to cry on, but who had offered her comfort when all hope had seemed lost. Phoebe had been sent to oversee one of the new clubs' IT department before everything had kicked off, and Wynter hadn't seen her since. Perhaps she had been spared after all. She sure hoped so.

"Welcome!" Marcus's deep voice then boomed from somewhere behind the stage, and the crowd went wild for him. There had to be well over two hundred humans there, and each began clapping and hollering as he mounted the steps and stood proudly over them.

It was the oddest sight, like she was at a show where a self-help guru was on stage talking into a microphone about his own brand of enlightenment or miracle cure, and Wynter watched as he grinned at the adoring welcome he'd received. Marcus was lapping up their adulation like she knew he'd always loved to, and when his eyes fell on hers, he simply winked and then carried on scanning his new team's many faces.

Bastard. She'd been right, of course. He'd known she was there.

He then shushed the crowd and waited a beat before getting right to the point. "I have some wonderful news. *Slave* is back up and running, as is *Bound*, and we have numerous other new locations opening within the coming weeks!" he told them, and the news was met with renewed cheers and applause. The old and human Wynter would have been devastated to hear that. She would've thought about the amount of poor Blood Slaves such an undertaking would require, but not anymore. She had thousands of vampires to feed, and so needed those slaves. She had cultivated her plan to have blood deposited in small quantities at each sitting, amounting to large amounts over the days, and so would be plentiful for her hordes. No one would have to die and at least that way her devoted soldiers would not go hungry.

The only thing in all this that Wynter didn't get yet was what these humans were doing in their home. It wasn't long until she got her answer. "And so, to your roles in this," Marcus told them, and each of the humans hung on his every word, "you have all been appointed as supervisor thanks to my meticulous standards. In this room sit two supervisors for each of my clubs around the world. Some of you are already in post and others are waiting to start, but for the time being, you will all stay here at the mansion while being trained. Plus, as an added bonus, you are all now tasked with personally serving my feeding needs."

Murmurs echoed through the crowd. Some of the humans seemed shocked, while others were confused, and Wynter could tell from that fact alone how there was a complete mix of older and new employees for Marcus to oversee. It was the older ones who knew he was indeed very particular in who he fed from, and so seemed surprised to hear he was ready to feed from them. He had changed his tune and while they could understand the alterations in the way, his clubs might work, they couldn't seem to grasp this change in how he himself chose to feed.

Wynter shot to her feet and saw how Marcus was just as surprised as the rest of them by her sudden movement. He scowled at her, clearly thinking she was about to storm off because he had run none of these plans by her, but instead she walked towards him.

They hadn't spoken in over two weeks. Not since he had ruined the work she had painstakingly undertaken at his behest, and there was a part of her that wanted to do the same to his. Maybe she could kill everyone in the room. Render him without his chosen 'Supervisors' and make him have to start all over again too?

No. She had told herself this wasn't the way she wanted to do this. He would only retaliate if she did, and Wynter knew she wasn't ready to keep a feud going. Marcus loved her, or so he had always said. He'd proven it in the way he'd acted, even when he was being cruel and unreasonable, and so she decided it was time she tried her best to care for him in return. To let go of the past and move forward, even if she had to force it.

Wynter said nothing as she moved through the crowd towards him, but she saw their guests each turn to stare at her in surprise and murmur to one another, asking what the hell she was doing. Even Phoebe seemed shocked, and while Wynter was pleased to find her alive, she didn't address her yet. Their reunion could wait.

"And what is my role in all of this, Marcus?" she whispered as she neared the stage, and she peered up at him with a gentle, innocent look on her face she hoped he knew was sincere. She wasn't there for a fight, just for the truth.

It was Bryn who decided to intercept her. He stood from his seat at the front and blocked her path, a sneer etched across his usually so stoic face.

"Well, seeing as Mr Cole has done away with his Managers and has chosen to feed from all us Supervisors instead, I think it's obvious—you've been demoted, Miss Armstrong…" he told her, and then sniggered, like he had just told the funniest little joke.

Something came over Wynter in that moment, and she wanted nothing more than to snap Bryn's neck in front of all these people. She wanted to hurt him. To tear that stupid grin from his face. She instead feigned upset, like he was right, but then started to laugh along with him. Her face spread with an even wider smile than his, and then on instinct, she lifted her hand and slapped him across the face with so much force he went flying to the floor and then slid another eight feet.

The room fell deathly silent, and all eyes were on her, but all Wynter could look at was Marcus. She needed him to be the one to say the words. To reveal all at long last.

And she would wait there as long as it took for him to validate her position in front of all his employees, both new and seasoned.

NINE

Marcus was suitably impressed. He had already spied his darling wife in the crowd, of course, but was well aware of her movements before seeing her, anyway. He always knew exactly what she was up to. Knew where she was and what she was doing, which was why it'd taken him so damn long to finally get his affairs in order in the first place.

Even now that she couldn't possibly escape, he still fretted night and day that she might try. The memories of her absence haunted him like a corpse rotting in the confines of his dark heart. And rather than breathing life into him, her return often felt like more torture, not less. Keeping tabs on Wynter was a necessary part of his daily struggle, and it was also the root of his problems. But he wouldn't stop his invasive adoration and the ways and means he had of getting his fix of her, no matter how much his work was suffering.

Because of course, he couldn't get enough. Of her smile and the way her body fit against his. Of the way she made him feel. Even her hate. He loved the fervent loathing she had for him, and even though he could no longer enjoy the taste of that harsh nectar for himself, he knew that bitterness still ran deep, despite the precious gift his priestess had given her.

Damn, he loved her. So much he'd kill every human in this room if she demanded it. His promises to the High Committee of Vampires meant nothing when compared to her needs. If she told him to burn it all down again, he would.

Something had changed in her now, though. His sweet little fighter somehow seemed as if she was ready and willing to become more than just his captive. She wanted her place by his side rather than accept it because she had no other choice, and he'd be lying if he didn't acknowledge her actions as both unexpected and delightful.

Their last six weeks together hadn't been the best, after all.

He had needed to get his head down and work, but all he'd been able to focus on was her, which was exactly why he'd given her the task of decorating their home in a bid to get her out of his sight and keep her nice and busy. But instead of working, he'd spent half the time either watching her or keeping tabs via his ever-loyal alpha soldier.

Wynter had done an amazing job on the house, but over the course of it had grown a tremendous deal of independence. Far too much autonomy for his liking. She had also somehow grown closer to the vampires he commanded and had given strength to form his own flesh and blood. The alpha and the rest of his comrades were not hers to oversee, and yet they doted on her. They assisted her and followed her commands without hesitation, and then, to top it all off, the alpha had gone and secured her place as their queen without so much as asking for Marcus's permission. He had led her to the hordes of his own accord and had dared let her kiss him.

It wasn't his place to take her there, or to instigate any of that. Marcus should've been the one to do it, and so, of course, he had been livid. He hadn't sought to trash the house, though. It'd been a knee-jerk reaction to ruin everything she had done, and he'd regretted it immediately, but couldn't tell her so. He had made strides in the right direction, sure, but he still couldn't admit to being wrong. And so, when she had returned, he'd attempted to turn things back around onto her as usual, but rather than fight him, or grin and bear it as normal, something had seemed to snap in her. Wynter hadn't fought or screamed at him. She hadn't called him names or begged him to stop being so cruel. She had simply surveyed the carnage behind him with a miserable and heartbroken look on her face, and then walked away without a word.

She had lost her fight, and Marcus knew then how he truly had failed at being a good husband to her. The silence was a hundred times worse than if she'd just bellowed and stormed at him. If she too had lashed out in her rage.

Instead, Wynter had taken herself away from him completely. But of course, she couldn't get far thanks to the magical barriers he commanded, and so she had climbed up into that tree, where she had remained for more than two weeks.

Marcus had watched her out the third-floor window for days. Watched as she had simply laid there, staring up into the sky as the world carried on turning without her. There was no emotion on her beautiful face, and he'd hated seeing her like that. She hadn't moved a muscle, even when the workmen had come and gone, or when their work had continued to go on beneath her. He'd wondered at length what was going through her mind. Was she plotting his demise? Trying to sever their connection by internally attempting to free herself of the magic his priestess had shared with her? Or perhaps he had pushed her one time too many, and she was thinking of all the ways in which she could hurt him in return. Planning a lifetime of hatred, when all he had ever wanted was for her to love him.

Yeah, he knew he had a funny way of showing it, but that didn't make it any less true.

And so, while she had clearly needed her space, he had finally gotten down to work. Marcus had already planned the fundamentals of his new regime, and he spent the days that followed, adding the final touches to the plan before sending out invitations to all his most trusted employees. He currently owned more than thirty clubs across the world, with another thirty due to open by the end of the year, and he'd decided that they each needed two supervisors to oversee the running of them.

He was no longer going to be based out of *Slave* or any other club. He was going to run his empire from the mansion alongside his wife, and they were going to be happy. He was going to make it so, but first, he had to rebuild his businesses from the ground up. The other clubs across the globe were running smoothly enough, and Marcus knew he could do the same here.

And so, two members of staff were to be put into the prime position and would be expected to work and live at their relative clubs, so they were there around the clock. One would be an older or more seasoned member of his current staff, who was experienced in his workings and the trade of Blood Slaves, and one would be a completely new employee, who would be trained by their senior counterpart. And Marcus was going to feed from them all. No longer would he select a few managers, and no more overseeing the day-to-day business himself. He would do it from afar, and they would take it in turns to come to him with their veins at the ready. In return, they would be offered amnesty from the other vampires, who were patrons of their clubs.

This also meant that Jack was affectively off the hook, but Marcus wasn't done with him yet. He would keep him at the mansion as a backup but would also let him be with his family. Marcella needed him, and although he hadn't liked the changes made in this generation of priestess, Marcus knew it was time he let them have a life of their own. Let them raise their new daughter together, rather than for him to take the child under his wing and then drink the mother dry, like he had with all his previous priestesses. They had gone willingly, of course, but this time was different. This time he had Wynter, and she needed him more than any witch progeny did.

With the room still deathly quiet, Marcus sent a wave of power throughout the group, commanding that they remain so, and that they watch him intently as he climbed down off the stage and went over to his wife's side.

"My sweet," he whispered, and he gathered her in his arms, placing kisses against her cheek and lips. "You came back to me," Marcus added, and he could sense her iciness beginning to thaw. In fact, she seemed like an open book. For the first time, he felt he knew exactly what she needed, and was relieved to discover that those needs involved him.

"Of course," Wynter whimpered, and she curled her body against his, driving him wild with desire for her. They had abstained for too long, and he was so full of lust he felt like taking her there and then, in front of the crowd, but forced himself to take a step backwards. He wanted her, like always, but wanted her in their new bed upstairs. Wanted her for hours, perhaps days. Not a quickie with an audience.

Marcus led her up onto the stage instead, their hands entwined, and once there he grinned down at his devoted followers, much like a cult leader might do with his flock. They were peering up at the two of them, their eyes wide with surprise and their ears trained solely on his voice. So ready for his commands. So eager to serve him.

He'd missed this. Nothing was more perfect.

"Ladies and gentlemen, pay no attention to what that fool dared say," he told them, and he saw the only just recovered Bryn turn a delightful shade of red at having been chastised in front of all the others. "None of you know this, but I have recently taken this incredible woman as my wife. She is mine, and she rules by my side. You will speak to her as you would me, and anything else will be dealt with harshly. I will not stand for anything less than perfection and devotion."

He revelled in the trepidation he felt emanating from his more seasoned members of staff. The new ones didn't know what he was capable of yet, but they would, and soon they too would watch him in fear. They wouldn't dare talk out of turn, and if they did, he was willing to bet they didn't do so a second time after he was done punishing them.

On his insistence, Wynter then stepped forward, and she eyed the crowd resolutely. He was about to say more when she surprised him by speaking up as well.

"I do not want your devotion, but your respect. I'll endeavour to talk with all of you in turn and learn your names and more about you. I would like to know each and every person here and will offer council to any who might need it. But please, do not fear me," she told them, and he sensed a shift happen among his loyal subjects. They somehow trusted her already, even after just a few seconds. "Not even when you discover what I am…"

Marcus didn't need to look. He felt Wynter's hand turn to mist in his, and the gasps from the crowd were enough to tell him how shocked the humans were to discover his wife was far more than she had once seemed. He grinned down at them and then turned to watch as Wynter reappeared, this time wearing one of her specially selected ball gowns.

His minions were beyond impressed, but they needed to get back to the task at hand, and so Marcus settled them back down with another wave of his magical hold on them.

"Now, each of you are to wait in your seats to be summoned by my assistant Bryn. Two names will be called at a time, and the person you are ushered forwards with is your fellow supervisor. He will inform you which location you are to serve in and will offer information to the new employees before sending you back to your seats together," he informed the large group, and then turned to Wynter with a smile. "And I will see you all later, when dinner will be served."

***

Damn, he was good. Marcus sure had everyone wrapped around his little finger, and Wynter knew that included her. She was pleased he had responded so well to her having effectively interrupted his little speech and was also glad to hear that he wasn't only going to take a step back from micromanaging the entire operation, but that he was also planning to stay at the mansion with her. In spite of everything, she still wanted the two of them to stay there. She also still felt desperate to have him hold her close and make love to her again and realised just how much she had indeed missed him.

Without another word, he led her off the stage, out of the hall, and into his office.

There, she perched against the solid wooden desk and watched him with a smile.

"I know what you want," she then whispered, watching as he delicately removed his jacket and tie, while she simply watched him, devouring the sight. Marcus was an older man, that much was true on many levels, but he was still well in his prime, and as he looked her up and down with those ice-blue eyes, Wynter knew she had been right.

After her break and the self-imposed solitary confinement of the tree, she had awoken a new woman. She was strong enough to be everything she needed to be, and more. And that included giving herself to her husband in far more ways than just physically. The witch's heart within her beat for him, and against all Wynter's previous promises to both him and herself, her own was slowly starting to follow suit.

"And what is it that I want?" he answered her, and then hissed when she transformed to her misty form for a second and then returned dressed in nothing but her high heels and a smile.

Marcus fell to his knees before her, and as he shuffled towards her on them, he continued to undress himself. When he reached the floor by her feet, the vampire lunged for her, kissing and lapping his way up her thigh, and soon Wynter was grabbing at him, pulling him harder against her core while crying out with the pleasure he readily gave.

When she came, he didn't stop, and soon Marcus had her screaming for him. He then pushed her back onto the desk and was inside her within seconds, pounding into her hard and at speeds no human could ever handle, and she adored it.

Their lovemaking was full of raw emotion and was the hardest he'd ever taken her, but it felt exactly what they both needed. And when they were eventually spent, he kissed her tenderly and then closed his eyes.

Wynter was about to ask what was wrong when Marcus whispered something she never thought she would hear. "I'm sorry…"

Damn. She hadn't expected that.

"Thank you," was all she could reply while forcing back her tears.

In all their time together and all the things Marcus had done, he had never once shown her any remorse for them. And yet, he wanted to say this now? It was almost too little too late, but she didn't want to make light of what it must have taken for him to finally say the words, and so she didn't tell him to shove his apology up his backside. Part of her wanted to, but instead Wynter bit her tongue.

"I mean it," Marcus continued, and she opened her eyes, his bright blue irises shining like lamps from behind. His soul was calling to her again, reaching out, and while she still wasn't used to accepting it, she didn't retreat like normal. She instead held his gaze and smiled. "Jealousy is an ugly trait, and on me it turns to violence and cruelty. I will stop it from ruling me, or I will at least try."

Wynter simply nodded. She would believe that when she saw it but was willing to take his words not as a promise, but a gesture. A sign that meant he was beginning to care properly. He was learning, just as she was, what it would take for them to finally make this marriage work.

All she had to learn for herself was how to truly stop hating him.

TEN

The next few weeks were like hell. Hundreds of humans were all milling around Marcus's home. His Priestess was locked away in her room. His wife was doing what she could to assist him, when all he wanted was to shut himself away with her in their bedroom and bolt the door. But it appeared Wynter had other ideas. She was talking to everyone. Every single person she could, like she was gathering some insight on the new members of his team. Creating a sort of knowledge base for herself, and then it was as if she was using that knowledge to exert control over the humans he had employed for his uses only. Wynter befriended them, and he often saw her congratulating them on a job well done.

She had to be playing at something.

Not once had she praised him for completing his work at last. Or for not taking just a few specially chosen managers to feed on like before but having added to his team by more than ten-times what he'd had previously. Never had she confided her feelings in him.

But with those strangers filling every spare room in their house? Oh, they got nothing but her openness and honesty. She counselled them relentlessly. Listened to their worries and settled their fears.

They loved her.

They fucking loved her.

His wife. His love. His one and only.

How dare they!

"You're letting your jealousy get the better of you again, Marcus. It is possible to share me, you know?" she chided him when he pressed the issue one night when they were finally alone. He'd outright demanded to know what she was up to, and instead she'd turned things around on him? Well, two could play that game.

"So, if I found myself a young, sexy, delicious new Blood Slave and doted on her like I did you, would you not feel jealous? Would you not seethe at the sight of her?" he tried, and didn't believe it when Wynter shook her head no. "You would snap her neck the moment you got her alone," he replied with a sneer, and noticed as his wife stood taller and regarded him with stoicism she was clearly forcing.

"I'd simply wish her well," she lied, and Marcus could see he was slowly getting under her skin.

She cared, it was obvious.

Was this the reason for her having insisted on his new supervisors staying at the mansion longer than the few days he'd initially planned? He had never been so well fed, and yet, it appeared there was a system to his feeding schedule. Only those she had vetted herself were sent to him. Only those she had met and gotten an insight of were allowed to be alone with her husband, and Marcus suddenly got it. Wynter was scared he might replace her.

She did love him and couldn't hide it. He was onto her, and so, Marcus being the same old deviant he'd always been, he decided to tease her some more. Even though he had secrets of his own and was being careful to keep things purely business, too. A simple transaction, rather than an intimate exchange. She didn't need to know how he was no longer taking his feeds directly from the vein, but from a blood bag hooked up to an IV. Yep, he was one of those. Like some kind of hipster drinking cold blood through a straw, he was acting just as any other monogamous male was more than willing to do. And it was all so that the love of his life didn't have to share him with those smitten by his bite. Not that she knew that, of course.

"Even if I kissed her? Or took the vein at the apex of her thighs while she writhed against me…"

Wynter was on him in a flash, and she pinned him down on the bed, her hands wrapped around his throat while she straddled him.

Marcus grinned and arched up against her. "You wouldn't care?"

"No," she hissed, and then tore away his clothes so she could sink down upon him, taking him inside her molten core. She could lie to herself all she wanted, but he knew the truth. The thought of him taking another woman the way he had taken her so very many times when she was human made her see red.

Was she jealous? Or was it simply that she couldn't bear to let him dare replace her? No matter her reasons, Wynter was his, and he was hers—and it appeared she was no longer against showing it.

***

She wasn't jealous. No fucking way. Not at all.

Nope.

She was just being clever. Making sure she figured them all out before sending them to her husband for dinner. Doing her due diligence, like any clever creature should.

After all, if he fell for someone new and turned them so that he could merge his soul with theirs, where would that leave her? With a witch's heart that beat solely for him, but a husband who no longer doted on her. That would be a hundred times worse than him loving her so intensely.

He had a funny way of showing it, but he still had his moments, and even though there might always be part of her that hated him, she couldn't help but hate the idea of his head ever being turned. Not that she felt like showing it right now.

She continued to choke him as she rode, thrusting harder and harder against him while being rough and taking her orgasms while enjoying the power it gave her to own him.

Wynter was screaming and bucking against him when she finally released her grip, and of course Marcus saw it as an invitation. He reached up and gripped her throat before wrenching her down for a kiss, and as their mouths tussled, she could feel the razor sharp tip of his tongue doing its dance. His instincts were to drink and kill, and even with her—a jinni whom he could draw no blood from—he was still trying.

And fuck, what a turn on that was. He still wanted to taste her. Could he close his eyes and remember the flavour of her blood with ease? Could he pick it out among all the others and readily leave all the rest?

"Do you still taste me on your lips, Marcus?" she groaned, "do you wish I was still your slave?"

"Some days," he whispered against her lips, "but I like the new you. The one I can properly enjoy." He then crushed her to him, and Wynter knew what he was getting at. The pair of them were far from perfect, but there were two things they knew how to do all too well.

"Fucking and fighting. Who knew we could find such common ground doing either," she replied, and then came again with a loud cry.

Marcus was close behind her, and when they were finally done, he peered into her eyes and shook his head.

"I love you, my sweet. I always will. We don't fuck, we make love. But yeah, we do still like a bit of a fight, don't we?" he teased, and he watched her with a smile as she dismounted him and then straightened and dressed herself with a mere blink of an eye.

"Whatever do you mean?" she joked, and then unlocked the door of his office and left before he could banter with her some more. She had work to do and needed to get on with it, and was all for getting down to business, when her darling husband threw yet another spanner in the works. It appeared he was ready for his next feed and had summoned someone in particular, rather than let Wynter continue sending him her chosen slaves.

Her old friend Phoebe was standing outside in the hallway. She was dressed in her usual relaxed gear, her hair a pastel shade of pink that suited her, and Wynter noticed right away how she had a new piercing in her nose. It looked nice, and while things felt a little awkward, when the two of them locked eyes, it was a relief when a wide smile spread across Phoebe's face.

"Hey, Wynter," she chimed, "I'd been hoping to get a chance to see you. Every time I've had a spare minute and came to find you, there's always been such a huge group hanging around I couldn't get a look in."

Wynter couldn't deny she was right. The new members of Marcus's merry team had needed far more guidance and nurturing than she'd imagined and being there to help them had filled her days and nights more than enough. So much so that she, too, had kept on thinking about catching up with Phoebe but failing miserably.

However, it wasn't like she was now here for a catch up.

Wynter looked over her shoulder to the open doorway behind where Marcus was dressed again and was stood watching them both expectantly.

"And it appears you're needed elsewhere too," she conceded before he even had to make a comment about her holding up his next meal. But this one was harder for her to accept. Marcus was going to bite Phoebe, and when he did, she would fall head over heels for him. She would try and touch him, or touch herself, and even though Wynter desperately wanted not to feel jealous because of it, she couldn't deny she was struggling.

And it wasn't like Phoebe would put her at ease afterwards. She had tried to counsel the others after their feeds too, but they'd told her nothing about their time with Marcus, and she knew he'd exerted his magical control over each of them to ensure it remained their secret. Regardless of them being friends, Phoebe would be no different.

Wynter simply stepped over to her and gave the poor girl a hug. "I'll catch up with you later. I'll make sure of it," she promised, and then walked away without looking back. She didn't need to see her vampire husband invite his chosen slave inside his office before closing the door behind her. Didn't want to imagine what was going to happen. Didn't need to remind herself how it felt to have his tongue lapping at her vein.

So why was that all she could bloody think about?

ELEVEN

Brodie couldn't remember ever being this happy. He was finally over his issues and had fallen in love. Given every part of himself to another after all this time. He'd let go of his grief and learned to let Archie in, and it felt amazing. Like he was free for the first time in over a thousand years.

And Archie truly was like a breath of fresh air. Brodie had learned a lot from Wynter and her outlook on life, but since being without her in his head he'd stopped and smelled the flowers, as it were, and had slowly come to terms with the new ways of the world in his own time.

His new boyfriend was the epitome of this generation's ethics. He was good and honest, but openly enjoyed his little quirks and showed them to all who cared to look without apology. Like his love of movies and lazing while binge watching TV shows, while on the flip side being a keen runner and climber, as well as being determined to get his pilot licence. Archie was modest about his toned body too, but when they were alone, Brodie could see he was growing more and more buff as the days went by. Plus, he was strong. Strong enough to playfully subdue even the all-powerful jinni when it came to their bedroom antics. Well, that was due to him allowing it, of course, but Archie certainly wasn't the delicate young man Brodie had imagined he'd be. Quite the contrary, he was a dominative and intense lover, and what once had scared him was now exciting and alluring.

They were mid-throes early one morning when a small tap on their bedroom door halted their antics. Rosalie had seemingly figured it was okay for her to intrude any time she liked, and while Brodie still found the practice rude, he was sure never to say so. She was still delicate, after all, and the two of them had promised to take care of her and the baby. If that meant not being selfish with their time together, then Brodie knew he would just have to accept it.

He transformed into his black smoke and then reappeared across the room, dressed and styled to perfection like always, and he saw something flash behind Archie's eyes. He was pissed off that the jinni had once again panicked and effectively run off, and he was proven right when Archie outright called him out on the instinct he had to hide whenever they were interrupted.

"Come in, Rosa," he called, and she appeared around the doorway a few seconds later. She crept inside and smiled at them both.

"Morning," she greeted.

"Hey, can I ask you something? Does it bother you that Brodie and I are together?" Archie replied, and she shook her head no.

"Of course not. Why would it?"

"Just proving a point," he answered, and offered Brodie a quick raise of his eyebrows before he then patted the bed so that she knew she was welcome to come and sit. "How are you feeling?"

"Good, and at least my sickness has passed now," she told him as she joined Archie on the bed, and Brodie stood and watched them. Like always, he wasn't sure what to say or do, and had a feeling it was just one of those things with him. He wondered if he would ever truly fit in with the humans he now lived with, and suddenly found himself missing Wynter. She was the only jinni he had ever sired, and he had failed her. She'd needed protecting and nurturing like any fledgling and they had only just scratched the surface thanks to him having been so preoccupied with avenging his past love rather than teach her. She had things she still needed to learn about herself and might never get to now that she was gone, and it was all thanks to him and his selfishness.

Well, he wasn't going to let the same thing happen again. Their circumstances were different, but Rosalie needed him. In just a few months, she would give birth to a baby. And not just any baby, but the child of a werewolf. Archie was just a young man, and he wouldn't know how to help should anything go wrong, and that was where Brodie was determined to step in. He could make the hard decisions. He could be strong when she might need it.

All he needed to do now was get over his damn awkward anxiety and learn to let the poor girl in.

Brodie started by taking a seat back down on his side of the bed beside Archie, who did a double take and grinned at him. He took Brodie's hand, and the jinni let him, and then he turned to Rosalie with a smile.

"You're glowing," he told her, and was rewarded with a coy grin. "But you are going to need to make a decision on where you want us to take you when the baby comes. And you'll be needing some supplies soon."

"Yeah, I've been doing a lot of thinking about that, too. I know I should really go and see a doctor, but I don't want to. I just want to stay here where it's safe," she replied resolutely, and Brodie could tell she had indeed been giving this a lot of thought. "I have no close family or anyone who would take us in if we went back to the mainland, plus I have no money. I wouldn't be able to survive on my own."

"I would help you," he told her, but Rosa shook her head again.

"Thank you, but I don't want that kind of help. I want us to stay together. All of us. We can be a family. If you'll have me…"

It was Archie who answered by dragging her into a tight bear hug, and while Brodie still felt awkward, he reached for her hand and smiled down at her.

"So, it's decided. We'll stay here," he replied when Archie finally let her go. They were both in tears, but at least they were the good kind. It'd been a long while since he'd seen happy tears and the hopeless romantic in him stirred. But then it was replaced by a voice of reason.

He needed to prepare. Rosa would require medical supplies and a sterile birthing area. She'd need medicine and baby clothes. And a contingency plan, should the worst happen.

There was no avoiding the outside world, but he wouldn't drag her to the mainland if he didn't have to. "I'll go across and get everything you need. Make a list and I'll buy everything," he then told her, and Rosalie nodded.

"Thank you so much. I'll get it done," she promised, and together the three of them then spent the entire day going over everything they would need, both for when the baby was here and for the rest of Rosalie's pregnancy.

There was so much to get, but Brodie knew he had more than enough money sat in his bank. His businesses were thriving, and he'd not needed to have any real input in them for years, which had been all well and good because he'd spent that time without being able to fully transform into his human guise, anyway. Good old email and the telephone. Business dealings were easier than ever now thanks to them, and so he'd expanded his portfolio more and more with each year that passed.

"I'll travel across the water in my misty form," he told Archie later that night as his beau prepared for bed, "and once I'm there, I'll buy a boat. We won't be able to transfer everything across via a new chopper plus there will be questions if I turn up out of the blue again and disappear with a second helicopter."

Archie nodded and then he offered Brodie a sheepish look, like there was something eating at him. The jinni stepped forward and gathered him up in his arms, where he held him for a moment. He'd done it to put Archie at ease, but then found himself settling a little too. He felt calmer and more determined to get everything in order. For Rosalie, and for her child. "What's wrong?" he asked when Archie, stayed silent.

"I was just wondering if I might be able to come with you?" he asked, but they both knew he couldn't leave Rosalie on the island with just Rafferty for invisible company.

"Why?" he asked rather than dismiss the idea too quickly.

"I was thinking I could hire a car and go visit my parents. Just to check in with them," he replied. "I know it's only been eight months, but I miss them. It'd be nice to go have just a quick catch up."

"It's a lovely idea," Brodie replied, but then he decided to be the voice of reason, rather than the bad guy. "But I think Rosalie will have to go with you. We can't leave her here."

"Rafferty can—"

"Rafferty can only do so much. His invisibility means he couldn't help her up if she fell or administer care should she need it. Only if she was unconscious," he cut in, and was pleased to see the realisation hit home. Archie nodded and shrugged, brushing the idea off seemingly without minding at all, but Brodie knew better. "Soon. I promise. I might even come with you…"

That seemed to ease his woes, and Archie grinned up at him.

"Don't think I won't be showing you off 'te everyone," he teased, his Scottish accent suddenly seeming more prevalent now that he was thinking of home. He was usually so well spoken it was easy to forget his Highland heritage, and Brodie found himself wondering what it might be like to go and meet his parents.

Right now, the idea filled him with nothing but dread, but he didn't show it. Instead, he simply grinned and then nodded.

"I'd best make sure I'm worthy of being shown off then," he said, making Archie laugh.

"A jinni boyfriend on my arm, that'll be more than noteworthy," he replied, and then creased up when Brodie took him seriously. "Just kidding, of course I'd never tell them!"

"No one would believe it if you tried," he joked in return, and Archie admitted he was right. Humans truly did think the tales of the paranormal were nothing more than a myth, when in reality, the creatures were indeed living among them. They were their friends and neighbours. Their colleagues and bosses. They outnumbered humans by a mile, and while Brodie had never agreed with the vampires' belief that they should be overthrown as rulers atop this planet they had ended up sharing, he couldn't deny thinking it would be nicer not to have to hide. Not to have to lurk in the shadows.

Which reminded him. "I'd best get going. Can't be having a black shadow cross the sea in the daytime now, can we?"

And then he went. He didn't make a song and dance of saying goodbye. They knew where he was heading and what for, and Brodie was just glad there was no risk in him returning to the mainland. Not now that Marcus had won his war and taken off with his spoils.

Theirs was a fight for another day. Perhaps even another century. Right now, he had to focus on his friends. His family.

Uncle Brodie. Yeah, he could handle that.

After Rosalie having checked and double checked he had all her lists, Brodie had to laugh to himself as he spirited across the small cluster of islands and over the land beyond. She was ever so particular and wanted only the best for her child. It was something he would gladly give her—give them both—and when he reached the closest big city; he took form in a quiet spot right beside the biggest department store he could find. This place had it all, from furniture to fancy wear, and he was sure he could tick off most, if not all, of the items Rosalie had requested. Yes, they might cost him more to buy there rather than shop around, but he wanted to be quick, and he was more than able to pay whatever the final price may be.

Brodie simply had to wait for the damn thing to open, but while he did, he slid inside as mist and then walked around the entire place twice in his invisible form. That passed the time nicely, as well as helped him find everything he needed, and once the huge store was open, he found an inconspicuous place to reappear and then started his mammoth task of gathering up everything he wanted. It took well over an hour, as well as three helpers from the store staffing team, but he left with almost everything on Rosalie's list and a few thousand pounds poorer—not that he cared. Brodie felt great being able to do this for her, and was glad he could show he cared, but as he was walking out of the department store, another idea struck him. She wasn't the only one he cared for, not by a long shot. Archie needed things, too. He was getting by on the few outfit choices he had available to him, and so Brodie decided his wardrobe would also be given a much-needed revamp.

It took the better part of the day, but soon he and his chosen helpers were loading up his newly hired van and Brodie checked off his list one last time. He had everything Rosalie had wanted, and then some. They would be unpacking and unboxing for hours upon his return, and for the first time, the old jinni stopped and took a deep inhale of the city air. He realised he felt good. Felt happy. It made a damn nice change.

But it didn't last long.

His mind immediately went from those he wasn't failing to the one person he had indeed let down. Wynter still needed him. He hadn't fought hard enough for her. Hadn't chased after her in the aftermath of their battle with the vampire fiend. Brodie vowed to himself he would avenge her. Wynter was a prisoner not of war, but of love. Marcus had waged his war because of his adoration for her, and he had won. She was his to command now and while Brodie doubted she would be in chains; she was still a captive.

He was going to find her. To help Wynter learn and make sure she understood that their kind were not slaves to any other, no matter how foreboding their warnings were or manipulative they could be. She was stronger than Marcus, and the vampire knew it, but he was more cunning and had beaten her down.

But she wouldn't stay down long.

And Brodie couldn't wait to see the day when she rose up and took everything from him, just like he had with her.

TWELVE

"So, tell me more about these new powers of yours," Phoebe asked when Wynter had finally got the chance to sit down and have some one-to-one time with her old friend, and she couldn't blame her for being interested in the unusual and unknown. It was a crazy thing indeed, this transformation she had made, and at times Wynter still had to remind herself that she was no longer human.

But like with Wentworth, she wasn't a performing monkey about to give Phoebe a show.

"You've seen enough to know I truly have changed, but haven't we all?" Wynter answered, and her friend nodded in answer. "Like you, Phoebe. You're here. You survived when so many others died, thanks to Marcus's insatiable thirst. How?"

"I honestly don't know," she answered, and then turned pale as her mind went elsewhere, undoubtedly back to whatever awful night it was that Marcus had laid waste to so many other lives. "He was tearing through everyone at the club. Not a soul was spared, but then he reached me, and it wasn't like he consciously chose not to feed, but as if he wasn't seeing me at all. He just looked right through me and carried onto the next poor soul."

"Like some kind of magical force had stopped him?" Wynter mused aloud.

"Maybe. But it was so terrifying I couldn't think straight. I could see then what Warren had been talking about all those times when he'd hated on the vampires who paid to feed on us. For me, I'd just kinda always gone along with the feeding because I knew it was required of me. I never even contemplated fighting back, and don't think I would have if Mr Cole had torn open my vein and drank me dry."

"You were under his spell, just like all the others who let him murder them," Wynter replied, and then dropped her voice. "You still are. He has that kind of power over every single one of you."

"I know, but that doesn't mean I cannot see the truth. I know it's wrong and that I shouldn't let him, but I just overlook it. My senses are altered by a more pressing desire."

"One that's telling you to serve him and do everything he says?"

"Right…" Phoebe confirmed.

Wynter leaned closer, peering into her friend's eyes. She had to know what was going on behind the closed doors of Marcus's office. No matter how many times she tried to convince herself it wasn't a big deal, it still was, and it was killing her seeing the humans come and go. Tearing her apart to know she could not satisfy him the way each of them were. Those days of her being his Blood Slave might be over, but there was something about it Wynter found she missed. Perhaps the closeness of the moments they'd shared, or the heat of knowing Marcus wanted her so much. Either way, it was a bittersweet victory to no longer have to let him feed on her blood.

"But he fed from you yesterday, didn't he?" she asked, and Phoebe frowned. Her brow furrowed, and she tried to answer, but couldn't. Not even a simple *yes* seemed to be able to leave her lips. "Show me your marks," she tried, and again her friend couldn't seem to respond.

"Stop, please," she eventually hissed, and Wynter could tell Marcus's hex truly was hard at work. He had made sure those who had fed him were sworn to secrecy regarding their time with their formidable leader, and she was desperate to know why.

"My love," a deep, throaty voice broke the intense silence that'd descended between Wynter and Phoebe, and they both turned to look at the redhead who had just arrived out of nowhere to join them.

"Marcella? I didn't realise you were here," Phoebe replied, and the witch shook her head but still offered her a small smile.

"She's not the woman you thought you knew, Phoebe. Marcella is Marcus's Priestess. She's his most loyal servant and the powerful witch behind everyone's curse," Wynter answered for her, and saw as her friend gulped hard and stared up at Marcella, as though looking for some sign that she was indeed so far from the façade she'd hidden behind back at *Slave*.

"Whoa, well, it's nice to see you anyway," Phoebe eventually answered.

"Did you have something to do with her surviving the cull?" Wynter interjected, and Marcella nodded.

"I saved her because I owed you both a life," she told them, and at first Wynter didn't know what she meant, but then it dawned on her. David. He was Phoebe's cousin, and she had murdered him.

She shook her head, trying to signal for Marcella not to say anything further, but it appeared the Priestess didn't care about saving her companion the hurt that would undoubtedly be caused by her revealing the truth. She evidently didn't need to worry herself with the dealings of the humans in Marcus's employ any longer, so had decided it was time the truth was out.

"Why?" Phoebe asked, clearly having figured out there was something going on, and once again, it was left to Wynter to explain on her behalf.

"Because of David. He didn't fall down those stairs. He was killed because he tried to attack me," she told her, and looked up at Marcella with a scowl.

"There was more to it. That day he attacked you, it was my doing. I sent him to you, thinking you'd welcome his advances, and then he took things too far. I took his life because the bruises he'd left on your body were my fault, and because if I hadn't intervened, he would've raped you."

Phoebe broke down in tears at hearing the news. She'd clearly mourned her cousin and had thought the best of him, and now she was being told a story quite to the contrary.

"Who are you people?" she finally spat and stood with haste before storming away. Wynter didn't even try to answer her or appease her poor friend. She simply looked up at Marcella and sneered.

"I don't think I know anymore, do you?" she seethed, and then stormed away as well, but Marcella wouldn't leave her alone. She followed Wynter out of the room and towards her newly appointed private office, keeping two steps behind her the entire way.

There, Wynter threw herself inside and felt glad she'd taken the tiny office towards the back of the mansion and made it her own. She'd warded it against any intruders and was glad she had. It was her small piece of solitude in an otherwise bustling house, and with her mind racing, thought nothing of slamming the door in the Priestess's face once she was inside.

"We need to talk, Wynter. Let me in," Marcella called from the other side, and she answered her with an expletive. It felt good telling the insensitive witch where to go, but that feeling didn't last long. A cold chill swept down her spine and she pulled her hand away from the door, feeling like it'd just burned her.

And then pain wracked through her chest like she'd just been stabbed through the heart. Wynter crumbled in a heap on the floor, clutching at her gut, just as the door burst open and flew right off its hinges.

Marcella was standing at the threshold with a sly smile curling at her lips. "Don't make me ask twice. I hate seeing you in pain, my love, but I am not against punishing you for your insolence," she demanded, and then stepped inside. She then offered Wynter a hand to help her up.

The pain subsided in an instant when she took it, and with her touch, the jinni's mind was filled with visions from their past. Of the numerous moments they had shared together both good and awful, and she saw red.

Wynter wasn't going to take that lying down, and so she wrapped her free hand up around Marcella's throat and pushed her backwards until the pair of them collided with the wall.

"I'm not your daughter, so don't think you can tell me what to do!" she bellowed, but it didn't matter what she said, because her hand was slowly unwrapping itself against her orders. Wynter had backed off before she was remotely ready, and she knew exactly why.

"What were you saying?" Marcella sneered, and Wynter decided to wipe that smug look off her face. She didn't understand these visions she'd been having, but there was one thing she had seen incredibly clearly indeed. A snippet of the future. This gift had to be of Mara's doing, and it was evident the witch's power inside of her was growing stronger if she was able to see not only what had been but also what was yet to come.

"You know you're having twins, right?" she replied, and the news had the desired effect. Marcella's smile faded in a second and she shook her head. "I wonder which one Marcus will let you keep..." she added spitefully.

"That's impossible," Marcella insisted, but Wynter didn't back down.

"I saw it. Two baby girls..." and she was telling the truth. Like a snapshot, she'd seen her. There had been two babes in Marcella's arms, each suckling at her breast.

Her shock soon turned to anger, and Marcella lashed out. She slapped Wynter across the face with the force of twenty men, but she barely flinched, and so the Priestess went for her again and again.

When she'd finally had enough, Marcella stormed away. As she did, she lifted her hand and snapped her fingers, and the door that'd laid there in pieces on the ground shot back up. It was repaired and on its hinges again a split-second later.

It was only when the door slammed shut and Wynter heard the distinct click of the lock that she reacted. She lunged for it and screamed with anger when she found her only exit magically welded closed.

Marcella knew she hated being confined. That it downright terrified her to have locked doors sealing her in, just like when Marcus had shut her away at the club. Wynter bellowed curses through the immovable blockade, but her anger soon turned to fear, and she crumbled into a heap when she heard nothing from the other side. No one was there. No one was coming to rescue her.

***

Marcus watched the fight via the house's many hidden cameras and couldn't deny being engrossed by the little show his two favourite women had put on for him. He'd never seen Marcella lash out like that before, not when she had only to click her fingers and render any foe powerless. With an entire magical arsenal in her back pocket to readily use on any whom she'd faced in the past, his priestess was a formidable adversary. But with Wynter, she'd been careful. And he knew why. Yes, her daughter's life had given his bride an unending source of strength, and she hadn't wanted to jeopardise things, but there was more than that.

His most loyal subject knew Marcus would make her pay for daring to hurt his wife. They had burned too many bridges to get her back, and despite his once dark urges, he himself hadn't laid a finger on Wynter since she'd returned to him. Mind games aside, he'd done nothing but love her, and so knew that this time he would not stand for anyone daring to do otherwise.

The Priestess came directly to his office without needing to be called, where she paced up and down in front of his desk, visibly shaking with rage. She knew she'd done wrong, and it was clear she thought he'd show mercy because of her honesty.

"My lady," he ground.

"My lord... please forgive me..."

"What possessed you to think I would forgive you for hurting and imprisoning my wife?"

"She lacks discipline," she tried, but Marcus was having none of it. He stood and stormed towards her, closing the gap effortlessly. Once there, he wrapped Marcella in his arms, like a father might do his daughter. But the pair of them were far from it. She bristled and he could sense her panic begin to rise. And rightly so.

"As do you," he whispered, his mouth pressed right against her ear. "You must be punished for your insolence, child."

"Do what you must, but please don't harm the baby," she pleaded, and Marcus leaned back to stare down into her soft face resolutely.

"I would never, ever harm her," he demanded, "which is why your husband will suffer the punishment in your stead. You must learn your place, my lady."

As if on cue, Jack arrived at the doorway to Marcus's office, where he stood awkwardly in wait for his master's orders. The vampire had summoned him without needing to say a word, and as Jack looked inside expectantly, Marcus could tell he already sensed that things were not right.

"Mr Cole?" Jack croaked, looking paler by the second.

Marcus didn't even reply. He sent silent word to his alpha soldier, who followed his order to drag the man outside and string him up beneath the branches of the sturdiest tree. This happened to be the old oak Wynter had found her solace in, but from now on, it was going to serve another purpose. Any and all who defied his orders or did something worthy of punishment were going to suffer the same fate as Jack, and it was going to be a public shame they would not easily live down.

The alpha knew exactly what Marcus wanted. A just and torturous punishment for his Priestess's emissary. Pain he would feel rattling through his bones long after it was over with, and a torture she would feel even though she was not the one enduring it.

Marcus dragged Marcella outside after them, and soon a small crowd also began to form. With the skill of a true sadist, they all watched as the alpha bound Jack's arms behind him and then fashioned a simple pulley, which he used to lift the human up off the ground from behind.

He screamed and writhed but was soon rendered speechless with fear when the bones began to twist behind him. Jack knew this would not end until Marcus was ready. And he knew by his master's devious smile that something terrible was yet to come.

Marcus made Marcella watch along with the other supervisors as Jack's shoulders popped out in turn with a tremendous crack. Each dislocated from their sockets thanks to the weight of him dragging his body down towards the ground, while the ropes kept his arms at his back so meant he could not escape the torture for even a second. It was an oldie, but a goodie—Strappado. One of his favourites from the dark days, and Marcus revelled in the heady air as those he'd summoned outside watched on in both fascination and horror.

Jack cried in agony just once more before he then passed out from the pain, and as tense silence descended, Marcus luxuriated in the fear and apprehension he could sense from those around him. The Supervisors each felt terrible for Jack but were also glad it wasn't them up there. His lesson was a warning to them all, and one which was readily heeded.

He loved it. This sense of power and magnificence. It was high time he got back to his old ways. No more Mr Nice Guy.

"Your husband will hang here for twenty-four hours. Do not attempt to help or free him. Offend me again and it'll be a week, understood?" he growled in his Priestess's ear.

"Yes, my lord," she whimpered back, tears rolling down her pale face as she stared up at the man she loved in dismay.

THIRTEEN

Wynter was still pacing her small office when the door swung open and Marcus strode inside with a satisfied smile on his face. At first, she thought he'd enjoyed having allowed her a small period of imprisonment, but soon realised there was a wholly different reason for his delight.

"Marcella has paid for her insubordination," he informed her, coming closer with great haste. Wynter backed up, trying to keep a clear head, but was soon overshadowed by his immense frame and suddenly felt tiny against him. Was he growing, or was it that she had transfigured smaller than before? She was sure she'd been taller when human, but now was slim and petite, her eyes barely reaching his chest. When had this become a thing? She wondered, but at the same time, Wynter liked it. And so did he. Marcus lifted her into his arms with ease and pinned her to the wall behind, his mouth trailing kisses up her neck and to her face. She melted against him, like always, and felt her heart begin to race. Damn, this witch adored him. Not her, or so she was still telling herself. Never.

"My lord, please put a stop to this…" a timid voice chimed from the doorway, and with a growl, Marcus let Wynter back down onto her feet and then stepped away.

"You slighted me, Marcella. That means he slighted me too. His punishment will not end, and you will not make any steps to help. Is that understood?" he demanded, and for the first time Wynter saw the Priestess properly cower before her master. She felt terrible for her, and for Jack, but knew she could not intervene. Marcus would never allow it, and so all they could do was ride out whatever punishment he had decided was fit. "He will endure, as will you. He will learn, as will you."

Marcella was nodding her head profusely, tears streaming down her soft face, and she too looked tiny against him. Small and slim, just like Wynter had become. And just like her daughter would've undoubtedly been as well.

It was strange, as if the witch was affecting her decision making in smaller, seemingly insignificant ways. Wynter didn't like it. Mara's heart was strong, perhaps strong enough to do more than give her power and strength and losing herself to the whims of a child was not where she wanted this immortal future to take her. She knew she had to be tougher, more resilient to those desires raging within her.

Marcus dismissed his priestess and then turned back to his wife, and Wynter couldn't help but smile over at him as a rush of gratification swept over her.

"You avenged my honour," she guessed, and Marcus shrugged coyly.

"No one raises a hand to you, my sweet. Not even her," he answered.

It was the nicest thing he had ever done for her, and there was no way she was going to let such a milestone pass them by without celebration.

It was her turn to thrust him against the wall and kiss every inch of him she could reach, and without a care in the world, she was soon tearing his clothes away, desperate to have her way with him.

***

Archie stood staring into his open closet with a frown. It was full at last. After all these months of him pretty much living in the same few pairs of trackies, it was now filled to the brim with a heap of new items. And all thanks to his quiet and brooding, yet also insanely generous, benefactor.

He'd unpacked the last of Rosa's baby bits with her a few days before, only to then find another set of bags at the back of the pile. Ones that weren't for their newest outcast or her baby but were instead for him. There was a completely new wardrobe in there. Everything he needed and more, and the extras. A watch that'd easily cost a thousand pounds, for starters. Brodie had gone all out to give Archie some incredible gifts, and if he were honest, he wasn't sure what to do about it. Part of him wanted to tell the jinni no. To tell him he had to send them back because he didn't need them. But the look on his face as Archie had opened them had said it all, and he knew he couldn't refuse his generosity.

Brodie said very little when it came to opening up. He'd given Archie snippets here and there about his past and the darkness that had driven him all these years, but not all that much. He and Rosa hardly talked at all, and yet he had gone above and beyond to provide her with the very best he could get her. Brodie had shown he cared, even if he couldn't say it.

And it felt to him like the same went for these gifts he'd picked up for Archie while he'd been at it. The clothes were sporting labels he'd never been able to afford before, and Brodie hadn't bought them to show off. There was no one on the island to show off to. No, Archie felt as if it was far more than him splashing the cash and buying his new boyfriend something pretty. It was his way of saying he cared. That he felt something he didn't know how to express with words.

He turned at the sound of his bedroom door opening and found Brodie standing in the doorway, watching him with a barely hidden look of worry.

"I love you, too," Archie told him with a smile.

Brodie let out a sigh and started to laugh.

"That obvious, huh?" he asked, and came closer. When he reached him, he gathered Archie up into his arms and looked down into his face with a strange look of wonder on his own.

"You look like you're seeing me for the first time?" he whispered and placed his palm against Brodie's black-skinned cheek.

"I think I am. Those words change everything, Archie. It's like you're saving my life with every moment you accept me into yours. I'd do anything for you. Anything," he demanded.

"Then say it," Archie whimpered, feeling incredibly naked all of a sudden.

"I love you…"

"Good, because there's no going back now. You know that, right?"

"I don't want to, and to prove it, I'm taking you on a date," Brodie answered, his smile returning. "A real date. On the mainland. Rosalie's fine and Rafferty can call me if he needs us to come back."

It was Archie's turn to laugh, but he didn't say no. He'd wanted this for a while now and was beyond ready to go and enjoy whatever the closest town or city had to offer them.

"But I don't have a stitch to wear," he teased, thinking one of the new shirts Brodie had bought would be ideal, but it appeared he'd planned everything. Even his ensemble for the evening.

Brodie pointed down at a box that Archie knew without a doubt had not been in his room before, and once the pair of them finally let one another go, he went to it with a coy smile. Maybe he was getting better at accepting gifts after all.

Inside the perfectly shaped and ridiculously heavy box sat a stunningly tailored tweed jacket and matching waistcoat. Archie had described such an outfit to Rafferty once as they'd sat watching one of their boxsets. He'd remarked on the main character's style and how he'd liked many of his outfits, such as a jacket and waistcoat combo exactly like the set he was now staring down at. "You remembered?" he remarked, thinking how Brodie hadn't even appeared to be listening at the time.

"I remember everything, foolish human," he teased, but Archie didn't take his banter to heart.

"I love them," he replied, and made quick work of trying the outfit on with a white shirt from his closet. The greys and blacks in the tweed matched his skin tone perfectly, and he knew he too would've chosen those colours over the typical browns. And then, of course, the pair were the perfect fit. "How did you get the measurements right?"

Brodie answered him with a coy shrug at first, but then spilled the beans when Archie pressed him.

"I transformed into your exact height and shape," he replied. "I know it's probably weird me changing, but I needed it to be perfect. And so, I walked into the tailors as close to your size as could be so that he could fit me with something which would fit like a glove. Are you pleased?"

"I truly am," Archie answered, and then he checked his watch. It was already getting late, and he wanted to have as much time as possible on their date, so wanted to get going sooner than later. "Give me fifteen minutes and I'll be good to go, okay?"

"Okay," Brodie replied, and then left him to get ready.

He met him by the front door in less than ten minutes and found Brodie dressed in nothing less than perfection. Archie had always envied his ability to dress himself magically, but tonight was different. Gone was his own sportswear and in its place was Brodie's equal. A well-dressed young man ready to wine and dine.

Archie's smiled faltered when Brodie led him out into the hall and turned right. He didn't know why he'd expected to turn left and out the cave as always, when the boat he'd bought to bring everything back from the mainland was clearly going to be moored down below. There was a dock Brodie had told him had been built hundreds of years previously by pirates who had used the island to hoard their wares. So, of course, the only way down to it was through the tunnels beneath them.

But he hadn't been down there since what'd happened. Since the sounds of scurrying bodies had come up through those same tunnels. From the time when their fortress had been invaded by thousands of hideous vampire soldiers. And since his friend had lost his life to their master.

"Brodie," he gulped, looking down into the darkness below.

He seemed confused at first, but then a look of realisation crossed his face and the jinni frowned.

"This is the only way down," he told Archie, "but if you can't do it, we'll try another time. We can have a picnic under the stars instead?" he offered, and while he appreciated the gesture, Archie shook his head no.

"I need to do this but might need a stiff drink once it's over with," he joked, trying to make light of the situation.

"You'll get one, and maybe we'll raise a glass to Jakob while we're at it," Brodie answered, and his sentiment brought a tear to Archie's eye. They'd had some serious ups and downs, but in the end, Brodie hadn't wanted the vampire assassin to die, he could tell.

Without another word, he then led the way, and the pair of them began the slow and steady descent to the dock with just a battery-powered lantern to light the way.

When they reached the small opening where the cells lay, Archie swallowed the lump that leapt up into his throat at the sight of the door hanging open, the key still in the lock from when Brodie had released Jakob to let him run from the horde with them. On the floor were the shattered remains of the coffee mug Archie had dropped, and he bent down to pick up a shard before tossing it away.

"Did he fight till the end?" he asked his companion, and Brodie nodded.

"He honoured his soul mate and refused to let go, even when death had him in her grasp."

"And what happened to his body?"

"Rafferty burned the pieces and then buried the ashes beneath the trunk of the oldest tree on this island," the jinni answered, and then hissed when he realised what awful detail he'd accidentally just given away. Jakob had left this world in pieces? Archie could think of nothing worse than being torn apart like that. It must've been awful. "He was given a warrior's farewell, Archie. The highest accolade for any immortal creature," Brodie assured him, but he wasn't sure whether it comforted him or not.

"And Wynter? How did she not die along with him?" he asked and realised then how he hadn't been told all that much about what'd actually gone down that day. In fact, he hadn't asked because he hadn't wanted to know. But now he needed to. He owed it to his friend, and to Wynter. She was his friend too, after all.

"The Priestess's magic was too strong for even the merging of two souls to overcome, and in the end, she gave Wynter something far more precious. She encased her within an impenetrable magic circle and gave her a heart— a witch's heart—and in doing so, saw to it she could never die. Not even when her soul mate passed over," he revealed, and Archie scowled.

"We're gonna get him, right?" he replied resolutely as he stood and went back to Brodie's side. "Promise me Marcus is gonna pay for what he did?"

"He will," Brodie replied with a frown, and then he took Archie's hands in his and stared down into his eyes. "But you cannot live your life fuelled by hate or driven by vengeance. Trust me…"

He knew exactly what the jinni was getting at. Brodie had lived that way for a thousand years and had wasted all that time, when he ought to have grieved the loss of his wife and found a way to move on without her. Archie would waste his life too if he refused to let go of the past, and he nodded in understanding.

"I won't, I promise."

They were down through the tunnels and to the dock a few minutes later, and the moment he saw the little boat that was their new link to the outside world, Archie felt better. They were going to the mainland. Going to enjoy a night out, just the two of them. A date. A real fucking date.

He didn't stop smiling the entire journey across.

When they reached the small marina on the other side, Brodie took care of everything, and Archie watched him move in awe. He did the work of ten men to get them properly moored up, and when he was done, he reached for Archie's hand and then actually kept hold rather than shy away from the public display of affection. He even held on as the pair of them walked up towards the bright lights of the town ahead, and Archie adored watching Brodie come further out the closet with every step they took.

"Damn, a guy could easily get used to this," he told the jinni, who beamed back at him. "So, where are we heading?"

"The pub, of course," Brodie answered, and Archie laughed. He'd remembered yet another passing comment he'd made about missing the nights spent down the local having a few beers and some 'pub-grub' for dinner.

"And what will you do while I devour the greasiest meal I can find?"

"Join you, of course," he answered, and Archie went to ask about the dynamics of that, but as they walked up over a ridge, found they'd arrived at their destination and figured he'd see for himself.

It was strange watching Brodie eat, but at the same time, Archie was glad he wasn't ending up eating alone. He thought it'd look very odd if the two of them had come for dinner and yet only one of them ate, but he noticed how the food didn't seem to taste of anything for the jinni. Archie groaned appreciatively at least ten times over the course of his meal, while Brodie simply seemed to be going through the motions.

But at least they were together. The conversation flowed with ease and the evening whizzed away as the two of them stared across the table into one another's eyes and really talked. Not about Rosa or the hardships ahead, but of their hopes and dreams, and their future they planned to spend together.

It was exactly what Archie had hoped for.

The date was over far too quickly, but as they meandered back to the marina, he was beaming. The handful of whisky's helped with that as well, but he didn't mind being a little tipsy. It was fun finally being able to just sit back and enjoy his new life a little. To discard the weight they were constantly carrying and allow themselves to do what new couples did.

"Well, ain't you just a tall glass of milk and honey," a small woman called to them as they reached the dock, and Archie laughed at first, but turned to Brodie with a confused frown when she hopped onto their boat.

"Who's this?" he whispered to him.

"She's a friend," Brodie told him, and the anxiety that'd just speared in Archie's gut immediately subsided. He hadn't realised just how tense their lives had gotten this past year, but he had gone straight to worrying, rather than to greet the woman like he knew he ought to.

"Don't worry, sugar, I ain't gonna hurt 'ya," she added in her southern American drawl as she eyed Archie up and down, "hey jinni, you didn't say he was such a cutie…"

"Ach, I know sweetheart. It's been a long time since a girl tried it on with me, but I'll tell you the same as I told all of them," Archie replied with a cheeky smile the woman seemed to lap up, and he found himself having fun with their little tête-à-tête. He then dropped his voice and spoke with a deep, Scottish twang. "I would ruin you…"

The woman burst out laughing and offered Archie a wink.

"Promises, promises," she teased, and then went over to Brodie and grinned up at him. "Nice to see you in the flesh. Been a long time."

"It sure has, Miss Vicki. Thank you for coming," he answered with a kind smile, "now, if you'll stop flirting with my boyfriend, maybe we can have a little chat in private?"

"You got it bad, boy. I like it," the woman, Miss Vicki, answered.

"Me too."

Archie watched their gentle back and forth with a smile. They were clearly old friends, and it was nice to meet someone from Brodie's past with whom he seemed to have a good history. He climbed onto the boat with them and carefully stashed the only two things he had insisted on buying while they had the chance—two bottles of perfectly aged Scotch whisky.

When he returned to the small seating area under the deck, he found the other two staring at him, all jokes seemingly forgotten.

"You ready, sugar?" she asked and beckoned him closer.

Archie sat down but looked at Brodie with a frown.

"For what?" he asked them both.

"For the sight, of course…" she answered, but he still had no idea what she was on about, and Brodie seemed to pick up on it.

"Miss Vicki is a voodoo priestess, Archie. She and I go way back, and she agreed to come and meet us so that she could give you the gift of sight. Remember how I told you before about Rafferty?" the jinni added, and now that he mentioned it, Archie did remember. The gift of sight from a witch would let him see the invisible goblin, and Archie knew it would make life far simpler if he could. Nicer to be able to converse with him properly and, if he wanted, high five the guy too.

He nodded and let Miss Vicki take his hand, but when she drew a dagger from her handbag, he had to look away. Archie knew he might not be as squeamish as he'd once been, but he still didn't want to see whatever it was she was planning to do with that knife and was glad he'd done so when she started slicing into his palm. Archie felt her draw a large circle and then lines within a pentagram, or so he guessed. He then wretched at the thought and forced himself to focus on the end result, not the method of getting to it.

Next, his strange companion began to growl and hiss, making guttural sounds as some kind of spell left her lips, and Archie finally cracked an eye open so he could see. Her eyes were closed, and she was holding his bloody hand in hers, channelling her power into him. Before long, he could feel himself growing hotter and hotter, and then suddenly, a rush of icy wind spread through him, and he was flung back in his seat.

Archie then opened his eyes wide and felt the icy heat seem to work its way up and settle inside them, like a shroud, and as the wave subsided, he slumped back and blacked out.

FOURTEEN

Archie barely remembered getting back to the house, but knew he'd needed Brodie's help. His date had carried him most of the way through the dark tunnels, and had then given him an arm inside, but he was slowly starting to feel better. Had the whisky really hit him that hard? He didn't feel drunk.

He went to the kitchen to pour himself a glass of water, and soon realised he wasn't more than tipsy. Maybe he'd just fallen asleep and was feeling out of sorts. That had to be it.

He finished the water and then decided it was time for something stronger. A glass of his new whisky would do nicely, and Archie grabbed a small tumbler from the cupboard.

"Hey Rafferty, we got any ice?" he shouted, his head in the freezer, and then he jumped back when an arm reached down and pulled open the bottom drawer to reveal a bag of the stuff. Archie stared at the pale limb and then followed it back up to a broad set of shoulders, followed by a squared jaw and eventually a blonde tuft of hair. "Holy shit!" he cried, it all coming back to him. "Raff?"

"In the flesh," Rafferty replied, grinning down at him.

Archie straightened up and took him in.

"Jeez, you're much better looking than I would've thought. Makes me feel a bit rotten for all the times I've walked round this house looking like trash," he joked. "And you're fucking tall. Aren't goblins meant to be little?"

"And aren't humans meant to be humble in the face of the supernatural?" Rafferty joked back.

"I've seen far too much shit this year to be humble, mate," he answered, and grabbed the offered ice and plopped it into his glass. "It's nice to finally see you, though," Archie added, and he poured a couple of shots worth of whisky over the ice before giving it a swirl.

"Nice to be seen," Rafferty answered with a smile, and Archie nodded. He figured it must be hard being invisible and raised his glass to him.

"Still think we need to ugly you up a bit. Don't let Rosa see you like this, she'll fall head over heels," he teased, making the goblin laugh.

"I think I liked it better when you couldn't see me," he joked in response, and Archie pouted up at him but was soon laughing off Rafferty's banter.

It was good to have a laugh, and in that moment, he felt right at home again. It was their corner of the world, just two humans and a pair of creatures he would've never even believed in a year before. Their life together was damn good. Maybe not be everyone's cup of tea, but it was fine by him.

***

Wynter was restless. There was nothing for her to do and no one to keep her busy. Marcus was working hard to train up his new supervisors and as the days passed, it felt like they were going slower and slower. As if her life was spent doing nothing more than standing still.

It was time she did more than just walk around chatting nonsense to the humans in her husband's keep. She was no psychologist and knew she wasn't helping them, not really. All she was doing was facilitating in them coming to terms with the inevitable. They were owned. Part of a team with a master who would never put their needs first, and then there was the feeding element of the role. All of them were stock. Cattle. A sure supply of the good stuff.

And she wasn't going to keep on shepherding them for Marcus.

She went to his office, where she not only found the door closed but also guarded. The alpha was blocking the entrance with his arms folded over his immense chest, and with a look she knew would ensure nobody dared try and get past him. Wynter didn't falter, though. She walked right up to him and sneered.

"Demoted back to doorman, I see," she teased, but the grey-skinned soldier didn't respond. She was about to throw another insult his way when he stepped aside and allowed her to pass, and Wynter couldn't hide her shock as she went around the behemoth and then turned the knob.

She'd guessed Marcus had to be done with his feed or else he wouldn't ever have allowed her in. She knew that much now at least but was surprised to find him still hunched over the young man he must've invited to his office to tend to his needs. At first, she figured he had to be drinking from the guy's wrist, but then she saw the plastic tube in her husband's mouth and did a double take.

He wasn't taking the vein. Wasn't forcing the Blood Slave at his mercy to succumb to the desires associated with his bite. Not imposing the effects upon him, and she had to wonder. Had it been the same for all the others? Strangely, she hoped so. Him sharing that experience with the other supervisors hadn't been something that'd come easily for her, and Wynter found herself feeling reassured at once. And sure enough, as she examined them further, there was a cannula in the young man's arm. Marcus was drinking from the tube like a straw, but there was more. He was also letting some of the blood trickle into a bag by their feet.

When he was finished, her husband offered her a bloody smile and then tossed her the still warm bag.

"Feed your hordes," he told her, and then pressed a button beneath his desk, which opened up some kind of hidden storage unit behind his drawers. It was refrigerated, and inside Wynter saw there were more than a dozen of the same red bags. "Take one per pit. They'll share and have just a few drops each. Keep them wanting, thirsty, and ready to serve you."

She simply nodded to him, thinking there was so much she could say, and yet wasn't ready to. Wynter felt like thanking Marcus for having respected her enough to not drink from the veins his slaves would so readily offer him but refused to give him the satisfaction. It was a quiet victory she would gladly not bring to light, because really, the idea made her feel incredible. There was no sharing him. No having to endure the connections he was cultivating with others like she had once been. The feed was merely a transaction now, and she adored it.

With her arms full, Wynter then crept away and back out into the hallway, where the alpha fell in step beside her and then escorted his so-called queen through the gardens to where the pits lay beneath the ground.

When she reached the first one, Wynter had the alpha lift the heavy manhole, and she spirited inside, and was met with the throb of a crowd rapidly forming around her. The soldiers were thirsty, but it appeared they were also desperate to see and touch her. To have Wynter reach for their hands like before, and so she did. She could read them all and sensed their desire like those needs were part of her own agenda somehow, and when she passed the closest vampire, the blood bag and placed the tube between his blue lips, even she felt hungry.

She then watched as he took a sip and passed it along, and the next vampire did the same before giving it to the next soldier in line. Not a single one of them had more than their fair share, and by the time they'd all been given a sip, Wynter was in awe. They were so dedicated it was astounding, and as she stood there feeling all sorts of things, she realised they were responding to her without her having to say a single word. The connection was there, no matter what, and a sense of pride swept through the throng like a wave of strength that then resonated through her army.

Damn, they truly were the ultimate fighting team, and she finally saw just why they were needed in this dark world. Should she give the word, humanity would fall. It was a power she hadn't asked for, but one she readily accepted because the alternative was the unthinkable. Marcus would've been the only other choice and with him at the helm, this same force would be unstoppable—making him unstoppable in return. He was bad enough as it was already. That much was true in how and where he'd utilised his army in the past. His personal vendettas had been fought and won thanks to the hordes, and she knew he would not have stopped there. At least this way, they would do no harm unless she commanded them to. Wrong no one without her say so. A far better alternative.

When she'd done the same with the other pits full of vampire soldiers, Wynter ghosted back up and out, where the alpha met her. He was looking down at her with that intense red stare again, and she glared back up at him.

"Why?" she asked incredulously. "Why me?"

He simply stared back at her and offered Wynter no response. There seemed to be no soul behind his dead eyes, and this time, he offered her nothing. No smile. No frown. Nothing but the look of a mindless, robotic, loyal minion, and not to her. Rage bubbled up inside of her and she shook her head. "You basically are just a fucking zombie, aren't you? Why don't you think for yourself? Say something? Be your own man?"

He simply continued to say and do nothing, and so Wynter turned and walked away. She headed straight for her little office so that she could be alone with her thoughts, even if they were what was driving her insane right now.

She sat at her desk a few minutes later, feeling sorry for herself, and decided it was time she truly took stock of her life. She wanted more. Not necessarily an empire like Marcus had built, but more than just the few thousand vampire soldiers. She barely had to lift a finger to command. Once again, those feelings of worthlessness were chiding her, and she felt lacking in purpose. She needed to learn more about what she truly was and knew the answer. She needed her mentor. Brodie had a lot left to teach her, and Wynter found herself missing him.

As if she knew, Marcella then appeared out of nowhere and, even though things had been stretched between them after their last altercation, it seemed she was ready to extend the proverbial olive branch. She reached out her hand and in her palm was the black and white bracelet Wynter had used to wear. The one she'd been led to believe had connected her to Brodie.

"I kept this, and didn't know why, but now I do. You need him, and he needs you," Marcella whispered and then, when she took it, disappeared without another word.

With a petulant huff, Wynter slipped the bracelet onto her wrist. She was sure nothing would happen, but the second she did, she realised it did indeed still connect her to the jinni who had later given her immortal life.

She closed her eyes and focussed and quickly found she could sense him. Her maker. They were bonded, just like vampires with their slaves.

Brodie was still on the island, Wynter could somehow tell, and he was happy. He was moving forward with his life and yet she knew he'd been thinking of her, too. Part of her wondered if maybe they'd been connected even without the material link? Like some kind of bond that'd linked them, even after all this time.

She still had so much left to learn from Brodie and found herself contemplating how she might go to him. How she could instigate some freedom from Marcus's prison and what she might have to sacrifice to make it happen. After all, this was the key to her finding herself, she realised.

Wynter needed to make amends and reconnect with her friends. She needed to learn everything she could and, most importantly, needed to find herself in the process. Thanks to the bracelet on her wrist, the pull to Brodie was as strong as when Marcus would call her to his side using his hex before. It was intense, and Wynter spent the rest of the day in a haze, focussed only on getting herself to her mentor's side.

And so, she thought how she might go about buttering her husband up. Her plans to behave and take her life for what it now was had done her well. She had earned Marcus's trust and now had an entire vampire army at her back, but she didn't need them for this task. No, this favour would need the oldest trick in the book—some good old-fashioned seduction.

As the humans in their keep finally began settling down for the evening, the constant flow of visitors to Marcus's office finally stemmed and Wynter crept inside, watching him work. He had his head down and seemed focussed on the papers in his hands, but she wasn't so convinced. She knew how susceptible he was to her lure, and so stepped over to him silently, her feet merely billowing on the ground like the cloud she often was.

She went around behind him and decided it was time he was wearing far less clothes, so made quick work of sliding loose his tie and then discarding it on the ground. Next, she plucked open the buttons on his crisp blue shirt. But rather than remove it, Wynter had another idea. She pulled the back taut and lifted it up over the back of his chair so that Marcus's hands and arms were forced backwards, and he dropped the paperwork down onto his desk.

"Oops," she whispered in his ear, earning herself a deep laugh, but he didn't stop her, so Wynter continued. She conjured away her own clothes and climbed across his lap, and it was her turn to laugh when she saw her husband lick his lips as he took in the sight before him. "Bet you wish you could still have a taste..." she teased.

"I can taste you any time I want, my sweet," he replied, and then wrenched his hands free in a flash. Marcus then gripped her behind and lifted Wynter up so that her shoulders hit the desk behind her, and her pussy came level with his mouth. True to his word, the vampire then demanded a taste, and Wynter let out a soft moan as he began working her body using his tongue.

Damn, he was good. Wynter was soon climbing her high and was quickly reminded of how she'd gone there to seduce him and not the other way around. But, like always, her husband had other ideas. And, like always, things went his way. Not that she minded on this occasion, of course.

By the time he was done, Wynter was on fire for him. She quickly ripped the remainder of his clothes free and lowered herself down onto his ever ready hard-on, her eyes on his as they began moving together in perfect harmony.

They carried on for hours, and Wynter let Marcus take her every which way he wanted.

She was still strewn over his desk on her belly, his hands around her neck and being pummelled from behind, when the sun rose the next morning.

Marcus pulled her upwards and nipped her ear with his teeth, relishing in her surprised cry. "I think it's time I sent you away, Wynter," he then whispered gruffly, still pounding into her and crushing her against him.

Panic rose within her, thinking she was being dismissed for negative reasons, but then it dawned on her. He knew. All this time, he knew exactly what she was planning and had let her try to seduce him, anyway. Of course he had.

Wynter turned her head back and caught the huge grin that was spread across her vampire husband's face.

"You knew?" she demanded and then shuddered as another climax echoed through her. Marcus was right there with her, and when they were both done, he stepped away and grabbed a fresh set of clothes from his closet.

"Of course. Who else do you think provided Marcella with the bracelet to give you?" he replied, laughing.

"But why?"

"Because I know this isn't enough for you, my sweet," he answered, turning oddly serious. "As in, this world I've brought you into. I know you wanted something different for your future and I like to think I've created a far better alternative, but of course I'm no fool. I know you need something more. There are things you must learn and, as frustrating it is for me to admit it, I know I cannot teach you."

Wynter was in shock. Not once in all their time together had Marcus flummoxed her so. Not even when he'd told her he loved her.

He'd finally made some mention of the life he had stolen from her. Some hint of the future with Jakob that had been ripped away. She had to force herself not to lash out at him. He'd 'created something different' all right! Damn, if there wasn't the chance of freedom on offer, Wynter knew she would've said something to rile him and cause an argument. But that was the old her. She didn't do that anymore. She fought in other ways and was clever now. Not blinded by hate and desperation, or the love for another she wanted to get back to. Marcus had quietened his little fighter's voice, but he hadn't quietened her soul. No, hers still screamed loudly from deep within, and for the first time in months, even Mara didn't seem to oppose her. In fact, the witch's heart beat as strong as ever, but her voice was unusually quiet. Did she agree that he was wrong? Or was she, too, just choosing not to fight? Yet again Wynter tried asking her and knew the witch's spirit heard her, but still refused her.

Coward, she thought, and then turned her attention back to her husband.

"Plus," he continued, "once you've got everything covered, I'll have an exceptionally trained and full powered Jinn by my side. We'll be unstoppable, my sweet."

She nodded but was still raging. She could see what he was up to. Marcus's quest for power was infallible, and it scared her. Wynter also had to wonder, was this the real reason why Mara was going along with her plan to get back to Brodie? She wanted her master to prevail against all odds and anyone who revolted against him and having Wynter at full strength was certainly a sure-fire way to do so.

And then something else occurred to her. By going to Brodie and the others, she was opening them up to more danger at the hands of their old foe.

"My friends owe you nothing. They will not be expected to follow your rules or else face any form of punishment," she demanded, and Marcus simply nodded. "I mean it. They have full amnesty. The past forgotten."

"Cross my heart," he told her, doing the action with the tip of his finger across the centre of his chest.

"And I can go, no caveats?"

"Just one," Marcus answered, and then the door beside him opened. In walked the alpha vampire and he stood there, looking anywhere but at her, and Wynter realised why when she looked down and remembered she was still naked. A second later, she was magically dressed and simply shrugged.

"I don't need a chaperone, but I get it. He can come on one condition—he does what I say. Got it?"

"Got it…"

FIFTEEN

As she climbed into her huge four-by-four, Wynter told herself over and over that things were going to be okay. She was going back to her friends, who would welcome her with open arms. She would train and then come back to Marcus without delay.

And without the others in tow.

Marcus had let slip how he felt about having a jinni in his team, so to give him two would be beyond foolish. But Brodie would know that as well, and he wouldn't let it happen either. She would make sure of it that they worked together and then she would go—end of story.

The alpha soldier climbed in beside her and Wynter tore away from the mansion before she could change her mind. However, this turned out, she knew it needed to happen. Every thought and feeling she had was drawing her back to that island, and she knew she wouldn't be able to silence those thoughts much longer.

The two of them reached the coast within a few hours and, once the car was safely locked away, she stood staring out at the grey sky ahead, which was broken only by the bright beam of the lighthouse one island over. Wynter was itching to get there. Her skin prickled like it was still real flesh, and she grimaced at her companion. It wasn't going to go down well that she'd brought one of the vampire soldiers along for the ride.

"I'll carry you across, but once we're there, you have to hold back. Let me talk to them and ease their fears," she told him, and the vampire simply nodded. Like always, he just followed along, but she was glad. It was easier not to have to fight.

Wynter checked they weren't being watched and then quickly dissipated into her misty form, and was soon carrying the huge, bulky soldier across the still water towards what looked like nothingness ahead. To the naked eye, the island was invisible, and to humans, the magic surrounding it would make it even less so.

Once they were far enough from the mainland, she saw Brodie's island appear out of the fog and made for the cliff edge. She knew the opening to the cave was there somewhere and soon found a clear path that led downwards towards a mossy shard of rock. She'd seen almost every inch of this island through her maker's eyes and yet as she came to land and transformed back into her human form, it felt brand new.

The travelling time had been a blur and Wynter hadn't thought to stop and smell the roses, as it were. But now that they were there, she took a moment to truly take it all in. The island was dreary and damp, but it was truly beautiful in its own way. The rocks were jagged and ugly, but they were also protective of those who resided within, and so she found the ancient landscape homely.

She'd never stopped to think about it much before. All she'd been focussed on was her time with Jak and their few stolen moments when she'd been strong enough to emerge from her hideaway.

Wynter suddenly felt dizzy and overcome with sadness at the thought of him. This was where he had spent his final days. As a prisoner. They ought to have had the most wonderful future together and instead he had been locked away, while she too had been shut inside the confines of her own cell. And then he had died here too.

"Wynter," the alpha hummed, and she knew she couldn't hide her upset from him. No matter how hard she was trying to overcome the emotions flooding through her, she just couldn't.

"I'm fine," she lied, shooing him away, but it was no use. All she could think about was how he, too, had played a part in the death of the vampire she had loved. She hated him. Hated all of them.

Wynter needed to get this over with. Needed to force away the thoughts that were overwhelming her and get in the cave. She needed to get to her friends. They would help.

She turned on her heel and stormed inside. Anything to get away from the vampire she'd been made to bring along and was still figuring out what to say when she collided with someone on their way out the entranceway.

It was Archie. He was in his gym gear and had headphones in, clearly heading out for a run, and he looked great. Slimmer than ever. Wynter was about to greet him and tell him so when he backed away and held his hands up to her in his panic.

"Please, don't hurt me," he whimpered, and she frowned.

"Archie, it's me," she said, but then realised he was looking over her shoulder to where the alpha was blocking the exit with his grey, brutish body, and insidious red eyes. Archie's MP3 player slipped from his hand, and his headphones fell to the ground with it. "Hey, trust me. We're not here to hurt anyone. It's me, Wynter," she told him, and saw the fear on his face slowly begin to subside.

He finally blinked and then looked into her face, which was when she realised he didn't know what she looked like. But he knew her voice, and that seemed to be what had triggered him to come back from whatever assumptions the sight of a vampire soldier had led him to.

"Wynter?" he whimpered, and she nodded.

"In the flesh," she joked, but then shook her head. "Not the time for jokes, but you know what I mean, right?" she added and then transformed into her white smoke for just a few seconds so that she could prove to him she was the same jinni he had slowly gotten to know months previously. Archie nodded, but his eyes were still wide.

"And what the fuck is he doing here?" he gulped, looking back at her chaperone, and Wynter sighed.

"Babysitting," she groaned, but then remembered how scary it had to have been for Archie. Having soldiers like the alpha swarm the island and take them down in that chopper. She'd tried her hardest to block out those memories, and it appeared so had he, but her return had to have taken him right back to that night too. Just like for her, those memories were doing a number on him, and Archie swayed on his feet, looking like he might be about to keel over.

She reached for him in time to stop him from slumping to the ground and then carried him over to the house as fast as she could without hurting him. The poor guy had to have had too much, and Wynter started to worry that things might not be the same between them after all.

She was met at the doorway by the jinni she had come looking for and let out a sigh when Brodie smiled and turned to let her pass.

"I've been expecting you," he told her, "but not him." He then pointed to the alpha.

"I know," she answered, and was just placing Archie down on the sofa when his eyes shot back open and he fought his way back up to his feet. "Please, both of you, hear me out. I wasn't allowed to come unless he was with me. I had no choice. Marcus trusted me to come, but only if—"

"Marcus what?!" Archie bellowed, surprising them all with his outburst. "He trusts you now? Wanna know what I imagined was going on? That he kept you prisoner, and you escaped, or that he got tired of your constant attempts to fight back and let you go. But no. You were off playing nice with him and earning his trust? I don't need to ask how," he seethed.

"Please don't," Wynter tried, but it appeared he was going to have his say no matter what.

"He killed Jakob. He murdered him right before your eyes and almost killed us all, and you've spent the last few months doing what? Playing happy families?"

"Archie!" she cried, feeling pain and anger beginning to rise within at his words, but she couldn't deny that he was right and so was filled with shame.

"How can you forgive him? How can you let that thing come here with you? Who the hell do you think you are?" he carried on and was on some kind of a roll. One that even Brodie didn't seem to want to put a stop to. She wondered, did he feel the same too, and that was why he was staying quiet?

Wynter started to feel hot. Her heart was racing and suddenly her hands felt like they were burning. She looked to Brodie for guidance on what was happening and saw his eyes widen with shock—or was it fear?

He leapt between her and Archie just in time to intercede as she lifted her palms and shot some kind of white bolts of power from them in the human's direction. She didn't even know what she was doing or why and was shocked to hear herself screaming as Brodie took the force directly to the chest and crumbled in a heap at Archie's feet.

He backed up, looking terrified, and Wynter wanted to tell him she was sorry. To say he was safe now. But then she felt a second round of the strange lightning begin to well up from within.

"Get back, Archie. Please! Get away. I can't control it," she begged him, and then realised her hands were coming up yet again, ready to deliver the poor boy with the hit he'd avoided the first time around.

He clambered to the ground and curled into a ball, begging for her to stop, but Wynter couldn't. This was Mara's doing, she knew, and no matter what she tried, the witch was clearly done with listening to Archie's account of how awful Marcus was and had been.

Wynter closed her eyes and screamed to Mara to stop and then felt the icy flesh of the alpha press against her red hot palms. She opened up, watching as he took the second jolt of magic as it burst out of her.

His body shook like he was being electrocuted and then he fell back with an almighty thud, and before Wynter could even think what to do next, she felt herself being lifted off the ground and carried away by the other magical male entity in residence at the island.

Rafferty took her across the other side of the house to the kitchen and sat her at the table with a thud, and Wynter stared up at him, tears streaming down her face.

"They're going to be okay," he told her, "but you need to calm down. And you need to calm *her* down…"

"I know," she replied, taking deep breaths. "I don't even know what the hell that was?" she admitted as he delivered her with a cup of tea. She went to refuse, seeing as she didn't need to eat at all, but he insisted.

"My special remedy," the goblin said, and as she took a sniff, Wynter somehow picked out exactly which herbs and spices he'd put in the tincture he'd mixed with the hot water. It was a harmless brew and one that'd calm a human's nerves readily, and as she took a sip, she realised how the drink wasn't there to calm her, but Mara. In focussing on the ingredients, he had distracted her long enough to calm the entire situation down, and Wynter was glad he'd known to not only remove her from the scene but also tackle the witch who was to thank for it.

"Works a treat," she told him with a smile, having had the smallest of sips, and Rafferty smiled.

"She's strong, isn't she?" he asked, taking a seat beside her, and Wynter nodded.

"And thanks to her power, I'm bound to Marcus forever. She won't let anyone come between us," she confessed. "I've done what I had to, become who he wanted me to, and all because I had no other choice. But I didn't know she'd use me like that simply because someone spoke against him. I never meant to hurt anyone," she cried, and had to stop herself from growing upset again.

"I had no idea," a soft voice said from behind her, and Wynter knew it was Archie. She risked a peek at him and was glad when Mara didn't try and hurt him again. The poor guy was trembling, but he stood tall, like he was trying to show her no fear, and she was impressed. It helped that Rafferty was there to come between them should something happen, but she felt fine. Mara had given her show of force and none of them needed reminding just what the young witch was capable of. She'd won, and Archie had clearly learned his lesson.

"Don't get me wrong, I get it," she replied, her head in her hands. "I'll never forget what he took from me, but I have no choice other than to move forward and accept my fate. He made sure of that when his priestess put this power inside of me."

"The witch's heart?" he asked, and she nodded, "Brodie told me."

"And did he tell you how I'm alive, but damned? I've got more than enough energy to live on, but it came at such a high price. I lost everything, Archie. Even the friends I have left can't talk to me because they're under his spell, or are loyal to him first and foremost. I knew something had to give. I need to have something to live for, which is why I begged Marcus to let me come here. I wanted to find you both and try to figure out a way to live with what I have become."

"We'll help you," a gruff voice replied, and she watched as a dishevelled-looking Brodie stumbled towards her with a frown. His eyes were only half open, and he was rubbing his chest as he then slid into one of the chairs at the table, but he seemed determined to be heard. Mara had given him a good beating, but at least he was still standing, and she was glad to see him back up and about. That blast would've undoubtedly killed Archie if he hadn't intervened, so it was clearly the better alternative.

The alpha wasn't far behind Brodie, and while Archie bristled, he didn't seem as scared as before. The vampire soldier had taken the second blast for him after all, and in doing so, had also saved his life.

"Damn right we're gonna help," Archie agreed, and he took a seat at the table.

"You need to get that witch under control, though," Brodie hissed, but then smiled at her. "It's good to have you back. I haven't missed your voice in my head, but I will admit it's not been the same without you here."

"What's going on out there—" a woman's voice then called from down the hall and Wynter did a double take. Someone else was here too?

She was about to ask the same question of her hosts when a tiny woman with a huge pregnant belly waddled in and looked around the room at the sorry group. She paled at the sight of the alpha, and understandably so, but smiled when she saw Wynter. "I've been expecting you," the young woman said, and as the surprised jinni stared back at her in surprise, so too did Brodie and Archie.

"What?" they both asked in unison, and the girl shrugged.

"I've been dreaming about her," she answered them and then waddled closer, clearly far from afraid even after all the commotion she'd heard. "Mara, isn't it?"

***

Archie stared at Wynter, who was looking over at Rosa with a confused look. In fact, looking around the room, everyone seemed confused. Except Rosalie. She was grinning, looking at Wynter like she was an old friend and couldn't believe she didn't recognise her.

"Who's Mara?" Archie finally broke the silence.

"She is, isn't she?" Rosa answered, and then suddenly, all eyes were back on Wynter. "Well, now that I think about it, she had red hair in my dreams. But it was definitely her."

"I...I..." Wynter was trying to say, but she couldn't seem to form a proper reply.

"No, this is Wynter. Remember, the jinni I was telling you about?" Brodie told Rosalie, who then frowned. "She used to live here but was taken away by the vampire who she used to work for."

"Yeah, Marcus. She told me all about how wonderful he is," Rosalie continued, and then stared at Wynter with such a sure look on her face Archie couldn't help but believe her. "I remember now. You're my cousin and you said we'd be together soon. That you'd be here in time for the baby coming because you said I could go and live with you and Uncle Jack?"

"What?" Brodie and Archie both asked again, looking from Rosa to the still bewildered looking Wynter.

They were looking back to Rosalie when a small giggle erupted from Wynter's chest, like she'd been trying to hold it back but couldn't do so any longer.

Archie turned to her and watched as her face lit up and, with another giggle, she swept her hands up over her hair, transforming it into a bright red shade right before their eyes.

"That's better," she said, still beaming up at Rosa.

"It can't be. You were just a baby when Marcella gave Wynter your heart," Brodie cried, shaking his head.

"I was indeed and was ready and willing to become little more than a battery for Wynter so that she could live the life my master wanted her to live, but then she started to feel sad for me. She tried to talk to me and guide me into thinking the way she did, but instead I realised it was me who needed to guide her. I helped her to forget the past and see my master the way I saw him. To want to serve him and be everything he needed for her to be," she told him with a coy smile, and Archie had to bite his tongue. He was about to start shouting again but remembered with ease just what the witch beside him was capable of and forced himself to calm down.

"You love him," Brodie replied, and Mara nodded.

"Of course. And it wasn't long before that love began pouring into Wynter, too. Thanks to me, she's grown so much since you last saw her. She's strong and powerful, the leader of an army!"

"Queen," the huge vampire soldier that'd been otherwise silent and motionless since coming to join them hissed, and Archie shuddered at the gravelly sound.

"Yes," Mara agreed, smiling up at him, "she's their queen now. Her fate is tied to theirs, and with her by my master's side, he cannot lose. You'd all do well to come and join us…"

Archie was livid. The poor girl was clearly insanely loyal to that asshole of a vampire. So much so that no matter what was said about him or the evidence she had to have seen for herself, she would never do a thing to hinder his rise to the top. Mara was merely a child, but she had to have been looking at the world through Wynter's eyes since having had her physical life snuffed out, and of course, that world had to have been intense.

"You're insane, Mara. Blinded by love and loyalty and you're dragging Wynter down with you. Marcus is your master, but not ours," he told her, forcing his voice to remain calm and even to not rile her. "You might be controlling Wynter and forcing her to stay with him, but you can't force us."

Mara began laughing.

"I might be forcing her to stay, but that's it. The rest is all on her," she told him, and then Archie watched as she blushed and ran her hand up her neck and to her lips, smiling at him. "I might be young, but I'm not naïve. I know how it feels to fuck him, and I also know how it feels when he makes love to me—I mean her…"

She then sat back in her seat and glowered across at the group, as if she was annoyed with herself having let slip how enamoured she was with her master, but it was obvious anyway. Archie felt like telling her so but knew there was nothing he could do to change things. All he could hope was that Wynter was strong enough to know her own mind when it came to her time with Marcus, and that she didn't forget who she was, even when Mara was holding the wheel.

SIXTEEN

That was it. Enough was bloody enough. Wynter had seen and heard more than she would've ever entertained under any other circumstances, and she wasn't going to let Mara use her body like a puppet any longer. Since when had she been able to talk and force herself out in such a way as she just had with Archie and the others? And where the hell had this plan involving the poor pregnant girl standing in the doorway come from? Somehow, she'd been left out of all this plotting and planning, and she was far from impressed.

Wynter knew she had to take the wheel again, and so began pushing against Mara's hold over her. But it was no use. The harder she pushed, the firmer the invisible yet impenetrable barrier surrounding her became, and so she tried another tactic. The power to transform belonged to her jinni side, of course. The witch needed to be put back in her box and so Wynter focused on her own power, not that which emanated from Mara's heart. She called to every cell in her body and commanded them to revert back to their natural form, and just as Mara opened her mouth to speak out of turn to Archie again, she instigated the change.

Her body turned to white smoke mid-sentence, and a split-second later Wynter was whole again, and herself.

She could sense Mara's rage within at being cast back inside her cell but didn't care. The insolent witch could scream and shout if she wanted too, Wynter wasn't listening.

"What the actual fuck?" she cried, staring at Brodie in shock as she settled back inside her own makeshift skin. "Did you know something like that could happen?" she asked and needed guidance from the mentor she had come to the island to find. But he couldn't seem to fathom an answer, which meant no.

"Maybe it's the same principle as two jinni's living as one? Each can come and go when strong enough?" Archie guessed, and Wynter wanted to throttle him purely because it looked like he might actually be right.

She climbed to her feet and stormed out, having suddenly felt overcome with sadness and rage. Just as she reached the opening that led out of the cave, she was wrenched back and turned to scowl at who had dared try and stop her. It was the alpha, and so she let him have it. She punched and kicked him to the ground without a care for any pain he might feel. In fact, she didn't think he could feel pain at all, and so gave him everything she had in a bid to quench the awful thoughts rising within her. She'd been played. Used by Mara to get her here and led to believe it was for her own reasons the entire time.

When she'd had enough, she started screaming and crying, holding herself in a ball on the ground.

"Wynter…" the vampire soldier groaned, still loyal as ever in spite of her viciousness.

"Why are we here?" she cried into her hands, "she did this. She made me think I had to come back, when actually she was drawing us here for something else."

Wynter snapped her head up and looked into the red eyes of her insanely devoted companion. Things finally falling into place. "Or *someone* else."

The still wide-eyed jinni climbed back up onto her feet and took a second to compose herself before skulking back into the house, and to the group she knew had to have seen her lose it just minutes before. She felt ashamed and confused but knew that it would not be like this forever. She was here to learn, and so she would. No matter Mara's real reasons for drawing her back to the island.

"Wynter, I—" Archie began, but she reached for his hand and shook her head.

"Later. I'm just trying to find my voice right now, and first thing's first," she interjected, and then turned to look at the young woman who had now taken a seat beside Rafferty at the kitchen counter—not that she could see him there of course. "Mara came to you? She said you're her cousin?" she asked, trying to get her head around what she'd said before Mara had broken through.

"Yes, my name's Rosalie Summers. A man called Jack Summers works for Mr Cole, and he's my uncle. He went to work at a nightclub when I was little and I haven't seen him since, but I remember my dad talking about him. He told us his brother chose a career over a family, but Mara told me differently. In my dreams she said he's married to a witch and that they were going to have her, but that she was chosen to save you instead," Rosalie answered, and Wynter's heart sank. "But she said that it was okay because her mother is having another baby?"

Wynter nodded and actually felt quite gobsmacked. She remembered Jack's surname from the nameplate on his door back at *Slave*, and it was indeed Summers.

Had Mara really known that this girl, Rosalie, was on the island with Brodie and the others? There was that one vision Wynter had of Marcella feeding two babies. Perhaps that prophecy also wasn't meant for her, but for Mara?

And of course, there was the issue of her having gone into Rosalie's dreams. If so, that had to mean there were other things Mara knew and was doing, and all without Wynter having any control over it.

Now that was a scary thought.

"It's true," she told the young woman, and then addressed the rest of their small group. "It appears there are other forces in play that I wasn't aware of, but please trust me when I assure you that I'm going to get a grip on things. And with that in mind, I'm gonna need your help." Wynter fixed her eyes on Brodie, who nodded.

"It's about time I taught you what it means to be a jinni and remind you who's more powerful between you and the witch who dared to take you for a test drive," he answered, his dark face lighting up as a far bigger smile began to dominate his features.

This was exactly what she'd been looking for and mirrored her maker's smile.

"When do we begin?" she asked, and Brodie didn't so much as look at the clock.

He climbed to his feet and offered her his hand.

"No time like the present."

***

"She knows," Marcus told his priestess when she appeared at his command and didn't need to elaborate. As always, his powerful companion was of the same mindset, and probably had more information than he did regarding his wife's exploits. But he didn't mind. She shared the pertinent details with him, and Marcus knew he could trust Marcella to have his interests at heart, no matter what the future entailed for her own offspring. She had proven so months previously by giving up the physical life of the child she had hoped to bear, and hundreds of times since.

But right now, it was his alpha who was serving him best. The soldier was coming back to him with increasingly regular updates on their progress at the island, and it was clear things hadn't taken long before they'd turned nasty. Marcella had warned him that Wynter wouldn't like being used, and he'd seen for himself just how she'd lashed out at the vampire soldier guarding her when realisation had struck. But it mattered naught. The end result was worth it, even if he despised having to be without his beloved wife in the interim.

"My lord, I had another vision," she replied, stepping closer.

"And?"

"She will bring them to us," Marcella informed him, "but there will be a price. An innocent life must be lost."

"It will be paid…" he answered. "Nothing can stop us. Not now we've gotten so far."

"So shall it be," the Priestess answered, and then she slowly retreated before disappearing into the shadows.

Marcus stood and peered out the window to the gardens that spread out all around the huge mansion he had taken and made a home. His Supervisors were slowly leaving now, except those remaining for their periods of servitude as his Blood Slaves, and it was nice having the house so quiet again now that their training was over with. Just the necessary few remained now, and Wynter was sure to find a huge difference when she returned.

He knew she liked the hustle and bustle, whereas he was the opposite and, of course, what he wanted was more important. She would honour his wishes, he was sure. Or at least, she would come to. Like in all things, she'd undoubtedly argue and perhaps say that his new employees should've stayed with them a while longer, but Marcus had finished playing his game over the bloodletting and didn't need, or want, them there any longer.

His heart ached, and it wasn't for blood or power, but for the closeness of the woman his soul had merged with. She was his now and forevermore, and being apart was agonising. Marcus remembered back to all those he had met before that were merged, and how he'd pitied them. But now, he was the poor wretch who was stuck pining for the woman he loved. Would she be angry if he took it upon himself to follow her to the island? Yes, he was sure she would. And, of course, it would alter the path of what he knew was to come, which was not an option.

He would simply have to endure.

Blood would help, and so he summoned his next feed and made quick work of setting the young offering up to a tube, which he sucked on like a straw. He felt pathetic and quelled those shameful inner taunts by gulping down the blood flowing into his mouth in droves, rather than stem it and sip gently as usual.

Marcus stopped with mere moments to spare before the young man laid out before him would be dead, but rather than care for his safety, the vampire simply summoned for Bryn to aide him with IV bags and his trusty nursing skills.

And then he simply summoned the next slave, and then the next.

By morning, every Blood Slave in the house was recuperating, and Marcus was still ill at ease. He wanted more and was about to start again on the first man, when Marcella appeared and blocked his path with her tiny frame.

"The trouble this would cause between you and the High Committee of Vampires would be catastrophic to our plight, my lord. Control your thirst. Remember where she has gone and why," she implored him, and Marcus was about to scurry around her when her words sunk in.

This was what being without Wynter did to him. The last time had seen him take hundreds of lives because of his unquenchable thirst, and this would be no different if he didn't get a grip of himself. He reminded himself that she hadn't left him. That she wasn't lost or had run away but was on a mission. One he had readily sent her on. And a mission that, when successful, would bring him something worth far more than an army of vampires or powerful coven could offer.

He decided to write her a letter instead. One he could burn the moment he'd finished it and never actually show her, but that would surely help him clear his head. The world wasn't right without her in it, and Marcus knew he had funny ways of showing or telling her so, but he did love her. With his entire being, not just his heart and soul.

SEVENTEEN

Twenty-four hours had passed and still, they were training. Brodie had at first taken Wynter out into the cave to get started, but it was clear from all the crashing and banging that'd quickly followed that they'd needed more space. Archie was glad for the quiet, but after they'd gone, all he could think about was how that witch had glared at him through Wynter's eyes. She had wanted him dead for daring to speak out about Marcus, even after everything he had done to those he cared about.

She was dangerous indeed, and he knew now to tread a lot more carefully with Wynter, because evidently Mara was watching the world through her eyes whether she liked it or not. And to that poor little witch, Marcus was everything. End of story.

"Hey Rosa, you doing okay?" he asked his fellow human, who hadn't said much in the aftermath of Mara's big reveal. She'd seemed to be taking it all in though, and hadn't gone running and hiding away, which was something at least.

"Yeah, just trying to get my head around it all," she answered, and then winced and repositioned herself. The baby had been giving her some serious jabs to the ribs lately and Archie smiled as he reached out his hand and gave her bump a gentle tap.

"Naughty," he whispered.

"Already giving me grief," she joked, "but I'm ready for more. I know what I need to do now, Archie. I'm going to live with my Uncle Jack."

He gulped and turned away in shock. He hadn't known what to expect, but it hadn't been for her to reveal that. He'd thought they were going to stay on the island together—him, Brodie and the two newcomers.

"They're bad people, Rosa. Can't you see? I know he's family, but that doesn't mean shit. He still gave his life to that vile vampire who has ruined Wynter's life. Brodie and me, we're the ones who've been here for you when it mattered. Can't you just stay with us?" he begged, and Rosalie simply smiled softly and shook her head. She was so calm. It was freaky, and Archie just couldn't believe her. He had to make her see. "Your baby will be born good. It will develop its powers over time and be a shifter. Brodie said it'll only become a werewolf if it isn't given a different path. A path anyone but Marcus can lead you both down."

"I trust you with my life, Archie. It's not that I don't want you to be with me in this, but it's the right thing to do," she answered, rubbing her belly thoughtfully. "I feel it in my bones. Wynter...Mara...whatever her name is, she was sent here to get me. To take us both where we're meant to be. I want you and Brodie to come too, but I know you can't let go of the past. So, when the time comes, we will have to all go our separate ways."

He wanted to cry. To scream and rant and rave. But it was no use. They had gotten inside her head and Rosalie seemed ready to go without so much as a backward glance at the two men who had saved her life and given her a safe home ever since. It was insane. Like some sort of cult mentality, but then, their nefarious leader hadn't even set eyes on the poor girl yet and she was already doing his bidding.

"Fuck this," he seethed, and shot to his feet. If they'd gotten to Rosalie, that was one thing, but he wasn't about to let Mara influence Brodie, too. He and Wynter were up on the summit training, but for all he knew, it might've all been a ruse to get him alone so she could dig her claws into him as well.

Archie ran for the door, and he grabbed his thick coat from the hook before taking off out the cave and up the cobbled path to the top of the island. He was just reaching the top when he heard Brodie screaming in pain.

"Control her..." he bellowed, and Archie was careful not to be spotted as he reached the top of the steps and took in what was going on before him.

Brodie was on the ground on his stomach and Wynter was straddling him, her hands around his neck as she tried to wrench him backwards. She looked up and locked eyes with Archie and had the audacity to wink at him before snapping Brodie's neck.

"No!" he cried, watching as his boyfriend slumped to the ground, and was about to make a run for him when Wynter clambered back and put her hands up.

"Stop, Archie. Stop!" she called, and it was the grey vampire soldier who then intercepted him and grabbed his arms, pulling Archie to a halt. He tried to fight, but it was no use. All he could do was watch as Brodie lay lifeless on the ground and Wynter stood staring down at him in shock.

Everything stilled for a few moments, and then Brodie suddenly turned to smoke before reappearing back in his usual fleshy form, much to Archie's immediate relief.

"Don't let her rule you, Wynter," he snapped at her, and then saw for himself that they now had a small audience. He simply offered Archie a swift nod to let him know everything was fine, and then turned his attention back to his fellow jinni.

"Make me force her away. Give me more, please," she begged, and Brodie let out a huff.

"I'm gonna go to places you don't want?" he replied, pacing around her.

"Do it," Wynter cried, her eyes wide, "I need to control her. I need to stay strong."

"Remember back to this time last year. Where were you? What were you doing?" he commanded, and Wynter didn't need long before she answered him.

"I was at the mansion with Jak. We talked for hours," she replied, tears falling from her eyes. "He took me for a drive and…and…" she couldn't seem to finish.

"And he fucked you over the bonnet of his car," Brodie carried on for her, and Archie remembered how he'd told him he was living within her at the time when all of this happened. He would've seen what she saw the entire time. He may not like women, but he had to admit that would've surely been hot. "What did he say? What did he make you see?"

"That I was nothing. Nothing worth loving. No one worth risking a single thing for. But that I could change it. I could find the woman worth all those things and become her," she whimpered, clutching at her chest, "he showed me I could start again. That I had to love myself before anyone was going to love me back."

"And do you love the woman you are today?" Brodie pressed.

"No," she answered gravely, and began to sob harder as tears wracked her body.

Archie went limp in the soldier's hold and felt him let go but knew he wouldn't let him go to the two Jinn before him. The soldier was watching too, but evidently had been tasked with letting whatever was going on play out.

"You loved Jakob, and Marcus took him away from you. He butchered him and even forced you to look upon the bloody mess that was once your soul mate. And all while Marcella was giving you a gift you never asked for. She was forcing Marcus's will upon you, and you never once said yes or agreed to it, did you?"

"No," Wynter answered, her tears of anguish turning to cries of anger.

"She never asked you to take the life of her unborn child in your hands, and she never asked if you wanted a gift which would leave you beholden to both her and Marcus forever."

"No," she growled, her eyes burning into his.

"And now you're supposed to be grateful? You didn't ask for this, so what are you gonna do about it? Are you gonna keep feeling guilty and letting Mara walk all over you, or are you gonna come back stronger than ever and stop her from saying or doing anything without your say so?"

Wynter's head shot back, and she started to giggle, just like she had in the kitchen before revealing she was in fact Mara. The same appeared to be happening now, and she glared up at Brodie, still sniggering like a child.

"She doesn't *let* me do anything, foolish jinni. I just do. I'm more powerful than she is, and she cannot stop me," she teased, but then started to shudder like some sort of jolt of energy was running through her.

"You're nothing but a battery pack, little witch. Get back in your box," Brodie answered, and then they all watched as Wynter fell on her knees and arched her back so that she was staring up into the sky.

Archie leaned forward, trying to see what she was doing, but then jumped out of his skin when she let out a piercing scream. It was so loud he couldn't think straight, and even the vampire beside him put his hands up over his ears at the bloodcurdling sound.

When she was finally done, Wynter seemed to somehow explode into a wave of white mist that then wafted across the entire plain and rolled around the acre or so of space. It was even billowing around his feet, and Archie watched her stretch out further, wrapping the landscape as far as he could see in white. It was as if a blizzard had just fallen, but instead of snow, it was thick, curling wisps of foggy white haze.

He started to wheeze as the smoke rose around him, stifling the air and blocking out any and all view that was left, and began to panic.

"Wynter," he choked, "you're loved. We all love you, including me. I'm sorry for judging you. Come back to us."

He was just starting to lose consciousness when the fog began to lower and slowly recede. It was still flowing back to the centre spot on the ground when Archie found his footing again, and he watched as Wynter transformed back into her usual guise.

She was sitting curled in a ball, her arms wrapped tightly around herself and the tears continued to fall, but at least she was herself again. Archie ran to her and was just wrapping his arms around her when Brodie did the same, followed quickly by the vampire who Archie wanted to push away, but instead forced himself to let play his part in her recovery. Wynter was cocooned within their grip and none of them were letting go. Not until she was ready.

***

Wynter felt reborn. As if her skin itself was new, not just her outlook and the driving force behind everything she thought, said, and did. Mara was still there, but she was quiet. Nothing more than a niggling voice in the back of her head that didn't need to be listened to, and as she lifted her head and peered into the eyes of those holding her in their arms, she knew who deserved to have their voices heard too. Not the infant witch forcing her to listen out of guilt, but the friends she held dear. Those who had guided her all this way without an ounce of selfishness, but for her own good.

Even the alpha was there, and as she watched him, she saw a light behind his otherwise cold, red, and dead eyes. Perhaps he wasn't soulless after all.

"Thank you," she told them, particularly Brodie, who had faced the brunt of it all and thankfully come through in one piece, but she knew it would've taken its toll on him. His days as an entire being would be shortened because of her, and she vowed to find him a way to survive longer before being forced back into a cage. One that didn't involve taking what he could from multiple sources.

She could feel Archie shivering with the cold against her and so clambered to her feet, nodding to her maker. "Let's get back," she said, and Brodie made quick work of leading the small group down the dark pathway and back to the cave, where the smell of food greeted them.

Archie was the only one to react to the scent, but Brodie grinned and she saw him watch the human jog away towards the beckoning smell of his dinner.

"I know," he then groaned, fixing his pale green eyes on hers. "I've got it bad."

"It's nice to see," Wynter replied, "and about time you let yourself feel something again."

"Speaking of…how do you feel?" he asked her, and Wynter had to stop and think before she answered.

"Like shit, but also really good—if that's a thing? The pain and guilt are still there, but mostly I just feel stronger in both my will and my abilities."

"I get it. And trust me when I tell you that those feelings might never go, but hopefully you'll figure out how to overcome those burdens sooner than later. They never got me anywhere," Brodie admitted, and Wynter knew all too well just how badly his grief had taken hold. She wouldn't let herself be the same. She would learn from his mistakes rather than repeat them, much like any apprentice from their mentor.

When they went back inside the main house, Archie was just finishing up his meal and he beckoned them both over to him with a frown.

"Rosa's dead set on taking the baby to the mansion with you," he told her, and Wynter grimaced. She'd been worrying about this ever since Mara's deception had been unveiled.

"I think that was always the plan, with or without any intervention from us," she replied.

"Does Marcus want her or the baby for any reason you might know of?" Brodie asked her, and Wynter wracked her brains trying to think of one but came up empty.

"No. But perhaps Marcella wants it?" she tried, thinking of the vision she'd had in which the Priestess was feeding two babies and Wynter had taken it as her having twins. Maybe it was Rosalie's baby in the vision instead?

"Either way, we can't let Rosa go without thinking this through. A shifter baby is bad enough, but having a full-blown werewolf for a father? Steps need to be taken, so that she keeps that child away from anyone who might want to have that sort of power at their command," Archie hissed, keeping his voice low on purpose because they all knew that if Rosalie overheard, then she wouldn't be happy.

"Agreed," she told him, and with a nod, they then finished their little huddle and parted ways.

When she was alone, though, Wynter struggled with her thoughts and urges. She reached for a nearby phone, thinking she might call Marcus and try and speak with him about what had happened with Mara. She wanted to know if he'd had any idea she was growing so strong, but knew there were other reasons, too. She found herself missing him. Now that she'd silenced the witch within, Wynter was left with an entirely different set of thoughts and feelings, and strangely, she was still thinking of her husband even without Mara's influence.

It was a welcome relief when Brodie came to find her before she could pick up that phone. He was followed quickly by Archie, and the pair of them took a seat on the sofas and began a debate over which movie they were going to watch that night.

Wynter smiled and set her things aside before snuggling down in her seat. It was nice to be home. Nice to be with her bickering friends, even if the dynamic between them had changed dramatically since the last time she saw them. The two of them were a couple now, she could tell. They were sat close to one another, and Archie had a fire in his eyes when he looked at Brodie that was simply unmistakeable. She had seen it up on the island's summit when he'd come to check on them, and even though Mara had been in charge at that point in time, it was easy to see that Archie had been terrified for his lover. He'd been scared to lose him and had tried charging at Wynter in a bid to stop her from hurting him.

"Promise me you won't ever take Mara on again, Archie," she groaned, abruptly halting their conversation. "She will kill you. I'm taking charge. Listening to Brodie and heeding his advice, but there will always be that one per-cent of the time that she might break through, and I do not want to risk your safety should that happen."

"I won't, or at least I'll try. I 'cannae help myself sometimes, but I'll learn too," he answered, and she smiled.

"A headstrong Scotsman, who would've thought," she teased, and then ducked the sofa cushion that came flying towards her. "Case and point!" Wynter giggled, sending one flying back at him.

Rosalie then popped her head around the doorway, as though checking the coast was clear, and came to join them.

"Hey," she said as she took the seat beside Wynter on the sofa. She was confused at first as to why the young woman would want to sit with a stranger, but then remembered that in her mind, they were already friends. And even more than that, they were family.

"Hey," she answered, and then reached over to put her hand on the large baby bump the small girl was negotiating. As she did, Wynter was bombarded with visions of Rosalie and the dreams she'd had with Mara in them. They washed over her, and Wynter couldn't help but jump back in shock. She then turned to the wide-eyed girl and smiled. The visions had put it all into perspective for her and she could finally see how there was, in fact, no ulterior motive behind Mara's visits. And it might be the best choice for her to come back to the mansion after all. "She meant every word, you know? You truly are family, Rosalie, and will be welcomed at the mansion with open arms. But you must know who you're dealing with once you get there, okay?"

"Okay," she replied timidly, "so tell me."

"There's the hordes of vampire soldiers, like my behemoth of a friend over there," she told her, pointing to the alpha, who didn't so much as flinch or grunt in greeting. "But they're locked away, so you don't need to worry about them. I command the armies for Marcus, who is my husband."

"And he's the vampire Brodie and Archie warned me about? The one who killed your ex-boyfriend because he was jealous?" Rosalie asked, and despite her gentle tone, the words were like a kick to Wynter's gut.

She choked on her reply and had to take a second to compose herself before trying again.

"Yes," she croaked and looked to her fellow jinni, who seemed just as surprised by Rosalie's candour.

"And you love him now?" she carried on, and Wynter suddenly felt like she was being interrogated, but figured it was best she tell them all the truth. She had come to realise a lot since Mara's awakening and knew that what she saw when she looked in the mirror now wasn't entirely pretty.

"When he killed Jak, I was in the midst of the magic that put Mara's heart inside mine. I wasn't myself and so he took advantage of the chance to tear me from my merged soul mate. Marcus then took me away and tried to make me love him, but I couldn't. Even Mara tried, and she brought us together. But it wasn't until his soul merged with the remains of mine that I was finally his. There was no acceptance, but the sheer force of his love overwhelmed me, and I was made to love him back."

The room fell utterly silent, and Wynter watched as Archie's face fell.

"I didn't realise you'd merged with him," he whispered.

"That's how she clawed her way to the surface. She merged with him too," Brodie added, and it made sense. Mara had wanted this all along and had pushed Wynter to accept Marcus's advances. Her soul was already his long before she was turned into a power source for his jinni lover and so when he was ready to finally let his soul merge, hers was ready and waiting, with or without Wynter's say so.

"So yeah, I love him in my own way while he loves me in his," she told Rosalie with a shrug.

"Good, because I want you both to raise the baby as your own," the girl replied resolutely, surprising them all. "Mara made me see that the best place for it is there with Uncle Jack, but I don't want my child being raised alongside a witch as an adopted sibling. They'll constantly be compared to one another, and my child will not fit in with them. Their powers will manifest in ways I won't even see coming, but if you take it, you can give it guidance. Raise the baby as Mara's cousin, but I don't feel like I can do it myself. This baby is going to need things I just know I won't be able to provide, but you will. And you've lost so much that you understand how I feel, don't you? I know you can give this baby the love it deserves."

"Rosa, no!" Archie cried, but she ignored him.

"Please, Wynter. Tell me you'll do this for me?"

"You can't know how you'll feel until the baby's here, Rosalie. Please, don't make any rash decisions," Wynter replied, but she was met with an utterly unyielding stare from the poor girl.

"I've been through hell and cannot spend the rest of my life looking at the reminder of it. Please…"

Wynter's heart broke for her, and all she could do was nod. She knew she had to take away this burden the poor girl felt. She had to help, and Rosalie was right. If her child was raised alongside a powerful young witch, they would always be compared to them. Always be second best. But with a different set of parents, they might just stand the chance of shining brighter. Of becoming something more than the lore dictated they would be.

"I'll do it," she promised Rosalie, who sat up higher in her seat and beamed.

"Thank you," she cried, and it was clear a huge weight had just lifted from her shoulders.

Rosa then put Wynter's hand back onto her round belly, and she was rewarded with a kick, which made her laugh. Damn, this was not at all what she'd expected from her trip to the island.

She looked across at the two men still watching them in shock and frowned, suddenly overcome with worry.

"How long have we got?" she asked them.

"Six weeks, give or take," Brodie replied, and he seemed to be on the same train of thought as her. "So, we'd better make sure you've got everything fully under control by then. This baby can have no ties to Mara. Only you."

"I agree," Wynter replied. There was no way the witch was having any kind of a say in this, and her strength of will intensified even further with that thought. Wynter decided she would train day and night if she had to. Anything to make sure she went back to the mansion in complete control of herself, and Brodie gave her a determined look that told her he was thinking the exact same thing.

EIGHTEEN

Rosalie was over a week late when her waters finally broke. Wynter had counted down the days and had checked in on her every chance she got, but nothing had prepared them for the moment it finally happened. The two of them had grown closer with every passing day and not once had the young girl shown any sign that she was having second thoughts regarding her decision. She had resigned herself to the fact that her baby was going to a better home than she could offer it, and Wynter knew she had to respect Rosa's wishes, as well as support her through the remainder of their time together.

Brodie had trained her hard in the interim but trained her well. She was in complete control of her jinni powers and even some magical abilities Mara's heart seemed to still be sharing with her, and by the time they were preparing for the new arrival, she felt stronger than ever.

The contractions came on quickly and were just a couple of minutes apart in no time at all, and Wynter tried her best to stop Rosalie going into shock with how fast things were progressing.

"Chillin' in there for ages and now they want out," she joked, and the panting woman laughed through gritted teeth as she endured another strong wave of pain.

"Almost there, Rosa. Almost there," Brodie called from his position between her legs on their makeshift delivery bed. He had prepared everything and seemed ready for every eventuality and was standing perched and ready when Rosalie screamed that she felt the urge to push.

Her baby was born within seconds, and while Brodie tended to it, Wynter held Rosalie's hand and stroked her face with a cool towel, mopping her brow as sweat poured down her cheeks and temples.

She was still whispering to her how everything was fine when it suddenly dawned how she hadn't heard a sound from the other end of the table.

Wynter looked down in horror to find the baby on the bed was blue.

Brodie was doing everything he could to rouse it, but nothing seemed to work.

"Give it to me," Rosalie cried, and he reacted by quickly placing the baby directly onto her naked stomach, where she cooed and whispered to it, running her hands up and down over the baby's back and legs.

Rosalie then looked up into Wynter's eyes and started to tremble. "Forgive me…" the new mother whimpered, and she tried to tell her there was nothing to forgive. That they had tried their best but clearly it wasn't meant to be, and the baby had gone on to a better place. But before she had the chance, there was a sudden jolt from them both, and then an almighty cry as the baby shot back to life and began screaming.

Rosalie shushed the babe and offered it her breast, but as her newborn latched on, her trembling returned and soon got worse.

It wasn't long before she was struggling to keep hold of the child in her arms, and Wynter reached for them both, which was when she realised Rosalie was burning up.

"Stay with us, Rosa," Brodie cried, but she was already losing consciousness. Her eyes rolled back into her head and her arms flopped down by her sides, leaving Wynter to have to grab the baby up off her chest to stop it from falling.

Brodie had already cut the cord, so she ran to the nearby bed and wrapped the baby—a girl—up in as many blankets as she could to keep her warm, and the little angel simply watched her. She wasn't crying any longer, nor did she seem to be in any danger, and was a beautiful shade of rosy pink now that she was breathing steadily.

"It's a girl, Rosa. A beautiful, healthy girl," she cried as she plucked the baby up into her arms and turned back to them, but then let out a cry when she saw the limp, lifeless body strewn on the bed before her.

As if out of nowhere, a woman was then suddenly standing over Rosalie. She was dressed all in white and had a gentle smile as she reached her hand out and placed it over Rosalie's chest.

"A life for a life, as agreed," she hummed, and Wynter was about to ask what she meant, when a white wisp seemed to rise out of Rosalie's chest and into the white woman's palm. "Her soul called to me, Wynter. She made me a deal, and I never go back on my deals…" the woman added, and then she smiled wider as she took in Wynter's confused expression. "Jakob was right about you being perfect for this task. He told me you would succeed where others have failed, but I will offer you one piece of advice. Take good care of that child, she'll save your life one day…"

And with that, she was gone, along with Rosalie's life.

The room fell silent, but then Brodie's voice was breaking through the bubble she'd found herself in.

"Wynter!" he cried. "Is the baby okay?"

"Yeah," she answered, nodding her head. She felt dumbstruck. Like she'd just been to hell and back herself, and when she finally tore her eyes away from where the woman in white had been, she found Brodie, Archie and Rafferty all watching her with fraught looks on their faces. She was about to ask them why when she looked down at where Rosalie's body had been and found the birthing bed empty. "Where's she gone?"

"Wynter, it's been over an hour. You've been standing there staring at the wall clutching the baby the entire time," Archie answered, and she shook her head.

"No, I was just watching the woman who appeared. It was only a minute or so?"

"Who?" he replied with a frown.

"She was here to take Rosalie's soul, and she told me...she told me..."

"That's between you and her, Wynter. The White Lady doesn't appear to just anyone," Brodie answered with a scowl, and she was reminded of the revelation Jakob had once made. The Lady of Death, that was her name. She had tasked Jak with taking the life of Brodie's wife. And then, of course, she had just mentioned him too. He was in the world beyond and was still rooting for her. Still sending messages and assurances that she could succeed, even in the face of all the obstacles that'd been and were still to come.

"Shit, as in the grim reaper?" Archie croaked, and both she and Brodie nodded.

She stepped away and out of the room, and the others all followed, looking at her with sour, sad faces. It hadn't really dawned on her yet, but now it began to suddenly sink in.

Rosalie was dead. She had given her life for her child in the end and had to have seen it coming. Maybe she had known long before Wynter had arrived on the island, or maybe it was more recently, but either way, she was gone. Rosalie had made the ultimate sacrifice and Wynter knew she would always honour it.

She sat down and finally released her grip of the sleeping child in her arms, who stirred but thankfully stayed asleep. She then showed her off to the others and both she and Archie began to cry.

"She's called Rosa," Wynter told them through the tears, and each of her friends nodded in agreement.

"Perfect," Archie replied, and then he put his hands forward, hoping for a cuddle, which she readily gave him. Once he was sitting back in his seat, staring down at the little bundle in his arms, Brodie stood and went to the doorway, beckoning for Wynter to follow him.

He led her out into the small bedroom they had put together for baby Rosa and started rooting through the drawers to find her some clothes and a nappy.

"We need to get her washed and dressed. And I'll have Rafferty make up some formula," he said, acting all business when she could tell he was in pain.

Wynter went to the stubborn jinni and wrapped her arms around him, which he entertained for all of three seconds before shooing her away. "Damn woman, you're always making me soft," he grumbled, gathering the last bits they needed, but Wynter refused to let him be.

"It's not soft to mourn, Brodie. Let yourself feel, no one is going to judge you," she told him, and then walked back to the living area to where Archie and Rafferty were talking softly to the newborn, and the alpha was stood staring down at the group with his usual scowl.

She went to her guard and looked him in the eye. "I know you're reporting back, so tell him I'll be home soon, okay? And Rosa's coming with me," she told him.

"Us too," Brodie added from the doorway, and she turned to him in surprise. This was not what she'd expected at all, and not what she had wanted either. She had told herself all along that Marcus wasn't going to have two jinni's living beneath his roof and had been foolish enough to believe she could see it through. But now things had changed for them all.

She went to tell him no, but then saw the way he was looking down at Archie, who was beaming. This was for him. Archie wanted to stay with baby Rosa and Brodie was going along with it for his sake, but he needed to know the risks.

Wynter went to her maker and wrapped her arms around him again but was only doing it so she could whisper in his ear.

"Don't let him get you," she told him, and as she pulled back, she knew he understood.

That night, Rafferty laid Rosalie's body out on a pyre, and they all watched as he lit it. Each took turns saying goodbye to their lost friend, and Wynter kept the baby strapped to her in a sling as they watched her body turn to ash and break down along with the wood.

The goblin then gathered the ash and buried it beneath one of the tallest trees she'd seen on the island, and he whispered ancient words as he covered them over and slowly retreated to the rest of the group.

Dawn was just approaching and as Wynter looked around at her downtrodden friends, she knew it was time they left this island and the awful memories made here behind.

Brodie had the same idea and told Archie as he took his hand in his.

"There's nothing here for us anymore," the human agreed, and as soon as they all returned to the house, they set about packing up their belongings, as well as those of the baby and a selection of Rosalie's things.

It was only Rafferty who chose not to gather any of his belongings, choosing to help the others, and Wynter went to the huge goblin and put her hand on his arm.

"Aren't you coming?" she asked, not having thought otherwise for even a minute, and she didn't know why it hadn't occurred to her sooner. The island was more than just his home. It was part of him. His life's work was to take care of it along with any inhabitants, and Wynter suddenly felt sad. "We'll be back before too long, I promise," she told him, and meant it. He couldn't come to them, but that didn't mean they wouldn't go to him.

"I'm used to it, honestly," he replied, "but thank you. It means a lot to know you'll miss me."

"We all will," Archie added, and Brodie gave his trusty comrade a nod. They had to have said goodbye so many times over the years it was merely part of their routine, but for Wynter, it was tough. The last time she'd gone, it was under duress and whilst out cold, but now she would have to see him as they packed up and left the goblin behind. It was awful.

Once they were packed and ready, the small sombre group climbed aboard Brodie's small boat. In it, they then sailed to the mainland and Wynter sent for her car, which she had thankfully placed in the care of a private company, to ensure it wasn't stolen or vandalised after her leaving it unattended in a parking lot for months. She'd stayed far longer than expected but didn't care one little bit. Of course, the pull back to Marcus had been strong, and every day she had needed to fight the urge to ring him or at least text, but she had managed it. She hadn't succumbed to yet another spell he had put her under and was proud of the leaps she had made in her bid to become her own person again.

She knew she would see him again before nightfall and was actually apprehensive about it. What would he make of Rosa? Would he agree to care for her and become a father? She sure hoped so. The alpha had to have forewarned him via their psychic link, so her arriving with a baby along with a bunch of misfits couldn't come as any surprise to her husband, but that didn't mean he would be there to permit them all back with open arms. Knowing Marcus, it'd be far from a warm welcome, just for the hell of it.

Wynter drove them north. Away from the coast and past too many cities and towns to count. She kept going and going, not tiring once, and only stopped when Archie grumbled his bladder needed emptying. When they came to a stop, Rosa too began to cry, and Wynter grabbed the babe so that she could change her nappy and give her some milk.

By the time she was done, Archie was sauntering back with a cheeseburger in one hand and a milkshake in the other.

"Looks like Rosa wasn't the only one grumpy and in need of food," she teased, making him laugh.

"Do you know how long it's been since I ate junk?" he demanded. "I can't even tell you! Too bloody long. And you did'ne tell me this mansion of yours was in Scotland. I'm not far from home."

Wynter was still laughing as she put Rosa back in her car seat and secured her in, and when she looked down, she was met with a wide toothless smile that melted her heart even more.

"Damn, girl. You're gonna break some hearts," she cooed, thinking it crazy how she could be smiling already, and Rosa's little blue eyes seemed to twinkle back at her.

Brodie noticed too, and he leaned over to get a look at the gorgeous little one. Wynter caught him grinning down at her, having clearly melted too, and the usually so grumpy jinni simply shrugged.

Wynter didn't say another word. She just slid back into the driver's seat and started the car back up. They weren't far from the mansion now at all, perhaps an hour, and Wynter could feel herself growing more and more anxious about seeing Marcus. She'd had a lovely break and didn't want him confusing her all over again, but at the same time, she was confusing herself. The anxiety she felt was tinged with excitement.

No, it couldn't be. Definitely not. She told herself over and over, but also couldn't deny the twinges in her gut as she grew nearer to the vampire she knew would be desperate to have her naked beneath him as soon as was possible upon her return.

Damn him, and the way he had clawed his way into her good graces.

***

They were close. He could sense it, and as Marcus reached out to his alpha vampire with his mind, he could tell the atmosphere in the car had been tense. The male jinni was apprehensive, while the human was nervous, and quite rightly so. Every other human who came and went from his mansion was a Blood Slave, and Marcus had already decided he wanted to play on the boy's fears of becoming one too. He could use that fear to make Archie do as he commanded—and readily would.

Or perhaps he would make him a sort of familiar. Someone who followed his commands without question and did as they were told, and all on the promise that they would one day be given the prestigious honour of becoming a vampire themselves. The alpha—his puppet—had listened in on Archie's conversations with Brodie at Marcus's request, and he knew they were planning an immortal life for the boy, but not that of a jinni. They were hoping for something else. A way in which they could stay together permanently, rather than share one source of power and life. And Marcus knew he could readily offer them it, but at a price, of course. Someone else would have to sire him, but he could make it happen. Ensure the right introductions were made.

And then there was his darling wife. She was returning to him after all these lonely, desolate weeks, and Marcus was beyond ravenous for her. She'd done him proud, though. So perfectly had she served him, and all without knowing she was. And so, his bidding had been done. Wynter was returning and had remained in his good graces, a fact that surprised him given their history, and she was bringing with her an entire trove of companions.

But of course, there was more. Wynter had acted exactly as his Priestess had foreseen she would and was now returning with the prize he was more than willing to let her believe was hers—the baby. Yes, having a second jinni was going to be a wonderful addition to his ever-growing foray of creatures working for him, but to nurture and groom a were-child? That was sheer gold dust.

Wolves kept to themselves and never, ever let their offspring fall into the hands of other creatures. Their young always started out as shifters and matured into werewolves only if led on the right path, and Marcus was going to see to it that Rosa became one of the strongest wolves to ever live. And she would be his to command.

Of course, shifter children could transform into anyone they wanted, even adults, and so with Rosa under his wing in whichever way she went, Marcus knew he would be unstoppable. All he had to do was make sure she made it through puberty without turning feral, but he would tackle that when the time came. For now, he would simply love and nurture her like she was his own, and the vampire looked forward to reaping the benefits later.

As soon as Wynter had driven inside the magical circle around the huge house, Marcus was on his feet and pacing his office. He felt like a tiger in a cage, eagerly awaiting the arrival of his next meal, and found himself staring at the camera feeds on his computer as the group arrived and began unloading. He watched as they made quick work of bringing in their bags and all the bits that came with the baby, and before he knew it, they were crossing the threshold and Wynter was showing the others inside with a timid smile.

Marcus wanted to rush out there and go to her, but he forced himself to hold back. She could wait just a couple more minutes. He didn't want to appear too eager, after all.

NINETEEN

Wynter's nerves were on fire as she stood and ushered the rest of their group inside, but she did her best to hide them as she gave the alpha the nod to go and fetch his master. She knew full well Marcus was aware they'd arrived, but he was busy playing it cool, no doubt. Too cool to come rushing out to greet them, or so it appeared.

She looked around and was disappointed to find the humans all gone. The noise and the busyness had been comforting before, but now the house was deathly quiet, and she had to wonder if there was anyone there at all. Even baby Rosa was strapped across her torso in her sling and had fallen back asleep, so she was adding to the quietness.

"Seriously? This is where you and Marcus live?" Archie asked, breaking the silence, and she was glad he did.

"Yep, plus a few choice others, of course, which now includes you," she answered, and Archie nodded, as if he'd forgotten.

"We'd like a room towards the back though, perhaps in the old servants' quarters?" Brodie asked, and while Wynter tried not to make a face, she forced herself to nod. There was no way she wanted to go back down there. She'd simply give them the go ahead and walk away.

"That can be arranged," she promised, but then Archie interjected, and she was beyond pleased that he did.

"Nah, I want one of the top rooms. After living in a cave for a year, we need a view."

Brodie grumbled, but he seemed ready and willing to give his beau whatever he wanted and shrugged.

"I'll show you the way," Wynter told them, and then shuddered when she felt an icy wave wash over her from across the huge hallway.

She turned to find Marcus standing watch over them all at the top of the first staircase, looking perfect as ever in his crisp grey suit and blue tie. He seemed utterly at ease with what he'd found, and yet was giving her one of his dangerous looks that meant he was willing to play whatever game she dared try. But today wasn't about games. It was about making things right and finding a way to instigate a new chapter in all their lives.

"Permit me," he called down to the others, who then turned and looked up at their vampire host in surprise. Marcus looked utterly impressed with himself, and Wynter watched as he descended the stairs with hardly a sound. "Welcome to our home. I trust you will both be very comfortable here."

"Forgo the formalities, Marcus," Brodie growled, and his unmasked hatred surprised Wynter. She had expected him to play nicely, when instead he'd gone straight on the offense.

"Nice to see you too, Brodie," her husband answered, and then fixed his icy blue stare on the human beside him. "And what do we have here?" he asked, taking a deep inhale of Archie's scent.

"Not supper, I hope," the human replied, always the jokester, and Marcus seemed to enjoy his jovial approach to breaking the tension. He stepped back and eyed Archie up and down with a smile, and Wynter found she was grinning along with them, until a second later when Marcus had her in his sights. She was soon peering up into his immense blue eyes and as their gazes connected, she felt as if everything within her shifted. Mara's influence or not, she gravitated towards him, and it was as if she was finally whole in his presence. No longer disjointed or unsure of anything, but completely driven towards one path and one goal for her future—and he was it.

Damn him for making her care so much. Their souls were truly united once again, and it was like a breath of fresh air, much like the two halves of the proverbial whole coming together at last.

"Welcome home, my sweet," he whispered before leaning in for a soft kiss, and despite their audience, it strangely didn't occur to Wynter to stop him.

After he pulled away, leaving her swooning, Marcus then took her hand and led the way. He took the group upstairs in silence and stopped outside what she knew was the largest of all their guest rooms. He was evidently being nice for a change.

Marcus pushed the handle and let the door swing open to reveal the huge space, complete with its high ceilings and ornate carvings, but which had been decorated with modern colours and textures. The room also had a huge four-poster bed in the centre made of black oak. "Archie, I trust this will suit?" he asked, and they watched as their guest stepped inside and took it all in with an open mouth. "This room has its own bathroom and closet, plus an incredible view…" Marcus continued, and Archie followed his cue and looked out at the astonishing scenery all around their magnificent home.

"It's perfect. Thank you," he answered.

"Excellent," Marcus replied with a smile, and then he turned to Brodie and Wynter's stomach dropped when she realised what he was about to do.

"And you requested a room in the servants' quarters, did you not?" he asked, putting him on the spot when she was sure he knew damn well they intended on sharing. Marcus also had to know this was all new to Brodie, and that he wasn't comfortable being so open about his relationship with Archie. Being together on that island had to have been one thing, but to be out and proud? She had the feeling he wasn't there yet.

In a surprise move, it was Archie who stepped forward and answered for the stunned jinni, and he looked thoroughly unimpressed by Marcus and his games.

"He'll be fine here with me," he demanded, and didn't seem to notice as her vampire husband drew in a deep breath, savouring his animosity. But she noticed. She always did, especially when it came to those she cared about, and Wynter felt the need to remind them all the terms she intended to lay out for their future together. However, she wouldn't do it in front of the others. Instead, she decided to distract them all by unwrapping the sling and unveiling the little bundle she had brought back with her.

"Marcus, this is Rosa," she told him, and could sense the tension in the room dissipate in an instant with the reminder of their precious cargo. Even Marcus thawed, and she watched him look the baby over with a gentle smile. He didn't say a word but leaned down to place a kiss against Rosa's forehead, and Wynter's heart leapt. He was so gentle it made her want to weep, and when his eyes locked with hers again, she saw warmth in them for the first time in what felt like forever.

"Please excuse us, gentlemen," he then told the others, and whisked Wynter away before she could add anything or direct her friends more.

Still clutching Rosa to her, she followed Marcus upstairs to where their bedroom dominated the top floor of the mansion and let out a cry when she saw that he'd had some work done while she was gone.

"You built her a nursery?" she cried, looking around at the new corner bedroom that was equipped with everything a newborn might need.

Marcus grinned as he took Rosa from her and hugged the baby to his chest, and Wynter's heart felt like it was going to burst at seeing him this way. "Marcus, does this mean…"

"You're going to make a wonderful mother, Wynter," he answered, and then laughed. "While I will strive to become as good of a father as I can."

"I'll settle for adequate," she joked, watching as he placed Rosa down into her new crib and then rocked it back and forth to soothe her.

Once she was back off to sleep, he was on his feet and standing over Wynter in a heartbeat, and she curled her body against his, feeling drawn to him. It was like they were starting over somehow, and despite all the wrongdoings and the games, she couldn't deny still wanting him.

"You seem different," Marcus whispered against her lips, and she smiled.

"I am. I went to that island to learn and grow and started by putting

Mara back in her box. Did you know what she was up to?" she asked and was surprised when he nodded. "And you didn't stop her?"

"Why would I? She was helping bring us together, and thanks to her, you've reunited Jack with his family. That was more important than me or Marcella putting a stop to the influx of power growing within you. Plus, I trusted you would get there in your own time. My little fighter," Marcus replied, and she knew he was goading her, but didn't take the bait.

"Thanks to Brodie I found the strength I needed, but in doing so I also had to own up to some things," she told him, "like how I feel about you…"

Marcus lifted Wynter off her feet and placed her down on the bed, where he joined her and nestled himself between her thighs, his eyes roving over her face as he pressed their still clothed bodies together.

"And?" he asked when she didn't elaborate.

"I thought it was her influence making me love you. I always felt so sure of it until her voice went quiet and I was left with my own. And…I found myself missing you. I lost count of how many times I picked up the phone with the intention of calling."

"I felt the same, my sweet. I wrote to you every day and then burned the letter afterwards because I was ashamed to miss you so damn much," he admitted, and the revelation only made Wynter burn harder for him. "I was so lost without you I couldn't stand the noise of all the humans here, so I sent most of them away."

"I noticed," she joked, but Marcus shook his head solemnly.

"I almost drank dry those who remained. It was Marcella who had to stop me before I got in even more trouble with the Committee."

He began peeling away at her clothes, turning them to smoke as they left her body, and soon she was tearing his away too, feeling desperate to reconnect.

When he entered her, the world seemed to fall away and all Wynter could see was him. Marcus was everything, and she peered up at him in awe as he made love to her. "I love you," he whispered in her ear, and Wynter felt her body sing with the notion of it. She'd wanted this her entire life, to be loved so powerfully that she was everything to the man behind those words, and now that she had it, she realised just how important those words were.

Marcus had given her everything in his quest to make her his and had stripped her life bare in the process of rebuilding it. She would hate that part of their history forever, but that didn't stop things from having changed this past year.

"I…I love you too," she whimpered, her voice little more than a whisper, but he heard, and Wynter was rewarded with the most genuine smile she thought she'd ever seen on his darkly handsome face.

The next morning, as Rosa roused and began grumbling for her feed, Wynter watched with a smile as Marcus gathered her up out of her crib and brought her to bed with them. He was still cooing at her with a soft smile when the door to their bedroom opened and the alpha walked in, a bottle of formula in his hands at the ready.

He handed it to Wynter, but she passed it over to her husband, and then showed him how to feed the babe in his arms, who readily sucked down her breakfast and then fell back into a food-induced doze.

"She's such a gentle baby," Marcus said as he watched her, and Wynter nodded.

"And alert. It's like she knows exactly what's going on already."

"Maybe she does," he mused, and Wynter simply shrugged. She then showed him how to change and dress her, and together the three of them headed downstairs to see how Archie and Brodie were settling in.

They found them in the kitchen, where Archie had found the stash of human food and was enjoying some breakfast, and he took one look at hers and Marcus's formal wear and laughed.

"Not even nine-am and the ball gowns are out?" he teased, but she paid him no mind. Wynter simply handed baby Rosa to Brodie so he could have a cuddle, and then she turned back to find Marcus staring at Archie with a serious, intense look on his face. At first, she panicked, thinking he was going to face the consequences for speaking to them both so casually, but then Marcus smiled.

"Would you like to come and work for me, Archie?" he asked, taking them all by surprise, and Wynter wasn't the least bit shocked when Brodie jumped to his feet and start spewing profanities at the vampire he clearly still detested. And she couldn't blame him, either. It had taken a lot for her to move on without wanting to murder Marcus every time he gave her that sly smile of his, whereas for Brodie he was on day two and was understandably at odds with their host.

Marcus simply continued to smile, clearly relishing in her maker's reaction. "Relax, jinni. I don't mean as a Blood Slave. I mean, as an assistant of sorts. A familiar."

Wynter had heard the term before in the movies and such and didn't know if it had the same meaning she presumed or not, but she knew one thing for sure. If Archie signed on that fateful dotted line, he would belong to Marcus entirely. She couldn't allow that. Not after everything she'd seen and lived through as one of those elite few who were close to the powerful vampire.

"Let's not discuss it now, surely? Let him think it over and figure out the terms," she tried, and was met with nothing but stony silence from them all.

Marcus then drew in a deep breath and smiled across at their human guest.

"You don't hide your resentment very well, Archie. I can taste it from here. Let me guess, you despise me for what I did to the assassin? He was your friend," he surmised, and then approached at superhuman speed before pinning Archie to the refrigerator door. Marcus lifted his prey's hands and inspected the cuts to his palms. Cuts from where he had bled for Jakob. "You didn't let him feed from the vein. Good choice. Things get messy very quickly that way. And if you chose to serve me, I would protect you from any other vampire who might want a sip of this precious blood."

"He doesn't need your protection, Marcus," Brodie seethed from his spot a few feet away. "I'll make sure he's safe."

"I know…I can smell your stench all over the poor boy. But I'm willing to overlook it if you serve me. To fall for a jinni is a foolish thing indeed, Archie. He will need a host and when that time comes, you'll of course offer yourself to him, and will pay the ultimate price for doing so. But I can offer you something more," Marcus carried on, and Wynter could see for herself how none of this seemed new to Archie. He'd clearly been thinking about this himself and had perhaps been plotting ways in which he and Brodie could make this work using another way.

And Marcus had to know. He was playing on his fears in an attempt to lure him in, and so she stepped out of Brodie's way so that the jinni could intervene on Archie's behalf. If something was going to be done about their predicament, then it would be thought out and planned. Not rushed or forced. They had time yet.

Her maker passed Rosa to her and then wrenched Marcus away and lifted him off the ground by his neck, and at first Wynter hung back, thinking he deserved it, but then she found herself moving forward on instinct. Her husband was doing nothing to stop Brodie, and then she found herself reaching up with one hand and wrapping it around his neck, mirroring him.

"Let's not do this," she growled.

"Don't let Mara control you, Wynter," he tried, but still dropped Marcus and stepped away, which in turn made her release her grip on him. She stared at them all and shook her head. It wasn't Mara who had made her move, but some other instinctual need to protect her husband.

Something more powerful than any gift his priestess could offer her.

"He's the other half of my soul, Brodie. You can't hurt him without hurting me. We've played this game before with disastrous consequences, remember?" she reminded him, and then stormed away, clutching Rosa to her as she headed for the door and out into the cool morning sunshine.

She needed some space from them all, and so took her daughter for a walk around the grounds, muttering the entire time about how much of a pain in the arse they all were—especially the men.

TWENTY

Wynter ended up taking baby Rosa on a long walk that took a good couple of hours, and by the time she returned to the house was feeling much calmer than when she left it. On the way in, she came to a stop below the tree in which she had lost herself for days. It'd taken a lot for her to come away from that as strong as she'd felt, and she vowed to herself that she wouldn't ever let herself feel so lost again.

"I'm going to stay calm, for you," she told the tiny babe in her arms, who was looking up into the branches of the huge oak with awe. "Wanna see?" she then cooed and began climbing the branches to the spot she'd laid in before. At first, it was wonderful looking out at the lands all around them, but then a vision began creeping in around the edges of Wynter's conscious thought. Much like when she had touched items before, she was seeing a memory that had been ingrained in the ancient wood. And a recent one.

Jack had been tortured in this tree. Her tree. Marcus had let him suffer and had offered the poor man no mercy, not even when he had screamed in agony. And all for a crime he hadn't even committed. "Yes," she told Rosa again, and herself. "We're going to stay calm and focussed. We've got an entire household in there who needs us to take charge and stop them from killing each other…"

"Easier said than done," someone answered, and Wynter looked down to find Marcella standing beneath the tree with two babies in her arms—her twins. "But I'll help."

Given their history, Wynter's first instinct was not to trust Marcella, but then she remembered everything that the witch had done for her these past few months. Everything she had given her. The heart she shared with Marcella's daughter fluttered, and she nodded.

Wynter smiled and climbed down to greet her, and she marvelled at how well the Priestess looked. She'd given birth in secret just days before and yet looked radiant. It was the first time Wynter had seen her since their return home, and the first time she had laid eyes on the twins, and so she glided down to greet her, grinning from ear to ear. The two newest additions to their household were fast asleep in their mother's arms, and Wynter ran her hand over each of their heads. The tiny witches had bright red hair like their mother, already growing in abundance, and seemed utterly at ease with the world.

"What are their names?" she asked, and Marcella smiled.

"Well, you know the tradition," she reminded her, and Wynter nodded. Each witch in their powerful line had Marcus's name in theirs, and the two new arrivals would be no exception. "Marlee and Marceline."

"Beautiful," she replied with a warm and genuine smile, and then frowned. "You're going to help me keep everyone here safe?" Wynter added, thinking back to the reason Marcella had apparently come to find her in the first place.

"Of course. It's what family does…"

"Where do we start?" she asked.

"By giving him an army," the Priestess answered cryptically, and Wynter went to answer that Marcus already had one. He had entire hordes of soldier vampires that she had taken command of for him. And that was when Marcella's eyes dropped to the three babies they were holding between them. She didn't need to say another word.

"No," Wynter whispered.

"Yes," Marcella countered, turning serious. "I've seen them all grown up. These girls of ours will be loyal to their master and beyond powerful. They will become the first in his legion, his army of unique and formidable progeny, and he will never be thwarted again. He will reign supreme with you at his side and his family at his back. It will be beautiful, my love."

"And the alternative?" Wynter tried, but Marcella shook her head.

"There isn't one. You know my visions are true, but can be brutally so, and there is no future for our children other than in his keep, and his command. They can never leave him, just like you cannot. Like Rosa, my children now bear his name and were born to serve his cause. There is no other way. You need to know this now and remember it every time you decide to defy him. Because it's not a decision you make solely for yourself, but for them too," she warned, and an icy shudder went down Wynter's spine. She knew all too well what that meant, and how she could not let it happen. They couldn't lose another child, not after Mara's sacrifice, and she couldn't let another soul die because of her selfishness.

It would hurt her to follow him without question, but at the same time, Wynter knew it was already too late for second-guessing the decisions she had made and the influence she'd exerted over the others. She had returned to Marcus willingly and had brought with her a trio of new additions to her husband's pack of unsuspecting comrades. She was already doing what he wanted, already stopping with her own defiance because she feared the repercussions for those same people. He had already won her over.

And now, she would have to keep it that way, because the alternative didn't even bear thinking about.

***

Marcus watched as Wynter walked back into the house, and then he intercepted Marcella before she could do the same.

"Did you do it?" he asked, and his priestess nodded.

"Yes, my lord," she replied with a soft smile. "I gave her what you asked. She will not defy you again."

"Good," he answered, and then stroked her twins' foreheads with his fingertips. "How did you do it?"

"I lied," she replied with a frown. "I told her there was only one vision for both her own future, and the future of the next generations being born into this family of yours. She'd do anything to save the life of her new adopted child, and I think she feels the same about these two," Marcella added, and looked down at her babies and smiled.

Marcus knew then and there that he'd been right. Wynter was coming around. She was finally bending to his will, and when she did, she was going to realise just how much they were capable of together. Marcella had indeed seen a vision of their future, but of course it wasn't just about the children they were bringing into their world, but also about the two figureheads who were to run his empire—him and Wynter. They were going to conquer the world, and there would be no one who could stop them.

It was going to be magnificent.

The end of book four in the Blood Slave series...

BLOOD SLAVE

The Complete series

#5 Carnival of Souls

By

Eden Wildblood

ONE

The first wedding anniversary for any couple ought to have been something for both parties to want to celebrate, but as hers approached, Wynter couldn't help but feel sad. She had lost so much that day, and as her memories of Jakob and the love she had borne him came creeping back into her usually so carefully locked inner core, she wanted to weep. They had been torn apart, literally, by the vampire who had then forced her to be his, and now he wanted her to commemorate the day?

"Let's just stay home. I don't want to leave Rosa," she tried, but like in all things, Marcus Cole was resolute. She had learned the hard way how he always got what he wanted, and even though that had evidently appeared to be her, he sure wasn't smitten enough to let his wife bat her lashes and get her way. If anything, the less she fought, the more likely he was to yield, but even after all this time, Wynter still didn't have him sussed. There was only one time she had gotten what she wanted—when she'd turned up with a motherless child and told him in no uncertain terms that it was theirs. And, of course, she now knew why. He had welcomed baby Rosa into their home and openly adored the young child, and it wasn't because Wynter had asked him to.

Marcella, his priestess, had warned her of Marcus and his intentions for the future of their extended family. He was growing it with a purpose, and now had two Jinn beneath his roof as well as a powerful witch and her twin babies, plus Rosa who was going to become something else entirely. She was the offspring of a human and a werewolf and was inevitably going to follow in her father's footsteps. The bloodline was too strong, so she would one day turn lycan herself. It was inescapable without some sort of miracle.

Plus, of course, there was Marcus's vampire army who were now under her command, yet undoubtedly still at his mercy. But he apparently also had plans that didn't seem to include the hordes of soulless vampires she now had a strange maternal connection with. Plans that involved the children in his keep, rather than the forces by his side. Marcella's words regarding his brood still echoed through Wynter's mind, and she knew without a doubt that she was a big a part of it all as well as her darling husband. Without her, his world would crumble, and if he was ever going down, she knew he would take them all with him. That was not allowed to happen. Wynter had been forced to accept her fate, and now it appeared she was responsible for the next generations' survival too.

Fucking vampires. Why had she ever said yes to that job? She knew why. Like now, she had always been too weak to say no. Always ended up getting herself into trouble rather than be an adult and make the hard choice even if it was also the right one.

"My sweet," Marcus simply said, his voice hard and low. A shudder went through her when she made eye contact with his incredible icy blues, and she shot cold, and then hot as the heart beating within her fluttered hard because of his intense scrutiny. As always, she was torn thanks to the heart that always had two ideas on how to proceed at any given time. Torn between wanting to tell him where to go and wanting to fall at his feet and offer her unending service to whatever his cause may be. The witch Mara was to thank for the latter, but at the same time, she knew now how it wasn't all her doing. Wynter's soul was merged with that of the vampire standing before her, so of course she wanted to give him everything he desired. Against all odds, and her better judgement, she loved him. The swine.

He wasn't going to budge on this, and so Wynter nodded in acceptance of his offer to take her away for the night. And actually, she figured it'd probably be quite nice to get a break from the mansion for a short while. Life with Rosa and the others was wonderful, but even in a huge house they could get on top of each other, and Wynter still felt as if Archie and Brodie were judging her. She was sure they talked behind her back about how weak she was and how she'd let Marcus have his way so readily and had caught the sideways glances they each often gave her whenever she showed any type of affection to her husband in their presence. They hadn't said anything in a long while to warrant it, but Wynter still had the feeling the pair thought she had let them down, and it was a tough one to shake because ultimately, she felt it too.

"Just a couple of days?" she double-checked, peering down at the little angel in her arms. Rosa was blossoming from a newborn into an alert and interesting little child and was beautiful with her bright eyes and the blonde ringlets that were beginning to grow at the back of her head. She didn't want to miss a moment of her development.

"She won't even have the chance to miss us," he promised, and Wynter looked up to find a gentle smile on Marcus's face. He was looking down at Rosa too and, as always when it came to her, he seemed to soften. Wynter had never experienced much of his softer side, if he even had one, and once again thought how strange it was that the ancient vampire had taken to the newborn so quickly.

"Okay," she replied, and then stood and headed for the doorway. Outside in the hall, she went straight down the stairs to Brodie and Archie's room. She found the door ajar and crept inside and was glad to find just her fellow Jinni there. Archie was still the more judgemental of the pair, and it was a relief not to have to explain to him where she was going and why.

The thought made Wynter laugh to herself. Out of all the creatures that lived in this huge mansion, after her vampire husband, it was the human who intimidated her the most. He truly was domineering, and not only with his boyfriend, but with them all.

"Hey, what's up?" Brodie asked, taking Rosa from her without question.

"Nothing, it's just that Marcus has asked me to join him on his business trip, so I wondered if you could look after the baby?" she answered, telling a white lie she knew Brodie could see right through. He didn't call her out on it, though. The two of them shared a bond no one could ever break, and because of that, Brodie knew her inside and out, and vice versa. He knew she was embarrassed about this stuff, and so let her be.

"Sure," he simply answered, "Rosa's welcome to stay with her uncles anytime."

"You're the best," she replied before forcing herself away. But Wynter only made it as far as the doorway before she turned back with a frown. "We won't be gone long. Two days max."

"And we'll miss you, but we'll be fine," he pressed, and then looked down at the babe in his arms. "She'll be fine."

"I know," Wynter answered, and then forced herself away. There was no packing she needed to do, and of course Marcus had known it, so he was waiting for her at the top of the stairs leading down again to the ground floor.

"Come," he commanded, and just like before, something stirred within her. Mara's heart adored the vampire standing before her and the magic power they shared did very little to close the void, bridging their combined consciousness. Wynter was in control now and forever, or so she had been assured, but as always there remained a burning desire to obey him. To give Marcus everything he demanded of her, and then some.

She faltered for the slightest second, thinking she might go and offer Rosa one last hug before leaving, and the vampire before her was on her like a viper who had been poised ready to attack his prey. Marcus was beside his wife in a second, and when he had her in his grasp, she sensed his impending rage. His skin was icy cold, as were his blue eyes, and she peered up into his face without faltering. She was a jinni who could take him down in a fight without question, but there would be the worst of prices to pay for doing so. Marcus never lost. Never let anyone stop him from having his way, and Wynter once again backed down.

"Let's go," she whispered against his cool skin, and peered up into his face resolutely. "Before I change my mind…" Wynter added, and then gave him a playful smile so that Marcus didn't think she was being serious, even if she was just a little.

She then turned into her misty form and evaded his grip, before returning to her whole state a few feet away. "Catch me if you can," she teased, and then took off down the stairs like a cloud speeding through the breeze. She was at the front door in half a second and took her human shape right before going through it, but he was still faster than her. Somehow, Marcus had made it outside before she could transform and make it across the magical threshold, which would've stopped her if she were still in her misty form.

"After you, my sweet," he replied, opening the car door for her, and Wynter climbed inside what she knew was one of the vampire's most expensive and fully armoured vehicles. It didn't matter how powerful he was. Marcus had enemies, and she didn't need to ask to know he wanted to keep as much distance between him and them as possible. Her too. She could see it in his eyes.

The car in front held his handful of top soldiers, but in their vehicle and with his back to them sat his assistant Bryn. It appeared Marcus had promoted another of his Blood Slaves. This time to driver. Last she'd checked, he hadn't had a dedicated chauffeur, and yet she could sense the guy was warded with magic. Much like those who ran his clubs and had blood that was magically poisonous to vampires in a bid to keep them safe from harm, the man in the front seat was utterly off limits to all who might wish to feast on him. And Wynter was glad. At least he couldn't be turned against Marcus using the effects of a bite, and also that no one could ground them by incapacitating his driver.

"Mr Cole," Bryn welcomed his boss with a smile, before dropping it, along with his courteous tone of voice, "Mrs Cole."

She knew why he still hated her. She'd made him feel small in front of all the others back when Marcus had summoned his Blood Slaves to the mansion. Plus, there was the fact that he was clearly in love with his dastardly boss. He wasn't the first, though, and definitely wouldn't be the last. She pitied him. Which, of course, Bryn knew.

Wynter didn't respond. She simply watched out the window as the small convoy drove away and was grateful when Marcus took out his laptop and got to work during their long drive south to the London club.

It took hours, but she didn't care. She zoned out and left him to his work, but the entire time, she had this increasing sense of foreboding. Something was going to happen, she could tell, but her senses were unusually off and Wynter was sure it was Marcus's doing. Even though he took no notice of her and focussed solely on his workload and the assistant he was keeping on his toes in the front seat, her husband kept his hand on her thigh for the full duration of their drive. At first, it irked her, but then after a while she took a strange sort of comfort from his hold. The small show of dominance over her that proved to all who dared to look that she was his. That he owned her.

Ordinarily she would've hated it, but not today. All apprehension aside, Wynter knew she was his and couldn't bear the thought of him taking his hand away. She might loathe him at times but hated the notion of ever being cast aside even more.

By the time they eventually pulled up outside the most prestigious of all Marcus's clubs, Wynter was desperate for some attention, and when he then denied her, it was with a grin that told her he knew exactly what she was feeling. The torment was exquisite and as they made their way inside the unnamed nightclub that held no pretence of being a real human haunt, Marcus held her closer still, clearly hoping to heighten her desire even more. He was a fiend, through and through, but she couldn't deny she loved it.

Wynter played him at his own game, and when he started talking 'shop' the moment they'd walked in the door, she sauntered away in the direction of the loud music playing within.

"Find me when you're done working," she whispered, but knew he could hear her clearly thanks to his keen vampire senses and didn't look back when the doormen opened the blackened entrance up and welcomed her inside, after a nod from their master, of course.

She couldn't deny feeling right at home there on the club floor. It was dark and loud, and there wasn't a human in sight who wasn't being fed from, but this was still a club. An establishment servicing the needs of its patrons, and for many, it was so that they could entertain themselves without having to keep up the old facade of being human.

She joined the foray of creatures on the dance floor and let her body feel the music blasting from all around her. Wynter lost herself to it and found a smile creeping onto her face. It'd been so long since she'd danced. So long since she had let herself go.

Damn, it felt good to be free again. Free from the onlookers at the mansion who seemed to want things from her she couldn't fathom. Free from the torture of knowing she had failed those she had fought so hard to keep living. All that was left was bliss, and when she opened her eyes and looked around, Wynter felt truly at home.

She soon realised why.

Marcus was standing not twenty feet away and as their eyes locked on one another's, the entire world seemed to fall away. He was ignoring the men and women talking at him and seemed to be watching her rather than continue his work. Wynter smiled and danced on, and in the blink of an eye, Marcus was directly in her line of sight yet again. His blue eyes were shining brightly and when she blinked and turned, he was there again and again.

Eventually, she came to a stop and glared back at him. How was he doing this? How did he seem to be everywhere at once? It had to be some sort of trick. Wynter moved forward, and Marcus mirrored her, and when they reached each other, he surprised her by being the one to speak first.

"What are you doing to me?" he asked, and she was so shocked she couldn't answer. Wynter simply shook her head and stared up into his face in a strange kind of awe. She wasn't doing anything. It was him. Wasn't it? She was still deliberating when Marcus then did the unthinkable. He began to dance with her.

He took her hand and then started to move, and it was so out of character she felt self-conscious at first. Wynter took in a deep, steadying breath. She tasted blood in the air but didn't focus on that. There was something else, something primal. Him. His scent was heightened, as if he might be nervous, but Marcus didn't show it for a second. Wynter let everything go as she got into the swing of it. She even let her husband take the lead as he moved them into the centre of the strange crowd.

Marcus's moves were old-fashioned and far from her usual style, but she liked it. Liked being there with him. And with every turn she made, she peered back into his eyes, watching them grow steadily brighter. They were shining more than ever, and as the two of them continued to dance, Wynter felt something start to shift within her again. But this time, it wasn't Mara's doing. It had nothing to do with magic, but with fate. She hadn't thought it possible before, but it was like they were somehow merging more. As if their souls were forging an even stronger bond, and when she finally came to a stop in his arms, Wynter was met with the craziest of notions. She was married to the most powerful man on Earth. And the most vigilant. He would never be thwarted. Even Marcella had told her so, and he would never die. And there she was, at his side. That made her the most powerful woman in the world, surely?

It was time she truly stopped fighting him. That she began to embrace his darkness rather than run from it. To allow herself to be his true equal and reap the benefits of his reign, rather than resist.

As Wynter began to succumb to her soul and its desperation to merge with his even more, she felt a wave of strength pass through her, and smiled up at her husband as they continued to dance. But then, the same wave seemed to continue out and through the crowds all around them, and suddenly those close by moved in tighter, and those next to them closed the gaps. Before they knew it, everyone was tightly packed onto the dance floor, and even as the vampires continued to feed on the human slaves they'd brought with them, there was nothing but calm. She could sense it and yet knew it was thanks to her. Wynter was relaxed and at ease, and she was somehow influencing those around them to be the same, no matter what was happening to them.

"What is this?" she whimpered, peering up into Marcus's eyes, and he smiled.

"Magic, but all of your own, my sweet," he answered, and then parted the crowd with ease and led her away.

He didn't stop until they were alone in his office, where he showered her with forceful kisses and tore away her clothes. "I always knew you were the one, Wynter. The one who would become powerful enough to have everyone around you at your mercy," he growled, and then cried out as he ditched his own clothes and finally took her. "You're the key, my sweet. I always knew it…"

And she did too. Wynter had been warned so many times, and now it was clearer than ever before. They were going to make an unstoppable duo, and for the first time, she wasn't scared to revel in that knowledge. A tide had turned, and she wasn't too terrified of both him and his love to accept it.

TWO

He'd done it. Her master had ended the internal battle his wife had struggled with, and the way Marcella knew was through her visions of the future. She had been plagued with various outcomes lately, both excellent and awful, but now the future was clear. There was one path. She couldn't see the small steps they would each have to take to get there, but she could see the end result. One ruler who presided overall. A king of kings. A master for not only the supernatural, but also for the entire world. Humans would cower before him. Vampires would bow and do as he commanded. The other creatures were his minions, too, and none were strong enough to stop him.

And by his side was the other half of his soul. His immortal bride still needed a little more convincing, but she had made huge strides in just the last few days, and so Marcella knew what she had to do next. She needed to give her one final gift.

She left her husband and children to sleep and tiptoed across the hallway to where Brodie and Archie's room lay. The human of the duo was out for his morning run and Brodie was in charge of little Rosa, which was perfect. It wasn't Archie she needed to talk with, not yet, at least.

Marcella tapped on the door and then let herself inside, and she found the jinni standing vigil over the baby's bedside. He looked at her in surprise at first and then sneered.

"Let me guess, they're staying longer?" he presumed, and Marcella forced herself to smile across at him sweetly. She still wasn't all that keen on Brodie and would rather rip his heart out and force him back into the blackness of his misty form than offer him eternity in his human likeness, but the needs of the many outweighed her personal views about him. So, she forced away the urge she had to shut him up.

"Quite the contrary, Brodie," she replied. "Mr Cole and his wife will return shortly. I only came to see you because I had a vision of your future and wanted to share it with you."

"Oh, and since you're here in person, I bet it wasn't good?" he replied, and she shook her head.

"Always so dismissive—typical jinni. I see two options for you. One path leads to isolation and fear, while the other will secure your place in this household and give you the power to live forever in your human form. But the path you take is yours to decide upon, and yours alone."

"And Archie?" he demanded, clearly seething.

Marcella waited a beat before she answered and was pleased when she could see just how much that moment of silence had affected the jinni standing before her. He seemed desperate to know, and so Marcella gave him the answer she knew he wouldn't like.

"He will stand by Wynter's side and watch you leave..."

"Shit!" he spat, and the witch quickly intercepted his next train of thought.

"But you have another option," she promised, and stepped closer. "I can initiate you both into this family and ensure your safety."

"And if we accept, what will it entail?" Brodie asked and was right to believe there had to be a caveat.

"Archie must become a vampire. I offer this gift to him, but also to you, because this way you will have a host strong enough to give you everything you'll ever need to remain whole," she answered, and could tell that was what he wanted. She also wondered if perhaps the two of them had discussed the possibility already. "Without it, there is no hope for you, jinni."

The door then opened behind her and in walked the human in question. He was dripping with sweat and looked good, and Marcella caught herself watching him a little too intently. He truly was a sight though, and she wasn't ashamed to admit she felt a stirring in her belly as she watched him. It was no wonder the jinni was so smitten. "Come to me when you're ready," she told him, and while he was clearly confused, Archie didn't ask her what she meant. It was obvious that Brodie was going to fill him in on her behalf, and so she left them to talk it over.

***

"What did she mean by that?" Archie asked his wide-eyed beau, and Brodie quickly told him what Marcella had offered.

"We have to think about it. Figure out what her game is," he said, but Archie shook his head.

"This is exactly what we wanted, Brodie. We were hoping this offer would someday be on the table, and now that she's come and delivered it, you wanna wait? Nah, we need to tell her yes before she changes her mind!" he demanded, and Brodie suddenly grabbed him by the shoulders like he was trying to shake some sense into him.

Archie responded by pushing him away, and, as usual, Brodie didn't back down. It didn't matter the strength Archie had built up since working out more regularly; he was no match for the jinni, but he gave it his best shot, like always. The two of them squared up to one another. However, the problem with their tussles was that they always ended in bed, and so Archie forced himself away. He was still panting when Brodie closed the gap again, and this time, offered him a gentle kiss.

"Don't you see?" Brodie then whispered, "this is what she wants, which is why we need to question it. Nothing is free, especially in Marcus's world."

"I don't care," Archie replied, staring back into the jinni's incredible green eyes. "The risks are worth the reward."

Brodie then backed off, and while Archie hated seeing him admit defeat, he was glad. This was the right path for them both. He could feel it.

***

Marcella listened in on their conversation from outside and smiled to herself. Everything was falling into place perfectly, and she was glad. At last, the future was looking more certain, and she knew her master would be pleased with her efforts. After all, her number-one job was to ensure the longevity of his reign. She was his Priestess, but also the witch responsible for furthering the bloodline tasked with remaining so, and she had finally done that. She had given him not one, but two witches next in line who would serve him without question. Just like she and all the witches who had come before her, the twins were his to command, but they would also learn when to take matters into their own hands as they saw fit. And now was that time.

In all the visions she had seen and the various futures that lay ahead, there was one dominant theme. Wynter. Everything relied on her. In the visions where Marcus failed, it was purely because she had left him or pushed him away, and then there was the catastrophic vision in which Wynter had died, taking him with her. The stories were true, after all, and her master had been unable to carry on without the other half of his soul, so had perished right before Marcella's third eye. It had been awful, and something she never wanted to have to witness ever again.

With his bride at his side, the visions were quite the opposite, and he thrived because of her. Marcus was destined for greatness and his future had changed thanks to Wynter, and for the better. He would never take another lover as long as they both lived, and Marcella wanted that particular path to play out more than any other. So much so that she would pay whatever price she had to if it meant she could make it happen, and the Priestess smiled to herself as she walked back into her bedroom to prepare to pay it.

After all, there was a ritual she needed to complete. One Marcella knew would commence almost as soon as Archie had showered and readied himself to come and accept her offer. It was only a matter of time.

When he came to her as anticipated, she was surprised to find him still doubtful, and so played the other hand she'd been concealing until the opportune moment.

"Your parents will be proud of you, Archie," she told him with a sly smile, and she watched as he gulped with clear unease. "They weren't all that impressed to find me on their doorstep a few weeks ago, especially when I told them what you were really up to on that island. But, once they had signed their lives away, they finally understood."

"Understood what?" he demanded. "What did you tell them?" he added, and Marcella revelled in the worry she could see in his stare. Poor Archie hated to think he had disappointed his parents, and she knew she had been right to pre-empt his arrival by telling them lies and forcing them to become Blood Slaves.

"They are under my spell now, Archie. But I was honest. I told your mother all about how your new job was nothing more than an offer made at the whim of a billionaire who whisked you away to become his whore. And your father…" she sucked in a breath and shook her head, "he wasn't happy to hear that you ran away from a fight rather than stay and protect your friends. I believe he used the word 'coward', but Mr Cole helped them to see the truth."

Archie was shaking with rage, and rightly so. Marcella had pushed his buttons on purpose and could see her words were having the desired effect on him.

"I'm not a coward," he seethed, and the Priestess laid her hand on his cheek to gently caress his soft face.

"I know, and so do your parents. Once they were under my hex, I revealed the world in which you now live. They accept you and are beholden to my master now as Blood Slaves. However, their contracts will pass to you when the transition is complete. You may decide their fate, and who does or does not feed on them." She knew he'd never allow them to become mindless slaves driven by a lust for a vampire's bite and had said the words purely as bait.

"Then what are we waiting for?" Archie demanded, and Marcella grinned.

Right answer.

THREE

As Wynter came down from her final climax, she draped herself across her husband's body and let him cradle her in his arms. They'd just shared a passionate and highly charged night together, and she smiled to herself as her high finally began to wane.

She felt rather serene as she lay there, and closed her eyes, listening to the sounds all around them. The throng down in the club was still going strong, and Wynter listened for a moment before focussing her attention on a different kind of noise. It was odd, more like a calling than an audible sound, and as she listened, she realised her entire being was reacting to it. Wynter reached for the sensation with her mind and then turned to mist on a strange kind of autopilot.

She lifted above the ground and peered down at her husband in shock, only to find him smiling. As though he had felt it too, or perhaps, had been the one doing the calling.

"Go on," he whispered, and at first, she had no idea what he meant, but then a split-second later she felt herself sinking downwards over him. Moving through the layers of skin and bone, and into a magical void the likes she hadn't needed to utilise in over a year now. Not since having been given a constant source of power to remain whole, rather than by needing to cling onto a host and utilise theirs.

Nevertheless, Marcus welcomed her into his heart, and as she settled there, she could suddenly sense exactly what he was thinking and how he was feeling. It was just like when she had been a newly made jinni and had needed to live inside of Brodie's body to survive. There, she had grown stronger, but with Marcus, it was entirely different. His thoughts were not necessarily a conscious stream, but more of an overriding driving force, and all she could make out from within the cacophony was her name. Her face was all she could see. His times with her the only images replaying through his thoughts. It was then Wynter realised just how much Marcus loved her. And also how intense that love was, and she called out to him in astonishment.

Her husband stood, and he moved across the room in a flash so that he could stare into the nearby mirror and allow Wynter to watch through his eyes as he answered her.

"I don't know why you're surprised, my sweet. I've told you so a hundred times and shown you even more. And now that we've fully merged our souls, we are one. You might not need a host to give you strength, but you'll always have one, regardless. I will give you shelter any time. What's mine is yours, Wynter. Always," he demanded, rendering her speechless. She could tell he wasn't lying either, thanks to not only their bond but also the truthfulness a host was forced to share with a jinni who took up residence within them.

She wanted to answer him in person and went to leave again, there being no need for her to have a host after all, but he stopped her. Marcus's thoughts were as forceful as his words, and so Wynter had no choice but to wait at his command. She wanted to see what he was up to and was then surprised to sense it as he called out to his alpha soldier using their mental link. Theirs truly was an odd bond, but it was revealed to her now that Marcus enjoyed it and wanted to keep him and the others at his command, and it was clear why. He had made a point of surrounding himself with women who obeyed his every command, but things had changed and he had those in his life who couldn't do so without answering back. Even Marcella had a mind of her own now as well, and it was clear that he was changing the way he ruled them. He had raised witches for hundreds of generations, treating them like his daughters and nurturing them as they grew and became his next Priestess, but never like with her. She'd been granted a life and had been allowed to take a husband.

And now he had three more girls to raise. Three children whom he hoped would see him as a father, just like the witches before them had. And through it all, he had often yearned for a son. Someone he could treat like a true protégé.

When the alpha entered the office and Marcus peered into his red eyes, Wynter sensed that the strange creature was her husband's second-best alternative. The soldier nodded to his master and then did a double take, staring into Marcus's eyes with a frown for just a second before storming to the back of the room with a grunt. She wondered if he'd known she was in there. Whether he'd sensed her watching and had stopped to look because he was wondering why she was hiding away. But, like the good and loyal soldier she knew he was, the alpha did nothing. He simply followed his orders and took his place at the centre of the small group he was leader of.

Wynter let out a gasp when she properly took in the sight from her spot within her husband's body. Through his eyes, she could see blood dripping from the alpha's chin, and saw in Marcus's mind as his number-one then relayed to his master an account of the feeding frenzy they and the others had partaken in downstairs. It had been carnage. The vampires had been relentless with their bites, and yet not even one of the human guests had fought back. They'd all remained calm and at ease, even as they'd been drained dry, and Wynter suspected that it was somehow because of her. She had felt the changes in herself and knew she'd affected those on the dance floor with her and Marcus, and hated how her influence had later resulted in their deaths.

While Wynter was lost in her guilty thoughts, she realised she'd closed herself off for a few seconds to the real world outside of her small makeshift home within Marcus's heart. She came back around in time to watch through her husband's eyes as he greeted another guest into their midst. It was a woman, and not someone Wynter had seen before.

"A pleasure, as always," the newcomer chimed, and through their bond she knew Marcus could tell the woman was being fake. Inside his mind, her husband was plotting, and Wynter couldn't deny wanting to know more as she saw for herself how his sly inner workings played out.

When the woman's fake smiled dropped entirely and she sucked in a pained breath, Wynter was enthralled. It was then that she realised the newcomer was looking across the room at the handful of vampire soldiers lying in wait. She figured it had to be a show of her terror at what she was seeing, but then the woman looked back into Marcus's eyes pleadingly, and Wynter felt as if she was looking at her too. "Please no… not now. Not like this…" she croaked, but he shook his head.

"This is not the time for negotiation, but for action—on your part. There will be no mercy," he replied icily, and Wynter quickly went to ask him what he and the woman had meant. Marcus saw it coming though and answered her with a memory. A vision that was played out especially for her in his mind's eye, and in it she was seeing through his perspective, watching a scene play out before her like a movie.

It had to be hundreds of years ago. Marcus was staring down at the same woman who was visiting with him now. The two of them were archenemies, though, and she had bravely fought against him and his tyranny. The woman was a lot like Wynter, but unlike her, she had not succumbed to any attraction she might have for him. And neither had he. The woman, whom she now knew was named Audrina, was a vampire hunter. She had set her sights on the big, bad Marcus Cole, but had failed repeatedly, and had fallen into his trap one time too many. This time, he wasn't going to let it go. Audrina had killed an entire horde of the soulless soldier army, and so a debt was to be paid. A debt the huntress would pay for, not with her life, but with her heart and soul. The Priestess at the time, another red-haired witch, was straddling her on the ground, and was holding her down seemingly without any effort at all. She then began cutting some sort of symbols into Audrina's skin, scarring her while chanting strange, guttural words, before coming to a stop and letting out a bloodcurdling scream, and then she went eerily still.

A man was then led into the room, and while Audrina was filling the air with screams and hardly coherent begging, Wynter watched him curiously. She recognised the man but couldn't quite place him. His dark hair and eyes were full of sorrow, but he was merely a human, and his captors forced him to his knees beside the two women at Marcus's command. He tried to fight but was no match for his paranormal guards and was soon lying face down on the ground in a pool of his own blood.

"Love is the greatest power on this Earth, my dear," the Priestess then whispered to Audrina, and Wynter watched as a callous smile spread across her face. One she herself had seen on the face of this woman's great, great granddaughter many times. "And your lover is ours now. My master will keep him safe, he promises…" she told her, and then climbed up and stood over the man. Audrina continued to beg for mercy, tears streaming down her temples and onto the ground.

Wynter knew there would be no mercy for either of them. She might've met Marcus years later, but he was the same ruthless vampire as always. The Priestess then leaned down and shushed the man's whimpers, while Audrina remained glued to the floor by a kind of magical force. She could only look on as the witch performed a ritual. She was halfway through before Wynter realised she was making him a vampire.

She finished up by feeding him her blood, and then she slit his throat to relieve him of his own. Bucket loads of the stuff poured from his wound, covering the ground, and Audrina too. She was clearly terrified, and yet still unable to move away.

As the blood drained from the man's face, Wynter suddenly realised why she recognised him. He turned whiter and whiter, and then his hair turned grey and fell out. The last to change were his eyes, which were soon red and devoid of any kind of soul. It was the alpha.

"What the hell?" she cried, but Marcus didn't answer her. He simply let the rest of his memory speak for itself and Wynter watched as the exsanguinated corpse then suddenly came back to life before their eyes. He twitched on the ground, and when he sat up and stared into the face of the witch hunter who was crying out what had to be his name, it was with an empty look that made Wynter feel sorry for them both. "You had him turned to punish her?" Wynter called to her husband, and he answered simply—

"No. I had him turned to spite her. The punishment came after," Marcus replied, and then Wynter continued to watch the memory as the Priestess leaned down and scooped her fingertip through the pool of blood on the ground that'd once belonged to her new vampire soldier. She then pushed it into Audrina's mouth, forcing her to ingest it, and the poor woman understandably gagged and retched.

"You are cursed to live forever. Not as a vampire, but as a lost soul. Yours is connected to his—" the witch pointed at the new vampire soldier she'd just created, and Audrina let out a howl of pain — "and if he lives, so too shall you. There is nothing that can break this curse, not even the Lady of Death herself. Try all you wish, but you will remain in this form until your debt is paid."

"And how will I pay it?" the woman cried, but the Priestess didn't answer. She instead stared up at her master, but was looking through him, and when she spoke again, it was with that voice which sounded like a hundred women at once. A voice Wynter herself had heard many times, and yet still it gave her the creeps.

"When two suns rise and the half-moon wanes, your greatest foe will give you an heir," she told him, and Marcus nodded. He hadn't understood it at the time, but had trusted in the prophecy to be true, just like all the others his numerous Priestesses had delivered over his very many years. And just like that, he had cursed the poor woman, not that Wynter was surprised. She'd seen him do much worse.

In the blink of an eye, they were back in the present, and Marcus was looking down into the fearful face of the same woman who had wronged him all those years before.

"Take her," he told the alpha, who nodded and then stormed towards Audrina, and when she screamed at his touch, it was almost too much for Wynter to bear. She thought how awful it must be for the huntress to see the man she loved like this. How devastated she had to be at reuniting this way after all the years she had spent without him.

The alpha silenced the poor woman with a bite to the neck, and as Audrina melted against him, Wynter figured he was merely forcing her compliance before feeding on her, but then he began unbuckling his belt. He tore away her dress and was inside of her a second later.

"Look away," Wynter implored her husband, but he refused, and so she tried to rise out of the sanctuary of his heart so that she could walk out of her own accord. But instead, found herself unable to leave. "Please, Marcus! She cannot give you an heir this way, so why put her through it?" she cried, getting angrier by the moment.

"Why not?" his inner voice countered, rendering her speechless. "Who told you that vampires could not procreate? On what authority do you have it that she cannot give me the heir that was promised?"

"Because... well..." Wynter stumbled, and realised she had no answer at all. Movies and television had said so—yeah, she wasn't about to answer that! "And the prophecy? Two suns and a half-moon?"

Three images flashed through her husband's mind in response. Twin witches, and a baby half-werewolf. Damn.

"Magic is what created the vampire, and magic is also what brings children into this world. Audrina was purely cursed with immortality, not infertility. Her body was frozen in time until she was reunited with her soul mate, and as you can see, they're reunited all right."

She could see too bloody well and swore at both Marcus and his morally inept protégé. She tried again to leave and cursed her husband when he laughed. "I command the magic that drives you too, my sweet. Don't forget it," he said, and continued to make her watch as his soldier did his bidding.

FOUR

Marcella looked down into Archie's face and smiled as he settled on his knees before her. It was pleasing to know how much he wanted this, and just how ready he'd been when the offer had come. The witch had the sneaking suspicion that this was what all the working out had been for and found herself impressed that Archie was going to spend his immortality with a figure he'd worked hard to achieve. She might be married, but she had still seen plenty of proof for herself and part of her wanted to tell him well done. But of course, she did no such thing.

Instead, she focussed on the matter at hand and began speaking the ancient enchantment that would bind Archie's soul to the power her coven commanded. She could also sense his willingness for the gift she was bestowing on him increase as the spell began to take hold of the life force within him. Marcella had to call upon every one of her ancestors to remind her of the words, but they came through for her, just as she had known they would. It had been centuries since any Priestess serving Marcus had created a new fully fledged vampire to walk the Earth beside him, and that was because each time since the ceremony would only be half-completed. None but the soulless soldiers had been sired. Not a single full vampire had been created by their coven since him—their master—and he was undoubtedly going to be angry that she'd made another without his say so. But this needed to be done. Marcella's visions were true and just, and she was utterly certain of the necessity for Archie to become her master's immortal brother.

After all, Marcus needed Wynter, and she considered Brodie indispensable. Which, of course, meant he needed —

"Archie," she whispered, and took his hand in hers. Before he could respond, she then placed a knife in his grip and used it to slice open her palm, which quickly oozed with blood. Marcella cupped it and then pushed her hand to his mouth, and Archie dutifully swallowed it down, even if he looked sick to his stomach in doing so.

Next, it was her turn to do the same with him, and once their blood flowed through one another's veins, Marcella recited her spell. She then shared their blood again, truly combining it between the two bodies, and didn't stop even when Archie began screaming with pain as his human essence became overwhelmed by her magical power. The back and forth had to continue. But it wasn't like in the movies, where after a few seconds the person transitioning was reborn and forgot all about the pain of their resurrection. Instead, it was more like he'd just been set on fire from within by the power her blood was giving to him, and nothing could quell the flames. All Archie could do was ride it out. And as he battled those demons, Marcella looked up at the jinni, who was watching over the entire thing in brooding silence.

Brodie was stood with his arms folded, staring down at the ground, and Marcella was surprised he hadn't come to his lover's side. Hadn't tried to help Archie during the transition.

"How long?" was all he asked, clearly having sensed her gaze on him. He didn't tear his eyes away from the man he loved for even a second, though, and Marcella admired him for that. He might not fully approve—yet—but he was standing by Archie, regardless. Plus, she could sense there was something else driving him to support the change. The jinni was losing his power. His hold over his human form was already waning, and before long, he'd be forced back into the blackness of his misty being. He needed a host, and who better than the man who loved him? Especially once that man became an immortal who would not be weakened by the parasite drawing strength from his heart.

"An hour, maybe two. I cannot leave his side during his transition, but perhaps you could go to the blood stores and bring him back some provisions for after? I will give Archie my blood while the magic takes hold," she informed him, and Brodie genuinely seemed shocked to see what the process actually involved. But what she had said was true. Archie needed her blood, and a lot of it, so Marcella cut her other palm open and encouraged the poor boy to drink.

This time, he didn't hesitate. The thirst was already within him, and Archie took everything she offered before falling back onto the ground and curling into a ball as he writhed and bellowed in agony.

The two of them continued the cycle until he finally came to rest, and Marcella took a moment to lie beside him on the hard ground and give her own body the chance to recuperate for a few seconds. Like with any intense spell work, she was depleted and in need of rest, and when she looked up to find her master standing over her with a smile, she too felt reborn.

Marcus had returned in time to help her with this final step, and Marcella was overcome with joy. She needed his strength to help her carry on.

The Priestess immediately climbed up on to her knees and then bowed at his feet.

"My lady," he greeted her, his hand grazing her cheek gently.

"My lord," she answered, bowing deeper.

"Your ancestors vowed they would never make another vampire but me…" he sighed, and Marcella nodded. It was true, and she had gone against the ruling, but for good reason.

"I know," was all she answered, and when Marcus stilled, she lifted her face to his. He looked pained, and she knew why.

"And you'll pay the price?" he whispered, and she didn't hesitate.

"Yes."

"Excellent," he replied, with what she had learned over the years was a fake smile, but it didn't matter. Their deal was done. Marcella knew she wasn't in any trouble, but instead she owed her master a debt. A debt that he would call in imminently, but she was ready.

The Priestess looked to the future and saw but one vision now. It was clear and without any other variances. She had done the right thing in turning Archie, and even her master knew it.

Marcella couldn't be prouder.

Her life's work was complete, and when Marcus settled himself behind her, cradling her in his hold, she smiled. He didn't have to be there for this final step, but she was glad he was.

It was time. "Brother…you must finish your transition," he whispered, and Archie nodded. The final stage was about to commence, and Marcella settled back and stared up into Marcus's face. She knew she didn't need to tell him goodbye, or to tell her children and husband she loved them. Marcella knew she would be with them always, just as her ancestors were with her, and so she relaxed against her master, feeling glad he was there to hold her.

Archie buried his face in her hair, and as she felt the sharp sting of his tongue against her neck, Marcella cried out. The lure of a vampire bite did not work on witches after all, and so she was forced to endure it as he drew the life from her, one gulp at a time. The only thing she clung onto was the hold her master kept her in, and the hand he was cradling with his own.

As she succumbed to the call of death, she heard him whisper her name and knew, once and for all, that she had not failed him. Her master was proud of her. He called her his greatest victory, and as she fell into the nothingness of the beyond, it was with the lightest of hearts.

She would not grieve. Would not beg to be returned. Her job as Priestess was done, and Marcella took great strength in knowing she was the first to leave behind not one, but two heirs to the great fortune she had beheld for a quarter of a century.

And as she took her place among the dead, she watched the living world with a smile and offered them all a fond farewell.

FIVE

Wynter looked on in horror as she realised what was happening. Archie had just drained Marcella dry, and now she had to be dead. Her eyes rolled back and she let out a strange sort of sigh, and then didn't breathe back in. Marcella slumped back against Marcus, who scooped her into his arms as though she were simply napping. But they could all tell otherwise.

Archie propelled himself backwards in shock, his bloody mouth mumbling profuse apologies, but no one was truly listening. Even Brodie was staring at the witch in shock, and Wynter leaned down so that she could stroke her cheek with her fingertip. She wondered if perhaps they could do something to stop her from going but could already tell that it was too late.

An immense pain then began to radiate from her chest, and Wynter fell to her knees. Everything hurt, the heart of the witch inside her chest most of all, and she shuddered as a vision of Marcella's final hours magically came over her. She had known exactly what she was doing. The ancient laws dictated that any witch who sired a vampire would have to give their life as an offering to complete the rite, or else the vampire would remain soulless and devoid of all humanity. So much so that it would turn them into a mindless, immortal creature. A soldier.

It all made sense now.

"The price," she whispered, looking at the still horrified jinni opposite them. "This was the only way to give Archie a real future, and she knew it. A witch must offer their life in return for the immortal one's new life. She knew and did it anyway."

Wynter then pulled her hand away and clutched at her still aching chest and knew that it was Mara. She was mourning her mother.

"I had no idea that this was what it took," Brodie replied, his dark eyes pained. "If I had, I would've been kinder to her. I would have thanked her or tried to stop it."

"None of us knew, and I think she did that on purpose so we wouldn't try and stop her," she implored, but then Marcus turned to her, his blue eyes duller than she had ever seen them.

"I knew…" he countered and then climbed up onto his feet. Marcus was cradling Marcella like a child against him, and Wynter could tell he was sad to let her go. That he too, would mourn her.

"Then why let her do it?" Wynter begged.

"Because Marcella was wise and had visions that could be relied upon to come true. She saw you—the many versions of you—and how our future lay before us. She wouldn't have done this without the right reasons, and I have no doubt those reasons revolved around us."

"You mean me," she croaked, and Marcus didn't confirm or deny, but she knew she had to be right.

Wynter then watched him leave, and as silence descended between the three left behind, she decided to go too, thinking how Archie and Brodie had a lot they needed to figure out. The new vampire was drinking his way through a handful of blood bags, tears streaming down his face as the reality of what'd just happened seemed to be dawning on him. He had taken his first life. Had killed because of his new thirst, and Wynter could tell he wasn't taking things all that well. Archie would have to come to terms with what he had done, while learning to contend with what he had become, and she didn't envy him.

She made it as far as the door when she found her path blocked by Jack. His eyes were bloodshot red and streaming with tears. She went to comfort him, but then he shoved her away.

"You fucking happy now?" he spat and continued sobbing even in his rage. "What more do we have to give before you just stop? I lost my daughter because of you, and now my wife! You've not had to worry about a damn thing, while we've all had to sacrifice everything we have just so *he* could get the fucking girl…"

"Jack, please!" she tried, but it was no use. He was gone, lost in his grief, and seethed as he pushed her outstretched hand away yet again.

"She's gone because of you, Wynter. Gone, just so that you can get your goddam way yet again," Jack cried, swaying on the spot. He looked like he was about to crumble in a heap on the ground, and Wynter tried a third time to help him, but this time Brodie interceded.

"Leave him be," he told her as he grabbed the poor man and then helped him into a chair.

"I didn't mean for any of this," she replied, but her maker just shook his head as though dismayed with her. Wynter wanted to scream. She didn't need their guilt, not right now. She was suffering too, and yet they were all looking to her as the one and only place to lay the blame. It wasn't her doing; couldn't they see? It was Marcus. It was always Marcus.

But then why was her heart aching and her stomach churning with anxious shame that she couldn't force away?

Even Archie looked the other way when she peered down at him, seemingly unwilling to offer her any sort of comfort. He didn't even seem at all fazed by the human in their midst, and it appeared he was staying away not because of any lack of hunger, but out of respect. The newly created vampire looked almost bereft as he slumped back against the wall and took it all in, and Wynter stumbled away. "I didn't want any of this."

"Yeah, but you got it anyway," Brodie snapped as he wrapped a sympathetic arm around Jack's shoulders. "No matter your intentions, the outcome is always the same."

"And I'm done giving him everything, while you get the rewards," Jack then whimpered, glaring at her through his tears.

Wynter tried to think of a response. Tried to figure out a way to stick up for herself, but she realised she had nothing. All this time, she truly had been selfish. She'd ran for her own reasons and returned to Marcus because there was no other choice, and all the while, she had been fighting him. Pushing him away. And because of that, his Priestess had been forced to take matters into her own hands. It was apparent now that having Archie in her life as a vampire had meant she would need him in the future somehow, and while she couldn't fathom those reasons, Wynter knew she couldn't explain them away either. All she could do was accept yet another of Marcella's strange gifts. That didn't mean she would say goodbye lightly, though.

She took off out the door and away from the sullen atmosphere in the bedroom, and all the way downstairs Wynter tried to tell herself they were wrong. That they were all just in too much shock to stick up for her and that Jack was merely grieving. She remembered that feeling all too well and, of course, sympathised with him for lashing out. That's all this was. It had to be.

But she couldn't deny that he was right. The others had indeed all made sacrifices along the way. She had too, but even Jakob's death was her fault. The blame didn't lie easily on her shoulders, and as Wynter carried on towards the front garden in search of solace, she retreated further and further into herself. It was the only thing she could think to do to protect her aching heart and soul.

And as she withdrew, a strange sensation flooded through Wynter. She felt almost numb, but then on fire at the same time. And then there was the pain. An almighty thundering in her skull. It was as if someone was screaming in her head, and Wynter fell to the floor, covering her ears with her hands like it might somehow help. And then, the power Mara's witch heart gave her seeped away suddenly. She immediately returned to her pure jinni form and became nothing more than white mist. She'd need a host if she remained like this and cursed at her weakness. But at the same time, she understood. Mara was punishing her, too.

Was she no longer worthy of her gift? Was it gone now, and she'd be forced to go back to the old ways?

If so, then another idea overcame the bereft jinni. Maybe they were all better off without her.

She was weak without her heart. Dying. For the first time in over a year, she was a true Jinn again, and without a host, she would soon be gone forever.

"Let's do this then..." she called out loud to the witch, who had apparently tried to play chicken with her, but who clearly had no idea just how much of a fighter Wynter was. She was willing to die. Willing to end it all, because at least this way, she would take Marcus with her. And it would be all the witch's fault.

She stared up into the dull sky overhead and screamed into the nothingness. "I'll dance with the Lady of Death, Mara. I'll take her hand and let her have me."

Mara's power was back in less than a second, and as the incredible witch's strength washed over her again, Wynter was surprised that she felt relieved. Death wasn't something she regularly dallied with, and while she had been willing to take the white lady's hand should she appear, there was no doubt she was glad there had been no need.

She crumpled in a heap on the ground and then rolled onto her back, staring up into the night's sky, and realised she was laying over the first of her hordes' pits. Beneath her were hundreds of the soulless vampires she had once been fearful of, but not anymore. Wynter closed her eyes and called to them, seeking some warmth from the cold and pale soldiers in the depths below, but all she felt was emptiness. Their minds awaited her call to action, and their hearts held nothing but silence. There was no comfort to be found from them, but she knew that anyway. They were incapable of love, and Wynter envied them. She would do anything not to feel right now. Not to have shame burning at her gut and sorrow spearing in her heart.

If only she could find a way to turn it all off.

The sound of screams brought her back around, and Wynter jumped up on instinct. She then ran back towards the house in time to find the alpha vampire hoisting Jack up off the ground by the arms he'd also tied behind his back. With every yank upwards on the rope across her beloved oak tree's strongest branch, the poor man gave a pained cry, and Wynter shook her head. This couldn't be happening.

Marcus was watching the scene unfold from the doorway to the mansion, and she quickly ran to her husband's side. There, she reached for him, but couldn't take her eyes off Jack. She felt pained at watching him suffer and opened her mouth to try and plead for Marcus to have mercy on him when he immediately interjected.

"No one speaks to you like that, my sweet," he growled, and then stared into her eyes and frowned. "I can see how much the pain of losing Marcella agonises you. How you consider her actions your fault, and carry these burdens so tirelessly, but you must know that you're not alone. Not anymore. If you're hurt, then so am I," Marcus implored, and his were the first kind words anyone at the house had offered her since they had returned from London. Since Marcella had taken matters into her own hands yet again and she had been blamed for their loss.

But Marcus didn't blame her. He was the only one who understood, and the only person offering her any sort of comfort. She wanted to cry. All the times she had pushed him away and tried to blame him, and now here he was, the only one to have her back when everyone else had turned away.

"Thank you," she whimpered, and buried herself in his hold. For perhaps the first time ever, she considered herself lucky to have him. He had offered her comfort when all the others had turned their hatred towards her. He had wanted to shield her from it, or else exact revenge on her behalf.

Wynter had never cared for Marcus more.

"We don't need anyone else's permission to do the things we need to do or live the life we've chosen. All we need is each other, Wynter. Don't let them guilt you into choosing death over their shame," Marcus added, and she was surprised at how he could've possibly known. But then again, it wasn't as if she was being quiet with her turmoil and the struggles she was clearly having.

"I just needed someone to tell me I wasn't wrong, or selfish. That I wasn't to blame for the hurt and pain everyone around me is forced to deal with," she answered him honestly, and then leaned into Marcus's hold when she saw softness behind his usually so icy eyes.

"You've done nothing wrong. And you're not selfish. I'm the selfish one, but I don't care what anyone thinks, so they wouldn't dare try and guilt me like they did you. I'll have my way, and no one will stop me, and you have that same power. You're in a position to command them, not allow their blasphemy," he demanded, and then turned to look up at Jack, who had dislocated both of his shoulders and was out cold with the pain. "Which is why I did this. I don't care what grief or pain he feels, because all that matters is you've been hurt. He caused you pain with his careless words, and so now he will endure my wrath. As will the next person who dares try and hurt you."

"Marcus..." she whimpered, and he quietened her with a kiss.

"It's like that old saying. We can use the carrot or the stick, and I'm bored of using the carrot. What do you say?" he then whispered, and Wynter was surprised to find herself smile.

She didn't need anyone else to take away her pain. All she needed was the vampire who was strong enough to inspire hatred in others and then thrive on it. No matter what she tried, her friends and family had evidently come to hate her anyway, so Wynter decided it was high time she embraced it. Every decision she'd made went awry. Every choice she tried to instigate for the better had never worked. She had failed in every attempt she'd tried to make things better.

But Marcus didn't see her failures. He just saw her—the other half of his soul—and he had made sure she knew what that meant to him.

So, she finally stopped fighting, and it felt incredible to accept her fate at last. There was one man who would always have her back, and it wasn't the dead vampire she'd once loved, or the Jinn who had turned her into one of his kind. No, it was Marcus. She was his, and he was hers, and as she let go of the last thread of independence keeping them apart, Wynter smirked.

"I say yes. Fuck the carrot, bring on the stick," she joked, and then looked up at Jack again. "And you can leave him there as long as you want. He deserves everything he gets."

SIX

After the guilt of his first kill and the thirst that had accompanied it subsided, Archie had sat back and watched as the alpha soldier appeared and dragged Jack away, and he was glad. He didn't need the reminder either, and could understand why Wynter hadn't stuck around to let everyone have a go at her.

Now that the dust was settling, the new vampire could see things from an entirely different perspective, and he couldn't deny that he was glad for what had gone down. He could sense Marcella's power within him, her gift, and felt his entire body flood with it. He didn't need rest or time to recover from the transition, and he didn't need food either. Well, blood, but that thirst was currently quenched.

And so, he stood and took a proper look around. The world was entirely different now through his keen vampire eyes, and yet still the same. Archie knew it was he who had changed, and so he went in search of the one constant he hoped he could still rely on. Brodie.

He found him at the base of the stairs, watching out the open doorway as Marcus punished Jack for speaking out against his wife. Damn, that vampire was brutal.

"Hey," he said, taking a seat beside the jinni.

"Hey," was all Brodie answered, and it wasn't lost on Archie how his beau hadn't turned to look at him. He took his hand and kissed the back of it, but Brodie continued to look away.

"Come with me," he whispered, trying to pull him up, but still Brodie refused him. "What's wrong?"

"What's wrong?" the jinni echoed, finally turning to look at him, and Archie shrugged. He didn't see the problem. "Everything! That's what's wrong. We're surrounded by death and chaos, and we've now willingly brought Rosa into this home and made her a part of it. This is not okay, Archie."

Brodie then stormed off up the stairs, and Archie went to follow him, but was interrupted by Marcus and Wynter on their return. They had left Jack dangling from the tree like some sort of broken marionette, and yet Archie found he wasn't all that concerned for the human. He was more interested in the jinni.

She seemed different somehow, but he couldn't pinpoint why. And Archie found he simply accepted things this way. His focus was on Marcus anyway, who was peering across at him with a smile. Archie had never seen the guy smile before. In fact, he'd never really been on his radar all that much. Until now. But actually, it wasn't so bad at all. He was starting to like it. A bond had sprung to life between them. Something that hadn't remotely been there before, but now was burning brightly from deep inside his chest.

"Brother..." the new vampire whispered instinctively, and Marcus nodded.

"Indeed, and I have much to teach you," he replied, and then offered his wife a gentle kiss before letting her follow Brodie upstairs. He then led Archie down the hallway to his office and shut the door behind him.

The new vampire noticed everything. His senses were so heightened he could see and hear even the minuscule detail around them. His nose picked up the faintest of old scents that still lingered in Marcus's office. He could hear Jack still swinging beneath the tree and could hear the faint thrum of his heart as he endured his punishment. And there was something else afoot outside, too. The alpha was grunting, and Archie heard as he dragged a body out of the boot of his master's car. The same car the group had just returned in from London. It didn't occur to him to ask why an unconscious woman was being held captive. "First things first, let go of the life you knew before. The way forward requires a set of strengths you must embrace, and weaknesses you shall have to release."

"I already am," Archie admitted, and then told Marcus how he felt in the aftermath of the ceremony that had turned him. "I understand where she has gone and why, so I no longer feel any remorse for taking her life. Is that wrong?" he asked, feeling strangely comfortable in Marcus's presence now, and he took a seat opposite him beneath the huge window of his office. He could sense a kinship between them and wasn't ashamed to admit he liked it.

Marcus smiled and reached forward, placing a hand on Archie's shoulder tenderly.

"It's not wrong at all. In fact, it's natural selection. You have been given a gift, Archie. A power that now courses within you and sets you high above all others in the order of things. Some vampires take years to understand that, but luckily, you're not like any other vampire. You're my brother..." he told him, and the young vampire grinned. He felt like they truly were brothers now and was glad Marcus had said so.

"What else do I need to know?" he answered and felt ready for anything.

Marcus answered by telling him their fundamental laws, such as the sanctity of sex and how Archie was now tied to the same coven as he was. And that their fates were as aligned as his and Wynter's, plus how they needed to take care of each other more than ever. Everything felt right, and by the time Archie left the office, it was morning and his head was swimming. There was still so much he had to learn, but his mentor had done him well, and as he stalked upstairs, he knew what he had to do.

He went into the bedroom he shared with Brodie and found him sat on the bed staring out the window. Archie could sense the jinni's power waning and knew it was time they merged. His partner needed a host, and at last Archie could become one.

"Is that it, you're on his side now?" Brodie asked, his back still to Archie, who had to fend off a wave of rage. How dare he make assumptions based on the prejudice he had held onto for decades and not what he knew to be different now?

"Why won't you look at me?" he replied, changing the subject, and climbed onto the bed behind his jinni lover. "What have I done that's so wrong?"

"It's not what you've done, Archie, but what you are going to do," he replied, and the vampire answered by cradling Brodie in his arms. He placed kisses along his neck and jaw and smiled when he felt him begin to thaw.

"What am I going to do?" he asked, and got his answer when Brodie finally turned and faced him. The moment the jinni peered back into his eyes, Archie felt his entire being begin to stir. His heart pounded in his chest and without a sound, he felt himself calling to the man sitting before him with such intensity it took his breath away.

"You're going to make me yours, Archie," Brodie replied, looking into his eyes incredulously, which he could tell were now glowing. "Your soul is calling to mine, and it scares me how badly I want to say yes. How much I need this. Need you…"

Archie had him flat on his back in a heartbeat and began ripping away the jinni's clothes, which turned to mist and dissipated the moment they were free of Brodie's body. He then kissed every inch of his skin and stripped off. He was ready for what came next and understood what doing so would mean to them both.

"I love you," he whispered, and Archie knew his eyes were burning brightly again as he felt their souls connect, becoming one.

"I love you too," the jinni whimpered, and Archie crushed him against his chest, moving languidly as he made love to his one and only. The other half of his soul, and the man he loved with every fibre of his being.

It was then that Archie finally understood where Marcus had been coming from all this time. He got it and knew he would be the same should someone come and take Brodie away from him. And if his lover left of his own accord? Not a fucking chance. He would move heaven and earth to get him back, and as they whiled away the hours together in bed, Archie knew he could never let that happen. He would die without Brodie by his side—literally—and told him so. The jinni needed to know how he felt, and to remember it always.

"I'll see for myself," Brodie told him when dusk came and the pair of them were resting side by side on the huge bed, and Archie didn't need to ask how or why. It was time for the two of them to take one final step, and so the new vampire opened himself up, calling to Brodie and offering him a home in his heart. The jinni needed to rest and gather his strength, and finally, Archie was capable of giving a place in which to do so. His magic would heal his lover and keep him whole, while his now immortal body would suffer no ill effects from becoming his new host. It was ideal, and as Brodie turned to black smoke and disappeared inside his heart, Archie simply grinned.

"Welcome home," he then whispered, before climbing up and charging for the doorway. It was time he found Wynter and told her he was sorry for how he had treated her the night before. Brodie too. They had each let their emotions cloud their thoughts, and had lashed out, which wasn't fair on her.

He just prayed he wasn't too late.

SEVEN

Twenty years later

Rosa had made it into adulthood without turning full werewolf, but only barely. There had been times when her hormones had demanded blood, or the full moon had made her itch from the inside out. But every time, her father was there to help guide her through it. Marcus and Wynter were her adopted parents since her being orphaned at birth, she knew, but that hadn't stopped them from raising her as their own. And now, she wasn't only the eldest and had always been the favourite of their family, but she had grown to be the most powerful, too.

Her cousins, Marceline and Marlee, seemed barely human. They were born only to serve, and so Rosa had watched as her father had schooled them in an entirely different way to her and her younger adopted brother, Marc. The twin witches were taught about loyalty and servitude. They called him 'master' and bowed at his feet, whereas the two other children sat at his table and were taught about the art of war and how to command entire armies of the undead.

The one thing all four did have in common were the rules. They had never once left the confines of the mansion and its grounds, and whenever their father had visitors, the children were to be neither seen nor heard.

But that hadn't stopped Rosa from snooping. She knew the name of every man, woman or other creature who ever visited them, and was well versed in the mythologies that surrounded their kinds. As the years passed, she had learned about them all, and it helped that her mother was so open with her about them. Wynter had her flaws, but the jinni was loving and honest, and she adored her.

Rosa just wished she could at least make a decision without having to run to her husband first, but also wondered if she even knew she was doing it. After all, her mother was wise and had home-schooled all four children by herself, so knew her stuff, but when it came to even the smallest of things, it was Marcus who made the final call. He commanded their entire household, and Rosa knew as much as anyone not to defy him.

"We've had a lot more visitors to the house lately," she remarked one evening after a third procession of creatures had left, and her mother simply nodded. "Why is that?"

"Because we have recently taken command of the faeries, but they wouldn't give in so easily. Your father had many talks with their old leaders, and had to resort to traditional methods," Wynter answered honestly, and Rosa easily read between the lines.

"You mean, he killed them?" she enquired and didn't even flinch when her mother nodded in affirmation. She had grown up knowing all about death, and the necessity for it. She had seen her father slaughter entire families who'd tried to rise up against him, and had also welcomed her mother back from war with her hordes at her heels and blood covering her from head to toe.

Rosa could even remember back to the day when Marc had been born, tearing through his mother's belly and ripping her in two. Poor Audrina hadn't stood a chance and was merely the first in a long line of Marc's victims. The son of a soulless vampire and a cursed human had been born a monster and raised a brute. And even now, at eighteen years old, it was clear those tendencies were so engrained in his psyche that her brother would never change them. Plus, their father had welcomed it. A boy with the strength of a hundred vampires and loyalty to just the chosen few who had loved him since birth. Rosa counted herself lucky she had been included in that. The twin witches, too. Their father, Jack, hadn't been quite so lucky. He was her birth mother's uncle, and had been the last of Rosa's blood relatives, and Marc had dissected the man while he was still alive for the fun of it. He'd left Marceline and Marlee without their last remaining parent when they were only ten, but it hadn't mattered. Marcus had taken them under his wing and had groomed them to follow in their mother's footsteps. To become his Priestesses, and from what Rosa could tell, they were already serving him well.

Marceline was never seen without her red cape these days. She had no life of her own and no allegiance to anyone other than her master, whom Rosa had seen readily dote on his formidable young witch. Marlee, on the other hand, was still struggling with the path that had been chosen for her. Their uncle Archie had once told her all about the world outside their magical walls, and Marlee had begged to know more. Begged to see it someday, and while Marcus had always said no, Archie would tell her maybe. He had given Marlee hope, and it had been enough for her to rebel.

And that was Archie to a tee. He was a joker and was always getting them into trouble, but thankfully their other uncle, Brodie, would be on hand to help get them back out of it again. He would have a quiet word with whomever he needed to and was often the difference between them facing Marcus's wrath and getting off with a warning.

And yet lately, Rosa felt as if the scales were tipping. Trouble seemed at an all-time high, and it appeared to be affecting them all. The night before, she had seen Marlee out in the garden on her knees, her back red raw from the twenty lashings the alpha soldier was administering. Nothing could have stopped her from getting a beating this time though, not after she had tried to hide downstairs to sneak a few minutes with the vampire they all knew she had the biggest crush on. Ezra Dawson, the perfectly handsome one of the twins who sat on her father's High Committee of Vampires. He didn't even know she existed, and yet every time the committee were called to session, she'd tried to meet him. Tried getting a chance encounter, and all because she was convinced he was her soul mate.

"Witches don't have soul mates," Rosa had told her for the hundredth time, and yet Marlee still hadn't listened. She had gone downstairs and broken her father's rules regardless, and all for nothing more than a sound lashing and to remain, as always, a nobody in the beautiful vampire's eyes.

But she couldn't concern herself with such matters right now. That night, on the eve of her twenty-first birthday, Rosa went to bed feeling strange. She dreamt of blood and her teeth tearing through flesh, and of her bones breaking, but it feeling wonderful.

Natural.

Fated.

She woke with a start and knew she had to tell someone, and so headed straight to her mother, who went unusually quiet after she had revealed all.

"You need to keep yourself grounded, Rosa. You must remember who you are and what you want to become. Fight the desires inside of you to turn, and you will be rewarded," Wynter demanded, and then smiled resolutely. "In fact, I have an idea…" she added, and then climbed up onto her feet, heading for the doorway before the young woman could ask what she had meant.

EIGHT

Wynter headed for Marcus's office in a blind panic. The day had finally come that her daughter was turning, and she was terrified of what that meant. Rosa was coming of age and was changing, and not necessarily for the better.

"My sweet," Marcus called when Wynter entered, watching as she closed the door and then went to his side like always. When he saw how frazzled she was, he pulled her to him, nestling his wife in his hold. She felt better almost immediately. It hadn't mattered how much time had passed or the children who now shared his attention with her. She was still his first and only love, and she clung to him as if it were those first days all over again. "What's the matter?" he asked, and Wynter took a moment to calm herself before revealing what Rosa had said.

"I don't know what to do," she whimpered, and was surprised when he didn't answer her right away. The silence was intense, but she quickly realised why when a gentle knock came at the door and then a red-cloaked young woman entered a second later. It was Marceline, the now fully fledged Priestess of the Cole household. Marlee was still coming to terms with the life of servitude she had been taught to contend with, and there was a part of her fighting spirit that Wynter adored. She saw her old self in that young woman, and yet couldn't help but agree with her husband—she ought to stop. There was no life for Marlee that didn't involve her duties and nothing more, and to expect otherwise was merely causing her more pain.

"My lord," Marceline whispered, falling to her knees before them as was expected; and Wynter was reminded instantly of how her mother had looked in the same pose. A pang echoed through her chest at the thought of Marcella and their bond, and how much she missed her, but Wynter forced the hurt away. Like in all things, there was a reason for her life going the way it had, and the fates that had aligned to make it so. Wynter trusted in them, just like the witch's heart she had beating within her did.

"My lady," Marcus replied, and Wynter could sense just how impressed he was with the woman still bowed before him. She was his perfect student and had done them all proud with her accomplishments as both a witch and an acolyte, and her powers were growing with every passing day as testament to that. "Tell me what you see," he added, and reached forward with his hand.

Marceline took it and climbed back onto her feet. She then offered Wynter a respectful bow.

"I have seen many futures for Rosa in which she has been saved from becoming feral, but she will still need to transition into wolf form," she replied, and then flinched when Marcus shot to his feet and stepped forward so that he now towered over her.

Wynter couldn't tell if he was happy or sad to hear the news but knew she herself wasn't keen on having Rosa turn. They already had one child with a propensity for the macabre, and while Wynter had loved Audrina's abomination as best she could, she couldn't connect with the killer instinct that drove him. Marc was her husband's prized jewel, though, and so she had kept him under her wing all these years, albeit at arm's length.

However, she didn't want the same to become of Rosa. She had adored that girl since the moment she came into this world and would not be able to withstand losing her to the werewolves. Marcus commanded them, much like the majority of all the creatures across the globe, but there had been talks over the years. Ultimatums had been given, and Rosa's life hung in the balance because of them. If she turned, then she was to be married to another wolf, which would mean her leaving them. The leader of their pack had sniffed her out before getting within twenty miles of the mansion, and so he had tried to claim her, and had failed only because of Marcus and his ability to use his foes' weaknesses against them. But it had only been a temporary fix, and now fear speared in Wynter's gut at the thought of losing her.

She started to wonder what else might be done. Rosa had been raised amongst an array of creatures who had each taught her their strengths and ensured she emulated them as best she could, but there was more that could be done. There had to be.

Her mind went to the mother they had left behind so many years before. Rosalie had given her life for her child's, and Wynter wondered if perhaps she needed reminding that humans could be strong too.

Marceline then hissed and clutched at her chest, and she turned to Wynter, dropping the hood of her cloak to reveal her wide dark eyes.

"What?" Wynter insisted, stepping back.

"You just thought of something. What was it?" the witch replied, and even Marcus turned to his wife in surprise. She didn't blame him. It had been a long time since she had played a part in the decision making for their household, and it felt odd. As if she had forgotten how.

"I was just thinking about how Rosa could be reminded of her human strengths. In particular, the sacrifice Rosalie made for her..." she answered timidly, and quickly reached for her husband. She needed to know he wasn't mad with her for having the idea and breathed a sigh when she sensed his relief. Perhaps he truly had no idea what they might try, and that terrified Wynter more than she could say. After all, the idea had scared her enough to offer her first opinion in two decades.

"That's it!" Marceline then cried and turned to her master with a smile. "She now turns in all but one of my visions, master."

"And?" he demanded.

"Ashes that lay buried beneath the tallest tree…" she answered in the deep, multi-tonal voice of her ancestors. It dawned on Wynter right away, but Marcus didn't remember. He had been told but hadn't seen it for himself, and so his Priestess continued with her strange prophetic response. "With a lighthouse warded by a wolf across the sea, and a goblin tending for a home that no one has lived in for twenty years."

"She needs to visit Rosalie's grave," Marcus replied thoughtfully, and Marceline nodded. He then turned to Wynter and fixed his intense blue eyes on hers. "You will take her without delay, my sweet. Just the pair of you."

She shook her head no. She couldn't go alone, not after never leaving his side all this time.

"I can't, Marcus—"

"You can, and you will," he commanded, and all fight went when she saw the resolute determination in his stare. "It has to be you. You're her mother. Her guide and mentor. You must be by her side."

"And if it doesn't work?" she demanded, thinking the worst.

"It will," Marceline replied for her master, and then pressed a hand over Wynter's heart. The heart of her sister. "And you will know what to do when the time comes to show her the right path. Only you can help her decide."

Wynter didn't believe her. She hadn't decided anything on her own in what felt like forever and had grown afraid to. Not after all her decisions leading to disaster in the past, but it was what Marcus commanded of her, so she nodded. If this was what Rosa needed, then she was going to make sure she was there for her. That she would give everything to make it happen.

"When do we leave?" she asked her husband, who gulped, looking pained.

"Not a moment to lose…" he answered, and as much as she hated it, she agreed. Wynter gave Marceline a nod so that she knew to go and help Rosa get ready, and then she wrapped herself in Marcus's embrace.

It was going to take everything she had, but she knew there was no other choice. Rosa's life was at stake and so she was going to give her child this one chance to make it her own. And actually, it felt good to be reminded of the woman she had once been. The fighter.

Wynter forced herself away, and she didn't so much as look back as she tore out the door and headed straight for the garage.

It was time she remembered exactly what she was capable of. She was a jinni and a damn force to be reckoned with, and so it didn't matter what other forces were at play, she was going to win. For Rosa's sake, and especially her own.

NINE

Everything ached as Rosa and her mother drove for hours across the British countryside, and with every bump in the road, she flinched and cried out. It was like she was itching from the inside out, her body longing to transform.

And she knew exactly what was causing it.

They had become complacent. They had all considered the danger passed now that she was grown, and yet here she was, her entire body suddenly ready and eager to turn into the one thing she had dreaded her entire life. Rosa didn't understand any of it, but she knew one thing for sure, she had to fight it.

The moment she went to the other side, her real family would come for her. There were nights in her teens when she had felt them calling to her. When she'd heard their leader howling on the wind, desperate to reunite her with his people. And, just like now, she had been forced to shut him out.

But the call was in her blood, and the wolves who wanted her in their pack seemed to be stopping at nothing to ensure that her change happened.

The wolves hadn't counted on her new parents, though. Parents who, of course, had other plans. And it appeared desperate times had called for desperate measures, because she had never been allowed to leave the protective circle of the mansion. Not once in almost twenty-one years.

She was outside the walls she had stared at all that time. Across the barrier between her world and the real world. Rosa watched it all go by out the window of her mother's car, but she couldn't enjoy the view. She simply kept her head down and held onto her sanity, listening to her mum as she talked aloud to herself or sang along to the radio.

"Because, in all honesty, I'm scared," she was finishing, and Rosa turned to her with a frown.

"Scared of me?" she replied, and Wynter shook her head. She then turned to her with a soft smile.

"I could never be scared of you, Rosa," she insisted. "I'm scared of losing you. And I'm scared of you becoming something you don't want to be. And…"

"And what?" she demanded, feeling anger bubbling up inside.

"And I'm scared of your father," Wynter answered, and Rosa shook her head.

"He would never blame you," she replied, and then it dawned on her. Her mother hadn't said what she was afraid of, just that she feared him. Of her husband and the vampire Rosa had always called Dad. The incredible force of a man, myth, and monster, whom she had never once seen Wynter speak out of turn to.

And now she knew why. "You're afraid that if I turn and you have to go back without me, he'll think you failed him?" she asked, and her mother tried to laugh it off, but Rosa could see right through her façade. Underneath her living the life of the doting wife and perfect counterpart was a woman who had stood beside a dangerous man destined for greatness. She had been by his side through all the wars and the hostile takeovers and was clearly terrified of what he was capable of—both in battle and in life itself.

"It's more than me being worried about failing him. You know what he's like…" Wynter answered, and then began humming to the song on the stereo as though she didn't want to entertain their conversation any longer. But Rosa wanted to know more. For the first time in days, she felt a little better, and knew it was because she had something to focus on other than the ache in her bones.

"Why don't you tell me?" she asked, and then watched as her mother fidgeted with the steering wheel. "I remember when I was a toddler, and you used to leave the mansion sometimes. The alpha always went with you," she said, filling the heavy silence. "And I remember when Jack died, and you wanted to punish Marc for what he had done. Father would have none of it, even when you pleaded for him to show the boy the same repercussions as us girls would have received. He snapped you in two, forcing you to become your mist, and then pressed you into his chest. You stayed there for almost an entire week before he let you out…"

"You're very observant, Rosa," Wynter whispered, and then sighed dejectedly. "I cannot be trusted, which is why I always needed a chaperone or a place to cool off whenever I've tried to make the wrong decisions. Your father knows he has to make the decisions for me, otherwise bad things happen."

Now that got her attention. Rose turned in her seat and stared across at her mother incredulously. Had this been the reason for her doting wife routine all these years? She needed to know and wasn't going to rest until she did.

"What does that mean?" she demanded, and while hesitant at first, Wynter eventually listed off all the bad things that'd happened before Rosa was born. All the people they had lost and the lives she had torn apart. And, of course, the final nail in the coffin—Marcella.

"When she turned your uncle Archie, everyone hated me for it. No one cared for my pain, only that I had been selfish enough to take another life in my quest to find a way to be okay with the role Marcus wanted me to play at his side, and I couldn't bear it. I had failed her, just like all the others, and so retreated into myself," she admitted. "Marcus taught me to accept the pain and to trust his judgement, rather than question it any longer. He had my back, and always would, and so I gave him what he wanted. I gave him the life he desired and the wife at his side he deserved."

"And now you don't have a life outside the mansion, or an opinion of your own," Rosa replied, and could tell she was being cruel, but her mother didn't even seem to notice. Perhaps she had been on the receiving end of so many vile comments over the years that she truly had learned to simply ignore them.

And then it dawned on her. The stories finally began to add up. The hurt and the pain, and all eyes always on Wynter, but it wasn't her who had done any of it. No, it was the mastermind. The man at the top of the world who only went on to climb higher. Marcus. He was to blame for everything that'd gone wrong, not Wynter. Rosa adored her father, but she didn't see him with the same rose-tinted-glasses that the others seemed to. Archie was his brother by magic and there would be nothing that could break their bond. The twins were beholden to him, as was dictated years previously by their ancestors.

And of course, Wynter had once been the victim of free will. She'd tried and failed so badly she'd ended up broken down by it. Her will all but destroyed in her efforts to deny him, only to then be given a heart that would love him forever. "It's okay, Mum. There's no shame in loving him," she told her, thinking now was not the time or the way to talk about this. And really, she wondered if it would ever be. After all, Marcus Cole was infallible. He ruled all the magical creatures of this world and had the humans in his pockets, too. He was unstoppable, and even Rosa knew it was better to remain by his side than be crushed under his boot. Her mother might be seen to have taken the easy way out in the past, but it clearly hadn't been easy getting there.

When the car came to a stop a short while later, it was a relief. Rosa had been feeling dreadful again and was glad to be able to stretch her weary legs. She jumped out of the car and went for a short walk along the rocky beach her mother had driven them to, and it did the trick perfectly. Thanks to the cool morning air, she was finally able to take some deep breaths and enjoy the view, which was wonderful. Rosa had never seen the ocean in real life before. Never walked on a beach at dawn or listened as the waves hit the shore. She hadn't lived a normal life in the slightest but had never realised all that she'd missed out on until now. The movies and photos she'd seen throughout the years had felt real enough to quell her desire to see the world with her own eyes, but now that she was glimpsing the magic of nature for real, she wanted more.

It was a turning point for her, she was certain. But first, she had to get through her transition in one piece.

She was about to ask her mother where they were going next when she turned to find her gone. Nothing but a billowing cloud around her ankles, that then lifted her off the ground and floated out towards the islands ahead. The water was rough beneath her, and Rosa let out a few choice swearwords in surprise as they travelled over them, even more so when a waft of spray came up and hit her head on, almost soaking her. The cloud of mist beneath seemed to absorb the water instead, though, leaving Rosa clean and dry atop her mother's strange form. She might be pleased if she wasn't still so damn tender. Her pain was back and was resonating from the inside out. It felt like she might tear into a thousand scattered pieces at any moment, much like Wynter could do at will. Only, if those urges were to overcome Rosa, the pieces she transformed back into wouldn't be a cloud of mist, but a monstrous creature. A beast. And if she did so, she would lose everything. Everyone she cared about and the life she'd always known would be gone in a heartbeat and she would be forced into a life of subordination beneath her uncle's reign. Better the devil, or vampire, she knew.

Rosa couldn't let the change happen, and so she curled into a ball and pushed her hands into the mist, whispering to her mother to hurry.

They soon arrived at an island that from afar had appeared completely uninhabited. Far different to the next one over, which held a lighthouse and a garden that was clearly well tended. Someone lived there, but who would make such a remote place their home? And why did she like the idea so much?

Rosa was about to ask her mother more questions about it, having felt drawn to the island somehow, when her feet hit the ground and a wave of what felt like electricity shook her from head to toe. The sensation was odd, as if she were being jolted, but in a good way. Like she was being energised from the inside out. She felt like it was drawing out all her pain and the strange sensations that'd been clawing at her limbs for days. Like the island was curing her somehow. When it was over, she wanted to cry.

"Mum, I feel amazing! What is this place?" she asked and was surprised when Wynter seemed shocked by what'd just happened.

"I bought you here because this is where you were born, Rosa. Your birth mother's ashes are buried under that tree," she said, and pointed to the largest of all the oaks on the mostly flat plain atop the island. The tree, unlike the others around it, was green and lush. It appeared to be thriving despite the dull weather and lack of sunlight, and Rosa felt herself being drawn to it. She ran her hands over the bark and closed her eyes, and even though there wasn't a kind of spiritual awakening like she thought might happen, she felt warmer within.

"This is where I need to be…" she whispered to herself and felt as if everything might finally be falling into place. Had the pain been a test? If so, she hoped she had passed it by not giving in. "Who was she?" Rosa then asked.

"She was a human. Something each of us is guilty of overlooking and calling weak, but Rosalie Summers was the strongest human I had ever met. She loved you so much that she wanted you to come away with me. To live among your family and with parents who might understand you. We all wanted her to come too, but it wasn't meant to be," Wynter told her with tears in her eyes. Rosa had heard the story of her birth before, but now that she was actually on the island and standing at her birth mother's final resting place, it all finally felt real.

She could feel some sort of magic all around them and wondered if it had anything to do with Rosalie's sacrifice. Perhaps she had incited the magic with what she had done? Brought forth a power from another world?

There was definitely something going on, and whatever it was, it was helping her. Rosa felt a hundred times better than she had on the drive down. In fact, she felt better than she had in weeks, and took deep breaths of the salty, fresh air. And yet, while refreshing, she knew that wasn't what was making her feel better.

The sound of footsteps behind them made Rosa turn, and she found herself peering up into the face of the tallest man she had ever seen. He was broad and looked strong, and damn, he was handsome. Not that she even thought about such things. Of course not.

"Rosalie, is it really you?" he whispered, but then shook his head and smiled down at her as he neared, as though he'd just realised it couldn't be.

"Rosa, it's a pleasure to meet you," she answered, polite as always as per her father's teachings. She instinctually reached out her hand to shake his, and when he did, she saw stars. Rosa stumbled and almost keeled over, but the man caught her, and she knew then and there where the magic had come from. He was responsible for how she was feeling, and when they had touched it was as though she'd had a direct dose of the stuff. It felt wonderful.

"Whoa there," he cried, settling her, "you ok?" the man added, and she nodded timidly.

"Rafferty, put my daughter down will you," her mother's voice chimed, breaking their intense moment, and as Wynter approached, both she and the man righted themselves with shy smiles on both of their faces.

"It's been a long time," he replied, and Rosa watched her mother's smile falter ever so slightly.

"I know, old friend. I promised I'd be back sooner," she said, and Rosa could hear the guilt in her voice.

"You know time means nothing to a goblin. Come here, jinni," he answered, pulling her into a hug, and both women were surprised by his reaction. No one would dare touch her in that way at the mansion, but the man—or apparently goblin—had done so without a care. Yet another reason why Rosa liked him. He was unusual and didn't seem to play by the same rules she had lived by her entire life.

When he let her mother go, Wynter seemed lighter somehow. Rosa wondered if his touch had helped ease her pain, too. Not that she let on about having any, of course, but anyone close to her could see it. The problem was, no one seemed to want to address it. But then again, she got the feeling they had tried, which was how Wynter had become the shell of a woman Rosa instinctively knew she had once been. Because she had tried and failed, and because she had been given hopes that had been later quashed. She didn't need to guess whom by.

Silence fell between them all, and Rafferty couldn't seem to take his eyes off her. Rosa was glad when the huge goblin tore his gaze away and then stalked off, but as soon as he was out of reach, she suddenly felt a pang in her belly, and an ache that seemed to return with a bang.

"Come with me," Rafferty called when the pair of them didn't follow, and Rosa didn't need to be asked twice. She went down the small path and caught up with the still quiet goblin, and when he finally came to a stop, she stared up at him coyly while her mother disappeared inside a cave behind them. "You're wondering why you feel better, aren't you?" he then asked, his eyes staring off into the distance to where Rosa could make out the lighthouse through the mist.

"Is it you?" she asked. "Your magic?"

"Yes. And do you want to know why?" Rafferty answered, his tone solemn. Rosa nodded and gulped when he peered down at her again with such intensity it was as though his eyes were burning a hole in her skull.

"What is it?" she whimpered and was actually glad when Rafferty turned his attention back to the choppy waters.

"Across the sea is a lighthouse, and beneath that lighthouse lives a man. He tends his crops and milks his cow. He gathers eggs to eat from his chickens and bothers no one. He never leaves his post and always turns on his light at dusk…" he began, sounding like some sort of storybook narrator. "The man is called Kristian, and he is your betrothed."

Rosa sucked in a breath and shook her head. Her father had always told her there was no one chosen. No male worthy of her. She could choose when the time was right and would be allowed to follow her own path.

"No, my father—" she began, but Rafferty cut her off.

"Marcus Cole is not your real father, Rosa. You know this, and so you also know what your real dad was and how he became so."

"Yes, I know," she admitted, watching the sky as she tried to see across to the island she had spotted a few miles away.

"He died in that lighthouse, thanks to your uncle Brodie. His reign of violence and brutality towards his victims came to an end, but not before you were conceived," Rafferty continued, and Rosa nodded. She knew how her life had begun, which was why she didn't want to turn into a werewolf. She wanted to become a proper shifter and had enjoyed learning about her powers before the turn had threatened to take hold. "Your father had a pack. A family. And your uncle? Well, he was livid when he found out what'd happened. He tried to get you back, but Marcus killed his mate for daring to so much as suggest it. And then they made a deal."

"If I turn, then I'm theirs," she finished for him, and Rafferty nodded.

"Which is why Kristian is there. Waiting for you, hoping that you'll be his," he replied with a scowl. "He came here, your uncle. Tried to buy me off and when that didn't work, he tried threatening me. But goblins cannot be turned, and the magic I possess is unlike any other creature that walks this planet."

Rosa stumbled back and rested against the rocks beside the cave entrance, watching both Rafferty and the distant lighthouse with her hand clutched to her throat. It was all finally adding up.

"You protect things, don't you? Like this island and the people who lived here?"

"Yes, and I failed once before. I set my wards too weak, and we suffered an invasion, so I swore it would never happen again. I've strengthened it all, and in doing so I can give strength to the people who called this island their home," Rafferty admitted, and she smiled.

"Which is why I feel so much better for being here," she mused. "This place is in my blood. Your magic is in my bones."

"Perhaps," he answered, but she knew it to be true.

"Think about it. Why else would I feel instantly better? And when I touched you, it was like a hit from the source. Your magic helped me when I was an unborn child, and it will help me now. I don't care about the wolves or the man who calls himself my intended. I choose this life Marcus has given me, both the good and bad. Will you help me?"

"It's what I do, little Rose," Rafferty replied, and he turned to her with a smile that lit her up from the inside out.

TEN

Wynter watched the two of them through the cave entrance, and she smiled. Rosa really had no idea that what she was feeling towards Rafferty meant more than just his power, however, she wasn't about to tell her, and neither was he. Or so it seemed. The hundreds of years old goblin was remaining quiet and calm in the face of someone whom Wynter knew had shaken him, and she felt she might know why.

After twenty years and all that'd happened, the pair of them seemed destined to have crossed paths again. He liked her, the young half werewolf, and Wynter wasn't sure he knew what to do about that.

She moved away and went over to the house Rafferty had kept the same as she had always remembered. Nothing was different and there wasn't a thing out of place, and after a quick nostalgic wander around, she then went back out and turned to the right. A tunnel lay ahead, and Wynter needed to see what was there. Something was calling to her, like whispers guiding her down the path. She had to go to the place where Jakob had taken his last breath, and so crept down the tunnels and into the lower system of caves that ran through the depths of the small island. And all the while, sorrow was churning in her gut.

There was no light to guide her way and no trail to follow, but she knew the way. Despite her life since that day, she would always know this place. Always remember it with perfect, torturous clarity. But she hadn't been drawn back to that spot before, and at first wondered why now —

Two red eyes were the first thing she noticed, and they weren't the dull red of the vampire soldiers she commanded, but the piercing lasers of an animal. A predator.

And then she heard him growl.

"Fuck," she sighed.

"Stand aside," the werewolf hissed, but Wynter shook her head. Another five pairs of eyes then joined the first set, and a second voice came from the depths.

"Then you too shall die…" the voice growled, leading her to do a double take. What did he mean by that?

She got her answer when, like some kind of macabre copycat of the day she'd lost Jak, Rafferty's severed head was tossed towards her from the darkness and landed at her feet.

Rather than freak out like she might've done two decades before, Wynter let her impulses lead her. She turned and looked back up the tunnel to where Rosa was still talking with…

It was a shifter, and a damn good one at that. How hadn't she known? Why hadn't she realised it wasn't truly her friend?

Damn. She really had forgotten her old self.

She didn't hesitate and was up and out of the tunnels in a flash, but it was already too late.

"Mum, stop!" Rosa cried from the entrance above, and it took everything Wynter had not to charge straight for the imposter and rip his heart out.

"Rosa, he isn't Rafferty," she answered, and then let out a cry when her daughter nodded.

"I know, but it doesn't matter," she said, and was almost serene as she turned and looked up into the man's face. "This is Kristian. My soulmate."

"No, Rosa. It's a trick. They've been playing you since the moment we got back here," Wynter tried, but the young woman before her was having none of it.

"The reason I felt so much better wasn't because of goblin magic. It was because of Kristian and the magic he holds as a shifter. He's like me and hasn't turned, don't you see?" she implored, and while Wynter could see so for herself, she still didn't like any of this.

"Then why wasn't he honest from the very beginning?" she countered, "and he needs to show you his true face."

That seemed to work a bit better, and both watched him squirm a little.

"She's right, I need to see the real you. Show me…" Rosa asked him, and they watched as Kristian seemed to vibrate against the air around him. He altered right before their eyes and shifted to become a young man around the same age as Rosa, but Wynter could tell it still wasn't his true visage. She was about to say so when Rosa did it for her, and the jinni was proud of her for not simply falling for his lies. The fact remained that the werewolves had killed Rafferty and taken control of his island, lying in wait until Rosa returned for answers they'd known she would seek. They had employed devious tactics and had bided their time.

There had to be a reason.

The man continued to change at her daughter's insistence, and soon revealed himself to be not only a liar, but a conniving deviant too. The real Kristian had to be closer to sixty years old. He seemed to not only be controlling the magic of the island but also the wolves to her back, and Wynter quickly realised why.

"This man is the alpha—your uncle," she told Rosa, who immediately stepped away.

He didn't like that one little bit, and it was clear the rumours about inbreeding in the packs were true. He didn't see anything wrong in trying to wed his young niece, but the idea made Wynter sick to her stomach.

"This woman has lied to you your entire life, Rosa. She kept you from your true family and probably never even told you about us," Kristian tried, but Rosa shook her head. It didn't stop him from continuing. "This is why you needed to come back here, so that you could turn and be free of the pain and torment I know you feel. I am the only one who can help make it better."

"My mother has never lied, not to me," she replied tersely, stepping away, and even Wynter was surprised to hear her say so. She'd been far from perfect, but it was true, she'd never lied. And the reason why—guilt. She couldn't bear to hurt anyone else as a result of even the smallest lie, so had always remained completely honest, even if the truth might hurt at times. And anyway, Marcus was the one who did the lying and the manipulating, not her. She had lost her way since losing faith in herself but could feel that tide beginning to change. And she knew why. Rosa had spoken to her so openly before and it was like the breath of fresh air Wynter hadn't realised she needed. Ever since then she had begun to remember the old days, and wanted them back. To break through her timid shell and find her old self again, and to find her way back to the fighter she had once been.

"You remember?" Wynter asked, and Rosa nodded.

"I remember every day since the day I was born. All the promises you made me, and the words you spoke that day in the tree," she answered, taking her mother aback. "But you forgot, didn't you? It's time you remember who and what you are..."

Rosa then turned to her uncle, and they all watched as her skin began to ripple and change, just like his had done. She shifted, then and there. Rosa turned from one version of herself into another, but there were differences to her in the aftermath. She had a stronger, more determined aura about her, and it was clear she had made it through some sort of final transition. One that meant she wasn't going to become a werewolf but was going to remain as she had always been.

Wynter knew they had come to this island for a reason. One way or another, Rosa was going to finish her transformation and come away from it as her final self, and it appeared that wasn't going to be in werewolf form. Wynter hoped that she might end up the same too. Perhaps both could transform, much like they had done the last time they'd been on the island.

The air began to shift around them. Kristian was now holding Rosa tightly to him, and Wynter sensed the arrival of not only the handful of wolves she had previously encountered, but far more. Whilst everything had been going on and keeping them distracted, dozens had joined them and were now forming a semi-circle behind the jinni. It was clearer than ever just how devious the wolves were, their alpha most of all, and Wynter glowered at him but held her tongue. After all, it was Rosa's time to shine. To show them all what she was made of.

"Now that the deed is done, it's time you joined your true family," Kristian told her with a smile. "It doesn't matter what you have transformed into, you're still one of us. You're like me, a shifter, which means you're stronger than the others. It also means you've kept your mind free of the predatory thoughts that cloud the minds of our kind. You're a leader, child. An alpha…"

"I won't join you," she answered, but he simply laughed.

"You don't have a choice. You see, my pack here is going to do one of two things, but I'll let you decide which one," he began. "Marcus Cole will pay a high price to get his wife back, so we could take her prisoner and negotiate the terms of her release while starting our lives together, or you can walk away from me and she dies. Your choice."

"So obvious," Rosa answered, smirking back at him, and Wynter was impressed by her strength. The now fully-fledged shifter was doing her proud with every moment that passed, and she adored seeing her come into her own.

She remained perfectly still, following her daughter's lead, even as the wolves tightened their circle and began to close in. Whatever Rosa decided, she would do. No matter which route she took, Wynter was right there with her, just as she had always promised.

"It might be cliché, but it's what you've got, love. Now, make your choice. Come with us and she lives, or refuse and she dies," he demanded, clearly having grown unimpressed with his niece's unwillingness to play his game. "A jinni cannot win against an entire pack of wolves, so choose!"

Rosa responded by laughing in his face, and Wynter could sense his rage ripple through the pack at her heels. Shit was going to go down, and soon, so she readied herself for the fight that was clearly imminent.

The witch's heart that freely gave her power quickly joined the fray, and in less than a second, Wynter could feel her hands begin to tingle with it. Rosa seemed to know her mother was fit to burst, and so finally revealed her plan to them both.

"You're right. A jinni couldn't win against a pack of werewolves, but you see, she's not just a jinni—"

Sparks shot from Wynter's hands without warning, cutting off all negotiations, and the now practised jinni utilised Mara's power with ease. Her magic half didn't fail her, and despite their numbers, she quickly laid waste to the wolves closest to her, and then went after the others. Wynter tore out their hearts and ripped them limb from limb. She put her glowing hands straight into their open, snapping mouths as they tried to bite her, and ripped out their spines from the inside. She also grabbed their open jaws as they snapped at her and yanked them wide, tearing the beast's skull in two. She was a ruthless, violent killer, and didn't stop until every single one of them was dead.

And then she turned back to their leader and grinned, the blood of his minions dripping down her cheeks.

"Thanks, I needed that," she teased, stretching out her arms as though she were limbering up for more. "I'd forgotten what it was like to fight back purely because I wanted to, and now I am going to make it clear. You're going to die, and then Rosa and I are going to get the fuck back home."

Kristian was shaking with either rage or fear. She didn't know. Didn't care either. "You see, Marcus might be the worst of the worst. He never loses, and he never backs down, but I'll give him one thing. He surrounds himself with the best. You think you can take him on and win? Trust me, it's not possible. And the second you thought you could use either me or my daughter as leverage, you were already dead."

"Shit, she's good, isn't she?" Rosa then added, beaming over at her, and Wynter offered her a wink. Kristian didn't even get the chance to respond before Rosa ripped out his heart and tossed it over the cliff edge behind them, and then walked away like nothing had even happened. Kristian was coughing and spluttering, his body in shock as it came to terms with the end.

By the time his lifeless body slumped to the ground, Wynter was nothing but mist billowing around Rosa's feet, and she plucked her up off the ground and spirited her daughter away.

Back to the mainland, and the car she would drive them home in.

Like more than twenty years before, Wynter was taking her daughter to the mansion, but this time, she wasn't afraid to return as herself. Wasn't looking to fit in or blindly take care of the others in their keep. This time, she had her fighting spirit firmly back in place, and Marcus was going to have to like it or lump it. Because this time, it wasn't going anywhere.

ELEVEN

"Well?" Marcus demanded of his young Priestess, "what do you see?"

He knew without asking that Wynter was on her way home. Like always, the separation had been excruciating, and it'd been all he could do not to wreak havoc on his so carefully polished reign simply to keep himself from going crazy in her absence. But at least she hadn't been gone long. Not a day had gone by in the last two decades where they hadn't been together, and he hadn't allowed it easily. Especially as he'd also let her go without a chaperone. His trust wasn't earned with ease, and the vampire knew that without his wife having remained so compliant and in need of his guidance these past twenty years, she wouldn't have it now. Even still, he doubted his faith in her, though, and so glared down at the witch kneeling before him. "Answer me!"

"Rosa is an adult shifter now," Marceline finally replied, "she is counted as one of the wolves' most elite alphas and may take a pack of her own to lead."

"Never," he replied, and she nodded.

"She will not have a pack, but an army…" the Priestess replied, her voice deepening and turning wistful. She was having a vision. "Your daughter will raise an army, master. She will fight at your side, along with your wife and the hordes."

Marcus was pleased to hear it. This was exactly the outcome he had hoped for and so was even more pleased he'd sent the two of them away, rather than let Rosa succumb to her heritage and turn werewolf within the confines of their home. Whatever had happened on that island, it had forced the alternative and would yield wondrous consequences. He'd always known it would be worth keeping her. Even as a young girl, he'd remained unsure, but had trusted in the future Marcella had foreseen for them. The power that resided within the half human was his to command now, and he had strengthened that bond by ensuring Rosa had always believed he loved her like his own. And really, it was the greatest accolade the ancient vampire was able to give anyone. Marcus wasn't capable of loving anyone other than his bride. His soul was hers alone, and no matter those he held in the highest of regard, he could never love anyone else but her. Wynter. His doting wife and the other half of his heart.

When he closed his eyes, he could still remember the fighting spirit she'd once had. And the way she had tasted on his tongue as he'd fed from her vein. Those were good times, and he found he often missed them. Marcus missed the way she tried to tell him no or attempted in vain to refuse his commands. She was exciting back then, and he'd enjoyed the chase.

What he'd give to see her face full of spite once again. To smell her distain and taste it upon the air, or to have to hunt her down and have her at his mercy. But he had broken that spirit. He'd taken it for granted and pushed her one time too many, and ever since that day, she had become afraid. Too afraid to make her own choices because she knew what he'd do in retaliation. She'd been right, too. Marcus would've started by rehoming the baby she loved so damn much she had given up her life for it. And then he would've moved on to the next person she loved, and the next. All that would be left was him, as always, and while Marcus adored her submission, he also despised it.

But now, things were different. Their family was whole and, whether he had planned it that way or not, weren't going anywhere.

"And what of my future?" he asked his still kneeling Priestess.

"Unclear, master. There are too many who wish to challenge your reign for me to see clearly, but it is certain that with every passing day you grow stronger while they grow weaker…"

He didn't answer her. The future wasn't clear, but it was enough to know that he would remain strong, and that his family would continue to help him in his pursuit for ultimate control. Marcus would come to command all the magical creatures their world had to offer him, and then next would come the humans.

Marcus knew his darkness was spreading. His influence reached far and wide, and regardless of whether his people loved or hated him, he still had them in his pocket. Had control over them all and was becoming more than just an immortal. He was becoming a god.

The air shifted, as though the world had finally begun to turn again after its period of rest beneath his feet. He once again noticed the colours around him and the light. Where had that come from, and why hadn't he seen it before?

He knew why the moment he opened his mind and sensed her drawing nearer. The other half of his soul was within their grounds. She had returned to him, just as he'd known she would, and Marcus wasn't ashamed of how quickly he took for the doorway of their huge home. His brother was there too, having clearly sensed their return, and Archie turned to him with a smile.

"Rosa…I can sense the changes in her. She's a woman now. A shifter," he said, and Marcus nodded.

"We must celebrate," he told him. "I haven't held a proper party in decades but I'm sure I can remember how."

"Long overdue then," Archie agreed, and together they then watched Wynter's car as it sped up their driveway towards them. They had a matter of moments before the two women arrived, and it appeared Archie had one single piece of business to discuss with his brother before they did. "And Marlee, shall I free her?"

"No," Marcus answered, thinking the young witch should be kept in isolation a while longer. She most certainly did not deserve to attend their celebrations after defying his commands yet again.

"She listens to me," Archie tried. "We have a kinship. I can make her see."

"See what?" Marcus barked, but he knew exactly what was going on with the twins without anyone having to spell it out for him.

Marceline was his Priestess. When the two witches had been born, he'd thought the magic was doubly his, and yet, it was clear now that before Archie had even turned vampire, it had been fated. And so, Marcella had birthed two Priestesses. One for each of their coven's vampire progenies. Marlee didn't belong to him, but to Archie. They had a connection neither could comprehend, but Marcus could see it clearly. However, he would never tell. Better to keep the witch under his rule for as long as possible than lose her.

Like with all things, he didn't like to share.

"That you're a dickhead who cannot be refused, Marcus," Archie answered, clearing the air well in enough time before Wynter and Rosa reached them. He hadn't lost his humorous side, even after everything he had seen and done by Marcus's side, and the ancient vampire grinned across at his brother. Archie was the closest thing he had to a family after Wynter, but that didn't mean he got off lightly either. After all, this was no joking matter.

"Free the little witch but tell her the next time she tries to defy me, I'll do more than punish her. I'm not averse to other methods, which she knows. Humiliation is a good one. Remind her of all the times I strung her father up in that tree, and how I will readily do the same to her," he told him with a sly smile and a brief nod to the huge oak tree a small distance away, "so that everyone who visits will see who has served me well, and who has failed me…"

That certainly shut Archie up, and Marcus was glad. Now was not the time for jokes or for dwelling on the wrongdoings of a child.

His wife was back, and he was damn well going to celebrate it in style.

TWELVE

Wynter saw the two vampires waiting in the doorway, and her heart lurched. Marcus had never greeted her at the door before. He'd always played his games and toyed with her, but not this time. She initially wondered why, but then remembered that was a long time ago. They had all changed since those days, and yet, she was trying to find her way back to them. Foolish or not, she wanted just a small semblance of that independence back, and so revelled in her husband's greeting. It might be the first, and last, time he did so.

Despite herself, Wynter charged from the car the moment they'd parked and was in his arms a second later. She barely even noticed Archie and let Rosa greet her uncle while she reconnected with the other half of her entire being.

"Damn…" he whispered in her ear before planting the deepest of kisses against her lips.

"Did you miss me?" she asked when he broke the kiss, and Marcus beamed down at her. He was peering into her eyes as though seeing something different behind them, and she wondered if he could somehow sense her new resolve.

He didn't answer, but she knew, and so forced herself to take a step away. This was just the start of her renewed demeanour, and Wynter wasn't going to let him lead the way, but instead do some of the leading herself.

She reached across and grabbed Rosa's hand. "Your daughter is a full shifter now," Wynter added, and watched as he took a good look at the girl he had taken in and called his own. She could see for herself how impressed he was with her transition and smiled.

"I always knew you'd be strong enough," Marcus replied, and Rosa smiled up at him timidly.

"Damn right," Archie added, and then turned uncharacteristically serious. "What went down?" he asked, and the four of them took a slow walk inside while Rosa answered him.

They had seen the question coming, but it was still so fresh that when Rosa told the story of how they had taken down her uncle and his pack, Wynter stayed quiet. She knew what question would follow soon after the pair of them were caught up and was revving herself up to answering, but still, when Archie asked it sent a wave of grief through her. "And how's Raff?"

The two women fell silent, and it was Wynter who took charge of the situation.

"Where's Brodie?" she answered and was glad to see Archie had gotten the memo.

"Out the back, doing some training with Marc. Why?" he still asked, and she frowned.

"Go get him," was all she said, and then watched Archie go with an ache in her gut. He knew something was wrong, Wynter could tell, but the vampire also knew better than to challenge her. Not on something this important, and he probably had already guessed what she was about to tell them both, anyway.

Brodie was understandably grief-stricken to discover his oldest friend was dead. He and Rafferty had been a team, and now that he was gone, the jinni went into overdrive with his questions about how and why the goblin had met such an awful end.

"I converse with him almost daily," he told her. "So, was that really him the last time, or an imposter?"

"It was him," Wynter answered. "I saw for myself how the house was still perfectly tended to. The wolf wouldn't have done the same. I think they were lying in wait for us and managed to sneak in beneath the house while Rosa and I were travelling over. They must've grabbed Raff then, and Kristian quickly shifted to look like him before radiating his odd sort of magic all around the island. By the time we reached him, he was all set, while the real Rafferty was below with his pack."

"And you saw him dead? It couldn't have been a trick?" Archie asked, and Wynter paled.

"It wasn't a trick," she groaned.

"Then we need to go and give him a proper burial. He deserves to have the right send off," Brodie replied, and they all agreed. "We'll leave right away," he added, and went to go, but Wynter put her hand on his arm and peered up into his immense green eyes. She could feel him, her maker, and knew he was in an incredible amount of pain, but there was something he needed to know before he went back to the island.

"We fled in a hurry, Brodie…"

He frowned and then nodded. Of course, they hadn't had time to clear up the carnage and mess of bodies left behind after their fight, and she was glad he seemed to understand without her having to say so out loud.

"I'm coming with you," Rosa then piped up, and Wynter was about to tell her no. Or that she'd need Marcus's permission to leave again, who had gone to tend to some business. But then she remembered her new mantra. She was going to find herself again and would start by making some decisions—whether big or small.

"Why?" she asked, and they all seemed surprised to hear her challenge Rosa's request rather than blindly direct her to her father.

"I need closure. The island and our experience there gave me the strength I needed to become my true self, but I have this strange need to close that chapter of my life so I can move forward. And I want to help. I can be there for Brodie and Archie," Rosa replied. "Please, mum. I need to do this. It's my mess, and my fault Rafferty died. I need to pay my respects."

She had fought her corner well, and Wynter was all for helping her daughter move forward in her quest. It would scare the hell out of her to let Rosa out of her sight, but Wynter knew she had to. It was time she gave her some space.

"Then go," she whispered to her daughter, and then placed the lightest of kisses against her cheek. Wynter then had an idea, and she conjured up her old bracelet that'd connected her to Brodie. The white beads were still perfectly opaque, as was the single black bead in the centre, and she handed it to her daughter. "Take this. It will connect us."

"Mum, I can't..." Rosa tried, "this is yours," she added, but Wynter was adamant she take it. She had given her the bracelet on instinct and was convinced it was the right approach. The two of them were connected, after all.

"I'll know you're safe as long as you wear it," she answered, and hadn't known where the idea had come from, but knew it was the right thing to do because as soon as Rosa pushed the small, beaded bracelet onto her wrist, she could sense her. "This talisman will protect you."

"As will we," Brodie added, which made her feel even better.

"I know," she replied, and gave him a nod before she then stepped away. "So go. The sooner you get going, the quicker you'll return," Wynter added with a frown. She could tell it wouldn't be long before she lost her nerve and went running to her husband for guidance, but she wanted this for them. For Rosa. She was a woman now—an alpha—and had come into her own, and she deserved her closure.

Wynter watched them go with tears in her eyes, but she refused to let them fall. This was good. They were all taking steps forward to better themselves, and so when she turned and went back into the house, it was with her head held high.

She had just reached the stairs when one of the young house witches, Marlee, came bounding down them towards her. She seemed in an awful hurry, and Wynter reached out for her hand as she passed, which was when the young woman shared a vision with her. Whether accidentally or on purpose, she saw a glimpse of her future.

Wynter was locked away inside a cell made just for her. One of flesh, and inside the heart of the vampire she loved. She was a prisoner. A captive.

And her captor? The same as always.

"Run," Marlee hissed, but Wynter shook her head.

"Where would I go?" was her answer, and she let Marlee go before looking up the huge staircase at the master who had sent the young witch running in fear.

"My sweet," Marcus called down to her, and Wynter simply smiled up at him.

"Yes?"

"It didn't take you long to piss me off," he replied, taking a leisurely descent. She didn't need to ask why.

"I thought you wanted me to be more decisive?" she countered, her heart pounding in her chest as he neared.

"Yes, when the situation warrants it. However, allowing Rosa to leave is something you ought to have run by me," he said, and grabbed Wynter, pulling her into his tight embrace. "It's just a good thing she's with my brother, or else I would be forced to punish you, little fighter…"

"So, you're not?" she asked, trembling against him. There was no helping it, but Wynter didn't fight. She still wanted things to be good between them and hadn't been trying to annoy him. All she'd wanted was to decide on something without running to him for permission first.

"Not today, because I'm too damn glad to have you home," Marcus answered, "where you'll stay now. Forever."

She looked up into his intense blue eyes and saw danger behind them. It was the same danger she had tried to fight almost a quarter of a century before, and just like then, she buckled under the pressure.

"Forever," she whispered, and then let him carry her upstairs to their bedroom, where she showed him how much she had meant it.

THIRTEEN

The clean-up had been tough and disgusting work, but Rosa and her uncles had the island perfect again before long. The next job had been to burn the decapitated body of their friend, and she watched as they took turns telling stories about Rafferty and what he had meant to each of them. Rosa realised then how she hadn't had to go through the loss of a loved one before and began to comprehend then how evil the world could be. Just how hard it seemed to say goodbye, and she wondered if that were why Marcus had kept her so sheltered. And why Wynter had always been so afraid. By all accounts, her mother had lost everything she had once loved, and it was clear the trauma of those losses had never left her.

And yet, Wynter had still gone on to love her father and the children she had raised beneath his roof. She had made a life with him and a family. Their mansion had become a sort of citadel. A fortress surrounded by lush grounds laden with impenetrable magical force fields and teeming with creatures Rosa knew her father's enemies had no chance of thwarting.

Her uncles were two such creatures, and as she watched them, it was odd to her that they could each appear so human one minute, and then their true selves the next. Rosa had seen them kill. She had sneakily watched as Marcus had welcomed his foes into their home under the pretence of a parley, only to then set his minions on them. Her parents might have sheltered them from being part of the macabre display, but that hadn't stopped Rosa from sneaking a look wherever she could. There was also part of their grounds that was once a lush orchard but had now been named the 'dead man's forest' by those who lived at the mansion. None of them had needed to ask why. They could see the bodies that hung from the branches from their upstairs windows and knew the dark show of her father's force could be seen from outside their grounds too. It was a lesson to anyone who dared rise up or take arms against him. Not that many had in years. Not even the human populous, whom she knew had heard the rumours of a vampire king who had planned to take over the world. The very idea fascinated her, and she hoped to one day see it with her own eyes. To be at his side as Marcus took the world by storm—and force. He'd raised her in his shadow after all, so it stood to reason she would come to think much like he did, even with Wynter's more gentle input.

Rosa also wanted to know what was going on in the human world. To see what they saw and how they lived their lives. Were the rumours mere myth, or was there some truth to them? After all, given the numbers of humans in her father's employ, it stood to reason almost everyone knew someone who had gone into his service and never returned. Did they suspect anything?

"Uncle Archie, can I ask you something?" she probed when the funeral fire was out and the three of them had buried Rafferty's ashes beneath the same tree as her birth mother.

"Anything," he answered, and then put a protective arm around her. He had always been her closest confidant, and as much as she adored Brodie, there was just a more natural connection between the two of them. Archie had never fobbed her off when she'd asked silly questions, and she had never caught him in a lie. She had trusted the vampire time and again and wasn't about to stop now.

"When we go back, can we stop at a human city on the way? I want to see them. See how they live and listen to them talk," she replied, and was overjoyed when he nodded.

"I can go one better than that," he told her with a smile. "Your father trusts me to take care of you, and you know I'd never let any harm come 'te you. So, with absolutely no ulterior motive, of course, how about we go home via one of the biggest Pride communities you'll ever see? We can dance and sing, and just enjoy ourselves for one night away from it all. What 'ye say?" Archie added, his Scottish lilt making a comeback as he spoke. Perhaps reminiscent of old times.

Either way, Rosa was in and so nodded profusely. That sounded amazing, and actually, now that her transformation had happened, she was finally ready to take the next step in becoming a woman. She'd always been interested in sex and had found herself attracted to both men and women over her pubescent years but hadn't been afforded the chance to explore any of those feelings because her fears had always held her back. Pain had overridden everything, but now it was gone, and she was ready to try something new. What? She didn't know but was willing to go with the flow and figure things out once they got there. Something inside of her was screaming that it was time. She was twenty-one and still a virgin. Rosa wasn't ashamed of it, but she wanted to finally say goodbye to her tortured childhood and look to the future as a strong and powerful woman. And an alpha werewolf, after all.

The three of them left the island behind by nightfall, and Rosa got the impression it was for good this time. Brodie hadn't employed another goblin in Rafferty's place, and so the home there would go untended. Nature would take it all back, and the trees up on the summit would bloom in honour of their fallen friends and family.

But it was time to close that chapter of her life, and Rosa looked back just once as they sailed away. And it was the oddest thing. She was sure she saw a woman standing vigil on the highest point, silently watching them leave. She was dressed all in white and seemed to disappear the moment Rosa looked harder at her outline. Maybe she hadn't even been real at all, but whatever she was, she didn't seem to have any ill will towards them, and so Rosa turned back to the mainland and spoke of it to no one.

A couple of hours later, the three of them were dressed up and ready to hit the town. Archie had insisted they stop to buy some new clothes for their night out, Brodie excluded, of course, and Rosa had gladly indulged him. The vampire hadn't been away from the mansion for more than Marcus's bidding for years, and even Rosa enjoyed shopping for real, rather than simply wearing whatever her father allowed to be bought for her online.

And so, they stepped out into the real world, dressed to impress, and the young woman couldn't stop from staring at everything in awe. The human world had been busy carrying on without them all these years, and Rosa loved it. People were everywhere. In cars and busses on every street they went down, and on the pavements crammed into lines of foot traffic as shoppers wrapped up their late nights of spending, or partygoers got started for the evening ahead.

The three of them walked through it all, and Rosa stopped a few times en-route. Once, to draw her uncles aside so they could listen to a street performer sing, and another time she caught a smell she couldn't even begin to describe. It was the most delectable thing she had ever smelled before and soon tracked the source to a street vendor who was selling an entire array of incredibly flavoured donuts. Of course, she walked away with a salted caramel one already on the go, and another two varieties safely stashed away in a box for later. It was Brodie who paid, and as she watched him hand over the cash, Rosa realised she'd never even seen money before.

"We've got you, Rosie," Archie told her, having noticed, and while she grinned up at him, Rosa couldn't hide her embarrassment. As if she was so shielded from real life that she didn't even think about money when ordering food. There was so much she had to learn and was more thankful than ever for the family now willing to allow her to do so.

Her father's nightclub was in the centre of the city Archie had chosen, Manchester, and as they neared it, she could sense the magic he wielded there without having to be anywhere close by. Humans were flocking to *Slave* in droves, and while the three creatures weren't lured in by the same cunning magic, they still followed the crowds inside so that Archie could utilise his brother's services before they carried on to the LGBTQ village.

Rosa had no idea what to say or do there, but she let her uncles do the talking and then simply followed behind them. She got the shock of her life when a bouncer reached out and blocked her path with his chubby hand.

"No tailgating. How old are you anyway?" he demanded, and Rosa watched in horror as Archie and Brodie carried on forward, not realising she was no longer with them.

"Excuse me?" she answered, and hadn't done so with any kind of tone, but it appeared the man wasn't playing nice tonight, and he sneered at her.

"Get the hell out of here, girl," he told her, and then stared down at her tastefully covered body like a deviant. "Unless you're gonna make it worth my while…"

She gulped, feeling disgusted, and went to tell the guy off when everything suddenly fell silent around them. Rosa wasn't sure why at first, but then she realised a circle had closed in around the pair of them, blocking her and the bouncer from view of the onlookers. She looked away from his still probing gaze and was met with the red eyes of more than a dozen of her mother's guardsmen. Those chosen from her hordes to protect the clubs her father ran and ensure proper decorum was followed at all times. These were ruthless vampire soldiers who followed orders without fail or question and weren't the sort any human would dare mess with.

Rosa's first instinct was to worry she might be in trouble, but then she looked at the man who slowly seemed to be realising the precariousness of his situation and who foolishly attempted to step away.

The circle pressed in tighter around them, but Rosa wasn't the least bit fazed. She'd grown up with these soldiers around, but the human before her clearly wasn't used to such a close presence. She could see the sweat on his brow as his eyes darted between them all, and he shuddered as an icy wind echoed through the silent group of vampires.

She didn't know what to say and was just glad when Brodie appeared out of nowhere and grabbed the man by the back of his neck before dragging him inside the huge club. Rosa didn't need to ask whether she ought to follow, as the group of soldiers at her back pushed her forward without a sound, and only stopped when she reached an elevator that was waiting open for her. Brodie and the bouncer were inside, along with an older gentleman she had seen at the mansion before. He was one of the Supervisors, her father's elite chosen workers who ran his clubs, and the man simply nodded to Rosa in respect.

The group rode upstairs in silence, and when the doors opened on the fourth floor, they revealed a huge double office. An office that Brodie unceremoniously tossed the bouncer into, sending the man flying.

It was the Supervisor who went for him.

"Don't ever speak to my guests that way," he bellowed, and shocked Rosa by laying into the guy. He kicked him in the gut and continued with a few more, even when he curled into a ball in a bid to protect himself. She watched in shock but knew she mustn't intercede. The bouncer clearly deserved his punishment in the eyes of his boss, so she wasn't in a position to question how or why. A life under Marcus Cole's roof had taught her that much, and so she simply pressed herself into Brodie's hold.

When he was done, the Supervisor turned to them and offered her a small bow. "Miss Cole, I trust I have avenged your honour?"

"Cole?" the bouncer spluttered, writhing on the ground in pain, and it all seemed to sink in then. He ceased his groaning and instead dragged himself onto his knees. "Forgive me, my lady, I had no idea."

"And for your insolence, you should die," she replied, but then kneeled down in front of him, "however, I'm here to have fun, so I'm willing to settle for an apology."

His head jerked up and the poor man seemed surprised to find her with a soft smile rather than a venomous reaction. He clearly wasn't used to the gentler touch, but she'd meant what she'd said. This was hardly her idea of fun.

"I'm so sorry," he whimpered. "I will never speak to any of the customers in such a way again, and especially not you, Miss Cole. I endeavour to serve your father with every action I take, and to know I have failed will not rest easy in my gut."

"Then I can trust you not to step out of line again?" she asked, and the bouncer nodded profusely.

Rosa nodded and climbed back onto her feet. "Good, now get back to work and prove it."

Once the man was gone, along with his supervisor, Brodie let out a small laugh and nudged Rosa while leading her over to a set of windows they could use to look down on the crowd below.

"Well, that wasn't where I'd expected tonight to go," he joked, and then turned serious again, "but can you see now just what sort of business your father is in?"

"I've always been able to see, Brodie. I know how his mind works and he has taught me everything else I couldn't figure out on my own. Like how at least ten percent of those humans down there will end up ensnared as Blood Slaves by the year's end. And how just a few floors below us his workers are filling blood bags, one of which Archie is probably reaching the end of about now."

"And the bouncer?" he asked and hadn't given anything away. Rosa couldn't tell if he was impressed or not, but everything she'd said was true.

"I could've gladly watched him die, but at the same time, a little fear will do wonders for his productivity. I don't have spells and hexes on my side, but I can instil a little loyalty using other means," she told him, and was still scanning the crowd below when she saw a figure on the edge that appeared to be looking directly up at her. It was a woman, and she was dressed all in white, just like the apparition she had seen when leaving the island.

Rosa knew she had to go down there. This was no coincidence.

"Damn, I love your mother and her funny ways, and ought to have realised just how strong she still was under her armour," Brodie teased. "She taught you to be stronger than her. She taught you to be a leader, and a powerful ally to your father's cause."

He was right, and Rosa nodded. She then turned to her uncle and smiled.

"Now that's out of the way. How about you let me go for a walk among the humans down there?" she asked, and of course he didn't refuse.

She was downstairs and amidst the chaos in no time at all and quickly scanned the vast room. Rosa took it all in, but knew she was on the hunt for someone in particular. The girl dressed in white was there somewhere, and she was determined to find her. To figure out who the hell she was and why she had been following them.

There were humans everywhere, but Rosa could see the other creatures dotted around the room. Vampires mostly, of course, and as she took a slow walk around, she sensed the presence of a wolf. A loner with no pack, but he was there, and on the hunt. Rosa's alpha instincts kicked in and she focussed in on his scent with ease. The man was dancing with a human and appeared to have her exactly where he wanted her. The woman was under his spell, and Rosa watched as they smiled at each other and then shared a kiss. He was unlike any of the wolves she had encountered before, and he intrigued her. The man didn't appear to be a brute or a rapist. He wasn't feral, nor had he been driven insane without a pack, and she felt better after seeing him. As though she too might be okay going it alone.

"Intriguing, isn't he?" a soft voice said from beside her, and Rosa turned to see the woman she'd been searching for. She was still dressed all in white, her long ash coloured hair cascading in waves down her back, and when she turned to peer into Rosa's face, it was with the most beautifully deep turquoise eyes she had ever seen. They were an unnatural shade, but of course, it was obvious the woman wasn't human anyway, so Rosa wasn't surprised.

"Who are you?" she whispered, all thoughts of the wolf gone now that she was face to face with the strange apparition she'd seen twice that day.

"I am many things, Rosa. To some, I am terror, while others see me as bliss. I am the ultimate, the all-knowing, and all-seeing," she replied, and Rosa found herself laughing.

"All I wanted was a name," she joked, and was glad when the woman smiled back.

"I have many names, but you may call me Morana," she answered.

"It's lovely to meet you," Rosa replied, but her new friend shook her head.

"You and I met long before today. I took you in my arms the day you were born and was going to take you away with me, but then your mother offered her life for yours," Morana told her, and the world seemed to fall away at that moment.

Rosa could no longer hear the music or any of the chatter all around them. She was fixated on the woman before her, and it was slowly dawning on her who she might be. "Rosalie begged me to take her instead, and as I deliberated, I began to see that you indeed had a wondrous life ahead of you. A dark fate that would lead you back to me when the time was right, but not in the same way that I usually encounter people."

"Death?" Rosa whimpered and gulped when she nodded yes. "But you're not here to kill me?"

"Far from it," Morana replied with a smile, "I'm here to give you back something I took." She then opened her palm to reveal a glowing orb, and Rosa was immediately mesmerised by it. The ball was beautiful and seemed to shimmer in its own kind of light.

"What is it?"

"Your soul," Morana replied, and then closed her hands around it again and pulled them close to her body protectively, as though she wasn't quite ready to hand it back.

Rosa wanted to scream. She had no idea what was going on and was beginning to doubt herself, and the woman before her, but then thought about all the things she had seen and encountered over the years and knew she ought not to be surprised by this new development.

"Why?" was all she could ask.

"Because I discovered something that day and knew I had to keep your soul in my safekeeping until you completed your transition. I needed to know you wouldn't return to me a beast. If you turned, then my master vowed he would keep your soul safe and deliver it to the *After* once you died. We would keep your soul innocent, while your evil beastly urges did otherwise with your flesh, but now…"

"I'm not a wolf. I became a shifter instead."

"Yes, and that makes you worthy," Morana replied, and then she stepped forward and placed her cupped hands over Rosa's heart. "I helped keep you safe all these years. I watched over and cared for you, and now it's finally time for you to know how it feels to truly care for others, and especially how to love. You're destined for a love much stronger than you've ever known, and more powerful than fate itself."

"Who?" Rosa demanded, but Morana just shook her head. She then opened her hands and pushed against Rosa's chest, and the orb disappeared straight through her clothes and skin, going inside of her.

She immediately felt hot, and then cold, and could hardly breathe as the return of her soul began to radiate within her. It was the most intense flurry of emotion, empathy, and power she had ever felt, but when it was over, Rosa finally realised all the things she had been missing without it. Her heart pounded in her ears and when her eyes finally fell back on Morana, she had this incredible pang in her gut. A pang of longing and desperation, and one of love towards her friends and family back home. The Lady of Death had bound her to a life without those things, but why? And physically, her body screamed for that which Morana had stressed upon most—love.

All Rosa could think about was how she wanted to touch and kiss someone. Anyone. She was desperate to feel, and reached forward, but then pulled her hand away.

"I...I don't know what to think," she said, and then frowned. "You should never have taken this from me." All her life, something had been missing, and now she discovered it was this! She was livid. "How dare you?"

Rosa stormed away and was out in the foyer of the huge club in no time at all, and there she took the elevator back up to the main office, which was thankfully empty.

She paced up and down, her soul still settling within her, but couldn't quell her rage. It wasn't right that she'd had to live without a soul. It wasn't fair. It had to have affected her in ways she couldn't even begin to imagine. Had she lacked empathy, like she'd seen in movies when people sold their souls? Or perhaps the lack of a soul was to blame for her never having those impulses that drove people to act out, or to do rash things. Rosa had lived a sheltered, timid life. Always the good girl. Always being led by her father or mother, and never once even considering disobeying them. And now that her soul was returned to her, would she lose that gentle nature?

Morana appeared out of nowhere and simply watched her process, but Rosa wasn't done being angry. Not by a long shot. "Where do you get off doing this to me? And why did you do it? Who made you take such an important part of me away?"

"I didn't like it either, but destiny depended on it, Rosa. I wasn't the one to raise you, that was Wynter's task, but I'm the one to guide you now that you're a woman."

"And if I refuse?"

"Then we will both be punished and forced into the hellish afterlife," she answered with a sad frown, and it rocked Rosa to her core to see her that way. If the Lady of Death herself was afraid, then she wasn't sure she could refuse her. Rosa had never refused the people in her life a thing, but now that Morana was standing there before her, she knew she couldn't allow the strange reaper to dictate her future. She had taken charge of her own life and transformed mere days earlier, only to be told some other path was also destined for her?

No chance.

But before she told her so, Rosa needed to know more.

She reached for Morana's hand and couldn't help but notice she had gloves covering them, and layers of white clothing that flowed over the rest of her, like a second skin. It didn't matter though, the moment their bodies made contact, something inside of her seemed to snap. Whatever Morana was, she was more powerful than anyone else she'd ever known. But, like anyone, she had a master. Someone pulling her strings and dictating her actions.

Fear gripped her gut, and Rosa forced herself away. Whoever the puppet-master was, he was calling to her using Morana as his vessel. But Rosa was not ready or willing to serve him. Soul or no soul, she had her entire life ahead of her and there was only one man she'd been brought up to serve. The man she called her father. She had so much to offer him and was finally able to. Neither Morana or her master was going to take that opportunity away from her simply because they'd returned her soul. Something they'd had no right to take in the first place.

Thinking of the whole soul thing, she went over to where a mirror stood and checked her reflection but didn't seem any different. Not physically, anyway. But it was her eyes. They were the windows to the soul, after all, and as she stared at herself, Rosa saw her true self for the first time. She finally appreciated everything she had become and all the lessons she'd learned along the way and began to cry.

"What now?" she whimpered and turned back to Morana with a frown. "You chose me, why?"

"Because I saw in you a kindred spirit, Rosa. I found you worthy when I took you in my arms, and knew what had to be done," Morana replied cryptically, and Rosa took a step away.

"For what purpose? Don't just say love, because I have seen what it does to people. It can be devastating and inspiring all at the same time, but it isn't everything. There has to be more to life than that," she demanded, and Morana seemed surprised, but she didn't deny it.

"The love that awaits you will consume you whole. It will devour you and then turn everything you thought you knew on its head. You live within a carefully constructed cage, Rosa. One built by Marcus Cole to keep you at his mercy. You need to break free, which is why I want you to become my apprentice until you are ready. Only when you command the same power that seeks to devour you will you be worthy of his love, and I'm the only one who can help you. I'm willing to give you everything I have before I eventually fade into the same abyss I have been feeding souls to for centuries," she replied, taking Rosa aback. "I have reapers who do my bidding, but my successor must be someone special. Someone I believe in enough to give my entire self to, and someone I trust to follow in my footsteps."

"Me?" Rosa gulped. This wasn't at all what she'd expected.

"Yes, you…" she confirmed with a soft smile. "I'd hoped this conversation could happen later, but you're too intuitive for your own good." Rosa couldn't help but laugh. She knew that to be true as well and had almost gotten into trouble in the past for seeing through the nonsense those around her had tried to weave.

Morana closed the gap again, and she reached for Rosa's hands, gripping them with her own. "Share your life with me, and by the time you're done with this world, what's mine will all be yours. You will learn how to command death, honour fate, and have the love of the hand that guides the living into the *After*. He is your destiny. Your soul mate."

Rosa frowned. So, she had been right. The Lady of Death did indeed have a master. Someone who had to be a thousand times more powerful than she. And the person Rosa was apparently destined to fall in love with.

"I'm scared," she replied, and Morana smiled sweetly.

"Which is why I'm here. I gave your soul back at his command, and now I will guide and teach you to be his perfect mate," she insisted.

Rosa gulped. She then felt an overwhelming urge for connection and gave Morana's uncovered cheek the merest of touches. As she did, Rosa saw for herself just how powerful their connection was, and could be. And it was all thanks to the mystery man atop the deathly throne. She didn't even know his name but had felt his essence flowing through Morana into her and had the smallest of visions. Blackness engulfed her, and Rosa gasped. What she'd seen was dark and scary as hell, but also so alluring it brought heat to Rosa's cheeks and a stirring to her gut. She wanted more and felt desperate to touch Morana in other ways so she could get it, but the Lady of Death quickly pulled away.

"What's wrong?" Rosa asked, remorse spearing in her belly.

"We can't do that again," Morana replied gravely, and looked a little worse for wear as she stepped back.

"Why?" Rosa pleaded, watching as she stumbled away and leaned against the wall for support, as though weakened.

"This job has its blessings, and its curses," Morana replied, "and one is that you cannot be touched. Not unless the person is crossing over. I nearly took you into the *After*. In a flash, all our hard work could've been over. It can never happen again."

Well, that sucked, but at the same time, Rosa wasn't all too disappointed. Their touch had been nice, but it had also answered one of her previous uncertainties. She was a woman and had needs. Rosa finally felt ready to find herself a man and tick some firsts off her list. Fuck destiny and whoever the Lady of Death's puppet-master may be.

Her uncles took that moment to arrive in the elevator, and neither seemed surprised to find Rosa there. They greeted their niece and while both could clearly sense that something was up, they didn't appear to want to pry.

Rosa looked at Morana and then back to them with a frown. Why hadn't they said something about her presence?

"You ready for a real party?" Archie asked, and Rosa knew then that they couldn't see her.

So, the plot thickened, but she was glad. She didn't want to have to explain, and the last thing she needed was one of them to ask why there were still tears in her eyes. Rosa wanted to forget her troubles and have fun and decided that following their plan to have a wild night out on the town was the perfect way to do it.

FOURTEEN

The trio returned home by lunchtime the next day, and while Rosa was more than just a little hung over, Wynter didn't say a word about her first foray into the real world and more than overdue inaugural night out on the town. They'd clearly had a good time, and unlike the vampire and jinni, the newly transitioned alpha werewolf was more than able to drink and make merry when in the human world. But she was also not impervious to the effects a night like that could have on her the next day, so was obviously feeling it.

Marcus seemed completely oblivious to her sorry state, and he simply welcomed his family home with open arms, showing how much he truly cared about them. There were no punishments, partly due to her old friends being careful enough to have swung by *Slave* while they were out, and because thanks to such an act, Marcus was completely clued in on their exploits from there onwards.

It was Wynter who snuck Rosa away to the kitchen as soon as they could, where she began preparing her some bacon and eggs with toast slathered in butter. The perfect cure.

"Good night?" she asked, and watched her daughter remove her sunglasses with a smile.

"That obvious?" Rosa replied and thanked her for the food before devouring the first couple of bites. It was then that Wynter noticed something was wrong.

"Are you okay?" she asked and watched as a flurry of different emotions seemed to flit across her face. Rosa looked as though she might be about to hide behind a lie, but Wynter was glad when she evidently decided against it.

"No," Rosa replied, and while she appreciated her honesty, her heart broke at the word. She took another bite and seemed to think for a moment about how best to elaborate, but then opened her mouth and unleashed an entire stream of thoughts and explanations that took quite a bit of piecing together on Wynter's part.

Rosa told her everything about what'd gone down during her twenty-four hours away with Archie and Brodie. From the run-in with the bouncer to the insane altercation with the white Lady of Death herself.

When she was finished, the jinni was stunned. Rosa had been through so much the past few days it was unreal, and now she'd also reconnected with not only her soul, but its keeper too. Wynter had never realised she was even missing it, and now to hear this?

"Shit," was all she could reply.

"Yeah... tell me about it," came Rosa's response.

"Did she tell you what she told me?" Wynter replied and judging by the surprised look on her daughter's face, she clearly had no idea what she was on about, so she enlightened her. "You're going to save my life someday. She told me so when you were born."

"What?"

"That's all she said. Left me wondering how, when, and why, but over the years I'd forgotten all about it. About her. And now, here you are, telling me she's been part of our lives all this time. It's brought it all back," Wynter told her, and rubbed her aching chest. "My ex was an assassin. He answered to her, and eventually, she took him."

"I remember hearing about that," Rosa replied thoughtfully. "My father. He killed him..."

"Yes, and your new friend let him. When you were born, she spoke to me of Jak. She acted as though he had told her about me. I don't know how it works, but I like to think she was telling the truth. That he still has a life on the other side."

"It's called the *After*, and yes, I think there is a world beyond this one. Morana said she leads those who pass on, and she counsels them as they go into the abyss. She is apparently wise, just, and all knowing," Rosa replied, and then looked down at her hands, "but she isn't my friend."

"I thought you said—"

"I did, but I never said what that entails from my side of things. Or not, in this case," Rosa corrected her, and Wynter frowned. In every species she had encountered by Marcus's side, she had never once met a creature like Morana, and while Rosa finally had her soul back, it appeared it had come at a strange price.

"Did she say why?" she asked.

"Yes," Rosa replied, and reached up her fingertips to touch her lips. "Because I'm apparently destined for her master, but not unless I learn to control their power first. She wants me to become her apprentice and take her place when she eventually moves on. I'll die if I touch their kind as I am now, but I'm not going to become her protégé. I don't want any part of it."

Now that was interesting, and scary as hell to hear. Wynter had a feeling Marceline couldn't have seen any of that in her visions, otherwise surely it would change the future she was currently seeing?

"And what, you're supposed to sacrifice not only your freedom but also your chance to ever fall in love?"

"Apparently," Rosa croaked, and then focussed back on her food with a shrug.

Wynter's heart broke for her. To live without love was one thing, but to fight her destiny was going to be daily torture for her poor child. She only hoped Rosa would rethink her decision as time went on. That, or Morana, would release her from that fate, just as she had the grip she'd kept on her all these years.

She knew she had to tell Marcus what Rosa had told her, and so, after comforting her for as long as she could, Wynter took her leave. Her husband's soul was calling to hers and being away from him for so much as a minute longer felt like it would pain her greatly.

The jinni reached over and gave her daughter a hug.

"I'll support you whatever you decide, even if it means going to war with the Lady of Death herself," she whispered.

Wynter then pulled away and headed to her husband's office. She started to tell him what Rosa had said as soon as she found herself under his immense stare, but Marcus quieted her with a kiss and then smiled.

"You think I don't know everything that goes on in this family?" he teased. "I see all, and thanks to my new priestess, I can also see the future. Our daughter will be fine. In fact, better than fine. She will command an entire army in my name. Lover or no lover, she will be a fighter."

Wynter smiled, but actually, she wasn't sure whether to be pleased about that or not.

***

Rosa woke the next morning to find Morana sitting at the end of her bed, watching her sleep. She was smiling down at her with such reverence she couldn't stand it.

"Why are you here?" she croaked, rubbing the sleep from her eyes.

"I'm always here. I just chose to show myself now that you know the truth," Morana replied, only confusing Rosa further. "Fate brought us together, like I told you before," the Lady of Death added impatiently, "and your life will go on as normal, only with me in it now that I've revealed what you must do."

"But I'm not going to follow you, Morana. You must know that? I'm choosing a different path than you're saying I must lead," Rosa demanded, thinking that if she truly was always there, then she must have heard her the day before.

"We'll see," was all Morana replied, and then disappeared before Rosa could counter.

With a huff, she pulled the covers over herself and nestled back into her mountain of pillows. She was burying her head in the sand but didn't care. Her life was hers for living, not for the likes of Morana to dictate.

By the time she got out of bed, it was almost noon, and as she made her groggy way downstairs towards the kitchen, Rosa passed the ballroom and found it bustling with people. Humans were arranging tables and delivering ornamental flower arrangements, while her mother directed them. She was dressed in her usual finery and headed straight for Rosa when she found her spying.

"What's going on?" she asked and tried to bat her mother's hands away as Wynter began tiding up her clearly messy appearance. She was in trackies and a crop-top, and had scraped back her hair in a bun, but didn't think she was that bad. Not guest ready, but presentable nonetheless. "Mum!" she cried, having enough of her preening.

"We're obviously having a party," Wynter replied with a roll of her eyes. "Your father has invited only the highest in his esteem, and he hopes to present you to them."

"What do you mean, present me?" Rosa retorted, thinking the worst. She was currently in the midst of denying one fate and wasn't about to allow Marcus's friends the chance to eye her up like some prized pig. But at the same time, she didn't want to look a gift horse in the mouth. After all, this was the first get together she'd ever been invited to. Usually, she was upstairs with the other children, but evidently not tonight.

"He wants to show you off, but nothing more than that. Your father intends to let them all know how well you coped with your transition, Rosa, and wants them to see you at his side as he presents you as the alpha his team has been needing for decades."

Well, that certainly silenced her. The young woman gulped and tears sprung at her eyes.

"Dad said that?" she asked, and Wynter nodded. Rosa then stepped away before her tears could fall. They hadn't raised a sentimental fool, or a weak and tearful sort of woman. But today, she was bloody well feeling it. It'd been a hard few days, she told herself, that was all. With a nod, Wynter stalked off to tell some poor human boy he was doing things all kinds of wrong, and Rosa made for the kitchen. After raiding the fridge, she crept back up to her room, where she devoured her makeshift breakfast and let her mind wander.

She'd never been to a party before. She didn't know what was expected of her or how she should act. Didn't know the ins and outs of making small talk or what it took to work a crowd by her father's side. Rosa knew she would have to stick to him like glue. At least until she got a feel for how things were done.

Damn, she felt rather grown up suddenly. As if her childhood was over and she hadn't even thought to give it a proper send off. It didn't feel right not to have gone without a bang, and after some serious thought, she decided it was high time she listened to some of the urges she had buried down for so long. After all, Marc hadn't been denied from indulging any of his impulses. He had pillaged and murdered countless in his teens, and some even earlier than that. Even now, his darkness was unbridled, his evil nourished and its unleashing encouraged. Rosa wanted the same for her own urges, too. She was ready to see what the world had in store for her and figured she had better start sooner than later.

She wasn't even going to tell her parents, or the Lady of Death, who was apparently following her day and night. Rosa didn't want to answer to anyone other than herself. And anyway, wasn't it better to beg for forgiveness than have to grovel for permission? Living in the shadow of such a giant had taught Rosa a lot of things over her twenty-one years of life, and taking what you wanted was one of them. It was high time she learned some lessons from her father and accepted nothing less than what she deserved and had been denied all this time.

Rosa started by dressing herself up like some kind of starlet for the evening. Marlee came to her aid and magicked up a figure-hugging dress that the witch then helped take in to accentuate her curved waist, and together they wound her hair into a tight set of curls that then cascaded down her bare back. Her makeup was flawless, and her heels so high it took Rosa a few practice laps of her bedroom before she felt confident walking in them, but by the time she exited and made her way down to the now bustling hall, she was more than ready to take life by the throat.

FIFTEEN

Rosa followed closely as Marcus took her on a lap of the room at his side. He introduced her to countless men, women, and every kind of creature in between, and by the time she'd finished greeting them all, the young alpha was glad she had given each of the guests a moment of her time. She had evaluated them. Studied their body language and found herself becoming strangely in tune with the energies of some more than others. Rosa knew exactly why that was. Attraction.

When Wynter later appeared out of nowhere by her side, Rosa realised she had to have been with them that whole time and felt bad. Marcus was forcing her out of sight more and more lately, and while her mother seemed unperturbed on the outside, Rosa sensed her sadness. Wynter had given everything to her husband, including her mind, which he had controlled for decades. And now, just as she was slowly finding it again, he was asserting his dominance over her for seemingly the sheer fun of it. It was just another reason why Rosa didn't want what the two of them had. She refused to let Morana or her master rule her heart, and no one else, for that matter. She was going to be her own woman. Starting tonight.

And there was one man in the crowd who had particularly caught her attention. His name was Javi, and he was a hobgoblin. He wasn't the same sort of goblin as Rafferty had been, but more of a fun-loving and free-spirited type of guy. When they'd met, Rosa had been drawn to him right away. He had exuded charm and wit but had an energy to him that she particularly liked. And so, she sought him out. Javi was standing with some other goblins and they were chatting and laughing, but the moment Rosa stopped amidst their small group, every one of them fell silent. Presumably in shock.

"Miss Cole, what a pleasant surprise," Javi chimed in greeting, and Rosa smiled at him. He seemed pleased to see her, which was a bonus.

"Please, call me Rosa," she replied with a shake of her head, "no need for formalities."

Javi looked horrified at the thought and shook his head. The others around him mirrored his frown, and one of the women he'd been chatting to, another goblin named Sylvia, reached forward and put a hand on Rosa's arm.

"None of us would dream of it, Miss Cole. To be so informal with you would be to count ourselves as your equal, which we are not," she implored, and Rosa was about to argue when she sensed Sylvia's fear through her touch. None of them needed to mention her father, but they all knew that he had rules. Rules every single creature under his command had to follow, or else die. Rosa was different to those standing around her, but the fact remained that by flaunting the rules, she might put them in danger, and she couldn't allow that to happen.

Rosa simply smiled and nodded in understanding.

"All that matters is that you allow me the opportunity to join your conversation for a while," she replied, and the small group seemed impressed with her answer. Rosa had thought it obvious, but Javi and the others were clearly surprised by her effort to join them. The conversation started back up, albeit slowly, but it wasn't too long before the group settled to the presence of the newcomer. They talked about all sorts, including their adventures and the plans they had made for more, and Rosa was enthralled. She wanted to know every story they had the time to tell her and found herself genuinely sorry as the night began to wind down. But the one saving grace was that, even when his friends had gone, Javi stayed. The pair of them had disappeared off and were soon away from the crowd, growing closer by the second. Rosa could feel something brewing between them and wasn't afraid to tell Javi so. When those feelings were reciprocated, she was more than ready to act on them, and Javi ended up spending the night. Rosa was perfectly willing and able to finally give such a huge part of herself to another, and the goblin she'd chosen was gentle and kind, and he gave her a night she would never forget. It was a night of many firsts for her, but Javi was patient and caring, while also showing her all the things she had missed. And all the things she wanted more of.

The next morning, she waved him off from the back of the huge house with the biggest smile on her face. Rosa had finally given herself to another, and on her terms, too. It was a revelation. No longer the virgin daughter of the ruthless vampire king. She was truly a woman now, and it felt wonderful. So much so that she was already thinking of how to top the epic night she had shared with Javi. If only she could come and go from the mansion as she pleased, she could party the nights away and enjoy the company of whomever she chose, but instead she would have to wait. Or did she? There had to be a way she might instigate her freedom, and Rosa decided she would do whatever it took to persuade her father she could be trusted.

She turned to head back inside and found her mother standing watch. Wynter seemed stoic, and the jinni couldn't hide her unease as she passed one of the servants' rooms. Her eyes darted to the closed door as she neared it, and tears welled in her eyes. Something had happened in that room. Something big. Whether good or bad, Wynter didn't seem to enjoy being down in the depths of the mansion in the slightest, and so Rosa went to her and led the way back towards the main part of the house. Wynter seemed to settle almost at once and finally revealed what she'd evidently come for.

"My sweet girl," she whispered, and stroked Rosa's cheek gently. "Not a girl anymore..."

Rosa blushed but didn't deny it. Their entire household was the open and honest sort, and she had grown up knowing to knock on closed doors before entering. Vampires and jinni's had sex drives to make the most promiscuous human blush, and the two couples who had raised her contained one of each. Two souls bound to one another's who adored their counterpart and were not afraid to show it. She knew all about sex and what it meant to them, but to her, it didn't hold the same lure. Javi had been an excellent lover, but she didn't feel the need to chase after him for more. In fact, she was excited by the idea of finding someone else to enjoy the practice with. Someone who could teach her more and show her the truly sensuous life she had missed out on.

"It was wonderful," she admitted, and Wynter grinned. The two of them chatted some more and her mother stressed again the importance of being careful, but Rosa was well prepared. She'd already started taking precautions and realised she'd been ready before even meeting Javi. It was nothing to do with Morana or her master, who would undoubtedly be pissed off that she'd given her virginity to someone else. But she didn't care. It had simply been time. An awakening had occurred, and the young wolf didn't regret it for a moment.

***

Wynter watched her daughter go with both a smile on her face and a pit in her stomach. Things were indeed changing for her, and while fate was trying to pull Rosa in one direction, some rebellious urges were pulling her in another. She didn't know which was the right or wrong path, but only hoped that Rosa would figure it all out before hurting herself or anyone else in the process of finding out what she wanted.

But at the same time, she deserved the chance to explore everything, including making the wrong decisions. They were hers to make and learn from, and Wynter vowed she would always stand by her no matter what Rosa decided. Marcus hadn't given them any indication of what he thought about the subject, and so Wynter went to him. She needed to know what he made of the night's events, and found him in his office, hard at work as usual.

"My sweet," he called, not looking up from his screen, "come, I need your opinion on something."

Wynter did as he asked but could sense that something was up. Marcus was his usual cryptic self, but there was an edge to his tone. One that always made a voice in the very back of her head scream at her to run. But of course, she never did. Like she had said to Marlee a few days ago on the stairs, where would she go? She was bound to Marcus forever. Her body and soul belonged to him and there was no undoing what had been done, or the past the two of them shared. Her life belonged to him now, and even though she was committed to finding her voice again, Wynter knew she would never be able to directly speak out against him. Her voice was not to be found to spite him, but to help her fall in line with his dictatorship and become his equal.

And then something struck her. How hadn't she seen it before? The same could be said for the witch who had shown her that vision. She too was constantly trying to deny his rulings, but not because she actively wanted to defy him. No, it was due to the fact she was destined for something else. And that could only mean one thing. Marlee didn't belong to him, which was why she always acted out. Marcella had given him two witches before she'd died, one for him and the other for the vampire she was destined to create. A brother for the vampire king. A protégé and prince to become his right-hand man. Archie.

Wynter stepped forward and reached her husband's side, which was when she saw what it was he was poring over. It was footage from all around their home, and at first Wynter thought he must be angry at Rosa and Javi for their exploits, but instead he was watching her recent conversation with Rosa on repeat.

"No," she whispered, and could feel herself shaking as she dared utter the word.

"No what?" Marcus demanded. He clearly hadn't reacted to it well, and she knew why. After all, it had to be an absolute age since he was last told no.

"No, you don't get to scrutinise my conversations with my daughter any longer. You did the same when I came to tell you about her fate, didn't you? This is how you already knew, because you sit and spy on us rather than let me tell you myself. It stops now, Marcus. Rosa is going through a transition all of her own and she deserves her privacy," she demanded, and was met with not only an icy stare from her husband, but an immensely cold blast as his rage understandably consumed him. Marcus Cole wasn't used to being told off.

"A transition. Is that what you're calling it?" he spat, and with a flick of his fingers against the touch screen, opened a clip from Rosa's room the night before. Wynter didn't need to look. It was an invasion of their daughter's privacy, and she refused to give Marcus the satisfaction of watching it.

"Yeah, that's what I'm calling it," she replied, and went to move away, but Marcus was up on his feet in a flash. He reached out and grabbed her around the neck from behind, his tongue pressing against what used to be one of his favourite veins. But those same veins had long since dried up, and so Wynter merely grinned. "You cannot tame me with your bite any longer," she taunted him, knowing full well he had other ways he was more than ready to utilise should he need to force her submission.

Wynter spun to face him, and rather than be angry, she opted to try and figure out why he was acting so strangely. Marcus gave her nothing, and so she turned into her misty form and took her place within his heart. She knew that was where things were heading anyway, so saved him the bother of forcing her. But this time, she called to him from within the confines of her home, that was both a sanctuary and a prison cell. "Give Rosa the freedom to find herself, Marcus. Watch as she lives and learns, and she will be much better for it."

"She can fuck everyone she sees for all I care," he grunted aloud in response, and sat back down at his huge desk. There, the vampire flicked back to his work, and as he began to settle, Wynter called out to him again. She couldn't sit back while others were getting hurt, not any longer.

"And Marlee?" she tried, "give her to Archie. Let her fulfil her destiny."

"No," was all Marcus ground in response, although he didn't deny that Wynter was right.

"He's your brother!"

"That doesn't make him worthy. Plus, I don't want to share. She's mine until I decide otherwise, end of discussion."

Silence then descended between the two of them, and Wynter settled in for the long haul. She had a feeling this was going to be the imprisonment Marlee had foreseen, and rather than fight it, the jinni decided she would use it to her advantage. She would meditate and ground herself.

Wynter decided it was high time she called upon the dual powers within her to rekindle her relationship with her true self. The one she'd lost amidst the chaos that had been her life beneath the vampire's shadow. It was time she took a good hard look in the mirror and uncovered both the good and the bad. Marcus might own her, but he didn't own her thoughts or her emotions. Her soul was bound to his, and she loved him, right or wrong, and it was high time he accepted her flaws the way she'd been forced to accept his.

SIXTEEN

It was later that morning when Rosa was presented with an opportunity she had never thought was possible. Her father came to tell her he was going to Edinburgh to oversee the renovations at one of his clubs, *Zeal*, and that he wanted her to accompany him. They would be gone for weeks, and the entire time, she would be living and working from the club by his side.

A chance to properly go and experience the real world was at her fingertips, ready for her at long last, and so Rosa jumped at it. She packed in no time at all and was already in the car when Marcus left the house and took his seat beside her.

His assistant Bryn then started the car, and they were soon heading east towards the huge city not far from their home. Surprisingly, her father didn't open a laptop and start working, nor did he sit in contemplative silence, as was his usual way. Instead, Marcus turned to her, and Rosa wilted beneath his intense stare. Those eyes of his were like black holes, and she had always struggled to peer back into them. Even as a child, she had looked away, and now she felt that same fear she had back then.

"Dad?" she whimpered, staring down at the hands in her lap.

"I want you to shift," he answered, getting straight to the real reason why he'd brought her along.

"I don't know… it's not a fine art…" she stammered and jumped when the vampire slammed his hand down onto the leather seat between them.

"Then you will make it so!" he bellowed. "I haven't spent the last twenty years grooming a shifter, only to have you chicken out on me now that you have taken your rightful place as an alpha at my side. I need you to look like someone, and I need it now."

Rosa gulped. Her father had never spoken to her like this before, and she didn't know how to handle it.

She opened her mouth to apologise, but Marcus cut her off. "I let you go off with your mother to finish your transition, and when you returned a fully-fledged alpha shifter, did you come to me and pledge your fealty? Did you promise me you would fight by my side forever? Did you learn and develop your power so as best to help our cause?"

"No," she replied, and she could have kicked herself. She hadn't done any of those things, when actually, they ought to have been first on her list.

"No. You've spent the days since fighting with your destiny and fucking around with hobgoblins," he demanded, making her blush.

"I'm sorry, Dad. I know it's no excuse, but I just thought you knew how loyal I am to you. I would never deny you the use of my power and absolutely pledge to serve you in whatever way you command," she tried, but knew she was getting the words all wrong. She had never had to do any of this before and was painfully aware that she still had a lot to learn.

Marcus softened a little, the giveaway being the increase of temperature in the car, and Rosa finally lifted her gaze to look into her father's eyes. She forced herself not to look away, and realised then that her mother was behind them, too. Rosa felt embarrassed that Wynter had been there to witness her being told off but reminded herself to stop it. She needed to deliver, and so forced her shame away. "Who do you need me to become?" she asked, hoping to God she could come through for him after all this.

"Let's start with someone you know well; someone you should be able to conjure the image of from memory. Wynter…" he replied and rubbed his chest thoughtfully. He didn't seem to realise he was even doing it, but Rosa knew she was there, anyway. She often was, and in the back of her mind, the young wolf made a decision. She didn't want love the likes they had. It was brutal and often violent and had even caused wars in the past. If love meant being imprisoned or manipulated, then she didn't want any part of it.

Rosa forced herself to concentrate back on the task her father had given her and focused on her mother's face. She imagined herself as her exact likeness and willed it so. It took a lot out of her, but soon the air around Rosa began to hum and power resonated within the particles of her makeup, which seemed as though they were clinging to her aura. With their help, she transitioned from her usual self to that of another. Wynter's face and body were hers now, and she wore them like a mask that clung so tightly across the entirety of her skin that once the deed was done, it was without any effort at all.

Marcus leaned closer, studying her with a smile. "Very good. You could easily pass for her."

"Thank you," Rosa replied, and realised it was in her own voice. Of course, she was still herself beneath a façade, and so would be discovered by anyone who knew the true voice of whomever she was portraying, but she promised herself she would practice. Accents and dialects could easily be taught, and she would do so. Her father needed her to prove herself to him, and she would.

"And so, to the real task at hand," Marcus told her, and he sat back in his seat to watch the world go by outside. The ride had been so intense Rosa had almost forgotten they were en-route to the club, and when she looked up, she realised they were almost there. "I want to test them. To see if someone with the means to infiltrate my domain could do serious damage to everything I have built."

He turned back to her and handed Rosa a USB stick. "I want you to walk right inside, power up the computer in my office and plug this in. A virus will be planted and everything will go down across all my clubs. If and when that happens, I will systematically beat the shit out of everyone in charge of my security, and you can help me. Got it?"

Strangely, she did get it. And there was something else, too. She didn't feel bad for the people her father had just threatened to hurt should she be successful. More fool those who thought they were safe in the Cole's employ.

Rosa had but one question.

"Yes, but does my mother have the authority to access your office without you?"

Marcus seemed impressed, and when he turned to her, he did a double take, as though he'd forgotten she was still wearing his wife's guise.

"Usually, however, I don't want you to go in there as Wynter," he answered. "I want you to go in as me."

Rosa gulped. That was going to take some effort, but she was ready to try. Just like with Wynter, she knew his face well. She knew his mannerisms and traits, even if she wasn't as well versed with him as she was her mother. She stared at Marcus for a second, and then closed her eyes and focused solely on his likeness in her mind. She willed herself to become him and felt herself shift from one façade to another as his likeness settled across her skin just as it had before.

When she opened her eyes again, her father was beaming. It felt so strange to see him that way, but Rosa liked it and she smiled back at him.

"Will I do?" she asked, and he nodded.

"Yes, but you'll have to keep quiet," he reminded her, and Rosa agreed. "Good thing I'm not well known for making small talk."

She laughed. That much was true at least.

Rosa then peered down at herself. It was the oddest thing. She was herself underneath her shifted skin, but right then and there she was a man. She had pecs instead of breasts and didn't even want to think about what was going on between her legs. When she swallowed, there was a lump in her throat that had to be an Adam's apple, and she was taller somehow. And broader. This whole shifting thing was going to take some getting used to, but at the same time felt completely natural.

The car began to slow, and Rosa had a moment of panic. There wasn't long until they would arrive at the club, and she didn't feel ready to take on her task. She'd had hardly any time to prepare, plus she was still wearing her normal clothes.

Marceline answered her unspoken question by appearing between the two Marcus's at that very moment, an outfit at the ready in her hands. With a snap of her fingers, she transferred them with the clothes from Rosa's body, and once again the shifter looked down at herself in awe.

She and her father were dressed in entirely matching suits. She doubted any human would notice the difference, but of course there was one problem.

"I won't have the same lure over them," she said, and once again Marceline was at the ready. She handed Rosa a vial filled with blood and herbs, and for an awful moment she thought she might need to drink it.

"Pocket," the Priestess informed her, and Rosa gladly tucked the small bottle into her breast pocket. And then, just like that, Marceline was gone again.

"Bryn will accompany you inside, and I will be watching via a button-hole camera. I will instruct him how to guide you, and when he whispers in your ear, merely nod and follow his guidance."

Rosa nodded. This was going to be simple. In and out, do the job and then be back in her own skin in no time at all.

She hadn't a moment to spare, because with that, they had arrived. Marcus said nothing more as Bryn opened the door and followed Rosa inside, and she took every step as carefully as though it were her most important task yet. Each of her movements was carefully planned and perfectly timed, and when she was inside the club, Bryn at her side, the human populous inside each stopped what they were doing and jumped to attention.

"Stare at them, give nothing away, and then simply nod," Bryn advised, and Rosa did as he said. Once they'd had their nod from the boss they thought had come to check in, each of the workers got back to their jobs, and Bryn led the way over to an awaiting elevator, which Rosa gladly took up to the top floor.

Once they were there, she knew she was moments away from completing her task, and almost ran to the PC her father had installed for his personal use only. It was still firing up when a huge human man appeared at the doorway to Marcus's office. He frowned and called to her, but Rosa didn't know what to do. She simply stood there, staring back at him.

"Umm... Ryker, is it?" Bryn piped up, and the man nodded.

"Yeah," he hummed, still staring at her. "And who the fuck is this, 'cos it ain't Mr Cole?"

Shit. She quickly fumbled with the USB and stuck it in the machine, hoping there wasn't anything else she needed to do to get the virus uploaded, and it appeared Ryker was a fast learner. He realised she was up to no good and bolted for them, taking Bryn out with ease, who curled up in a ball on the ground and started whimpering like the coward Rosa had always heard her mother refer to him as. "I asked who the fuck you are…" the burly man asked, but Rosa remained silent.

She answered by punching him straight in the throat, earning herself a moment to duck the blow he was about to deliver, but not enough to get away. Ryker was quick and powerful for a human. He turned and grabbed her, taking Rosa down. He punched her and within seconds, the pair of them were having a full on brawl on the floor of her father's new office.

Rosa loved it. She let loose on the man and didn't care for the blows he returned. It was when alarms started going off around them they both returned to the matter at hand, and Rosa pinned Ryker down, straddling him on the ground.

"This was fun," she then teased, relishing in his surprise at hearing a woman's voice coming from the guise of his boss. "If my father lets you live, perhaps we can do this again sometime."

Rosa then took off for the stairs and was out of the building mere moments later. She ran to the car and threw herself inside, where she found Marcus amid chaos, yet with the biggest grin on his face.

He ended the call he'd been on and took a good look at his daughter, who peered down at the bloody suit Marceline had given her. "I ruined your outfit," she joked, and was glad to see her father didn't bat an eye.

"And completed the mission I gave you, well done," he answered, and she saw his eyes dart around her face, taking in her bloody nose and swelling lip. "Ryker?"

"Yeah, who is that guy?"

"Head of security. I hired him to stop this exact thing from happening and can see he tried. He still failed, though," he replied, and showed Rosa the tablet in his palm. It was going crazy, flashing with errors and warnings. The virus she had planted was wiping every server they had across the entire world, and Marcus was monitoring everything. He had masterminded this coup somehow, and Rosa was desperate to know why, but was also aware she couldn't directly ask.

"He definitely tried," she agreed, and looked down at the bruises on her knuckles, "but I gave him worse. He knew it wasn't you."

"And for that, I won't kill him," Marcus replied, and then he focused back on the matter at hand while Rosa cleaned herself up with a simple transformation back to her real likeness. She stretched her limbs and was amazed at how good she felt. There were no remnants of the beating she'd just taken, only the strength that seemed to emanate from within, and she watched with a grin as Ryker then came charging out the door with Bryn in his grasp, dragging her father's assistant by the scruff of his neck.

Rosa climbed out of the car, watching him with a smile as he did another double take. She was still wearing the bloody suit, which now swamped her smaller frame, and Ryker dropped Bryn, who went running for the driver's seat so that he could not only hide, but no doubt debrief her father.

"You're the…" Ryker gulped, watching as Rosa took off the suit jacket and tie. She then went around to the boot of the car, looking for her suitcase, and found Marceline had left her clothes in a neat little pile at the ready for her. With Ryker still watching her in shock, Rosa quickly changed, being careful not to show off too much flesh in the process, and as she did, she finally spoke to the poor man standing dumbfounded a few feet away.

"The shifter, yes. Rosa Cole, it's a pleasure to make your acquaintance," she told him with a wry smile. "You did well, Ryker. You realised it wasn't my father, but still didn't manage to stop me. It was fun being on the receiving end as you tried though, and I can't lie. I enjoyed our tussle very much."

When Ryker gulped, Rosa only smiled wider. He was big and burly, and a proper brute, and yet she was somehow making him blush. How cute indeed.

She threw the bloody clothes in a heap, slammed the boot of the car closed, and wandered over to him.

"I'm sorry if I hurt you, Miss Cole," the guardsman insisted, and Rosa just laughed.

"If you survive the night, maybe you can make it up to me?" she answered, and of course saw the panic start to set in. Ryker had failed the big, bad Marcus Cole. He was going to answer for his failings, presumably with blood, and even after whatever time he had already served, the poor guy didn't seem at ease with his fate in the slightest. Perhaps, like her mother had once done, he was fighting it?

Marcus took that moment to finally step out of the car, and when he found the two of them staring into each other's faces so intently, the vampire didn't seem to mind one bit. Rosa hoped she was going to see more of this side of him during their stay. She wanted to see and do everything she had her mind set on. To have it all and then some, and to return home with an abundance of stories to tell her family.

"Take my daughter inside and keep her company while I deal with the rest," Marcus told Ryker, who nodded to his master and quickly led Rosa away. She wondered if he realised he'd just received a pardon, but rather than question him, she simply enjoyed the view. He was built like a behemoth and covered in tattoos, and the moment they were alone, she pinned him against the wall of her father's office.

"We shouldn't…" he tried, and then kissed her anyway. "Your dad…"

"My father told you to keep me company, and there's only one sort of company I want," Rosa demanded, and she unbuckled his jeans as she did so. Ryker was on her in a heartbeat, and he didn't so much as hesitate this time. Rosa made it clear what she wanted and by the time they were done, she was more than satisfied with how he had delivered it. Javi had been a wonderful and gentlemanly first, but the burly human had given her something darker and more carnal. Something raw and exciting.

And Rosa wanted more.

She spent the next ten days taking a different lover each night. While Marcus worked his minions hard to ensure the nightclub came together around them, she went wild. Her passion was unhindered, her inhibitions non-existent. Rosa loved and explored in abundance, and by the time they got back in the car to head home, she knew exactly who and what she wanted to be.

SEVENTEEN

Marcus was sitting at his home office desk, poring over yet another set of blueprints, when he felt someone watching him. The room had been warded against prying eyes of all magical ability, and so if it were the case, even he knew whoever it was had to be on a whole different playing field to those he encountered in his everyday life.

"Always so wrapped up in your work, Marcus Cole. Finish one project only to start another. Tested the humans in your keep, only to beat their loyalty for you back into them when they failed. Forced the woman you loved to love you back. Forced the children who call this house home to bend to your will…"

It was a woman, and as Marcus lifted his head towards the sound of her voice, she revealed herself.

"The Lady of Death, to what do I owe the honour?" he asked but had his suspicions already. He had taken Rosa away with him for this very reason. Morana wanted her and had told her she was fated to be with the reaper's master. And yet, his daughter had refused, and so Marcus had encouraged her frivolity. He had actively put suitors in Rosa's path to tempt her, and boy, had she been tempted. So much so that this master of death had sent Morana to negotiate. Not with the young shifter he supposedly loved, but with her keeper, and the only being she obeyed. He had some sense, at least.

"You know what they say about history repeating itself?" Morana replied thoughtfully, and she stepped into the light so that Marcus could finally see her gentle features up close. She was still cloaked and covered entirely in white, but her sad smile seemed innocent, and she reeked of sincerity.

Marcus nodded. "It's true, you know? Kingdoms fall, only to be replaced by a bigger, better keep. Dictators are massacred and their deaths celebrated, only for other more dangerous monsters to rise up in their place. My job is to make sure there is balance to this chaos, but of course, every once in a while, someone or something gets out of control. Their flame burns too bright and needs extinguishing."

"My lady, I hope you're not referring to me?" he asked, mocking her threat. If she wanted to take him into the *After* she would've done it already. No, she wasn't there to take him, but to bargain.

"After wiping out entire civilisations repeatedly, we vowed never to have another extinction level event, however, there needs to be a natural order. Creatures become more powerful than humans—so we knock them back down. And vice versa. You, Marcus Cole, are shifting those tides. I am supposed to stop you…"

"And yet?"

Morana smiled and shrugged her shoulders.

"And yet my master has changed tactics again. He wants something you have and is willing to make you an offer for it." It was obvious what the 'something' was, and if he were a lesser man, Marcus knew he might have been more concerned about his lack of heart on the subject. But instead, he focused on what he wanted from the proposed deal. Rosa was important to him, sure, but she was also an asset. And one he would readily cash in for the right price.

"It had better be worth my while," he grumbled, and sat back in his chair thoughtfully. It was that age old debate. That fateful moment he had been fighting since becoming a vampire all those years ago. There was such a thing as too much power, and Marcus had sensed he was getting too close, but could never stop. He wanted it all and smiled. "I will never die. I will not fail, and I will rule it all. The oceans and every country this planet holds. Every creature will be mine to command."

"Yes," was all Morana replied.

"And those I love will remain by my side," he added, and it wasn't lost on him how they were an afterthought. Not Wynter, of course. If he was alive, then so too would his bride, but everyone else was out of want, not need.

"Of course."

"And what do you require of me in return?" he asked, not committing to anything until he had heard her terms.

"Your daughter's hand, of course. But first, my master demands the deaths of those who have wronged us," she replied, and Marcus grinned. Whoever she was talking about killing, it was personal. No doubt unjustified and therefore impossible for Morana to carry out herself. She needed someone to do it for her. Someone with questionable morals and a penchant for murder.

"I'm listening…" was his immediate reply, and he sat back in his seat as he did just that. Marcus didn't even so much as argue, and as the dastardly plan began to come together, all he could think about was getting what he wanted out of it.

***

When Rosa was summoned via text to her father's office later the next evening, she didn't think anything of it at first. Marcus often commanded them to his side, and without a magical hold over her, he usually opted for a more modern approach than hollering up the stairs or sending one of his minions to find her.

Nothing felt off in the slightest, at least not until she reached the doorway and found the office empty.

"Dad?" she called and was greeted by a grunt from behind her. The alpha vampire was standing a few feet away, and Rosa didn't need to ask why. He'd been sent to escort her somewhere, and a chill suddenly swept over her. "Where is he?" she asked the mountainous vamp, and the guy simply gave another grunt and walked away. He led Rosa out the huge house and across the gardens towards the forest she'd been warned never to enter. The one where the bodies of her father's enemies swung for all to see.

It was eerily silent within. No animal sounds greeted them from the treetops. Even the wind stayed quiet, rather than whistle through the trees. Rosa was shaking by the time they reached a building she didn't even know existed there, and refused when her guide insisted she go in. His answer was to simply yank her by the arm and throw Rosa inside the dark doorway, and she responded with an expletive or two before immediately falling silent at what lay before her. The alpha slammed the door closed behind them, making her jump, and drew Rosa closer to the macabre display inside.

People were strung up there in rows. Their arms were tied above their heads, which, on most, were hung low. She wondered if this might be a sort of blood farm, but then spotted someone she knew there and paled. "Ryker?" she cried and ran to him. The burly bouncer had been beaten black and blue, but was still conscious, and had been testing his binds when she found him. "What the hell is going on?" she hissed, and he looked up into her face with a pained frown.

"I dunno. One minute I was in work as usual, and the next I was here," he replied. Rosa was about to hunt for some more clues, when she looked at the next person in line and realised she knew them, too. And the person next to them.

"Figured it out yet?" her father's voice called from somewhere at the back of the huge room. Rosa was still piecing things together, and her hand flew to her mouth when Marceline appeared out of thin air beside Ryker.

"Javi?" she whimpered and fell to the floor in front of him. The hobgoblin didn't look at all well, and he was turning greener by the second. He opened his mouth and looked as if he was trying to say her name, but instead coughed up thick, black blood that then spewed out of his mouth and down his chest. Rosa screamed and turned to glare up at her father, who had now joined them. "Why?" she demanded and began to cry harder when the alpha vampire started stringing Javi up by his wrists, just like the others.

"Surely you've worked it out by now?" Marcus replied, brushing away her tears. And she had indeed. They were all the lovers she had known in her short time so far since Javi. All the men who had delivered her pleasure when she had asked for it, and who had let themselves be seduced by her newly sparked libido. None of them had asked for this, and she pleaded for her father to let them go, but of course he refused.

He didn't seem sorry in the slightest, and Rosa felt rage begin to rise in her chest. She nodded, thinking her father would then let her go, but instead he held her to him. He stared into her eyes, and for a moment, he seemed sad. Not for the others, but for her.

"Morana put you up to this, didn't she? You don't have to do as she asks. I refused her, and so can you," she tried, but the ancient vampire shook his head.

"I don't care about them," he replied, "I just care about you."

"Then stop this!" she interjected, but Marcus shook his head.

"In the last thirty days, you have let all these men defile you. Let them have what is not theirs, nor is yours to give. The God of Death demands they pay their debts..."

Rosa did a double take. So, he was in cahoots with the master manipulator now? Not just Morana, but the puppeteer pulling her strings, too.

"What's he offered you?" she ground, shoving Marcus by the shoulders so that he was forced back just enough to drop his hands from her cheeks. "You, who has it all, and it is never enough. The vampire who encouraged me to have a life and to live it to the fullest. The man who took me in your arms and called me yours... And now, you sell me out. For what?" Rosa bellowed, and while she could tell her words had affected him, her father still refused to back down. He seemed sad for a second, but then his face turned icily resolute.

"For everything!" Marcus bellowed, opening out his arms as if to justify him wanting more than he already had. More than the world already at his fingertips and the people who remained loyal through thick and thin.

"I can see it now. Why Wynter tried so hard to run from you. She knew she could never love you without being forced, and of course you knew that too. The only reason you could make her stay was out of fear," she croaked, and a wave of satisfaction spread through her when a pained look shot across the usually so stoic vampire's face.

However, Marcus was quick to force it away. But it was enough to know she had given him a taste of his own medicine, even if it was merely a drop in the ocean compared to his wrongdoings.

"I will allow you one kindness. One life spared from all of those strung up around you. Who will it be, child?" he asked, clearly choosing not to respond to her taunt. Her father then walked her to the end of the line, past all the poor men who had dared to have her these past few weeks.

Rosa paled. How could she choose? How could one life possibly be worth more than any of the others?

"I can't," she pleaded, and Marcus's response was to slit the throat of the man at the other end of the line, her most recent conquest, Jamie. He was a bartender at the club and a truly sweet guy, but now he was gone because of her.

When she still didn't answer, her father lifted his blade and sliced through the next three victims' necks one after the other, and Rosa watched in horror as the blood poured down onto the ground and then ran into small grates set in the floor. The place was like some human abattoir. She imagined there were huge barrels beneath them, catching up the offering ready for drinking by his many clients, and Marcus grinned as he watched her process it all.

"Waste not, want not," he chimed, and then murdered the next three humans on the row without batting an eye. It was when there were just two left that Rosa finally caved.

"Stop please," she tried, and Marcus paused with his blade pressed precariously over Ryker's neck.

"Which one will it be?" he asked, but she already knew. She'd known right from the word go.

Rosa looked into Ryker's eyes and smiled—or at least tried to. She had hoped to offer him a thank you, but of course there was no way to convey such a thing. A glimmer of hope swept across his face, and she knew he'd thought for a moment that he'd been saved, but then realisation came over him. The human nodded, but then looked from her to Marcus and sneered.

"Fuck you both," he mumbled, and then was gone in a flash thanks to Marcus's swiftness with the blade.

Before she could even blink, Marceline reappeared, and she teleported Javi away. Rosa hadn't even had the chance to tell him she was sorry and felt utterly miserable. She and Marcus were alone once again and surrounded by corpses.

She began heaving and ran straight for the door, thundering out into the now black forest where she puked everything her body could find to throw up. She was still gagging on bile when a white hand passed her a perfectly crisp silk hanky.

"You think this is bad, you should've seen what my master was like in the dark ages..." Morana told her, and while Rosa didn't want to hear her excuses or her dark jokes, she was glad of the supportive hand. Despite their minimal ups but epic downs, it was nice to have her there.

But as she righted herself, Rosa realised they were not alone. Marcus was standing at the base of the stairs that led into the strange room, and beside him was another man. Someone tall and broad. In fact, he had to be the biggest guy she had ever seen, and Rosa's instincts kicked in, so she found herself drawing closer to him with intrigue.

"The infamous Marcus Cole, a pleasure," the guy was saying, and was clearly pleased with the outcome of her father's recent game.

She could only see the man from the side but noticed a thick dark brown beard on his jaw, and then he had a neatly plaited kind of Mohawk on top with shaved sides. Rosa gulped. He was all kinds of perfect, and she turned to share the briefest of looks with Morana, wondering if the man was who she'd thought it had to be. The White Lady simply offered her a wry smile.

The breath rushed from her lungs then and there. He was *him*. The one Rosa had been running from. The man who had orchestrated this entire thing.

She was livid. There the two men were, bigging each other up and acting like they'd just come to some kind of perfect conclusion, while completely ignoring the two women standing just a few feet away. How dare he?

Rosa decided she'd seen enough. The some kind of Viking-looking Adonis could go to hell, especially after orchestrating a stunt like that. She hadn't been interested before and wasn't about to change her mind now just because he was all kinds of hot.

She stepped away and was about to turn and run from them all when the man shot his hand out and grabbed her by the arm. His grip was so firm she yelped and stared down at the offending article angrily. By the time she looked back up, the man had turned towards her at last and when his eyes darted her way; her legs buckled. His gaze was so intense Rosa saw stars, and when he offered the tiniest of smiles, she flushed with heat from head to toe.

"Rosa," he whispered, and seemed to like watching her squirm, so kept her tightly in his grasp. She realised then that, unlike Morana, he wasn't wearing gloves. He was touching her. Their contact was skin-to-skin, which could only mean one thing. He was there to take her. Was she going into the *After*? Was she fated to leave this world already, or was he forcing her?

"No," was all she managed to reply. No, what? Rosa didn't want to die, and she also didn't want to go with him. Was that it? Or was she also saying she didn't want him at all?

She couldn't actually get her mouth round more words to elaborate anyway, but he didn't seem to care.

The man moved in closer and stared so intensely into her eyes it was as if he were looking into her soul. As if he were reading her thoughts while simultaneously ridding her of all conscious will.

"No is not a word I hear very often, and yet you do like to repeat it so," he replied.

He was being playful, after everything he and her father had just put her through. The fucking swine. Rosa tried again to wrestle herself out of his grip and was taken off guard when he reached out with his other hand and grabbed her by the throat. It hurt like hell, but she refused to show it, and continued to fight his hold. "Enough!" he roared, and yet still Rosa couldn't let herself succumb so easily. She'd tried to deny him. Tried to outsmart and outrun him and had failed miserably at her attempt to have her own life. She also despised having basically been moved from one dictator's hold to another. She simply couldn't and wouldn't allow it.

She glowered up at him and then looked over at the man who'd raised her. Marcus was staring right through her like some sort of robot, and she sneered.

"I hope you're happy now, you fucking monster," Rosa croaked.

It was the huge man before her who answered.

"He'll never be happy, Rosa. But until he realises that, I can bend him to my will and exploit him in any way I see fit. I can take what I want and do it all with his blessing, because there will always be something he wants that I can gladly offer. If he were strong enough to deny me, I wouldn't be standing here now. But he's not like you."

With that, the man then slung her up and over his shoulder and carried her back out of the forest. Rosa kicked and screamed, but of course, it did nothing to deter him. Whoever he was, her shifter strength meant nothing in comparison to his.

He came to a stop only when he was ready and put the still wriggling woman down on the grass with a thud. The mansion was a few hundred feet to her right, and she contemplated running for it, but the moment the thought even crossed her mind, the strange man grabbed her waist and pulled her back to him. He pinned himself to her, and Rosa felt engulfed by his aura, both physically and spiritually. She shuddered with both fear and rage.

"Why me?" she whispered, and instead of answering he began mumbling something in a guttural language she'd never heard before. He then gave a swish of his hand and snapped his fingers, and out of nowhere, a small wooden hut appeared on what had moments earlier been a large patch of empty grass before them.

He led her inside, revealing the hut to be not much more than a huge room with a fire pit in the centre and a basic kitchen to one side. There was a huge bed on the other end, and a small bathroom sectioned off. The bed was the only place to properly sit and had been laden with furs. Rosa's thoughts once again went to his Viking appearance. The home was rustic and cosy. Very old fashioned and minimalistic. It suited its purpose, and nothing more.

631

EDEN WILDBLOOD

She watched as the strange giant wandered the open space. His boots were heavy, and the boards beneath his feet creaked under his weight, but they held. As did the beam he leaned on as he lit the fire and then put a kettle over it.

"Tea?" the man asked, and Rosa just stared back at him. He was offering her tea? Something as simple as that after the shit he'd just orchestrated!

She moved away from him, her own feet silent on the boards beneath her. Rosa wanted to put as much distance between them as she could and simply watched as he brewed up a pot and then poured her a cup, regardless of not having been given an answer. "You know, you can talk to me," he teased, and set the cup down before heading over to the bed, where he sat cross-legged atop it.

Rosa went around to where he had been, and she took her full mug from the counter but didn't join him. She held back and instead stared into the flames as she took the first few sips of the deliciously calming brew.

"Who are you?" she asked and watched the man smile. Yep, she was fully aware she was caving. Whether she liked it or not, Rosa needed to know more about him, and told herself it was merely a case of gathering intel so she could find a way to escape. She did really want to know.

"That's a question I have many answers to," he eventually replied, and paused. He then watched her intently while he considered his next words. "Most recent cultures may refer to me as the Grim Reaper. The Black God who isn't merely a reaper, but who watches over the souls of all that have passed on from this realm."

"And is it true?" she asked, and he nodded.

"I came into existence the same time as life began to form on this planet, and savour both the light and dark this world has to offer me. I'm an impartial entity. Beholden to none, and neither good nor evil."

Considering his most recent escapades, Rosa considered that debatable, but at the same time, it made sense. She didn't know if heaven or hell existed, but knew there were creatures aplenty in this world, and thanks to Morana had learned first-hand that there was indeed an *After*.

"And your name?" she asked, having realised he'd never actually told her it.

"I have had many over the years. The Norse referred to me as Hel, and ancient Slavic people called me Chernobog, while the Egyptians opted for Anubis. I'm called Baron Samedi in some cultures and was given the name Thanatos by the ancient Greeks."

"And to me?" she pleaded, her head swimming. All she wanted was a name, and now he'd reeled off a list that was incomprehensible to her. It was all too much to take in, and Rosa couldn't even fathom how this man—this God—had been around for so long and yet had appeared to her in such a normal guise.

"Many of my modern day followers now call me by any name that has connotations to darkness, but my favourite is Onyx. Nyx for short," he told her, and Rosa almost snorted. Talk about coincidences that were now seeming anything but.

She had always been drawn to gemstones and crystals and had put it down to the bracelet and charms her mother and the witches often had with them. In fact, Rosa had been drawn to the black onyx stones in various forms over the years. There was the small, rounded pebble that resided in a purse Marceline had given her to help ward off the negative energies from her previous full moon experiences, and, of course, the black beaded bracelets Brodie had made for her as a child.

"Why me, Nyx?" she asked him again, and the giant took a moment to finish his tea before answering.

"I've had many lovers over the various millennia, but not once have I found *the one*," he began, and Rosa had to force herself not to roll her eyes. After all that he had done to instigate their meeting, he was going to finish it with a cliche? She wanted to try and storm off, but knew such a dramatic reaction would be pointless, anyway. The doorway was no doubt warded shut, plus she knew she couldn't get far. "But not any longer. I knew the moment Morana took you in her arms that you were different, and it was on my say so that we let your birth mother take your place."

"Nyx, I'm literally just beginning my life after putting everything on hold because of my transition. I had just a few weeks to find myself, and now you plan to take it all away from me because of some prophetic nonsense about soul mates? You instigated the murder of anyone who came anywhere near me. You ruined my life, and now you propose that we simply live happily ever after... The answer is no. A hundred times, no."

Rosa finished her tea and set the mug down, and she turned to the doorway, staring at it longingly. "Please just let me go," she whimpered, yet Nyx remained silent and still. She went to plead with him some more, but then began to feel woozy. Lights shot across her vision, and as she sat there, Rosa was magically transported to a whole different world, time, and place.

She watched as some kind of memory played out before her. Morana was handing a glowing orb to Nyx—Rosa's soul. He thanked the White Lady and then punched a hole in his chest before he then pushed the orb inside. It had clearly pained him to do so, but then the strange being had smiled. He seemed somehow satisfied and came to rest with his hand over the spot where he'd just pushed the orb inside.

"I was the one who kept you safe all this time. Morana delivered you to me when she discovered you were worthy, and she brought your soul back only at my command. But for the two decades in between, your life was tied to my essence. You shared parts of me that no one has ever been allowed to, and you opened my eyes to what I was missing," Nyx told her, his voice narrating the scene playing out before her eyes. "It all started millennia ago. I needed something to pass the time, and one day I started to notice the variances between the millions of souls passing through my world and into the *After*. Some were light, while others were dark. Their lives were not like that of the first men. They had changed. Their deeds had become less about survival and more about desire. But there were some souls who were simply sublime. The pure were like a drug to me, and I devoured them. I began searching for more, and when I couldn't find them in death, I started taking the souls of the living. I did so without a thought for the soulless life that person then led, or the emptiness of death that came when their physical body failed and they were presented with nothingness. No hand to hold. No guide. That deed had already been done, and yet I didn't care. I didn't want or need to, but then you came along, Rosa. Your soul was my undoing. Like some sort of lightning bolt, you clung to me rather than submit to my hunger. You needed something else from me, and so I started to give rather than take. I started to love..."

Rosa's vision returned, and she almost fell to the ground as the real world forced itself back into her consciousness. That day when Morana had given her soul back had been surreal, and while she had felt differently for it, Rosa had no idea at the time just what that act had meant. What she'd had taken and then strangely returned years later, and what else had accompanied her soul when Morana had placed that glowing orb back inside her chest. "That's why I asked Morana to train you. I wanted her to teach you who and what I am, so that when the time came for us to finally become one, you would be ready. I was going to wait for you and had it all perfectly planned out in my head. But then you just had to keep refusing me."

"Damn right. I think you need to get with the times a little," she replied, only half joking. "When was the last time you made an effort to truly get to know someone?"

"I *know* every single person who moves on from this world, Rosa. I know them intimately. Their hopes and dreams, those that were dashed, and those they had fulfilled. I can see the life they have lived and the choices they made to get to their final chapter. To reach my lair is to proceed to the final step, and I give every soul the opportunity to reveal all before they cross over. I have been regaled by some wonderful accounts of people's lives and have been granted a glimpse into the minds of men and women like no other. And when they are done, they take my hand and willingly leave all thought behind in my safekeeping," he said, leaving Rosa in awe. Was he for real? "I'm not the monster you seem to think I am," Nyx then told her solemnly, and she immediately softened a little.

Damn him for breaking through her resolve.

She stood and stared across at him, moving closer on instinct, but was still wary. He had done monstrous things to those poor people who had dared share a bed with her. It didn't matter that Marcus had been his conduit, Nyx was to blame for them having been taken too soon.

"And yet you actively arranged some of those deaths," she snapped, and Nyx sighed. He nodded and looked to Rosa with tears in his eyes.

"For which I will pay. Like I said, every single soul finishes in my keep. Each and every one is mine to watch safely to the *After*, including your friends. I will answer to them when their time comes and will be honest when they ask how and why they were taken. I let my jealousy rule me, but I'm hoping I will be able to tell them their sacrifice was worth it. That we made it through. And that we're happy together, like it was always fated to be..."

"You think rather highly of yourself," she replied, and then came to a stop right before Nyx on the bed. She hadn't even realised she'd moved that much closer, and fear rippled through her when she saw the lust in his eyes.

"No, I think very highly of you," he croaked, and reached for her before she could even process what he'd said. Nyx pulled Rosa down and into his lap, where he cradled her, wrapping himself around her like some sort of shield. His touch drove her wild. And what the hell was that scent? He smelled earthy, like smoke and wood, but then there was something else. It was sweet and as she breathed him in, Rosa felt warmth spreading through her.

Home.

Shit. This really was it. He'd been right about the two of them being connected by some kind of fate. Time seemed to slow down as Rosa peered up at Nyx's chiselled face. She could sense the pain and guilt he was wearing without shame. He was ready and willing to repent for his evil deeds.

He then began speaking in that strange language again. But this time, she understood it. "I will weather any storm for you. You are mine as I am yours until the end of days..."

Oh no, she thought. This was happening. Rosa didn't know what was more terrifying—that she was starting to bend to Nyx's will by the forces of fate, or that she was starting to want to.

EIGHTEEN

Wynter watched out the window for days, her eyes across the gardens to where the mysterious cabin lay, and she couldn't help the dread churning in her belly. Marcus tried numerous times to persuade her everything had worked out for the best, but she was having none of it. Something wasn't right, and the jinni couldn't deny doubting her husband's word.

It was never going to be so simple as love at first sight. Never going to be a case of Rosa just accepting what had happened. The carnage she had seen, and the brutality. And all directed from the man who had raised her but orchestrated by the being who supposedly loved her. It wasn't right. Any of it.

When the two of them were called upon at last, Wynter was surprised to find an invitation to tea on Marcus's desk. It was so formal. And so cold. Nothing like her daughter in the slightest, and she rushed over to the small dwelling with haste. If something was wrong, then Rosa would find a way to tell her, and Wynter vowed she would pay her fullest attention to any signal her daughter might try and give her.

Instead of a tense, forced atmosphere, though, Rosa and Nyx seemed perfectly at ease with each other. They were smiling coyly and sharing lusty glances as they prepared a kind of herbal tea in the small kitchen area of their cabin. The two of them appeared intimately acquainted, and Marcus didn't seem to notice at all. This was unlike him, but Wynter sensed he was completely at ease with the situation this strange God of Death had lured their daughter into. When she finally got Rosa alone, she was sure to quiz the young alpha about what had happened between them.

"Come sit with me," was all she answered, and led her mother away from the other two with a soft smile. The pair of them took a seat beside the fire, and Wynter turned towards Rosa so she could take a good look at her as she divulged their tale. "Mum, I'm honestly fine. Nyx hasn't hurt me or forced me into anything, but he has shown me the truth about everything I ever wondered about. Things like life and death, and what happens to souls when they pass on."

"It's only been a few days," Wynter intervened, but Rosa shook her head.

"Time works differently around him. For us, it's been months. He opened up in ways I've never imagined one person could do for another, and thanks to me seeing him laid bare, I could make my own decisions about whether or not to follow him. His world is fascinating, and my eyes are open for the first time in more than twenty years."

"And?" she demanded, watching as Nyx and Marcus took a seat on the log opposite them by the huge fire pit. She was drawn to her husband, as always, but couldn't take her eyes off the strange master of death sitting across from her. Was he for real, or was there some kind of foul game at play here?

"And I'm happy. Truly happy. I can see the life I'm destined to lead, and who I shall be taking forward with me..."

Her words brought back Wynter's dread. What the hell did that mean? "When was the last time you were happy, Mum?"

The jinni went cold. When she really stopped to think about it, there was only one clear answer. And it was one she would never dare say out loud.

She looked over at her husband and could just about make out his face through the flames. He, too, was staring straight ahead, his eyes glaring into the flames almost possessively. Whatever Nyx was saying, he wasn't impressed by it.

"Happiness is overrated, Rosa. I've been satisfied for many years. I had a family to raise and a man to love," she began, but then stopped when she saw a look of terror go across Marcus's face. She'd never seen him so afraid. Not once in all their years together.

Before she could so much as react, she was forced to watch as Nyx shot his hand up and through Marcus's chest. It was quick, and the move impossible to outmanoeuvre. The vampire seemed surprised. His mouth fell open in disbelief, but all shock was over with when Nyx tore out his bloody, and still beating, heart.

Pain wracked through her at the sight, and Wynter knew it was because of their merged souls. If one should die, then so would the other. It was fated. And so, Rosa had indeed chosen who she was taking into the *After* alongside her new beau. It appeared it was their time—her and Marcus—and Wynter knew she ought to be furious, but instead she was relieved.

Death would mean an end to this awful life she'd been forced to live in.

It might feel warm. Maybe even inviting, rather than scary.

She was ready.

"Breathe and relax. Trust me," Rosa whispered in her ear, and before Wynter could ask why, she watched as her daughter did the same to her chest. She punched a hole directly in her sternum, and before Wynter could turn to mist on instinct and evade the intrusion, Rosa ripped the heart straight from her too.

She slumped down onto the ground, watching as Rosa and Nyx both stood. She could feel her life ebbing away but was somehow alert enough to watch as they pushed the two hearts together, turning each to mush, before then dropping them into the flames.

It was agonising, and Wynter knew right away that she was done for. Marcus was gone. He was dead and cold, his body lying on the floor just feet away, his once vibrant blue eyes now pale. The witch's heart was no more, and while it felt freeing to release Mara's hold on her, Wynter couldn't help but be scared.

Her hands and feet were turning to mist already, her body going into shock, and she looked up to find the Lady of Death looking down at her with a smile.

"Are you here to collect me?" she asked Morana and was surprised when she shook her head.

"I'm here to remind you of something I once told you," she answered, and then turned her face away, looking instead over to where Rosa was patiently watching them.

"She'll save my life one day," Wynter whimpered.

"Yes," the reaper replied, and then sighed as she climbed down onto her knees beside her. "Plus, you can't die yet. I have a gift for you."

Wynter's eyes rolled into the back of her skull, inside of which she saw nothing but thin, delicate wisps of white smoke. She was about to ask Morana what gift she could've possibly brought her, when she felt herself being lifted off the ground and cradled against someone's chest. She presumed it was Rosa, but then forced her eyes to open and looked up into the face of a man she hadn't seen in more than twenty years.

"Jakob?" she whimpered and started to sob when he peered down into her face and nodded.

"First thing is first, you need a home," he told her, and as Wynter reached for him with what remained of her body, the vampire she had loved and lost all those years ago responded by opening not only his arms but also his heart and soul. She seeped inside of him and found her place, and then watched through his eyes as Jakob looked around at the cabin and its inhabitants.

His thoughts were chaotic, but somehow focussed on the tasks ahead. He had been returned to her, and while there was a lot of work to be done if they had any hope of clearing up Marcus's mess, he was more than ready.

Ready to start again.

Ready to bring order to the chaos her dead husband had created.

Ready to stand and serve by Rosa's side as she inherited her father's legacy, and more than willing to help her tear his regime down inch by goddamn inch.

It was time to start over. A redress if the balance was overdue, and this time, they were going to do it together. As a real family.

***

Rosa and Jak walked back towards the house, and all the way she could sense he was having his all-important inner talk with Wynter. No doubt telling his love all about how Morana had kept him separate from all the other souls reaped that fateful day two decades earlier. The Lady of Death had known then how important he was but had no idea just how much. When Rosa had been born, Morana's words to Wynter had been true. Rosa was going to save her life one day.

Today.

She had figured out that her soul and Marcus's couldn't possibly have fully merged. The scenario went against all laws of their kinds. Her soul had been merged with Jakob's. She had willingly accepted his, and Marcus had then changed the rules without asking anyone for permission. When Nyx had removed his heart, it had killed him. It should've killed her too, and yet Wynter had merely been wounded. Perhaps fatally if she didn't find a host pretty sharpish, yes, but Rosa had trusted in her mother to stay strong.

And, of course, she had done so thanks to Jakob. She deserved to have him back and having a place in his heart was exactly what she needed. The chance to live a real life with the man she loved. The true other half of her heart.

It was Mara's heart that had done the deed. She was the one who loved Marcus, and her magic had Wynter fooled all this time that it was her soul and not the witches which had merged with the vampire's. Whether Marcus knew or not, he didn't put a stop to it.

And that had left a loophole. One Rosa and Nyx could exploit.

She and Jak reached the mansion and found the place in uproar. Inside, Marcus's followers had sensed an epic change, and yet knew nothing of what had gone down. But there was one witch who knew exactly what fate had befallen her master.

Marceline was outside on the ground beneath the tree her human father had been strung up in time and again. She was on her knees, a rope in her hand which she was using to flagellate herself. The poor girl was clearly distraught, and Rosa wasn't surprised when Jak stopped and stared.

"She wants me to go to her," he whispered, and Rosa knew he meant Wynter, and agreed.

"Don't stop her, though. She needs this. Just stay by her side while Marceline does what she feels she must."

And with that, Rosa headed inside to where she knew a hundred questions awaited her.

Archie was at the base of the grand staircase, his eyes wide and full of fear.

"What's going on?" he asked, and Rosa answered by taking his hand, along with the witch standing by his side—Marlee. She then placed them together and smiled.

"Twins, one for one vampire master, and the other destined for someone else..." she replied, and Archie seemed genuinely shocked. He looked at Marlee and shook his head.

"How did I never see it before?" he cried and pulled the young witch into his embrace. The poor girl didn't seem to know what to do with herself at first, but then she settled into Archie's hold and smiled the first genuine smile Rosa had seen on her face in a very long time.

"You are the vampire master of this family now, Archie. You have a Priestess at your side and an empire to run. My only hope is that you choose a different path to that of your late brother."

It took the vampire a moment to comprehend what she'd said, but when the penny finally dropped, Archie seemed genuinely sad.

"Marcus is dead?" he asked, his voice soft and low.

"Yes," Rosa answered, and while the jinn, who then appeared from upstairs, seemed glad, his smile soon faded.

"Wynter," Brodie bellowed, sinking to his haunches on the bottom step. "That means..." he surmised, and all eyes turned to him. Rosa was sure she even heard Archie gasp.

"She lives. Thanks to the God of Death, and to Rosa, his bride," a husky voice then called from the doorway. Even after all this time, Jak's distinctive Russian accent was still strong, and couldn't belong to any other than he. Archie bound for the door and threw himself at Jak. He wrapped him in his arms, and Rosa was sure she even heard him sob. His friend was back from the grave, after all, and it was clearly a fine end to a miserable day.

When the pair finally parted, Jakob looked down at Brodie, who was still sitting on the step, his face like that of a child. There was no hatred between them now. No anger. Only respect and perhaps even admiration.

"I should've always known you'd do right by her," he said solemnly, and stood with his hand outstretched. Jak reached forward and shook it with his own, and the two men smiled.

"Miserable old jinni," Jak joked, making Brodie laugh.

"Yeah, some things never change," he answered.

All eyes were then suddenly on Rosa.

"What now?" Archie asked, and she shrugged.

"Balance has been restored, so it's time to start over. Time for us all to move on. Me included," she told them, and Nyx seemed to take that as his cue. He appeared out of nowhere beside her and took his new wife's hand.

The deed had been done simply and without any of the usual human proceedings, and Rosa had loved it. Loved him too, despite his wrongdoings. But, unlike the misguided mother she had helped save, she hadn't forgiven or forgotten. Tides were indeed changing, and so too was the way deeds were done. Nyx had done things neither of them were proud of, and Rosa had vowed she would help him atone. Help him become more than a God. And he would help her, too.

"It's the first day of the rest of our lives. Let's start by cleaning up this mess and beginning again," Marlee declared, much to the surprise of the group.

"Sounds good to me," Archie replied, and he clapped Jakob on the back as he embraced his old friend again.

This time, it was going to be different. They had each other and were all stronger for it. No longer was their dictatorial leader suffocating them with his rules. Each one of them was free, and Rosa knew that together they were going to finally achieve their greatest accomplishment yet.

Life. Ones worth living and without fear.

Forever.

Together.

Unbound, unburdened, and free.

The End of the Blood Slave series

About the Author

Eden Wildblood is setting out on a journey to tell these dark stories to the world. She devours horror movies and books, and listens to heavy metal, and yet always wonders why people are still surprised when she reveals her dark side.

But now, she's using that part of herself to bring that darkness to life. To share her soul with the world…

Find out more about Eden by following her on Facebook
www.facebook.com/edenwildblood

Or check out Eden's other alias's via:
www.lmauthor.com

Printed in Great Britain
by Amazon